Grant Allen

This Mortal Coil

A novel

Grant Allen

This Mortal Coil
A novel

ISBN/EAN: 9783337045449

Printed in Europe, USA, Canada, Australia, Japan

Cover: Foto ©Andreas Hilbeck / pixelio.de

More available books at **www.hansebooks.com**

THIS MORTAL COIL

𝔄 𝔑𝔬𝔳𝔢𝔩

By GRANT ALLEN

AUTHOR OF "IN ALL SHADES," "THE DEVIL'S DIE," ETC.

A NEW EDITION

𝔏𝔬𝔫𝔡𝔬𝔫
CHATTO & WINDUS, PICCADILLY
1895

CONTENTS.

CONTENTS.

THIS MORTAL COIL.

CHAPTER I.

BOHEMIA.

WHOEVER knows Bohemian London, knows the smoking-room of the Cheyne Row Club. No more comfortable or congenial divan exists anywhere between Regent Circus and Hyde Park Corner than that chosen paradise of unrecognized genius. The Cheyne Row Club is not large, indeed, but it prides itself upon being extremely select—too select to admit upon its list of members peers, politicians, country gentlemen, or inhabitants of eligible family residences in Mayfair or Belgravia. Two qualifications are understood to be indispensable in candidates for membership: they must be truly great, and they must be unsuccessful. Possession of a commodious suburban villa excludes *ipso facto*. The Club is emphatically the head-quarters of the great Bohemian clan; the gathering-place of unhung artists, unread novelists, unpaid poets, and unheeded social and political reformers generally. Hither flock all the choicest spirits of the age during that probationary period when society, in its slow and lumbering fashion, is spending twenty years in discovering for itself the bare fact of their distinguished existence. Here Maudle displays his latest designs to Postlethwaite's critical and admiring eye; here Postlethwaite pours his honeyed sonnets into Maudle's receptive and sympathetic tympanum. Everybody who is anybody has once been a member of the "dear old Cheyne Row:" Royal Academicians and Cabinet Ministers and Society Journalists and successful poets still speak with lingering pride and affection of the days when they lunched there, as yet undiscovered, on a single chop and a glass of draught claret by no means of the daintiest.

B

Not that the Club can number any of them now on its existing roll-call: the Cheyne Row is for prospective celebrity only; accomplished facts transfer themselves at once to a statelier site in Pall Mall near the Duke of York's Column. Rising merit frequents the Tavern, as scoffers profanely term it: risen greatness basks rather on the lordly stuffed couches of Waterloo Place. No man, it has been acutely observed, remains a Bohemian when he has daughters to marry. The pure and blameless ratepayer avoids Prague. As soon as Smith becomes Chancellor of the Exchequer, as soon as Brown takes silk, as soon as Robinson is elected an Associate, as soon as Tompkins publishes his popular novel, they all incontinently with one accord desert the lesser institution in the Piccadilly byway, and pass on their names, their honours, their hats, and their subscriptions to the dignified repose of the Athenæum. For them, the favourite haunt of judge and bishop: for the young, the active, the struggling, and the incipient, the chop and claret of the less distinguished but more lively caravanserai by the Green Park purlieus.

In the smoking-room of this eminent and unsuccessful Bohemian society, at the tag-end of a London season, one warm evening in a hot July, Hugh Massinger, of the Utter Bar, sat lazily by the big bow window, turning over the pages of the last number of the *Charing Cross Review.*

That he was truly great, nobody could deny. He was in very fact a divine bard, or, to be more strictly accurate, the author of a pleasing and melodious volume of minor poetry. Even away from the Cheyne Row Club, none but the most remote of country-cousins—say from the wilder parts of Cornwall or the crofter-clad recesses of the Isle of Skye—could have doubted for a moment the patent fact that Hugh Massinger was a distinguished (though unknown) poet of the antique school, so admirably did he fit his part in life as to features, dress, and general appearance. Indeed, malicious persons were wont at times unkindly to insinuate that Hugh was a poet, not because he found in himself any special aptitude for stringing verses or building the lofty rhyme, but because his face and bearing imperatively compelled him to adopt the thankless profession of bard in self-justification and self-defence. This was ill-natured, and it was also untrue; for Hugh Massinger had lisped in numbers—at least in penny ones—ever since he was able to lisp in print at all. Elizabethan or nothing, he had taken to poetry almost from his very cradle; and had astonished his father at sixteen by a rhymed version of an ode of Horace, worthy the inspiration of the great Dr. Watts himself, and not, perhaps, far below the poetic standard of Mr. Martin Farquhar Tupper. At Oxford he had perpetrated a capital Newdigate;

and two years after gaining his fellowship at Oriel, he had published anonymously, in parchment covers, "Echoes from Callimachus, and other Poems"—in the style of the early romantic school—which had fairly succeeded by careful nursing in attaining the dignity of a second edition under his own name. So that Massinger's claim to the sodality of the craft whose workmen are "born not made" might perhaps be considered as of the genuine order, and not entirely dependent, as cynics averred, upon his long hair, his pensive eyes, his dark-brown cheek, or the careless twist of his necktie and his shirt-collar.

Nevertheless, even in these minor details of the poetical character, it must candidly be confessed that Hugh Massinger outstripped by several points many of the more recognized bards whose popular works are published in regulation green-cloth octavos, and whose hats and cloaks, of unique build, adorn with their presence the vestibule pegs of the Athenæum itself. He went back to the traditions of the youth of our century. The undistinguished author of "Echoes from Callimachus" was tall and pale, and a trifle Byronic. That his face was beautiful, extremely beautiful, even a hostile reviewer in the organ of another clique could hardly venture seriously to deny: those large grey eyes, that long black hair, that exquisitely chiselled and delicate mouth, would alone have sufficed to attract attention and extort admiration anywhere in the universe, or at the very least in the solar system.

Hugh Massinger, in short, was (like Coleridge) a noticeable man. It would have been impossible to pass him by, even in a crowded street, without a hurried glance of observation and pleasure at his singularly graceful and noble face. He looked and moved every inch a poet; delicate, refined, cultivated, expressive, and sicklied o'er with that pale cast of thought which modern æstheticism so cruelly demands as a proof of attachment from her highest votaries. Yet at the same time, in spite of deceptive appearances to the contrary, he was strong in muscular strength: a wiry man, thin, but well knit: one of those fallacious, uncanny, long-limbed creatures, who can scale an Alp or tramp a score or so of miles before breakfast, while looking as if a short stroll through the Park would kill them outright with sheer exhaustion. Altogether, a typical poet of the old-fashioned school, that dark and handsome Italianesque man: and as he sat there carelessly, with the paper held before him, in an unstudied attitude of natural grace, many a painter might have done worse than choose the author of "Echoes from Callimachus" for the subject of a pretty Academy pot-boiler.

So Warren Relf, the unknown marine artist, thought to himself in his armchair opposite, as he raised his eyes by chance from the etchings in the *Portfolio*, and glanced across casually with a hasty look at the undiscovered poet.

"Has the *Charing Cross* reviewed your new volume yet?" he asked politely, his glance meeting Massinger's while he flung down the paper on the table beside him.

The poet rose and stood with his hands behind his back in an easy posture before the empty fireplace. "I believe it has deigned to assign me half a column of judicious abuse," he answered, half yawning, with an assumption of profound indifference and contempt for the *Charing Cross Review* and all its ideas or opinions collectively. "To tell you the truth, the subject's one that doesn't interest me. In the first place, I care very little for my own verses. And in the second place, I don't care at all for reviewers generally, or for the *Charing Cross Snarler* and its kind in particular. I disbelieve altogether in reviews, in fact. Familiarity breeds contempt. To be quite candid, I've written too many of them."

"If criticism in literature's like criticism in art," the young painter rejoined, smiling, "why, with the one usual polite exception of yourself, Massinger, I can't say I think very much of the critics.—But what do you mean, I should like to know, by saying you don't care for your own verses? Surely no man can do anything great, in literature or art—or in shoe-blacking or pig-sticking, if it comes to that—unless he thoroughly believes in his own vocation."

Massinger laughed a musical laugh. "In shoe-blacking or pig-sticking," he said, with a delicate curl of his thin lips, "that's no doubt true; but in verse-making, query? Who on earth at the present day could even pretend to himself to believe in poetry? Time was, I dare say—though I'm by no means sure of it—when the bard, hoary old impostor, was a sort of prophet, and went about the world with a harp in his hand, and a profound conviction in his innocent old heart that when he made 'Sapphic' rhyme to 'traffic,' or produced a sonnet on the theme of 'Catullus,' 'lull us,' and 'cull us,' he was really and truly enriching humanity with a noble gift of divine poesy. If the amiable old humbug could actually bring himself to believe in his soul that stringing together fourteen lines into an indifferent piece, or balancing 'mighty' to chime with 'Aphrodite,' in best Swinburnian style, was fulfilling his appointed function in the scheme of the universe, I'm sure I should be the last to interfere with the agreeable delusion under which (like the gentlemen from Argos in Horace) he must have been labouring. It's so delightful to believe in anything, that for my own part I wouldn't attempt to insinuate doubts into the mind of a contented Buddhist or a devout worshipper of Mumbo Jumbo."

"But surely you look upon yourself as a reaction against this modern school of Swinburnians and ballad-mongers, don't you?" Relf said, with a shrug.

"Of course I do. Byron's my man. I go back to the original divine inspiration of the romantic school. It's simpler, and it's easier. But what of that? Our method's all the same at bottom, after all. Who in London in this nineteenth century can for a moment affect to believe in the efficacy of poetry? Look at this last new volume of my own, for example!—You won't look at it, of course, I'm well aware, but that's no matter: nobody ever does look at my immortal works, I'm only too profoundly conscious. I cut them myself in a dusty copy at all the libraries, in order to create a delusive impression on the mind of the public that I've had at least a solitary reader. But let that pass. Look, metaphorically, I mean, and not literally, at this last new volume of mine! How do you think a divine bard does it? Simply by taking a series of rhymes—'able,' and 'stable,' and 'table,' and 'cable;' 'Mabel,' and 'Babel,' and 'fable,' and 'gable'—and weaving them all together cunningly by a set form into a Procrustean mould to make up a poem. Perhaps 'gable,' which you've mentally fixed upon for the fourth line, won't suit the sense. Very well, then; you must do your best to twist something reasonable, or at least inoffensive, out of 'sable' or 'label,' or 'Cain and Abel,' or anything else that will make up the rhyme and complete the metre."

"And is that your plan, Massinger?"

"Yes, all this last lot of mine are done like that: just *bouts rimés*—I admit the fact; for what's all poetry but *bouts rimés* in the highest perfection? Mechanical, mechanical. I draw up a lot of lists of rhymes beforehand: 'kirtle,' and 'myrtle,' and 'hurtle,' and 'turtle' (those are all original); 'pæan,' 'Ægean,' 'plebeian,' and 'Tean' (those are fairly new); 'battle,' and 'cattle,' and 'prattle,' and 'rattle' (those are all commonplace); and then, when the divine afflatus seizes me, I take out the lists and con them over, and weave them up into an undying song for future generations to go wild about and comment upon. 'What profound thought,' my unborn Malones and Furnivalls and Leos will ask confidingly in their learned editions, 'did the immortal bard mean to convey by this obscure couplet?'—I'll tell you in confidence. He meant to convey the abstruse idea that 'passenger' was the only English word he could find in the dictionary at all like a rhyme to the name of 'Massinger.'"

Warren Relf looked up at him a little uneasily. "I don't like to hear you run down poetry like that," he said, with an evident tinge of disapprobation. "I'm not a poet myself, of course; but still I'm sure it isn't all a mere matter of rhymes and refrains,

of epithets and prettinesses. What touches our hearts lies
deeper than mere expression, I'm certain. It lies in the very
core and fibre of the man. There are passages even in your
own poems—though you're a great deal too cynical to admit
it now—that came straight out of the depths of your own heart,
I venture to conjecture—those 'Lines on a Lock of Hair,' for
example.—Aha, cynic! there I touched you on the raw.—But
if you think so lightly of poetry as a pursuit, as you say, I
wonder why you ever came to take to it."

"Take to it, my dear fellow! What an Arcadian idea! As
if men nowadays chose their sphere in life deliberately. Why,
what on earth makes any of us ever take to anything, I should
like to know, in this miserable workaday modern world of ours?
Because we're simply pitchforked into it by circumstances.
Does the crossing-sweeper sweep crossings, do you suppose, for
example, by pure preference for the profession of a sweep?
Does the milkman get up at five in the morning because he sees
in the purveying of skim-milk to babes and sucklings a useful,
important, and even necessary industry to the rising generation
of this great Metropolis? Does the dustman empty the domestic
bin out of disinterested regard for public sanitation? or the
engine-driver dash through rain and snow in a drear-nighted
December like a Comtist prophet, out of high and noble enthusiasm of humanity?" He snapped his fingers with an emphatic
negative.—"We don't choose our places in life at all, my dear
boy," he went on after a pause: "we get tumbled into them by
pure caprice of circumstances. If I'd chosen mine, instead of
strictly meditating the thankless Muse, I'd certainly have
adopted the exalted profession of a landed proprietor, with the
pleasing duty of receiving my rents (by proxy) once every
quarter, and spending them royally with becoming magnificence,
in noble ways, like the Greek gentleman one reads about in
Aristotle. I always admired that amiable Greek gentleman—
the *megaloprepês*, I think Aristotle calls him. His berth would
suit me down to the ground. He had nothing at all of any sort
to do, and he did it most gracefully with princely generosity on
a sufficient income."

"But you *must* write poetry for something or other, Massinger; for if it isn't rude to make the suggestion, you can hardly
write it, you know, for a livelihood."

Massinger's dark face flushed visibly. "I write for fame," he
answered majestically, with a lordly wave of his long thin hand.
"For glory—for honour—for time—for eternity. Or, to be more
precisely definite, if you prefer the phrase, for filthy lucre. In
the coarse and crude phraseology of political economists, poetry
takes rank nowadays, I humbly conceive, as a long investment.
I'm a journalist by trade—a mere journeyman journalist; the

gushing penny-a-liner of a futile and demoralized London press. But I have a soul within me above penny-a-lining; I aspire ultimately to a pound a word. I don't mean to live and die in Grub Street. My soul looks forward to immortality, and a footman in livery. Now, when once a man has got pitchforked by fate into the rank and file of contemporary journalism, there are only two ways possible for him to extricate himself with peace and honour from his unfortunate position. One way is to write a successful novel. That's the easiest, quickest, and most immediate short-cut from Grub Street to Eaton Place and affluence that I know of anywhere. But unhappily it's crowded, immensely overcrowded—vehicular traffic for the present entirely suspended. Therefore, the only possible alternative is to take up poetry. The Muse must descend to feel the pulse of the market. I'm conscious of the soul of song within me; that is to say, I can put 'Myrrha' to rhyme with 'Pyrrha,' and alliterate *p*s and *q*s and *w*s with any man living (bar Algernon) in all England. Now, poetry's a very long road round, I admit —like going from Kensington to the City by Willesden Junction; but in the end, if properly worked, it lands you at last by a circuitous route in fame and respectability. To be Poet Laureate is eminently respectable. A man can live on journalism meanwhile; but if he keeps pegging away at his Pegasus in his spare moments, without intermission, like a costermonger at his donkey, Pegasus will raise him after many days to the top of Parnassus, where he can build himself a commodious family residence, lighted throughout with electric lights, and commanding a magnificent view in every direction over the Vale of Tempe and the surrounding country. Tennyson's done it already at Aldworth; why shouldn't I, too, do it in time on Parnassus?"

Relf smiled dubiously, and knocked the ash off his cigar into the Japanese tray that stood by his side. "Then you look upon poetry merely as an ultimate means of making money?" he suggested, with a deprecatory look.

"Money! Not money only, my dear fellow, but position, reputation, recognition, honour. Does any man work for anything else? Any man, I mean, but cobblers and enthusiasts?"

"Well, I don't know. I may be an enthusiast myself," Relf answered slowly; "but I certainly do work at art to a great extent for art's sake, because I really love and admire and delight in it. Of course I should like to make money too, within reasonable limits—enough to keep myself and my people in a modest sort of way, without the footman or the eligible family residence. Not that I want to be successful, either: from what I've seen of successful men, I incline to believe that success as a rule has a very degenerating effect upon character.

Literature, science, and art thrive best in a breezy, bracing air. I never aim at being a successful man myself; and if I go on as I'm doing now, I shall no doubt succeed in not succeeding. But apart from the money and the livelihood altogether, I love my work as an occupation. I like doing it; and I like to see myself growing stronger and freer at it every day."

"That's all very well for you," Massinger replied, with another expansive wave of his graceful hand. "You're doing work you care for, as I play lawn-tennis, for a personal amusement. I can sympathize with you there. I once felt the same about poetry myself. But that was a long time ago: those days are dead—dead—hopelessly dead, as dead as Mad Margaret's affidavit. I'm a sceptic now: my faith in verse has evaporated utterly. Have I not seen the public devour ten successive editions of the 'Epic of Washerwomen,' or something of the sort? Have I not seen them reject the good and cleave unto the evil, like the children of Israel wandering in the Wilderness? I know now that the world is hollow, and that my doll is stuffed with sawdust.—Let's quit the subject. It turns me always into a gloomy pessimist.—What are you going to do with yourself this summer?"

"Me? Oh, just the usual thing, I suppose. Going down in my tub to paint sweet mudbanks off the coast of Suffolk."

"Suffolk to wit! I see the finger of fate in that! Why, that's just where I'm going too. I mean to take six or eight weeks' holiday, if a poor drudge of a journalist can ever be said to indulge in holidays at all—with books for review, and proofs for correction, and editorial communications for consideration, always weighing like a ton of lead upon his unhappy breast: and I propose to bury myself alive up to the chin in some obscure, out-of-the-way Suffolk village they call Whitestrand.— Have you ever heard of it?"

"Oh, I know it well," Relf answered, with a smile of delightful reminiscence. "It's grand for mud. I go there painting again and again. You'd call it the funniest little stranded old-world village you ever came across anywhere in England. Nothing could be uglier, quainter, or more perfectly charming. It lies at the mouth of a dear little muddy creek, with a funny old mill for pumping the water off the sunken meadows; and all around for miles and miles is one great flat of sedge and seapink, alive with water-birds and intersected with dikes, where the herons fish all day long, poised on one leg in the middle of the stream as still as mice, exactly as if they were sitting to Marks for their portraits."

"Ah, delightful for a painter, I've no doubt," Hugh Massinger replied, half yawning to himself, "especially for a painter to whom mud and herons are bread and butter, and brackish water is Bass and Allsopp; but scarcely, you'll admit, an attractive picture to the inartistic public, among whom I take the liberty, for this occasion only, humbly to rank myself. I go there, in fact, as a martyr to principle. I live for others. A member of my family—not to put too fine a point upon it, a lady—abides for the present moment at Whitestrand, and believes herself to be seized or possessed by prescriptive right of a lien or claim to a certain fixed aliquot portion of my time and attention. I've never admitted the claim myself (being a legally-minded soul); but just out of the natural sweetness of my disposition, I go down occasionally (without prejudice) to whatever part of England she may chance to be inhabiting, for the sake of not disappointing her foregone expectations, however ill-founded, and be the same more or less.—You observe, I speak with the charming precision of the English statute-book."

"But how do you mean to get to Whitestrand?" Relf asked suddenly, after a short pause. "It's a difficult place to reach, you know. There's no station nearer than ten miles off, and that a country one, so that when you arrive there, you can get no conveyance to take you over."

"So my cousin gave me to understand. She was kind enough to provide me with minute instructions for her bookless wilds. I believe I'm to hire a costermonger's cart or something of the sort to convey my portmanteau; and I'm to get across myself by the aid of the natural means of locomotion with which a generous providence or survival of the fittest has been good enough to endow me by hereditary transmission. At least, so my cousin Elsie instructs me."

"Why not come round with me in the tub?" Relf suggested good-humouredly.

"What? your yacht? Hatherley was telling me you were the proud possessor of a ship.—Are you going round that way any time shortly?"

"Well, she's not exactly what you call a yacht," Relf replied, with an apologetic tinge in his tone of voice. "She's only a tub, you know, an open boat almost, with a covered well and just room for three to sleep and feed in. 'A poor thing, but mine own,' as Touchstone says; as broad as she's long, and as shallow as she's broad, and quite flat-bottomed, drawing so little water at a pinch that you can sail her across an open meadow when there's a heavy dew on.—And if you come, you'll have to work your passage, of course. I navigate her myself, as captain, crew, cabin-boy, and passenger, with one other painter fellow to share watches with me. The fact is, I got her built as a substitute for rooms, because I found it cheaper than taking lodgings at a seaside place and hiring a rowboat whenever one wanted one. I cruise about the English coast with her

in summer; and in the cold months, I run her round to the
Mediterranean. And, besides, one can get into such lovely little
side-creeks and neglected channels, all full of curious objects of
interest, which nobody can ever see in anything else. She's
a perfect treasure to a marine painter in the mud-and-buoy
business. But I won't for a moment pretend to say she's comfortable for a landsman. If you come with me, in fact, you'll
have to rough it."

"I love roughing it.—How long will it take us to cruise round
to Whitestrand?"

"Oh, the voyage depends entirely upon the wind and tide.
Sailing-boats take their own time. The *Mud-Turtle*—that's
what I call her—doesn't hurry. She's lying now off the Pool at
the Tower, taking care of herself in the absence of all her regular
crew; and Potts, my mate, he's away in the north, intending to
meet me next week at Lowestoft, where my mother and sister
are stopping in lodgings. We can start on our cruise whenever
you like—say, if you choose, to-morrow morning."

"Thanks, awfully," Hugh answered, with a nod of assent.
"To tell you the truth, I should like nothing better. It'll be
an experience, and the wise man lives upon new experiences.
Pallas, you remember, in Tennyson's 'Œnone,' recommended to
Paris the deliberate cultivation of experiences as such.—I'll
certainly go. For my own part, like Saint Simon, I mean in my
time to have tried everything. Though Saint Simon, to be sure,
went rather far, for I believe he even took a turn for a while at
picking pockets."

CHAPTER II.

DOWN STREAM.

TIDE served next morning at eleven; and punctual to the
minute—for, besides being a poet, he prided himself on his
qualities as a man of business—Hugh Massinger surrendered
himself in due course by previous appointment on board the
Mud-Turtle at the Pool by the Tower. But his eyes were
heavier and redder than they had seemed last night; and his
wearied manner showed at once, by a hundred little signs, that
he had devoted but small time since Relf left him to what Mr.
Herbert Spencer periphrastically describes as "reparative pro-
cesses."

The painter, attired for the sea like a common sailor in jersey
and trousers and knitted woollen cap, rose up from the deck to
greet him hospitably. His whole appearance betokened serious

business. It was evident that Warren Relf did not mean to play at yachting.

"You've been making a night of it, I'm afraid, Massinger," he said, as their eyes met. "Bad preparation, you know, for a day down the river. We shall have a loppy sea, if this wind holds, when we pass the Nore. You ought to have gone straight to bed when you left the club with me last evening."

"I know I ought," the poet responded with affected cheerfulness. "The path of duty's as plain as a pikestaff. But the things I ought to do I mostly leave undone; and the things I ought not to do, I find, on the contrary, vastly attractive. I may as well make a clean breast of it. I strolled round to Pallavicini's after you vacated the Row last night, and found them having a turn or two at lansquenet. Now, lansquenet's an amusement I never can resist. The consequence was, in three hours I was pretty well cleaned out of ready cash, and shall have to keep my nose to the grindstone accordingly all through what ought by rights to have been my summer holiday. This conclusively shows the evils of high play, and the moral superiority of the wise man who goes home to bed and is sound asleep when the clock strikes eleven."

Relf's face fell several tones. "I wish, Massinger," he said very gravely, "you'd make up your mind never to touch those hateful cards again. You'll ruin your health, your mind, and your pocket with them. If you spent the time you spend upon play in writing some really great book now, you'd make in the end ten times as much by it."

The poet smiled a calm smile of superior wisdom. "Good boy!" he cried, patting Relf on the back in mock approbation of his moral advice. "You talk for all the world like a Sunday-school prize-book. Honest industry has its due reward; while pitch-and-toss and wicked improper games land one at last in prison or the workhouse. The industrious apprentice rises in time to be Lord Mayor (and to appropriate the public funds *ad libitum*); whereas, the idle apprentice, degraded by the evil influences of ha'penny loo, ends his days with a collar of hemp round his naughty neck in an equally exalted but perhaps less dignified position in life—on a platform at Newgate. My dear Relf, how on earth can you, who are a sensible man, believe all that antiquated nursery rubbish? Cast your eyes for a moment on the world around you, here in the central hub of London, within sight of all the wealth and squalor of England, and ask yourself candidly whether what you see in it at all corresponds with the idyllic picture of the little-Jack-Horner school of moralists. As a matter of fact, is it always the good boys who pull the plums with self-appreciative smile out of the world's pudding? Far from it: quite the other way. I have seen the wicked flourishing in my time like a green bay-tree. Honest industry breaks stones on the road, while successful robbery or successful gambling rolls by at its ease, cigar in mouth, lolling on the cushions of its luxurious carriage. If you stick to honest industry all your life long, you may go on breaking stones contentedly for the whole term of your natural existence. But if you speculate boldly with your week's earnings and land a haul, you may set another fellow to break stones for you in time, and then you become at once a respectable man, a capitalist, and a baronet. All the great fortunes we see in the world have been piled up in the last resort, if you'll only believe it, by successful gambling."

"Every man has a right to his own opinion," Warren Relf answered with a more serious air, as he turned aside to look after the rigging. "I admit there's a great deal of gambling in business; but anyhow, honest industry's a simple necessary on board the *Mud-Turtle.*—Come aft, here, will you, from your topsy-turvy moral philosophy, and help me out with this sheet and the mainsail. Before we reach the German Ocean, you'll have the whole art of navigation at your fingers' ends—for I mean to sketch while you manage the ship—and be in a position to write an ode in a Catalonian metre on the Pleasures of Luffing, and the True Delight of the Thames Waterway."

Massinger turned to do as he was directed, and to inspect the temporary floating hotel in which he was to make his way contentedly down to the coast of Suffolk. The *Mud-Turtle* was indeed as odd-looking and original a little craft as her owner and skipper had proclaimed her to be. A centre-board yawl, of seventeen tons registered burden, she ranked as a yacht only by courtesy, on the general principle of what the logicians call excluded middle. If she wasn't that, why, then, pray what in the world was she? The *Mud-Turtle* measured almost as broad across the beam as she reckoned feet in length from stem to stern; and her skipper maintained with profound pride that she couldn't capsize in the worst storm that ever blew out of an English sky, even if she tried to. She drew no more than three feet of water at a pinch; and though it was scarcely true, as Relf had averred, that a heavy dew was sufficient 'to float her, she could at least go anywhere that a man could wade up to his knees without fear of wetting his tucked-up breeches. This made her a capital boat for a marine artist to go about sketching in; for Relf could lay her alongside a wreck on shallow sands, or run her up a narrow creek after picturesque waterfowl, or approach the riskiest shore to the very edge of the cliffs, without any reference to the state of the tide, or the probable depth of the surrounding channel.

"If she grounds," the artist said enthusiastically, expatiating on her merits to his new passenger, "you see it doesn't really matter twopence ; for the next high tide'll set her afloat again within six hours. She's a great opportunist : she knows well that all things come in time to him who can wait. The *Mud-Turtle* positively revels in mud; she lies flat on it as on her native heath, and stays patiently without one word of reproach for the moon's attraction to come in its round to her ultimate rescue."

The yawl's accommodation was opportunist too : though excellent in kind, it was limited in quantity, and by no means unduly luxurious in quality. She was a working-man's yacht, and she meant business. Her deck was calculated on the most utilitarian principles—just big enough for two persons to sketch abreast; her cabin contained three wooden bunks, with their appropriate complement of rugs and blankets; and a small and primitive open stove devoted to the service of the ship's cookery, took up almost all the vacant space in the centre of the well, leaving hardly room for the self-sacrificing volunteer who undertook the functions of purveyor and bottle-washer to turn about in. But the lockers were amply stored with fresh bread, tinned meats, and other simple necessaries for a week's cruise; while food for the mind existed on a small shelf at the stern in the crude shape of the " Coaster's Companion," the Sailing Directions issued by Authority of the Honourable Brethren of the Trinity House, and the charts of the Thames, constructed from the latest official surveys of her Majesty's Board of Admiralty. Thus equipped and accoutred Warren Relf was accustomed to live an outdoor life for weeks together with his one like-minded chum and companion ; and if the spray was sometimes rather moist, and the yellow fog rather thick and slabby, and the early mornings rather chill and raw, and the German Ocean rather loppy and aggressive on the digestive faculties, yet the good dose of fresh air, the delicious salty feeling of the free breeze, and the perpetual sense of ease and lightness that comes with yachting, were more than enough fully to atone to an enthusiastic marine artist for all these petty passing inconveniences.

As for Hugh Massinger, a confirmed landsman, the first few hours' sail down the crowded Thames appeared to him at the outset a perfect phantasmagoria of ever-varying perils and assorted terrors. He composed his soul to instant death from the very beginning. Not, indeed, that he minded one bit for that : the poet dearly loved danger, as he loved all other forms of sensation and excitement : they were food for the Muse ; and the Muse, like Blanche Amory, is apt to exclaim, " Il me faut des émotions ! " But the manifold novel forms of enterprise as the lumbering little yawl made her way clumsily among the great East-Indiamen and big ocean-going steamers, darting boldly now athwart the very bows of a huge Monarch-liner, insinuating herself now with delicate precision between the broadsides of two heavy Rochester barges, and just escaping collision now with some laden collier from Cardiff or Newcastle, were too complicated and too ever-pressing at the first blush for Massinger fully to take in their meaning at a single glance.

The tidal Thames is the Cheapside of the ocean, a mart of many nations, resorting to it by sea and by land. It's all very well going down the river on the Antwerp packet or the outward-bound New-Zealander; you steam then at your ease along the broad unencumbered central channel, with serene confidence that a duly qualified pilot stands at your helm, and that everybody else will gladly give way to you, for the sake of saving their own bacon. But it's quite another matter to thread your way tortuously through that thronged and bustling highway of the shipping interest in a centre-board yawl of seventeen tons registered burden, manned by a single marine artist and an amateur passenger of uncertain seamanship. Hugh Massinger was at once amused and bewildered by the careless confidence with which his seafaring friend dashed boldly in and out among brigs and schooners, smacks and steamships, on port or starboard tack, in endless confusion, backing the little *Mud-Turtle* to hold her own in the unequal contest against the biggest and swiftest craft that sailed the river. His opinion of Relf rose rapidly many degrees in mental register as ho watched him tacking and luffing and scudding and darting with cool unconcern in his toy tub among so many huge and swiftly moving monsters.

"Port your helm!" Relf cried to him hastily once, as they crossed the channel just abreast of Greenwich Hospital. "Here's another sudden death down upon us round the Reach yonder!" And even as he spoke, a big coal-steamer, with a black diamond painted allusively on her bulky funnel, turning the low point of land that closed their view, bore hastily down upon them from the opposite direction with menacing swiftness. Massinger, doing his best to obey orders, grew bewildered after a time by the glib rapidity of his friend's commands. He was perfectly ready to act as he was bid when once he understood his instructions; but the seafaring mind seems unable to comprehend that landsmen do not possess an intuitive knowledge of the strange names bestowed by technical souls upon ropes, booms, gaffs, and mizzen-masts; so that Massinger's attempts to carry out his orders in a prodigious hurry proved productivo for the most part rather of blank confusion than of the effect intended by the master skipper. After passing Greenhithe, however, they began to find the channel somewhat clearer, and Relf ceased for a while to skip about the deck like the little

hills of the Psalmist, while Massinger felt his life comparatively
safe at times for three minutes together, without a single danger
menacing him ahead in the immediate future from port or starboard, from bow or stern, from brig or steamer, from grounding
or collision.

About two o'clock, after a hot run, they cast anchor awhile
out of the main channel, where traders ply their flow of intercourse, and stood by to eat their lunch in peace and quietness
under the lee of a projecting point near Gravesend.

"If wind and tide serve like this," Relf observed philosophically, as he poured out a glassful of beer into a tin mug—
the *Mud-Turtle's* appointments were all of the homeliest—"we
ought to get down to Whitestrand before an easy breeze with
two days' sail, sleeping the nights in the quiet creeks at Leigh
and Orfordness."

"That would exactly suit me," Massinger answered, drain-
ing off the mugful at a gulp after his unusual exertion. "I
wrote a hasty line to my cousin in Suffolk this morning telling
her I should probably reach Whitestrand the day after to-
morrow, wind and weather permitting.—I approve of your ship,
Relf, and of your tinned lobster too. It's fun coming down to
the great deep in this unconventional way. The regulation
yacht, with sailors and a cook and a floating drawing-room, my
soul wouldn't care for. You can get drawing-rooms galore any
day in Belgravia; but picnicking like this, with a spice of
adventure in it, falls in precisely with my own view of the ends
of existence."

"It's a cousin you're going down to Suffolk to see, then?"

"Well, yes; a cousin—a sort of a cousin; a Girton girl; the
newest thing out in women. I call her a cousin for convenience'
sake. Not too nearly related, if it comes to that; a surfeit of
family's a thing to be avoided. But we're a decadent tribe, the
tribe of Massinger; hardly any others of us left alive; when I
put on my hat, I cover all that remains of us; and cousinhood's a capital thing in its way to keep up under certain
conditions. It enables a man to pay a pretty girl a great deal
of respectful attention, without necessarily binding himself down
in the end to anything definite in the matrimonial direction."

"That's rather a cruel way of regarding it, isn't it?"

"Well, my dear boy, what's a man to do in these jammed
and crushed and overcrowded days of ours? Nature demands
the safety-valve of a harmless flirtation. If one can't afford to
marry, the natural affections *will* find an outlet, on a cousin or
somebody. But it's quite impossible, as things go nowadays,
for a penniless man to dream of taking to wife a penniless
woman and living on the sum of their joint properties. According to Cocker, nought and nought make nothing. So one must

just wait till one's chance in life turns up, one way or the other. If you make a fluke some day, and paint a successful picture, or write a successful book, or get off a hopeless murderer at the Old Bailey, or invent a new nervous disease for women, or otherwise rise to sudden fortune by any one of the usual absurd roads, then you can marry your pretty cousin or other little girl in a lordly way out of your own resources. If not, you must just put up with the plain daughter of an eminent alderman in the wine and spirit business, or connected with tallow, or doing a good thing in hides, and let her hard cash atone vicariously for your own want of tender affection. When a man has no patrimony, he must obviously make it up in matrimony. Only, the great point to avoid is letting the penniless girl meanwhile get too deep a hold upon your personal feelings. The wisest men—like me, for example—are downright fools when it comes to high play on the domestic instincts. Even Achilles had a vulnerable point, you know. So has every wise man. With Achilles, it was the heel; with us, it's the heart. The heart will wreck the profoundest and most deliberate philosopher living. I acknowledge it myself. I ought to wait, of course, till I catch the eminent alderman's richly endowed daughter. Instead of that, I shall doubtless fling myself away like a born fool upon the pretty cousin or some other equally unprofitable investment."

"Well, I hope you will," Relf answered, cutting himself a huge chunk of bread with his pocket clasp-knife. "I am awfully glad to hear you say so. For your own sake, I hope you'll keep your word. I hope you won't stifle everything you've got that's best within you for the sake of money and position and success. —Have a bit of this corned beef, will you?—A woman who sells herself for money is bad enough, though it's woman's way— they've all been trained to it for generations. But a man who sells himself for money—who takes himself to market for the highest bidder—who makes capital out of his face and his manners and his conversation—is absolutely contemptible, and nothing short of it.—I could never go on knowing you, if I thought you capable of it. But I don't think you so. I'm sure you do yourself a gross injustice. You're a great deal better than you pretend yourself. If the occasion ever actually arose, you'd follow your better and not your worse nature.—I'll trouble you for the mustard."

Massinger passed it, and pretended to feel awfully bored. "I'm sure I don't know," he answered; "I shall wait and see. I don't undertake either to read or to guide my own character. According to the fashionable modern doctrine, it was all settled for me irrevocably beforehand by my parents and grandparents in past generations. I merely stand by and watch where it leads me, with passive resignation and silent curiosity. The attitude's not entirely devoid of plot-interest. It's amusing to sit, like the gods of Epicurus, enthroned on high, and look down from without with critical eyes upon the gradual development on the stage of life of one's own history and one's own idiosyncrasy."

CHAPTER III.

ARCADIA.

THE village of Whitestrand, on the Suffolk coast—an oasis in a stretch of treeless desert—was, and is, one of the remotest and most primitive spots to be found anywhere on the shores of England. The railways, running inland away to the west, have left it for ages far in the lurch; and even the two or three belated roads that converge upon it from surrounding villages lead nowhere. It is, so to speak, an absolute terminus. The World's End is the whimsical title of the last house at Whitestrand. The little river Char that debouches into the sea just below the church, with its scattered group of thatched cottages, cuts off the hamlet effectually with its broad estuary from the low stretch of reclaimed and sluice-drained pasture-land of wiry grass that rolls away to southward. On the north, a rank salt marsh hems it in with broad flats of sedge and thrift and wan sea-lavender; and eastward, the low line of the German Ocean spreads dimly in front its shallow horizon on the very level of the beach and the village. Only to the west is there any dry land, a sandy heath across whose barren surface the three roads from the neighbouring hamlets meander meaninglessly by tortuous curves towards the steeple of Whitestrand. All around, the country lies flat, stale, and singularly unprofitable. The village, in fact, occupies a tiny triangular peninsula of level ground, whose isthmus is formed by the narrow belt of heath-clad waste which alone connects it with the outer universe.

The very name Whitestrand, as old as the days of the Danish invasion of the East Anglian plain, at once describes the one striking and noteworthy feature of the entire district. It has absolutely no salient point of its own of any sort, except the hard and firm floor of pure white sand that extends for miles and miles on either side of the village. The sands begin at the diked land south of the river—rescued from the tide by Oliver's Dutch engineers—and narrowing gradually as they pass northward, disappear altogether into low muddy cliff some four or five miles beyond the church of Whitestrand. No strip of coast anywhere in England can boast such a splendid beach of uniform whiteness, firmness, and solidity. At Whitestrand itself, the sands extend for three-quarters of a mile seaward at low tide, and are so smooth and compact in their consistent level, that a horse can gallop over them at full speed without leaving so much as the mark of a hoof upon the even surface of that natural arena. Whitestranders are enormously proud of their beach; the people of Walberswick, a rival village some miles off, with a local reputation for what passes in Suffolk as rural picturesqueness, maliciously declare this is because the poor Whitestranders—heaven help them!—have nothing else on earth to be proud of. Such remarks, however, savour no doubt of mere neighbourly jealousy; the Walberswick folk, having no beach at all of their own to brag about, are therefore naturally intolerant of beaches in other places.

All Whitestrand—what there was left of it—belonged to Mr. Wyville Meysey. His family had bought the manor and estate a hundred years before, from their elder representatives, when the banking firm of Meysey's in the Strand was in the first heydey of its financial glory. Unhappily for him, his particular ancestor, a collateral member of the great house, had preferred the respectable position of a country gentleman to an active share in the big concern in London. From that day forth the sea had been steadily eating away the Meysey estate, till very little was left of it now but salt marsh and sandhills and swampy pasture-lands.

It was Tuesday when Hugh Massinger and Warren Relf set sail from the Tower on their voyage in the *Mud-Turtle* down the crowded tidal Thames; on Thursday morning, two pretty girls sat together on the roots of an old gnarled poplar that overhung the exact point where the Char empties itself into the German Ocean. The Whitestrand poplar, indeed, had formed for three centuries a famous landmark to seafaring men who coast round the inlets of the Eastern Counties. In the quaint words of the old county historian, it rose "from the manor of Whitestrand straight up towards the kingdom of heaven;" and round its knotted roots and hollow trunk the current ran fierce at the turn of the tides, for it formed the one frail barrier to the encroachment of the sea on that portion of the low and decaying Suffolk coast-line. Everybody had known the Whitestrand poplar as a point to sail by ever since the spacious days of great Elizabeth. When you get in a line with the steeple of Walberswick, with the windmill on Snade Hill opening to the right, you can run straight up the mouth of Char towards the tiny inland port of Woodford. Vessels of small burden in distress off the coast in easterly gales often take shelter in this little creek as a harbour of refuge from heavy weather on the German Ocean.

The elder of the two girls who sat together picturesquely on this natural rustic seat was dark and handsome, and so like Hugh Massinger himself in face and feature, that no one would have had much difficulty in recognizing her for the second cousin of whom he had spoken, Elsie Challoner. Her expression was more earnest and serious, to be sure, than the London poet's; her type of beauty was more tender and true; but she had the same large melting pathetic eyes, the same melancholy and chiselled mouth, the same long black wiry hair, and the same innate grace of bearing and manner in every movement as her Byronic relative. The younger girl, her pupil, was fairer and shorter, a pretty and delicate blonde of eighteen, with clear blue eyes and wistful mouth, and a slender but dainty girlish figure. They sat hand in hand on the roots of the tree, half overarched by its hollow funnel, looking out together over the low flat sea, whose fresh breeze blew hard in their faces, with the delicious bracing coolness and airiness peculiar to the shore of the German Ocean. There is no other air in all England to equal that strong air of Suffolk; it seems to blow right through and through one, and to brush away the dust and smoke of town from all one's pores with a single whiff of its clear bright purity.

"How do you think your cousin'll come, Elsie?" the younger girl asked, twisting her big straw hat by its strings carelessly in her hands. "I expect he'll drive over in a carriage from Daw's from the Almundham Station."

"I'm sure I don't know, dear," the elder and darker answered with a smile.—"But how awfully interested you seem to be, Winifred, in this celebrated cousin of mine! What a thing it is for a man to be a poet! You've talked of nothing else the whole morning."

Winifred laughed. "Cousins are so very rare in this part of the country, you see," she said apologetically. "We don't get sight of a cousin, you know—or, for the matter of that, of any other male human being, erect upon two legs, and with a beard on his face—twice in a twelvemonth. The live young man is rapidly becoming an extinct animal in these parts, I believe. He exists only in the form of a photograph. We shall soon have him stuffed, whenever we catch him, or exhibit a pair of his boots, with a label attached, in a glass case at all the museums, side by side with the dodo, and the something-or-other-osaurian. A live young man in a tourist suit is quite a rarity, I declare, nowadays.—And then a poet too! I never in my life set eyes yet upon a genuine all-wool unadulterated poet. —And you say he's handsome, extremely handsome! Handsome, and a poet, and a live young man, all at once, like three gentlemen rolled into one, as Mrs. Malaprop says: that's really something to make one's self excited about."

"Winifred! Winifred! you naughty bad girl!" Elsie laughed out, half in jest and half in earnest, "moderate your transports. You've got no sense of propriety in you, I do believe—and no respect for your instructress's dignity either. I oughtn't to let you talk on like that. It isn't becoming in the guardian of youth. The guardian of youth ought sternly to insist on due reticence in speaking of strangers, especially when they belong to the male persuasion.—But as it's only Hugh, after all, I suppose it really doesn't matter. I look upon Hugh, Winnie, like my own brother."

"What a jolly name, Hugh!" Winifred cried, enthusiastically. "It goes so awfully well together, too, Hugh Massinger. There's a great deal in names going well together. I wouldn't marry a man called Adair, now, Elsie, or O'Dowd, either, not if you were to pay me for it (though why you should pay me, I'm sure I don't know), for Winifred Adair doesn't sound a bit nice; and yet Elsie Adair goes just beautifully.—Winifred Challoner— that's not bad, either. Three syllables, with the accent on the first. Winifred Massinger—that sounds very well too; best of all, perhaps. I shouldn't mind marrying a man named Massinger."

"Other things equal," Elsie put in, laughing.

"Oh, of course he must have a moustache," Winifred went on in quite a serious voice. "Even if a man was a poet, and was called Massinger, and had lovely eyes, and could sing like a nightingale, but hadn't a moustache—a beautiful, long, wiry, black moustache, like the curate's at Snade—I wouldn't for the world so much as look at him. No close-shaven young man need apply. I insist upon a moustache as absolutely indispensable. Not red: red is quite inadmissible. If ever I marry— and I suppose I shall have to, some day, to please papa—I shall lay it down as a fixed point in the settlements, or whatever you call them, that my husband must have a black moustache, and must bind himself down by contract beforehand as long as I live never to shave it."

Elsie shaded her eyes with her hand and looked out seaward. "I shan't let you talk so any more, Winnie," she said, with a vigorous effort to be sternly authoritative. "It isn't right; and you know it isn't. The instructress of youth must exert her authority. We ought to be as grave as a couple of church owls.—What a funny small sailing-boat that is on the sea out yonder! A regular little tub! So flat and brong! She's the roundest boat I ever saw in my life. How she dances about like a walnut-shell on the top of the water!"

"Oh, that's the *Mud-Turtle!*" Winifred cried eagerly, anxious to display her nautical knowledge to the full extent before Elsie, the town-bred governess. "She's a painter's yawl, you know. I've seen her often. She belongs to an artist, a marine artist, who comes this way every summer to sketch and paint mud-banks. He lies by up here in the shallows of the creek, and does, oh, the funniest little pictures you ever saw, all full of nothing—just mud and water and weeds and herons—or else a great dull flat stretch of calm sea, with a couple of gulls and a buoy in the foreground. They're very clever, I suppose, for people who understand those things ; but, like the crater of Vesuvius, there's nothing in them. She can go anywhere, though, even in a ditch—the *Mud-Turtle* can ; and she sails like a bird, when she's got all her canvas on. You should just see her in a good breeze, putting out to sea before a fresh sou'-wester ! "

" She's coming in here now, I think," Elsie murmured, half aloud.—" Oh no, she's not; she's gone beyond it, towards the point at Walberswick."

" That's only to tack," Winifred answered, with conscious pride in her superior knowledge. " She's got to tack because of the wind, you know. She'll come up the creek as soon as she catches the breeze. She'll luff soon.—Look there, now ; they're luffing her. Then in a minute they'll put her about a bit, and tack again for the creek's mouth.—There you are, you see : she's tacking, as I told you.—That's the artist, the shorter man in the sailor's jersey. He looks like a common A.B. when he's got up so in his seafaring clothes; but when you hear him speak, you can tell at once by his voice he's really a gentleman. I don't know who the second man is, though, the tall man in the tweed suit : he's not the one that generally comes—that's Mr. Potts. But, oh, isn't he handsome ! I wonder if they're going to sail close alongside ? I do hope they are. The water's awfully deep right in by the poplar here. If they turn up the creek, they'll run under the roots just below us.—They seem to be making signs to us now.—Why, Elsie, the man in the tweed suit's waving his hand to you ! "

Elsie's face was crimson to look upon. As the instructress of youth, she felt herself distinctly discomposed. " It's my cousin," she cried, jumping up in a tremor of excitement, and waving back to him eagerly with her tiny handkerchief. " It's Hugh Massinger ! How very delightful ! He must have come down by sea with the painter."

" They're going to run in just close by the tree," Winifred exclaimed, quite excited also at the sudden apparition of the real live poet. " Oh, Elsie, doesn't he just look poetical ! A man with a face and eyes like that couldn't help writing poetry, even if he didn't want to. He must be a friend of Mr. Relf's, I suppose. What a lovely, romantic, poetical way to come down from London—tossing about at sea in a glorious breeze on a wee bit of a tub like that funny little *Mud-Turtle* ! "

By this time, the yawl, with the breeze in her sails, had run rapidly before the wind for the mouth of the river, and was close upon them by the roots of the poplar. As it neared the tree, Hugh stood up on the deck, bronzed and ruddy with his three days' yachting, and called out cheerily in a loud voice, " Hullo, Elsie, this is something like a welcome ! We arrive at the port, after a stormy passage on the high seas, and are met at its mouth by a deputation of the leading inhabitants. Shall we take you on board with your friend at once, and carry you up the rest of the way to Whitestrand ? "

Elsie's heart came up into her mouth. She would have given the world to be able to cry out cordially, " Oh, Hugh, that'd be just lovely ; " but propriety and a sense of the duties of her position compelled her instead to answer in a set voice, " Well, thank you ; it's ever so kind of you, Hugh ; but we're here in our own grounds, you know, already.—This is Miss Meysey, Winifred Meysey : Winnie, this is my cousin Hugh, dear. Now you know one another.—Hugh, I'm so awfully glad to see you ! "

Warren Relf turned the bow toward the tree, and ran the yawl close alongside till her tiny taffrail almost touched the roots of the big poplar. " That's better," he said.—" Now, Massinger, introduce us. You do it like a Lord Chamberlain, I know.—You won't come up with us, then, Miss Challoner ? "

Elsie bent her head. " We mustn't," she said candidly, " though I own I should like it.—It's so very long since I've seen you, Hugh. Where are you going to stop at in the village ? You must come up this very afternoon to see me."

Hugh bowed a bow of profound acquiescence. " If you say so," he answered with less languor than his wont, " your will is law. We shall certainly come up.—I suppose I may bring my friend Relf with me—the owner and skipper of this magnificent and luxurious vessel ?—We've had the most delightful passage down, Elsie. In future, in fact, I mean to live permanently upon a yawl. It's glorious fun. You sail all day before the free, free breeze ; and you dodge the steamers that try to run you down ; and you put up at night in a convenient creek ; and you sleep like a top on the bare boards ; and you live upon seabiscuit and bottled beer and the fresh sea-air ; and you feel like a king or a Berserker or a street arab ; and you wonder why the dickens you were ever such a stupid fool before as to wear black clothes, and lie on a feather-bed, and use a knife and fork, and eat olives and *pâté de foie gras*, and otherwise give way to the ridiculous foibles of an effete and superannuated western civilization. I never in my life felt anything like it. The blood of the old Sea-kings comes up in my veins, and I've been rhyming 'viking' and 'liking,' and 'striking' and 'diking,' ever since we got well clear of London Bridge, till this present moment.—I shall write a volume of Sonnets of the Sea, and dedicate them duly to you—and Miss Meysey."

As for Winifred, with a red rose spreading over all her face, she said nothing; but twirling her hat still in her hand, she gazed and gazed open-eyed, and almost open-mouthed—except that an open mouth is so very unbecoming—upon the wonderful stranger with the big dark eyes, who had thus dropped down from the clouds upon the manor of Whitestrand. He was handsome, indeed—as handsome as her dearest dreams; he had a black moustache, strictly according to contract; and he talked with an easy offhand airy grace—the easy grace of the Cheyne Row Club—that was wholly foreign to all her previous experience of the live young men of the county of Suffolk. His tongue was the pen of a ready writer. He poured forth language with the full and regular river-like flow of a practised London journalist and first-leader hand. Crisp adjectives to him came easy as Yes or No, and epigram flowed from his lips like water.

"I'll put her in nearer," Warren Relf said quietly, after a few minutes, glancing with mute admiration at Elsie's beautiful face and slim figure.—"We're in no hurry to go, of course, Massinger; we've got the whole day all free before us.—That's the best of navigating your own craft you see, Miss Challoner; it makes you independent of all the outer world beside. Bradshaw ceases to exercise over you his iron tyranny. You've never to catch the four-twenty. You go where you like; you stop when you please; you start when you choose; and if, when you get there, you don't like it, why you simply go on again till you reach elsewhere. It's the freest life, this life on the ocean wave, that ever was imagined; though I believe Byron has said the same thing already.—We'll lie by here for half an hour, Hugh, and if you prefer it, I'll put you ashore, and you can walk up through the grounds of the Hall, while I navigate the ship to the Fisherman's Rest, up yonder at Whitestrand."

As he spoke, he put over the boom for a moment, to lay her in nearer to the roots of the tree. It was an unlucky movement. Winifred was sitting close to the water's edge, with her hat in her hand, dangling over the side. The boom, flapping suddenly in the wind with an unexpected twirl, struck her wrist a smart blow, and made her drop the hat with a cry of pain into the current of the river. Tide was on the ebb; and almost before they had time to see what had happened, the hat had floated on the swift stream far out of reach, and was careering hastily in circling eddies on its way seaward.

Hugh Massinger was too good an actor, and too good a swimmer into the bargain, to let slip such a splendid opportunity for a bit of cheap and effective theatrical display. The

eyes of Europe and of Elsie were upon him—not to mention the
unknown young lady, who, for aught he knew to the contrary,
might perhaps turn out to be a veritable heiress to the manor
of Whitestrand. He had on his old gray tourist knickerbocker
suit, which had seen service, and would be none the worse, if it
came to that, for one more wetting. In a second, he had
pulled off his coat and boots, sprung lightly to the further deck
of the *Mud-Turtle*, and taken a header in his knickerbockers and
stockings and flannel shirt into the muddy water. In nothing
does a handsome man look handsomer than in knickerbockers
and flannels. The tide was setting strong in a fierce stream
ound the corner of the tree, and a few stout strokes, made all
the stouter by the consciousness of an admiring trio of specta-
tors, brought the eager swimmer fairly abreast of the truant hat
in mid-current. He grasped it hastily in his outstretched hand,
waved it with a flourish high above his head, and gave it a
twist or two of playful triumph, all wet and dripping, in his
graceful fingers, before he turned. An act of daring is nothing
if not gracefully or masterfully performed.—And then he
wheeled round to swim back to the yawl again.

In that, however, he had reckoned clearly without his host.
The water proved in fact a most inhospitable entertainer. Hand
over hand, he battled hard against the rapid current, tying the
recovered hat loosely around his neck by its ribbon strings, and
striking out vigorously with his cramped and trammelled legs
in the vain effort to stem and breast the rushing water. For a
minute or so he struggled manfully with the tide, putting all
his energy into each stroke of his thighs, and making his
muscles ache with the violence of his efforts. But it was all to
no purpose. The stream was too strong for him. Human thews
could never bear it down. After thirty or forty strokes, he
looked in front of him casually, and saw, to his surprise, not to
say discomfiture, that he was farther away from the yawl than
ever. This was distressing—this was even ignominious; to any
other man than Hugh Massinger, it would indeed have been
actually alarming. But to Hugh the ignominy was far more
than the peril: he was so filled with the sentimental and
personal side of the difficulty—the consciousness that he was
showing himself off to bad advantage before the eyes of two
beautiful girls—that he never even dreamt of the serious danger
of being swept out to sea and there drowned helplessly. He
only thought to himself how ridiculous and futile he must needs
look to that pair of womankind in having attempted with so
light a heart a feat that was utterly beyond his utmost powers.

Vanity is a mighty ruler of men. If Hugh Massinger had
stopped there till he died, he would never have called aloud for
help. Better death with honour, on the damp bed of a muddy

stream, than the shame and sin of confessing one's self openly beaten in fair fight by a mere insignificant tidal river. It was Elsie who first recognized the straits` he was in—for though love is blind, yet love is sharp-eyed—and cried out to Warren Relf in an agony of fear : " He can't get back! The stream's too much for him ! Quick, quick ! You've not a moment to lose ! Put about the boat at once and save him ! "

With a hasty glance, Relf saw she was right, and that Hugh was unable to battle successfully with the rapid current. He turned the yawl's head with all speed outward, and took a quick tack to get behind the baffled swimmer and intercept him, if possible, on his way towards the sea, whither he was now so quickly and helplessly drifting.

CHAPTER IV.

BURIDAN'S ASS.

For a minute the two girls stood in breathless suspense : then Warren Relf, cutting in behind with the yawl, flung out a coil of rope in a ring towards Hugh with true seafaring dexterity, so that it struck the water straight in front of his face flat like a quoit, enabling him to grasp it and haul himself in without the slightest difficulty. The help came in the nick of time, yet most inopportunely. Hugh would have given worlds just then to be able to disregard his proffered aid, and to swim ashore by the tree in lordly independence without extraneous assistance. It is grotesque to throw yourself wildly in, like a hero or a Leander, and then have to be tamely pulled out again by another fellow. But he recognized the fact that the struggle was all in vain, and that the interests of English literature and of a well-known insurance office in which he held a small life policy, imperatively demanded acquiescence on his part in the friendly rescue. He grasped the rope with a very bad grace indeed, and permitted Relf to haul him in, hand over hand, to the side of the *Mud-Turtle*.

Yet, as soon as he stood once more on the yawl's deck, dripping and unpicturesque in his clinging clothes, but with honour safe, and the lost hat now clasped tight in his triumphant right hand, it began to occur to him that, after all, the little adventure had turned out in its way quite as romantic, not to say effective, as could have been reasonably expected. He did not know the current ran so fast, or perhaps he would never have attempted the Quixotic task of recovering that plain straw hat with the blue ribbon—worth at best half a crown net—from its angry eddics; yet the very fact that he had exposed himself to danger, real danger, however unwittingly, on a lady's behalf, for so small a cause, threw a not unpleasing dash of romance and sentiment into his foolish and foolhardy bit of theatrical gallantry. To risk your life for a plain straw hat—and for a lady's sake—smacks, when one comes to think of it, of antique chivalry. He forgave himself his wet and unbecoming attire, as he handed the hat, with as graceful a bow as circumstances permitted, from the yawl's side to Winifred Meysey, who stretched out her hands, all blushes and thanks and apologetic regrets, from the roots of the poplar by the edge, to receive it.

"And now, Elsie," Hugh cried, with such virile cheerfulness as a man can assume who stands shivering in wet clothes before a keen east wind, "perhaps we'd better make our way at once up to Whitestrand without further delay to change our garments. Hood makes garments rhyme under similar conditions to 'clinging like cerements,' and I begin to perceive now the wisdom of his allusion. A very bad rhyme, but very good reason. They *do* cling, if you'll permit me to say so—they cling, indeed, a trifle unpleasantly.—Good-bye for the present. I'll see you again this afternoon in a drier and, I hope, a more becoming costume.—Miss Meysey, I'm afraid your hat's spoiled. —Put her about now, Relf. Let's run up quick. I don't mind how soon I get to Whitestrand."

Warren Relf headed the yawl round with the wind, and they ran merrily before the stiff breeze up stream towards the village. Meanwhile, Hugh stood still·on the deck in his dripping clothes, smiling as benignly as if nothing had happened, and waving farewell with one airy hand—in spite of chattering teeth—to Elsie and Winifred. The two girls, taken aback by the incident, looked after them with arms clasped round one another's waists. Winifred was the first to break abruptly the hushed silence of their joint admiration.

"Oh, Elsie," she cried, "it *was* so grand! Wasn't it just magnificent of him to jump in like that after my poor old straw? I never saw anything so lovely in my life. Exactly like the sort of things one reads about in novels!"

Elsie smiled a more sober smile of maturer appreciation. "Hugh's always so," she answered, with proprietary pride in her manly and handsome and chivalrous cousin. "He invariably does just the right thing at just the right moment; it's a way he has. Nobody else has such splendid manners. He's the dearest, nicest, kindest-hearted fellow——" She checked herself suddenly, with a flushed face, for she felt her own transports needed moderating now, and her praise was getting perhaps somewhat beyond the limits of due laudation as expected from cousins. A governess, even when she comes from Girton, must rise, like Cæsar's wife, above suspicion. It must be generally understood in her employer's family, that, though apparently possessed of a circulating fluid like other people's, she carries no such compromising and damaging an article as a heart about with her. And yet, if, as somebody once observed, there's " a deal of human nature in man," is it not perhaps just equally true that there's a deal of the self-same perilous commodity in woman also?

The men made their way up stream to Whitestrand, and landed at last, with an easy run, beside the little hithe. At the village inn—the Fisherman's Rest, by W. Stannaway—Hugh Massinger, in spite of his disreputable dampness, soon obtained comfortable board and lodging, on Warren Relf's recommendation. Relf was in the habit of coming to Whitestrand frequently, and was "well-beknown," as the landlord remarked, to the entire village, children included, so that any of his friends were immediately welcome at the quaint old public-house by the water's edge. For his own part the painter preferred the freedom of the yawl, where he paid of course neither rent nor taxes, and came and went at his own free-will; but as Massinger, not being a " vagrom man," meant to spend his entire summer holiday in harness at Whitestrand, he desired to have some more settled *pied-à-terre* for his literary labours than the errant *Mud-Turtle.*

"I'll change my clothes in a jiffy," the poet cried to his friend as he leapt ashore, " and be back with you at once, a new creature.—Relf, you'll stop and have some lunch, of course. —Landlord, we'd like a nice tender steak—you can raise a steak at Whitestrand, I suppose ?—That's well. Underdone, if you please.—Just hand me out my portmanteau there.—Thank you, thank you." And with a graceful bound, he was off to his room—a low-roofed old chamber on the ground-floor—as airy and easy as if nothing had ever occurred at all to ruffle his temper or disturb the affectedly careless set of his immaculate collar and his loosely knotted necktie.

In ten minutes he emerged again, as he had predicted, in the front room, another man—an avatar of glory—resplendent in a light-brown velveteen coat and Rembrandt cap, that served still more obviously than ever to emphasize the full nature and extent of his poetical pretensions. It was a coat that a laureate might have envied and dreamt about. The man who could carry such a coat as that could surely have written the whole of the " Divina Commedia " before breakfast, and tossed off a book or two of " Paradise Lost " in a brief interval of morning leisure.

"Awfully pretty girl that!" he said as he entered, and drummed on the table with impatient forefinger for the expected steak;—" the little one, I mean, of course—not my cousin. Fair, too. In some ways I prefer them fair. Though dark girls have more go in them, after all, I fancy; for dark and true and tender is the North, according to Tennyson. But fair or dark, North or South, like Horniman's teas, they're 'all good alike,' if you take them as assorted. And she's charmingly fresh and youthful and naive."

"She's pretty, certainly," Warren Relf replied, with a certain amount of unusual stiffness apparent in his manner; "but not anything like so pretty, to my mind, or so graceful either, as your cousin, Miss Challoner."

"Oh, Elsie's well enough in her own way, no doubt," Hugh went on, with a smile of expansive admiration. "I like them all in their own way. I'm nothing, indeed, if not catholic and eclectic. On the whole, one girl's much the same as another, if only she gives you the true poetic thrill. As Alfred de Musset calmly puts it, with delicious French bluntness, 'Qu'importe le goblet pourvu qu'on a l'ivresse?' Do you remember that delightful student song of Blackie's?—

> " 'I can like a hundred women;
> I can love a score;
> Only one with heart's devotion
> Worship and adore.'

I subscribe to that: all but the last two verses; about those I'm not quite so certain. As to loving a score, I've tried it experimentally, and I know I can manage it. But anyway, Elsie's extremely pretty. I've always allowed she's extremely pretty. The trouble of it is that she hasn't, unfortunately, got a brass farthing. Not a sou, not a cent, not a doit, not a stiver. I don't myself know the precise exchange value of doits and stivers, but I take them to be something exceptionally fractional. I could rhyme away (without prejudice) to Elsie and Chelsea and braes of Kelsie, or even at a pinch could bring in Selsey—you must know Selsey Bill, as you go in for yachting —if it weren't that I feel how utterly futile and purposeless it all is when a girl's fortune consists altogether of a negative quantity in doits and stivers. But the other—Miss Meysey, now—who's she, I wonder?—Good name, Meysey. It sounds like money, and it suggests daisy. There was a Meysey a banker in the Strand, you know—not very daisy-like, that, is it?—and another who did something big in the legal way—a judge, I fancy.—He doubtless sat on the royal bench of British Themis with immense applause (which was instantly suppressed), and left his family a pot of money. Meysey—lazy— crazy—hazy. None of them'll do, you see, for a sonnet but daisy. How many more Miss Meyseys are there, if any? I wonder. And if not, has she got a brother? So pretty a girl deserves to have tin. If I were a childless, rich old man, I

think I'd incontinently establish and endow her, just to improve
the beauty and future of the race, on the strictest evolutionary
and Darwinian principles."

"Her father's the Squire here," Warren Relf replied, with a
somewhat uneasy glance at Hugh, shot sideways. "He lords
the manor and a great part of the parish. Wyville Meysey's his
full name. He's rich, they [say, tolerably rich still; though a
big slice of the estate south of the river has been swallowed up
by the sea, or buried in the sand, or otherwise disposed of. The
sea's encroaching greatly on this coast, you know; some places,
like Dunwich, have almost all toppled over bodily into the
water, churches included; while in others, the shifting sand of
the country has just marched over the ground like a conquering
army, pitching its tent and taking up its quarters, to stay, in
the meadows. Old Meysey's lost a lot of land that way, I
believe, on the south side; it's covered by those pretty little
wave-like sandhills you see over yonder. But north of the river
they say he's all right. That's his place, the house in the fields,
just up beyond the poplar. I dare say you didn't notice it as
we passed, for it's built low—Elizabethan, half hidden in the
trees. All the big houses along the East Coast are always
planned rather squat and flat, to escape the wind, which runs
riot here in the winter, the natives say, as if it blew out of the
devil's bellows! But it's a fine place, the Hall, for all that, as
places go, down here in Suffolk. The old gentleman's connected
with the bankers in the Strand—some sort of a cousin or other,
more or less distantly removed, I fancy."

"And the sons?" Hugh asked, with evident interest, tracking
the subject to its solid kernel.

"The sons? There are none. They had one once, I believe
—a dragoon or hussar—but he was shot, out soldiering in Zululand or somewhere; and this daughter's now the sole living
representative of the entire family."

"So she's an heiress?" Hugh inquired, getting warmer at
last, as children say at Hide-and-seek.

"Ye-es. In her way—no doubt, an heiress.—Not a very big
one, I suppose, but still what one might fairly call an heiress.
She'll have whatever's left to inherit.—You seem very anxious
to know all about her."

"Oh, one naturally likes to know where one stands—before
committing one's self to anything foolish," Hugh murmured
placidly. "And in this wicked world of ours, where heiresses
are scarce—and actions for breach of promise painfully common
—one never knows beforehand where a single false step may
happen to land one. I've made mistakes before now in my
life; I don't mean to make another one through insufficient
knowledge, if I can help it."

He took up a pen that lay upon the table of the little sitting-room before him, and began drawing idly with it some curious characters on the back of an envelope he pulled from his pocket. Relf sat and watched him in silence.

Presently, Massinger began again. "You're very much shocked at my sentiments, I can see," he said quietly, as he glanced with approval at his careless hieroglyphics.

Relf drew his hand over his beard twice. "Not so much shocked as grieved, I think," he replied after a moment's pause.

"Why grieved?"

"Well, because, Massinger, it was impossible for any one who saw her this morning to doubt that Miss Challoner is really in love with you."

Hugh went on fiddling with the pen and ink and the envelope nervously. "You think so?" he asked, with some eagerness in his voice, after another short pause. "You think she really likes me?"

"I don't merely think so," Relf answered with confidence; "I'm absolutely certain of it—as sure as I ever was of anything. Remember, I'm a painter, and I have a quick eye. She was deeply moved when she saw you come. It meant a great deal to her.—I should be sorry to think you would play fast and loose with any girl's affections."

"It's not the girl's affections I play fast and loose with," Massenger retorted lazily. "I deeply regret to say it's very much more my own I trifle with. I'm not a fool; but my one weak point is a too susceptible disposition. I can't help falling in love—really in love—not merely flirting—with any nice girl I happen to be thrown in with. I write her a great many pretty verses; I send her a great many charming notes; I say a great many foolish things to her; and at the time I really mean them all. My heart is just at that precise moment the theatre of a most agreeable and unaffected flutter. I think to myself, 'This time it's serious.' I look at the moon, and feel sentimental. I apostrophize the fountains, meadows, valleys, hills, and groves to forebode not any severing of our loves. And then I go away and reflect calmly, in the solitude of my own chamber, what a precious fool I've been—for, of course, the girl's always a penniless one—I've never had the luck or the art yet to captivate an heiress; and when it comes to breaking it all off, I assure you it costs me a severe wrench, a wrench that I wish I was sensible enough to foresee or adequately to guard against, on the prevention-better-than-cure principle."

"And the girl?" Relf asked, with a growing sense of profound discomfort, for Elsie's face and manner had instantly touched him.

"The girl," Massinger replied, putting a finishing stroke or

two to the queer formless sketch he had scrawled upon the
envelope, and fixing it up on the frame of a cheap lithograph
that hung from a nail upon the wall opposite; "well, the girl
probably regrets it also, though not, I sincerely trust, so profoundly as I do. In this case, however, it's a comfort to think
Elsie's only a cousin. Between cousins there can be no harm,
you will readily admit, in a little innocent flirtation."

"It's more than a flirtation to her, I'm sure," Relf answered,
with a dubious shake of the head. "She takes it all *au grand
sérieux.*—I hope you don't mean to give her one of these horrid
wrenches you talk so lightly about?—Why, Massinger, what
on earth is this? I—I didn't know you could do this sort of
thing!"

He had walked across carelessly, as he paced the room, to the
lithograph in whose frame the poet had slipped the back of his
envelope, and he was regarding the little addition now with eyes
of profound astonishment and wonder. The picture was a
coarsely executed portrait of a distinguished statesman, reduced
to his shirt-sleeves, and caught in the very act of felling a tree;
and on the scrap of envelope, in exact imitation of the right
honourable gentleman's own familiar signature, Hugh had
written in bold free letters the striking inscription, "W. E.
Gladstone."

The poet laughed. "Yes, it's not so bad," he said, regarding
it from one side with parental fondness. "I thought they'd probably like to have the Grand Old Man's own genuine autograph;
so I've turned one out for them off-hand, as good as real, and twice
as legible. I flatter myself it's a decent copy. I can imitate
anybody's hand at sight.—Look here, for example; here's your
own." And taking another scrap of paper from a bundle in his
pocket, he wrote with rapid and practised mastery, "Warren H.
Relf" on a corner of the sheet in the precise likeness of the
painter's own large and flowing handwriting.

Relf gazed over his shoulder in some surprise, not wholly
unmingled with a faint touch of alarm. "I'm an artist, Massinger," he said slowly, as he scanned it close; "but I couldn't
do that, no, not if you were to pay me for it. I could paint
anything you chose to set me, in heaven above, or earth beneath,
or the waters that are under the earth; but I couldn't make a
decent fac-simile of another man's autograph.—And, do you
know, on the whole, I'm awfully glad that I could never possibly learn to do it."

Massinger smiled a languid smile. "In the hands of the
foolish," he said, addressing his soul to the beefsteak which had
at last arrived, "no doubt such abilities are liable to serious
abuse. But the wise man is an exception to all rules of life: he
can safely be trusted with edge-tools. We do well in refusing

firearms to children: grown people can employ them properly.
I'm never afraid of any faculty or knowledge on earth I possess.
I know seventeen distinct ways of cheating at loo, without the
possibility of a moment's detection, and yet that doesn't prevent
me, whenever I play, from being most confoundedly out of
pocket by it. The man who distrusts himself must be conscious
of weakness. Depend upon it, no amount of knowledge ever
hurts those who repose implicit confidence in their own prudence
and their own sagacity."

CHAPTER V.

ELECTIVE AFFINITIES.

THE Girton governess of these latter days stands on a very
different footing indeed in the family from the forty-pound-a-
year-and-all-found young person who instructed youth as a final
bid for life in the last generation. She ranks, in fact, in the
unwritten table of precedence with the tutor who has been a
university man; and, as the outward and visible sign of her
superior position, she dines with the rest of the household at
seven-thirty, instead of taking an early dinner in the school-
room with her junior pupils off hashed mutton and rice-
pudding at half-past one. Elsie Challoner had been a Girton
girl. She was an orphan, left with little in the world but her
brains and her good looks to found her fortune upon; and she
had wisely invested her whole small capital in getting herself an
education which would enable her to earn herself in after life a
moderate livelihood. In the family at Whitestrand, where she
had lately come, she lived far more like a friend than a governess: the difference in years between herself and Winifred was
not extreme; and the two girls, taking a fancy to one another
from the very first, became companions at once, so intimate
together that Elsie could hardly with an effort now and again
bring herself to exert a little brief authority over the minor
details of Winifred's conduct. And, indeed, the modern
governess, though still debarred the possession of a heart, is
now no longer exactly expected to prove herself in everything a
moral dragon: she is permitted to recognize the existence of
human instincts in the world we inhabit, and not even forbidden
to concede at times the abstract possibility that either she or
her pupils might conceivably get married to an eligible person,
should the eligible person at the right moment chance to
present himself, with the customary credentials as to position
and prospects.

“ I wonder, Elsie,” Winifred said, after lunch, “ whether your cousin will really come up this afternoon? Perhaps he won’t now, after that dreadful wetting. I dare say, as he only came down in the yawl, he hasn’t got another suit of clothes with him. I shouldn’t be surprised if he had to go to bed at the inn, as Mr. Relf does, while they dry his things for him by the kitchen fire! Mr. Relf never brings more, they say, than his one blue jersey.”

“ That’s not like Hugh,” Elsie answered confidently. “ Hugh wouldn’t go anywhere, by sea or land, without proper clothes for every possible civilized contingency. He’s not a fop, you know—he’s a man all over—but he dresses nicely and appropriately always. You should just see him in evening clothes; he’s simply beautiful then. They suit him splendidly.”

“ So I should think, dear,” Winifred answered with warmth. —“ I wonder, Elsie, whether papa and mamma will like your cousin ? ”

“ It’s awfully good of you, darling, to think so much of what sort of reception my cousin gets,” Elsie replied, with a kiss, in perfect innocence. (Winifred blushed faintly.) “ But, of course, your papa and mamma are sure to like him. Everybody always does like Hugh. There’s something about him that insures success. He’s a universal favourite, wherever he goes. He’s so clever and so nice, and so kind and so sympathetic. I never met anybody else so sympathetic as Hugh. He knows exactly beforehand how one feels about everything, and makes allowances so cordially for all one’s little private sentiments. I suppose that’s the poetic temperament in him. Poetry must mean at bottom, I should think, keen insight into the emotions of others.”

“ But not always power of responding sympathetically to those emotions.—Look, for example, at such a case as Goethe’s,” a clear voice said from the other side of the hedge. They were walking along, as they often walked, with arms clasped round one another’s waists, just inside the grounds, close to the footpath that led across the fields; and only a high fence of privet and dog-rose separated their confidences from the ear of the fortuitous public on the adjoining footpath. So Hugh had come up, unawares from behind, and overheard their confidential chit-chat! How far back had he overheard? Elsie wondered to herself. If he had caught it all, she would be so ashamed of herself!

“ Hugh ! ” she cried, running on to the little wicket gate to meet him. “ I’m so glad you’ve come. It’s delightful to see you. But oh, you must have thought us two dreadful little sillies. —How much of our conversation did you catch, I wonder ? ”

“ Only the last sentence,” Hugh answered lightly, taking both her hands in his and kissing her a quiet cousinly kiss on her

D

smooth broad forehead. "Just that about poetry meaning keen insight into the emotions of others ; so, if you were saying any ill about me, my child, or bearing false witness against your neighbour, you may rest assured at any rate that I didn't hear it.—Good-morning, Miss Meysey. I'm recovered, you see : dried and clothed and in my right mind—at least, I hope so. I trust the hat is the same also."

Winifred held out a timid small hand. "It's all right, thank you," she said, with a sudden flush; "but I shall never, never wear it again, for all that. I couldn't bear to. I don't think you ought to have risked your life for so very little."

"A life's nothing where a lady's concerned," Hugh answered airily, with a mock bow. "But indeed you give me credit for too much gallantry. My life was not in question at all; I only risked a delightful bath, which was somewhat impeded by an unnecessarily heavy and awkward bathing-dress.—What a sweet place this is, Elsie; so flowery and bowery, when you get inside it. The little lane with the roses overhead seems created after designs by Birket Foster. From outside, I confess, to a casual observer the first glimpse of East Anglian scenery is by no means reassuring."

They strolled up slowly together to the Hall door, where the senior branches were seated on the lawn, under the shade of the one big spreading lime-tree, enjoying the delicious coolness of the breeze as it blew in fresh from the open ocean. Elsie wondered how Hugh and the Squire would get on together; but her wonder indeed was little needed; for Hugh, as she had said, always got on admirably with everybody everywhere. He had a way of attacking people instinctively on their strong point; and in ten minutes, he and the Squire were fast friends, united by firm ties of common loves and common animosities. They were both Oxford men—at whatever yawning interval of time, that friendly link forms always a solid bond of union between youth and age; and both had been at the same college, Oriel. "I dare say you know my old rooms," the Squire observed, with a meditative sigh. "They looked out over Fellows' Quad, and had a rhyming Latin hexameter on a pane of stained glass in one of the bay windows."

"I know them well," Hugh answered, with a rising smile of genuine pleasure—for he loved Oxford with a love passing the love of her ordinary children. "A friend of mine had them in my time. And I remember the line: 'Oxoniam quare venisti premeditare.' An excellent leonine, as leonines go, though limp in its quantity.—Do you know, I fell in love with that pane so greatly, that I had a wire framework made to put over it, for fear some fellows should smash it some night, flinging about oranges at a noisy wine-party."

From Oxford, they soon got off upon Suffolk, and the encroachment of the sea, and the blown sands; and then the Squire insisted upon taking Hugh for a *tour du propriétaire* round the whole estate, with running comments upon the wasting of the foreshore and the abominable remissness of the Board of Admiralty in not erecting proper groynes to protect the interests of coast-wise proprietors. Hugh listened to it all with his grave face of profound sympathy and lively interest, putting in from time to time an acquiescent remark confirmatory of the wickedness of government officials in general, and of the delinquent Board of Admiralty in particular.

"Æolian sands!" he said once, with a lingering cadence, rolling the words on his tongue, as the Squire paused by the big poplar of that morning's adventure to point him out the blown dunes on the opposite shore—"Æolian sands! Is that what they call them? How very poetical! What a lovely word to put in a sonnet! Æolian—just the very thing of all others to go on all-fours with an adjective like Tmolian?—So it swallowed up forty acres of prime salt-marsh pasture—did it, really? That must have been a very serious loss indeed. Forty acres of prime salt-marsh! I suppose it was the sort of land covered with tall rank reedy grasses, where you feed those magnificent rough-coated, long-horned, Highland-looking cattle we saw this morning? Splendid beasts: most picturesque and regal. 'Bulls that walk the pastures in kingly-flashing coats,' George Mere.ith would call them. We passed a lot of them as we cruised ip stream to-day to Whitestrand.—And the sand has absolutely ᴜverwhelmed and wasted it all? Dear me! dear me! What a terrible calamity! It was the Admiralty's fault! Might make a capital article out of that to bully the government in the *Morning Telephone.*"

"If you did, my dear sir," the Squire said warmly, with an appreciative nod, "you'd earn the deepest gratitude of every owner of property in the county of Suffolk, and indeed along the whole neglected East Coast. The way we've been treated and abused, I assure you, has been just scandalous—simply scandalous. Governments, buff or blue, have all alike behaved to us with incredible levity. When the present disgraceful administration, for example, came into power—— "

Hugh never heard the remainder of that impassioned harangue, long since delivered with profound gusto on a dozen distinct election platforms. He was dimly aware of the Squire's voice, pouring forth denunciation of the powers that be in strident tones and measured sentences; but he didn't listen; his soul was occupied in two other far more congenial pursuits: one of them, watching Elsie and Winifred with Mrs. Meysey; the other, trying to find a practical use for Æolian sands in connection

with his latest projected eroic poem on the Burial of Alaric.
Æolian; dashes: Tmolian; abashes: not a bad substratum, that,
he flattered himself, for the thunderous lilt of his opening
stanza.

It was not till the close of the afternoon, however, that he
could snatch a few seconds alone with Elsie. They wandered
off by themselves then, near the water's edge, among the thick
shrubbery ; and Hugh, sitting down in a retired spot under the
lee of a sheltering group of guelder-roses, took his pretty cousin's
hands for a moment in his own, and looking down into her great
dark eyes with a fond look, cried laughingly, " Oh, Elsie, Elsie,
this is just what I've been longing for all day long. I thought
I should never manage to get away from that amiable old bore,
with his encroachments, and his mandamuses, and his groynes,
and his interlocutors. As far as I could understand him, he
wants to get the Board of Admiralty, or the Court of Chancery,
or somebody else high up in station, to issue instructions to the
east wind not to blow Æolian sands in future over his sacred
property. It's too grotesque: quite, quite too laughable. He's
trying to bring an action for trespass against the German Ocean.

' Will ye bridle the deep sea with reins ? will ye chasten the high sea with
　　rods ?
　Will ye take her to chain her with chains who is older than all ye gods ? '

Or will you get an injunction against her in due form on
stamped paper from the Lord Chief Justice of England ? Canute
tried it on, and found it a failure. And all the time, while the
good old soul was moaning and droning about his drowned
land, there was I, just sighing and groaning to get away to a
convenient corner with a pretty little cousin of mine with whom
I had urgent private affairs of my own to settle.—My dear Elsie,
Suffolk agrees with you. You're looking this moment simply
charming."

" It's your own fault, Hugh," Elsie answered, with a blush,
never heeding overtly his last strictly personal observation.
" You shouldn't make yourself so universally delightful. I'm
sure· I thought, by the way you talked with him, you were
absolutely absorbed in the wasting of the cliff, and personally
affronted by the aggressive east wind. I was just beginning to
get quite jealous of the encroachments.—For you know, Hugh,
it's such a real pleasure to me always to see you."

She spoke tenderly, with the innocent openness of an old
acquaintance; and Hugh, still holding her hand in his own,
leaned forward with admiration in his sad dark eyes, and put
out his face close to hers, as he had always done since they were
children together. " One kiss, Elsie," he said persuasively.—
" Quick, my child; we may have no other chance. Those

dreadful old bores will stick to us like leeches. 'Gather ye roses while you may: Old Time is still a-flying.'"

Elsie drew back her face half in alarm. "No, no, Hugh," she cried, struggling with him for a second. "We're both growing too old for such nonsense now. Remember, we've ceased long ago to be children."

"But as a cousin, Elsie," Hugh said, with a wistful look that belied his words.

Else preferred in her own heart to be kissed by Hugh on different grounds; but she did not say so. She held up her face, however, with a rather bad grace, and Hugh pressed it to his own tenderly. "That's paradise, my houri," he murmured low, looking deep into her beautiful liquid eyes.

"O son of my uncle, that was paradise indeed; but that was not like a cousin," she answered, with a faint attempt to echo his playfulness, as she withdrew, blushing.

Hugh laughed, and glanced idly round him with a merry look at the dancing water. "You may call it what you like," he whispered, with a deep gaze into her big dark pupils. "I don't care in what capacity on earth you consider yourself kissed, so long as you still permit me to kiss you."

For ten minutes they sat there talking—saying those thousand-and-one sweet empty things that young people say to one another under such circumstances—have not we all been young, and do not we all well know them?—and then Elsie rose with a sigh of regret. "I think," she said, "we mustn't stop here alone any longer; perhaps Mrs. Meysey wouldn't like it."

"Oh, bother Mrs. Meysey!" Hugh cried, with an angry side-ward toss of his head. "These old people are a terrible nuisance in the world. I wish we could get a law passed by a triumphant majority that at forty everybody was to be promptly throttled, or at least transported. There'd be some hope of a little peace and enjoyment in the world then."

"Oh, but, Hugh, Mrs. Meysey's just kindness itself, and I know she'll let you come and see me ever so often. She said at lunch I might go out on the water or anywhere I liked, whenever I chose, any time with my cousin."

"A very sensible, reasonable, intelligent old lady," Hugh answered approvingly, with a mollified nod. "I wish they were all as wise in their generation. The profession of chaperon, like most others, has been overdone, and would be all the better now for a short turn of judicious thinning.—But, Elsie, you've told them I was a cousin, I see. That's quite right. Have you explained to them in detail the precise remoteness of our actual relationship?"

Elsie's lip quivered visibly. "No, Hugh," she answered. "But why? Does it matter?"

"Not at all—not at all. Very much the contrary. I'm glad you didn't. It's better so. If I were you, my child, I think, do you know, I'd allow them to believe, in a quiet sort of way—unless, of course, they ask you point-blank, that you and I are first-cousins. It facilitates social intercourse considerably. Cousinhood's such a jolly indefinite thing, one may as well enjoy as long as possible the full benefit of its charming vagueness."

"But, Hugh, is it right? Do you think I ought to?—I mean, oughtn't I to let them know at once, just for that very reason, how slight the relationship really is between us?"

"The relationship is *not* slight," Hugh answered with warmth, darting an eloquent glance deep down into her eyes. "The relationship's a great deal closer, indeed, than if it were a much nearer one.—That may be paradox, but it's none the less true, for all that.—Still, it's no use arguing a point of casuistry with a real live Girton girl. You know as much about ethics as I do, and a great deal more into the bargain. Only, a cousin's a cousin anyhow; and I for my part wouldn't go out of my way to descend gratuitously into minute genealogical particulars of once, twice, thrice, or ten times removed, out of pure puritanism. These questions of pedigree are always tedious. What subsists all through is the individual fact that I'm Hugh, and you're Elsie, and that I love you dearly—of course with a purely cousinly degree of devotion."

"Hugh, you needn't always flourish that limitation in my face, like a broomstick."

"Caution, my dear child—mere ingrained caution—the solitary resource of poverty and wisdom. What's the good of loving you dearly on any other grounds, I should like to know, as long as poetry, divine poetry, remains a perfect drug in the publishing market? A man and a girl can't live on bread and cheese and the domestic affections, can they, Elsie? Very well, then, for the present we are both free. If ever circumstances should turn out differently—— " The remainder of that sentence assumed a form inexpressible by the resources of printer's ink, even with the aid of a phonetic spelling.

When they turned aside from the guelder-roses at last with crimson faces, they strolled side by side up to the house once more, talking about the weather or some equally commonplace and uninteresting subject, and joined the Meyseys under the big tree. The Squire had disappeared, and Winifred came out to meet them on the path. "Mamma says, Mr. Massinger," she began timidly, "we're going a little picnic all by ourselves on the river to-morrow—up among the sandhills papa was showing you. They're a delicious place to picnic in, the sandhills; and mamma thinks perhaps you wouldn't mind coming to join us, and

bringing your friend the artist with you. But I dare say you won't
care to come : there'll be only ourselves—just a family party."

"My tastes are catholic," Hugh answered jauntily. "I love
all innocent amusements—and most wicked ones. There's
nothing on earth I should enjoy as much as a picnic in the sandhills.—You'll be coming too, of course, won't you, Elsie ?—Very
well, then. I'll bring Relf, and the *Mud-Turtle* to boot. I know
he wants to go mud-painting himself. He may as well take us
all up in a body."

"We shall do nothing, you know," Winifred cried apologetically. "We shall only just sit on the sandhills and talk, or
pick yellow horned-poppies, and throw stones into the sea, and
behave ourselves generally like a pack of idlers."

",That'll exactly suit me," Hugh replied, with a smile. "My
most marked characteristics are indolence and the practice of
the Christian virtues. I hate the idea that when people invite
their friends to a feast they're bound to do something or other
definite to amuse them. It's an insult to one's intelligence; it's
degrading one to the level of innocent childhood, which has to
be kept engaged with Blindman's Buff and an unlimited supply
of Everton toffee, for fear it should bore itself with its own in-
anity. On that ground, I consider music and games at suburban
parties the resource of incompetence. Sensible people find
enough to amuse them in one another's society, without playing
dumb crambo or asking riddles. Relf and I will find more than
 nough, I'm sure, to-morrow in yours and Elsie's."

He shook hands with them all round and raised his hat in
farewell with that inimitable grace which was Hugh Massinger's
peculiar property. When he left the Hall that afternoon, he
left four separate conquests behind him. The Squire thought
this London newspaper fellow was a most sensible, right-minded,
intelligent young man, with a head on his shoulders, and a complete comprehension of the rights and wrongs of the intricate
riparian proprietors' question. Mrs. Meysey thought Elsie's
cousin was most polite and attentive, as well as an extremely
high-principled and excellent person. (Ladies of a certain age
are always strong on the matter of principles, which they discuss
as though they were a definitely measurable quantity, like money
or weight or degrees Fahrenheit.) Winifred thought Mr.
Massinger was a born poet, and oh, so nice and kind and
appreciative. Elsie thought dear darling Hugh was just the
same good, sweet, sympathetic old friend and ally and comforter
as ever. And they all four united in thinking he was very
handsome, very clever, very brilliant, and very delightful.

As for Hugh, he thought to himself, as he sauntered back by
the rose-bordered lane to the village inn, that the Squire was a
most portentous and heavy old nuisance; that Mrs. Wyville

Meysey was a comic old creature ; that Elsie was really a most charming girl ; and that Winifred, in spite of her bread-and-butter blushes, wasn't half bad, after all—for an heiress.

The heiress is apt to be plain and forbidding. She is not fair to outward view, as many maidens be. Her beauty has solid, not to say strictly metallic qualities, and resides principally in a safe at her banker's. To have tracked down an heiress who was also pretty was indeed, Hugh felt, a valuable discovery.

When he reached the inn, he found Warren Relf just returned from a sketching expedition up the tidal flats. " Well, Relf," he cried, " you see me triumphant. I've been reconnoitring Miss Meysey's outposts, with an ultimate view to possible siege operations. To judge by the first results of my reconnaissance, she seems a very decent sort of little girl in her own way. If sonnets will carry her by storm, I don't mind discharging a few cartloads of them from a hundred-ton-gun point-blank at her outworks. Most of them can be used again, of course, in case of need, in another campaign, if occasion offers."

" And Miss Challoner ? " Relf suggested, with some reproof in his tone. " Was she there too ? Have you seen her also ? "

" Yes, Elsie was there," the poet answered unconcernedly, as he rang the bell for a glass of soda-water. " Elsie was there, looking as charming and as piquante and as pretty as ever; and, by Jove ! she's the cleverest and brightest and most amusing girl I ever met anywhere up and down in England. Though she's my own cousin, and it's me that says it, as oughtn't to say it, she's a credit to the family. I like Elsie. At times, I've almost half a mind, upon my soul, to fling prudence to the winds, and ask her to come and accept a share of my poor crust in my humble garret.—But it won't do, you know—it won't do. *Sine Cerere et Baccho, friget Venus.* Either I must make a fortune at a stroke, or I must marry a girl with a fortune ready made to my hand already. Love in a cottage is all very well in its way, no doubt, with roses and eglantine—whatever eglantine may be—climbing round the windows; but love in a hovel— which is the plain prose of it in these hard times—can't be considered either pretty or poetical. Unless some Columbus of a critic, cruising through reams of minor verse, discovers my priceless worth some day, and divulges me to the world, there's no chance of my ever being able to afford anything so good and sweet as Elsie.—But the other one's a nice small girl of her sort too. I think for my part I shall alter and amend those quaint little verses of Blackie's a bit—make 'em run :

> 'I can like a hundred women ;
> I can love a score ;
> Only with a heart's devotion
> Worship three or four.' "

Relf laughed merrily in spite of himself.

Massinger went on musing in an undertone : " Not that I like the first and third lines as they stand, at all : a careful versifier would have insisted upon rhyming them. I should have made ' devotion ' chime in with ' ocean,' or ' lotion,' or ' Goshen,' or ' emotion,' or something of that sort, to polish it up a bit. There's very good business to be got out of ' emotion,' if you work it properly ; but ' ocean ' comes in handy, too, down here at Whitestrand. I'll dress it up into a bit of verse this evening, I think, for Elsie—or the other girl.—Winifred's her Christian name. Hard case, Winifred. ' Been afraid ' is only worthy of Browning, who'd perpetrate anything in the way of a rhyme to save himself trouble. Has a false Ingoldsby gallop of verse about it that I don't quite like. Winnie's comparatively easy, of course : you've got ' skinny ' and ' finny,' and ' Minnie ' and ' spinney.' But Winifred's a very hard case indeed. ' Winnie ' and ' guinea ' are good enough rhymes ; but not quite new : they've been virtually done before by Rossetti, you know :

> 'Lazy, laughing, languid Jenny,
> Fond of a kiss and fond of a guinea.'

But I doubt if I could ever consent to make love to a girl whose name's so utterly and atrociously unmanageable as plain Winifred.—Now, Mary—there's a name for you, if you like : with ' fairy ' and ' airy,' and ' chary ' and ' vagary,' and all sorts of other jolly old-world rhymes to go with it. Or, if you want to be rural, you can bring in ' dairy '—do the pretty-milkmaid business to perfection. But ' Winifred '—' bin afraid '—the thing's impossible. It compels you to murder the English language. I wouldn't demean myself—or I think it ought to be by rights bemean myself—by writing verses to her with such a name as that.—I shall send them to Elsie, who, after all, deserves them more, and will be flattered with the attention into the bargain."

At ten o'clock, he came out once more from his own room to the little parlour, where Warren Relf was seated " cooking " a sky in one of his hasty seaside sketches. He had an envelope in his hand, and a hat on his head. " Where are you off ? " Relf asked carelessly.

" Oh, just to the post," Hugh Massinger answered, with a gay nod. " I've finished my new batch of verses on the ocean— emotion—potion—devotion theme, and I'm sending them off, all hot from the oven, to my cousin Elsie.—They're not bad in their way. I like them myself. I shall print them, I think, in next week's *Athenæum.*

CHAPTER VI.

WHICH LADY?

HUGH found the day among the sandhills simply delightful. He had said with truth he loved all innocent pleasures, for his was one of those sunny, many-sided, æsthetic natures, in spite of its underlying tinge of pessimism and sadness, that throw themselves with ardour into every simple country delight, and find deep enjoyment in trees and flowers and waves and scenery, in the scent of new-mown hay and the song of birds, and in social intercourse with beautiful women. Warren Relf had readily enough fallen in with Hugh's plan for their day's outing; for Warren Relf in his turn was human too, and at a first glance he had been greatly taken with Hugh's pretty cousin, the dark-eyed Girton girl. His possession of the *Mud-Turtle* gave him for the moment a title to respect, for a yacht's a yacht, however tiny. So he took them all up together in the yawl to the foot of the sandhills; and while Mrs. Meysey and the girls were unpacking the hampers and getting lunch ready on the white slopes of the drifted dunes, he sat down by the shore and sketched a little bit of the river foreground that exactly suited his own peculiar style—an islet of mud, rising low from the bed of the sluggish stream, crowned with purple sea-aster and white-flowered scurvy-grass, and backed by a slimy bed of tidal ooze, that shone with glancing rays of gold and crimson in the broad flood of the reflected sunlight.

Elsie was very happy, too, in her way; for had she not Hugh all the time by her side, and was she not wearing the ardent verses she had received from him by post that very morning, inside her dress, pressed close against her heart, and rising and falling with every pulse and flutter of her bosom? To him, the handicraftsman, they were a mere matter of ocean, and potion, and lotion, and devotion, strung together on a slender thread of pretty conceit; but to her, in the innocent ecstasy of a first great love, they meant more than words could possibly utter.

She could not thank him for them; her pride and delight went too deep for that; and even were it otherwise, she had no opportunity. But once, while they stood together by the sounding sea, with Winifred by their side, looking critically at the picture Warren Relf had sketched in hasty 'outline, and began to colour, she found an occasion to let the poet know, by a graceful allusion, she had received his little tribute of verse in safety. As the painter with a few dainty strokes filled in the floating iridescent tints upon the sunlit ooze, she murmured aloud, as if quoting from some well-known poem

> " Red strands that faintly fleck and spot
> The tawny flood thy banks enfold ;
> A woof of Tyrian purple, shot
> Through cloth of gold."

Hugh looked up at her appreciatively with a smile of recognition. They were his own verses, out of the Song of the Char he had written and posted to her the night before. " Mere faint Swinburnian echoes, nothing worth," he murmured low in a deprecating aside; but he was none the less flattered at the delicate attention, for all that. " And how clever of her, too," he thought to himself with a faint thrill, " to have pieced them in so deftly with the subject of the picture! After all, she's a very intelligent girl, Elsie! A man might go further and fare worse—if it were not for that negative quantity in doits and stivers."

Warren Relf looked up also with a quick glance at the dark-eyed girl. " You're right, Miss Challoner," he said, stealing a lover's side-look at the iridescent peacock hues upon the gleaming mud. " It shines like opal. No precious stone on earth could be lovelier than that. Few people have the eye to see beauty in a flat of tidal mud like the one I'm painting; but cloth of gold and Tyrian purple are the only words one could possibly find to express in fit language the glow and glory of its exquisite colouring. If only I could put it on canvas now, as you've put it in words, even the Hanging Committee of the Academy, I believe—hard-hearted monsters—would scarcely be stony enough to dream of rejecting it."

Elsie smiled. How every man reads things his own way, by the light of his own personal interests! Hugh had seen she was trying to thank him unobtrusively for his copy of verses; Warren Relf had only found in her apt quotation a passing criticism on his own little water-colour.

After lunch, the two seniors, the Squire and Mrs. Meysey, manifested the distinct desire of middle age for a quiet digestion in the shade of the sandhills; and the four younger folks, nothing loth to be free, wandered off in pairs at their own sweet will along the bank of the river. Hugh took Elsie for his companion at first, while Warren Relf had to put himself off for the time being with the blue-eyed Winifred. Now Relf hated blue eyes. " But we must arrange it like a set of Lancers," Hugh cried with an easy flourish of his graceful hand; " at the end of the figure, set to corners and change partners." Elsie might have felt half jealous for a moment at this equitable suggestion, if Hugh hadn't added to her in a lower tone, and with his sweetest smile: " I mustn't monopolize you all the afternoon, you know, Elsie; Relf must have his innings too; I can see by his face he's just dying to talk to you."

"I'd rather a great deal talk with you, Hugh," Elsie murmured gently, looking down at the sands with an apparently sudden geological interest in their minute composition.

"I'm proud to hear it; so would I," Hugh answered gallantly. "But we mustn't be selfish. I hate selfishness. I'll sacrifice myself by-and-by on the altar of fraternity to give Relf a turn in due season. Meanwhile, Elsie, let's be happy together while we can. Moments like these don't come to one often in the course of a lifetime. They're as rare as rubies and as all good things. When they do come, I prize them far too much to think of wasting them in petty altercation."

They strolled about among the undulating dunes for an hour or more, talking in that vague emotional way that young men and maidens naturally fall into when they walk together by the shore of the great deep, and each very much pleased with the other's society, as usually happens under similar circumstances. The dunes were indeed a lovely place for flirting in, as if made for the purpose—high billowy hillocks of blown sand, all white and firm, and rolling like chalk downs, but matted together underfoot with a tussocky network of spurges and campions and soldanella convolvulus. In the tiny combes and valleys in between, where tall reed-like grasses made a sort of petty imitation jungle, you could sit down unobserved under the lee of some mimic range of mountains, and take your ease in an enchanted garden, like sultans and sultanas of the "Arabian Nights," without risk of intrusion. The sea tumbled in gently on one side upon the long white beach; the river ran on the other just within the belt of blown sandhills; and wedged between the two, in a long line, the barrier ridge of miniature wolds stretched away for miles and miles in long perspective towards the southern horizon. It was a lotus-eating place, to lie down and dream and make love in for ever. As Hugh sat there idly with Elsie by his side under the lee of the dunes, he wondered the Squire could ever have had the bad taste to object to the generous east wind which had overwhelmed his miserable utilitarian salt-marsh pastures with this quaint little fairyland of tiny knolls and Liliputian valleys. For his own part, Hugh was duly grateful to that unconscious atmospheric landscape gardener for his admirable additions to the flat Suffolk scenery; he wanted nothing better or sweeter in life than to lie here for ever stretched at his ease in the sun, and talk of poetry and love with Elsie.

At the end of an hour, however, he roused himself sturdily. Life, says the philosopher, is not all beer and skittles; nor is it all poetry and dalliance either. "Stern duty sways our lives against our will," say the " Echoes from Callimachus." It's all very well, at odd moments, to sport with Amaryllis in the shade, or with the tangles of Neæra's hair—for a reasonable period. But if Amaryllis has no money of her own, or if Neæra is a penniless governess in a country-house, the wise man must sacrifice sentiment at last to solid advantages; he must quit Amaryllis in search of Phyllis, or reject Neæra in favour of Vera, that opulent virgin, who has lands and houses, messuages and tenements, stocks and shares, and is a ward in Chancery. Face to face with such a sad necessity, Hugh now found himself. He was really grieved that the circumstances of the case compelled him to tear himself unwillingly away from Elsie; he was so thoroughly enjoying himself in his own pet way; but duty, duty—duty before everything! The slave of duty jumped up with a start.

"My dear child," he exclaimed, glancing hastily at his watch, "Relf will really never forgive me. I'm sure it's time for us to set to corners and change partners. Not, of course, that I want to do it myself. For two people who are *not* engaged, I think we've had a very snug little time of it here together, Elsie. But a bargain's a bargain, and Relf must be inwardly grinding his teeth at me.—Let's go and meet them."

Elsie rose more slowly and wistfully. "I'm never so happy anywhere, Hugh," she said with a lingering cadence, "as when you're with me."

"And yet we are *not* engaged," Hugh went on in a meditative murmur—"we're not engaged. We're only cousins! For mere cousins, our cousinly solicitude for one another's welfare is truly touching. If all families were only as united as ours, now! interpreters of prophecy would not have far to seek for the date of the millennium. Well, well, instructress of youth, we must look out for these other young people; and if I were you, experience would suggest to me the desirability of not coming upon them from behind too unexpectedly or abruptly. A fellow-feeling makes us wondrous kind. Relf is young, and the pretty pupil is by no means unattractive."

" I'd trust Winifred as implicity—— " Elsie began, and broke off suddenly.

"As you'd trust yourself," Hugh put in, with a little quiet irony, completing her sentence. " No doubt, no doubt; I can readily believe it. But even you and I—who are staider and older, and merely cousins—wouldn't have cared to be disturbed too abruptly just now, you know, when we were pulling soldanellas to pieces in concert in the hollow down yonder. I shall climb to the top of the big sandhill there, and from that specular mount—as Satan remarks in " Paradise Regained "—I shall spy from afar where Relf has wandered off to with the immaculate

Winifred.—Ah, there they are, over yonder by the beach, looking for pebbles or something—I suppose amber. Let's go over to them, Elsie, and change partners. Common politeness compels one, of course, to pay some attention to one's host's daughter."

As they strolled away again, with a change of partners, back towards the spot where Mrs. Meysey was somewhat anxiously awaiting them, Hugh and Winifred turned their talk casually on Elsie's manifold charms and excellences. "She's a sweet, isn't she?" Winifred cried to her new acquaintance in enthusiastic appreciation. "Did you ever in your life meet anybody like her?"

"No, never," Hugh answered with candid praise. Candour was always Hugh's special cue. "She's a dear, good girl, and I like her immensely. I'm proud of her too. The only inheritance I ever received from my family is my cousinship to Elsie; and I duly prize it as my sole heirloom from fifty generations of penniless Massingers."

"Then you're very fond of her, Mr. Massinger?"

"Yes, very fond of her. When a man's only got one relative in the world, he naturally values that unique possession far more than those who have a couple of dozen or so of all sexes and ages, assorted. Some people suffer from too much family; my misfortune is that, being a naturally affectionate man, I suffer from too little. It's the old case of the one ewe lamb; Elsie is to me my brothers and my sisters, and my cousins and my aunts, all rolled into one, like the supers at the theatre."

"And are you and she——" Winifred began timidly. All girls are naturally inquisitive on that important question.

Hugh broke her off with a quick, little laugh. "Oh dear no, nothing of the sort," he answered hastily, in his jaunty way. "We're not engaged, if that's what you mean, Miss Meysey; nor at all likely to be. Our affection, though profound, is of the brotherly and sisterly order only. It's much nicer so, of course. When people are engaged, they're always looking forward with yearning and longing and other unpleasant internal feelings, much enlarged upon in Miss Virginia Gabriel's songs, to a delusive future. When they're simply friends, or brothers and sisters, they can enjoy their friendship or their fraternity in the present tense, without for ever gazing ahead with wistful eyes towards a distant and ever-receding horizon."

"But why need it recede?" Winifred asked innocently.

"Why need it recede? Ah, there you pose me. Well, it needn't, of course, among the rich and the mighty. If people are swells, and amply provided for by their godfathers and godmothers at their baptism, or otherwise, they can marry at once; but the poor and the struggling—that's Elsie and me, you know, Miss Meysey—the poor and the struggling get engaged foolishly, and hope and hope for a humble cottage—the poetical cottage, all draped with roses and wild honeysuckle, and the well-attired woodbine—and toil and moil and labour exceedingly, and find the cottage receding, receding, receding still, away off in the distance, while they plough their way through the hopeless years, just as the horizon recedes for ever before you when you steer straight out for it in a boat at sea. The moral is—poor folk should not indulge in the luxury of hearts, and should wrap themselves up severely in their own interests, till they're wholly and utterly and irretrievably selfish."

"And are you selfish, I wonder, Mr. Massinger?"

"I try to be, of course, from a sense of duty; though I'm afraid I make a very poor hand at it. I was born with a heart, and do what I will, I can't quite stifle that irrepressible natural organ.—But I take it all out, I believe, in the end, in writing verses."

"You sent Elsie some verses this morning," Winifred broke out in an artless way, as if she were merely stating a common fact of every-day experience.

Hugh had some difficulty in suppressing a start, and in recovering his composure so as to answer unconcernedly: "Oh, she showed them to you, then, did she?" (How thoughtless of him to have posted those poor rhymes to Elsie, when he might have known beforehand she would confide them at once to Miss Meysey's sympathetic ear!)

"No, she didn't show them to me," Winifred replied, in the same careless easy way as before. "I saw them drop out of the envelope, that's all; and Elsie put them away as soon as she saw they were verses; but I was sure they were yours, because I know your handwriting—Elsie's shown me bits of your letters sometimes."

"I often send copies of my little pieces to Elsie before I print them," Hugh went on casually, in his most candid manner. "It may be vain of me, but I like her to see them. She's a capital critic, Elsie; women often are: she sometimes suggests to me most valuable alterations and modifications in some of my verses."

"Tell me these ones," Winifred asked abruptly, with a little blush.

It was a trying moment. What was Hugh to do? The verses he had actually sent to Elsie were all emotion and devotion, and hearts and darts, and fairest and thou wearest, and charms and arms; amorous and clamorous chimed together like old friends in one stanza, and sorrow dispelled itself to-morrow with its usual cheerful punctuality in the next. To recite them to Winifred as they stood would be to retire at once from his

half-projected siege of the pretty little heiress's heart and han
For that decisive step Hugh was not at present entirely prepared. He mustn't allow himself to be beaten by such a
scholar's mate as this. He cleared his throat, and began boldly
on another piece, ringing out his lines with a sonorous lilt—a
set of silly, garrulous, childish verses he had written long since,
but never published, about some merry sea-elves in an enchanted submarine fairy country.

> A tiny fay
> At the bottom lay
> Of a purple bay
>   Unruffled,
> On whose crystal floor
> The distant roar
> From the surf-bound shore
>   Was muffled.
>
> With his fairy wife
> He passed his life
> Undimmed by strife
>   Or quarrel ;
> And the livelong day
> They would merrily play
> Through a labyrinth gay
>   With coral.
>
> They loved to dwell
> In a pearly shell,
> And to deck their cell
>   With amber ;
> Or amid the caves
> That the riplet laves
> And the beryl paves
>   To clamber.

He went on so, with his jigging versicles, line after line, as they
walked along the firm white sand together, through several
foolish sing-song stanzas; till at last, when he was more than
half-way through the meaningless little piece, a sudden thought
pulled him up abruptly. He had chosen, as he thought, the
most innocent and non-committing bit of utter trash in all his
private poetical repertory ; but now, as he repeated it over to
Winifred with easy intonation, swinging his stick to keep time
as he went, he recollected all at once that the last rhymes flew
off at a tangent to a very personal conclusion—and what was
worse, were addressed, too, not to Elsie, but very obviously to
another lady ! The end was somewhat after this wise :

> On a darting shrimp
> Our quaint little imp
> With bridle of gimp
>   Would gambol ;

> Or across the back
> Of a sea-horse black
> As a gentleman's hack
>   He'd amble.
>
> Of emerald green
> And sapphire's sheen
> He made his queen
>   A tiar ;
> And the merry two
> Their whole life through
> Were as happy as you
>   And I are.

And then came the seriously compromising bit :

> But if you say
> You think this lay
> Of the tiny fay
>   Too silly,
> Let it have the praise
> My eye betrays
> To your own sweet gaze,
>   My Lily.
>
> For a man he tries,
> And he toils and sighs
> To be very wise
>   And witty ;
> But a dear little dame
> Has enough of fame
> If she wins the name
>   Of pretty.

Lily! Lily! Oh, that discomposing, unfortunate, compromising Lily! He had met her down in Warwickshire two seasons since, at a country-house where they were both staying, and had fallen over head and ears in love with her—then. Now, he only wished with all his heart and soul she and her fays were at the bottom of the sea in a body together. For of course she was penniless. If not, by this time she would no doubt have been Mrs. Massinger.

Hugh Massinger was a capital actor; but even he could hardly have ventured to pretend with a grave face that those Lily verses had ever been addressed to Elsie Challoner. Everything depended upon his presence of mind and a bold resolve. He hesitated for a moment at the "emerald green and sapphire's sheen," and seemed as though he couldn't recall the next line. After a minute or two's pretended searching he recovered it feebly, and then he stumbled again over the end of the stanza.

"It's no use," he cried at last, as if angry with himself. "I should only murder them if I were to go on now. I've forgotten the rest. The words escape me. And they're really not worth your seriously listening to."

"I like them," Winifred said in her simple way. "They're so easy to understand : so melodious and meaningless. I love verse that you don't have to puzzle over. I can't bear Browning for that—he's so impossible to make anything sensible out of. But I adore silly little things like these, that go in at one ear and out of the other, and really sound as if they meant something.—I shall ask Elsie to tell me the end of them."

Here was indeed a dilemma! Suppose she did, and suppose Elsie showed her the real verses! At all hazards, he must extricate himself somehow from this impossible situation.

"I wish you wouldn't," he said gently, in his softest and most persuasive voice. "Elsie mightn't like you to know I sent her my verses—though there's nothing in it—girls are so sensitive sometimes about these matters.—But I'll tell you what I'll do, if you'll kindly allow me; I'll write you out the end of them when I get home to the inn, and bring them written out in full, a nice clear copy, the next time I have the pleasure of seeing you." ("I can alter the end somehow," he thought to himself with a sudden inspiration, "and dress them up innocently one way or another with fresh rhymes, so as to have no special applicability of any sort to anybody or anything anywhere in particular.")

"Thank you," Winifred replied, with evident pleasure. "I should like that ever so much better. It'll be so nice to have a poet's verses written out for one's self in his own hand-writing."

"You do me too much honour," Hugh answered, with his mock little bow. "I don't pretend to be a poet at all; I'm only a versifier."

They joined the old folks in time by the yawl. The Squire was getting anxious to go back to his garden now—he foresaw rain in the sky to westward.

Hugh glanced hastily at his watch with a sigh. "I must be going back too," he cried. "It's nearly five now; we can't be up at the village till six. Post goes out at nine, they say, and I have a book to review before post-time. It must positively reach town not later than to-morrow morning. And what's worse, I haven't yet so much as begun to dip into it."

"But you can never read it, and review it too, in three hours!" Winifred exclaimed, aghast.

"Precisely so," Hugh answered in his jaunty way, with a stifled yawn; "and therefore I propose to omit the reading as a very unnecessary and wasteful preliminary. It often prejudices one against a book to know what's in it. You approach a work you haven't read with a mind unbiased by preconceived impressions. Besides, this is only a three-volume novel; they're all alike; it doesn't matter. You can say the plot is crude and ill-constructed, the dialogue feeble, the descriptions vile, the situations borrowed, and the characters all mere conventional puppets. The same review will do equally well for the whole stupid lot of them. I usually follow Sydney Smith's method in that matter; I cut a few pages at random, here and there, and then smell the paper-knife."

"But is that just?" Elsie asked quietly, a slight shade coming over her earnest face.

"My dear Miss Challoner," Warren Relf put in hastily, "have you known Massinger so many years without finding out that he's always a great deal better than he himself pretends to be? I know him well enough to feel quite confident he'll read every word of that novel through to-night, if he sits up till four o'clock in the morning to do it; and he'll let the London people have their review in time, if he telegraphs up every blessed word of it by special wire to-morrow morning. His wickedness is always only his brag; his goodness he hides carefully under his own extremely capacious bushel."

Hugh laughed. "As you know me so much better than I know myself, my dear boy," he replied easily, "there's nothing more to be said about it. I'm glad to receive so good a character from a connoisseur in human nature. I really never knew before what an amiable and estimable member of society hid himself under my rugged and unprepossessing exterior." And as he said it, he drew himself up, and darting a laugh from the corner of those sad black eyes, looked at the moment the handsomest and most utterly killing man in the county of Suffolk.

When Elsie and Winifred went up to their own rooms that evening, the younger girl, slipping into Elsie's bedroom for a moment, took her friend's hands tenderly in her own, and looking long and eagerly into the other's eyes, said at last in a quick tone of unexpected discovery: "Elsie, he's awfully nice-looking and awfully clever, this Oxford cousin of yours. I like him immensely."

Elsie brought back her eyes from infinity with a sudden start. "I'm glad you do, dear," she said, looking down at her kindly. "I wanted you to like him. I should have been dreadfully disappointed, in fact, if you didn't. I'm exceedingly fond of Hugh, Winnie."

Winifred paused for a second significantly; then she asked point-blank: "Elsie, are you engaged to him?"

"Engaged to him! My darling, what ever made you dream of such a thing?—Engaged to Hugh!—engaged to Hugh Massinger!—Why, Winnie, you know, he's my own cousin."

"But you don't answer my question plainly," Winifred per-

sisted with girlish determination. "Are you engaged to him or
are you not?"

Elsie, mindful of Hugh's frequent declarations, answered
boldly (and not quite untruthfully): "No, I'm not, Winifred."

The heiress of Whitestrand stroked her friend's hair with a
sigh of relief. That sigh was blind. Girl though she was, she
might clearly have seen with a woman's instinct that Elsie's
flushed cheek and downcast eyes belied to the utmost her spoken
word. But she did not see it. All preoccupied as she was with
her own thoughts and her own wishes, she never observed at all
those mute witnesses to Elsie's love for her handsome cousin.
She was satisfied in her heart with Hugh's and Elsie's double
verbal denial. She said to herself with a thrill in her own soul,
as a girl will do in the first full flush of her earliest passion:
"Then I may love him if I like! I may make him love me! It
won't be wrong to Elsie for me to love him!"

CHAPTER VII.

FRIENDS IN COUNCIL.

THAT same night, as the Squire and Mrs. Meysey sat by themselves towards the small-hours—after the girls had unanimously
evacuated the drawing-room—discussing the affairs of the
universe generally, as then and there envisaged, over a glass of
claret-cup, the mother looked up at last with a sudden glance
into the father's face, and said in a tone half-anxious, half-
timid: "Tom, did it happen to strike you this afternoon that
that handsome cousin of Elsie Challoner's seemed to take a
great fancy to our Winifred?"

The Squire stirred his claret-cup idly with his spoon. "I
suppose the fellow has eyes in his head," he answered bluntly.
"No man in his senses could ever look at our little Winnie, I
should think, Emily, and not fall over his ears in love with her."

Mrs. Meysey waited a minute or two more in silent suspense
before she spoke again; then she said once more, very tentatively: "He seems a tolerably nice young man, I think, Tom."

"Oh, he's well enough, I dare say," the Squire admitted
grudgingly.

"A barrister, he says. That's a very good profession," Mrs.
Meysey went on, still feeling her way by gradual stages.

"Never heard so in my life before," the Squire grunted out.
"There are barristers and barristers. He gets no briefs.
Lives on literature, by what he tells me: next door to living
upon your wits, I call it."

"But I mean, it's a gentleman's profession, anyhow, Tom, the bar."

"Oh, the man's a gentleman, of course, if it comes to that—a perfect gentleman; and an Oxford man, and a person of culture, and all that sort of thing—I don't deny it. He's a very presentable fellow, too, in his own way; and most intelligent: understands the riparian proprietors' question as easy as anything.—You can ask him to dinner whenever you choose, if that's what you're driving at."

Mrs. Meysey called another halt for a few seconds before she reopened fire, still more timidly than ever. "Tom, do you know I rather fancy he really likes our Winifred?" she murmured, gasping.

"Of course he likes our Winifred," the Squire repeated, with profound conviction in every tone of his voice. "I should like to know who on earth there is that doesn't like our Winifred! Nothing new in that. I could have told you so myself. Go ahead with it, then.—What next, now, Emily?"

"Well, I think, Tom, if I'm not mistaken, Winifred seemed rather inclined to take a fancy to him too, somehow."

Thomas Wyville Meysey laid down his glass incredulously on the small side-table. He didn't explode, but he hung fire for a moment. "You women are always fancying things," he said at last, with a slight frown. "You think you're so precious quick, you do, at reading other people's faces. I don't deny you often succeed in reading them right. You read mine precious often, I know, when I don't want you to—that I can swear to. But sometimes, Emily, you know you read what isn't in them. That's the way with all decipherers of hieroglyphics. They see a great deal more in things than ever was put there. You remember that time when I met old Hillier down by the copse yonder——"

"Yes, yes, I remember," Mrs. Meysey admitted, checking him at the outset with an astute concession. She had cause to remember the facts, indeed, for the Squire reminded her of that one obvious and palpable mistake about the young fox-cubs at least three times a week, the year round, on an average. "I was wrong that time; I know I was, of course. You weren't in the least annoyed with Mr. Hillier. But I think—I don't say I'm sure, observe, dear—but I think Winifred's likely to take a fancy in time to this young Mr. Massinger. Now, the question is, if she does take a fancy to him—a serious fancy—and he to her—what are you and I to do about it?"

As she spoke, Mrs. Meysey looked hard at the lamp, and then at her husband, wondering with what sort of grace he would receive this very revolutionary and upsetting suggestion. For herself—though mothers are hard to please—it may as well be admitted off-hand, she had fallen a ready victim at once to Hugh Massinger's charms and brilliancy and blandishments. Such a nice young man, so handsome and gentlemanly, so adroit in his talk, so admirable in his principles, and though far from rich, yet, in his way, distinguished! A better young man, darling Winifred was hardly likely to meet with. But what would dear Tom think about him? she wondered. Dear Tom had such very expansive not to say utopian ideas for Winifred —thought nobody but a Duke or a Prince of the blood half good enough for her: though, to be sure, experience would seem to suggest that Dukes and Princes, after all, are only human, and not originally very much better than other people. Whatever superior moral excellence we usually detect in the finished product may no doubt be safely set down in ultimate analysis to the exceptional pains bestowed by society upon their ethical education.

The Squire looked into his claret-cup profoundly for a few seconds before answering, as if he expected to find it a perfect Dr. Dee's divining crystal, big with hints as to his daughter's future; and then he burst out abruptly with a grunt: "I suppose we must leave the answering of that question entirely to Winnie."

Mrs. Meysey did not dare to let her internal sigh of relief escape her throat; that would have been too compromising, and would have alarmed dear Tom. So she stifled it quietly. Then dear Tom was not wholly averse, after all, to this young Mr. Massinger. *He*, too, had fallen a victim to the poet's wiles. That was well; for Mrs. Meysey, with a mother's eye, had read Winifred's heart through and through. But we must not seem to give in too soon. A show of resistance runs in the grain with women. "He's got no money," she murmured suggestively.

The Squire flared up. "Money!" he cried, with infinite contempt, "money! money! Who the dickens says anything to me about money? I believe that's all on earth you women think about.—Money indeed! Much I care about money, Emily. I dare say the young fellow hasn't got money. What then? Who cares for that? He's got money's worth. He's got brains; he's got principles; he's got the will to work and to get on. He'll be a judge in time, I don't doubt. If a man like that were to marry our Winifred, with the aid we could give him and the friends we could find him, he ought to rise by quick stages to be—anything you like—Lord Chancellor, or Postmaster-General, or Archbishop of Canterbury, for the matter of that, if your tastes happen to run in that direction."

"He hasn't done much at the bar yet," Mrs. Meysey continued, playing her fish dexterously before landing it.

“Hasn’t done much! Of course he hasn’t done much! How the dickens could he? Can a man make briefs for himself, do you suppose? He’s given himself up, he tells me, to earning a livelihood by writing for the papers. Penny-a-lining; writing for the papers. He had to do it. It’s a pity, upon my word, a clever young fellow like that—he understands the riparian proprietors’ question down to the very ground—should be compelled to turn aside from his proper work at the bar to serve tables, so to speak—to gain his daily bread by penny-a-lining. If Winifred were to take a fancy to a young man like that, now——” The Squire paused, and eyed the light through his glass reflectively.

“He’s very presentable,” Mrs. Meysey went on, rearranging her workbox, and still angling cleverly for dear Tom’s indignation.

“He’s a man any woman might be perfectly proud of,” the Squire retorted in a thunderous voice with firm conviction.

Mrs. Meysey followed up her advantage persistently for twenty minutes, insinuating every possible hint against Hugh, and leading the Squire deeper and deeper into a hopeless slough of unqualified commendation. At the end of that time she said quietly: “Then I understand, Tom, that if Winifred and this young Massinger take a fancy to one another, you don’t put an absolute veto on the idea of their getting engaged, do you?”

“I only want Winnie to choose for herself,” the Squire answered with prompt decision. “Not that I suppose for a moment there’s anything in this young fellow’s talking a bit to her. Men *will* flirt, and girls *will* let ’em. Getting engaged, indeed! You count your chickens before the eggs are laid. A man can’t look at a girl nowadays, but you women must take it into your precious heads at once he wants to go straight off to church and marry her. However, for my part, I’m not going to interfere in the matter one way or the other. I’d rather she’d marry the man she loves, and the man who loves her, whenever he turns up, than marry fifty thousand pounds and the best estate in all Suffolk.”

Mrs. Meysey had carried her point with honours. “Perhaps you’re right, dear,” she said diplomatically, as who should yield to superior wisdom. It was her policy not to appear too eager.

“Perhaps, I’m right!” the Squire echoed, half in complacency and half in anger. “Of course I’m right. I know I’m right, Emily. Why, I was reading in a book the other day a most splendid appeal from some philosophic writer or other about making fewer marriages in future to please Mamma, and more to suit the tastes of the parties concerned, and subserve the good of coming generations. I think it was an article in one of the magazines. It’s the right way, I’m sure of that; and in Winifred’s case I mean to stick to·

So, from that day forth, if it was Hugh Massinger's intention or desire to prosecute his projected military operations against Winifred Meysey's hand and heart, he found at least a benevolent neutral in the old Squire, and a secret, silent, but none the less powerful domestic ally in Mrs. Meysey. It is not often that a penniless suitor thus enlists the sympathies of the parental authorities, who ought by precedent to form the central portion of the defensive forces, on his own side in such an aggressive enterprise. But with Hugh Massinger, nobody ever even noticed it as a singular exception. He was so clever, so handsome, so full of promise, so courteous and courtly in his demeanour to young and old, so rich in future hopes and ambitious, that not the Squire alone, but everybody else who came in contact with his easy smile, accepted him beforehand as almost already a Lord Chancellor, or a Poet Laureate, or an Archbishop of Canterbury, according as he might choose to direct his talents into this channel or that; and failed to be surprised that the Meyseys or anybody else on earth should accept him with effusion as a favoured postulant for the hand of their only daughter and heiress. There are a few such universal favourites here and there in the world : whenever you meet one, smile with the rest, but remember that his recipe is a simple one—Humbug.

CHAPTER VIII.

THE ROADS DIVIDE.

HUGH stopped for two months or more at Whitestrand, and during all that time he saw much both of Elsie and of Winifred. The Meyseys introduced him with cordial pleasure to all the melancholy gaieties of the sleepy little peninsula. He duly attended with them the somnolent garden-parties on the smooth lawns of neighbouring Squires: the monotonous picnics up the tidal stream of the meandering Char; the heavy dinners at every local rector's and vicar's and resident baronets; with all the other dead-alive entertainments of the dullest and most stick-in-the-mud corner of all England. The London poet enlivened them all, however, with his never-failing flow of exotic humour, and his slow, drawled-out readiness of Pall-Mall repartee. It was a comfort to him, indeed, to get among these unspoiled and unsophisticated children of nature; he could palm off upon them as original the last good thing of that fellow Hatherley's from the smoking-room of the Cheyne Row Club, or fire back upon them, undetected, dim reminiscences of pungent chaff overheard in brilliant West-end drawing-rooms. And then, there were Elsie and Winifred to amuse him; and Hugh, luxurious, easy-going, epicurean philosopher that he was, took no trouble to decide in his own mind even what might be his ultimate intentions towards either fair lady, satisfied only, as he phrased it to his inner self, to take the goods the gods provided him for the passing moment, and to keep them both well in hand together. "How happy could I be with either," sings Captain Macheath in the oft-quoted couplet, "were t'other dear charmer away." Hugh took a still more lenient view of his personal responsibilities than the happy-go-lucky knight of the highway; he was quite content to be blest, while he could, with both at once, asking no questions, for conscience' sake, of his own final disposition, marital or otherwise, towards one or the other, but leaving the problem of his matrimonial arrangements for fate, or chance, to settle in its own good fashion.

It was just a week after his arrival at Whitestrand that he went up one morning early to the Hall. Elsie and Winifred were seated together on a rug under the big tree, engaged in reading one novel between them.

"You must wish Winifred many happy returns of the day," Elsie called out gaily, looking up from her book as Hugh approached them. "It's her birthday, Hugh; and just see what a lovely delightful present Mr. Meysey's given her!"

Winifred held out the present at arm's length for his admiraion. It was a pretty little watch, in gold and enamel, with her nitials engraved on the back on a broad shield. "It's just a veauty! I should love one like it myself!" Elsie cried enthusiastically. "Did you ever see such a dear little thing? It's keyless too, and so exquisitely finished. It really makes me feel quite ashamed of my own poor old battered silver one."

Hugh took the watch and examined it carefully. He noted the maker's name upon the dial, and, opening the back, made a rapid mental memorandum of the number. A sudden thought had flashed across him at the moment. He waited only a few minutes at the Hall, and then asked the two girls if they could walk down into the village with him. He had a telegram to send off, he said, which he had only just that moment remembered. Would they mind stepping over with him as far as the post-office?

They strolled together into the sleepy High Street. At the office, Hugh wrote and sent off his telegram. It was addressed to a well-known firm of watchmakers in Ludgate Hill. "Could you send me by to-morrow evening's post, to address as below, a lady's gold and enamel watch, with initials 'E. C., from H. M,' engraved on shield on back, but in every other respect precisely similar to No. 2479 just supplied to Mr. Meysey, of Whitestrand

Hall ?   If so, telegraph back cash-price at once, and cheque for
amount shall be sent immediately.   Reply paid.—Hugh Massinger, Fisherman's Rest, Whitestrand, Suffolk."

Before lunch-time the reply had duly arrived : " Watch shall
be sent on receipt of cheque.   Price twenty-five guineas."   So
far, good.   It was a fair amount for a journeyman journalist to
pay for a present ; but, as Hugh shrewdly reflected, it would
kill two birds with one stone.   Day after to-morrow was Elsie's
birthday.   The watch would give Elsie pleasure ; and Hugh, to
do him justice, thoroughly loved giving pleasure to anybody,
especially a pretty girl, and above all Elsie.   But it could also
do him no harm in the Meyseys' eyes to see that, journeyman
journalist as he was, he was earning enough to afford to throw
away twenty-five guineas on a mere present to a governess-cousin.
There is a time for economy, and there is a time for lavishness.
The present moment clearly came under the latter category.

On the second morning, true to promise, the watch arrived by
the early post ; and Hugh took it up with pride to the Hall, to
bestow it in a casual way upon poor breathless and affectionate
Elsie.   He took it up for a set purpose.   He would show these
purse-proud landed aristocrats that his cousin could sport as
good a watch any day as their own daughter.   The Massingers
themselves had been landed aristocrats—not presumably purse-
proud—in their own day in dear old Devonshire ; but the
estates had disappeared in houses and port and riotous living
two generations since ; and Hugh was now proving in his own
person the truth of the naif old English adage—" When land is
gone and money spent, then larning is most excellent."   Journalism is a poor sort of trade in its way ; but at any rate an able
man can earn his bread and salt at it somehow.   Hugh didn't
grudge those twenty-five guineas ; he regarded them, as he
regarded his poems, in the light of a valuable long investment.
They were a sort of indirect double bid for the senior Meyseys'
respect, and for Winifred's fervent admiration.   When a man is
paying attentions to a pretty girl, there's nothing on earth
he desires so much as to appear in her eyes lavishly generous.
A less abstruse philosopher, however, might perhaps have
bestowed his generosity direct upon Winifred *in propriâ
personâ :* Hugh, with his subtler calculation of long odds and
remote chances, deemed it wiser to display it in the first
instance obliquely upon Elsie.   This was an acute little piece
of psychological byplay.   A man who can make a present like
that to a poor cousin, with whom he stands upon a purely
cousinly footing, must be, after all, not only generous, but a
ripping good fellow into the bargain.   How would he not
comport himself under similar circumstances to the maiden of
his choice, and to the wife of his bosom ?

Elsie took the watch, when Hugh produced it, with a little cry of delight and surprise; then, looking at the initials so hastily engraved in neat Lombardic letters on the back, the tears rose to her eyes irrepressibly as she said, with a gentle pressure of his hand in hers: "I know now, Hugh, what that telegram was about the other morning. How very, very kind and good of you to think of it. But I almost wish you hadn't given it to me. I shall never forgive myself for having said before you I should like one the same sort as Winifred's. I'm quite ashamed of your having thought I meant to hint at it."

"Not at all," Hugh answered, with just the faintest possible return of her gentle pressure. "I was twisting it over in my own mind what on earth I could ever find to give you. I thought first of a copy of my last little volume; but then that's nothing—I'm only too sensible myself of its small worth. A book from an author is like spoiled peaches from a market-gardener: he gives them away only when he has a glut of them. So, when you said you'd like a watch of the same sort as Miss Meysey's, it seemed to me a perfect interposition of chance on my behalf. I knew what to get, and I got it at once. I'm only glad those London watchmaker fellows, whose respected name I've quite forgotten, had time to engrave your initials on it."

"But, Hugh, it must have cost you such a mint of money."

Hugh waved a deprecatory hand with airy magnificence over he broad shrubbery. "A mere trifle," he said, as who could ommand thousands. "It came just to the exact sum the *Contemporary* paid me for that last article of mine on 'The Future of Marriage.'" (Which was quite true, the article in question having run to precisely twenty-five pages, at the usual honorarium of a guinea a page.) "It took me a few hours only to dash it off." (Which was scarcely so accurate, it not being usual for even the most abandoned or practised of journalists to "dash off" articles for a leading review; and the mere physical task of writing twenty-five pages of solid letterpress being considerably greater than most men, however rapid their pens, could venture to undertake in a few hours.)

Winifred looked up at him with a timid glance. "It's a lovely watch," she said, taking it over with an admiring look from Elsie: "and the inscription makes it ever so much nicer. One would prize it, of course, for that alone. But if I'd been Elsie, I'd a thousand times rather have had a volume of poems, with the author's autograph dedication, than all the watches in all England."

"Would you?" Hugh answered, with an amused smile. "You rate the autographs of a living versifier immensely above their market value. Even Tennyson's may be bought at a shop in the Strand, you know, for a few shillings. I feel this indeed fame. I shall begin to grow conceited soon at this rate.—And by the way, Elsie, I've brought you a little bit of verse too. Your Laureate has not forgotten or neglected his customary duty. I shall expect a butt of sack in return for these: or may I venture to take it out instead in nectar ?" They stood all three behind a group of syringa bushes. He touched her lips with his own lightly as he spoke. "Many happy returns of the day —as a cousin," he added, laughing.—"And now, what's your programme for the day, Elsie ?"

"We want you to row us up the river to Snade, if it's not too hot, Hugh," his pretty cousin responded, all blushes.

"'Tuus, O Regina, quid optes, Explorare labor; mihi jussa capessere fas est," Hugh quoted merrily. "That's the best of talking to a Girton girl, you see. You can fire off your most epigrammatic Latin quotation at her, as it rises to your lips, and she understands it. How delightful that is, now. As a rule, my Latin quotations, which are frequent and free, as Truthful James says, besides being neat and appropriate, like after-dinner speeches, fall quite flat upon the stony ground of the feminine intelligence—which last remark, I flatter myself, in the matter of mixed metaphor, would do credit to Sir Bôyle Roche in his wildest flight of Hibernian eloquence. I made a lovely Latin pun at a picnic once. We had some chicken and ham sausage—a great red German sausage of the polony order, in a sort of huge boiled-lobster-coloured skin; and towards the end of lunch, somebody asked me for another slice of it. 'There isn't any,' said I. 'It's all gone. Finis Poloniæ!' Nobody laughed. They didn't know that 'Finis Poloniæ' were the last words uttered by a distinguished patriot and soldier, 'when Freedom shrieked as Kosciusko fell.' That comes of firing off your remarks, you see, quite above the head of your respected audience."

"But what does that mean that you just said this minute to Elsie ?" Winifred asked doubtfully.

"What! A lady in these latter days who doesn't talk Latin !" Hugh cried, with pretended rapture. "This is too delicious! I hardly expected such good fortune. I shall have the well-known joy, then, of explaining my own feeble little joke, after all, and grimly translating my own poor quotation. It means, 'Thy task it is, O Queen, to state thy will: Mine, thy behests to serve for good or ill.' Rough translation, not necessarily intended for publication, but given merely as a guarantee of good faith, as the newspapers put it. Æolus makes the original remark to Juno in the first 'Æneid,' when he's just about to raise the wind—literally, not figuratively—on her behalf, against the unfortunate Trojans. He was then occupying the same post as clerk of the weather, that is now filled jointly by the correspondent of the *New York Herald* and Mr. Robert Scott of the Meteorological Office. I hope they'll send us no squalls to-day, if you and Mrs. Meysey are going up the river with us."

On their way to the boat, Hugh stopped a moment at the inn to write hastily another telegram. It was to his London publisher: "Please kindly send a copy of 'Echoes from Callimachus,' by first post to my address as under." And in five minutes more, the telegram despatched, they were all rowing up stream in a merry party toward Snade meadows. Hugh's plan of campaign was now finally decided. He had nothing to do but to carry out in detail his siege operations.

In the meadows he had ten minutes or so alone with Winifred. "Why, Mr. Massinger," she said, with a surprised look, "was it you, then, who wrote that lovely article, in the *Contemporary*, on 'The Future of Marriage,' we've all been reading?"

"I'm glad you liked it," Hugh answered, with evident pleasure; "and I suppose it's no use now trying any longer to conceal the fact that I was indeed the culprit."

"But there's another name to it," Winifred murmured in reply. "And Mamma thought it must be Mr. Stone, the novelist."

"Habitual criminals are often wrongly suspected," Hugh answered, with a languid laugh. "I didn't put my own name to it, however, because I was afraid it was a trifle sentimental, and I hate sentiment. Indeed, to say the truth—it was a cruel trick, perhaps, but I imitated many of Stone's little mannerisms, because I wanted people to think it was really Stone himself who wrote it. But for all that, I believe it all—every word of it, I assure you, Miss Meysey."

"It was a lovely article," Winifred cried, enthusiastically. "Papa read it, and was quite enchanted with it. He said it was so sensible—just what he's always thought about marriage himself, though he never could get anybody else to agree with him. And I liked it too, if you won't think it dreadfully presumptuous of a girl to say so. I thought it took such a grand, beautiful, ethereal point of view, all up in the clouds, you know, with no horrid earthy materialism or nonsense of any sort to clog and spoil it. I think it was splendid, all that you said about its being treason to the race to take account of wealth or position, or prospects or connections, or any other worldly consideration, in choosing a husband or wife for one's self—and that one ought rather to be guided by instinct alone, because instinct—or love, as we call it—was the voice of nature speaking within us.—Papa said that was beautifully put. And I thought it was really true as well. I thought it was just what a great prophet would have said if he were alive to say it; and that the man who wrote it——" She paused, breath-less, partly because she was quite abashed by this time at her own temerity, and partly because Hugh Massinger, wicked man! was actually smiling a covert smile through the corners of his mouth at her youthful enthusiasm.

The pause sobered him. "Miss Meysey," he broke in, with unwonted earnestness, and with a certain strange tinge of sub-dued melancholy in his tremulous voice, "I didn't mean to laugh at you. I really believe it. I believe in my heart every single word of what I said there. I believe a man—or a woman either—ought to choose in marriage just the one other special person towards whom their own hearts inevitably lead them. I believe it all—I believe it without reserve. Money or rank, or connection or position, should be counted as nothing. We should go simply where nature leads us; and nature will never lead us astray. For nature is merely another name for the will of heaven made clear within us."

Ingenuous youth blushed itself crimson. "I believe so too," the timid girl answered in a very low voice and with a heaving bosom.

He looked her through and through with his large dark eyes. She shrank and fluttered before his searching glance. Should he put out a velvet paw for his mouse now, or should he play with it artistically a little longer? Too much precipitancy spoils the fun. Better wait till the " Echoes from Callimachus " had arrived. They were very fetching. And then, besides— besides, he was not entirely without a conscience. A man should think neither of wealth nor position, nor prospects nor connections, in choosing himself a partner for life. His own heart led him straight towards Elsie, not towards Winifred. Could he turn his back upon it, with those words on his lips, and trample poor Elsie's tender heart under foot ruthlessly? Principle demanded it; but he had not the strength of mind to follow principle at that precise moment. He looked long and deep into Winifred's eyes. They were pretty blue eyes, though pale and mawkish by the side of Elsie's. Then he said with a sudden downcast, half-awkward glance—that consum-mate actor—"I think we ought to go back to your mother now, Miss Meysey."

Winifred sighed. Not yet! Not yet! But he had looked at her hard! he had fluttered and trembled! He was sum-moning up courage. She felt sure of that. He didn't venture as yet to assault her openly. Still, she was certain he did really like her; just a little bit, if only a little.

Next morning, as she strolled alone on the lawn, a village boy in a corduroy suit came lounging up from the inn, in rustic *insouciance*, with a small parcel dangling by a string from his little finger. She knew the boy, and called him quickly towards her. "Dick," she cried, "what's that you've got there?"

The boy handed it to her with a mysterious nod. "It's for you, miss," he said, in his native Suffolk, screwing up his face sideways into a most excruciating pantomimic expression of the profoundest secrecy. "The gentleman at our house,—him wooth the black moostosh, ye know—he towd me to give it to yow, into yar own hands, he say, if I could manage to ketch ye aloon anyhow. He fared partickler about yar own hands. I heen't got to wait, cos he say, there oon't be noo answer."

Winifred tore the packet open with trembling hands. It was a neat little volume, in a dainty delicate sage-green cover—"Echoes from Callimachus, and other Poems;" by Hugh Massinger, sometime Fellow of Oriel College, Oxford. She turned at once with a flutter from the title-page to the fly-leaf: "A Mlle. Winifred Meysey; Hommage de l'auteur." She only waited a moment to slip a shilling into Dick's hand, and then rushed up, all crimson with delight, into her own bed-room. Twice she pressed the flimsy little sage-green volume in an ecstasy to her lips; then she laid it hastily in the bottom of a drawer, under a careless pile of handkerchiefs and lace bodices. She wouldn't tell even Elsie of that tardy much-prized birthday gift. No one but herself must ever know Hugh Massinger had sent her his volume of poems.

When Dick returned to the inn ten minutes later, environed n a pervading odour of peppermint, the indirect result of Vinifred Meysey's shilling, Hugh called him in lazily with his quiet authoritative air to the prim little parlour, and asked him in an undertone to whom he had given the precious parcel.

"To the young lady harself," Dick answered confidentially, thrusting the bull's-eye with his tongue into his pouched cheek. "I give it to har behind the laylacs, too, where noo'one coon't see us."

"Dick," Hugh Massinger said, in a profoundly persuasive and sententious voice, laying his hand magisterially on the boy's shoulder, "you're a sharp lad; and if you develop your talents steadily in this direction, you may rise in time from the distinguished post of gentleman's gentleman to be a private detective or confidential agent, with an office of your own at the top of Regent Street. Dick, say nothing about this on any account to anybody; and there, my boy—there's half a crown for you."

"The young lady ha' gin me one shillen a'ready," Dick replied with alacrity, pocketing the coin with a broad grin. Business was brisk indeed this morning.

"The young lady was well advised," Hugh answered grimly. "They're cheap at the price—dirt cheap, I call it, those immortal poems—with an autograph inscription by the bard in person.—And I've done a good stroke of business myself too. The 'Echoes from Callimachus' are a capital landing-net. If they don't succeed in bringing her out, all flapping, on the turf, gaffed and done for, a pretty speckled prey, why, no angler on earth that ever fished for women will get so much as a tiny rise out of her.—It's a very fair estate still, is Whitestrand. 'Paris vaut bien une messe,' said Henri. I must make some little sacrifices myself if I want to conquer Whitestrand fair and even."

"Paris vaut bien une messe," indeed. Was Whitestrand worth sacrificing Elsie Challoner's heart for?

CHAPTER IX.

HIGH-WATER.

MEANWHILE, Warren Relf, navigating the pervasive and ubiquitous little *Mud-Turtle*, had spent his summer congenially in cruising in and out of Essex mud-flats and Norfolk broads, accompanied by his friend and chum Potts, the marine painter—now lying high and dry with the ebbing tide on some broad bare bank of ribbed sand, just relieved by a battle-royal of gulls and rooks from the last reproach of utter monotony ; now working hard at the counterfeit presentment of a green-grown wreck, all picturesque with waving tresses of weed and sea-wrack, in some stranded estuary of the Thames backwaters ; and now again tossing and lopping on the uneasy bosom of the German Ocean, whose rise and fall would seem to suggest to a casual observer's mind the physiological notion that its own included crabs and lobsters had given it a prolonged and serious fit of marine indigestion. For a couple of months at a stretch the two young artists had toiled away ceaselessly at their labour of love, painting the sea itself and all that therein is, with the eyots, creeks, rivers, sands, cliffs, banks, and inlets adjacent, in every variety of mood or feature, from its glassiest calm to its angriest tempest, with endless patience, delight, and satisfaction. They enjoyed their work, and their work repaid them, It was almost all the payment they ever got, indeed, for, like loyal sons of the Cheyne Row Club, the crew of the *Mud-Turtle* were not successful. And now, as September was more than half through, Warren Relf began to bethink him at last of Hugh Massinger, whom he had left in rural ease on dry land at Whitestrand under a general promise to return for him "in the month of the long decline of roses," some time between the 15th and the 20th. So,

on a windy morning, about that precise period of the year, with
a north-easterly breeze setting strong across the North Sea, and
a falling barometer threatening squalls, according to the printed
weather report, he made his way out of the mouth of the Yare,
and turned southward before the flowing tide in the direction
of Whitestrand.

The sea was running high and splendid, and the two young
painters, inured to toil and accustomed to danger, thoroughly
enjoyed its wild magnificence. A storm to them was a study in
action. They could take notes calmly of its fiercest moments.
Almost every wave broke over the deck; and the patient little
Mud-Turtle, with her flat bottom and centre-board keel, tossed
about like a walnut shell on the surface of the water, or drove
her nose madly from time to time into the crest of a billow, to
emerge triumphant one moment later, all shining and dripping
with sticky brine, in the deep trough on the other side. Painting
in such a sea was of course simply impossible; but Warren Relf,
who loved his art with supreme devotion, and never missed an
opportunity of catching a hint from his ever-changing model
under the most unpromising circumstances, took out pencil and
paper a dozen times in the course of the day to preserve at least
in black and white some passing aspect of her mutable features.
Potts for the most part managed sheet and helm; while Relf,
in the intervals of luffing or tacking, holding hard to the mainmast with his left arm, and with the left hand just grasping his
drawing-pad on the other side of the mast, jotted hastily down
with his right whatever peculiar form of spray or billow happened for the moment to catch and impress his artistic fancy.
It was a glorious day for those who liked it; though a land-
lubber would no doubt have roundly called it a frightful
voyage.

They had meant to make Whitestrand before evening; but
half-way down, an incident of a sort that Warren Relf could
never bear to miss intervened to delay them. They fell in
casually with a North Sea trawler, disabled and distressed by
last night's gale, now scudding under bare poles before the free
breeze, that churned and whitened the entire surface of the
German Ocean. The men on board were in sore straits, though
not as yet in immediate danger; and the yawl gallantly stood in
close by her, to pick up the swimmers in case of serious accident.
The shrill wind tore at her mainmast; the waves charged her in
vague ranks; the gaff quivered and moaned at the shocks; and
ever and anon, with a bellowing rush, the resistless sea swept
over her triumphantly from stem to stern. Meanwhile, Warren
Relf, eager to fix this stray episode on good white paper while it
was still before his eyes, made wild and rapid dashes on his pad
with a sprawling hand, which conveyed to his mind, in strange

shorthand hieroglyphics, some faint idea of the scene as it passed before him.

"She's a terrible bad sitter, this smack," he observed in a loud voice to Potts, with good-humoured enthusiasm, as they held on together with struggling hands on the deck of the *Mud-Turtle.* "The moment you think you've just caught her against the skyline on the crest of a wave, she lurches again, and over she goes, plump down into the trough, before you've had a chance to make a single mark upon your sheet of paper. Ships are always precious bad sitters at the best of times; but when you and your model are both plunging and tossing together in dirty weather on a loppy channel, I don't believe even Turner himself could make much out of it in the way of a sketch from nature—Hold hard, there, Frank! Look out for your head! She's going to ship a thundering big sea across her bows this very minute.—By Jove! I wonder how the smack stood that last high wave!—Is she gone? Did it break over her? Can you see her ahead there?"

"She's all right still," Potts shouted from the bow, where he stood now in his oilskin suit, drenched from head to foot with the dashing spray, but cheery as ever, in true sailor fashion. "I can see her mast just showing above the crest. But it must have given her a jolly good wetting. Shall we signal the men to know if they'd like to come aboard here?"

"Signal away," Warren Relf answered good-humouredly above the noise of the wind. "No more sketching for me to-day, I take it. That last lot she shipped wet my pad through and through with the nasty damp brine. I'd better put my sketch, as far as it goes, down below in the locker. Wind's freshening. We'll have enough to do to keep her nose straight in half a gale like this. We're going within four or five points of the wind now, as it is. I wish we could run clear ahead at once for the poplar at Whitestrand. I would, too, if it weren't for the smack. This is getting every bit as hot as I like it. But we must keep an eye upon her, if we don't want her crew to be all dead men. She can't live six hours longer in a gale like to-day's, I'll bet you any money."

They signalled the men, but found them unwilling still, with true seafaring devotion, to abandon their ship, which had yet some hours of life left in her. They'd stick to the smack, the skipper signalled back in mute pantomime, as long as her timbers held out the water. There was nothing for it, therefore, but to lie hard by her, for humanity's sake, as close as possible, and to make as slowly as the strength of the wind would allow, by successive tacks, for the river-mouth at Whitestrand.

All day long, they held up bravely, lurching and plunging on the angry waves; and only towards evening did they part company with the toiling smack, as it was growing dusk along the low flat stretch of shore by Dunwich. There, a fish-carrier from the North Sea, one of those fast long steamers that plough the German|Ocean on the look-out for the fishing fleet—whose catches they take up with all speed to the London market, fell in with them in the very nick of time, and transferring the crew on board with some little difficulty, made fast the smack —or rather her wreck—with a towline behind, and started under all steam to save her life for the port of Harwich. Warren Relf and his companion, despising such aid, and preferring to live it out by themselves at all hazards, were left behind alone with the wild evening, and proceeded in the growing shades of twilight to find their way up the river at Whitestrand.

"Can you make out the poplar, Frank?" Warren Relf shouted out, as he peered ahead into the deep gloom that enveloped the coast with its murky covering. "We've left it rather late, I'm afraid, for pushing up the creek with a sea like this! Unless we can spot the poplar distinctly, I should hardly like to risk entering it by the red light on the sandhills alone. Those must be the lamps at Whitestrand Hall, the three windows to starboard yonder. The poplar ought to show by rights a point or so west of them, with the striped buoy just a little this side of it."

"I can make out the striped buoy by the white paint on it," his companion answered, gazing eagerly in front of him; "but I fancy it's a shade too dark now to be sure of the poplar. The lights of the Hall don't seem quite regular. Still, I should think we could make the creek by the red lantern and the beacon at the hithe, without minding the tree, if you care to risk it. You know your way up and down the river as well as any man living by this time; and we've got a fair breeze at our backs, you see, for going up the mouth to the bend at White-strand."

The wind moaned like a woman in agony. The timbers creaked and groaned and crackled. The black waves lashed savagely over the deck. The *Mud-Turtle* was almost on the shore before they knew it.

"Luff, luff!" Relf called out hastily, as he peered once more into the deepening gloom with all his eyes. "By George! we're wrong. I can see the poplar—over yonder; do you catch it? We're out of our bearings a quarter of a mile. We've gone too far now to make it this tack. We must try again, and get our points better by the high light. That was a narrow squeak of it, by Jove! Frank. I can twig where we've got to now, distinctly. It's the lights in the house that led us astray. That's not the Hall: it's the windows of the vicarage."

They ran out to eastward again, for more sea-room, a couple of hundred yards, or farther, and tacked afresh for the entrance of the creek, this time adjusting their course better for the open mouth by the green lamp of the beacon on the sandhills. The light fixed on their own masthead threw a glimmering ray ahead from time to time upon the angry water. It was a hard fight for mastery with the wind. The waves were setting in fierce and strong towards the creek now; but the tide and stream on the other hand were ebbing rapidly and steadily outward. They always ebbed fast at the turn of the tide, as Relf knew well: a rushing current set in then round the corner by the poplar-tree, the same current that had carried out Hugh Massinger so resistlessly seaward in that little adventure of his on the morning of their first arrival at Whitestrand. Only an experienced mariner dare face that bar. But Warren Relf was accustomed to the coast, and made light of the danger that other men would have trembled at.

As they neared the poplar a second time, making straight for the mouth with nautical dexterity, a pale object on the port bow, rising and falling with each rise or fall of the waves on the bar, attracted Warren Relf's casual attention for a single moment by its strange weird likeness to a human figure. At first, he hardly regarded the thing seriously as anything more than a stray bit of floating wreckage; but presently, the light from the masthead fell full upon it, and with a sudden flash he felt convinced at once it was something stranger than a mere plank or fragment of rigging.

"Look yonder, Frank," he called out in echoing tones to his mate; "that can't be a buoy upon the port bow there!"

The other man looked at it long and steadily. As he looked, the *Mud-Turtle* lurched once more, and cast a reflected pencil ray of light from the masthead lamp over the surface of the sea, away in the direction of the suspicious object. Both men caught sight at once of some floating white drapery, swayed by the waves, and a pale face upturned in ghastly silence to the uncertain starlight.

"Port your helm hard;" Relf cried in haste. "It's a man overboard. Washed off the smack perhaps. He's drowned by this time, I expect, poor fellow."

His companion ported the helm at the word with all his might. The yawl answered well in spite of the breakers. With great difficulty, between wind and tide, they lay up towards the mysterious thing slowly in the very trough of the billows that roared and danced with hoarse joy over the shallow bar; and Relf, holding tight to the sheet with one hand, and balancing himself as well as he was able on the deck, reached out with the other a stout boathook to draw the tossing body

alongside within hauling dis ance of the *Mud-Turtle*. As he
did so, the body, eluding his grasp, rose once more on the crest
of the wave, and displayed to their view an open bosom and a
long white dress, with a floating scarf or shawl of some thin
material still hanging loose around the neck and shoulders.
The face itself they couldn't as yet distinguish; it fell back
languid beneath the spray at the top, so that only the throat
and chin were visible; but by the dress and the open bosom
alone, it was clear at once that the object they saw was not the
corpse of a sailor. Warren Relf almost let drop the boathook in
horror and surprise.

"Great heavens!" he exclaimed, turning round excitedly,
"it's a woman—a lady—dead—in the water!"

The billow broke, and curled over majestically with resistless
force into the trough below them. Its undertow sucked the
Mud-Turtle after it fiercely towards the shore, away from the
body. With a violent effort, Warren Relf, lunging forward
eagerly at the lurch, seized hold of the corpse by the floating
scarf. It turned of itself as the hook caught it, and displayed
its face in the pale starlight. A great awe fell suddenly upon
the astonished young painter's mind. It was indeed a woman
that he held now by the dripping hair—a beautiful young girl,
in a white dress; and the wan face was one he had seen before.
Even in that dim half-light he recognized her instantly.

"Frank!" he cried out in a voice of hushed and reverent
surprise—"never mind the ship. Come forward and help me.
We must take her on board. I know her! I know her! She's
a friend of Massinger's."

The corpse was one of the two young girls he had seen that
day two months before sitting with their arms round one
another's waists, close to the very spot where they now lay up,
on the gnarled and naked roots of the famous old poplar.

CHAPTER X.

SHUFFLING IT OFF.

THE day had been an eventful one for Hugh Massinger: the
most eventful and pregnant of his whole history. As long as
he lived, he could never possibly forget it. It was indeed a
critical turning-point for three separate lives—his own, and
Elsie's, and Winifred Meysey's. For, as Hugh had walked that
morning, stick in hand and orchid in buttonhole, down the rose-
embowered lane in the Squire's grounds with Winifred, he had
asked the frightened, blushing girl, in simple and straight-

forward language, without any preliminary, to become his wife. His shy fish was fairly hooked at last, he thought now: no need for daintily playing his catch any longer; it was but a question, as things stood, of reel and of landing-net. The father and mother, those important accessories, were pretty safe in their way too. He had sounded them both by unobtrusive methods, with dexterous plummets of oblique inquiry, and had gauged their profoundest depths of opinion with tolerable accuracy, as to settlements and other ante-nuptial precontracts of marriage. For what is the use of catching an heiress on your own rod, if your heiress's parents, upon whose testamentary disposition in the last resort her entire market value really depends, look askance with eyes of obvious disfavour upon your personal pretensions as their future son-in-law? Hugh Massinger was keen enough sportsman in his own line to make quite sure of his expected game before irrevocably committing himself to duck-shot cartridge. He was confident he knew his ground now; so, with a bold face and a modest assurance, he ventured, in a few plain and well-chosen words, to commend his suit, his hand, and his heart to Winifred Meysey's favourable attention.

It was a great sacrifice, and he felt it as such. He was positively throwing himself away upon Winifred. If he had followed his own crude inclinations alone, like a romantic schoolboy, he would have waited for ever and ever for his cousin Elsie. Elsie was indeed the one true love of his youth. He had always loved her, and he would always love her. 'Twas foolish, perhaps, to indulge overmuch in these personal preferences, but after all it was very human; and Hugh acknowledged regretfully in his own heart that he was not entirely raised in that respect above the average level of human weaknesses. Still, a man, however humanesque, must not be governed by impulse alone. He must judge calmly, deliberately, impersonally, disinterestedly of his own future, and must act for the best in the long-run by the light of his own final and judicial opinion. Now, Winifred was without doubt a very exceptional and eligible chance for a briefless barrister: your sucking poet doesn't get such chances of an undisputed heiress every day of the week, you may take your affidavit. If he let her slip by on sentimental grounds, and waited for Elsie—poor, dear old Elsie—heaven only knew how long they might both have to wait for one another—and perhaps even then be finally disappointed. It was a foolish dream on Elsie's part; for, to say the truth, he himself had never seriously entertained it. The most merciful thing to Elsie herself would be to snap it short now, once for all, before things went further, and let her stand face to face with naked facts: ah, how hideously naked!—let her know she must either look out another husband somewhere for herself, or go on earning her own livelihood in maiden meditation, fancy free, for the remaining term of her natural existence. Hugh could never help ending up a subject, however unpleasant, even in his own mind, with a poetical tag: it was a trick of manner his soul had caught from the wonted peroration of his political leaders in the first editorial column of that exalted print, the *Morning Telephone.* So he made up his mind; and he proposed to Winifred.

The girl's heart gave a sudden bound, and the red blood flushed her somewhat pallid cheek with hasty roses as she listened to Hugh's graceful and easy avowal of the profound and unfeigned love that he proffered her. She thought of the poem Hugh had read her aloud in his sonorous tones the evening before—much virtue in a judiciously selected passage of poetry, well marked in delivery:

> " ' He does not love me for my birth,
>   Nor for my lands so broad and fair:
>   He loves me for my own true worth,
>   And that is well,' said Lady Clare,"

That was how Hugh Massinger loved her, she was quite sure. Had he not trembled and hesitated to ask her? Her bosom fluttered with a delicious fluttering; but she cast her eyes down, and answered nothing for a brief space. Then her heart gave her courage to look up once more, and to murmur back, in answer to his pleading look: "Hugh, I love you." And Hugh, carried away not ungracefully by the impulse of the moment, felt his own heart thrill responsive to hers in real earnest, and in utter temporary forgetfulness of poor betrayed and abandoned Elsie. They walkèd back to the Hall together next minute, whispering low, in the fool's paradiso of first young love—a fool's paradise, indeed, for those two poor lovers, whose wooing set out under such evil auspices.

But when Hugh had left his landed prey at the front door of the square-built manor-house, and strolled off by himself towards the village inn, the difficulty about Elsie for the first time began to stare him openly in the face in all its real and horrid magnitude. He would have to confess and to explain to Elsie. Worse still, for a man of his mettle and his sensitiveness, he would have to apologise for and excuse his own conduct. That was unendurable—that was ignominious—that was even absurd. His virility kicked at it. There is something essentially insulting and degrading to one's manhood in having to tell a girl you've pretended to love, that you really and truly don't love her— that you only care for her in a sisterly fashion. It is practically to unsex one's self. A pretty girl appeals quite otherwise to the man that is in us. Hugh felt it bitterly and deeply—for him- self, not for Elsie. He pitied his own sad plight most sincerely.

But then, there was poor Elsie to think of too. No use in the
world in blinking that. Elsie loved him very, very dearly. True,
they had never been engaged to one another—so great is the
love of consistency in man, that even alone in his own mind
Hugh continued to hug that translucent fiction; but she had
been very fond of him, undeniably fond of him, and he had
perhaps from time to time, by overt acts, unduly encouraged
the display of her fondness. It gratified his vanity and his sense
of his own power over women to do so: he could make them
love him—few men more easily—and he liked to exercise that
dangerous faculty on every suitable subject that flitted across
his changeful horizon. The man with a mere passion for making
conquests affords no serious menace to the world's happiness;
but the man with an innate gift for calling forth wherever he
goes all the deepest and truest instincts of a woman's nature is,
—when he abuses his power—the most deadly, terrible, and
cruel creature known in our age to civilized humanity. And
yet he is not always deliberately cruel; sometimes, as in Hugh
Massinger's case, he almost believes himself to be good and
innocent.

He had warned Winifred to whisper nothing for the present
to Elsie about this engagement of theirs. Elsie was his cousin,
he said—his only relation—and he would dearly like to tell her
the secret of his heart himself in private. He would see her
that evening and break the news to her. "Why *break* it?"
Winifred had asked in doubt, all unconscious. And Hugh,
a strange suppressed smile playing uneasily about the corners
of his thin lips, had answered with guileless alacrity of speech:
"Because Elsie's like a sister to me, you know, Winifred; and
sisters always to some extent resent the bare idea of their
brothers marrying."

For as yet Elsie herself suspected nothing. It was best, Hugh
thought, she should suspect nothing. That was a cardinal
point in his easy-going practical philosophy of life. He never
went half-way to meet trouble. Till Winifred had accepted
him, why worry poor dear Elsie's gentle little soul with what
was, after all, a mere remote chance, a contingent possibility?
He would first make quite sure, by actual trial, where he stood
with Winifred; and then—and then, like a thunderbolt from a
clear sky, he might let the whole truth burst in full force at
once upon poor lonely Elsie's devoted head. Meanwhile, with
extraordinary cleverness and care, he continued to dissemble.
He never made open love to Winifred before Elsie's face; on
the contrary, he kept the whole small comedy of his relations
with Winifred so skilfully concealed from her feminine eyes,
that to the very last moment Elsie never even dreamt of her
pretty pupil as a possible rival, or regarded her in any other

conceivable light than as the nearest of friends and the dearest of sisters. Whenever Hugh spoke of Winifred to Elsie at all, he spoke of her lightly, almost slightingly, as a nice little girl, in her childish way—though much too blue-eyed—with a sort of distant bread-and-butterish schoolroom approbation, which wholly misled and hoodwinked Elsie as to his real intentions. And whenever he spoke of Elsie to Winifred, he spoke of her jestingly, with a good-humoured, unmeaning, brotherly affection that made the very notion of his ever contemplating marriage with her seem simply ridiculous. She was to him indeed as the deceased wife's sister is in the eye of the law to the British widower. With his easy, off-hand London cleverness, he had baffled and deceived both those innocent, simple-minded, trustful women; and he stood face to face now with a general *éclaircissement* which could no longer be delayed, but whose ultimate consequences might perhaps prove fatal to all his little domestic arrangements.

Would Elsie in her anger set Winifred against him? Would Winifred, justly indignant at his conduct to Elsie, refuse, when she learned the whole truth, to marry him?

Nonsense—nonsense. No cause for alarm. He had never really been engaged to Elsie—he had said so to her face a thousand times. If Elsie chose to misinterpret his kind attentions, bestowed upon her solely as his one remaining cousin and kins-woman, the only other channel for the blood of the Massingers, surely Winifred would never be so foolish as to fall blindly into Elsie's self-imposed error, and to hold him to a bargain he had over and over again expressly repudiated. He was a barrister, and he knew his ground in these matters. Chitty on Contract lays it down as an established principle of English law that free consent of both parties forms a condition precedent and essential part of the very existence of a compact of marriage.

With such transparent internal sophisms did Hugh Massinger strive all day to stifle and smother his own conscience; for every man always at least pretends to keep up appearances in his private relations with that inexorable domestic censor. But as evening came on, cigarette in mouth, he strolled round after dinner, by special appointment, to meet Elsie at the big poplar. They often met there, these warm summer nights; and on this particular occasion, anticipating trouble, Hugh had definitely arranged with Elsie beforehand to come to him by eight at the accustomed trysting-place. The Meyseys and Winifred had gone out to dinner at a neighbouring vicarage; but Elsie had stopped at home on purpose, on the hasty plea of some slight passing headache. Hugh had specially asked her to wait and meet him. Better get it all over at once, he thought to himself, in his shortsighted wisdom—like the measles or the chicken-pox

·—and know straight off exactly where he stood in his new position with these two women.

Women were the greatest nuisance in life. For his own part, now he came to look the thing squarely in the face, he really wished he was well quit of them all for good and ever.

He was early for his appointment ; but by the tree he found Elsie, in her pretty white dress, already waiting for him. His heart gave a jump, a pleased jump, as he saw her sitting there before her time. Dear, dear Elsie; she was very, very fond of him ! He would have given worlds to fling his arms tight around her then, and strain her to his bosom and kiss her tenderly. He would have given worlds, but not his reversionary chances in the Whitestrand property. Worlds don't count; the entire fee-simple of Mars and Jupiter would fetch nothing in the real-estate market. He was bound by contract to Winifred now, and he must do his best to break it gently to Elsie.

He stepped up and kissed her quietly on the forehead, and took her hand in his like a brother. Elsie let it lie in her own without remonstrance. They rose and walked in lovers' guise along the bank together. His heart sank within him at the hideous task he had next to perform—nothing less than to break poor Elsie's heart for her. If only he could have shuffled out of it sideways anyhow! But shuffling was impossible. He hated himself; and he loved Elsie. Never till that moment did he know how he loved her.

This would never do ! He was feeling like a fool. He crushed down the love sternly in his heart, and began to talk about indifferent subjects—the wind, the river, the rose-show at the vicarage. But his voice trembled, betraying him still against his will ; and he could not refrain from stealing sidelong looks at Elsie's dark eyes now and again, and observing how beautiful she was, after all, in a rare and exquisite type of beauty. Winifred's blue eyes and light-brown hair, Winifred's small mouth and moulded nose, Winifred's insipid smile and bashful blush, were cheap as dirt in the matrimonial lottery. She had but a doll-like, Lowther Arcade styles of prettines. Maidenly as she looked, one twist more of her nose, one shade lighter in her hair, and she would become simply bar-maidenly. But Elsie's strong and powerful, earnest face, with its serious lips and its long black eyelashes, its profound pathos and its womanly dignity, its very irregularity and faultiness of outline, pleased him ten thousand times more than all your baby-faced beauties of the conventional, stereotyped, ballroom pattern. He looked at her long and sighed often. Must he really break her heart for her? At last he could restrain that unruly member, his tongue, no longer. " Elsie," he cried, eyeing her full in a genuine outburst of spontaneous admiration, " I never

In my life saw any one anywhere one-half so beautiful and graceful as you are!"

Elsie smiled a pleased smile. "And yet," she murmured,
with a half malicious, teasing tone of irony, "we're not engaged,
Hugh, after all, you remember."

Her words came at the very wrong moment; they brought
the hot blood at a rush into Hugh's cheek. "No," he answered
coldly, with a sudden revulsion and a spasmodic effort; "we're
not engaged—nor ever will be, Elsie!"

Elsie turned round upon him with sudden abruptness in
blank bewilderment. She was not angry; she was not even
astonished; she simply failed altogether to take in his meaning.
It had always seemed to her so perfectly natural, so simply
obvious that she and Hugh were sooner or later to marry one
another; she had always regarded Hugh's frequent reminder
that they were not engaged as such a mere playful warning
against too much precipitancy; she had always taken it for
granted so fully and unreservedly that whenever Hugh was rich
enough to provide for a wife he would tell her so plainly, and
carry out the implied engagement between them—that this
sudden announcement of the exact opposite meant to her ears
less than nothing. And now, when Hugh uttered those cruel,
crushing, annihilating words, "Nor ever will be, Elsie," she
couldn't possibly take in their reality at the first blush, or be-
ieve in her own heart that he really intended anything so
vicked, so merciless, so unnatural.

"Nor ever will be!" she cried, incredulous. "Why, Hugh,
Hugh, I—I don't understand you."

Hugh steeled his heart with a violent strain to answer back
in one curt, killing sentence: "I mean it, Elsie; I'm going to
marry Winifred."

Elsie gazed back at him in speechless surprise. "Going to
marry Winifred?" she echoed at last vaguely, after a long pause,
as if the words conveyed no meaning to her mind. "Going to
marry Winifred? To marry Winifred!—Hugh, did you really
and truly say you were going to marry Winifred?"

"I proposed to her this morning," Hugh answered outright,
with a choking throat and a glassy eye; "and she accepted me,
Elsie; so I mean to marry her."

"Hugh!"

She uttered only that one short word, in a tone of awful and
unspeakable agony. But her bent brows, her pallid face, her
husky voice, her startled attitude, said more than a thousand
words, however wild, could possibly have said for her. She
took it in dimly and imperfectly now; she began to grasp what
Hugh was talking about; but as yet she could not understand
to the full all the man's profound and unfathomed infamy. She

looked at him feebly for some word of explanation. Surely he must have some deep and subtle reason of his own for this astonishing act and fact of furtive treachery. Some horrible combination of adverse circumstances, about which she knew and could know nothing, must have driven him against his will to this incredible solution of an insoluble problem. He could not of his own mere motion have proposed to Winifred. She looked at him hard : he quailed before her scrutiny.

"I love you, Elsie," he burst out with an irresistible impulse at last, as she gazed through and through him from her long black lashes.

Elsie laid her hand on his shoulder blindly. "You love me," she murmured. "Hugh, Hugh, you still love me ? "

"I always loved you, Elsie," Hugh answered bitterly with a sudden pang of abject remorse; "and as long as I live I shall always love you."

"And yet—you are going to marry Winifred ! "

"Elsie ! We were never, never engaged."

She turned round upon him fiercely with a burst of horror. He, to take refuge in that hollow excuse ! "Never engaged !" she cried, aghast. "You mean it, Hugh?—you mean that mockery ?—And I, who would have given up my life for love of you ! "

He tried to assume a calm judicial tone. "Let us be reasonable, Elsie," he said, with an attempt at ease, "and talk this matter over without sentiment or hysterics. You knew very well I was too poor to marry; you knew I always said we were only cousins; you knew I had my way in life to make. You could never have thought I really and seriously dreamt of marrying you ! "

Elsie looked up at him with a scared white face. That Hugh should descend to such transparent futilities ! "This is all new to me," she moaned out in a dazed voice. "All, all—quite, quite new to me."

"But, Elsie, I have said it over and over a thousand times before."

She gazed back at him like a stone. "Ah, yes; but till to-day," she murmured slowly, "you never, never, never meant it."

He sat down, unmanned, on the grass by the bank. She seated herself by his side, mechanically as it were, with her hand on his arm, and looked straight in front of her with a vacant stare at the angry water. It was growing dark. The shore was dark, and the sea, and the river. Everything was dark and black and gloomy around her. She laid his hand one moment in her own. "Hugh!" she cried, turning towards him with appealing pathos, "you don't mean it now: you will never mean it. You're only saying it to try and prove me. Tell me it's that. You're yourself still. O Hugh, my darling, you can never mean it!"

Her words burnt into his brain like liquid fire; and the better self within him groaned and faltered; but he crushed it down with an iron heel. The demon of avarice held his sordid soul. "My child," he said, with a tender inflection in his voice as he said it, "we must understand one another. I do seriously intend to marry Winifred Meysey."

"Why?"

There was a terrible depth of suppressed earnestness in that sharp short *why*, wrung out of her by anguish, as of a woman who asks the reason of her death-warrant. Hugh Massinger answered it slowly and awkwardly with cumbrous, round-about, self-exculpating verbosity. As for Elsie, she sat like a statue and listened: rigid and immovable, she sat there still; while Hugh, for the very first time in her whole experience, revealed the actual man he really was before her appalled and horrified and speechless presence. He talked of his position, his prospects, his abilities. He talked of journalism, of the bar, of promotion. He talked of literature, of poetry, of fame. He talked of money, and its absolute need to man and woman in these latter days of ours. He talked of Winifred, of Whitestrand, and of the Meysey manor-house. "It'll be best in the end for us both, you know, Elsie," he said argumentatively, in his foolish rigmarole, mistaking her silence for something like unwilling acquiescence. 'Of course I shall still be very fond of you, as I've always been fond of you—like a cousin only—and I'll be a brother to you now as long as I live; and when Winifred and I are really married, and I live here at Whitestrand, I shall be able to do a great deal more for you, and help you by every means in my power, and introduce you freely into our own circle, on different terms, you know, where you'll have chances of meeting—well, suitable persons. You must see yourself it's the best thing for us both. The idea of two penniless people like you and me marrying one another in the present state of society is simply ridiculous."

She heard him out to the bitter end, revealing the naked deformity of his inmost nature, though her brain reeled at it, without one passing word of reproach or dissent. Then she said in an icy tone of utter horror: "Hugh!"

"Yes, Elsie."

"Is that all?"

"That is all."

"And *you* mean it?"

"I mean it."

"Oh, for heaven's sake, before you kill me outright, Hugh, Hugh! is it really true? Are you really like that? Do you really mean it?"

"I really mean to marry Winifred."

Elsie clasped her two hands on either side of her head, as if to hold it together from bursting with her agony. "Hugh," she cried, "it's foolish, I know, but I ask you once more, before it's too late, in sight of heaven, I ask you solemnly, are you seriously in earnest? Is that what you're made of? Are you going to desert me? To desert and betray me?"

"I don't know what you mean," Hugh answered stonily, rising as if to go—for he could stand it no longer. "I've never been engaged to you. I always told you so. I owe you nothing. And now I mean to marry Winifred."

With a cry of agony, she burst wildly away from him. She saw it all now; she understood to the full the cruelty and baseness of the man's innermost underlying nature. Fair outside; but false, false, false to the core! Yet even so, she could scarcely believe it. The faith of a lifetime fought hard for life in her. He, that Hugh she had so loved and trusted—he, the one Hugh in all the universe—he to cast her off with such callous selfishness! He to turn upon her now with his empty phrases! He to sell and betray her for a Winifred and a manor-house! Oh, the guilt and sin of it! Her head reeled and swam round deliriously. She hardly knew what she felt or did. Mad with agony, love, and terror, she rushed away headlong from his polluted presence—not from Hugh, but from this fallen idol. He saw her white dress disappearing fast through the deep gloom in the direction of the poplar-tree, and he groped his way after her, almost as mad as herself, struck dumb with remorse and awe and shame at the ruin he had visibly and instantly wrought in the fabric of that trustful girl's whole being.

One moment she fled and stumbled in the dark along the grassy path toward the roots of the poplar. Then he caught a glimpse of her for a second, dimly silhouetted in the faint starlight, a wan white figure with outstretched arms against the black horizon. She was poising, irresolute, on the gnarled roots. It was but for the twinkling of an eye that he saw her; next instant, a splash, a gurgle, a shriek of terror, and he beheld her borne wildly away, a helpless burden, by that fierce current towards the breakers that glistened white and roared hoarsely in their savage joy on the bar of the river.

In her agony of disgrace, she had fallen, rather than thrown herself in. As she stood there, undecided, on the slippery roots, with all her soul burning within her, her head swimming and her eyes dim, a bruised, humiliated, hopeless creature, she had missed her foothold on the smooth worn stump, slimy with lichens, and raising her hands as if to balance herself, had thrown herself forward, half wittingly, half unconsciously, on

the tender mercies of the rushing stream. When she returned
for a moment, a little later, to life and thought, it was with a
swirling sense of many waters, eddying and seething in mad
conflict round her faint numb form. Strange roaring noises
thundered in her ear. A choking sensation made her gasp for
breath. What she drank in with her gasp was not air, but
water—salt, brackish water, an overwhelming flood of it. Then
she sank again, and was dimly aware of the cold chill ocean
floating around her on every side. She took a deep gulp, and
with it sighed out her sense of life and action. Hugh was lost
to her, and it was all over. She could die now. She had
nothing to live for. There was no Hugh; and she had not
killed herself.

Those two dim thoughts were the last she knew as her eyes
closed in the rushing current: there had never been a Hugh;
and she had fallen in by accident.

CHAPTER XI.

SINK OR SWIM?

HUGH was selfish, heartless, and unscrupulous; but he was not
physically a coward, a cur, or a palterer. Without one second's
hought, he rushed wildly down to the water's edge, and
)alancing himself for a plunge, with his hands above his head,
on the roots of the big tree, he dived boldly into that wild
current, against whose terrific force he had once already
struggled so vainly on the morning of his first arrival at
Whitestrand. Elsie had had but a few seconds' start of him;
with his powerful arms to aid him in the quest, he must surely
overtake and save her before she could drown, even in that
mad and swirling tidal torrent. He flung himself on the water
with all his force, and goaded by remorse, pity, and love—for,
after all, he loved her, he loved her—he drew unwonted strength
from the internal fires, as he pushed back the fierce flood on
either side with arms and thews of feverish energy. At each
strong push, he moved forward apace with the gliding current,
and in the course of a few stout strokes he was already many
yards on his way seaward from the point at which he had
originally started. But his boots and clothes clogged his
movements terribly, and his sleeves in particular so impeded
his arms that he could hardly use them to any sensible
advantage. He felt conscious at once that, under such
hampering conditions, it would be impossible to swim for
many minutes at a stretch. He must find Elsie and save

her almost immediately, or both must go down and drown together.

He wanted nothing more than to drown with her now. "Elsie, Elsie, my darling Elsie!" he cried aloud on the top of the wave. To lose Elsie was to lose everything. The sea was running high as he neared the bar, and Elsie had disappeared as if by magic. Even in that dark black water on that moonless night he wondered he couldn't catch a single glimpse of her white dress by the reflected starlight. But the truth was, the current had sucked her under—sucked her under wildly with its irresistible force, only to fling her up again, a senseless burden, where sea and river met at last in fierce conflict among the roaring breakers that danced and shivered upon the shallow bar.

He swam about blindly, looking round him on every side through the thick darkness with eager eyes for some glimpse of Elsie's white dress in a stray gleam of starlight; but he saw not a trace of her presence anywhere. Groping and feeling his way still with numbed limbs, that grew weary and stiff with the frantic effort, he battled on through the gurgling eddy till he reached the breakers on the bar itself. There, his strength proved of no avail—he might as well have tried to stem Niagara. The great waves, rolling their serried line against the stream from the land, caught him and twisted him about resistlessly, raising him now aloft on their foaming crest, dashing him now down deep in their hollow trough, and then flinging him back again over some great curling mountain of water far on to the current from which he had just emerged with his stout endeavour. For ten minutes or more he struggled madly against those titanic enemies; then his courage and his muscle failed together, and he gave up the unequal contest out of sheer fatigue and physical inability to continue it longer. It was indeed an awful and appalling situation. Alone there in the dark, whirled about by a current that no man could stem, and confronted with a rearing wall of water that no man could face, he threw himself wearily back for a moment at full length, and looked up in his anguish from his floating couch to the cold stars overhead, whose faint light the spray every instant hid from his sight as it showered over him from the curling crests of the great billows beyond him. And it was to this that he had driven poor innocent, trustful, wronged Elsie! the one woman he had ever truly loved! the one woman who, with all the force of a profound nature—profounder ten thousand times than his own—had truly loved him!

Elsie was tossing up and down there just as hopelessly now, no doubt. But Elsie had no pangs of conscience added to torment her. *She* had only a broken heart to reckon with.

He let himself float idly where wind and waves might happen

to bear him. There was no help for it: he could swim no
farther. It was all over, all over now. Elsie was lost, and for
all the rest he cared that moment less than nothing. Winifred!
He scorned and hated her very name. He might drown at his
ease, for anything he would ever do himself to prevent it. The
waves broke over him again and again. He let them burst
across his face or limbs, and floated on, without endeavouring
to swim or guide himself at all. Would he never sink? Was
he to float and float and float like this to all eternity?

Roar—roar—roar on the bar, each roar growing fainter and
fainter in his ears. Clearly receding, receding still. The
current was carrying him away from it now, and whirling him
along in a back eddy, that set strongly south-westward towards
the dike of the salt marshes.

He let himself drift wherever it might take him. It took
him back, back, back, steadily, till he saw the white crest of
the breakers on the ridge extend like a long gray line in the
dim distance upon the sea beyond him. He was well into safer
water by this time: the estuary was only very rough here. He
might swim if he chose. But he did not choose. He cared
nothing for life, since Elsie was gone. In a sudden revulsion of
wild despair, a frantic burst of hopeless yearning, he knew, for
the first time in his whole life, now it was too late, how truly
and deeply and intensely he had loved her. As truly and
deeply as he was capable of loving anybody or anything on
earth except himself. And that, after all, was nothing much to
boast of.

Still, it was enough to overwhelm him for the moment with
agonies of remorse and regret and pity, and to make him long
just then and there for instant death, as the easiest escape from
his own angry and accusing conscience. He wanted to die; he
yearned and prayed for it. But death obstinately refused to
come to his aid. He turned himself round on his face now, and
striking out just once with his wearied thighs, gazed away
blankly towards the foam on the bar, where Elsie's body must
still be tossing in a horrible ghastly dance of death among the
careering breakers.

As he looked, a gleam of ruddy light showed for a second
from a masthead just beyond the bar. A smack—a smack!
coming in to the river! The sight refilled him with a faint
fresh hope. That hope was too like despair; but still it was
something. He swam out once more with the spasmodic
energy of utter despondency. The smack might still be in time
to save Elsie! He would make his way out to it, though it ran
him down; if it ran him down, so much the better! he would
shout aloud at the top of his voice, to outroar the breakers: "A
lady is drowning! Save her!—save her!"

He struck out again with mad haste through the back current. This time, he had to fight against it with his wearied limbs, and to plough his way by prodigious efforts. The current was stronger, now he came to face it, than he had at all imagined when he merely let himself drift on its surface. Battling with all his might against the fierce swirls, he hardly seemed to make any headway at all through the angry water. His strength was almost all used up now; he could scarcely last till he reached the smack.—Great heavens, what was this? She was turning!—she was turning! The surf was too much for her timbers to endure. She couldn't make the mouth of the creek. She was luffing seaward again, and it was all up, all up with Elsie.

It was Warren Relf's yawl, bearing down from Lowestoft, and trying for the first time to enter the river through the wall of breakers.

Oh, if only he had lain right in her path just then, as she rode over the waves, that she might run him down and sink him for ever, with his weight of infamy, beneath those curling billows! He could never endure to go ashore again—and to feel that he had virtually murdered Elsie.

Elsie, Elsie, poor murdered Elsie! He should hate to live, now he had murdered Elsie!

And then, as he battled still fiercely with the tide, in a flash of his nerves, he felt suddenly a wild spasm of pain seize on both his thighs, and an utter disablement affect his entire faculty of bodily motion. It was a paroxysm of cramp—overwhelming—inexpressible—and it left him in one second powerless to move or think or act or plan, a mere dead log, incapable of anything but a cry of pain, and helpless as a baby in the midst of that cruel and unheeding eddy.

He flung himself back for dead on the water once more. A choking sensation seized hold of his senses. The sea was pouring in at his nostrils and his ears. He knew he was going, and he was glad to know it. He would rather die than live with that burden of guilt upon his black soul. The waves washed over his face in serried ranks. He didn't mind; he didn't struggle; he didn't try for one instant to save himself. He floated on, unconscious at last, back, slowly back, towards the bank of the salt marsh.

When Hugh Massinger next knew anything, he was dimly conscious of lying at full length on a very cold bed, and fumbling with his fingers to pull the bed-clothes closer around him But there were no bed-clothes, and everything about was soaking wet. He must be stretched in a pool of water, he thought—so damp it was all round to the touch—with a soft

mattress or couch spread beneath him. He put out his hands
to feel the mattress. He came upon mud, mud, deep layers
of mud; all cold and slimy in the dusk of night. And then
with a flash he remembered all—Elsie dead! Elsie drowned!
—and knew he was stranded by the ebbing tide on the edge
of the embankment. No hope of helping Elsie now. With a
violent effort, he roused himself to consciousness, and crawled
feebly on his knees to the firm ground. It was difficult work,
floundering through the mud, with his numb limbs; but he
floundered on, upon hands and feet, till he reached the shore,
and stood at last, dripping with brine and crusted with soft
slimy tidal ooze, on the broad bank of the moated dike that
hemmed in the salt marshes from the mud-bank of the estuary.
It was still dark night, but the moon had risen. He could
hardly say what the time might be, for his watch had stopped, of
course, by immersion in the water; but he roughly guessed, by
the look of the stars, it was somewhere about half-past ten. We
have a vague sense of the lapse of time even during sleep or
other unconscious states; and Hugh was certain he couldn't
have been floating for much more than an hour or thereabouts.

He gazed around him vaguely at the misty meadows. He was
a mile or so from the village inn. The estuary, with its acrid
flats of mud, lay between him and the hard at Whitestrand.
Sheets of white surf still shimmered dimly on the bar far out to
~ea. And Elsie was lost—lost to him irrevocably.

He sat down and pondered on the bank for a while. Those
ive minutes were the turning-point of his life. What should he
do and how comport himself under these sudden and awful and
unexpected circumstances? Dazed as he was, he saw even then
the full horror of the dilemma that hedged him in. Awe and
shame brought him back with a rush to reason. If he went
home and told the whole horrid truth, everybody would say
he was Elsie's murderer. Perhaps they would even suggest
that he pushed her in—to get rid of her. He dared not tell
it; he dared not face it. Should he fly the village—the county
—the country?—That would be foolish and precipitate indeed,
not to say wicked: a criminal surrender. All was not lost,
though Elsie was lost to him. In his calmer mood, no longer
heroic with the throes of despondency, sitting shivering there
with cold in the keen breeze, between his dripping clothes, upon
the bare swept bank, he said to himself many times over that
all was not lost; he might still go back—and marry Winifred.

Hideous—horrible—ghastly—inhuman: he reckoned even so
his chances with Winifred.

The shrewd wind blew chill upon his wet clothes. It bellowed and roared with hoarse groans round the stakes on the
dike-sluices. His head was whirling still with asphyxia and

numbness. He felt hardly in a condition to think or reason. But this was a crisis, a life-and-death crisis. He must pull himself together like a man, and work it all out, his doubtful course for the next three hours, or else sink for ever in a sea of obloquy, remembered only as Elsie's murderer. Everything was at stake for him—live or die. Should he jump once more into the cold wild stream—or go home quietly like a sensible man, and play his hand out to marry Winifred?

If he meant to go, he must go at once. It was no use to think of delaying or shilly-shallying. By eleven o'clock, the inn would be closed. He must steal in, unperceived, by the open French windows before eleven, if he intended still to keep the game going. But he must have his plan of action definitely mapped out none the less beforehand; and to map it out, he must wait a moment still; he must sum up chances in this desperate emergency.

Life is a calculus of varying probabilities. Was it likely he had been perceived at the Hall that evening? Did anybody know he had been walking with Winifred?

He fancied not—he believed not.—He was certain not, now he came to think of it. Thank heaven, he had made the appointment verbally. If he'd written a note, that damning evidence might have been produced against him at the coroner's inquest. Inquest? Unless they found the body—Elsie's body—pah! how horrible to think of—but still, a man must steel himself to face facts, however ghastly and however horrible. Unless they found the body, then, there would be no inquest; and if only things were managed well and cleverly, there needn't even be any inquiry. Unless they found the body—Elsie's body—poor Elsie's body, whirled about by the waves!—But they would never find it—they would never find it. The current had sucked it under at once, and carried it away careering madly to the sea. It would toss and whirl on the breakers for a while, and then sink unseen to the fathomless abysses of the German Ocean.

He hated himself for thinking all this—with Elsie drowned—or not yet drowned even—and yet he thought it, because he was not man enough to face the alternative.

Had Elsie told any one she was going to meet him? No; she wouldn't even tell Winifred of that, he was sure. She met him there often by appointment, it was true, but always quietly: they kept their meetings a profound secret between them.

Had any one seen them that evening together? He couldn't remember noticing anybody.—How shrill the wind blew through his dripping clothes. It cut him in two; and his head reeled still.—No; nobody, nobody. He was quite safe upon that score at least. Nobody knew he was out with Elsie.

Could he go back, then, and keep it all quiet, saying nothing himself, but leaving the world to form its own conclusions? A sudden thought flashed in an intuitive moment across his brain. A Plan!—a Plan! How happy! A Policy! He saw his way out of it all at once. He could set everything right by a simple method. Yes, that would do. It was bold, but not risky. He might go now: the scheme for the future was all matured. Nobody need ever suspect anything. A capital idea! Honour was saved ; and he might still go back and marry Winifred.

Elsie dead! Elsie drowned! The world lost, and his life a blank ! But he might still go back and marry Winifred.

He rose, and shook himself in the wind like a dog. The Plan was growing more definite and rounded in his mind each moment. He turned his face slowly towards the lights at Whitestrand. The estuary spread between him and them with its wide mud-flats. Cold and tired as he was, he must make at all speed for the point where it narrowed into the running stream near Snade meadows. He must swim the river there, with what legs he had left, and cross to the village. There was no time to be lost. It was neck or nothing. At all hazards, he must do his best to reach the inn before the doors were shut and locked at eleven.

When he left the spot where he had been tossed ashore, his idea for the future was fully worked out. He ran along the bank with eager haste in the direction of Whitestrand. Once nly did he turn and look behind him. A ship's light gleamed ebly in the offing across the angry sea. She was beating up gainst a head wind to catch the breeze outside towards Lowestoft or Yarmouth.

CHAPTER XII.

THE PLAN IN EXECUTION.

Hugh hurried along the dike that bounded the salt-marsh meadows seaward, till he reached the point in his march up where the river narrowed abruptly into a mere third-class upland stream. There he jumped in, and swam across, as well as he was able in the cold dark water, to the opposite bank. O .ce over, he had still to straggle as best he might through two or three swampy fields, and to climb a thickset hedge or so— regular bullfinches—before he fairly gained the belated little high-road. His head swam. Wet and cold and miserable without, he was torn within by conflicting passions ; but he walked firm and erect now along the winding road in the deep gloom, fortunately never meeting a soul in the half-mile or so of lonely way that lay between the point where he had crossed the stream and the Fisherman's Rest by the bank at Whitestrand. He was glad of that, for it was his cue now to escape observation. In his own mind, he felt himself a murderer; and every flicker of the wind among the honeysuckle in the hedge, every rustle of the leaves on the trees overhead, every splash of the waves upon the distant shore, made his heart flutter, and his breath stop short in response, though he gave no outer sign of fear or compunction in his even tread and erect bearing—the even tread and erect bearing of a proud, self-confident, English gentleman.

How lucky that his rooms at the inn happened to be placed on the ground-floor, and that they opened by French windows down to the ground on to the little garden! How lucky, too, that they lay on the hither side of the door and the taproom, where men were sitting late over their mug of beer, singing and rollicking in vulgar mirth with their loud half-Danish, East-Anglian merriment! He stole through the garden on tiptoe, unperceived, and glided like a ghost into the tiny sitting-room. The lamp burned brightly on the parlour table, as it had burnt all evening, in readiness for his arrival. He slipped quietly, on tiptoe still, into the bedroom behind, tossed off a stiff glassful of brandy-and-water cold, and changed his clothes from head to foot with as much speed and noiselessness as circumstances permitted. Then, treading more easily, he went out once more with a bold front into the other room, flung himself down at his ease in the big armchair, took up a book, pretending to read, and rang the bell with ostentatious clamour for the good landlady. His plan was mature; he would proceed to put it into execution.

The landlady, a plentiful body of about fifty, came in with evident surprise and hesitation. "Lord a mussy, sar," she cried aloud in a slight flurry, "I thowt yow wor out; an' them min a-singin' and a-bellerin' like that oover there in the bar! Stannaway'll be some riled when he find yow're come in an' all that noise gooin' on in the house! 'Teen't respectable. But we din't hear ye. I hoop yow'll 'scuse 'em: they're oonly the fishermen from Snade, enjoyin' theirselves in the cool of the evenin'."

Hugh made a manful effort to appear unconcerned. "I came in an hour ago or more," he replied, smiling—a sugar-of-lead smile.—"But, pray don't interfere with these good people's merriment for worlds, I beg of you. I should be sorry, indeed, if I thought I put a stopper upon anybody's innocent amusement anywhere. I don't want to be considered a regular kill-joy.—I rang the bell, Mrs. Stannaway, for a bottle of seltzer."

It was a simple way of letting them know he was really there; and though the lie about the length of time he had been home was a fairly audacious one—for somebody might have come in meanwhile to trim the lamp, or look if he was about, and so detect the falsehood—he saw at once, by Mrs. Stannaway's face, that it passed muster without rousing the slightest suspicion.

"Why, William," he heard her say when she went out, in a hushed voice to her husband in the taproom, "Mr. Massinger hev bin in his own room the whool time while them chaps hev bin a-shoutin' an' swearin' suffin frightful out here, more like heathen than human critters."

Then, they hadn't noticed his absence, at any rate! That was well. He was so far safe. If the rest of his plan held water equally, all might yet come right—and he might yet succeed in marrying Winifred.

To save appearances—and marry Winifred! With Elsie still tossing on the breakers of the bar, he had it in his mind to marry Winifred!

When Mrs. Stannaway brought in the seltzer, Hugh Massinger merely looked up from the book he was reading with a pleasant nod and a murmured "Thank you." 'Twas the most he dared. His teeth chattered so he could hardly trust himself to speak any further; but he tried with an agonized effort within to look as comfortable under the circumstances as possible. As soon as she was gone, however, he opened the seltzer, and pouring himself out a second strong dose of brandy, tossed it off at a gulp, almost neat, to steady his nerves for serious business. Then he opened his blotting-book, with a furtive glance to right and left, and took out a few stray sheets of paper—to write a letter. The rst sheet had some stanzas of verse scribbled loosely upon it, 'ith many corrections. Hugh's eyes unconsciously fell upon une of them. It read to him just then like an act of accusation. They were some simple lines describing some ideal utopian world—a dream of the future—and the stanza on which his glance had lighted so carelessly ran thus—

> "But, fairer and purer still,
>   True love is there to behold;
> And none may fetter his will
>   With law or with gold:
> And none may sully his wings
>   With the deadly taint of lust;
> But freest of all free things
>   He soars from the dust."

"With law or with gold," indeed! Fool! Idiot! Jackanapes! He crumpled the verses angrily in his hand as he looked, and flung them with clenched teeth into the empty fireplace. His own words rose up in solemn judgment against him, and condemned him remorselessly by anticipation. He had sold Elsie for Winifred's gold, and the Nemesis of his crime was already pursuing him like a deadly phantom through all his waking moments.

With a set cold look on his handsome dark face, he selected another sheet of clean white note-paper from the morocco-covered blotting-book, and then pulled a bundle of old, worn-edged letters from his breast-pocket—a bundle of letters in a girl's handwriting, secured by an elastic india-rubber band, and carefully numbered with red ink from one to seventy, in the order they had been received. Hugh was nothing, indeed, if not methodical. In his own way, he had loved Elsie, as well as he was capable of loving anybody: he had kept every word she ever wrote to him; and now that she was gone—dead and gone for ever—her letters were all he had left that belonged to her. He laid one down on the table before him, and yielding to a momentary impulse of ecstasy, he kissed it first with reverent tenderness. It was Elsie's letter—poor dead Elsie's.—Elsie dead! He could hardly realize it.—His brain whirled and swam with the manifold emotions of that eventful evening. But he must brace himself up for his part like a man. He *must* not be weak. There was work to do; he must make haste to do it.

He took a broad-nibbed pen carefully from his desk—the broadest he could find—and fitted it with pains to his ivory holder. Elsie always used a broad nib—poor drowned Elsie— dear, martyred Elsie! Then, glancing sideways at her last letter, he wrote on the sheet, in a large flowing angular hand, deep and black, most unlike his own, which was neat and small and cramped and rounded, the two solitary words, " My darling," He gazed at them when done with evident complacency. They would do very well : an excellent imitation !

Was he going, then, to copy Elsie's letter? No; for its first words read plainly, " My own darling Hugh." He had allowed her to address him in such terms as that; but still, he muttered to himself even now, he was never engaged to her—never engaged to her. In copying, he omitted the word " own." That, he thought, would probably be considered quite too affectionate for any reasonable probability. Even in emergencies he was cool and collected. But " My darling," was just about the proper mean. Girls are always stupidly gushing in their expression of feeling to one another. No doubt Elsie herself would have begun, " My darling."

After that, he turned over the letters with careful scrutiny, as if looking down the pages one by one for some particular phrase or word he wanted. At last he came upon the exact thing , " Mrs. Mersey and Winifred are going out to-morrow."—That'll do," he said in his soul to himself: "a curl to the *w* "—and laying the blank sheet once more before him, he wrote down boldly, in the same free hand, with thick black down-strokes, " My darling Winifred."

The Plan was shaping itself clearly in his mind now. Word

by word he fitted in so, copying each direct from Elsie's letters, and dovetailing the whole with skilled literary craftsmanship into a curious cento of her pet phrases, till at last, after an hour's hard and anxious work, round drops of sweat standing meanwhile cold and clammy upon his hot forehead, he read it over with unmixed approbation—to himself—an excellent letter both in design and execution.

"Whitestrand Hall, September 17.

"MY DARLING WINIFRED,

"I can hardly make up my mind to write you this letter; and yet I must: I can no longer avoid it. I know you will think me so wicked, so ungrateful: I know Mrs. Meysey will never forgive me; but I can't help it. Circumstances are too strong for me. By the time this reaches you, I shall have left Whitestrand, I fear for ever. Why I am leaving, I can never, never, never tell you. If you try to find out, you won't succeed in discovering it. I know what you'll think; but you're quite mistaken. It's something about which you have never heard; something that I've told to nobody anywhere; something I can never, never tell, even to you, darling. I've written a line to explain to Hugh; but it's no use either of you trying to trace me. I shall write to you some day again to let you know how I'm getting on — but never my whereabouts.— Darling, for heaven's sake, do try to hush this up as much as you can. To ave myself discussed by half the county would drive me mad ith despair and shame. Get Mrs. Meysey to say I've been called away suddenly by private business, and will not return. If only you knew all, you would forgive me everything.— Good-bye, darling. Don't think too harshly of me.

"Ever your affectionate, but heart-broken

"ELSIE."

His soul approved the style and the matter. Would it answer his purpose? he wondered, half tremulously. Would they really believe Elsie had written it, and Elsie was gone? How account for her never having been seen to quit the grounds of the Hall? For her not having been observed at Almundham Station? For no trace being left of her by rail or road, or sea or river? It was a desperate card to play, he knew, but he held no other; and fortune often favours the brave. How often at loo had he stood against all precedent upon a hopeless hand, and swept the board in the end by some audacious stroke of inspired good play, or some strange turn of the favouring chances! He would stand to win now in the same spirit on the forged letter. It was his one good card. Nobody could ever prove he wrote it. And perhaps, with the unthinking readiness of the world at large, they would all accept it without further question.

If ever Elsie's body were recovered! Ah, yes: true: that would indeed be fatal. But then, the chances were enormously against it. The deep sea holds its own: it yields up its dead only to patient and careful search; and who would ever dream of searching for Elsie? Except himself, she had no one to search for her. The letter was vague and uncertain, to be sure; but its very vagueness was infinitely better than the most definite lie: it left open the door to so much width of conjecture. Every man could invent his own solution. If he had tried to tell a plausible story, it might have broken down when confronted with the inconvenient detail of stern reality: but he had trusted everything to imagination. And imagination is such a charmingly elastic faculty! The Meyseys might put their own construction upon it. Each, no doubt, would put a different one; and each would be convinced that his own was the truest.

He folded it up and thrust it into an envelope. Then he addressed the face boldly, in the same free black hand as the letter itself, to "Miss Meysey, The Hall, Whitestrand." In the corner he stuck the identical little monogram, E. C., written with the strokes crossing each other, that Elsie put on all her letters. His power of imitating the minutest details of any autograph stood him here in good stead. It was a perfect facsimile, letter and address: and tortured as he was in his own mind by remorse and fear, he still smiled to himself an approving smile as he gazed at the absolutely undetectable forgery. No expert on earth could ever detect it. "That'll clinch all," he thought serenely. "They'll never for a moment doubt that it comes from Elsie."

He knew the Meyseys had gone out to dinner at the vicarage that evening, and would not return until after the hour at which Elsie usually retired. As soon as they got back, they would take it for granted she had gone to bed, as she always did, and would in all probability never inquire for her. If so, nothing would be known till to-morrow at breakfast. He must drop the letter into the box unperceived to-night, and then it would be delivered at Whitestrand Hall in due course by the first post to-morrow.

He shut the front window, put out the lamp, and stole quietly into the bedroom behind. That done, he opened the little lattice into the back garden, and slipped out, closing the window closely after him, and blowing out the candle. The post-office lay just beyond the church. He walked there fast, dropped his letter in safety into the box, and turned, unseen, into high-road once more in the dusky moonlight.

Wearied and faint and half delirious as he was after his long immersion, he couldn't even now go back to the inn to rest quietly. Elsie's image haunted him still. A strange fascination led him across the fields and through the lane to the Hall —to Elsie's last dwelling-place. He walked in by the little side-gate, the way he usually came to visit Elsie, and prowled guiltily to the back of the house. The family had evidently returned, and suspected nothing: no sign of bustle or commotion or disturbance betrayed itself anywhere: not a light showed from a single window: all was dark and still from end to end, as if poor dead Elsie were sleeping calmly in her own little bedroom in the main building. It was close on one in the morning now. Hugh skulked and prowled around the east wing on cautious tiptoe, like a convicted burglar.

As he passed Elsie's room, all dark and empty, a mad desire seized upon him all at once to look in at the window and see how everything lay within there. At first, he had no more reason for the act in his head than that: the Plan only developed itself further as he thought of it. It wouldn't be difficult to climb to the sill by the aid of the porch and the clambering wistaria. He hesitated a moment; then remorse and curiosity finally conquered. The romantic suggestion came to him, like a dream, in his fevered and almost delirious condition: like a dream, he carried it at once into effect. Groping and feeling his way with numb fingers, dim eyes, and head that still reeled and swam in terrible giddiness from his long spell of continued asphyxia, he raised himself cautiously to the level of the sill, and prised the window open with his dead white hand. The lamp on the table, though turned down so low that he hadn't observed its glimmer from outside, was still alight and burning faintly. He turned it up just far enough to see through the gloom his way about the bedroom. The door was closed, but not locked. He twisted the key noiselessly with dexterous pressure, so as to leave it fastened from the inside.—That was a clever touch!—They would think Elsie had climbed out of the window.

A few letters and things lay loose about the room. The devil within him was revelling now in hideous suggestions. Why not make everything clear behind him? He gathered them up and stuck them in his pocket. Elsie's small black leather bag stood on a wooden frame in the far corner. He pushed into it hastily the nightdress on the bed, the brush and comb, and a few selected articles of underclothing from the chest of drawers by the tiled fireplace. The drawers themselves he left sedulously open. It argued haste. If you choose to play for a high stake, you must play boldly, but you must play well. Hugh never for a moment concealed from himself the fact that the adversary against whom he was playing now was the public hangman, and that his own neck was the stake at issue.

If ever it was discovered that Elsie was drowned, all the world, including the enlightened British jury—twelve butchers and bakers and candlestick-makers, selected at random from the Whitestrand rabble, he said to himself angrily—would draw the inevitable inference for themselves that Hugh had murdered her. His own neck was the stake at issue—his own neck, and honour and honesty.

He glanced around the room with an approving eye once more. It was capital! Splendid! Everything was indeed in most admired disorder. The very spot it looked, in truth, from which a girl had escaped in a breathless hurry. He left the lamp still burning at half-height: that fitted well; lowered the bag by a piece of tape to the garden below; littered a few stray handkerchiefs and lace bodices loosely on the floor; and crawling out of the window with anxious care, tried to let himself down hand over hand by a branch of the wistaria.

The branch snapped short with an ugly crack; and Hugh found himself one second later on the shrubbery below, bruised and shaken.

CHAPTER XIII.

WHAT SUCCESS?

AT the Meyseys' next morning, all was turmoil and surprise. The servants' hall fluttered with unwonted excitement. No less an event than an elopement was suspected. Miss Elsie had not come down to breakfast; and when Miss Winifred went up, on the lady's-maid's report, to ask what was the matter, she had found the door securely locked on the inside, and received no answer to her repeated questions. The butler, hastily summoned to the rescue, broke open the lock; and Winifred entered, to find the lamp still feebly burning at half-height, and a huddled confusion everywhere pervading the disordered room. Clearly, some strange thing had occurred. Elsie's drawers had been opened and searched: the black bag was gone from the stand in the corner; and the little jewel-case with the silver shield on the top was missing from its accustomed place on the dressing-table.

With a sudden cry, Winifred rushed forward, terrified. Her first idea was the usual feminine one of robbery and murder. Elsie was killed—killed by a burglar. But one glance at the bed dispelled that illusion; it had never been slept in. The nightdress and the little embroidered nightdress-bag in red silk were neither of them there in their familiar fashion. The brush and comb had disappeared from the base of the looking-glass. The hairpins even had been removed from the glass hair-pin box. These indications seemed frankly inconsistent with the theory of mere intrusive burglary. The enterprising burglar doesn't make up the beds of the robbed and murdered, after pocketing their watches; nor does he walk off, as a rule, with ordinary hairbrushes and embroidered nightdress-bags. Surprised and alarmed, Winifred rushed to the window: it was open still: a branch of the wistaria lay broken on the ground, and the mark of a falling body might be easily observed among the plants and soil in the shrubbery border.

By this time, the Squire had appeared upon the scene, bringing in his hand a letter for Winifred. With the cool common sense of advancing years, he surveyed the room in its littery condition, and gazed over his daughter's shoulder as she read the shadowy and incoherent jumble of phrases Hugh Massinger had strung together so carefully in Elsie's name last night at the Fisherman's Rest. " Whew ! " he whistled to himself in sharp surprise as the state of the case dawned slowly upon him. "Depend upon it, there's a young man at the bottom of this. 'Cherchez la femme,' says the French proverb. When a young woman's in question, ' Cherchez l'homme ' comes very much nearer it. The girl's run off with *somebody*, you may be sure. I only hope she's run off all straight and above-board, and not gone away with a groom or a gamekeeper or a married clergyman."

" Papa ! " Winifred cried, laying down the letter in haste and bursting into tears, " do you think Mr. Massinger can have anything to do with it ? "

The Squire had been duly apprised last night by Mrs. Meysey —in successive instalments—as to the state of relations between Hugh and Winifred; but his blunt English nature cavalierly rejected the suggested explanation of Elsie's departure, and he brushed it aside at once after the fashion of his kind with an easy " Bless my soul ! no, child. The girl's run off with some fool somewhere. It's always fools who run off with women. Do you think a man would be idiot enough to "—he was just going to say, " propose to one woman in the morning, and elope with another the evening after ! " but he checked himself in time, before the faces of the servants, and finished his sentence lamely by saying instead, " commit himself so with a girl of that sort ? "

" That wasn't what I meant, papa," Winifred whispered low. " I meant, could she have fancied ?—— You understand me."

The Squire gave a snort in place of *No*. Impossible, impossible; the young man was so well connected. She could never have thought he meant to make up to *her* Much more likely, if it came to that, the girl would run away *with* him than *from* him. Young women don't really run away from a man because their hearts are broken. They go up to their own bedrooms instead, and muse and mope over it, and cry their eyes red.

And indeed, the Squire remarked to himself inwardly on the other hand, that if Hugh were minded to elope with any one, he would be far more likely to elope with the heiress of Whitestrand than with a penniless governess like Elsie Challoner. Elopement implies parental opposition. Why the deuce should a man take the trouble to run away with an undowered orphan, whom nobody on earth desires to prevent him from marrying any day, in the strictly correctest manner, by banns or license, at the parish church of her own domicile? The suggestion was clearly quite quixotic. If Elsie had run away with any one, it was neither from nor with this young man of Winifred's, the Squire felt sure, but with the gardener's son or with the under-gamekeeper.

Still, he felt distinctly relieved in his own mind when, at half-past ten, Hugh Massinger strolled idly in, a rose in his button-hole and a smile on his face—though a little lame of the left leg—all unconscious, apparently, that anything out of the common had happened since last night at the great house.

Hugh was one of the very finest and most finished actors then performing on the stage of social England; but even he had a difficult part to play that stormy morning, and he went through his rôle, taking it altogether, with but indifferent success, though with sufficient candour to float him through unsuspected somehow. The circumstances, indeed, were terribly against him. When he fell the night before from Elsie's window, he had bruised and shaken himself, already fatigued as he was by his desperate swim and his long unconsciousness; and it was with a violent effort, goaded on by the sense of absolute necessity alone, that he picked himself up, black bag and all, and staggered home, with one ankle strained, to his rooms at the Stannaways'. Once arrived there, after that night of terrors and manifold adventures, he locked away Elsie's belongings cautiously in a back cupboard—incriminating evidence, indeed, if anything should ever happen to come out—and flung himself half undressed at last in a fever of fatigue upon the bed in the corner.

Strange to say he slept—slept soundly. Worn out with overwork and exertion and faintness, he slept on peacefully like a tired child, till at nine o'clock Mrs. Stannaway rapped hard at the door to rouse him. Then he woke with a start from a heavy sleep, his head aching, but drowsy still, and with feverish pains in all his limbs from his desperate swim and his long immersion.

He was quite unfit to get up and dress; but he rose for all that,
as if all was well, and even pretended to eat some breakfast,
though a cup of tea was the only thing he could really gulp
down his parched throat in his horror and excitement. Last
night's events came clearly home to him now in their naked
ghastliness, and with sinking heart and throbbing head, he
realized the full extent of his guilt and his danger, the depth
of his remorse, and the profundity of his folly.

Elsie was gone—that was his first thought. There was no
more an Elsie to reckon with in all this world. Her place was
blank—how blank he could never before have truly realized.
The whole world itself was blank too. What he loved best in
it all was gone clean out of it.

Elsie, Elsie, poor drowned, lost Elsie! His heart ached as he
thought to himself of Elsie, gasping and struggling in that cold,
cold sea, among those fierce wild breakers, for one last breath—
and knew it was he who had driven her, by his baseness and
wickedness and cruelty, to that terrible end of a sweet young
existence. He had darkened the sun in heaven for himself
henceforth and for ever. He had sown the wind, and he should
reap the whirlwind. He hated himself; he hated Winifred ; he
hated everybody and everything but Elsie. Poor martyred
Elsie! Beautiful Elsie! His own sweet, exquisite, noble Elsie!
He would have given the whole world at that moment to bring
her back again. But the past was irrevocable, quite irrevocable.
There was nothing for a strong man now to do but to brace
himself up and face the present.

"If not, what resolution from despair?"—That was all the
comfort his philosophy could give him.

Elsie's things were locked up in the cupboard. If suspicion
lighted upon him in any way now, it was all up with him.
Elsie's bag and jewel-case and clothing in the cupboard would
alone be more than enough to hang him. Hang him! What
did he care any longer for hanging? They might hang him
and welcome, if they chose to try. For sixpence he would save
them the trouble, and drown himself. He wanted to die. It
was fate that prevented him. Why hadn't he drowned when he
might, last night? An ugly proverb that, about the man who
is born to be hanged, etc., etc. Some of these proverbs are downright rude—positively vulgar in the coarse simplicity and
directness of their language.

He gulped down the tea with a terrible effort : it was scald-
ing hot, and it burnt his mouth, but he scarcely noticed it.
Then he pulled about the sole on his fork for a moment, to dirty
the plate, and boning it roughly, gave the flesh to the cat, who
ate it purring on the rug by the fireplace. He waited for a
reasonable interval next before ringing the bell—it takes a lone

man ten minutes to breakfast—but as soon as that necessary time had passed, he put on his hat, crushing it down on his head, and with fiery soul and bursting temples, strolled up, with the jauntiest air he could assume, to the Meyseys' after breakfast.

Winifred met him at the front door. His new sweetheart was pale and terrified, but not now crying. Hugh felt himself constrained to presume upon their novel relations and insist upon a kiss—she would expect it of him. It was the very first time he had ever kissed her, and, oh evil omen, it revolted him at last that he had now to do it—with Elsie's body tossed about that very moment by the cruel waves upon that angry bar or on the cold sea-bottom. It was treason to Elsie —to poor dead Elsie—that he should ever kiss any other woman. His kisses were hers, his heart was hers, for ever and ever. But what would you have? He looked on, as he had said, as if from above, at circumstances wafting his own character and his own actions hither and thither wherever they willed—and this was the pass to which they had now brought him. He must play out the game—play it out to the end, whatever it might cost him.

Winifred took the kiss mechanically and coldly, and handed him Elsie's letter—his own forged letter—without one word of preface or explanation. Hugh was glad she did so at the very first moment—it allowed him to relieve himself at once from the terrible strain of the affected gaiety he was keeping up just to save appearances. He couldn't have kept it up much longer. His countenance fell visibly as he read the note—or pretended to read it, for he had no need really to glance at its words— every word of them all now burnt into the very fibres and fabric of his being.

"Why, what does this mean, Miss Meysey—that is to say, Winifred?" he corrected himself hurriedly. "Elsie isn't gone? She's here this morning as usual, surely?"

As he said it he almost hoped it might be true. He could hardly believe the horrible, horrible reality. His face was pale enough in all conscience now—a little too pale, perhaps, for the letter alone to justify. Winifred, eyeing him close, saw at a glance that he was deeply moved.

"She's gone," she said, not too tenderly either. "She went away last night, taking her things with her—at least some of them.—Do you know where she's gone, Mr. Massinger? Has she written to you, as she promises?"

"Not Mr. Massinger," Hugh corrected gravely, with a livid white face, yet affecting jauntiness. "It was agreed yesterday it should be 'Hugh' in future.—No; I don't at all know where she is, Winifred; I wish I did." He said it seriously. "She hasn't written a single line to me."

Hugh's answer had the very ring of truth in it—for indeed it was true; and Winifred, watching him with a woman's closeness, felt certain in her own mind that in this at least he was not deceiving her. But he certainly grew unnecessarily pale. Cousinly affection would hardly account for so much disturbance of the vaso-motor system. She questioned him closely as to all that had passed or might have passed between them these weeks or earlier. Did he know anything of Elsie's movements or feelings? Hugh, holding the letter firmly in one hand, and playing with the key of that incriminating cupboard, in his waistcoat pocket, loosely with the other, passed with credit his examination. He had never, he said, with gay flippancy almost, been really intimate with Elsie, talked confidences with Elsie, or received any from Elsie in return. She did not know of his engagement to Winifred. Yet he feared, whatever her course might be, some man or other must be its leading motive. Perhaps—but this with the utmost hesitation—Warren Relf and she might have struck up a love affair.

He felt, of course, it was a serious ordeal. Apart from the profounder background of possible consequences—the obvious charge of having got rid of Elsie—two other unpleasant notions stared him full in the face. The first was, that the Meyseys might suspect him of having driven Elsie to run away by his proposal to Winifred. But supposing even they never thought of that—which was highly unlikely, considering the close sequence of the two events and the evident drift of Winifred's questions—there still remained the second unpleasantness—that his cousin, through whom alone he had been introduced to the family, should have disappeared under such mysterious circumstances. Was it likely they would wish their daughter to marry a man among whose relations such odd and unaccountable things were likely to happen?

For, strangely enough, Hugh still wished to marry Winifred. Though he loathed her in his heart just then for not being Elsie, and even, by some illogical twist of thought, for having been the unconscious cause of Elsie's misfortunes; though he would have died himself far rather than lived without Elsie; yet, if he lived, he wished for all that to marry Winifred. For one thing, it was the programme; and because it was the programme, he wanted, with his strict business habits, to carry it out to the bitter end. For another thing, his future all depended upon it; and though he didn't care a straw at present for his future, he went on acting, by the pure force of habit in a prudent man, as deliberately and cautiously as if he had still the same serious stake in existence as ever. He wasn't going to chuck up everything all at once, just because life was now an utter blank to him. He would go on as usual in the regular groove, and pretend to the world he was still every bit as interested and engaged in life as formerly.

So he brazened things out with the Meyseys somehow, and to his immense astonishment, he soon discovered they were ready dupes, in no way set against him by this untoward accident. On the contrary, instead of finding, as he had expected, that they considered this delinquency on the part of his cousin told against himself as a remote partner of her original sin, by right of heredity, he found the Squire and Mrs. Meysey nervously anxious for their part lest he, her nearest male relative, should suspect them of having inefficiently guarded his cousin's youth, inexperience, and innocence. They were all apology, where he had looked for coldness; they were all on the defensive, where he had expected to see them vigorously carrying the war into Africa. One thing, above all others, he noted with profound satisfaction—nobody seemed to doubt for one second the genuineness and authenticity of the forged letter. Whatever else they doubted, the letter was safe. They all took it fully for granted that Elsie had gone, of her own free-will, gone to the four winds, with no trace left of her; and that Hugh, in the perfect innocence of his heart, knew no more than they themselves about it.

Nothing else, of course, was talked of at Whitestrand that livelong day; and before night, the gossips and quidnuncs of the village inn and the servants' hall had a complete theory of their own to account for the episode. Their theory was simple, romantic, and improbable. It had the dearly-loved spice of mystery about it. The coastguard had noticed that a ship, name unknown, with a red light at the masthead and a green on the port bow, had put in hastily about nine o'clock the night before, near the big poplar. The Whitestrand cronies had magnified this fact before nightfall, through various additions of more or less fanciful observers or non-observers—for fiction, too, counts for something—into a consistent story of a most orthodox elopement. Miss Elsie had let herself down by a twisted sheet out of her own window, to escape observation—some said a rope, but the majority voted for the twisted sheet, as more strictly in accordance with established precedent—she had slipped away to the big tree, where a gentleman's yacht, from parts unknown, had put in cautiously, before a terrible gale, by previous arrangement, and had carried her over through a roaring sea across to the opposite coast of Flanders. Detail after detail grew apace; and before long there were some who even admitted to having actually seen a foreign-looking gentleman in a dark cloak—the cloak is a valuable romantic property upon such occasions— catch a white-robed lady in his stout arms as she leaped a wild leap into an open boat from the spray-covered platform of the gnarled poplar roots. Hugh smiled a grim and hideous smile of

polite incredulity as he listened to these final imaginative em-
bellishments of the popular fancy; but he accepted in outline
the romantic tale as the best possible version of Elsie's disappearance for public acceptance. It kept the police at least from
poking their noses too deep into this family affair, and it freed
him from any possible tinge of blame in the eyes of the Meyseys.
Nobody can be found fault with for somebody else's elopement.
Two points at least seemed fairly certain to the Whitestrand
intelligence: first, that Miss Elsie had run away of her own
accord, in the absence of the family; and second, that she neither
went by road nor rail, so that only the sea or river appeared to
be left by way of a possible explanation.

The Meyseys, of course, were less credulous as to detail; but
even the Meyseys suspected nothing serious in the matter.
That Elsie had gone was all they knew; why she went, was a
profound mystery to them.

CHAPTER XIV

LIVE OR DIE?

AND all this time, what had become of Elsie and the men in
the *Mud-Turtle?*

Hugh Massinger, for his part, took it for granted, from the
moment he came to himself again on the bank of the salt
marshes, that Elsie's body was lying unseen full fathoms five
beneath the German Ocean, and that no tangible evidence of his
crime and his deceit would ever be forthcoming to prove the
naked truth in all its native ugliness against him. From time
to time, to be sure, one disquieting thought for a moment occurred
to his uneasy mind: a back-current might perhaps cast up the
corpse upon the long dike where he had himself been stranded,
or the breakers on the bar might fling it ashore upon the great
sands that stretched for miles on either side of the river mouth
at Whitestrand. But to these terrible imaginings of the night-
watches, the more judicial functions of his waking brain refused
their assent on closer consideration. He himself had floated
through that seething turmoil simply because he knew how to
float. A woman, caught wildly by the careering current in its
headlong course, would naturally give a few mad struggles for
life, gasping and gulping and flinging up her hands, as those
untaught to swim invariably do; but when once the stream had
carried her under, she would never rise again from so profound
and measureless a depth of water. He did not in any way
doubt that the body had been swept away seaward with irre-

sistible might by the first force of the outward flow, and that it now lay huddled at the bottom of the German Ocean in some deep pool, whence dredge or diver could never by human means recover it.

How differently would he have thought and acted all along nad he only known that Warren Relf and his companion on the *Mud-Turtle* had found Elsie's body floating on the surface, a limp burden, not half an hour after its first immersion.

That damning fact rendered all his bold precautions and daring plans for the future worse than useless. As things really stood, he was plotting and scheming for his own condemnation. Through the mere accident that Elsie's body had been recovered, he was heaping up suspicious circumstantial evidence against himself by the forged letter, by the night escapade, by the wild design of entering Elsie's bedroom at the Hall, by the mad idea of concealing at his own lodgings her purloined clothes and jewelry and belongings. If ever an inquiry should come to be raised into the way that Elsie met her death, the very cunning with which Hugh had fabricated a false scent would recoil in the end most sternly against himself. The spoor that ho scattered would come home to track him. Could any one believe that an innocent man would so carefully surround himself with an enveloping atmosphere of suspicious circumstances out of pure wantonness?

And yet, technically speaking, Hugh was in reality quite innocent. Murderer as he felt himself, he had done no murder. Morally guilty though he might be of the causes which led to Elsie's death, there was nothing of legal or formal crime to object against him in any court of so-called justice. Every man has a right to marry whom he will; and if a young woman with whom he has cautiously and scrupulously avoided contracting any definite engagement, chooses to consider herself aggrieved by his conduct, and to go incontinently, whether by accident or design, and drown herself in chagrin and despair and misery, why, that is clearly no fault of his, however much she may regard herself as injured by him. The law has nothing to do with sentiment. Judges quote no precedent from Shelley or Tennyson. If Hugh had told the whole truth, he would at least have been free from legal blame. By his extraordinary precautions against possible doubts, he had only succeeded in making himself seem guilty in the eyes even of the unromantic lawyers.

When Warren Relf drew Elsie Challoner, a huddled mass, on board the *Mud-Turtle*, the surf was rolling so high on the bar that, with one accord, he and Potts decided together it would be impossible for them, against such a sea, to run up the tidal mouth to Whitestrand. Their piteous little dot of a craft could never face it. Wind had veered to the south-east. The only way possible now was to head her round again, and make before the shifting breeze for Lowestoft, the nearest northward harbour of refuge.

It was an awful moment. The sea roared onward through the black night; the cross-drift whirled and wreathed and eddied; the blinding foam lashed itself in volleys through the dusk and gloom against their quivering broadside. And those two men, nothing daunted, drove the *Mud-Turtle* once more across the flank of the wind, and fronted her bows in a direct line for the port of Lowestoft, in spite of wind and sea and tempest.

But how were they to manage meanwhile, in that tossing cockleshell of a boat, about the lady they had scarcely rescued? That Elsie was drowned, Warren Relf didn't for a moment doubt; still, in every case of apparent drowning, it is a duty to make sure life is really extinct before one gives up all hope; and that duty was a difficult one indeed to perform on board a tiny yawl, pitching and rolling before a violent gale, and manned against the manifold dangers of the sea by exactly two amateur sailors. But there was no help for it. The ship must drift with one mariner only. Potts did his best for the moment to navigate the dancing little yawl alone, now that they let her scud before the full force of the favouring wind, under little canvas; while Warren Relf, staggering and steadying himself in the cabin below, rolled the body round in rugs and blankets, and tried his utmost to pour a few drops of brandy down the pale lips of the beautiful girl who lay listless and apparently lifeless before him.

It was to him indeed a terrible task; for from the first moment when the painter set eyes on Elsie Challoner, he had felt some nameless charm about her face and manner, some tender cadence in her musical voice, that affected him as no other face and no other voice had ever affected him or could ever affect him. He was not exactly in love with Elsie—love with him was a plant of slower growth—but he was fascinated, impressed, interested, charmed by her. And to sit there alone in that tossing cabin, with Elsie cold and stiff on the berth before him, was to him more utterly painful and unmanning than he could ever have imagined a week or two earlier.

He did not doubt one instant the true story of the case. He felt instinctively in his heart that Hugh Massinger had shown her his inmost nature, and that this was the final and horrible result of Hugh's airy easy protestations.

As he sat there, watching by the light of the one oil lamp, and rubbing her hands and arms gently with his rough hard palms, he saw a sudden tumultuous movement of Elsie's bosom, a sort of gasp that convulsed her lungs—a deep inspiration, with a gurgling noise; and then, like a flash, it was borne in upon him suddenly that all was not over—that Elsie might yet be saved— that she was still living.

It was a terrible hour, a terrible position. If only they had had one more hand on board, one more person to help him with the task of recovering her! But how could he ever hope to revive that fainting girl, alone and unaided, while the ship drifted on, single-handed, tossing and plunging before that stiffening breeze? He almost despaired of being able to effect anything. Yet life is life, and he would nerve himself up for it. He would try his best, and thank heaven this boisterous wind that roared through the rigging would carry them quick and safe to Lowestoft.

His mother and sister were still there. If once he could get Miss Challoner safe to land, they might even now hope to recover her. Where there's life, there's hope. But what hope in the dimly lighted cabin of a toy yawl, just fit for two hardy weather-beaten men to rough it hardly in, and pitching with wild plunges before as fierce a gale as ever ploughed the yeasty surface of the German Ocean?

He rushed to the companion-ladder as well as he was able, steadying himself on his sea-legs by the rail as he went, and shouted aloud in breathless excitement: "Potts, she's alive! she's not drowned! Can you manage the ship anyhow still, while I try my best to bring her round again?"

Potts answered back with a cheery: "All right. There's nothing much to do but to let her run. She's out of our hands, for good or evil. The admiral of the fleet could do no more for her. If we're swamped, we're swamped; and if we're not, we're running clear for Lowestoft harbour. Give her sea-room enough, and she'll go anywhere. The storm don't live that'll founder the *Mud-Turtle*. I'll land you or drown you, but any-how I'll manage her."

With that manful assurance satisfying his soul, Warren Relf turned back, his heart on fire, to the narrow cabin and flung himself once more on his knees before Elsie.

A more terrible night was seldom remembered by the oldest sailors on the North Sea. Smacks were wrecked and colliers foundered, and a British gunboat, manned by the usual com-plement of scientific officers, dashed herself full tilt in mad fury against the very base of a first-class lighthouse; but the taut little *Mud-Turtle*, true to her reputation as the staunchest craft that sailed the British channels, rode it bravely out, and battled her way triumphantly, about one in the morning, through the big waves that rolled up the mouth of Lowestoft harbour. Potts had navigated her single-handed amid storm and breakers, and Warren Relf, in the cabin below, had almost succeeded in making Elsie Challoner open her eyes again.

But as soon as the excitement of that wild race for life was fairly over, and the *Mud-Turtle* lay in calm water once more, with perfect safety, the embarrassing nature of the situation, from the conventional point of view, burst suddenly for the first time upon Warren Relf's astonished vision; and he began to reflect that for two young men to arrive in port about the small hours of the morning, with a young lady very imperfectly known to either of them, lying in a dead faint on their cabin bunk, was, to say the least of it, a fact open to social and even to judicial misconstruction. It's all very well to say offhand, you picked the lady up in the German Ocean; but Society is apt to move the previous question, how did she get there? Still, something must be done with the uncovenanted passenger. There was nothing for it, Warren Relf felt, even at that late season of the night, but to carry the half-inanimate patient up to his mother's lodgings, and to send for a doctor to bring her round at the earliest possible opportunity.

When Elsie was aware of herself once more, it was broad daylight; and she lay on a bed in a strange room, dimly conscious that two women whom she did not know were bending tenderly and lovingly over her. The elder, seen through a haze of half-closed eyelashes, was a sweet old lady with snow-white hair, and a gentle motherly expression in her soft gray eyes: one of he few women who know how to age graciously—

> " Whose fair old face grew more fair
> As Point and Flanders yellow."

The younger was a girl about Elsie's own time of life, who looked as sisterly as the other looked motherly; a pleasant-faced girl, not exactly pretty, but with a clear brown skin, a cheek like the sunny side of peaches, and a smile that showed a faultless row of teeth within, besides lighting up and irradiating the whole countenance with a charming sense of kindliness and girlish innocence. In a single word it was a winning face. Elsie lay with her eyes half open, looking up at the face through her crossed eyelashes, for many minutes, not realizing in any way her present position, but conscious only, in a dimly pleased and dreamy fashion, that the face seemed to soothe and comfort and console her.

Soothe and comfort and console her for what? She hardly knew. Some deep-seated pain in her inner nature—some hurt she had had in her tenderest feelings—a horrible aching blank and void.—She remembered now that something unspeakable and incredible had happened.—The sun had grown suddenly dark in heaven.— She   been sitting by the waterside with dear

Hugh—as she thought of the name, that idolized name, a smile played for a moment faintly round the corners of her mouth; and the older lady, still seen half unconsciously through the chink in the eyelids, whispered in an audible tone to the younger and nearer one : "She's coming round, Edie. She's waking now. I hope, poor dear, she won't be dreadfully frightened, when she sees only two strangers by the bed beside her."

"Frightened at you, mother," the other voice answered, soft and low, as in a pleasant dream. "Why, nobody on earth could ever be anything but delighted to wake up anywhere and find you, with your dear sweet old face, sitting by their bedside."

Elsie, still peering with half her pupils only through the closed lids, smiled to herself once more at the gentle murmur of those pleasant voices, both of them tender and womanly and musical, and went on to herself placidly with her own imaginings.

——Sitting by the waterside with her dear Hugh—dear, dear Hugh—that prince of men. How handsome he was; and how clever, and how generous! And Hugh had begun to tell her something. Eh! but something! What was it? What was it? She couldn't remember; she only knew it was something terrible, something disastrous, something unutterable, something killing. And then she rushed away from him, mad with terror, towards the big tree, and——

Ah!

It was an awful, heart-broken, heart-rending cry. Coming to herself suddenly, as the whole truth flashed like lightning once more across her bewildered brain, the poor girl flung up her arms, raised herself wildly erect in the bed, and stared around her with a horrible vacant, maddened look, as if all her life were cut at once from under her. Both of the strangers recognized instinctively what that look meant. It was the look and the cry of a crushed life. If ever they had harboured a single thought of blame against that poor wounded, bleeding, torn heart for what seemed like a hasty attempt at self-murder, it was dissipated in a moment by that terrible voice—the voice of a goaded, distracted, irresponsible creature, from whom all consciousness or thought of right and wrong, of life and death, of sense and movement, of motive and consequence, has been stunned at one blow by some deadly act of undeserved cruelty and unexpected wickedness.

The tears ran unchecked in silent sympathy down the women's flushed cheeks.

Mrs. Relf leant over and caught her in her arms. "My poor child," she whispered, laying Elsie's head with motherly tenderness on her own soft shoulder, and soothing the girl's pallid white face with her gentle old hand, " cry, cry, cry if you can! Don't hold back your tears ; let them run, darling. It'll do you good.—Cry, cry, my child—we're all friends here. Don't be afraid of us."

Elsie never knew, in the agony of the moment, where she was or how she came there; but nestling her head on Mrs. Relf's shoulder, and fain of the sympathy that gentle soul extended her so easily, she gave free vent to her pent-up passion, and let her bosom sob itself out in great bursts and throbs of choking grief; while the two women, who had never till that very morning seen her fair face, cried and sobbed silently in mute concert by her side for many, many minutes together.

"Have you no mother, dear?" Mrs. Relf whispered through her tears at last; and Elsie, finding her voice with difficulty, murmured back in a choked and blinded tone: "I never knew my mother."

"Then Edie and I will be mother and sister to you," the beautiful old lady answered, with a soft caress. "You mustn't talk any more now. The doctor would be very, very angry with me for letting you talk and cry even this little bit. But crying's good for one when one's heart's sore. I know, my child, yours is sore now. When you're a great deal better, you'll tell us all about it.—Edie, some more beef-tea and brandy.—We've been feeding you with it all night, dear, with a wet feather.—You can drink a little, I hope, now. You must take a good drink, and lie back quietly."

Elsie smiled a faint sad smile. The world was all lost and one for her now; but still she liked these dear souls' sweet uiet sympathy. As Edie glided across the room noiselessly to .etch the cup, and brought it over and held it to her lips and made her drink, Elsie's eyes followed every motion gratefully.

"Who are you?" she cried, clutching her new friend's plump soft hand eagerly. "Tell me where I am. Who brought me here? How did I get here?"

"I'm Edie Relf," the girl answered in the same low silvery voice as before, stooping down and kissing her. "You know my brother, Warren Relf, the artist whom you met at Whitestrand. You've had an accident—you fell into the water—from the shore at Whitestrand. And Warren, who was cruising about in his yawl, picked you up and brought you ashore here. You're at Lowestoft now. Mamma and I are here in lodgings. Nobody at Whitestrand knows anything about it yet, we believe. —But darling," and she held poor Elsie's hand tight at this, and whispered very low and close in her ear, "we think we guess all the rest too. We think we know how it all happened.—Don't be afraid of us. You may tell it all to us by-and-by, when you're quite strong enough. Mother and I will do all we can to make you better. We know we can never make you forget it."

Elsie's head sank back on the pillow. It was all terrible—

terrible—terrible.　But one thought possessed her whole nature now.　Hugh must think she was really drowned : that would grieve Hugh—dear affectionate Hugh.—He might be cruel enough to cast her off as he had done—though she couldn't believe it—it must surely be a hideous, hideous dream, from which sooner or later she would be certain to have a happy awakening—but at any rate it must have driven him wild with grief and remorse and horror to think he had killed her—to think she was lost to him.—Oughtn't she to telegraph at once to Hugh—to dear, dear Hugh—and tell him at least she was saved, she was still living ?

CHAPTER XV.

THE PLAN EXTENDS ITSELF.

FOR three or four days, Elsie lay at the Relfs' lodgings at Lowestoft, seriously ill, but slowly improving; and all the time, Mrs. Relf and Edie watched over her tenderly with unceasing solicitude, as though she had been their own daughter and sister. Elsie's heart was torn every moment by a devouring desire to know what Hugh had done, what Hugh was doing, what they had all said and thought about her at Whitestrand.　She never said so directly to the Relfs, of course; she couldn't bring herself yet to speak of it to anybody; but Edie perceived it intuitively from her silence and her words; and after a time, she mentioned the matter in sisterly confidence to her brother Warren.　They had both looked in the local papers for some account of the accident—if accident it were—and saw, to their surprise, that no note was taken anywhere of Elsie's sudden disappearance.

This was curious, not to say ominous; for in most English country villages a young lady cannot vanish into space on a summer evening, especially by flinging herself bodily into the sea—as Warren Relf did not doubt for a second Elsie had done in the momentary desperation of a terrible awakening—without exciting some sort of local curiosity as to where she has gone or what has become of the body.　We cannot emulate the calm social atmosphere of the Bagdad of the Califs, where a mysterious disappearance on an enchanted carpet aroused but the faintest and most languid passing interest in the breasts of the bystanders.　With us, the enchanted carpet explanation has fallen out of date, and mysterious disappearances, however remarkable, form a subject rather of prosaic and prying inquiry

on the part of those commonplace and unromantic myrmidons,
the county constabulary.

So the strange absence of any allusion in the Whitestrand
news to what must needs have formed a nine days' wonder in the
quiet little village, quickened all Warren Relf's profoundest suspicions as to Hugh's procedure.   At Whitestrand, all they could
possibly know was that Miss Challoner was missing—perhaps
even that Miss Challoner had drowned herself.   Why should it
all be so unaccountably burked, so strangely hushed up in the
local newspapers?   Why should no report be divulged anywhere?   Why should nobody even hint in the *Lowestoft Times*
or the *Ipswich Chronicle* that a young lady, of considerable
personal attractions, was unaccountably missing from the family
of a well-known Suffolk landowner?

Already on the very day after his return to Lowestoft,
Warren Relf had hastily telegraphed to Hugh Massinger at
Whitestrand that he was detained in the Broads, and would be
unable to carry out his long-standing engagement to take him
round in the *Mud-Turtle* to London.   But as time went on, and
no news came from Massinger, Warren Relf's suspicions deepened
daily.   It was clear that Elsie, too, was lingering in her con-
valescence from suspense and uncertainty.   She couldn't make
up her mind to write either to Hugh or Winifred, and yet she
couldn't bear the long state of doubt which silence entailed
upon her.   So at last, to set to rest their joint fears, and to make
ure what was really being said and done and thought at
Vhitestrand, Warren Relf determined to run over quietly for
an afternoon's inquiry, and to hear with his own ears how
people were talking about the topic of the hour in the little
village.

He never got there, however.   At Almundham Station, to
his great surprise, he ran suddenly against Mr. Wyville
Meysey.   The Squire recognized him at a glance as the young
man who had taken them in his yawl to the sandhills, and
began to talk to him freely at once about all that had since
happened in the family.   But Relf was even more astonished
when he found that the subject which lay uppermost in Mr.
Meysey's mind just then was not Elsie Challoner's mysterious
disappearance at all, but his daughter Winifred's recent engagement to Hugh Massinger.   The painter was still some years too
young to have mastered the profound anthropological truth
that, even with the best of us, man is always a self-centred
being.

"Well, yes," the Squire said, after a few commonplaces of
conversation had been interchanged between them.   "You
haven't heard, then, from your friend Massinger lately, haven't
you?   I'm surprised at that.   He had something out of the

common to communicate. I should have thought he'd have
been anxious to let you know at once that he and my girl
Winifred had hit things off amicably together.—Oh yes, it's
announced, definitely announced: Society is aware of it. Mrs.
Meysey made it known to the county, so to speak, at Sir
Theodore Sheepshanks's on Wednesday evening. Your friend
Massinger is not perhaps quite the precise man we might have
selected ourselves for Winifred, if we'd taken the choice into
our own hands: but what I say is, let the young people settle
these things themselves—let the young people settle them
between them. It's they who've got to live with one another,
after all, not we; and they're a great deal more interested in it
at bottom, when one comes to think of it, than the whole of the
rest of us put together."

"And Miss Challoner?" Warren asked, as soon as he could
edge in a word conveniently, after the Squire had dealt from
many points of view—all equally prosy—with Hugh Massinger's position, character, and prospects—"is she still with you?
I'm greatly interested in her. She made an immense impression on me that day in the sandhills."

The Squire's face fell somewhat. "Miss Challoner?" he
echoed. "Ah, yes; our governess. Well, to tell you the truth
—if you ask me point-blank—Miss Challoner's gone off a little
suddenly.—We've been disappointed in that girl, if you *will*
have it. We don't want it talked about in the neighbourhood
more than we can help, on Hugh Massinger's account, more than
anything else, because, after all, she was a sort of a cousin of his
—a sort of a cousin, though a very remote one; as we learn now,
an extremely remote one. We've asked the servants to hush it
all up as much as they can, to prevent gossip; for my daughter's
sake, we'd like to avoid gossip; but I don't mind telling you, in
strict confidence, as you're a friend of Massinger's, that Miss
Challoner left us, we all think, in a most unkind and ungrateful
manner. It fell upon us like a thunderbolt from a clear sky.
She wrote a letter to Winifred the day before to say she was
leaving for parts unknown, without grounds stated. She slipped
away, like a thief in the night, as the proverb says, taking just
a small handbag with her, one dark evening; and the only other
communication we've since received is a telegram from London
—sent to Hugh Massinger—asking us, in the most mysterious,
romantic school-girlish style, to forward her luggage and belongings to an address given."

"A telegram from London!" Warren Relf cried in blank
surprise. "Do you think Miss Challoner's in London, then?
That's very remarkable.—A telegram to Massinger! asking you
to send her luggage on to London!—You're quite sure it came
from London, are you?"

"Quite sure!—Why, I've got it in my pocket this very moment, my dear sir," the Squire replied somewhat testily. (When an elder man says "My dear sir" to a very much younger one, you may take it for granted he always means to mark his strong disapprobation of the particular turn the talk has taken.) "Here it is—look: 'To Hugh Massinger, Fisherman's Rest, Whitestrand, Suffolk.—Ask Winifred to send the rest of my luggage and property to 27, Holmbury Place, Duke Street, St. James's. Explanations by post hereafter.—ELSIE CHALLONER.' —And here's the letter she wrote to Winifred: a very disappointing, disheartening letter. I'd like you to read it, as you seem interested in the girl. It's an immense mistake ever to be interested in anybody anywhere! A very bad lot, after all, I'm afraid; though she's clever, of course, undeniably clever.—We had her with the best credentials, too, from Girton. We're only too thankful now to think she should have associated for so very short a time with my daughter Winifred."

Warren Relf took the letter and telegram from the Squire's hand in speechless astonishment. This was evidently a plot—a dark and extraordinary plot of Massinger's. Just at first he could hardly unravel its curious intricacies. He knew the address in Holmbury Place well; it was where the club porter of the Cheyne Row lived. But he read the letter with utter bewilderment. Then the whole truth dawned piecemeal upon his astonished mind as he read it over and over slowly. It was all a lie—a hideous, hateful lie. Hugh Massinger believed that Elsie was drowned. He had forged the letter to Winifred to cover the truth, and, incredible as it seemed to a straightforward, honest nature like Warren Relf's, he had managed to get the telegram sent from London by some other person, in Elsie's name, and to have Elsie's belongings forwarded direct to the club porter's, as if at her own request, by Miss Meysey. Warren Relf stood aghast with horror at this unexpected revelation of Massinger's utter baseness and extraordinary cunning. He had suspected the man of heartlessness and levity; he had never suspected him of anything like so profound a capacity for serious crime—for forgery and theft and concealment of evidence.

His fingers trembled as he held and examined the two documents. At all hazards, he must show them to Miss Challoner. It was right she should know herself for exactly what manner of man she had thrown herself away. He hesitated a moment, then he said boldly: "These papers are very important to me, as casting light on the whole matter. I'm an acquaintance of Massinger's, and I'm deeply interested in the young lady. It's highly desirable she should be traced and looked after. I have some reason to suspect where she is at present. I want to ask a favour of you now. Will you lend me these documents, for three days only, and will you kindly mention to nobody at present the fact of your having seen me or spoken to me here this morning?" To gain time at least was always something.

The Squire was somewhat taken aback at first by this unexpected request; but Warren Relf looked so honest and true as he asked it, that, after a few words of hesitation and explanation, the Squire, convinced of his friendly intentions, acceded to both his propositions at once. It flashed across his mind as a possible solution that the painter had been pestering Elsie with too-pressing attentions, and that Elsie, with hysterical girlish haste, had run away from him to escape them—or perhaps only to make him follow her. Anyhow, there would be no great harm in his tracking her down. "If the girl's in trouble, and you think you can help her," he said good-naturedly, "I don't mind giving you what assistance I can in this matter. You can have the papers. Send them back next week or the week after. I'm going to Scotland for a fortnight's shooting now—at Farquharson's of Invertanar—and I shan't be back till the 10th or 11th. But I'm glad somebody has some idea where the girl is. As it seems to be confidential, I'll ask no questions at present about her; but I do hope she hasn't got into any serious mischief."

"She has got into no mischief at all of any sort," Warren Relf answered slowly and seriously. "You are evidently labouring under a complete misapprehension, Mr. Meysey, as to her reasons for leaving you. I have no doubt that misapprehension will be cleared up in time. Miss Challoner's motives, I can assure you, were perfectly right and proper; only the action of another person has led you to mistake her conduct in the matter."

This was mysterious, and the Squire hated mystery; but after all, it favoured his theory—and besides, the matter was to him a relatively unimportant one. It didn't concern his own private interest. He merely suspected Warren Relf of having got himself mixed up in some foolish love affair with Elsie Challoner, his daughter's governess, and he vaguely conceived that one or other of them had taken a very remarkable and romantic way of wriggling out of it. Moreover, at that precise moment his train came in; and since time and train wait for no man, the Squire, with a hasty farewell to the young painter, installed himself forthwith on the comfortable cushions of a first-class carriage, and steamed unconcernedly out of Almundham Station.

It was useless for Warren Relf now to go on to Whitestrand. To show himself there would be merely to display his hand openly before Hugh Massinger. The caprice of circumstances had settled everything for him exactly as he would have wished it. It was lucky indeed that the Squire would be away for a whole fortnight; his absence would give them time to concert a connected plan of action, and to devise means for protecting Elsie. For to Warren Relf that was now the one great problem in the case—how to hush the whole matter up, without exposing Elsie's wounded heart to daws and jays—without making her the matter of unnecessary suspicion, or the subject of common gossip and censorious chatter. At all costs, it must never be said that Miss Challoner had tried to drown herself in spite and jealousy at Whitestrand poplar, because Hugh Massinger had ventured to propose to Winifred Meysey.

That was how the daws and jays would put it, after their odious kind, over five o'clock tea, in their demure drawing-rooms.

What Elsie herself would say to it all, or think of doing in these difficult circumstances, Warren Relf did not in the least know. As yet, he was only very imperfectly informed as to the real state of the case in all its minor details. But he knew this much—that he must screen Elsie at all hazards from the slanderous tongues of five o'clock tea-tables, and that the story must be kept as quiet as possible, safeguarded by himself, his mother, and his sister.

So he took the next train back to Lowestoft, to consult at leisure on these new proofs of Hugh Massinger's guilt with his domestic counsellors.

CHAPTER XVI.

FROM INFORMATION RECEIVED.

At Whitestrand itself, that same afternoon, Hugh Massinger sat in his own little parlour at the village inn, feverish and eager, as he had always been since that terrible night when "Elsie was drowned," as he firmly believed without doubt or question; and in the bar across the passage, a couple of new-comers, rough waterside characters, were talking loudly in the seafaring tongue about some matter of their own over a pint of beer and a pipe of tobacco. Hugh tried in vain for many minutes to interest himself in the concluding verses of his "Death of Alaric"—anything for an escape from this gnawing remorse—but his Hippocrene was dry, his Pegasus refused to budge a feather : he could find no rhymes and grind out no sentiments; till, angry with himself at last for his own unproductiveness, he leant back in his chair with profound annoyance and listened listlessly to the strange disjointed echoes of gossip that came to him in fragments through the half-open door from the adjoining taproom. To his immense surprise, the talk was not now of topsails or of spinnakers: conversation seemed to have taken a literary turn; he caught more than once through a haze of words the unexpected names of Charles Dickens and Rogue Riderhood.

The oddity of their occurrence in such company made him prick up his ears. He strained h's hearing to catch the context.

"Yis," the voice was drawling out, in very pure Suffolk, just tinged with the more metropolitan Wapping accent; "I read that there book, 'Our Mutual Friend,' I think he call it. A mate o' mine, he say to me one day, 'Bill,' he say, 'he ha' bin a-takin' yow off, bor. He ha' showed yow up in print, under the naame o' Roogue Ridenhood,' he say, 'and yow owt to read it, if oonly for the likeness. Blow me if he heen't got yow what ye call proper.' 'Yow don't mean that?' I say, 'cos I thowt he was a-jookin', ye know. 'I dew, though,' he answer; 'and yow must look into it.' Well, I got howd o' the book, an' I read it right throu'; leastways, my missus, she read it out loud to me; she ha' got more larnin' than me, ye know; and the whool lot is what I call a bargain o' squit. It's noo more like me than chalk's like cheese."

"The cap doon't fare to fit yow, then," the other voice retorted, with a gurgle of tobacco. "He heen't drew yow soo any one would know who it is?"

"Know me? I should think not. What he say 's a parcel of rubbidge. This here Roogue Ridenhood, accordin' to the tale, ye see, he used to row about Limehouse Reach, a-searchin' for bodies."

"Searchin' for bodies!" the second man repeated, with an incredulous whiff. "Why, what the deuce and turfy did he want to do that for?"

"Well, that's jest where it is, doon't ye see? He done it for a livin'. 'For a livin',' I say, when my missus up an' read that part out to me; 'why, what manner o' livin' could a poor beggar make out o' that?' I say. 'It een't as though a body was wuth anything nowadays, as a body,' I say, argifyin' like. 'A man what knew anything about the riverside wouldn't a wroot such rubbidge as that, an' put it into a printed book, what ought to be ackerate. My belief is,' I say, 'that that there Dickens is an ooverrated man. In fact, the man's a fule. A body nowadays, whether it be a drownded body or a nat'ral one, een't wuth nothin', not the clothes it stand upright in, as a body,' I put it. 'Times goon by,' I say to har, 'a body was actshally a body, an' wuth savin' for itself, afore body-snatchin' was done away wooth by that there 'Natomy Ack. But what is it now? Wuth half a crown for landin' it, paid by the parish, if it's landed in Essex, or five bob if yow tow it oover Surrey side of river. Not but what I grant yow there's bodies an' bodies. If a nob drownd hisself, why then, in course, there's sometimes as much as fifty pound, or maybe a hundred, set on the body. His friends are glad to get the corpse back, an' prove his death, an' hev it buried reglar in the family churchyard. Saves a deal in lawyer's expenses, that do. I doon't deny but what they offer free enough for a nob. But how many nobs goo and drownd their-selves in a season, do yow suppose? And who that knew any-thing about the river would goo a-lookin' for nobs in Limehouso Reach or down about Bermondsey way?'"

" It stand to reason they woon't, Bill," the other voice answered with a quiet chuckle.

" In course it stand to reason," Bill replied warmly with an emphatic expletive. " When a nob drownd hisself, he doon't hull hisself off London Bridge; no, nor off Blackfriars nather, I warrant ye. He doon't put hisself out aforehand for nothin' like that, takin' a 'bus into the City out o' pure fulishness. He jest clap bis hat on his hid an' stroll down to Westminister Bridge, or to Charen Cross or Waterloo—a lot on 'em goo oover Waterloo, pleece or no pleece ; an' he jump in cloose an' handy to his own door, in a way of speakin', and a done wooth it. But what's the use of lookin' for him arter that below bridge, down Limehouse way? Anybody what know tho river know well enough that a body startin' from Waterloo, or maybe from Westminister, doon't goo down to Limehouse, ebb or flow, nor nothing like it. It get into the whirlpool off Saunders's wharf, an' ketch the back-current, and turn round and round till it's flung up by the tide, as yow may say, upward, on the mud at Milbank, or by Lambeth Stangate. Soo there een't a livin' to be made anyhow by pickin' up bodies down about Limehouse ; an' it's allus been my opinion ever since then that that there Dickens is a very much ooverrated pusson."

" There een't the least doubt about that," the other answered. " If he said soo, yow can't be far wrong there nather."

To Hugh Massinger, sitting apart in his own room, these strange scraps of an alien conversation had just then a ghastly and horrible fascination. These men were accustomed, then, to drowned corpses ! They were connoisseurs in drowning. They knew the ways of bodies like regular experts. Ho listened, spellbound, to catch their next sentences. There was a short pause, during which—as he judged by the way they breathed —each took a long pull at the pewter mug, and then the last speaker began again. "Yow owt to know," he murmured musingly, " for I s'pose there een't any man on the river any-where what 'a had to do wooth as many bodies as yow hev !"

" Yow're right, bor," the first person assented emphatically.

"Thutty year I ha' sarved the Trinity House, sunshine or rain, an' yow doon't pervision lightships that long woothout larnin' a thing or two on the way about corpsus. The current carry 'em all one way round. A body what start on its jarney at Westminister, as it may be here, goo ashore at Milbank. A body which begin at London Bridge, come out, as reglar as clock-wuck, on the fudder ind o' the Isle o' Dogs.—It's jest the same along this here east coost. I picked up that gal I ha' come about to-day on the north side o' the Orfordness Light, by the back o' the Trinity groyne or cloose by. A body which come up on the north side of Orfordness has allus drifted down from the nor'-west'ard. Soo it stand to reason this here gal I ha' got layin' up there in the dead-house must ha' come wooth the ebb from Walzerwig or Aldeburgh or maybe Whitestrand. There een't another way out of it anyhow. Well, they towd me at Walzerwig there was a young lady missin' oover here at White-strand—a young lady from the Hall—a nob, niver doubt : an' as there might be money in it, or agin there mightn't, why, in course, I come up here to make all proper enquiries."

Hugh Massinger's heart gave a terrible bound. Oh, heavens! that things should have come to this pass. That wretch had found Elsie's body!

In what a tangled maze of impossibilities had he enmeshed himself for ever by that one false step of the forged letter. This wretch had found Elsie's body—the body that he loved with all his soul—and he could neither claim it himself nor look upon it, bury it nor show the faintest interest in it, without involving his case still further in endless complications, and rousing suspicions of fatal import against his own character.

He waited breathless for the next sentence. The second speaker went on once more. "And it doon't fit?" he suggested, inquiringly.

"No, it doon't fit, drot it," the man called Bill answered in an impatient tone. "She een't drownded at all, wuss luck, the young lady what's missin' from the Hall. They ha' had letters an' talegraphs from har, dated later'n the day I found har. I ha' handed oover the body to the county pleece; it's in the dead-house at the Low Light : an' I shan't hev noo more than half a crown from the parish arter all for all my trouble. Suffolk an' Essex are half a crown counties ; Surrey's more liberal ; it goo to five bob on 'em. Why, I'm more'n eight shillins out o' pocket by that there gal a'ready, what wooth loss o' time an' travellin' expenses an' soo on. Next time I ketch a body knockin' about on a lee shore, wooth the tide runnin', an' the breakers poundin' it on its face on the shingle, they may whistle for it theirselves, that's what they may doo ; I een't a-gooin' to trouble my hid about it. Make a livin' out on it, indeed! Why, it's all

rubbidge, nothin' more or less. It's my opinion that there
Dickens is a very much ooverrated pusson."

Hugh Massinger rose slowly, like one stunned, walked across
the room, as in a dream, to the door, closed it noiselessly, for he
could contain himself no longer, and then, burying his face
silently in his arms, cried to himself a long and bitter cry, the
tears following one another hot and fast down his burning
cheeks, while his throat was choked by a rising ball that seemed
to check his breath and impede the utterance of his stifled sobs.
Elsie was dead, dead for him as if he had actually seen her
drowned body cast up, unknown, as the man so hideously and
graphically described it in his callous brutality, upon the long
spit of the Orfordness lighthouse. He didn't for one moment
doubt that it was she indeed whom the fellow had found and
placed in the mortuary. His own lie reacted fatally against
himself. He had put others on a false track, and now the false
track misled his own spirit. From that day forth, Elsie was
indeed dead, dead, dead for him. Alive in reality, and for all
else save him, she was dead for him as though he had seen her
buried. And yet, most terrible irony of all, he must still pretend before all the world strenuously and ceaselessly to believe
her living. He must never in a single forgetful moment display
his grief and remorse for the past; his sorrow for the loss of the
one woman he had really loved—and basely betrayed; his profound affection for her now she was gone and lost to him for
ver. He dare not even inquire—for the present at least—
'here she would be laid, or what would be done with her poor
dishonoured and neglected corpse. It must be buried, unheeded, in a pauper's nameless grave, by creatures as base and
cruel as the one who had discovered it tossing on the shore, and
regarded it only as a lucky find to make half a crown out of.
Hugh's inmost soul was revolted at the thought. And yet——
And yet, even so, he was not man enough to go boldly down to
Orfordness and claim and rescue that sacred corpse, as he truly
and firmly believed it to be, of Elsie Challoner's. He meant still
in his craven soul to stand well with the world, and to crown his
perfidy by marrying Winifred.

CHAPTER XVII.

BREAKING A HEART.

WHEN Warren Relf returned to Lowestoft, burning with news
and eager at his luck, his first act was to call his sister Edie
hurriedly out of Elsie's room, and proceed to a consultation

with her upon the strange evidence he had picked up so unexpectedly at Almundham Station.　Should they show it to Elsie,
or should they keep it from her?　That was the question.　Fortune had indeed favoured the brave; but how now to utilize
her curious information?　Should they let that wronged and
suffering girl see the utter abysses of human baseness yawning
in the man she once loved and trusted, or should they sedulously
and carefully hide it all from her, lest they break the bruised
reed with their ungentle handling?　Warren Relf himself, after
thinking it over in his own soul—all the way back to Lowestoft
in his third-class carriage—was almost in favour now of the
specious and futile policy of concealment.　Why needlessly
harrow the poor child's feelings?　Why rake up the embers of
her great grief?　Surely she had been wounded and lacerated
enough already.　Let her rest content with what she knew so
far of Massinger's cruel and treacherous selfishness.

But Edie met this plausible reasoning, after a true women's
fashion, with an emphatic negative.　She stood out for the
truth, the whole truth, and nothing but the truth, come what
might of it.

"Why?" Warren asked with a relenting eye.

"Because," Edie answered, looking up at him resolutely, "it
would be better she should get it all over at once.　It's like
pulling a tooth—one wrench, and be done with it!　What a pity
she should spend her whole life long in mourning and wailing
over this wicked man, who isn't and never was in any way
worthy of her!—Warren, she's a dear, sweet, gentle girl.　She
takes my heart.　I love her dearly already.—She'll mourn and
wail for him enough anyhow.　I want to disenchant her as
much as I can before it's too late.　The sooner she learns to
hate and despise him as he deserves, the better for everybody."

"Why?" Warren asked once more, with a curious side-glance.

"Because," Edie went on, very earnestly, "she may some day
meet some other better man, who could make her ten thousand
times happier as his wife, than this wretched, sordid, money-
hunting creature could ever make any one.　If we disenchant
her at once, without remorse, it'll help that better man's case
forward whenever he presents himself.　If not——' She paused
significantly.　Their eyes met; Warren's fell.　They understood
one another.

"But isn't it selfish?" Warren asked wistfully.

Edie looked up at him with a profoundly meaningless expression on her soft round face.　"Selfish!" she cried, making
her mouth small.　"I don't understand you.　What on earth
has selfishness to do with it any way?　Nobody spoke about
any particular truer and better man.　You jump too quick.　I
merely laid on a young man in the abstract.　From the point of

view of a young man in the abstract, I'm sure I'm right, absolutely right. I always am. It's a way I have, and I can't help it."

"Besides which," Warren Relf interposed suddenly, "if Massinger really did write that forged letter, she'll have to arrange something about it, you see, sooner or later. She'll want to set herself right with the Meyseys, of course, and she'll probably make some sort of representation or proposition to Massinger."

"She'll do nothing of the kind, my dear," Edie answered promptly with brisk confidence.—"You're a goose, Warren, and you don't one tiny little bit understand the inferior creatures. You men always think you know instinctively all about us women, and can read us through and through at a single glance, as if we were large print on a street-poster; while, as a matter of fact, you never really see an inch deep below the surface.— I'll tell you what she'll do, you great blind creature: she'll accept the forgery as if it were in actual fact her own letter; she'll never write a word, for good or for evil, to contradict it or confirm it, to any of these horrid Whitestrand people; she'll allow this hateful wretch Massinger to go on believing she's really dead; and she'll cease to exist, as far as he's concerned, in a passive sort of way, henceforth and for ever."

"Will she?" Warren Relf asked dubiously. "How on earth do you know what she'll do, Edie?"

"Why, what else on earth *could* she do, silly?" his sister nswered, with the same perfect conviction in her own inbred ıgacity and perspicacity as ever. "Could she go and say to ıim, with tears in her eyes and a becoming smile on her pretty little lips: 'My own heart's darling, I love you devotedly—and I know you signed my name to that forged letter?' Could she fling herself on these Moxies, or Mumpsies, or Mixies, or Meyseys, or whatever else you call them, and say sweetly: 'I didn't run away from you; I wasn't in earnest? I only tried ineffectually to drown myself, for love of this dear, sweet, charming, poetical cousin of mine, who disgracefully jilted me in order to propose to your own daughter; and then, believing me to have killed myself for shame and sorrow, has trumped up letters and telegrams in my name, of malice prepense, on purpose to deceive you. He's a mean scoundrel, and I hate his very name; and I want him for myself; so I won't allow him to marry your Winifred, or whatever else her precious new-fangled high-faluting name may be.' Could any woman on earth so utterly efface herself and her own womanliness as to go and say all that, do you suppose, to anybody anywhere?—*You* may think so in your heart, I dare say, my dear boy; but you won't get a solitary woman in the world to agree with you on the point for one single minute."

The painter drew his hand slowly across his cold brow. "I suppose you're right, Edie," he answered, bewildered. "But what'll she do with herself, then, I wonder?"

"Do?" Edie echoed. "As if *do* were the word for it? Why, do nothing, of course—be; suffer; exist; mourn over it. She'd like, if she could, poor, tender, bruised, broken-hearted thing, to creep into a hole, with her head hanging down, and die quietly, like a wounded creature, with no one on earth to worry or bother her. She mustn't die; but she won't *do* anything. All we've got to do ourselves is just to comfort her: to be silent and comfort her. She'll cease to live now; she'll annihilate herself; she'll retire from life; and that horrid man'll think she's dead; and that'll be all. She'll accept the situation. She won't expose him; she loves him too much a great deal for that. She won't expose herself; she's a great deal too timid and shrinking and modest for that. She'll leave things alone; that's all she can do.—And on the whole, my dear, if you only knew, it's really and truly the best thing possible."

So Edie took the letter and telegram pitifully in her hand, and went with what boldness she could muster up into Elsie's bedroom. Elsie was lying on the sofa, propped up on pillows, in the white dress she had worn all along, and with her face and hands as white as the dress stuff; and as Edie held the incriminating documents, part hidden in her gown, to keep them from Elsie, she felt like the dentist who hides behind his back the cruel wrenching instrument with which he means next moment in one fierce tug to drag and tear your very nerves out. She stooped down and kissed Elsie tenderly. "Well, darling," she said—for illness makes women wonderfully intimate—"Warren's come back.—Where do you think he's been?—He's been over to-day as far as Almundham."

"Almundham!" Elsie repeated, with cheek more blanched and pale than ever. "Why, what was he doing over there to-day, dear? Did he hear anything about—about—— Were they all inquiring after me, I wonder?—Was there a great deal of talk and gossip abroad?—Oh, Edie, tell me quick all about it!"

"No, darling," Edie answered, pressing her hand tight, and signing to her mother, who sat by the bed, to clasp the other one; "nobody's talking. You shall not be discussed. Warren met Mr. Meysey himself at the Almundham Station; and Mr. Meysey was going to Scotland; and he said they'd heard from you twice already, to explain it all; and nobody seemed to think that—that anything serious in any way had happened."

"Heard from me twice!" Elsie cried, puzzled. "Heard from me twice—to explain it all! Why, what on earth did he mean, Edie? There must be some strange mistake somewhere."

Edie leant over her with tears in her eyes. It was a horrible wrench, but come it must, and the sooner the better. They should understand where they stood at once. "No, no mistake, darling," she answered distinctly. "Mr. Meysey gave Warren the letter to read.—He's brought it back. I've got it here for you. It's in your own hand, he says.—Would you like to see it this moment, darling?"

Elsie's cheek showed pale as death now; but she summoned up courage to murmur "Yes."

It seemed the mere unearthly ghost of a *yes*, so hollow and empty was it; but she forced it out somehow, and took the letter. Edie watched her with bent brows and trembling lips. How would she take it? Would she see what it meant? Would she know who wrote it? Could she ever believe it?

Elsie gazed at it in dumb astonishment. So admirable was the imitation, that for a moment's space she actually thought it was her own handwriting. She scanned it close. "My darling Winifred," it began as usual, and in her own hand too. Why, this must be just an old letter of her own to her friend and pupil; what possible connection could Mr. Meysey or Mr. Relf imagine it had with the present crisis? But then the date—the date was so curious: "September 17,"—that fatal evening! She glanced through it all with a burning eye. Great heavens, what was this? "So wicked, so ungrateful: I know Mrs. Meysey will never forgive me."—"By the time this reaches you I shall have left Whitestrand, I fear for ever." "Darling, for eaven's sake, do try to hush this up as much as you can."— Ever your affectionate, but broken-hearted ELSIE."

A gasp burst from her bloodless lips. She laid it down, with both hands on her heart. That signature, ELSIE, betrayed the whole truth. She was white as a sheet now, and trembling visibly from head to foot. But she would go right through with it; she would not flinch; she would know it all—all—all, utterly.

"I never wrote it," she cried to Edie with a choking voice.

"I know you didn't, darling," Edie whispered in her ear.

"And you know who did?" Elsie sobbed out, terrified.

Elsie nodded. "I know who did—at least, I suspect.—Cry, darling, cry. Never mind us. Don't burst your poor heart for want of crying."

But Elsie couldn't cry yet. She put her white hand, trembling, into her open bosom, and pulled out slowly, with long lingering reluctance—a tiny bundle of water-stained letters. They were Hugh's letters, that she had worn at her breast on that terrible night. She had dried them all carefully one by one here in bed at Lowestoft; and she kept them still next the broken heart that Hugh had so lightly sacrificed to mammon. Smudged and half-erased by immersion as they were, she could still read them in their blurred condition; and she knew them by heart already, for the matter of that, if the water had made them quite illegible.

She drew the last one out of its envelope with reverent care, and laid it down side by side with the forged letter to Winifred. Paper for paper, they answered exactly, in size and shape and glaze and quality. Hugh had often shown her how admirably he could imitate any particular handwriting. The suspicion was profound; but she would give him at least the full benefit of all possible doubts. She held it up to the light and examined the water-mark. Both were identical—an unusual paper; bought at a fantastic stationer's in Brighton. It was driving daggers into her own heart; but she would go right through with it: she must know the truth. She gave a great gasp, and then took three other letters singly from the packet. Horror and dismay were awakening within her the instincts and ideas of an experienced detective. They were the three previous letters she had last received from Hugh, in regular order. A stain caused by a drop of milk or grease, as often happens, ran right through the entire quire. It was biggest on the front page of the earliest letter, and smallest and dimmest on its back fly-leaf. It went on decreasing gradually by proportionate gradations through the other three. She looked at the letter to Winifred with tearless eyes. It corresponded exactly in every respect; for it had been the fifth and middle sheet of the original series.

Elsie laid them all down on the sofa by her side with an exhausted air and turned wearily to Edie. Her face was flushed and feverish at last. She said nothing, but leaned back with a ghastly sob on her pillow. She knew to a certainty now it was Hugh who had done this nameless thing—Hugh who had done it, believing her, his lover, to be drowned and dead—Hugh who had done it at the very moment when, as he himself supposed, her lifeless body was tossing and dancing among the mad breakers, that roared and shivered with unholy joy over the hoarse sandbanks of the bar at Whitestrand. It was past belief —but it was Hugh who had done it.

She could have forgiven him almost anything else save *that*; but *that*, never, ten thousand times never! She could have forgiven him even his cold and cruel speech that last night by the river near the poplar: "I have never been engaged to you. I owe you nothing. And now I mean to marry Winifred." She could have forgiven him all, in the depth of her despair.—She could have loved him still, even—so profound is the power of first-love in a true pure woman's inmost nature—if only she could have believed he had melted and repented in sackcloth and ashes for his sin and her sorrow. If he had lost his life in trying to save her! If he had roused the county to search for her body! Nay, even if he had merely gone home, remorseful and self-reproaching, and had proclaimed the truth and his own shame in an agony of regret and pity and bereavement.—For her own sake, she was glad, indeed, he had not done all this; or at least she would perhaps have been glad if she had had the heart to think of herself at all at such a moment. But for him—for him—she was ashamed and horrified and stricken dumb to learn it.

For, instead of all this, what nameless and unspeakable thing had Hugh Massinger really done? Gone home to the inn, at the very moment when she lay there senseless, the prey of the waves, that tossed her about like a plaything on their cruel crests—gone home to the inn, and without one thought of her, one effort to rescue her—for how could she think otherwise?— full only of vile and craven fears for his own safety, sat down at his desk and deliberately forged in alien handwriting that embodied Lie, that visible and tangible documentary Meanness, that she saw staring her in the face from the paper before her! It was ghastly; it was incredible; it was past conception; but it was, nevertheless, the simple fact. As she floated insensible down that hideous current, for the sea and the river to fight over her blanched corpse, the man she had loved, the man who had so long pretended to love her, had been quietly engaged in his own room in forging her name to a false and horrible and misleading letter, which might cover her with shame in the unknown grave to which his own cruelty and wickedness and callousness had seemingly consigned her! No wonder the tears stood back unwillingly from her burning eyeballs. For grief and horror and misery like hers, no relief can be found in mere hysterical weeping.

And who had done this heartless, this dastardly, this impossible thing? Hugh Massinger—her cousin Hugh—the man she had set on such a pinnacle of goodness and praise and affection— the man she had worshipped with her whole full heart—the man she had accepted as the very incarnation of all that was truest and noblest and best and most beautiful in human nature. Her idol was dethroned from its shrine now; and in the empty niche from which it had cast itself prone, she had nothing to set up instead for worship. There was not, and there never had been, a Hugh. The universe swam like a frightful blank around her. The sun had darkened itself at once in her sky. The solid ground seemed to fail beneath her feet, and she felt herself suspended alone above an awful abyss, a seething and tossing and eddying abyss of utter chaos.

Edie Relf held her hand still; while the sweet gentle motherly old lady with the snow-white hair and the tender eyes put a cold

palm up against her burning brow to help her to bear it. But
Elsie was hardly aware of either of them now. Her head swam
wildly round and round in a horrible phantasmagoria, of which
the Hugh that was not and that never had been formed the
central pivot and main revolving point; while the Hugh that
was just revealing himself utterly in his inmost blackness and
vileness and nothingness whirled round and round that fixed
centre in a mad career, she knew not how, and she asked not
wherefore. "Cry, cry, darling, do try to cry," both the other
women urged upon her with sobs and tears; but Elsie's eyeballs
were hard and tearless, and her heart stood still every moment
within her with unspeakable awe and horror and incredulity.

Presently she stretched out a vague hand towards Edie.
"Give me the telegram, dear," she said in a cold hard voice, as
cold and hard as Hugh Massinger's own on that fearful evening.

Edie handed it to her without a single word.

She looked at it mechanically, her lips set tight; then she
asked in the same cold metallic tone as before: "Do you know
anything of 27, Holmbury Place, Duke Street, St. James's?"

"Warren says the club porter of the Cheyne Row lives there,"
Edie answered softly.

Elsie fell back upon her pillows once more. "Edie," she cried,
"oh, Edie, Edie, hold me tight, or I shall sink and die!—If only
he had been cruel and nothing more, I wouldn't have minded
it; indeed, I wouldn't. But that he should be so cowardly, so
mean, so unworthy of himself—it kills me, it kills me—I couldn't
have believed it!"

"Kiss her, mother," Edie whispered low. "Kiss her, and lay
her head, so, upon your dear old shoulder! She's going to cry
now! I know she's going to cry! Pat her cheek: yes, so. If
only she can cry, she can let her heart out, and it won't quite
kill her."

At the words, Elsie found the blessed relief of tears; they rose
to her eyes in a torrent flood. She cried and cried as if her
heart would burst. But it eased her somehow. The two other
women cried in sympathy, holding her hands, and encouraging
her to let out her pent-up emotions to the very full by that
natural outlet. They cried together silently for many minutes.
Then Elsie pressed their two hands with a convulsive grasp; and
they knew she would live, and that the shock had not entirely
killed out the woman within her.

An hour later, when Edie, with eyes very red and swollen, went
out once more into the little front parlour to fetch some needle-
work, Warren Relf intercepted her with eager questioning.
"How is she now?" he asked with an anxious face. "Is she
very ill? And how did she take it?"

"She's crying her eyes out, thank heaven," Edie answered

fervently. "And it's broken her heart. It's almost killed her, but not quite. She's crushed and lacerated like a wounded creature."

"But what will she do?" Warren asked, with a wistful look.

"Do? Just what I said. Nothing at all. Annihilate and efface herself. She'll accept the position, leaving things exactly where that wretched being has managed to put them; and so far as he's concerned, she'll drop altogether out of existence."

"How?"

"She'll go with mamma and me to San Remo."

"And the Meyseys?"

"She'll leave them to form their own conclusions. Henceforth, she prefers to be simply nobody."

CHAPTER XVIII.

COMPLICATIONS.

ELSIE spent a full fortnight, or even more, at Lowestoft; and before she vacated her hospitable quarters in the Relfs' rooms, it was quite understood between them all that she was to follow out the simple plan of action so hastily sketched by Edie to Warren. Elsie's one desire now was to escape observation. Eyes seemed to peer at her from every corner. She wanted to fly for ever from Hugh—from that Hugh who had at last so unconsciously revealed to her the inmost depths of his own abject and self-centred nature; and she wanted to be saved the hideous necessity for explaining to others what only the three Relfs at present knew—the way she had come to leave White-strand. Hungering for sympathy, as women will hunger in a great sorrow, she had opened to Edie, bit by bit, the floodgates of her grief, and told piecemeal the whole of her painful and pitiable story. In her own mind, Elsie was free from the reproach of an attempt at self-murder; and Edie and Mrs. Relf accepted in good faith the poor heart-broken girl's account of her adventure; but she could never hope that the outer world could be induced to believe in her asserted innocence. She dreaded the nods and hints and suspicions and innuendoes of our bitter society; she shrank from exposing herself to its sneers or its sympathy, each almost equally distasteful to her delicate nature. She was threatened with the pillory of a news-paper paragraph. Hugh Massinger's lie afforded her now an easy chance of escape. She accepted it willingly, without after-thought. All she wanted in her trouble was to hide her poor head where none would find it; and Edie Relf's plan enabled her to do this in the surest and safest possible manner.

Besides, she didn't wish to make Winifred unhappy. Winifred loved her cousin Hugh. She saw that now; she recognized it distinctly. She wondered she hadn't seen it plainly long before. Winifred had often been so full of Hugh; had asked so many questions, had seemed so deeply interested in all that concerned him. And Hugh had offered his heart to Winifred—be the same more or less, he had at least offered it. Why should she wish to wreck Winifred's life, as that cruel, selfish, ambitious man had wrecked her own? She couldn't tell the whole truth now without exposing Hugh. And for Winifred's sake at least she would not expose him, and blight Winifred's dream at the very moment of its first full ecstasy.

For Winifred's sake? Nay, rather for his own. For in spite of everything, she still loved him. She could never forgive him, but she still loved him. Or if she didn't love the Hugh that really was, she loved at least the memory of the Hugh that was not and that never had been. For his dear sake, she could never expose that other base creature that bore his name and wore his features. For her own love's sake, she could never betray him. For her womanly consistency, for her sense of identity, she couldn't turn round and tell the truth about him. To acquiesce in a lie was wrong, perhaps; but to tell the truth would have been more than human.

"I wish," she cried in her agony to Edie, "I could go away at once and hide myself for ever in America or Australia, or somewhere like that—where *he* would never know I was really living."

Edie stroked her smooth black hair with a gentle hand; she had views of her own already, had Edie. "It's a far cry to Loch Awe, darling," she murmured softly. "Better come with mother and me to San Remo."

"San Remo?" Elsie echoed. "Why, San Remo?"

And then Edie explained to her in brief outline that she and her mother went every winter to the Riviera, taking with them a few delicate English girls of consumptive tendency, partly to educate, but more still to escape the bitter English Christmas. They hired a villa—the same every year—on a slope of the hills, and engaged a resident governess to accompany them. But, as chance would have it, their last governess had just gone off, in the nick of time, to get married to her faithful bank clerk at Brixton; so here was an opportunity for mutual accommodation. As Edie put the thing, Elsie might almost have supposed, were she so minded, she would be doing Mrs. Relf an exceptional favour by accepting the post and accompanying them to Italy. And, to say the truth, a Girton graduate who had taken high honours at Cambridge was certainly a degree or two better than anything the delicate girls of consumptive tendency could reasonably have expected to obtain at San Remo. But none the less the offer was a generous one, kindly meant; and Elsie accepted it just as it was intended. It was a fair exchange of mutual services. She must earn her own livelihood wherever she went; trouble, however deep, has always that special aggravation and that special consolation for penniless people; and in no other house could she possibly have earned it without a reference or testimonial from her last employers. The Relfs needed no such awkward introduction. This arrangement suited both parties admirably; and poor heart-broken Elsie, in her present shattered condition of nerves, was glad enough to accept her new friends' kind hospitality at Lowestoft for the present, till she could fly with them at last, early in October, from this desecrated England and from the chance of running up against Hugh Massinger.

Her whole existence summed itself up now in the one wish to escape Hugh. He thought her dead. She hoped in her heart he might never again discover she was living.

On the very first day when she dared to venture out in a Bath-chair, muffled and veiled, and in a new black dress—lest any one perchance should happen to recognize her—she asked to be wheeled to the Lowestoft pier; and Edie, who accompanied her out on that sad first ride, walked slowly by her side in sympathetic silence. Warren Relf followed her too, but at a safe distance; he could not think of obtruding as yet a male presence upon her shame and grief; but still he could not wholly deny himself either the modest pleasure of watching her from afar, unseen and unsuspected. Warren had hardly so much as caught a glimpse of Elsie since that night on the *Mud-Turtle*; but Elsie's gentleness and the profundity of her sorrow had touched him deeply. He began indeed to suspect he was really in love with her; and perhaps his suspicion was not entirely baseless. He knew too well, however, the depth of her distress to dream of pressing even his sympathy upon her at so inopportune a moment. If ever the right time for him came at all, it could come, he knew, only in the remote future.

At the end of the pier, Elsie halted the chair, and made the chairman wheel it as she directed, exactly opposite one of the open gaps in the barrier of woodwork that ran round it. Then she raised herself. up with difficulty from her seat. She was holding something tight in her small right hand; she had drawn it that moment from the folds of her bosom. It was a packet of papers, tied carefully in a knot with some heavy object. Warren Relf, observing cautiously from behind, felt sure in his own mind it was a heavy object by the curve it described as it wheeled through the air when Elsie threw it. For Elsie had risen now, pale and red by turns, and was flinging it out with feverish energy in a sweeping arch far, far into the water. It struck the surface with a dull thud—the heavy thud of a stone or a metallic body. In a second it had sunk like lead to the bottom, and Elsie, bursting into a silent flood of tears, had ordered the chairman to take her home again.

Warren Relf, skulking hastily down the steps behind that lead to the tidal platform under the pier, had no doubt at all in his own mind what the object was that Elsie had flung with such fiery force into the deep water; for that night on the *Mud-Turtle*, as he tried to restore the insensible girl to a passing gleam of life and consciousness, two distinct articles had fallen, one by one, in the hurry of the moment, out of her loose and dripping bosom. He was not curious, but he couldn't help observing them. The first was a bundle of water-logged letters in a hand which it was impossible for him not to recognize. The second was a pretty little lady's watch, in gold and enamel, with a neat inscription engraved on a shield on the back, " E. C. from H. M.," in Lombardic letters. It wasn't Warren Relf's fault if he knew then who H. M. was; and it wasn't his fault if he knew now that Elsie Challoner had formally renounced Hugh Massinger's love, by flinging his letters and presents bodily into the deep sea, where no one could ever possibly recover them.

They had burnt into her flesh, lying there in her bosom. She could carry them about next her bruised and wounded heart no longer. And now, on this very first day that she had ventured out, she buried her love and all that belonged to it in that deep where Hugh Massinger himself had sent her.

But even so, it cost her hard. They were Hugh's letters— those precious much-loved letters. She went home that morning crying bitterly, and she cried till night, like one who mourns her lost husband or her lost children. They were all she had left of Hugh and of her day-dream. Edie knew exactly what she had done, but avoided the vain effort to comfort or console her. " Comfort—comfort scorned of devils! " Edie was woman enough to know she could do nothing. She only held her new friend's hand tight clasped in hers, and cried beside her in mute sisterly sympathy.

It was about a week later that Hugh Massinger, goaded by remorse, and unable any longer to endure the suspense of hearing nothing further, directly or indirectly, as to Elsie's fate, set out one morning in a dogcart from Whitestrand, and drove along the coast with his own thoughts, in a blazing sunlight, as far as Aldeburgh. There, the road abruptly stops. No highway spans the ridge of beach beyond: the remainder of the

distance to the Low Light at Orfordness must be accomplished
on foot, along a flat bank that stretches for miles between sea
and river, untrodden and trackless, one bare blank waste of
sand and shingle. The ruthless sun was pouring down upon it
in full force as Hugh Massinger began his solitary tramp along
that uneven road at the Martello Tower, just south of
Aldeburgh. The more usual course is to sail by sea; and
Hugh might indeed have hired a boat at Slaughden Quay if he
dared; but he feared to be recognized as having come from
Whitestrand to make inquiries about the unclaimed body; for
to rouse suspicion would be doubly unwise: he felt like a
murderer, and he considered himself one by implication already.
If other people grew to suspect that Elsie was drowned, it
would go hard but they would think as ill of him as he
himself thought of himself in his bitterest moments.

For, horrible to relate, all this time, with that burden of
agony and anguish and suspense weighing down his soul like a
mass of lead, he had had to play as best he might, every night
and morning, at the ardour of young love with that girl
Winifred. He had had to imitate with hateful skill the
wantonness of youth and the ecstasy of the happily betrothed
lover. He had had to wear a mask of pleasure on his pinched
face while his heart within was full of bitterness, as he cried
to himself more than once in his reckless agony. After such
unnatural restraint, reaction was inevitable. It became a
light to him to get away for once from that grim comedy, in
nich he acted his part with so much apparent ease, and to
race the genuine tragedy of his miserable life, alone and
undisturbed with his own remorseful thoughts for a few short
hours or so. He looked upon that fierce tramp in the eye of the
sun, trudging ever on over those baking stones, and through
that barren spit of sand and shingle, to some extent in the light
of a self-imposed penance—a penance, and yet a splendid
indulgence as well; for here there was no one to watch or
observe him. Here he could let the tears trickle down his face
unreproved, and no longer pretend to believe himself happy.
Here there was no Winifred to tease him with her love. He
had sold his own soul for a few wretched acres of stagnant salt
marsh: he could gloat now at his ease over his hateful bargain;
he could call himself "Fool" at the top of his voice; he could
groan and sigh and be as sad as night, no man hindering him.
It was an orgy of remorse, and he gave way to it with wild
orgiastic fervour.

He plodded, plodded, plodded ever on, stumbling wearily
over that endless shingle, thirsty and footsore, mile after mile,
yet glad to be relieved for awhile from the strain of his long
hypocrisy, and to let the tears flow easily and naturally one

after the other down his parched cheek. Truly he walked in
the gall of bitterness and in the bond of iniquity. The iron
was entering into his own soul; and yet he hugged it. The
gloom of that barren stretch of water-worn pebbles, the weird
and widespread desolation of the landscape, the fierce glare of
the mid-day sun that poured down mercilessly on his aching
head, all chimed in congenially with his present brooding and
melancholy humour, and gave strength to the poignancy of his
remorse and regret. He could torture himself to the bone in
these small matters, for dead Elsie's sake; he could do penance,
but not make restitution. He couldn't even so tell out the
truth before the whole world, or right the two women he had
cruelly wronged, by an open confession.

At last, after mile upon mile of weary staggering, he reached
the Low Light, and sat down, exhausted, on the bare shingle
just outside the lighthouse-keeper's quarters. Strangers are
rare at Orfordness; and a morose-looking man, soured by
solitude, soon presented himself at the door to stare at the new-
comer.

"Tramped it?" he asked curtly, with an inquiring glance
along the shingle beach.

"Yes, tramped it," Hugh answered, with a weary sigh, and
relapsed into silence, too utterly tired to think of how he had
best set about the prosecution of his delicate inquiry, now that
he had got there.

The man stood with his hand on his hip, and watched the
stranger long and close, with frank mute curiosity, as one
watches a wild beast in its cage at a menagerie. At last he
broke the solemn silence once more with the one inquisitive
word, " Why?"

"Amusement," Hugh answered, catching the man's laconic
humour to the very echo.

For twenty minutes they talked on, in this brief disjointed
Spartan fashion, with question and answer as to the life at
Orfordness tossed to and fro like a quick ball between them, till
at last Hugh touched, as if by accident, but with supreme skill,
upon the abstract question of provisioning lighthouses.

"Trinity House steam-cutter," the man replied to his short
suggested query, with a sidelong jerk of his head to southward.
"Twice a month. Pritty fair grub. Biscuit and pork an' tinned
meat an' soo on."

"Queer employment, the cutter's men," Hugh interposed
quietly. "Must see a deal of life in their way sometimes."

The man nodded. "Yis, an' death too," he assented with
uncompromising brevity.

"Wrecks?"

"*And* corpsus."

“ Corpses ? ”

“ Ah, corpsus, I believe you. Drownded ones. Plenty on 'em.”

“ Here ? ”

“ Sometimes. But moostly on the north side. Drift wooth the tide. Cutter’s man found one oonly a week agoo last Sarraday. Oover hinder aginst that groyne to windwud.”

“ Sailor ? ”

“ Not this time—gal— young woman.”

“ Where did she come from ? ” Hugh asked eagerly, yet suppressing his eagerness in his face and voice as well as he was able.

“ Doon’t know, u’m sure,” the man answered with something very like a shrug. “ They doon’t carry their naames and poorts wroot on their foreheads as though they wor vessels. Lowstof, Whitestrand, Southwold, Aldeburgh—might ha’ bin any on ’em.

Hugh continued his inquiries with breathless interest a few minutes longer, then he asked again in a trembling voice: “ Any jewelry on her ? ”

The man eyed him suspiciously askance. Detective in disguise, or what? he wondered. “ Ast the cutter’s man,” he drawled out slowly, after a long pause. “ If there was anything val’able on the corpse, t’een’t likely he’d leave it about har for the coroner to nail—not he ! ”

The answer cast an unexpected flood of light on the seafaring view of the treasure-trove of corpses, for which Hugh had hardly before been prepared in his own mind. That would account for her not having been recognized. “ Did they hold an inquest ? ” he ventured to ask nervously.

The lighthouse-man nodded. “ But whot’s the use o’ that ?— noo evidence,” he continued. “ Moost o’ these drownded bodies aren’t ’dentified. Jury browt it in ‘ Found drownded.’ Convenient vardick—save a lot o’ trouble.”

“ Where do you bury them ? ” Hugh asked, hardly able to control his emotion.

The man waved his hand with a careless dash towards a sandy patch just beyond the High Light. “ Oover hinder,” he answered. “ There’s shiploads on ’em there. Easy diggin’. Easier than the shingle. We buried the crew of a Hamburg brigantine there all in a lump last winter. They went ashore on the Oaze Sands. All hands drownded, about a baker’s dozen on ’em. Coroner came oover from Orford an’ set on ’em, here on the spot, as yow may say. That’s consecrated ground. Bishop came from Norwich and said his prayers oover it. A corpse coon’t lay better, nor more comforable, if it come to that, in Woodbridge Cemmetry.”

He laughed low to himself at his own grim wit; and Hugh,

unable to conceal his disgust, walked off alone, as if idly strolling in a solitary mood, towards that desolate graveyard. The lighthouse-man went back, rolling a quid in his bulged cheek, to his monotonous avocations. Hugh stumbled over the sand with blinded eyes and tottering feet till he reached the plot with its little group of rude mounds. There was one mound far newer and fresher than all the rest, and a wooden label stood at its head with a number roughly scrawled on it in wet paint—"240." His heart failed and sank within him. So this was *her* grave!—Elsie's grave! Elsie, Elsie, poor, desolate, abandoned, heart-broken Elsie.—He took off his hat in reverent remorse as he stood by its side. Oh, heavens, how he longed to be dead there with her! Should he fling himself off the top of the lighthouse now? Should ho cut his throat beside her nameless grave? Should he drown himself with Elsie on that hopeless stretch of wild coast? Or should he live on still, a miserable, wretched, self-condemned coward, to pay the penalty of his cruelty and his baseness through years of agony.

Elsie's grave! If only he could be sure it was really Elsie's! He wished he could. In time, then, he might venture to put up a headstone with just her initials—those sacred initials. But no; he dared not. And perhaps, after all, it might not be Elsie. Corpses came up here often and often. Had they not buried whole shiploads together, as the lighthouse-man assured him, after a terrible tempest?

He stood there long, bareheaded in the sun. His remorse was gnawing the very life out of him. He was rooted to the spot. Elsie held him spellbound. At length he roused himself, and with a terrible effort returned to the lighthouse. "Where did you say this last body came up?" he asked the man in as careless a voice as he could easily master.

The man eyed him sharp and hard. "Yow fare anxious about that there young woman," he answered coldly. "She flooted longside by the groyne oover hinder. Tide flung har up. That's where they moostly do come ashore from Lowstof or Whitestrand. Current sweep 'em right along the coost till they reach the ness : then it fling 'em up by the groyne as reg'lar as clockwork. There's a cross-current there; that's what make the point and the sandbank."

Hugh faltered. He knew full well he was rousing suspicion; yet he couldn't refrain for all that from gratifying his eager and burning desire to know all he could about poor martyred Elsie. He dared not ask what had become of the clothes, much as he longed to learn, but he wandered away slowly, step after step, to the side of the groyne. Its further face was sheltered by heaped-up shingle from the lighthouse-man's eye. Hugh sat down in the shade, close under the timber balks, and looked around him along the beach where Elsie had been washed ashore, a lifeless burden. Something yellow glittered on the sands hard by. As the sun caught it, it attracted for a second his casual attention by its golden shimmering. His heart came up with a bound into his mouth. He knew it—he knew it—he knew it in a flash. It was Elsie's watch! Elsie's! Elsie's! The watch he himself had given—years and years ago—no; six weeks since only—as a birthday present—to poor dear dead Elsie.

Then Elsie was dead! He was sure of it now. No need for further dangerous questioning. It was by Elsie's grave indeed he had just been standing. Elsie lay buried there beyond the shadow of a doubt, unknown and dishonoured. It was Elsie's grave and Elsie's watch. What room for hope or for fear any longer?

It was Elsie's watch, but rolled by the current from Lowestoft pier, as the lighthouse-man had rightly told him was usual, and cast ashore, as everything else was always cast, by the side of the groyne where the stream in the sea turned sharply outward at the extreme easternmost point of Suffolk.

He picked it up with tremulous fingers and kissed it tenderly; then he slipped it unobserved into his breast-pocket, close to his heart—Elsie's watch!—and began his return journey with an aching bosom, over those hot bare stones, away back to Aldeburgh. The beach seemed longer and drearier than before. The orgy of remorse had passed away now, and the coolness of utter despair had come over him instead of it. Half-way on, he sat down at last, wearier than ever, on the long pebble ridge, and gazed once more with swimming eyes at that visible token of Elsie's doom. Hope was dead in his heart now. Horror and agony brooded over his soul. The world without was dull and dreary; the world within was a tempest of passion. He would freely have given all he possessed that moment to be dead and buried in one grave with Elsie.

At that same instant at the Low Light the cutter's man, come across in an open boat from Orford, was talking carelessly to the underling at the lighthouse.

"Well, Tom, bor, how're things lookin' wi' yow?" he asked with a laugh.

"Middlin' like, an' that stodgy," the other answered grimly. "How do yow git on?"

"Well, we ha' tracked down that there body," the Trinity House man said casually; "the gal's, I mean, what I picked up on the ness; an' arter all my trouble, Tom, yow'll hardly believe it, but blow me if I made a penny on it."

"Yow din't?" the lighthouse-man murmured interrogatively.

"Not a farden," the fellow Bill responded in a disconsolate

voice. "The body worn't a nob's; so far, in that respeck, she worn't nobody arter all, but oonly one o' them there light-o'-loves down hinder at Lowstof. She was a sailor's moll, I reckon. Flung harself off Lowstof pier one dark night, maybe a fortnight agoo, or maybe three weeks. She'd bin hevin' some wuds wooth a young man she'd bin a-keepin' company wooth. I never see a more promisin' or more disappointin' corpse in my breathin' life. When I picked har up, I say to Jim, I say, 'Yow may take yar davy on't, bor, that this gal *is* a nob. I goo by har looks, an' I 'spect there's money on har.' Why, har dress aloon would ha' made any one take har for a real lady. And arter all, what do it amount to? Nothen at all! Jest the parish paay for har. That's Suffolk all oover, and rile me when I think on't. If it han't a bin for a val'able in the way o' rings what fell off har finger, in a manner of speakin', and dropped as yow may say into an honest man's pocket when he was a-takin' har to the dead-house—why, it fare to me, that there honest man would a bin out o' pocket a marter of a shillen or soo, and all thraow the interest he took in a wuthless an' good-for-nothen young woman. Corpsus may look out for theirselves in future, as far as I'm consarned, and that's to a sartinty. I ha' had too much on 'em. They're more bother than they're wuth. That's jest the long an' short on't—blow me if it een't."

CHAPTER XIX.

AU RENDEZVOUS DES BONS CAMARADES.

In the cosy smoking-room of the Cheyne Row Club, a group of budding geniuses, convened from the four quarters of the earth, stood once more in the bay-window, looking out on the dull October street, and discussing with one another in diverse tones the various means which each had adopted for killing time through his own modicum of summer holidays. Reminiscences and greetings were the order of the day. A buzz of voices pervaded the air. Everybody was full to the throat of fresh impressions, and everybody was laudably eager to share them all, still hot from the press, with the balance of humanity as then and there represented before him.—The mosquitoes at the North Cape were really unendurable: they bit a piece out of your face bodily, and then perched on a neighbouring tree to eat it; while the midnight sun, as advertised, was a hoary old impostor, exactly like any other sun anywhere, when you came to examine him through a smoked glass at close quarters.

Cromer was just the jolliest place to lounge on the sands, and the best centre for short excursions, that a fellow could find on a year's tramp all round the shores of England, Scotland, Wales, or Ireland.

Grouse were scanty and devilish cunning in Aberdeenshire this year; the young birds packed like old ones; and the accommodation at Lumphanan had turned out on nearer view by no means what it ought to be.

A most delightful time indeed at Beatenberg, just above the Lake of Thun, you know, with exquisite views over the Bernese Oberland; and *such* a pretty little Swiss maiden, with liquid blue eyes and tow-coloured hair, to bring in one's breakfast and pour out coffee in the thick white coffee-cups. And then the flowers!—a perfect paradise for a botanist, I assure you.

Montreal in August was hot and stuffy, but the Thousand Islands were simply delicious, and black-bass fishing among the back lakes was the only sport now left alive worthy a British fisherman's distinguished consideration.

Oh yes; the yacht behaved very well indeed, considering, on her way to Iceland—as well as any yacht that sailed the seas—but just before reaching Reykjavik—that's how they pronounce it, with the *j* soft and a falling intonation on the last syllable—a most tremendous gale came thundering down with rain and lightning from the Vatna Jökull, and, by George, sir, it nearly foundered her outright with its sudden squalls in the open cean. You never saw anything like the way she heeled over : ou could touch the trough of the waves every time from the gunwale.

Had anything new been going on, you fellows, while we were all away? and had anybody heard anything about the Bard, as Cheyne Row had unanimously nicknamed Hugh Massinger?

Yes, one budding genius in the descriptive-article trade—writer of that interesting series of papers in the *Charing Cross Review* on Seaside Resorts—afterwards reprinted in crown octavo fancy boards, at seven-and-sixpence, as "The Complete Idler"—had had a letter from the Bard himself only three days ago, announcing his intention to be back in harness in town again that very morning.

"And what's the Immortal Singer been doing with himself this hot summer?" cried a dozen voices—for it was generally felt in Cheyne Row circles that Hugh Massinger, though still as undiscovered as the sources of the Congo, was a coming man of proximate eventuality. "Has he hooked his heiress yet? He swore, when he left town in July, he was going on an angling expedition—as a fisher of women—in the eastern counties."

"Well, yes," the recipient of young love's first confidences responded guardedly; "I should say he had.—To be sure, the

Immortal One doesn't exactly mention the fact or amount of the young lady's fortune; but he does casually remark in a single passing sentence that he has got himself engaged to a Thing of Beauty somewhere down in Suffolk."

"Suffolk!—most congruous indeed for an idyllic, bucolic, impressionist poet.—He'll come back to town with a wreath round his hat, and his pockets stuffed with stanzas and sonnets to his mistress's eyebrow, where 'Suffolk punches' shall sweetly rhyme to 'the red-cheek apple that she gaily munches,' with slight excursions on lunches, bunches, crunches, and hunches, all à la Massinger, in endless profusion.—Now then, Hatherley; there's a guinea's worth ready made for you to your hand already. Send it by the first post yourself to the lady, and cut out the Bard on his own ground with the beautiful and anonymous East Anglian heiress.—I suppose, by the way, Massinger didn't happen to confide to you the local habitation and the name of the proud recipient of so much interested and anapæstic devotion ? "

"He said, I think, if I remember right, her name was Meysey."

"Meysey! Oh, then, that's one of the Whitestrand Meyseys, you may be sure; daughter of old Tom Wyville Meysey, whose estates have all been swallowed up by the sea. They lie in the prebend of Consumptum per Mare.—If he's going to marry her on the strength of her red, red gold, or of her vested securities in Argentine and Turkish, he'll have to collect his arrears of income from a sea-green mermaid—at the bottom of the deep blue sea; which will be worse than even dealing with that horrid Land League, for the Queen's writ doesn't run beyond the foreshore, and No Rent is universal law on the bed of the ocean."

"I don't think they've all been quite swallowed up," one of the bystanders remarked in a pensive voice; he was Suffolk born; "at least, not yet, as far as I've heard of them. The devouring sea is engaged in taking them a bite at a time, like Bob Sawyer's apple; but he's left the Hall and the lands about it to the present day—so Relf tells me."

"Has she money, I wonder?" the editor of that struggling periodical, the *Night-Jar*, remarked abstractedly.

"Oh, I expect so, or the Bard wouldn't ever have dreamt of proposing to her. The Immortal Singer knows his own worth exactly, to four places of decimals, and estimates himself at full market value. He's the last man on earth to throw himself away for a mere trifle. When he sells his soul in the matrimonial Exchange, it'll be for the highest current market quotation, to an eligible purchaser for cash only, who must combine considerable charms of body and mind with the superadded advantage of a respectable balance at Drummond's or at Coutts's. The Bard knows down to the ground the exact moneyworth of a handsome poet; he wouldn't dream of letting himself go dirt cheap, like a common every-day historian or novelist."

As the last speaker let the words drop carelessly from his mouth, the buzz of voices in the smoke-room paused suddenly: there was a slight and awkward lull in the conversation for half a minute; and then the crowd of budding geniuses was stretching out its dozen right hands with singular unanimity in rapid succession to grasp the fingers of a tall dark new-comer who had slipped in, after the fashion usually attributed to angels or their opposite, in the very nick of time to catch the last echoes of a candid opinion from his peers and contemporaries upon his own conduct.

"Do you think he heard us?" one of the peccant gossipers whispered to another with a scared face.

"Can't say," his friend whispered back uneasily. "He's got quick ears. Listeners generally hear no good of themselves. But anyhow, we've got to brazen it out now. The best way's just to take the bull by the horns boldly.—Well, Massinger, we were all talking about you when you came in. You're the chief subject of conversation in literary circles at the present day. Do you know it's going the round of all the clubs in London at this moment that you shortly contemplate committing matrimony?"

Hugh Massinger drew himself up stiff and erect to his full height, and withered his questioner with a scathing glance from his dark eyes such as only he could dart at will to scarify and annihilate a selected victim. "I'm going to be married in the course of the year," he answered coldly, "if that's what you mean by committing matrimony.—Mitchison," turning round with marked abruptness to an earlier speaker, "what have you been doing with yourself all the summer?"

"Oh, I've been riding a bicycle through the best part of Finland, getting up a set of articles on the picturesque aspect of the Far North for the *Porte-Crayon,* you know, and at the same time working in the Russian anarchists for the leader column in the *Morning Telephone.*—Bates went with me on the illegitimate machine—yes, that means a tricycle; the bicycle alone's accounted lawful: he's doing the sketches to illustrate my letterpress, or I'm doing the letterpress to illustrate his sketches—whichever you please, my little dear; you pays your money and you takes your choice, all for the small sum of sixpence weekly. The roads in Finland are abominably rough, and the Finnish language is the beastliest and most agglutinative I ever had to deal with, even in the entrancing pages of

Ollendorff. But there's good copy in it—very good copy.—The *Telephone* and the *Porte-Crayon* shared our expenses.—And where have you been hiding your light yourself since we last saw you?"

"My particular bushel was somewhere down about Suffolk, I believe," Hugh Massinger answered with magnificent indefiniteness, as though minute accuracy to the matter of a county or two were rather beneath his sublime consideration. "I've been stopping at a dead-alive little place they call Whitestrand : a sort of moribund fishing village, minus the fish. It's a lost corner among the mud-flats and the salt marshes; picturesque, but ugly, and dull as ditch-water. And having nothing else on earth to do there, I occupied myself with getting engaged, as you fellows seem to have heard by telegraph already. This is an age of publicity. Everything's known in London nowadays. A man can't change his coat, it appears, or have venison for dinner, or wear red stockings, or stop to chat with a pretty woman, but he finds a flaring paragraph about it next day in the society papers."

"May one venture to ask the lady's name?" Mitchison inquired courteously, a little apart from the main group.

Hugh Massinger's manner melted at once. He would not be chaffed, but it rather relieved him, in his present strained condition of mind, to enter into inoffensive confidences with a polite listener.

"She's a Miss Meysey," he said in a lower tone, drawing over towards the fireplace : "one of the Suffolk Meyseys—you've heard of the family. Her father has a very nice place down by the sea at Whitestrand. They're the banking people, you know : remote cousins of the old hanging judge's. Very nice old things in their own way, though a trifle slow and out of date—not to say mouldy.—But after all, rapidity is hardly the precise quality one feels called upon to exact in a prospective father-in-law : slowness goes with some solid virtues. The honoured tortoise has never been accused by its deadliest foes of wasting its patrimony in extravagant expenditure."

"Has she any brothers?" Mitchison asked with apparent ingenuousness, approaching the question of Miss Meysey's fortune (like Hugh himself) by obscure byways, as being a politer mode than the direct assault. "There was a fellow called Meysey in the fifth form with me at Winchester, I remember; perhaps he might have been some sort of relation."

Hugh shook his head in emphatic dissent. "No," he answered; "the girl has no brothers. She's an only child— the last of her family. There was one son, a captain in the Forty-fourth, or something of the sort; but he was killed in Zululand, and was never at Winchester, or I'm sure I should have heard of it.—They're a kinless lot, extremely kinless: in fact, I've almost realized the highest ambition of the American humorist, to the effect that he might have the luck to marry a poor lonely friendless orphan."

" She's an heiress, then ? "

Hugh nodded assent. " Well, a sort of an heiress," he admitted modestly, as who should say, " not so good as she might be." " The estate's been very much impaired by the inroads of the sea for the last ten years ; but there's still a decent remnant of it left standing. Enough for a man of modest expectations to make a living off in these hard times, I fancy."

" Then we shall all come down in due time," another man put in—a painter by trade—joining the group as he spoke, " and find the Bard a landed proprietor on his own broad acres, living in state and bounty in the baronial Hall, lord of Burleigh, fair and free, or whatever other name the place may be called by ! "

" If I invite you to come," Hugh answered significantly with curt emphasis.

" Ah yes, of course," the artist answered. " I dare say when you start your carriage, you'll be too proud to remember a poor devil of an oil and colour-man like me.—In those days, no doubt you'll migrate like all the rest to the Athenæum.—Well, well, the world moves—once every twenty-four hours on its own axis —and in the long run we all move with it and go up together.— Vhen I'm an R.A., I'll run down and visit you at the ancestral iansion, and perhaps paint your wife's portrait—for a thousand guineas, *bien entendu.*—And what sort of a body is the prospective father-in-law ? "

" Oh, just the usual type of Suffolk Squire, don't you know," Massinger replied carelessly. " A breeder of fat oxen and of pigs, a pamphleteer on Guano and on Grain, a quarter-sessions chairman, abler none ; but with faint reminiscences still of an Oxford training left in him to keep the milk of human kindness from turning sour by long exposure to the pernicious influence of the East Anglian sunshine. I should enjoy his society better, however, if I were a trifle deaf. He has less to say, and he says it more, than any other man of my acquaintance. Still, he's a jolly old boy enough, as old boys go. We shall rub along somehow till he pops off the hooks and leaves us the paternal acres on our own account to make merry upon."

So far Hugh had tried with decent success to keep up his usual appearance of careless ease and languid good-humour, in spite of volcanic internal desires to avoid the painful subject of his approaching marriage altogether. He was schooling himself, indeed, to face society. He was sure to hear much of his Suffolk trip, and it was well to get used to it as early as possible. But the next question fairly blanched his cheek, by leading up direct to the skeleton in the cupboard: "How did you first come to get acquainted with them?"

The question must inevitably be asked again, and he must do his best to face it with pretended equanimity. "A relation of mine—a distant cousin—a Girton girl—was living with the family as Miss Meysey's governess or companion or something," he answered with what jauntiness he could summon up. "It was through her that I first got to know my future wife. And old Mr. Meysey, the coming papa-in-law——"

He stopped dead short. Words failed him. His jaw fell abruptly. A strange thrill seemed to course through his frame. His large black eyes protruded suddenly from their sunken orbits; his olive-coloured check blanched pale and pasty. Some unexpected emotion had evidently checked his ready flow of speech. Mitchison and the painter turned round in surprise to see what might be the cause of this unwonted flutter. It was merely Warren Relf who had entered the club, and was gazing with a stony British stare from head to foot at Hugh Massinger.

The poet wavered, but he did not flinch. From the fixed look in Relf's eye, he felt certain in an instant that the skipper of the *Mud-Turtle* knew something—if not everything—of his fatal secret. How much did he know? and how much not?— that was the question. Had he tracked Elsie to her nameless grave at Orfordness? Had he recognized the body in the mortuary at the lighthouse? Had he learned from the cutter's man the horrid truth as to the corpse's identity? All these things or any one of them might well have happened to the owner of the *Mud-Turtle*, cruising in and out of East Anglian creeks in his ubiquitous little vessel. Warren Relf was plainly a dangerous subject. But in any case, Hugh thought with shame, how rash, how imprudent, how unworthy of himself thus to betray in his own face and features the terror and astonishment with which he regarded him! He might have known Relf was likely to drop in any day at the club! He might have known he would sooner or later meet him there! He might have prepared beforehand a neat little lie to deliver pat with a casual air of truth on their first greeting! And instead of all that, here he was, discomposed and startled, gazing the painter straight in the face like a dazed fool, and never knowing how or where on earth to start any ordinary subject of polite conversation. For the first time in his adult life he was so taken aback with childish awe and mute surprise that he felt positively relieved when Relf boarded him with the double-barrelled question: "And how did you leave Miss Meysey and Miss Challoner, Massinger?"

Hugh drew him aside towards the back of the room and lowered his voice still more markedly in reply. "I left Miss Meysey very well," he answered with as much ease of manner as he could hastily assume. "You may perhaps have heard from rumour or from the public prints that she and I have struck up an engagement. In the lucid language of the newspaper announcements, a marriage has been definitely arranged between us."

Warren Relf bent his head in sober acquiescence. "I had heard so," he said with grim formality. "Your siege was successful. You carried the citadel by storm that day in the sandhills.—I won't congratulate you. You know my opinion already of marriages arranged upon that mercantile basis. I told it you beforehand. We need not now recur to the subject. —But Miss Challoner?—How about her? Did you leave her well? Is she still at Whitestrand?" He looked his man through and through as he spoke, with a cold stern light in those truthful eyes of his.

Hugh Massinger shuffled uneasily before his steadfast glance. Was it only his own poor guilty conscience, or did Relf know all? he wondered silently. The man was eyeing him like his evil angel. He longed for time to pause and reflect; to think out the best possible non-committing lie in answer to this direct and leading question. How to parry that deadly thrust on the spur of the moment he knew not. Relf was gazing at him still intently. Hesitation would be fatal. He blundered into the first form of answer that came uppermost. "My cousin Elsie has gone away," he stammered out in haste. "She —she left the Meyseys quite abruptly."

"As a consequence of your engagement?" Relf asked sternly.

This was going one step too far. Hugh Massinger felt really indignant now, and his indignation enabled him to cover his retreat a little more gracefully. "You have no right to ask me that," he answered in genuine anger. "My private relations with my own family are surely no concern of yours or of any one's."

Warren Relf bowed his head grimly once more. "Where has she gone?" he asked in a searching voice. "I'm interested in Miss Challoner. I may venture to inquire that much at least. I'm told you've heard from her. Where is she now? Will you kindly tell me?"

"I don't know," Hugh answered angrily, driven to bay. Then with a sudden inspiration, he added significantly: "Do you either?"

"Yes," Warren Relf responded with solemn directness.

The answer took Massinger aback once more. A cold shudder ran down his spine. Their eyes met. For a moment they stared

one another out. Then Hugh's glance fell slowly and heavily.
He dared not ask one word more.—Relf must have tracked her,
for certain, to the lighthouse. He must have seen the grave,
perhaps even the body.—This was too terrible.—Henceforth, it
was war to the knife between them. "Hast thou found me, O
my enemy?" he broke out sullenly.

"I have found you, Massinger, and I have found you out,"
the painter answered in a very low voice, with a sudden burst
of unpremeditated frankness. "I know you now for exactly the
very creature you are—a liar, a forger, a coward, and only two
fingers' width short of a murderer.—There! you may make
what use you like of that.—For myself, I will make no use at all
of it.—For reasons of my own, I will let you go. I could crush
you if I would, but I prefer to screen you. Still, I tell you once
for all the truth. Remember it well.—I know it; you know it;
and we both know we each of us know it."

Hugh Massinger's fingers itched inexpressibly that moment to
close round the painter's honest bronzed throat in a wild death-
struggle. He was a passionate man, and the provocation was
terrible. The provocation was terrible because it was all true.
He was a liar, a forger, a coward—and a murderer!—But he
dared not—he dared not. To thrust those hateful words down
Relf's throat would be to court exposure, and worse than exposure; and exposure was just what Hugh Massinger could
never bear to face like a man. Sooner than that, the river, or
aconite. He must swallow it all, proud soul as he was. He
must swallow it all, now and for ever.

As he stood there irresolute, with blanched lips and itching
fingers, his nails pressed hard into the palms of his hands in the
fierce endeavour to repress his passion, he felt a sudden light
touch on his right shoulder. It was Hatherley once more. "I say,
Massinger," the journalist put in lightly, all unconscious of the
tragedy he was interrupting, "come down and knock about the
balls on the table a bit, will you?"

If Hugh Massinger was to go on living at all, he must go on
living in the wonted fashion of nineteenth-century literate humanity. Tragedy must hide itself behind the scenes; in public
he must still be the prince of high comedians. He unclosed his
hands and let go his breath with a terrible effort. Relf stood
aside to let him pass. Their glances met as Hugh left the room*
arm in arm with Hatherley. Relf's was a glance of contempt
and scorn; Hugh Massinger's was one of undying hatred.

He had murdered Elsie, and Relf knew it. That was the way
Massinger interpreted to himself the "Yes" that the painter had
just now so truthfully and directly answered him.

CHAPTER XX.

EVENTS MARCH.

"PAPA is still in Scotland," Winifred wrote to Hugh, "slaying many grouse; and mamma and I have the place all to ourselves now, so we're really having a lovely time, enjoying our holiday *immensely* (though you're not here), taking down everything, and washing and polishing, and rearranging things again, and playing havoc with the household gods generally. We expect papa back on Friday. His birds have preceded him. I *do* hope he remembered to send you a brace or two. I gave him your town address before he left, with *very* special directions to let you have some ; but, you know, you men always forget everything. As soon as he comes home, he'll make us take our alterations all down again, which will be a horrid nuisance, for the drawing-room *does* look so perfectly lovely. We've done it up exactly as you recommended, with the sage green plush for the old mantel-piece, and a red Japanese table in the dark corner; and I really think, now I see the effect, your taste's simply exquisite. But then, you know, what else can you expect from a distinguished poet! You always do everything beautifully—and I think you're a darling."

At any other time this naïve girlish appreciation of his decorative talents would have pleased and flattered Hugh's susceptible soul; for, being a man, he was of course vain ; and he loved a pretty girl's approbation dearly. But just at that moment he had no stomach for praise, even though it came from Sir Hubert Stanley; and whatever faint rising flush of pleasure he might possibly have felt at his little *fiancée's* ecstatic admiration was all crushed down again into the gall of bitterness by the sickening refrain of her repeated postscripts : " No further news yet from poor Elsie.—Has she written to you ? I shall be simply *frantic* if I don't hear from her soon. She can *never* mean to leave us all in doubt like this. I'm going to advertise to-morrow in the London papers. If only she knew the state of mind she was plunging me into, I'm sure she'd write and relieve my suspense, which is just *agonizing.*—A kiss from your little one : in the corner here. Be sure you kiss it where I've put the cross. Good-night, darling Hugh.—Yours ever, WINIFRED."

Hugh flung the letter down on the floor of his chambers in an agony of horror. Was his crime to pursue him thus through a whole lifetime? Was he always to hear surmises, conjectures, speculations, doubts as to what on earth had become of Elsie? Was he never to be free for a single second from the shadow of that awful pursuing episode? Was Winifred, when she became his wedded wife, to torture and rack him for years together with questions and hesitations about the poor dead child who lay, as he firmly and unreservedly believed, in her nameless grave by the lighthouse at Orfordness?—There was only one possible way out of it—a way that Hugh shrank from almost as much as he shrank from the terror and shame of exposure. It was ghastly: it was gruesome: it was past endurance; but it was the one solitary way of safety. He must write a letter from time to time, in Elsie's handwriting, addressed to Winifred, giving a fictitious account of Elsie's doings in an imaginary home, away over somewhere in America or the antipodes. He must invent a new life and a new life-history, under the Southern Cross, for poor dead Elsie: he must keep her alive like a character in a novel, and spin her fresh surroundings from his own brain, in some little-known and inaccessible quarter of the universe.

But then, what a slavery, what a drudgery, what a perpetual torture! His soul shrank from the hideous continued deceit. To have perpetrated that one old fatal forgery, in the first fresh flush of terror and remorse, was not perhaps quite so wicked, quite so horrible, quite so soul-destroying as this new departure. He had then at least the poor lame excuse of a pressing emergency; and it was once only. But to live a life of consistent lying—to go on fathering a perennial fraud—to forge pretended letters from mail to mail—to invent a long tissue of successful falsehoods—and that about a matter that lay nearest and dearest to his own wounded and remorseful heart—all this was utterly and wholly repugnant to Hugh Massinger's underlying nature. Set aside the wickedness and baseness of it all, the poet was a proud and sensitive man; and lying on such an extended scale was abhorrent to his soul from its mere ignominy and æsthetic repulsiveness. He liked the truth: he admired the open, frank, straightforward way. Tortuous cunning and mean subterfuges roused his profoundest contempt and loathing —when he saw them in others. Up till now, he had enjoyed his own unquestioning self-respect. Vain and shallow and unscrupulous as he was, he had hitherto basked serenely in the sunshine of his own personal approbation. He had done nothing till lately that sinned against his private and peculiar code of morals, such as it was. His proposal to Winifred had, for the first time, opened the sluices of the great unknown within him, and fathomless depths of deceit and crime were welling up now and crowding in upon him to drown and obliterate whatever spark or scintillation of conscience had ever been his. It was a hateful sight. He shrank himself from the effort to realize it.

And Warren Relf knew all! That in itself was bad enough.
But if he also invented a continuous lie to palm off upon Winifred and her unsuspecting people, then Warren Relf at least
would know it constantly for what it was, and despise him for it
even more profoundly than he despised him at present. All
that was horrible—horrible—horrible. Yet there was one person
whose opinion mattered to him far more that even Warren Relf's
—one person who would hate and despise with a deadly hatred
and an utter scorn the horrid perfidy of his proposed line of
conduct. That person was one with whom he sat and drank
familiarly every day, with whom he conversed unreservedly
night and morning, with whom he lived and moved and had his
being. He could never escape or deceive or outwit Hugh Massinger. Patriæ quis exsul se quoque fugit? Hugh Massinger
would dog him, and follow his footsteps wherever he went, with
his unfeigned contempt for so dirty and despicable a course of
action. It was vile, it was loathsome, it was mean, it was
horrible in its ghastly charnel-house falseness and foulness ; and
Hugh Massinger knew it perfectly. If he yielded to this last
and lowest temptation of Satan, he might walk about henceforth
with his outer man a whited sepulchre, but within he would
be full of dead men's bones and vile imaginings of impossible
evil.

Thinking which things definitely to himself, in his own tor-
mented and horrified soul, he—sat down and wrote another
forged letter.

It was a hasty note, written as if in the hurry and bustle of
departure, on the very eve of a long journey, and it told Winifred, in rapid general terms, that Elsie was just on her way to
the continent, *en route* for Australia—no matter where. She
would join her steamer (no line mentioned) under an assumed
name, perhaps at Marseilles, perhaps at Genoa, perhaps at
Naples, perhaps at Brindisi. Useless to dream of tracking or
identifying her. She was going away from England *for ever
and ever*—this last underlined in feminine fashion—and it
would be quite hopeless for Winifred to cherish the vain idea
of seeing her again in this world of misfortunes. Some day,
perhaps, her conduct would be explained and vindicated ; for
the present, it must suffice that letters sent to her at the address
as before—the porter's of the Cheyne Row Club, though Hugh
did not specifically mention that fact—would finally reach her
by private arrangement. Would Winifred accept the accompanying ring, and wear it always on her own finger, as a parting
gift from her affectionate and misunderstood friend,   ELSIE?

The ring was one from the little jewel-case he had stolen that
fatal night from Elsie's bedroom. Profoundly as he hated and
loathed himself for his deception, he couldn't help stopping half

way through to admire his own devilry of cleverness in sending
that ring back now to Winifred. Nothing could be so calculated to disarm suspicion. Who could doubt that Elsie was
indeed alive, when Elsie not only wrote letters to her friends,
but sent with them the very jewelry from her own fingers as
a visible pledge and token of her identity?—Besides, he really
wanted Winifred to wear it; he wished her to have something
that once was Elsie's. He would like the woman he was now
deceiving to be linked by some visible bond of memory to the
woman he had deceived and lured to her destruction.

He kissed the ring, a hot burning kiss, and wrapped it reverently and tenderly in cotton-wool. That done, he gummed and
stamped the letter with a resolute air, crushed his hat firmly
down on his head, and strode out with feverishly long strides
from his rooms in Jermyn Street to the doubtful hospitality of
the Cheyne Row.

Would Warren Relf be there again, he wondered? Was that
man to poison half London for him in future?—Why on earth,
knowing the whole truth about Elsie—knowing that Elsie was
dead and buried at Orfordness—did the fellow mean to hold his
vile tongue and allow him, Hugh Massinger, to put about this
elaborate fiction unchecked, of her sudden and causeless disappearance? Inexplicable quite! The thing was a mystery;
and Hugh Massinger hated mysteries. He could never know
now at what unexpected moment Warren Relf might swoop
down upon him from behind with a dash and a crash and an
explosive exposure.—He was working in the dark, like navvies
in a tunnel.—Surely the crash must come some day! The roof
must collapse and crush him utterly. It was ghastly to wait
in long blind expectation of it.

The forged letter still remained in his pocket unposted. He
passed a couple of pillar-boxes, but could not nerve himself up
to drop it in. Some grain of grace within him was fighting
hard even now for the mastery of his soul. He shrank from
committing himself irrevocably by a single act to that despicable
life of ingrained deception.

In the smoking-room at the club he found nobody, for it was
still early. He took up the *Times*, which he had not yet had
time to consult that morning. In the Agony Column, a familiar
conjunction of names attracted his eye as it moved down the
outer sheet. They were the two names never out of his thoughts
for a moment for the last fortnight. "Elsie," the advertisement
ran in clear black type, "Do write to me. I can stand this
fearful suspense no longer. Only a few lines to say you are
well. I am so frightened. Ever yours,　　　　Winifred."

He laid the paper down with a sudden resolve, and striding
across the room gloomily to the letter-box on the mantel-piece,

took the fateful envelope from his pocket at last, and held it dubious, between finger and thumb, dangling loose over the slit in the lid. Heaven and hell still battled fiercely for the upper hand within him. Should he drop it in boldly, or should he not? To be or not to be—a liar for life?—that was the question. The envelope trembled between his finger and thumb. The slit in the box yawned hungry below. His grasp was lax. The letter hung by a corner only. Nor was his impulse, even, so wholly bad: pity for Winifred urged him on; remorse and horror held him back feebly. He knew not in his own soul how to act; he knew he was weak and wicked only.

As he paused and hesitated, unable to decide for good or evil —a noise at the door made him start and waver.—Somebody coming! Perhaps Warren Relf.—That address on the envelope —"Miss Meysey, The Hall, Whitestrand, Suffolk."—If Relf saw it, he would know it was—well—an imitation of Elsie's handwriting. She had sent a note to Relf on the morning of the sandhills picnic. If any one else saw it, they would see at least it was a letter to his *fiancée*—and they would chaff him accordingly with chaff that he hated, or perhaps they would only smile a superior smile of fatuous recognition and smirking amusement. He could stand neither—above all, not Relf.— His fingers relaxed upon the cover of the envelope.—Half unconsciously, half unwillingly, he loosened his hold.—Plop! it fell through that yawning abyss, three inches down, but as deep s perdition itself.—The die was cast! A liar for a lifetime!

He turned round, and Hatherley the journalist stood smiling good-morning by the open doorway. Hugh Massinger tried his hardest to look as if nothing out of the common had happened in any way. He nodded to Hatherley, and buried his face once more in the pages of the *Times*. "The Drought in Wales "— "The Bulgarian Difficulty "—" Painful Disturbances on the West Coast of Africa."—Pah! What nonsense! What commonplaces of opinion! It made his gorge rise with disgust to look at them. Wales and Bulgaria and the West Coast of Africa, when Elsie was dead! dead and unnoticed!

A boy in buttons brought in a telegram—Central News Agency —and fixed it by the corners with brass-headed pins in a vacant space on the accustomed notice-board. Hatherley, laying down his copy of *Punch*, strolled lazily over to the board to examine it. "Meysey! Meysey!" he repeated musingly.—"Why, Massinger, that must be one of your Whitestrand Meyseys. Precious uncommon name. There can't be many of them."

Hugh rose and glanced at the new telegram unconcernedly. It couldn't have much to do with himself! But its terms brought the blood with a hasty rush into his pale cheek again "*Serious Accident on the Scotch Moors.*—Aberdeen, Thursday.

As Sir Malcolm Farquharson's party were shooting over the Glenbeg estate yesterday, near Kincardine-O'Neil, a rifle held by Mr. Wyville Meysey burst suddenly, wounding the unfortunate gentleman in the face and neck, and lodging a splinter of jagged metal in his left temple. He was conveyed at once from the spot in an insensible state to Invertanar Castle, where he now lies in a most precarious condition. His wife and daughter were immediately telegraphed for."

"Invertanar, 10.40 a.m.—Mr. Wyville Meysey, a guest of Sir Malcolm Farquharson's at Invertanar Castle, wounded yesterday by the bursting of his rifle on the Glenbeg moors, expired this morning very suddenly at 9.20. The unfortunate gentleman did not recover consciousness for a single moment after the fatal accident."

A shudder of horror ran through Hugh's frame as he realized the meaning of that curt announcement. Not for the mishap; not for Mrs. Meysey; not for Winifred: oh, dear no; but for his own possible or probable discomfiture.—His first thought was a characteristic one. Mr. Meysey had died unexpectedly. There might or there might not be a will forthcoming. Guardians might or might not be appointed for his infant daughter. The estate might or might not go to Winifred. He might or he might not now be permitted to marry her.— If she happened to be left a ward in Chancery, for example, it would be a hopeless business: his chance would be ruined. The court would never consent to accept him as Winifred's husband. And then—and then it would be all up with him.

It was bad enough to have sold his own soul for a mess of pottage—for a few hundred acres of miserable salt marsh, encroached upon by the sea with rapid strides, and half covered with shifting, drifting sandhills. It was bad enough to have sacrificed Elsie—dear, tender, delicate, loving-hearted Elsie, his own beautiful, sacred, dead Elsie—to that wretched, sordid, ineffective avarice, that fractional worship of a silver-gilt Mammon. He had regretted all that in sackcloth and ashes for one whole endless hopeless fortnight or more, already.—But to have sold his own soul and to have sacrificed Elsie for the privilege of being rejected by Winifred's guardian—for the chance of being publicly and ignominiously jilted by the Court of Chancery—for the opportunity of becoming a common laughing-stock to the quidnuncs of Cheyne Row and the five o'clock tea-tables of half feminine London—that was indeed a depth of possible degradation from which his heart shrank with infinite throes of self-commiserating reluctance. He could sell his own soul for very little, and despise himself well for the squalid ignoble bargain; but to sell his own soul for absolutely nothing, with a dose of well-deserved ridicule thrown in gratis, and no Elsie to console him for his bitter loss, was more than even Hugh Massinger's sense of mean self-abnegation could easily swallow.

He flung himself back unmanned, in the big leather-covered armchair, and let the abject misery of his own thoughts overcome him visibly in his rueful countenance.

" I never imagined," said Hatherley afterwards to his friends the Relfs, " that Massinger could possibly have felt anything so much as he seemed to feel the sudden death of his prospective father-in-law, when he read that telegram. It really made me think better of the fellow."

CHAPTER XXI.

CLEARING THE DECKS.

WARREN RELF had arranged for his mother and sister, with Elsie Challoner, to seek the friendly shelter of San Remo early in October. The sooner away from England the better. ;Before they went, however, to avert the chance of a disagreeable encounter, he met them on their arrival in town at Liverpool Street, and saw them safely across to the continental train at London Bridge. It chanced to be the very self-same day that Hugh Massinger had posted his second forged note to poor fatherless Winifred.

Elsie dared hardly look the young painter in the face even now, for shame and timidity; and Warren Relf, respecting her natural sensitiveness, concentrated most of his attention on his mother and Edie, scarcely allowing Elsie to notice by shy sideglances his unobtrusive preparations for her own personal comfort on the journey. But Elsie's quick eye observed them all, gratefully, none the less for that. She liked Warren : it was impossible for anybody not to like and respect the frank young painter, with his honest bronzed face, and his open, manly, outspoken manners. Timid as she was and broken-hearted still, she could not go away from England for ever and ever—for Elsie never meant to return again—without thanking him just once in a few short words for all his kindness. As they stood on the bare and windy platform with which the South-Eastern Railway Company woos our suffrages at London Bridge, she drew him aside for a moment from his mother and sister with a little hasty shrinking glance which Warren could not choose but follow. " Mr. Relf," she said, looking down at the floor and fumbling with her parasol, " I want to thank you; I can't go away without thanking you once."

He saw the effort it had cost her to say so much, and a wild
lump rose sudden in his throat for gratitude and pleasure.
"Miss Challoner," he answered, looking back at her with an
unmistakable light in his earnest eyes, "say nothing else. I
am more than sufficiently thanked already.—I have only one
thing to say to you now. I know you wish this episode kept
secret from every one: you may rely upon me and upon my
mate in the yawl. If ever in my life I can be of any service to
you, remember you can command me.—If not, I shall never
again obtrude myself upon your memory.—Good-bye, good-
bye." And taking her hand one moment in his own, he held it
for a second, then let it drop again. "Now go," he said in a
tremulous voice—"go back to Edie."

Elsie—one blush—went back as he bade her. "Good-bye,"
she said, as she glided from his side—"good-bye, and thank
you." That was all that passed between those two that day.
Yet Elsie knew, with profound regret, as the train steamed off
through the draughty corridors on its way to Dover, that
Warren Relf had fallen in love with her; and Warren Relf,
standing alone upon the dingy, gusty platform, knew with an
ecstasy of delight and joy that Elsie Challoner was grateful to
him and liked him. It is something, gratitude. He valued
that more from Elsie Challoner than he would have valued love
from any other woman.

With profound regret, for her part, Elsie saw that Warren
Relf had fallen in love with her; because he was such an honest,
manly, straightforward, good fellow, and because from the very
first moment she had liked him. Yet what to her were love
and lovers now? Her heart lay buried beneath the roots of the
poplar at Whitestrand, as truly as Hugh Massinger thought it
lay buried in the cheap sea-washed grave in the sand at Orfordness. She was grieved to think this brave and earnest man
should have fixed his heart on a hopeless object. It was well
she was going to San Remo for ever. In the whirl and bustle
and hurry of London life, Warren Relf would doubtless soon
forget her. But some faces are not easily forgotten.

From London Bridge, Warren Relf took the Metropolitan to
St. James's Park, and walked across, still flushed and hot, to
Piccadilly. At the club, he glanced hastily at that morning's
paper. The first paragraph on which his eye lighted was
Winifred Meysey's earnest advertisement in the Agony Column.
It gave him no little food for reflection. If ever Elsie saw that
advertisement, it might alter and upset all her plans for the
future—and all his own plans into the bargain. Already she
felt profoundly the pain and shame of her false position with
Winifred and the Meyseys: that much Warren Relf had learned
from Edie. If only she knew how eagerly Winifred pined for

news of her, she might be tempted after all to break her reserve, to abandon her concealment, and to write full tidings of her present whereabouts to her poor little frightened and distressed pupil. That would be bad; for then the whole truth must sooner or later come out before the world; and for Elsie's sake, for Winifred's sake, perhaps even a wee bit for his own sake also, Warren Relf shrank unspeakably from that unhappy exposure. He couldn't bear to think that Elsie's poor broken bleeding heart should be laid open to its profoundest recesses before the eyes of society, for every daw of an envious old dowager to snap and peck at. He hoped Elsie would not see the advertisement. If she did, he feared her natural tenderness and her sense of self-respect would compel her to write the whole truth to Winifred.

She might see it at Marseilles, for they were going to run right through to the Mediterranean by the special express, stopping a night to rest themselves at the Hôtel du Louvre in the Rue Cannebière. Edie would be sure to look at the *Times,* and if she saw the advertisement, to show it to Elsie.

But even if she didn't, ought he not himself to call her attention to it? Was it right of him, having seen it, not to tell her of it? Should he not rather leave to Elsie herself the decision what course she thought best to take under these special circumstances?

He shrank from doing it. It grieved him to the quick to strain her poor broken heart any further. She had suffered so much : why rake it all up again? And even as he thought all these things, he knew each moment with profounder certainty than ever that he loved Elsie. There is nothing on earth to excite a man's love for a beautiful woman like being compelled to take tender care for that woman's happiness—having a gentle solicitude for her most sacred feelings thrust upon one by circumstances as an absolute necessity.—Still, Warren Relf was above all things honest and trustworthy. Not to send that advertisement straight to Elsie, even at the risk of hurting her own feelings, would constitute in some sort, he felt, a breach of confidence, a constructive falsehood, or at the very best a *suppressio veri;* and Warren Relf was too utterly and transparently truthful to allow for a moment any paltering with essential verities.—He sighed a sigh of profound regret as he took his penknife with lingering hesitation from his waistcoat pocket. But he boldly cut out the advertisement from the Agony Column, none the less, thereby defacing the first page of the *Times,* and rendering himself liable to the censure of the committee for wanton injury to the club property; after the perpetration of which heinous offence he walked gravely and soberly into the adjoining writing-room and sat down to indite a hasty note intended for his sister at the Hôtel du Louvre:

"MY DEAR EDIE,

"Just after you left, I caught sight of enclosed advertisement in the second column of this morning's *Times*. Show it to Her. I can't bear to send it—I can't bear to cause her any further trouble or embarrassment of any sort after all she has suffered; and yet—it would be wrong, I feel, to conceal it from her. If she takes my advice, she will *not* answer it. Better let things remain as they are. To write one line would be to upset all. For heaven's sake, don't show Her this letter.

"With love to you both and kind regards to Her,

"Your affectionate brother,

"W. R."

He addressed the letter, "Miss Relf, Hôtel du Louvre, Marseilles," and went over with it to the box on the mantel-shelf, where Hugh Massinger's letter was already lying.

When Edie Relf received that letter next evening at the hotel in the Rue Cannebière, she looked at it once and glanced over at Elsie. She looked at it twice and glanced over at Elsie. She looked at it a third time—and then, with a woman's sudden resolve, she did exactly what Warren himself had told her not to do—she handed it across the table to Elsie.

Hugh's plot trembled indeed in the balance that moment; for if only Elsie wrote to Winifred, ignoring of course his last forged letter, then lying on the hall table at Whitestrand, all would have been up with him. His lie would have come home to him straight as a lie. The two letters would in all probability not have coincided. Winifred would have known him from that day forth for just what he was—a liar—and a forger.

And yet if, by that simple and natural coincidence, Elsie had sent a letter from Marseilles merely assuring Winifred of her safety and answering the advertisement, it would have fallen in completely with Hugh's plot, and rendered Winifred's assurance doubly certain. Elsie had sailed to Australia by way of Marseilles, then. In a novel, that coincidence would surely have occurred. In real life, it might easily have done so, but as a matter of fact it didn't; for Elsie read the letter slowly first, and then the advertisement.

"Poor fellow!" she said as she passed the letter back again to Edie. "It was very kind of him; and he did quite right.— I think I shall take his advice, after all.—It's terribly difficult to know what one ought to do. But I don't think I shall write to Winifred."

Not for herself. She could bear the exposure, if it was to

save Winifred. But for Winifred's sake, for poor dear Winifred's. She couldn't deprive her of her new lover.

Ought she to let Winifred marry him? What trouble might
not yet be in store for Winifred?—No, no. Hugh would surely
be kinder to *her*. He had sacrificed one loving heart for her
sake; he was not likely now to break another.

How little we all can judge for the best. It would have been
better for Elsie and better for Winifred, if Elsie had done as
Warren Relf did, and not as he said—if she had written the
truth, and the whole truth at once to Winifred, allowing her to
be her own judge in the matter. But Elsie had not the heart
to crush Winifred's dream; and very naturally. No one can
blame a woman for refusing to act with more than human
devotion and foresight.

Hugh Massinger had left the headquarters of Bohemia for
twenty minutes at the exact moment when Warren Relf entered
the Cheyne Row Club. He had gone to telegraph his respectful
condolences to Winifred and Mrs. Meysey at Invertanar Castle,
on their sad loss, with conventional politeness. When he came
back, he found, to his surprise, the copy of the *Times* still lying
open on the smoking-room table; but Winifred's advertisement
was cut clean out of the Agony Column with a sharp penknife.
In a moment he said to himself, aghast: "Some enemy hath
done this thing." It must have been Relf! Nobody else in the
lub knew anything. Such espionage was intolerable, unen-
lurable, not to be permitted. For three days he had been
trembling and chafing at the horrid fact that Relf knew all and
might denounce and ruin him. That alone was bad enough.
But that Relf should be plotting and intriguing against him!
That Relf should use his sinister knowledge for some evil end!
That Relf should go spying and eavesdropping and squirming
about like a common detective! The idea was fairly past
endurance. Among gentlemen such things were not to be permitted. Hugh Massinger was prepared not to permit them.

He passed a day and night of inexpressible annoyance. This
situation was getting too much for him. He was fighting in
the dark: he didn't understand Warren Relf's silence. If the
fellow meant to crush him, for what was he waiting? Hugh
could not hold all the threads in his mind together. He felt as
though Warren Relf was going to make, not only the Cheyne
Row Club, but all London altogether too hot for him. To have
drowned Elsie, to be jilted by Winifred, and to be baffled after
all by that creature Relf—this, this was the hideous and ignominious future he saw looming now visibly before him!

It was with a heavy heart that next evening at seven he
dropped into the club dining-room. Would Relf be there? he
wondered silently. And if so, what course would Relf adopt

towards him? Yes, Relf *was* there, at a corner table, as good luck would have it, with his back turned to him safely as he entered; and that fellow Potts, the other mudbank artist—they hung their wretched daubs of flat Suffolk seaboard side by side fraternally on the walls of the Institute—was dining with him and concocting mischief, no doubt, for the house of Massinger. Hugh half determined to turn and flee: then all that was manly and genuine within him revolted at once against that last disgrace. He would not run from this creature Relf. He would not be turned out of his own club—he was a member of the committee and a founder of the society. He would face it out and dine in spite of him.

But not before the fellow's very eyes; that was more than in his present perturbed condition Hugh Massinger could manage to stand. He skulked quietly round, unseen by Relf, into the side alcove—a recess cut off by an arched doorway—where he gave his order in a very low voice to Martin, the obsequious waiter. Martin was surprised at so much reserve. Mr. Massinger, he was generally the very freest and loudest-spoken gentleman in the whole houseful of 'em. He always talked, he did, as if the club and the kitchen and the servants all belonged to him.

From the alcove, by a special interposition of fate, Hugh could hear distinctly what Relf was saying. Strange—incredible—a singular stroke of luck: he had indeed caught the man in the very act and moment of conspiring.—They were talking of Elsie! Their conversation came to him distinct, though low. Unnatural excitement had quickened his senses to a strange degree. He heard it all—every sound—every syllable.

"Then you promise, Frank, on your word of honour as a gentleman, you'll never breathe a word of this or of any part of Miss Challoner's affair to anybody anywhere?"

"My dear boy, I promise, that's enough.—I see the necessity as well as you do.—So you've actually got the letter, have you?"

"I've got the letter. If you like, I'll read it to you. It's here in my pocket. I have to restore it by the time Mr. Meysey returns to-morrow."

Mr. Meysey! Restore it! Then, for all his plotting, Relf didn't know that Mr. Meysey was dead, and that his funeral was fixed to take place at Whitestrand on Monday or Tuesday!

There was a short pause. *What* letter? he wondered. Then Relf began reading in a low tone: "My darling Winifred, I can hardly make up my mind to write you this letter; and yet I must: I can no longer avoid it."

Great heavens, it was his own forged letter to Winifred! How on earth had it ever come into Relf's possession!

Plot, plot—plot and counterplot! Dirty, underhand, hole-and-corner spy-business! Relf had wheedled it out of the Meyseys somehow, to help him to track down and confront his enemy! Or else he had suborned one of the Whitestrand servants to steal or copy their master's correspondence!

He heard it through to the last word, " Ever your affectionate but heart-broken Elsie."

What were they going to say next?—Nothing. Potts just drew a long breath of surprise, and then whistled shortly and curiously. " The man's a blackguard, to have broken the poor girl's heart," he observed at last, " let alone this. He's a blackguard, Relf.—I'm very sorry for her.—And what's become of Miss Challoner now, if it isn't indiscreet to ask the question? "

" Well, Potts, I've only taken any other man into my confidence at all in this matter, because you knew more than half already, and it was impossible, without telling you the other half, fully to make you feel the necessity for keeping the strictest silence about it. I'd rather not tell either you or anybody exactly where Miss Challoner's gone now. But at the present moment, if you wan't to know the precise truth, I've no doubt she's at Marseilles, on her way abroad to a further destination which I prefer on her account not to mention. More than that it's better not to say. But she wishes it kept a profound secret, and she intends never to return to England."

As Hugh Massinger heard those words, those reassuring words, a sudden sense of freedom and lightness burst instantly over him in a wild rush of reaction. Aha! aha! poor feeble enemy! Was this all? Then Relf knew really nothing! That mysterious " Yes" of his was a fraud, a pretence, a mistake, a delusion! He was all wrong, all wrong and in error. Instead of knowing that Elsie was dead—dead and buried in her nameless grave at Orfordness—he fancied she was still alive and in hiding! The man was a windbag. To think he should have been terrified—he, Hugh Massinger—by such a mere empty boastful eavesdropper!—Why, Relf, after all, was himself deceived by the forged letters he had so cleverly palmed off upon them. The special information he pretended to possess was only the special information derived from Hugh Massinger's own careful and admirable forgeries. He hugged himself in a perfect transport of delight. The load was lifted as if by magic from his breast. There was nothing on earth for him, after all, to be afraid of!

He saw it all at a glance now.—Relf was in league with the servants at the Meyseys'. Some prying lady's-maid or dishonest flunkey must have sent him the first letter to Winifred, or at least a copy of it: nay, more; he or she must have intercepted the second one, which arrived while Winifred was on her way

to Scotland—else how could Relf have heard this last newly
fledged fiction about the journey abroad—the stoppage at Marseilles—the determination never to return to England ?—And
how greedily and eagerly the man swallowed it all—his nasty
second-hand servants'-hall information !   Hugh positively
despised him in his own mind for his ready credulity and his
mean duplicity.   How glibly he retailed the plausible story,
with nods and hints and additions of his own : " At the present
moment, I've no doubt she's at Marseilles, on her way abroad
to a further destination, which I prefer on her account not to
mention."   What airs and graces and what comic importance
the fellow put on, on the strength of his familiarity with this
supposed mystery !   Any other man with a straightforward
mind would have said outright plainly, " to Australia ; " but
this pretentious jackanapes with his stolen information must
make up a little mystification all of his own, to give himself
importance in the eyes of his greedy gobemouche of a companion.
It was too grotesque ! too utterly ridiculous !   And this was the
man of whom he had been so afraid !   His own dupe ! the ready
fool who swallowed at second-hand such idle tattle of the
servants' hall, and employed an understrapper or a pretty
soubrette to open other people's letters for his own information !
From that moment forth, Hugh might cordially hate him, Hugh
might freely despise him; but he would never, never, never be
afraid of him.

One only idea left some slight suspicion of uneasiness on his
enlightened mind.   He hoped the lady's-maid—that hypothetical
lady's-maid—had sent on the forged letter—after reading it—to
Winifred.   Not that poor Winifred would have time to think
much about Elsie at present, in the midst of this sudden and
unexpected bereavement : she would be too full of her own dead
father, no doubt, to pay any great attention to her governess's
misfortunes.   But still, one doesn't like one's private letters to
be so vulgarly tampered with.   And the worst of it was, he
could hardly ask her whether she had received the note or not.
He could hardly get at the bottom of this low conspiracy.   It
was his policy now to let sleeping dogs lie.   The less said about
Elsie the better.

Yet in his heart he despised Warren Relf for his meanness.
He might forge himself : nothing low or ungentlemanly or degrading in forgery.   Dishonest, if you life ; dishonest, not vulgar.
But to open other people's letters—pah !—the disgusting small-
ness and lowness and vulgarity of it !   A sort of under-footmanish
type of criminality.   *Pecca fortiter*, if you will, of course, but
don't be a cad and a disgrace to your breeding.

CHAPTER XXII.

HOLY MATRIMONY.

THE way of the transgressor went easy for a while with Hugh Massinger. His sands ran smoother than he could himself have expected. His two chief bugbears faded away by degrees before the strong light of facts into pure nonentity. Relf did *not* know that Elsie Challoner lay dead and buried in a lonely grave at Orfordness; and Winifred Meysey was *not* left a ward in Chancery, or otherwise inconvenienced and strictly tied up in her plans for marrying him. On the contrary, the affairs of the deceased were arranged exactly as Hugh himself would have wished them to be ordered. The will in particular was a perfect gem: Hugh could have thrown his arms round the blameless attorney who drew it up: Mrs. Meysey appointed sole executrix and guardian of the infant; the estate and Hall bequeathed absolutely and without remainder to Winifred in person; a life-interest in certain specified sums only, as arranged by settlement, to the relict herself; and the coast all clear for Hugh Massinger. Everything indeed had turned out for the best. The late Squire had chosen the happiest possible moment for dying. The infant and the guardian were on Hugh's own side. There need be no long engagement, no tremulous expectation of dead men's shoes now: nor would Hugh have to put up for an indefinite term of years with the nuisance of a father-in-law's perpetual benevolent interference and well-meant dictation. Even the settlements, those tough documents, would be all drawn up to suit his own digestion. As Hugh sat, decorously lugubrious, in the dining-room at Whitestrand with Mr. Heberden, the family solicitor, two days after the funeral, he could hardly help experiencing a certain subdued sense of something exceedingly akin to stifled gratitude in his own soul towards that defective breech-loader which had relieved him at once of so many embarrassments, and made him practically Lord of the Manor of Consumptum per Mare, in the hundred of Dunwich and county of Suffolk, containing by admeasurement so many acres, roods, and perches, be the same more or less—and mostly less, indeed, as the years proceeded.

But for that slight drawback, Hugh cared as yet absolutely nothing. One only trouble, one visible kill-joy, darkened his view from the Hall windows. Every principal room in the house faced due south. Wherever he looked, from the drawing-room or the dining-room, the library or the vestibule, the boudoir or the billiard-room, the Whitestrand poplar rose straight and sheer, as conspicuous as ever, by the brink of the Char, where sea and stream met together on debatable ground in angry encounter. Its rugged boles formed the one striking and beautiful object in the whole prospect across those desolate flats of sand and salt marsh, but to Hugh Massinger that ancient tree had now become instinct with awe and horror—a visible memorial of his own crime—for it *was* a crime—and of poor dead Elsie in her nameless grave by the Low Lighthouse. He grew to regard it as Elsie's monument. Day after day, while he stopped at Whitestrand, he rose up in the morning with aching brows from his sleepless bed—for how could he sleep, with the breakers that drowned and tossed ashore his dear dead Elsie thundering wild songs of triumph from the bar in his ears?—and gazed out of his window over the dreary outlook, to see that accusing tree with its gnarled roots confronting him ever, full in face, and poisoning his success with its mute witness to his murdered victim. Every time he looked out upon it, he heard once more that wild, wild cry, as of a stricken life, when Elsie plunged into the careeing current. Every time the wind shrieked through its creaking branches in the lonely night, the shrieks went to his heart like so many living human voices crying for sympathy. He hated and dispised himself in the very midst of his success. He had sold his own soul for a wasted strip of swamp and marsh and brake and sandhill, and he found in the end that it profited him nothing.

Still, time brings alleviation to most earthly troubles. Even remorse grows duller with age—till the day comes for it to burst out afresh in fuller force than ever and goad its victim on to a final confession. Days and weeks and months rolled by, and Hugh Massinger by slow degrees began to feel that Othello was himself again. He wrote, as of old, his brilliant leaders every day regularly for the *Morning Telephone:* he slashed three-volume novels with as much vigour as ever, and rather more cynicism and cruelty than before, in the *Monday Register* : he touched the tender stops of various quills, warbling his Doric lay to Ballade and Sonnet, in the wonted woods of the *Pimlico Magazine* with endless versatility. Nor was that all. He played high in the evening at Pallavicini's, more recklessly even than had been his ancient use; for was not his future now assured to him? and did not the horrid picture of his dead drowned Elsie, tossed friendless on the bare beach at Orfordness, haunt him and sting him with its perpetual presence to seek in the feverish excitement of roulette some momentary forgetfulness of his life's tragedy? True, his rhymes were sadder and gloomier now than of old, and his play wilder : no more of the rollicking, humorous, happy-go-lucky ballad-mongering that alternated in the " Echoes from Callimachus" with his more serious verses: his sincerest laughter, he knew himself, with some pain was fraught, since Elsie left him. But in their lieu had come a reckless abandonment that served very well at first sight instead of real mirth or heartfelt geniality. In the old days, Hugh had always cultivated a certain casual vein of cheerful pessimism: he had posed as the man who drags the lengthening chain of life behind him good-humouredly: now, a grim sardonic smile usurped the place of his pessimistic *bonhomie*, and filled his pages with a Carlylese gloom that was utterly alien to his true inborn nature. Even his lighter work showed traces of the change. His wayward article, "Is Death Worth Dying?" in the *Nineteenth Century*, was full of bitterness; and his clever skit on the Blood-and-Thunder school of fiction, entitled "The Zululiad," and published as a Christmas "shilling shocker," had a sting and a venom in it that were wholly wanting to his earlier performances in the same direction. The critics said Massinger was suffering from a shallow spasm of Bryonic affectation. He knew himself he was really suffering from a profound fit of utter self-contempt and wild despairing carelessness of consequence.

The world moves, however, as Galileo remarked, in spite of our sorrows. Three months after Wyville Meysey's death, Whitestrand received its new master. It was strange to find any but Meyseys at the Hall, for Meyseys had dwelt there from time immemorial; the first of the bankers, even, though of a younger branch, having purchased the estate with his newly-gotten gold from an elder and ruined representative of the main stock. The wedding was a very quiet affair, of course: half-mourning at best, with no show or tomfoolery; and what was of much more importance to Hugh, the arrangements for the settlements were most satisfactory. The family solicitor wasn't such a fool as to make things unpleasant for his new client. Winifred was a nice little body in her way, too; affectionately proud of her captive poet: and from a lordly height of marital superiority, Hugh rather liked the pink and white small woman than otherwise. But he didn't mean to live much at Whitestrand either—"At least while your mother lasts, my child," he said cautiously to Winifred, letting her down gently by gradual stages, and saving his own reputation for kindly consideration at the same moment. "The good old soul would naturally like still to feel herself mistress in her own house. It would be cruel to mothers-in-law to disturb her now. Whenever we come down, we'll come down strictly on a visit to her. But for ourselves, we'll nest for the present in London."

Nesting in London suited Winifred, for her part, excellently well. In poor papa's day, indeed, the Meyseys had felt themselves of late far too deeply impoverished—since the sandhills

swallowed up the Yondstream farms—even to go up to town in
a hired house for a few weeks or so in the height of the season,
as they had once been wont to do, during the golden age of the
agricultural interest. The struggle to keep up appearances in
the old home on a reduced income had occupied to the full their
utmost energies during these latter days of universal depression.
So London was to Winifred a practically almost unknown
world, rich in potentialities of varied enjoyment. She had been
there but seldom, on a visit to friends; and she knew nothing
as yet of that brilliant circle that gathers round Mrs. Bouverie
Barton's Wednesday evenings, where Hugh Massinger was able
to introduce her with distinction and credit. True, the young
couple began life on a small scale, in a quiet little house—most
æsthetically decorated on economical principles—down a side-
street in the remote recesses of Philistine Bayswater. But
Hugh's coterie, though unsuccessful, was nevertheless *ex officio*
distinguished: he was hand-in-glove with the whole Cheyne
Row set—the Royal Academicians still in embryo; the Bishops
Designate of fate who at present held suburban curacies; the
Cabinet Ministers whose budget yet lingered in domestic
arrears; the germinating judges whose chances of the ermine
were confined in near perspective to soup at sessions, or the
smallest of small devilling for rising juniors. They were not
rich in this world's goods, those discounted celebrities; but
they were a lively crew, full of fun and fancy, and they delighted Winifred by their juvenile exuberance of wit and eloquence. She voted the men with their wives, when they had
and—which wasn't often, for Bohemia can seldom afford the
luxury of matrimony—the most charming society she had
ever met; and Bohemia in return voted "little Mrs. Massinger," in the words of its accepted mouthpiece and spokes-
man, Hatherley, "as witty a piece of Eve's flesh as any in
Illyria." The little "arrangement in pink and white" became,
indeed, quite a noted personage in the narrow world of Cheyne
Row society.

To say the truth, Hugh detested Whitestrand. He never
wanted to go near the place again, now that he had made
himself in very deed its lord and master. He hated the
house, the grounds, the river; but above all he hated that
funereal poplar, that seemed to rise up and menace him each
time he looked at it with the pains and penalties of his own evil
conscience. At Easter, Winifred dragged him home once more,
to visit the relict in her lonely mansion. The Bard went, as in
duty bound; but the duty was more than commonly distasteful. They reached Whitestrand late at night, and were shown
upstairs at once into a large front bedroom. Hugh's heart
leaped up in his mouth when he saw it. It was Elsie's room:

the room into which he had climbed on that fateful evening; the room bound closest up in his memory with the hideous abiding nightmare of his poisoned life; the room he had never since dared to enter; the room he had hoped never more to look upon.

"Are we to sleep here, Winnie?" he cried aghast, in a tone of the utmost horror and dismay. And Winifred, looking up at him in silent surprise, answered merely in an unconcerned voice: "Why, yes, my dear boy; what's wrong with the room? It's good enough. We're to sleep here, of course—certainly."

He dared say no more. To remonstrate would be madness. Any reason he gave must seem inadequate. But he would sooner have slept on the bare ground by the river-side than have slept that night in that desecrated and haunted room of Elsie's.

He did *not* sleep. He lay awake all the long hours through, and murmured to himself, ten thousand times over, "Elsie, Elsie, Elsie, Elsie!" His lips moved as he murmured sometimes. Winifred opened her eyes once—he felt her open them, though it was as dark as pitch—and seemed to listen. One's senses grow preternaturally sharp in the night watches. Could she have heard that mute movement of his silent lips? He hoped not. Oh no; it was impossible. But he lay awake till morning in a deadly terror, the cold sweat standing in big drops on his brow, haunted through the long vigils of the dreary night by that picture of Elsie, in her pale white dress, with arms uplifted above her helpless head, flinging herself wildly from the dim black poplar, through the gloom of evening, upon the tender mercies of the swift dark water.

Elsie, Elsie, Elsie, Elsie! It was for this he had sold and betrayed his Elsie!

In the morning when he rose, he went over to the window—Elsie's window, round whose sides the rich wistaria clambered so luxuriantly—and looked out with weary sleepless eyes across the weary dreary stretch of barren Suffolk scenery. It was still winter, and the wistaria on the wall stood bald and naked and bare of foliage. How different from the time when Elsie lived there! He could see where the bough had broken with his weight that awful night of Elsie's disappearance. He gazed vacantly across the lawn and meadow towards the tumbling sandhills. "Winifred," he said—he was in no mood just then to call her Winnie—"what a big bare bundle of straight tall switches that poplar is! So gaunt and stiff! I hate the very sight of it. It's a great disfigurement. I wonder your people ever stood it so long, blocking out the view from their drawing-room windows."

Winifred rose from the dressing-table and looked out by his side in blank surprise. "Why, Hugh," she cried, noting both his unwonted tone and the absence of the now customary pet form of her name, "how *can* you say so? I call it just lovely. Blocking out the view, indeed! Why, it *is* the view. There's nothing else. It's the only good point in the whole picture. I love to see it even in winter—the dear old poplar—so tall and straight—with its twigs etched out in black and gray against the sky like that. I love it better than anything else at Whitestrand."

Hugh drummed his fingers on the frosted pane impatiently. "For my part, I hate it," he answered in a short but sullen tone. "Whenever I come to live at Whitestrand, I shall never rest till I've cut it down and stubbed it up from the roots entirely."

"Hugh!"

There was something in the accent that made him start. He knew why. It reminded him of Elsie's voice as she cried aloud "Hugh!" in her horror and agony upon that fatal evening by the grim old poplar.

"Well, Winnie," he answered much more tenderly. The tone had melted him.

Winifred flung her arms around him with every sign of grief and dismay and burst into a sudden flood of tears. "Oh, Hugh," she cried, "you don't know what you say: you can't think how you grieve me.—Don't you know why? You must surely guess it.—It isn't that the Whitestrand poplar's a famous tree—a sea-mark for sailors—a landmark for all the country round—historical almost, not to say celebrated! It isn't that it was mentioned by Fuller and Drayton, and I'm sure I don't know how many other famous people—poor papa knew, and was fond of quoting them. It's not for all that, though for that alone I should be sorry to lose it, sorrier than for anything else in all Whitestrand. But, oh, Hugh, that *you* should say so! That *you* should say, 'For my part, I hate it.'—Why, Hugh, it was on the roots of that very tree, you know, that you saw me for the very first time in my life, as I sat there dangling my hat—with Elsie. It was from the roots of that tree that I first saw you and fell in love with you, when you jumped off Mr. Relf's yawl to rescue my poor little half-crown hat for me.—It was there you first won my heart—you won my heart—my poor little heart.—And to think you really want to cut down that tree would nearly, very nearly break it.—Hugh, dear Hugh, never, never, never say so!"

No man can see a woman cry unmoved. To do so is more or less than human. Hugh laid her head tenderly on his big shoulder, soothed and kissed her with loving gentleness, swore he was speaking without due thought or reflection, declared that he loved that tree every bit as much in his heart as she herself did, and pacified her gradually by every means in his large repertory of masculine blandishments. But deep down in his bosom, he crushed his despair. If ever he came to live at Whitestrand, then, that hateful tree must for ever rise up in mute accusation to bear witness against him!

It could not! It should not! He could never stand it. Either they must never live at Whitestrand at all, or else—or else, in some way unknown to Winifred, he must manage to do away with the Whitestrand poplar.

CHAPTER XXIII.

UNDER THE PALM-TREES.

A LONE governess, even though she be a Girton girl, vanishes readily into space from the stage of society. It's wonderful how very little she's missed. She comes and goes and disappears into vacancy, almost as the cook and the housemaid do in our modern domestic phantasmagoria; and after a few months, everybody ceases even to inquire what has become of her. Our round horizon knows her no more. If ever at rare intervals she appens to flit for a moment across our zenith again, it is but as *revenant* from some distant sphere. She has played her part in life, so far as we are concerned, when she has " finished the education " of our growing girls, as we cheerfully phrase it— what a happy idea that anybody's education could ever be finished!—and we let her drop out altogether from our scheme of things accordingly, or feel 'her, when she invades our orbit once more, as inconvenient as all other *revenants* proverbially find themselves. Hence, it was no great wonder indeed that Elsie Challoner should subside quietly into the peaceful routine of her new residence at the Villa Rossa at San Remo, with " no questions asked," as the advertisements frankly and ingenuously word it. She had a few girl-friends in England—old Girton companions—who tracked her still on her path through the cosmos, and to these she wrote unreservedly as to her present whereabouts. She didn't enter into details, of course, about the particular way she came to leave her last temporary home at the Meyseys' at Whitestrand : no one is bound to speak out every-thing; but she said in plain and simple language she had accepted a new and she hoped more permanent engagement on the Riviera. That was all. She concealed nothing and added nothing. Her mild deception was purely negative. She had

M

no wish to hide the fact of her being alive from anybody on earth but Hugh and Winifred; and even from them, she desired to hide it by passive rather than by active concealment.

But it is an error of youth to underestimate in the long run the interosculation of society in our modern Babylon. You may lurk and languish and lie obscure for a while; but you do not permanently evade anybody: you may suffer eclipse, but you cannot be extinguished. While we are young and foolish, we often think to ourselves, on some change in our environment, that Jones or Brown has now dropped entirely out of our private little universe—that we may safely count upon never again happening upon him or hearing of him anyhow or anywhere. We tell Smith something we know or suspect about Miss Robinson, under the profound but, alas, too innocent conviction that they two revolve in totally different planes of life, and can never conceivably collide against one another. We leave Mauritius or Eagle City, Nebraska, and imagine we are quit for good and all of the insignificant Mauritians or the free-born, free-mannered, and free-spoken citizens of that far western mining camp. Error, error, sheer juvenile error! As comets come back in time from the abysses of space, so everybody always turns up everywhere. Jones and Brown run up against us incontinently on the King's Road at Brighton; or occupy the next table to our own at Delmonico's; or clap us on the shoulder as we sit with a blanket wrapped round our shivering forms, intent upon the too wintry sunrise on the summit of the Rigi. Miss Robinson's plane bisects Smith's horizon at right angles in a *dahabeeyah* on the Upper Nile, or discovers our treachery at an hotel at Orotava in the Canary Islands. Our Mauritian sugar-planter calls us over the coals for our pernicious views on differential duties and the French bounty system among the stormy channels of the Outer Hebrides; and Colonel Bill Manningham, of the *Eagle City National Banner*, intrudes upon the quiet of our suburban villa at remote Surbiton to inquire, with Western American picturesqueness and exuberance of vocabulary, what the Hades we meant by our casual description of Nebraskan society as a den of thieves, in the last number of the St. Petersburg *Monitor?* Oh no; in the pre-Columban days of Boadicea, and Romulus and Remus, and the Twenty-first Dynasty, it might perhaps have been possible to mention a fact at Nineveh or Pekin with tolerable security against its being repeated forthwith in the palaces of Mexico or the huts of Honolulu; but in our existing world of railways and telegraphs and penny postage, and the great ubiquitous special correspondent, when Morse and Wheatstone have wreaked their worst, and whosoever enters Jerusalem by the Jaffa Gate sees a red-lettered notice-board staring him in the face, "This way to Cook's Excursion Office"—the attempt to

conceal or hush up anything has become simply and purely a
ridiculous fallacy. When we go to Timbuctoo, we expect to
meet with some of our wife's relations in confidential quarters;
and we are not surprised when the aged chief who entertains us
in Parisian full dress at an eight o'clock dinner in the Fiji
Islands relates to us some pleasing Oxford anecdotes of the
missionary bishop whom in unregenerato days he assisted to
eat, and under whom we ourselves read Aristotle and Tacitus
as undergraduates at dear sleepy old Oriel. More than ever
nowadays is the proverb true, "Quod tacitum velis nemini
dixeris."

It was ordained, therefore, in the nature of things, that sooner
or later Hugh Massinger must find out Elsie Challoner was
really living. No star shoots ever beyond the limits of our
galaxy. But the discovery might be postponed for an indefinite
period; and besides, so far as Elsie herself was concerned, her
only wish was to keep the fact secret from Hugh in person, not
from the rest of the world at large; for she knew everybody
else in her little sphere believed her merely to have left the
Meyseys' in a most particular and unexplained hurry. Now,
Hugh for his part, even if any vague rumour of her having been
sighted here or there in some distant nook of the Riviera by So-
and-so or What's-his-name might happen at any time to reach
his ear, would certainly set it down in his own heart as one
more proof of the signal success of his own clever and cunningly
designed deception. As a matter of fact, more than one person
did accidentally, in the course of conversation, during the next
few years mention to Hugh that somebody had said Miss Challoner had been seen at Marseilles or Cannes, or Genoa or somewhere; and Hugh in every case did really look upon it only as
another instance of Warren Relf's blind acceptance of his bland
little fictions. The more people thought Elsie was alive, the
more did Hugh Massinger in his own heart pride himself inwardly on the cleverness and far-sightedness of the plot he had
laid and carried out that awful evening at the Fisherman's Rest
at Whitestrand in Suffolk.

Thus it happened that Elsie was not far wrong, for the present
at least, in her calculation of chances as to Hugh and Winifred.

The very day Elsie reached San Remo, news of Mr. Meysey's
death came to her in the papers. It was a sudden shock, and
the temptation to write to Winifred then was very strong; but
Elsie resisted it. She had to resist it—to crush down her sympathy for sympathy's sake. She couldn't bear to break poor
Winifred's heart at such a moment by letting her know to the
full all Hugh's baseness. It was hard indeed that Winifred
should think her unfeeling, should call her ungrateful, should
suppose her forgetful; but she bore even that—for Winifred's

sake—without murmuring. Some day, perhaps, Winifred would know; but she hoped not. For Winifred's sake, she hoped Winifred would never find out what manner of man she proposed to marry.

And for Hugh's, too. For with feminine consistency and steadfastness of feeling, Elsie even now could not learn to hate him. Nay, rather, though she recognized how vile and despicable a thing he was, how poor in spirit, how unworthy of her love, she loved him still—she could not help loving him. For Hugh's sake, she wished it all kept secret for ever from Winifred, even though she herself must be the victim and the scapegoat. Winifred would think harshly of *her* in any case: why let her think harshly of Hugh also?

And so, in the little Villa Rossa at San Remo, among that calm reposeful scenery of olive groves and lemon orchards, Elsie's poor wounded heart began gradually to film over a little with external healing. She had the blessed deadening influence of daily routine to keep her from brooding; those six pleasant, delicate, sensitive, sympathetic consumptive girls to teach and look after and walk out with perpetually. They were bright young girls, as often happens with their type; extremely like Winifred herself in manner—too like, Elsie sometimes thought in her own heart with a sigh of presentiment. And Elsie's heart was still young, too. They clambered together, like girls as they were, among the steep hills that stretch behind the town; they explored that pretty coquettish country; they wandered along the beautiful olive-clad shore; they made delightful excursions to the quaint old villages on the mountain sides— Taggia and Ceriana, and San Romolo and Perinaldo—mouldering gray houses perched upon pinnacles of mouldering gray rock, and pierced by arcades of Moorish gloom and medieval solemnity. All alike helped Elsie to beat down the memory of her grief, or to hold it at bay in her poor tortured bosom. That she would ever be happy again was more than in her most sanguine moments she dared to expect; but she was not without hope that she might in time grow at least insensible.

One morning in December, at the Villa Rossa, about the hour for early breakfast, Elsie heard a light knock at her door. It was not the cook with the *café-au-lait* and roll and tiny pat of butter on the neat small tray for the first breakfast : Elsie knew that much by the lightness of the knock. "Come in," she said; and the door opened and Edie entered. She held a letter in her right hand, and a very grave look sat upon her usually merry face. "Somebody dead?" Elsie thought with a start. But no; the letter was not black-bordered. Edie opened it and drew from it slowly a small piece of paper, an advertisement from the *Times.* Then Elsie's breath came and went hard. She knew now what the letter portended. Not a death: not a death—but a marriage!

"Give it me, dear," she cried aloud to Edie. "Let me see it at once. I can bear it—I can bear it."

Edie handed the cutting to her, with a kiss on her forehead, and sat with her arm round Elsie's waist as the poor dazed girl, half erect in the bed, sat up and read that final seal of Hugh's cruel betrayal: "On Dec. 17th, at Whitestrand Parish Church, Suffolk, by the Rev. Percy W. Bickersteth, M.A., cousin of the bride, assisted by the Rev. J. Walpole, vicar, HUGH EDWARD DE CARTERET MASSINGER, of the Inner Temple, Barrister-at-law, to WINIFRED MARY, only daughter of the late Thomas Wyville Meysey, of Whitestrand Hall, J.P."

Elsie gazed at the cutting long and sadly; then she murmured at last in a pained voice: "And he thought I was dead! He thought he had killed me!"

Edie's fiery indignation could restrain itself no longer. "He's a wicked man," she cried: "a wicked, bad, horrible creature; and I don't care what you say, Elsie; I hope he'll be punished as he well deserves for his cruelty and wickedness to you, darling."

"I hope not—I pray not," Elsie answered solemnly. And as she said it, she meant it. She prayed for it profoundly.

After a while, she set down the paper on the table by her bed-ide, and laying her head on Edie's shoulder, burst into tears— torrent of relief for her burdened feelings. Edie soothed her nd wept with her, tenderly. For half an hour Elsie cried in silence; then she rose at last, dried her eyes, burnt the little slip of paper from the *Times* resolutely, and said to Edie: "Now it's all over."

"All over?" Edie echoed in an inquiring voice.

"Yes, darling, all over," Elsie answered very firmly. "I shall never, never cry any more at all about him. He's Winifred's now, and I hope he'll be good to her.—But, oh, Edie, I *did* once love him so!"

And the winter wore away slowly at San Remo. Elsie had crushed down her love firmly in her heart now—crushed it down and stifled it to some real purpose. She knew Hugh for just what he was; she recognized his coldness, his cruelty, his little care for her; and she saw no sign—as how should she see it?—of the deadly remorse that gnawed from time to time at his tortured bosom. The winter wore away, and Elsie was glad of it. Time was making her regret less poignant.

Early in February, Edie came up to her room one afternoon, when the six consumptive pupils were at work in the school-room below with the old Italian music-master, under Mrs. Relf's direction, and seating herself, girl-fashion, on the bed, began to talk about her brother Warren.

Edie seldom talked of Warren to Elsie: she had even ostentatiously avoided the subject hitherto, for reasons of her own which will be instantly obvious to the meanest intelligence. But now, by a sort of accident of design, she mentioned casually something about how he had always taken them, most years, for so many nice trips in his yawl to the lovely places on the coast about Bordighera and Mentone, and even Monte Carlo.

"Then he sometimes comes to the Riviera with you, does he?" Elsie asked listlessly. She loved Edie and dear old Mrs. Relf, and she was grateful to Warren for his chivalrous kindness; but she could hardly pretend to feel profoundly interested in him. There had never been more than one man in the world for her, and that man was now Winifred's husband.

"He always comes," Edie answered, with a significant stress on the world *always*. "Indeed, this is the very first year he's ever missed coming since we first wintered here. He likes to be near us while we're on the coast. It gives him a chance of varying his subjects. He says himself, he's always inclined to judge of genius by its power of breaking out in a fresh place— not always repeating its own successes. In summer he sketches round the mouth of the Thames and the North Sea, but in winter he always alters the venue to the Mediterranean. Variety's good for a painter, he thinks: though, to be sure, that doesn't really matter very much to *him*, because nobody ever by any chance buys his pictures."

"Can't he sell them, then?" Elsie asked more curiously.

"My dear, Warren's a born artist, not a picture-dealer; therefore, of course, he never sells anything. If he were a mere dauber, now, there might be some chance for him. Being a real painter, he paints, naturally enough, but he makes no money."

"But the real painter always succeeds in the end, doesn't he?"

"In the end, yes; I don't doubt that: within a century or two. But what's the good of succeeding, pray, a hundred years after you're dead and buried? The bankers won't discount a posthumous celebrity for you. I should like to succeed while I was alive to enjoy it. I'd rather have a modest competence in the nineteenth century than the principal niche in the Temple of Fame in the middle of the twentieth. Besides, Warren doesn't want to succeed at all, dear boy—at least. not much. I wish to goodness he did. He only wants to paint really great pictures."

"That's the same thing, isn't it?—or very nearly."

"Not a bit of it. Quite the contrary in some cases.

Warren's one of them. He'll never succeed while he lives, poor child, unless his amiable sister succeeds in making him. And that's just what I mean to do in time, too, dear.—I mean to make Warren earn enough to keep himself—and a wife and family."

Elsie looked down at the carpet uneasily. It wanted darning. "Why didn't he come this winter as usual?" she asked in haste, to turn the current of the conversation.

"Why? Well, why? What a question to ask!—Just because *you* were here, Elsie."

Elsie examined the holes in the Persian pattern on the floor by her side with minuter care and precision than ever. "That was very kind of him," she said after a pause, defining one of them with the point of her shoe accurately.

"Too kind," Edie echoed—"too kind, and too sensitive."

"I think not," Elsie murmured low. She was blushing visibly, and the carpet was engrossing all her attention.

"And *I* think *yes*," Edie answered in a decisive tone. "And when I think yes, other people ought as a matter of course to agree with me. There's such a thing as being too generous, too delicate, too considerate, too thoughtful for others. You've no right to swamp your own individuality. And I say, Warren ought to have brought the yawl round to San Remo long ago, to give us all a little diversion, and not gone skulking like a ickpocket about Nice and Golfe Jouan, and Toulon and t. Tropez, for a couple of months together at a stretch, with- ut so much as ever even running over here to see his own mother and sister in their winter-quarters. It's not respectful to his own relations."

Elsie started. "Do you mean to say," she cried, "he's been as near as Nice without coming to see you?"

Edie nodded. "Ever since Christmas."

"No! Not really?"

"Yes, my child. Really, or I wouldn't say so. It's a practice of mine to tell the truth and shame a certain individual. Warren couldn't stop away from us any longer; so he took the yawl round by Gibraltar after—after the 17th of December, you know."—Elsie smiled sadly.—"And he's been knocking about along the coast round here ever since, afraid to come on—for fear of hurting your feelings, Elsie."

Elsie rose and clasped her hands tight. "It was very kind of him," she said. "He's a dear good fellow.—I think I could bear to meet him now. And in any case, I think he ought at least to come over and see you and your mother. It would be very selfish of me, very wrong of me to keep you all out of so much pleasure.—Ask him to come, Edie.—Tell him—it would not hurt me very much to see him."

Edie's eyes flashed mischievous fire. "That's a pretty sort of message to send any one," she cried, with some slight amusement. "We usually put it in a politer form. May I vary it a little and tell him, Elsie, it will give you great pleasure to see him?"

"If you like," Elsie answered, quite simply and candidly. He was a nice fellow, and he was Edie's brother. She must grow accustomed to meeting him somehow. No man was anything at all to her now.—And perhaps by this time he had quite forgotten his foolish fancy.

The celebrated centreboard yawl *Mud-Turtle*, of the port of London, Relf, master, seventeen tons registered burden, was at that moment lying up snugly by a wooden pier in the quaint little French harbour of St. Tropez, just beyond the blue peaks of the frontier mountains. When Potts next morning early brought a letter on board, addressed to the skipper, with an Italian stamp duly stuck in the corner, Warren Relf opened it hastily with doubtful expectations. Its contents made his honest brown check burn bright red. "My dear old Warren," the communication ran shortly, "you may bring the yawl round here to San Remo as soon as you like. She says you may come; and what's more, She authorizes me to inform you in the politest terms that it will give her very great pleasure indeed to see you. So you can easily imagine the pride and delight with which I am ever, Your affectionate and successful sister, Edie."

"Edie's a brick!" Warren said to himself with a bound of his heart; "and it's really awfully kind of—Elsie."

Before ten o'clock that same morning, the celebrated centreboard yawl *Mud-Turtle*, manned by her owner and his constant companion, was under way with a favouring wind, and scudding like a seabird, with all canvas on, round the spit of Bordighera, on her voyage to the tiny harbour of San Remo.

CHAPTER XXIV.

THE BALANCE QUIVERS.

MARCH, April, May passed away: anemones and asphodels came and went; narcissus and globeflower bloomed and withered; and Warren Relf, cruising about in the *Mud-Turtle* round the peacock-blue bays and indentations of the Genoese Riviera, had spent many cloudless days in quiet happiness at the pretty little villa among the clambering olive terraces on the slopes at San Remo. Elsie had learnt at least to tolerate his presence now: she no longer blushed a vivid crimson when she saw him coming up the zigzag roadway; she wasn't much more awkward before him, in fact, than with other creatures of his sex in general; nay, more, as a mere friend she rather liked and enjoyed his society than otherwise. Not to have liked Warren Relf, indeed, would have been quite unpardonable. The Relfs had all shown her so much kindness, and Warren himself had been so chivalrously courteous, that even a heart of stone might surely have melted somewhat towards the manly young painter. And Elsie's heart, in spite of Hugh's unkindness, was by no means stony. She found Warren, in his rough sailor clothes, always gentle, always unobtrusive, always thoughtful, always considerate; and as Edie's brother, she got on with him quite as comfortably in the long run as could be expected of anybody under such trying circumstances.

At first, to be sure, she couldn't be induced to board the deck of the busy little *Mud-Turtle*. But as May came round with its warm Italian sunshine, Edie so absolutely insisted on her taking a trip with them along that enchanted coast towards Monaco and Villefranche, beneath the ramping crags of the Tête du Chien, that Elsie at last gave way in silence, and accompanied them round the bays and headlands and roadsteads of the Riviera on more than one delightful outing. Edie was beginning, by her simple domestic faith in her brother's profound artistic powers, to inspire Elsie, too, with a new sort of interest in Warren's future. It began to dawn upon her slowly, in a dim chaotic fashion, that Warren had really a most unusual love for the byways of nature, and a singular faculty for reading and interpreting with loving skill her hidden hieroglyphics. "My dear," Edie said to her once, as they sat on deck and watched Warren labouring with ceaseless care at the minute growth of a spreading stain on a bare wall of seaward rock, "he *shall* succeed—he *must* succeed! I mean to make him. He shall be hung. A man who can turn out work like that must secure in the end his recognition."

"I don't want recognition," Warren answered slowly, putting a few more lingering microscopic touches to the wee curved frondlets of the creeping lichen. "I do it because I like to do it. The work itself is its own reward. If only I could earn enough to save you and the dear old Mater from having to toil and moil like a pair of galley-slaves, Edie, I should be amply satisfied, and more than satisfied.—I confess, I should like to do that, of course. In art, as elsewhere, the labourer is worthy of his hire, no doubt: he would prefer to earn his own bread and butter. It's hard to work and work, and work and work, and get scarcely any sale after all for one's pictures."

"It'll come in time," Edie answered, nodding sagaciously. "People will find out they're compelled at last to recognize

your genius. And that's the best success of all, in the long run
—the success that comes without one's ever seeking it. The
men who aim at succeeding, succeed for a day. The men who
work at their art for their art's sake, and leave success to mind
its own business, are the men who finally live for ever."

"It doesn't do them much good, though, I'm afraid," Warren
answered, with a sigh, hardly looking up from his fragments of
orange-brown vegetation. " They seldom live to see their final
triumph.

> 'For praise is his who builds for his own age ;
> But he that builds for time, must look to time for wage !'"

As he said it, he glanced aside nervously at Elsie. What a slip
of the tongue! Without remembering for a moment whom he
was quoting, he had quoted with thoughtless ease a familiar
couplet from the " Echoes from Callimachus."

Elsie's face showed no passing sign of recognition, however.
Perhaps she had never read the lines he was thinking of;
perhaps, if not, she had quite forgotten them. At any rate, she
only murmured reflectively to Edie: "I think, with you, Mr.
Relf *must* succeed in the end. But how soon, it would be
difficult to say. He'll have to educate his public, to begin with,
up to his own level. When I first saw his work, I could see
very little myself to praise in it. Now, every day, I see more
and more. It's like all good work; it gains upon you as you
study it closely."

Warren turned round to her with a face like a girl's.
" Thank you," he said gently, and said no more. But she
could see that her praise had moved him to the core. For two
or three minutes, he left off painting ; he only fumbled with a
dry brush at the outline of the lichens, and pretended to be
making invisible improvements in the petty details of his
delicate foreground. She observed that his hand was trembling
too much to continue work. After a short pause he laid down
his palette and colours. " I shall leave off now," he said, " till
the sun gets lower ; it's too hot just at present to paint properly."

Elsie pitied the poor young man from the bottom of her soul.
She was really afraid he was falling in love with her. And if
only he knew how hopeless that would be! She had a heart
once ; and Hugh had broken it.

That evening, in the sacred recess of Elsie's room, Edie and
Elsie talked things over together in girlish confidence. The
summer was coming on apace now. What was Elsie to do
when the Relfs returned, as they must return, to England?

She could never go back. That was a fixed point, round
which as pivot the rest of the question revolved vaguely. She

could never expose herself to the bare chance of meeting Hugh
and—and Mrs. Massinger. She didn't say so, of course; no
need to say it; she was far too profoundly wounded for that.
But Edie and she both took it for granted in perfect silence.
They understood one another, and wanted no language to
communicate their feelings.

Suddenly, Edie had a bright idea: why not go to St. Martin
Lantosque?

Where's St. Martin Lantosque?" Elsie asked languidly. Her
own future was not a subject that aroused in her mind any
profound or enthusiastic interest.

"St. Martin Lantosque, my dear," Edie answered with her
brisker, more matter-of-fact manner, "is a sort of patent safety-
valve or overflow cistern for the surplus material of the Nice
season. As soon as the summer grows unendurably hot on the
Promenade des Anglais, the population of the *pensions* and
hotels on the sea-front manifest a mutually repulsive influence
—like the particles of a gas, according to that prodigiously
learned book you teach the girls elementary physics out of.
The heat, in fact, acts expansively; it drives them forcibly
apart in all directions—some to England, some to St. Petersburg, some to America, and some to the Italian lakes or the
Bernese Oberland. Well, that's what becomes of most of them:
they melt away into different atmospheres; but a few visitors—
he people with families who make Nice their real home, not
he mere sun-worshippers who want to loll on the chairs on the
Quai Masséna or in the Jardin Public—retire for the summer
only just as far as St. Martin Lantosque. It's a jolly little
place, right up among the mountains, thirty miles or so behind
Nice, as beautiful as a butterfly, and as cool as a cucumber, and
supplied with all the necessaries of life, from afternoon tea to a
consular chaplain. It's surrounded by the eternal snows, if you
like them eternal; and well situated for penny ices, if you prefer
your glaciers in that mitigated condition. And if you went
there, you might manage to combine business with pleasure,
you see, by giving lessons to the miserable remnants of the
Nice season. Lots of the families must have little girls: lots
of the little girls must be pining for instruction: lots of the
mammas must be eager to find suitable companionship; and a
Girton graduate's the very person to supply them all with just
what they want in the finest perfection. We'll look the matter
up, Elsie. I spy an opening."

" Will your brother come here next winter, Edie?"

"I know no cause or impediment why he shouldn't, my dear.
He usually does one winter with another. It's a way he has, to
follow his family. He takes his pleasure out in the exercise of
the domestic affections.—But why do you ask me?"

"Because"—and Elsie hesitated for a moment—"I think—if he does—I oughtn't to say here."

"Nonsense, my dear," Edie answered promptly. It was the best way to treat Elsie. "You needn't be afraid. I know what you mean. But don't distress yourself: men's hearts will stand a fearful deal of breaking. It doesn't hurt them. They're coarse earthenware to our egg-shell porcelain. He must just pine away with unrequited affection in his own way as long as he likes. Never mind *him*. It'll do him good. It's yourself and ourselves you've got to think of. He's quite happy as long as he's allowed to paint his own unsaleable pictures in peace and quietness."

"I wish he could sell them," Elsie went on reflectively. "I really do. It's a shame a man who can paint so beautifully and so poetically as he does should have to wait so long and patiently for his recognition. He strikes too high a note; that's what's the matter. And yet I wouldn't like to see him try any lower one. I didn't understand him at first, myself; and I'm sure I find as much in nature as most people.—But you want to have looked at things for some time together, through his pair of spectacles, before you can catch them exactly as he does. The eye that sees is half the vision."

"My dear," Edie answered in her cheery way, "we'll make him succeed. We'll push him and pull him. He'll never do it if he's left to his own devices, I'm sure. He's too utterly wrapped up in his work itself to think much of the reception the mere vulgar picture-buying world accords it. The chink of the guinea never distracts his ear from higher music. But I'm a practical person, thank heaven—a woman of affairs—and I mean to advertise him. They ought to hang him, and he shall be hung. I'm going to see to it. I shall get Mr. Hatherley to crack him up—Mr. Hatherley has such a lot of influence, you know, with the newspapers. Let's roll the log with cheerful persistence. We shall float him yet; you see if we don't. He shall be Warren Relf, R.A., with a tail to his name, before you and I have done launching him."

"I hope so," Elsie murmured with a quiet sigh.

If Warren Relf could have heard that conversation, he might have plucked up heart of grace indeed for the future. When a woman begins to feel a living interest in a man's career, there's hope for him yet in that woman's affections. Though, to be sure, Elsie herself would have been shocked to believe it. She cherished her sorrow still in her heart of hearts as her dearest chattel, her most sacred possession. She brought incense and tears to it daily with pious awe. Woman-like, she loved to take it out of its shrine and cry over it each night in her own room alone, as a religious exercise. She was faithful to the Hugh that had never been, though the Hugh that really was had proved so utterly base and unworthy of her. For that first Hugh's sake, she would never love any other man. She could only feel for Warren Relf the merest sisterly interest and grateful friendship.

However, we must be practical, come what may; we must eat and drink though our hearts ache. So it was arranged at last that Elsie should retire for the summer to the cool shades of St. Martin Lantosque; while the Relfs returned to their tiny house at 128, Bletchingley Road, London, W A few pupils were even secured by hook and by crook for the off-season, and a home provided for Elsie with an American family, in search of culture in the cheapest market, who had hired a villa in the patent safety-valve, to avoid the ever unpleasant necessity for returning to the land of their birth, across the stormy millpond, for the hot summer. The day before the Relfs took their departure from San Remo, Elsie had a few words alone with Warren in the pretty garden of the Villa Rossa. There was one thing she wanted to ask him particularly—a special favour, yet a very delicate one. "Shall you be down about the coast of Suffolk much this year?" she asked timidly. And Warren gathered at once what she meant. "Yes," he answered in almost as hesitating a voice as her own, looking down at the prickly-pears and green lizards by his feet, and keeping his eyes studiously from meeting hers; "I shall be cruising round, no oubt, at Yarmouth and Whitestrand, and Lowestoft and .ldeburgh."

She noticed how ingeniously he had mixed them all up together in a single list, as if none were more interesting to her mind than the other; and she added in an almost inaudible voice: "If you go to Whitestrand, I wish very much you would let me know about poor dear Winifred."

"I will let you know," he answered, with a bound of his heart, proud even to be entrusted with that doubtful commission. "I'll make it my business to go there almost at once.—And I may write and tell you how I find her, mayn't I?"

Elsie drew back, a little frightened at his request. "Edie could tell me, couldn't she? That would save you the trouble," she murmured after a pause, not without some faint undercurrent of conscious hypocrisy.

His face fell. He was disappointed that he might not write to her himself on so neutral a matter. "As you will," he answered, with a downcast look. "Edie shall do it, then."

Elsie's heart was divided within her. She saw her reply had hurt and distressed him. He was *such* a good fellow, and he would be so pleased to write. But if only he knew how hopeless it was! What folly to encourage him, when nothing on earth could ever come of it! She wished she knew what she ought to do under these trying circumstances. Gratitude would urge her to say "Yes, of course;" but regard for his own happiness would make her say "No" with crushing promptitude. It was better he should understand at once, without appeal, that it was quite impossible—a dream of the wildest. She glanced at him shyly and caught his eye; she fancied it was just a trifle dimmed. She was *so* sorry for him. "Very well, Mr. Relf," she murmured, relenting and taking his hand for a moment to say good-bye. "You can write yourself, if it's not too much trouble."

Warren's heart gave a great jump. "Thank you," he said, wringing her hand, oh, so hard! "You are very kind.—Good-bye, Miss Challoner." And he raised his hat and departed all tremulous. He went down that afternoon to the *Mud-Turtle* in the harbour the happiest man alive in the whole of San Remo.

CHAPTER XXV.

CLOUDS ON THE HORIZON.

THE Massingers pitched their tent at Whitestrand again for August. Hugh did his best indeed to put off the evil day; but if you sell your soul for gold, you must take the gold with all its encumbrances; and Winifred's will was a small encumbrance that Hugh had never for one moment reckoned upon in his ante-nuptial calculations of advantages and drawbacks. He took it for granted he was marrying a mere girl, whom he could mould and fashion to his own whim and fancy. That simple, childish, blushing little thing had a will of her own, however—ay, more, plenty of it. When Hugh proposed with an insinuating smile that they should run down for the summer to Barmouth or Aberystwith—he loved North Wales—Winifred replied with quiet dignity: "Wales is stuffy. There's nothing so bracing as the east coast. After a London season, one needs bracing. I feel pulled down. We'll go and stop with mamma at Whitestrand." And she shut her little mouth upon it with a snap like a rat-trap. Against that solid rock of sheer resolution, Hugh shattered himself to no purpose in showery spray of rhetoric and reasoning. Gibraltar is not more disdainful of the foam that dashes upon its eternal cliffs year after year than Winifred was to her husband's running fire of argument and expostulation. She never deigned to argue in return; she merely repeated with naked iteration ten thousand times over the categorical formula, "We'll go to Whitestrand."

And to Whitestrand they went in due time. The plastic male character can no more resist the ceaseless pressure of feminine persistence than clay can resist the hands of the potter, or wood the weeping effect of heat and dryness. Hugh took his way obediently to dull flat Suffolk when August came, and relinquished with a sigh his dreams of delicious picnics by the Dolgelly waterfalls, and his mental picture of those phenomenally big trout—three pounds apiece, fisherman's weight—that lurk uncaught in the deep green pools among the rocks and stickles of the plashing Wnion. The Bard had sold himself for prompt cash to the first bidder: he found when it was too late he had sold himself unknown into a mitigated form of marital slavery. The purchaser made her own terms: Hugh was compelled meekly to accept them.

Two strong wills were clashing together. In serious matters, neither would yield. Each must dint and batter the other.

They did *not* occupy Elsie's room this time. Hugh had stipulated with all his might for that concession beforehand. He would never pass a night in that room again, he said: the paint or the woodwork or the chairs or something made him hopelessly sleepless. In these old houses, sanitary arrangements were always bad. Winifred darted a piercing look at him as he shuffled uneasily over that lame excuse. Already a vague idea was framing itself piecemeal in her woman's mind—a very natural idea, when she saw him so moody and preoccupied and splenetic—that Hugh had been really in love with Elsie, and was in love with Elsie still, even now that Elsie was away in Australia—else why this unconquerable and absurd objection to Elsie's room? Did he think he had deceived and ill-treated Elsie?

A woman's mind goes straight to the bull's-eye. No use pretending to mislead her with side-issues; she flings them aside with a contemptuous smile, and proceeds at once to worm her way to the kernel of the matter.

August wore away, and September came in; and Hugh continued to mope and to bore himself to his heart's content at that detestable Whitestrand. To distract his soul, he worked hard at his "Ode to Manetho;" but even Manetho, audacious theme, gave him scanty consolation. Nay, his quaint "Legend of Fee-Faw-Fum," that witty apologue, with its grimly humorous catalogue of all possible nightly fears, supplied him with food but for one solitary morning's meditation. You can't cast out your blue-devils by poking fun at them; those cerulean demons will not be laughed down or rudely exorcised by such simple means. They recur in spite of you with profound regularity. The *fons et origo mali* was still present. That hateful poplar still fronted his eyes wherever he moved: that window with the wistaria still haunted his sight whenever he tried to lounge at his ease on the lawn or in the garden. The river, the sand-hills, the meadows, the walks, all, all were poisoned to him: all spoke of Elsie. Was ever Nemesis more hideous or more complete? Was ever punishment more omnipresent? He had gained all he wished, and lost his own soul; at every turn of his own estate some horrible memento of his shame and his guilt rose up to confuse him. He wished he was dead every day he lived: dead, and asleep in his grave, beside Elsie.

As that dreaded anniversary, the seventeenth of September, slowly approached—the anniversary, as Hugh felt it, of Elsie's murder—his agitation and his gloom increased visibly. Winifred wondered silently to herself what on earth could ail him. During the last few weeks, he seemed to have become another man. An atmosphere of horror and doubt surrounded him. On the fifteenth, two days before the date of Elsie's disappearance, she went up hastily to their common room. The door was half-locked, but not securely fastened: it yielded to a sudden jerk of her wrist, and she entered abruptly—to find Hugh, with a guilty red face, pushing away a small bundle of letters and a trinket of some kind into a tiny cabinet which he always mysteriously carried about with him. She had hardly time to catch them distinctly, but the trinket looked like a watch or a locket. The letters, too, she managed to note, were tied together with an elastic band, and numbered in clear red ink on the envelopes. More than that she had no chance to see. But her feminine curiosity was strongly excited; the more so as Hugh banged down the lid on its spring-lock with guilty haste, and proceeded with hot and fiery fingers to turn the key upon the whole set in his own portmanteau.

"Hugh," she cried, standing still to gaze upon him, "what do you keep in that little cabinet?"

Hugh turned upon her as she had never before seen him turn. No longer clay in the hands of the potter, he stood stiff and hard like adamant then. "If I had meant you to know," he said coldly, "I would have told you long ago. I did not tell you, therefore I do not mean you to know. Ask me no questions. This incident is now closed. Say nothing more about it." And he turned on his heel, and left her astonished.

That was all. Winifred cried the night through, but Hugh remained still absolute adamant. Next morning, she altered her tactics completely, and drying her eyes once for all, said never another word on the subject. She even pretended to be cheerful and careless. When a woman pretends to be cheerful and careless after a domestic scene, the luckless man whose destiny she holds in the hollow of her hand may well tremble, especially if there is something he wants to conceal from her.

She means to egg it all out, and egged out it will all be, as
certainly as the sun will rise to-morrow. It may take a long
time, but it will come for all that. A woman on the track of a
secret, pretending carelessness, is a dangerous animal. She will
go far. *Hanc tu, Romane, caveto.*

On the sixteenth, Winifred formed a little plan of her own,
which she ventilated with childish effusion at lunch-time.
"Hugh, dear," she said in her most winning voice, "do you
happen to remember—if you've time for such trifles—that to-
morrow's a very special anniversary?"

Hugh's cheek blanched as if by magic. What devilry was
this? What deliberate cruelty? For the moment his usual
courage and presence of mind forsook him. Had Winifred,
then, found out everything?—A special anniversary, indeed!
As if he could forget it!—And that she, for whose sake—with
the manor of Whitestrand thrown in—he had done it all and
made himself next door to a murderer—that she, of all people
in the world, should cast it in his teeth, and make bitter game
of him about Elsie's death! "Well, Winifred," he answered in
a strange low voice, looking hard at her eyes: "I suppose I'm
not likely to forget it, am I?"

Winifred noted the tone, silently. Aloud, she gave no token
in any way of having observed his singular manner.—"It's a
year to-morrow since Hugh proposed to me, you know, mamma
ear," she went on, in her quietest and most cutting voice,
urning round to her mother, "and he does me the honour to
.ay politely he isn't likely to forget the occasion.—For a whole
year, he's actually remembered it. But it seems to make him
terribly grumpy.—Never mind, Hugh; I'll let you off. I'm a
sweet little angel, and I'm not going to be angry with my great
bear: so there, Mr. Constellation, you see I've forgiven you.—
Now, what I was going to say's just this. As to-morrow's a
special anniversary in our lives, I propose we should celebrate it
with becoming dignity."

"Which means, I suppose, the ordinary British symbol of
merry-making, a plum-pudding for dinner," Hugh interposed
bitterly. He saw his mistake with perfect clearness now, but
he hadn't the tact or the grace to conceal it, with a woman's
cleverness, under a show of good-humour.

"A plum-pudding is *banal*," Winifred answered with a smile
—"distinctly *banal*. I'm surprised a member of the Cheyne
Row set should even dream of suggesting it. What would Mr.
Hatherley say if he heard the Immortal One make such a proposition? He'd detect in it the strong savour of Philistia; he'd
declare you'd joined the hosts of Goliath.—No. It isn't a plum-
pudding. My idea's this. Why shouldn't we go for a family
picnic, just our three selves, in honour of the occasion?"

"A picnic!" Hugh cried, aghast—" a picnic to-morrow!—
On the seventeenth !"—Then recollecting himself once more, he
added hastily : "In this unsettled weather! The sandhills are
soaked. There isn't a place on the whole estate one could arrange
to seat one's self down on comfortably."

"I hadn't thought of the sandhills," Winifred answered with
quiet dignity. "I thought it'd be awfully nice if we all bespoke
a dry seat in Mr. Relf's yawl——"

"Relf's yawl!" Hugh cried aloud, with increasing excitement.
"You don't mean to say that creature's here again!"

"That creature, I'm in a position to state without reserve,"
Winifred answered chillily, "ran up the river to the Fisherman's
Rest late last night, as lively as ever. I saw the *Mud-Turtle*
come in myself, before a chipping breeze! And Mrs. Stannaway
told me this morning Mr. Relf was a-lying off the hard, just
opposite Stannaway's. So I thought it'd be a capital plan, in
memory of old times, if we got Mr. Relf to take us down in the
yawl to Orfordness, land us comfortably at the Low Light, and
let us picnic on the nice dry ridge of big shingle just above the
graveyard where they bury the wretched sailors."

Hugh's whole soul was on fire within him ; but his face was
pale, and his hands deadly cold. Was this pure accident, mere
coincidence, or was it designed and deliberate torture on
Winifred's part, he wondered? To picnic in sight of Elsie's
nameless grave, on the very anniversary of Elsie's death, with
every concomitant of pretended rejoicing that could make that
ghastly act more ghastly still than it would otherwise be in its
own mere naked brutality! It was too sickening to think upon.
But did Winifred know? Could Winifred mean it as a punishment for his silence? Or had she merely blundered upon that
horrible proposition as a sheer coincidence out of pure
accident?

As a matter of fact, the last solution was the true and simple
one. The sandhills, or Orfordness, were the two recognized
alternative picnicking places where all Whitestrand invariably
disported itself. If you didn't go to the one, you went as a
matter of course to the other. There was no third way open to
the most deliberate and statesmanlike of mortals. The Meyseys
had gone to Orfordness for years. Why not go there on the
anniversary of Winnie's engagement? To Winifred, the proposal
seemed simplicity itself; to Hugh, it seemed like a strangely
perverse and cunning piece of sheer feminine cruelty.

"There's nothing to see at Orfordness," he said shortly—
"nothing but a great bare bank of sand and shingle, and a
couple of lighthouses, standing alone in a perfect desert of
desolation.—Besides, the weather's just beastly.—Much better
·stop at home as usual by ourselves, and eat our dinner here

in peace and quietness! This isn't the sort of season for picnicking."

"Oh! but Hugh," Mrs. Meysey put in, with her maternal authority, "you know we always go to Orfordness. It's really quite a charming place in its way. The sands are so broad and hard and romantic. We sail down, and picnic at the lighthouse; and then we get a man to row us across the river at the back to Orford Castle—there's a splendid view from Orford Castle—and altogether it makes a delightful excursion, of its kind, for Suffolk. We ought to do something to commemorate the day.— If we weren't in such deep mourning still "—and Mrs. Meysey glanced down with a conventional sigh at her crape excrescences —" we'd ask a few friends in to dinner; but I'm afraid it's a little too soon for that. Still, at any rate, there could be no harm —not the slightest harm—in our just running down to Orford-ness for a family picnic. It's precisely the same as lunching at home here together."

"Do you remember, Hugh," Winifred went on, musingly, putting the screw on, "how we walked out that morning, a year ago, by the water-side; and how you picked a bit of forget-me-not and meadow-sweet from the bank and gave it me; and what pretty verses about undying love you repeated as you gave it? —And in the evening, mamma, I had to go out to dinner, all ʌlone with you and poor dear papa, to Snade vicarage! I ecollect how angry and annoyed I was because I had to go out ınd leave Hugh that particular evening! and because I'd worn that same dinner dress at Snade vicarage three parties running!"

"Yes," Mrs. Meysey continued, with another deep-drawn sigh; "and what a night that was, to be sure! So full of surprises! It was the night, you know, when poor Elsie Challoner ran away from us. *You* got engaged to Hugh in the morning, and in the evening Elsie disappeared as if by magic! Such a coincidence! Poor dear Elsie! Not a year ago! A year, to-morrow!"

"No, mother dear. That was the eighteenth. I was engaged on the Wednesday, you recollect, and it was the Thursday when we found out Elsie had gone away from us."

"Thursday, the eighteenth, when we found it out, dear," Mrs. Meysey repeated in a decisive voice (the maternal mind is strong on dates); "but Wednesday, the seventeenth, late in the evening, of course, when she went away from us.—Poor dear Elsie! I wonder what's become of her! It's curious she doesn't write to you oftener, Winifred."

Were they working upon his feelings, of *malice prepense?* Were they trying to make him blurt out the truth? he wondered. Hugh Massinger in his agony could stand it no longer. He rose from the table and went over to the window. There, the poplar stared him straight in the face. He turned around and looked hard at Winifred. Her expressionless blue eyes were placid as usual. "Then, if it's fine," she said, in an insipid voice, "we'll ask Mr. Relf to give us a lift down to Orfordness to-morrow in the *Mud-Turtle.*"

"No!" Hugh thundered in an angry tone. "However you go, Relf shan't take you. I don't want to see any more of Relf. I dislike Relf; I object to Relf. He's a mean cur! I won't go anywhere with Relf in future."

"But, children, you should never let your angry passions rise," Winifred murmured provokingly. "'Your little hands were never meant to tear each other's eyes.' If he doesn't want to go in Mr. Relf's boat, he shan't be made to, then, poor little fellow. He shall do exactly as he likes himself. He shall have another boat all of his own. I'll order one this evening for him at Martin's or at Stannaway's."

"If it's fine," Mrs. Meysey interposed parenthetically.

"If it's fine, of course," Winifred answered, rising. "We don't want to picnic in a torrent of rain.—Whatever else we may be, we're rational animals.—But how do you know, Hugh, what Orfordness is like? You can't tell. You've never been there."

"I went there once alone last year," Hugh answered sulkily; "and I saw enough of the beastly hole then to know very well I don't desire its further acquaintance."

"But you never told me you'd been over there."

Hugh managed to summon up a sardonic smile. "I wasn't married to you then, Winnie," he answered, with a savage snarl, that showed his projecting canines with most unpleasant distinctness. "My goings-out and my comings-in were not yet a matter of daily domestic inquisition. I hadn't to report myself every time I came or went, like a soldier in barracks to his commanding officer.—I went to Orfordness one day for a walk—by myself—unbidden—for my own amusement."

All that afternoon and late into the evening, Hugh watched the clouds and the barometer eagerly. His fate that day hung upon a spider's web. If it rained to-morrow, all might yet be well; if not, he felt in his own soul they stood within measurable distance of a domestic cataclysm. He would not go to Orfordness with Winifred. He could not go to Orfordness with Winifred. That much was certain. He could not picnic, on the anniversary of Elsie's death, within sight of Elsie's nameless grave, in company with those two strange women—his wife and his mother-in-law. Ugh! how he hated the bare idea! If it came to the worst—if it was fine to-morrow—he must either

break for ever with Winifred—for she would never give in—or
else he must fling himself off the roots of the poplar, where
Elsie had flung herself off that day twelve months ago, and
drown as she had drowned among the angry breakers.

There would be a certain dramatic completeness and round-
ness about that particular fate which commended itself especially
to Hugh Massinger's poetical nature. It would read so like a
Greek tragedy—a tale of Atè and Hubris and Nemesis. Even
from the point of view of the outer world, who knew but the
husk, it would seem romantic enough to 'drown one's self,' disconsolate, on the very anniversary of one's first engagement to
the young wife one meant to leave an untimely widow. But to
Hugh Massinger himself, who knew the whole kernel and core
of the story, it would be infinitely more romantic and charming
in its way to drown one's self off the self-same poplar on the
self-same day that Elsie had drowned herself. No bard could wish
for a gloomier or more appropriate death. Would it rain or
shine? On that slender thread of doubt his whole future now
hung and trembled.

The morning of the seventeenth dawned at last, and Hugh
rose early, to draw aside the bedroom blinds for a moment. A
respite! a respite! It was pouring a regular English downpour.
There was no hope—or no danger, rather—of a picnic to-day.
Thank Heaven for that. It put off his fate. It saved him the
inconvenience and worry of having to drown himself this
particular morning. And yet the *dénouement* would have been
so strictly dramatic that he almost regretted a shower of rain
should intervene to spoil it.

At ten o'clock he started out alone in the blinding downpour
and took the train as far as Aldeburgh. Thence he followed
the shingle beach to Orfordness, plodding' on, as he had done a
year before, over the loose stones, but through drenching rain,
instead of under hot and blazing sunlight. When he reached
the lighthouse, he sat himself down in pilgrim guise beside
Elsie's grave in the steady drip, and did penance once more by
that unknown tomb in solemn silence. Not even the lighthouse-
man came out this time to gaze at him in wonder; it poured
too hard and too persistently for that. He sat there alone for
half an hour, by Elsie's watch; for he had wound it that
morning with reverent hands, and brought it away with him for
that very purpose. A little rusty, perhaps, from the sea, it
would keep good time enough still for all he needed. At the
end of the half-hour he rose once more, plodded back again over
the shingle in his dripping clothes, and catching the last train
home to Almundham, reached Whitestrand just in time to dress
for dinner.

Winifred was waiting for him at the front door, white with

emotion—not so much anger as slighted affection. "Where have you been?" she asked, in a cold voice, as he arrived at the porch, a dripping, draggled, wearied pedestrian, in a soaking suit of last year's tweeds.

"Didn't I say well I was bound to report myself to my commanding officer?" Hugh answered tauntingly. "All right, then; I proceed at once to report myself. I may as well tell you as leave you to worry. I've been to Orfordness—alone—tramped it."

"To Orfordness!" his wife echoed in profound astonishment. "You didn't want to go with us there if it was fine. Why, what on earth, Hugh, did you ever go there in this pelting rain for?"

"Your mother recommended it," Hugh answered sullenly, "as a place of amusement. She said it was altogether a most delightful excursion. She praised the sands as firm and romantic. So I thought I'd try it on her recommendation. I found it damp, decidedly damp.—Send me my shoes, please!" And that was all the explanation he ever vouchsafed her.

CHAPTER XXVI.

REPORTING PROGRESS.

WARREN RELF spent many days that summer at Whitestrand, cruising vaguely about the mouth of the Char, or wandering and sketching among the salt-marsh meadows; but he never happened to come face to face, by accident or design, with Hugh Massinger. Fate seemed persistently to interpose between them. Once or twice, indeed, Winifred said with some slight asperity to her husband, "Don't you think, Hugh, if it were only for old acquaintance' sake, we ought to ask that creature Relf some day to dinner?"

But Hugh, who was yielding enough in certain matters, was as marble here: he could never consent to receive his enemy, of his own accord, beneath his own roof—for Whitestrand, after all, was his own in reality. "No," he growled out, looking up from his paper testily. "I don't like the fellow. I've heard things about him that make me sorry I ever accepted his hospitality. If you happen to meet him, Winifred, prowling about the place and trying to intercept you, I forbid you to speak to him."

"You forbid me, Hugh?"

"Yes,"—coldly—"I forbid you."

Winifred bit her lip, and was discreetly silent. No need to

answer. Those two proud wills were beginning already to clash more ominously one against the other. " Very well," the young wife thought in silence to herself; " if he means to mew me up, seraglio and zenana fashion, in my own rooms, he should hire a guard and some Circassian slaves, and present me with a *yashmak* to cover my face with."

A day or two later, as she strolled on some errand into the placid village, she came suddenly upon Warren Relf, in his rough jersey and sailor cap, hanging about the lane, sketch-book in hand, not without some vague expectation, as Hugh had said, of accidentally intercepting her. It was a painful duty, but Elsie had laid it upon him; and Elsie's will was law now. Naturally, he had never told Elsie about the meeting with Hugh at the Cheyne Row Club. If he had, she would never have imposed so difficult, delicate, and dangerous a task upon him. But she knew nothing; and so she had sent him on this painful errand.

Winifred smiled a frank smile of recognition as she came up close to him. The painter pulled off his awkward cap awkwardly and unskilfully.

" You were going to pass me by, Mr. Relf," she said, with a good-humoured nod. " You won't recognize me or have anything to do with me, perhaps, now I'm married and done for! "

The words gave him an uncomfortable thrill; they seemed so minous, so much truer than she thought them.

" I hardly *did* know you," he answered with a forced smile. I've not been accustomed to see you in black before, Mrs. Massinger.—And to say the truth, when I come to look at you, you're paler and thinner than when I last met you."

Winifred coughed—a little dry cough. Women always take sympathetic remarks about their ill health in a disparaging sense to their personal appearance. " A London season! " she answered, smiling; yet even her smile had a certain unwonted air of sadness about it. " Too many of Mrs. Bouverie Barton's literary evenings have unhinged me, I suppose. My small brains have been over-stimulated.—You've not been up to the Hall yet to see us, Mr. Relf. I saw the *Mud-Turtle* come ploughing bravely in some three or four days ago, and I wondered you'd never looked up old friends.—For of course you know I owe you something: it was you who first brought dear Hugh to Whitestrand."

How Warren ever got through the remainder of that slippery interview, gliding with difficulty over the thin ice, he hardly knew. He walked with Winifred to the end of the lane, talking in vague generalities of politeness; and then, with some lame excuse of the state of the tide, he took a brusque and hasty leave of her. He felt himself guilty for talking to her at all, considering the terms on which he stood with her husband. But

Elsie's will overrode everything. When he wrote to Elsie, that
letter he had looked forward to so long and eagerly, it was with
a heavy heart and an accusing conscience; for he felt somehow,
from the forced gaiety of Winifred's ostentatiously careless manner, that things were not going quite so smoothly as a wedding-
bell at the Hall already. That poor young wife was ill at ease.
However, for Elsie's sake, he would make the best of it. Why
worry and trouble poor heart-broken Elsie more than absolutely
needful with Winifred's possible or actual misfortunes ?

"I didn't meet your cousin himself," he wrote with a very
doubtful hand—it was hard to have even to refer to the subject
at all to Elsie; " but I came across Mrs. Massinger one afternoon, strolling in the lane, with her pet pug, and looking very
pretty in her light half-mourning, though a trifle paler and
thinner than I had yet known her. She attributes her paleness,
however, to too much gaiety during the London season and to
the late hours of our Bohemian society. I hope a few weeks at
Whitestrand will set her fully up again, and that when I have
next an opportunity of meeting her, I may be able to send you
a good report of her health and happiness."

How meagre, how vapid, how jejune, how conventional! Old
Mrs. Walpole of the vicarage herself could not have worded it
more baldly or more flabbily. And this was the letter he had
been burning to write: this the opportunity he had been so
eagerly awaiting! What a note to send to his divine Elsie! He
tore it up and wrote it again half a dozen times over, before he
was finally satisfied to accept his dissatisfaction as an immutable,
inevitable, and unconquerable fact. And then, he compensated
himself by writing out in full, for his own mere subjective grati-
fication, the sort of letter he would have liked to write her, if
circumstances permitted it—a burning letter of fervid love,
beginning, " My own darling, darling Elsie," and ending, with
hearts and darts and tears and protestations, " Yours ever devotedly and lovingly, WARREN." Which done, he burned the
second genuine letter in a solemn holocaust with a lighted fusee,
and sent off that stilted formal note to " Dear Miss Challoner,"
with many regrets and despondent aspirations. And as soon as
he had dropped it into the village letter-box, all aglow with
shame, the *Mud-Turtle* was soon under way, with full canvas
set, before a breathless air, on her voyage once more to Lowestoft.

But Winifred never mentioned to Hugh that she had met and
spoken to "that creature Relf," with whom he had so sternly
and authoritatively forbidden her to hold any sort of communication. That was bad—a beginning of evil. The first great
breach was surely opening out by slow degrees between them.

A week later, as the yawl lay idle on her native mud in Yar-

mouth harbour, Warren Relf, calling at the post-office for his
expected budget, received a letter with a French stamp on it,
and a postmark bearing the magical words, "St. Martin Lantosque, Alpes Maritimes," which made his quick breath come
and go spasmodically. He tore it open with a beating heart.

"DEAR MR. RELF" (it said simply),
"How very kind of you to take the trouble of going to
Whitestrand and sending me so full and careful an account of
dear Winifred. Thank you ever so much for all your goodness.
But you are always kind. I have learnt to expect it.
"Yours very sincerely,
"ELSIE CHALLONER."

That was all : those few short words; but Warren Relf lived
on that brief note night and morning, till the time came when
he might return once more in his small craft to the South and
to Elsie.

When he did return, with the southward tide of invalids and
swallows, Elsie had left the first poignancy of her grief a year
behind her; but Warren saw quite clearly still, with a sinking
heart, that she was true as ever to the Hugh that was not and
that never had been. She received him kindly, like a friend and
a brother; but her manner was none the less the cold fixed
manner of a woman who has lived her life out to the bitter end,
nd whose heart has been broken once and for ever. When
Varren saw her, his soul despaired. He felt it was cruel even
to hope. But Edie, most cheerful of optimists, laughed him to
scorn. "If *I* were a man," she cried boldly, and then broke off.
That favourite feminine aposiopesis is the most cutting known
form of criticism. Warren noted it, and half took heart, half
desponded again more utterly than ever.

Still, he had one little buttress left for his failing hopes : there
was no denying that Elsie's interest in his art, as art, increased
daily. She let him give her lessons in water-colours now, and
she watched his own patient and delicate work with constant
attention and constant admiration, among the rocks and bays of
the inexhaustible Riviera. During that second sunny winter at
San Remo, in fact, they grew for the first time to know one
another. Warren's devotion told slowly, for no woman is wholly
proof in some lost corner of her heart against a man's determined
and persistent love. She could not love him in return, to be
sure : oh no ; impossible : all that was over long ago, for ever :
an ingrained sense of womanly consistency barred the way to
love for the rest of the ages. But she liked him immensely; she
saw his strong points ; she admired his earnestness, his goodness,
his singleness of purpose, his worship of his art, and his hopeless

and chivalrous attachment to herself into the bargain. Its very hopelessness touched her profoundly. He could never expect her to return his love; of that she was sure; but he loved her for all that; and she acknowledged it gratefully. In one word, she liked him as much as it is possible for a woman to like a man she is not and cannot ever be in love with.

"Is that right yet, Miss Challoner?" Warren asked one day, with a glance at his canvas, as he sat with Edie and Elsie on the deck of the *Mud-Turtle*, painting in a mass of hanging ruddy-brown seaweed, whose redness of tone Elsie thought he had somewhat needlessly exaggerated.

"Why 'Miss Challoner'?" Edie asked with one of her sudden arch looks at her brother. "We're all in the family, now, you know, Warren. Why not 'Elsie'? She's Elsie of course to all the rest of us."

Warren glanced into the depths of Elsie's dark eyes with an inquiring look. "May it be, Elsie?" he asked, all tremors.

She looked back at him, frankly and openly. "Yes, Warren, if you like," she said in a simple straightforward tone that disarmed criticism. The answer, in fact, half displeased him. She granted it too easily, with too little reserve. He would have preferred it even if she had said "No," with a trifle more coyness, more maidenly timidity. The half is often better than the whole. She assented like one to whom assent is a matter of slight importance. He had leave to call her Elsie in too brotherly a fashion. It was clear the permission meant nothing to her. And to him it might have meant so much, so much! He bit his lip, and answered shyly, "Thank you."

Edie noted his downcast look and his suppressed sigh. "You goose!" she said afterwards. "Pray, what did you expect? Do you think the girl's bound to jump down your throat like a ripe gooseberry? If she's worth winning, she's worth waiting for. A woman who can love as Elsie has loved can't be expected to dance a polka at ten minutes' notice on the mortal remains of her dead self. But then, a woman who can love as Elsie has loved must love in the end a man worth loving.—I don't say I've a very high opinion of you in other ways, Warren. As a man of business, you're simply nowhere; you wouldn't have sold those three pictures in London, you know, last autumn if it hadn't been for your amiable sister's persistent touting; but as a marrying man, I consider your'e A1, eighteen carat, a perfect hundred-guinea prize in the matrimonial market."

Before the end of the winter, Elsie and Warren found they had settled down into a quiet brotherly and sisterly relation, which to Elsie's mind left nothing further to be desired; while to Warren it seemed about as bad an arrangement as the nature of things could easily have permitted.

"It's a pity he can't sell his pictures better," Elsie said one day confidentially to Edie. "He does so deserve it; they're really lovely. Every day I watch him, I find new points in them. I begin to see now how really great they are."

"It *is* a pity," Edie answered mischievously. "He must devote his energies to the harmless necessary pot-boiler. For until he finds his market, my dear, he'll never be well enough off to marry."

"Oh, Edie, I couldn't bear to think he should sink to pot-boiling. And yet I should like to see him married some day to some nice good girl who'd make him happy," Elsie assented innocently.

"So should I, my child," Edie rejoined with a knowing smile. "And what's more, I mean to arrange it too. I mean to put him in a proper position for asking the nice good girl's consent. Next summer and autumn, I shall conspire with Mr. Hatherley to boom him."

"To what?" Elsie asked, puzzled.

"To boom him, my dear. *B, double o, m*—boom him. A most noble verb, imported, I believe, with the pickled pork and the tinned peaches, direct from Chicago. To boom means, according to my private dictionary, to force into sudden and almost explosive notoriety.—That's what I'm going to do with Warren. I intend, by straightforward and unblushing adver-'ising—in short by log-rolling—to make him go down next eason with the money-getting classes as a real live painter. Their gold shall pour itself into Warren's pocket. If he wasn't a genius, I should think it wrong; but as I know he is one, why shouldn't I boom him?"

"Why not, indeed?" Elsie answered all unconscious. "And then he might marry that nice good girl of yours, if he can get her to take him."

"The nice good girl will have to take him," Edie replied with a nod. "When I puts my foot down, I puts it down. And I've put it down that Warren shall succeed, financially, artistically, and matrimonially. So there's nothing more to be said about it."

And indeed when Warren returned to England in the spring, to be boomed, it was with distinct permission this time from Elsie to write to her as often and as much as he wanted—in a strictly fraternal and domestic manner

CHAPTER XXVII.

ART AT HOME.

THAT same winter made a sudden change in Hugh Massinger's financial position. He found himself the actual and undoubted possessor of the Manor of Whitestrand. Winter always tried Mrs. Meysey. Like the bulk of us nowadays, her weak points were lungy. Of late, she had suffered each season more and more from bronchitis, and Hugh had done his disinterested best to persuade her to go abroad to some warmer climate. His solicitude for her health, indeed, was truly filial, and not without reason. If she chose Madeira or Algiers or Egypt, for example, she would at least be well out of her new son's way for six months of the year; and Hugh was beginning to realize, as time went on, a little too acutely that he had married the estate and manor of Whitestrand with all its encumbrances, a mother-in-law included; while if, on the other hand, she preferred Nice or Cannes or Pau, or even Florence, or any nearer continental resort, they would at any rate have an agreeable place to visit her in, if they were suddenly summoned away to her side by the telegraphic calls of domestic piety. But Mrs. Meysey, true metal to the core, wouldn't hear of wintering away from Suffolk. She clung to Whitestrand with East Anglian persistence. Where was one better off, indeed, than in one's own house, with one's own people to tend and comfort one? If the March winds blew hard at the Hall, were there not deadly mistrals at Mentone and gusts of foggy Föhn at dreary Davos Platz? If you gained in the daily tale of registered sunshine at Hyères or at Bordighera, did not a superabundance of olive oil diversify the stew at the *table-d'hôte*, and a fatal suspicion of Italian garlic poison the *fricandeau* of the second breakfast? Mrs. Meysey, in her British mood, would stand by Suffolk bravely while she lived; and if the hard gray weather killed her at last, as it killed its one literary apologist in our modern England, she would acquiesce in the decrees of Fate, and be buried, like a Briton, by her husband's side in Whitestrand churchyard. Elizabethan Meyseys of the elder stock—in frilled ruffs and stiff starched head-dresses—smiled down upon her resolution from their niched tomb in Whitestrand church every Sunday morning: never should it be said that this, their degenerate latter-day representative, ran away from the east winds of dear old England to bask in the sunlight at Malaga or Seville, among the descendants of the godless Armada sailors, from whose wreckage and pillage those stout old squires had built up the timbers of that very Hall which she herself still worthily inhabited.

So Mrs. Meysey stopped sturdily at home; and the east wind wreaked its vengeance upon her in its wonted fashion. Early in March, Winifred was summoned by telegram from town: "Come at once. Much worse. May not live long. Bring Hugh with you." And three weeks later, another fresh grave rose eloquent in Whitestrand churchyard; and the carved and painted Elizabethan Meyseys, smiling placidly as ever on the empty seat in the pew below, looked forward with confidence to the proximate addition of another white marble tablet with a black epitaph to the family collection in the Whitestrand chancel.

The moment was a specially trying one for Winifred. A month later, a little heir to the Whitestrand estates was expected to present himself on the theatre of existence. When he actually arrived upon the stage of life, however, poor frail little waif, it was only just to be carried across it once, a speechless super-numerary, in a nurse's arms, and to breathe his small soul out in a single gasp before he had even learnt how to cry aloud like an English baby. This final misfortune, coming close on the heels of all the rest, broke down poor Winifred's health terribly. A new chapter of life opened out before her. She ceased to be the sprightly, lively girl she had once been. She felt herself left alone in the big wide world, with a husband who, as she was now beginning to suspect, had married her for the sake of her money only, while his heart was still fixed upon no one but Elsie. Poor lonely child: it was a dismal outlook for her. Her soul was sad. She couldn't bear to brazen things out any longer in London—to smile and smile and be inwardly miserable. She must come back now, she said plaintively, to her own people in dear old Suffolk.

To Hugh, this proposition was simply unendurable. He shrank from Whitestrand with a deadly shrinking. Every-thing about the estate he had made his own was utterly dis-tasteful to him and fraught with horror. The house, the grounds, the garden, the river, above all that tragic, accusing poplar, were so many perpetual reminders of his crime and his punishment. Yet he saw it would be useless to oppose Wini-fred's wish in such a matter—the whole idea was so simple, so natural. A squire ought to live on his own land, of course; he ought to occupy the ancestral Hall where his predecessors have dwelt before him for generations. Had not he himself fulmi-nated in his time in the gorgeous periods of the *Morning Tele-phone* against the crying sin and shame of absenteeism? But if he went there, he could only go on three conditions. The Hall itself must be remodelled, redecorated, and refurnished throughout, till its own inhabitants would hardly recognize it:

the grounds must be replanted in accordance with his own cultivated and refined taste : and last of all—though this he did not venture to mention to Winifred—by fair means or by foul, the Whitestrand poplar—that hateful tree—must be levelled to the soil, and its very place must know it no longer. For the first two conditions he stipulated outright : the third he locked up for the present quietly in the secret recesses of his own bosom.

Winifred, for her part, was not wholly averse, either, to the remodelling of Whitestrand. The house, she admitted, was old-fashioned and dowdy. Its antiquity went back only to the "bad period." After the æsthetic drawing-rooms of the Cheyne Row set, she confessed to herself, grudgingly—though not to Hugh—that the blue satin and whitey-gold paint of the dear old place seemed perhaps just a trifle dingy and antiquated. There were tiny cottages at Hampstead and Kensington that White-strand Hall could never reasonably expect to emulate. She didn't object to the alterations, she said, so long as the original Elizabethan front was left scrupulously intact, and no incongruous meddling was allowed with the oaken wainscot and carved ceiling of the Jacobean vestibule. But where, she asked, with sound Suffolk common-sense, was the money for all these improvements to come from ? A season of falling rents, and encroaching sea, and shifting sands, and agricultural depression, with Hessian fly threatening the crops, and obscure bacteria fighting among themselves for possession of the cattle, was surely not the best chosen time in the world for a country gentleman to enlarge and complete and beautify his house in.

"Pooh ! " Hugh answered, in one of his heroically sanguine moods, as he sat in the dining-room with his back to the window and the hated poplar, and his face to the ground-plans and estimates upon the table before him. "I mean to go up to town for the season always, and to keep up my journalistic connection in a general way ; and in time, no doubt, I shall begin to get work at the bar also. I shall make friends assiduously with what a playful phrase absurdly describes as 'the lower branch of the profession.' I shall talk my nicest to every dull solicitor I meet anywhere, and do my politest to the dull solicitor's stupid wife and plain daughters. I'll fetch them ices at other people's At Homes, and shower on them tickets for all the private views we don't care about, and all the first nights at uninteresting theatres. That's the way to advance in the profession. Sooner or later, I'll get on at the bar. Meanwhile, as the estate's fortunately unencumbered, and there's none of that precious nonsense about entail, or remainders, or settlements, or so forth, we can raise the immediate cash for our present need on short mortgages."

“I hate the very name of mortgages,” Winifred cried impatiently. “They suggest brokers’ men and bailiffs, and bankruptcy and beggary.”

“And everything else that begins with a B,” Hugh continued, smiling a placid smile to himself, and vaguely reminiscent of “Alice in Wonderland.” “Why with a B!” Alice said musingly. —“Why not?” said the March Hare.—Alice was silent.—“Now, for my own part, I confess, on the contrary, Winifred, to a certain sentimental liking for the mortgage as such, viewed in the abstract. It’s a document intimately connected with the landed interest and the feudal classes; it savours to my mind of broad estates and haughty aristocrats, and lordly rent-rolls and a baronial ancestry. I will admit that I should feel a peculiar pride in my connection with Whitestrand if I felt I had got it really with a mortgage on it. How proud a moment, to be seised of a mortgage! The poor, the abject, the lowly, and the landless don’ go in heavily for the luxury of mortgages. They pawn their watches, or raise a precarious shilling or two upon the temporary security of Sunday suits, kitchen clocks, and second-hand flat-irons. But a mortgage is an eminently gentlemanly form of impecuniosity. Like gout and the lord-lieutenancy of your shire, it’s incidental to birth and greatness.—Upon my word, I’m not really certain, Winnie, now I come to think upon it, that a gentleman’s house is ever quite complete without a History of England, a billiard table, and a mortgage. Unencumbered estates suggest Brummagem: they bespeak the vulgar affluence of the *nouveau riche*, who keeps untold gold lying idle at his bankers on purpose to spite the political economists. But a loan of a few thousands, invested with all the glamour of deposited title-deeds, foreclosing, engrossed parchment, and an extremely beautiful and elaborate specimen of that charming dialect, conveyancers’ English, carries with it an air of antique respectability and county importance that I should be loth to forego, even if I happened to have the cash in hand otherwise available, for carrying out the necessary improvements.”

“But how shall we ever pay it back?” Winifred asked, with native feminine caution.

Hugh waved his hands expansively open. When he went in for the sanguine, he did it thoroughly. “One thing at a time, my child,” he murmured low. “First borrow; then set your wits to work to look around for a means of repayment.—In the desk at home in London this very moment lies an immortal epic, worth ten thousand pounds if it’s worth a penny, and cheap at the price to a discerning purchaser. Ormuz and Ind are perfect East Ends to it. It teems with Golcondas and Big Bonanzas. In time the slow world must surely discover that this England of ours still encloses a great live poet. The blind and battling must open their eyes and look at last placidly about them. They'll then be glad to buy fifty editions of that divine strain, varying in character from the large paper *édition de luxe* in antique vellum at ten guineas—five hundred numbered copies only printed, and issued to subscribers upon conditions which may be learnt on application at all libraries—to the school selection at popular prices, intended to familiarize the ingenuous youth of this nation with the choicest thoughts of a distinguished and high-minded living author.—Winnie, I'm tired to death of hearing people say when I'm introduced to them: 'Oh, Mr. Massinger, I've often wanted to ask, are you descended from the poet Massinger?' I mean the time to arrive before long when I can answer them plainly with a bold face: 'No, my dear sir, or madam, I am not; but I *am* the poet Massinger, if you care to be told so.'—When that time comes, we'll pay off the mortgages and build a castle—in Spain or elsewhere—with the balance of our fortune. Meanwhile, we have always the satisfaction of knowing that nothing on earth could be more squirearchical in its way than a genuine mortgage."

"I'm not so sure as I once was, Hugh, that you'll ever make much out of your kind of poetry."

"Of course not, my child; because now I happen to be only your husband. A prophet, we know on the best authority, is not without honour, et cætera, et cætera. But I mean to make my mark yet for all that; ay, and to make money out of it, too, into the bargain."

So, in the end, Winifred's objections were over-ruled—since this was not a matter upon which that young lady felt strongly —and the money for "improving and developing the estate" having been duly raised by the aid, assistance, instrumentality, or mediation of that fine specimen of conveyancers' English aforesaid, to which Hugh had so touchingly and professionally alluded, a fashionable architect was invited down from town at once to inspect the Hall and to draw up plans for its renovation as a residential mansion of the most modern pattern.

The fashionable architect, after his kind, performed his work well—and expensively. He spared himself no pains (and Hugh no money) on rendering the Hall a perfect example on a small scale of the best Elizabethan domestic architecture. He destroyed ruthlessly and repaired lavishly. He put mullions to the windows, and pillars to the porch, and moulded ceilings to the chief reception-rooms, and oaken balustrades to either side of the wide old rambling Tudor staircase. He rebuilt whatever Inigo had defaced, and pulled down whatever of vile and shapeless Georgian contractors had stolidly added. He "restored" the building to what it had never before been: a fine squat old-fashioned country mansion of the low wind-swept East Anglian

type, a House Beautiful everywhere, without and within, and as
unlike as possible to the dingy Hall that Hugh Massinger had
seen and mentally discountenanced on the occasion of his first
visit to Whitestrand. "You give an architect money enough,"
says Colonel Silas Lapham in the greatest romance—bar one—
in the English language, "and he'll build you a fine house
every time." Hugh Massinger gave his architect money enough,
or at least credit enough—which comes at first to the same
thing—and he got a fine house, as far as the means at his disposal went, on that ugly corner of flat sandy waste at forsaken
Whitestrand.

When the building was done and the papering finished, they
set about the furnishing proper. And here, Winifred's taste
began to clash with Hugh's; for every woman, though she may
eschew ground-plans, elevations, and estimates, has at least
distinct ideas of her own on the important question of internal
decoration. The new Squire was all for oriental hangings,
Turkey carpets, Indian durrees, and Persian tiling. But Mrs.
Massinger would have none of these heathenish gewgaws, she
solemnly declared; her tastes by no means took a Saracenic
turn. Mr. Hatherley and the Cheyne Row men would make
fun of her, and call her house Liberty Hall, if she furnished it
throughout with such Mussulman absurdities. For her own
part, she renounced Liberty and all his works: she eschewed
everything east of longitude thirty degrees: inlaid coffee-tables
were an abomination in her eyes; pierced Arabic lamps roused
no latent enthusiasm: the only real thing in decoration was
Morris; and on Morris she pinned her faith unreservedly. She
would be utterly utter. She had a Morris carpet and Morris
curtains; white ivory paint adorned her lop-sided overmantels,
and red De Morgan ware with opalescent hues ranged in long
straight rows upon her pigeon-hole cabinets. To Hugh's
poetical mind this was all too plaguy modern; out of keeping,
he thought, with the wide oaken staircase and the punctilious
Elizabethanism of the eminent architect's façade and ceilings.
Winifred, however, laughed his marital remonstrances to utter
scorn. She hated an upholsterer's house, she said, all furnished
alike from end to end with servile adherence to historical
correctness. Such Puritanical purism was meant for slaves.
Why pretend to be living in Elizabethan England or Louis
Quinze France, when we're really vegetating, as we all know,
in the marshy wilds of nineteenth-century Suffolk? Let your
house reflect your own eclecticism—a very good phrase, picked
up from a modern handbook of domestic decoration. She
liked a little individuality and lawlessness of purpose. "Your
views, you know, Hugh," she cried with the *ex cathedrâ*
conviction of a woman laying down the law in her own house-

hold, "are just the least little bit in the world pedantic. You
and your architect want a stiff museum of Elizabethan art. It
may be silly of me, but I prefer myself a house to live in."

"'The drawing-room does look so perfectly lovely,' you remember," Hugh quoted quietly from her own old letters. "'We've
done it up exactly as you recommended, with the sage-green
plush for the old mantel-piece, and a red Japanese table in the
dark corner; and I really think, now I see the effect, your
taste's simply exquisite. But then, you know, what else can you
expect from a distinguished poet! You always do everything
beautifully!' Can you recollect, Mrs. Massinger, down the dim
abyss of twelve or eighteen months, who wrote those touching
words, and to whom she addressed them?"

"Ah, that was all very fine then," Winifred answered with a
pout, arranging Hugh's Satsuma jars with Japanesque irregularity on the dining-room overmantel. "But you see that was
before I'd been about much in London, and noticed how other
people smarten up their rooms, and formed my own taste in the
matter of decoration. I was then in the frankly unsophisticated
state. I'd studied no models. I'd never seen anything beautiful
to judge by."

"You were then Miss Meysey," her husband answered, with
a distantly cold inflexion of voice. "You're now Mrs. Hugh de
Carteret Massinger. It's that that makes all the difference, you
know. The reason there are so many discordant marriages, says
Dean Swift, with more truth than politeness, is because young
women are so much more occupied in weaving nets than in
making cages."

"I never wove nets for you," Winifred cried angrily.

"Nor made cages either, it seems," Hugh answered with pro-
voking calmness, as he sauntered off by himself, cigar in hand,
into the new smoking-room.

Their intercourse nowadays generally ended in such little
amenities. They were beginning to conjugate with alarming
frequency that verb to nag, which often succeeds in becoming
at last the dominant part of speech in conjugal conversation.

One portion of the house at least, Hugh succeeded in remodelling entirely to his own taste, and that was the bedroom which
had once been Elsie's. By throwing out a large round bay window,
mullioned and decorated out of all recognition, and by papering,
painting, and refurnishing throughout with ostentatious novelty
of design and detail, he so completely altered the appearance of
that hateful room that he could hardly know it again himself
for the same original square chamber. Moreover, that he might
never personally have to enter it, he turned it into the Married
Guest's Bedroom. There was the Prophet's Chamber on the
Wall for the bachelor visitors—a pretty little attic under the

low caves, furnished, like the Shunammite's, with "a bed, and a table, and a stool, and a candlestick;" and there was the Maiden's Bower on the first floor, for the young girls, with its dainty pale-green wardrobe and Morris cabinet; and there was the Blue Room for the prospective heir, whenever that hypothetical young gentleman from parts unknown proceeded to realize himself in actual humanity; so Hugh ventured to erect the remodelled chamber next door to his own into a Married Guest's Room, where he himself need never go to vex his soul with unholy reminiscences. When he could look up at the Hall with a bold face from the grass plot in front, and see no longer that detested square window, with the wistaria festooning itself so luxuriantly round the corners, he felt he might really perhaps after all live at Whitestrand. For the wistaria, too, that grand old climber, with its thick stem, was ruthlessly sacrificed; and in its place on the left of the porch, Hugh planted a fast-growing new-fangled ampelopsis, warranted quickly to drape and mantle the raw stone surfaces, and still further metamorphose the front of the Hall from what it had once been—when dead Elsie lived there. All was changed, without and within. The Hall was now fit for a gentleman to dwell in.

Only one eyesore still remained to grieve and annoy him. The Whitestrand poplar yet faced and confronted him wherever he looked. It turned him sick. It poisoned Suffolk for him. The poplar must go! He could never endure it. Life would indeed be a living death, in sight for ever of that detested and grinning memorial. For it grinned at him often from the gnarled and hollow trunk. A human face seemed to laugh out upon him from its shapeless boles—a human face, fiendish in its joy, with a carbuncled nose and grinning mouth. He hated to see it, it grinned so hideously. So he set his wits to work to devise a way for getting rid of the poplar, root and branch, without unnecessarily angering Winifred.

CHAPTER XXVIII.

REHEARSAL.

MEANWHILE, when the house was all finished and decorated throughout, Hugh turned his thoughts once more, on fame intent, to his great forthcoming volume of verses. Since he married Winifred, he had published little, eschewing journalism and such small tasks as unworthy the dignity of accomplished squiredom; but he had been working hard from time to time at polishing and repolishing his *magnum opus*, "A Life's Philosophy" —a lengthy poem in a metre of his own, more or less novel, and embodying a number of moral reflections, more or less trite, on the youth, adolescence, maturity, and decrepitude of the human subject. It exactly suited Mr. Matthew Arnold's well-known definition, being, in fact, an exhaustive criticism of life, as Hugh Massinger himself had found it. He meant to print it in time for the autumn book-season. It was the great stake of his life, and he was confident of success. He had worked it up with ceaseless toil to what seemed to himself the highest possible pitch of artistic handicraft; and he rolled his own sonorous rhymes over and over again with infinite satisfaction upon his literary palate, pronouncing them all, on impartial survey, of most excellent flavour. Nothing in life, indeed, can be more deceptive than the poetaster's confidence in his own productions. He mistakes familiarity for smoothness of ring, and a practised hand for genius and originality. It is his fate always to find his own lines absolutely perfect; in which cheerful personal creed the rest of the world mostly fails altogether to agree with him.

In such a self-congratulatory and hopeful mood, Hugh sat one morning in the new drawing-room, holding a quire of closely written sermon-paper stitched together in his hand, and gazing affectionately with parental pride at his last-born stanzas. Winifred had only returned yesterday from a shopping expedition up to town, and was idling away a day in rest and repair after her unwonted exertion among the crowded bazaars of the modern Bagdad. So Hugh leaned back in his chair at his ease, and, seized with the sudden thirst for an audience, began to pour forth in her ear in his rotund manner the final finished introductory prelude to his "Life's Philosophy." His wife, propped up on the pillows of the sofa and lolling carelessly, listened and smiled as he read and read, with somewhat sceptical though polite indifference.

"Let me see, where had I got to?" Hugh went on once, after one of her frequent and trying critical interruptions. "You put me out so, Winnie, with your constant fault-finding! I can't recollect how far I'd read to you."

"'Begotten unawares:' now go ahead," Winifred answered carelessly—as carelessly as though it was some other fellow's poems he had been pouring forth to her.

"'Or bastard offspring of unconscious nature, Begotten unawares,'" Hugh repeated pompously, looking back with a loving eye at his much-admired manuscript. "Now listen to the next good bit, Winifred; it's really impressive.—

XXXII.

"When chaos slowly set to sun or planet,
    And molten masses hardened into earth ;
When primal force wrought out on sea and granite
    The wondrous miracle of living birth ;

Did mightier Mind, in clouds of glory hidden,
  Breathe power through its limbs to feel and know,
Or sentience spring, spontaneous and unbidden,
  With feeble steps and slow?

XXXIII.

" Are sense and thought but parasites of being?
  Did Nature mould our limbs to act and move,
But some strange chance endow our eyes with seeing,
  Our nerves with feeling, and our hearts with love?
Since all alone we stand, alone discerning
  Sorrow from joy, self from the things without;
While blind fate tramples on the spirit's yearning,
  And floods our souls with doubt.

XXXIV.

" This very tree, whose life is our life's sister,
  We know not if the ichor in her veins
Thrill with fierce joy when April dews have kissed her,
  Or shrink in anguish from October rains;
We search the mighty world above and under,
  Yet nowhere find the soul we fain would find;
Speech in the hollow rumbling of the thunder,
  Words in the whispering wind.

XXXV.

" We yearn for brotherhood with lake and mountain,
  Our conscious soul seeks conscious sympathy;
Nymphs in the coppice, Naiads in the fountain,
  Gods on the craggy height or roaring sea.
We find but soulless sequences of matter;
  Fact linked to fact in adamantine rods;
Eternal bonds of former sense and latter;
  Dead laws for living gods.

" There, Winifred, what do you say to that now? Isn't that calculated to take the wind out of some of these pretentious fellows' sails? What do you think of it?"

" Think?" Winifred answered, pursing up her lips into an expression of the utmost professional connoisseurship. " I think ' granite ' doesn't rhyme in the English language with ' planet '; and I consider ' sentience ' is a horribly prosaic word of its sort to introduce into serious poetry.—What's that stuff about liquor, too? ' We know not if the liquor in her something.' I don't like ' liquor.' It's not good: bar-room English, only fit for a public-house production."

" I didn't say ' liquor,'" Hugh cried indignantly. " I said ' ichor,' which of course is a very different matter. ' We know not if the ichor in her veins.' Ichor's the blood of the gods in Homer. That's the worst of reading these things to women: classical allusion's an utter blank to them.—If you've got nothing better than that to object, have the kindness, please, not to interrupt me."

Winifred closed her lips with a sharp snap; while Hugh went on, nothing abashed, with the same sonorous metre-marked mouthing—

XXXVI.

" They care not any whit for pain or pleasure
　　That seem to men the sum and end of all.
　Dumb force and barren number are their measure :
　　What can be, shall be, though the great world fall.
　They take no heed of man, or man's deserving,
　　Reck not what happy lives they make, or mar,
　Work out their fatal will, unswerved, unswerving,
　　And know not that they are.

"Now, what do you say to that, Winifred ? Isn't it just hunky?"

" I don't like interrupting," Winifred snapped out savagely. "You told me not to interrupt, except for a good and sufficient reason."

" Well, don't be nasty," Hugh put in, half smiling. " This is business, you know—a matter of public appreciation—and I want your criticism: it all means money. Criticism from anybody, no matter whom, is always worth at least something."

"Oh, thank you, *so* much. That *is* polite of you. Then if you want criticism, no matter from whom, I should say I fail to perceive, myself, the precise difference you mean to suggest between the two adjectives 'unswerved' and 'unswerving.' To the untutored intelligence of a mere woman, to whom classical allusion's an utter blank, they seem to say exactly the same thing twice over."

"No, no," Hugh answered, getting warm in self-defence. "'Unswerved' is passive; 'unswerving' is active, or at least middle: the one means that they swerve themselves; the other, that somebody or something else swerves them."

" You do violence to the genius of the English language," Winifred remarked curtly. " I may not be acquainted with Latin and Greek, but I talk at least my mother-tongue. Are you going to print nothing but this great, long, dreary incomprehensible ' Life's Philosophy ' in your new volume ? "

" I shall make it up mainly with that," Hugh answered, crestfallen, at so obvious a failure favourably to impress the domestic critic. " But I shall also eke out the title-piece with a lot of stray occasional verses—the ' Funeral Ode for Gambetta,' for example, and plenty of others that I haven't read you. Some of them seem to me tolerably successful." He was growing modest before the face of her unflinching criticism.

" Read me ' Gambetta,' Winifred said with quiet imperiousness. "I'll see if I like that any better than all this foolish maundering ' Philosophy.' "

Hugh turned over his papers for the piece " by request," and after some searching among quires and sheets, came at last upon a clean-written copy of his immortal threnody. He began reading out the lugubrious lines in a sufficiently grandiose and sepulchral voice. Winifred listened with careless attention, as to a matter little worthy her sublime consideration. Hugh cleared his throat and rang out magniloquently—

> " She sits once more upon her ancient throne,
>   The fair Republic of our steadfast vows :
>   A Phrygian bonnet binds her queenly brows ·
> Athwart her neck her knotted hair is blown.
> A hundred cities nestle in her lap,
>   Girt round their stately locks with mural crowns :
> The folds of her imperial robe enwrap
>   A thousand lesser towns."

" ' Mural crowns ' is good," Winifred murmured satirically : " it reminds one so vividly of the stone statues in the Place de la Concorde."

Hugh took no notice of her intercalary criticism. He went on with ten or twelve stanzas more of the same bombastic, would-be sublime character, and wound up at last in thunderous 'ones with a prophetic outburst as to the imagined career of ome future Gambetta—himself possibly—

> " He still shall guide us toward the distant goal ;
>   Calm with unerring tact our weak alarms ;
>   Train all our youth in skill of manly arms,
> And knit our sires in unity of soul :
> Till bursting iron bars and gates of brass
>   Our own Republic stretch her arm again
> To raise the weeping daughters of Alsace,
>   And lead thee home, Lorraine.

" Well, what do you think of *that*, Winnie ? " he asked at last triumphantly, with the air of a man who has trotted out his best war-horse for public inspection and has no fear of the effect he is producing.

" Think ? " Winifred answered. " Why, I think, Hugh, that if Swinburne had never written his Ode to Victor Hugo, *you* would never have written that Funeral March for your precious Gambetta."

Hugh bit his lip in bitter silence. The criticism was many times worse than harsh : it was true ; and he knew it. But a truthful critic is the most galling of all things.

" Well, surely, Winifred," he cried at last, after a long pause, " you think those other lines good, don't you ?—

> "And when like some fierce whirlwind through the land
> The wrathful Teuton swept, he only dared
> To hope and act when every heart and hand,
> But his alone, despaired."

"My dear Hugh," Winifred answered candidly, "don't you see in your own heart that all this sort of thing may be very well in its own way, but it isn't original—it isn't inspiration; it isn't the true sacred fire: it's only an echo. Echoes do admirably for the young beginner; but in a man of your age—for you're getting on now—we expect something native and idiosyncratic.—I think Mr. Hatherley called it idiosyncratic.—You know Mr. Hatherley said to me once you would never be a poet. You have too good a memory. 'Whenever Massinger sits down at his desk to write about anything,' he said in his quiet way, 'he remembers such a perfect flood of excellent things other people have written about the same subject, that he's absolutely incapable of originality.' And the more I see of your poetry, dear, the more do I see that Mr. Hatherley was right—right beyond question. You're clever enough, but you know you're not original."

Hugh answered her never a single word. To such a knock-down blow as that, any answer at all is clearly impossible. He only muttered something very low to himself about casting one's pearls before some creature inaudible.

Presently, Winifred spoke again. "Let's go out," she said, rising from the sofa, "and sit by the sea on the roots of the poplar."

At the word, Hugh flung down the manuscript in a heap on the ground with a stronger expression than Winifred had ever before heard fall from his lips. "I hate the poplar!" he said angrily; "I detest the poplar! I won't have the poplar! Nothing on earth will induce me to sit by the poplar!"

"How cross you are!" Winifred cried with a frown. "You jump at me as if you'd snap my head off! And all just because I didn't like your verses.—Very well then; I'll go and sit there alone.—I can amuse myself, fortunately, without your help. I've got Mr. Hatherley's clever article in this month's *Contemporary*."

That evening, as they sat together silently in the drawing-room, Winifred engaged in the feminine amusement of casting admiring glances at her own walls, and Hugh poring deep over a serious-looking book, Winifred glanced over at him suddenly with a sigh, and murmured half aloud: "After all, really I don't think much of it."

"Much of what?" Hugh asked, still bending over the book he was anxiously consulting.

"Why, of that gourd I brought home from town yesterday.

You know Mrs. Walpole's got a gourd in her drawing-room;
and every time I went into the vicarage I said to myself: 'Oh,
how lovely it is! How exquisite! How foreign-looking! If
only I had a gourd like that, now, I think life would be really
endurable. It gives the last touch of art to the picture. Our
new drawing-room would look just perfection with such a
gourd as hers to finish the wall with.' Well, I saw the exact
counterpart of that very gourd the day before yesterday at a
shop in Bond Street. I bought it, and brought it home with
exceeding great joy. I thought I should then be quite happy.
I hung it up on the wall to try, this morning. And sitting here
all evening, looking at it with my head first on one side and
then on the other, I've said to myself a thousand times over:
'It doesn't look one bit like Mrs. Walpole's. After all, I don't
know that I'm so much happier, now I've got it, than I was
before I had a gourd of my own at all to look at."

Hugh groaned. The unconscious allegory was far too obvious
in its application not to sink into the very depths of his soul.
He turned back to his book, and sighed inwardly to think for
what a feeble, unsatisfactory shadow of a gourd he had sacrificed his own life—not to speak of Winifred's and Elsie's.

By-and-by Winifred rose and crossed the room. " What's
that you're studying so intently? " she asked, with a suspicious
glance at the book in his fingers.

Hugh hesitated, and seemed half inclined for a moment to
hut the book with a bang and hide it away from her. Then he
made up his mind with a fresh resolve to brazen it out.
" Gordon's ' Electricity and Magnetism,' he answered quietly,
as unabashed as possible, holding the volume half-closed with
his forefinger at the page he had just hunted up. " I'm—I'm
interested at present to some extent in the subject of electricity.
I'm thinking of getting it up a little."

Winifred took the book from his hand, wondering, with a
masterful air of perfect authority. He yielded like a lamb.
On immaterial questions it was his policy not to resist her.
She turned to the page where his finger had rested and ran it
down lightly with her quick eye. The key-words showed in
some degree at what it was driving: " Franklin's Experiment "
—" Means of Collection "—" Theory of Lightning Rods "—
" Ruhmkorff's Coils "—" Drawing down Electric Discharges
from the Clouds."—Why, what was all this? She turned
round to him inquiringly. Hugh shuffled in an uneasy way in
his chair. The husband who shuffles betrays his cause. " We
must put up conductors, Winnie," he said hesitatingly, with a
hot face, " to protect those new gables at the east wing.—It's
dangerous to leave the house so exposed. I'll order them down
from London to-morrow."

"Conductors! Fiddlesticks!" Winifred answered in a breath, with wifely promptitude. "Lightning never hurt the house yet, and it's not going to begin hurting it now, just because an Immortal Poet with a fad for electricity has come to live and compose at Whitestrand. If anything, it ought to go the other way. Bards, you know, are exempt from thunderbolts. Didn't you read me the lines yourself, 'God's lightnings spared, they said, Alone the holier head, Whose laurels screened it,' or something to that effect? *You're* all right, you see. Poets can never get struck, I fancy."

"But 'Mr. Hatherley said to me once you would never be a poet,'" Hugh repeated with a smile, exactly mimicking Winifred's querulous little voice and manner. "As my own wife doesn't consider me a poet, Winifred, I shall venture to do as I like myself about my private property."

Winifred took up a bedroom candle and lighted it quietly without a word. Then she went up to muse in her own bedroom over her new gourd and other disillusionments.

As soon as she was gone, Hugh rose from his chair and walked slowly into his own study. Gordon's "Electricity" was still in his hand, and his finger pointed to that incriminating passage. He sat down at the sloping desk and wrote a short note to a well-known firm of scientific instrument makers whose address he had copied a week before from the advertisement sheet of *Nature.*

"Whitestrand Hall, Almundham, Suffolk.

"GENTLEMEN,

"Please forward me to the above address, at your earliest convenience, your most powerful form of Ruhmkorff Induction Coil, with secondary wires attached, for which cheque will be sent in full on receipt of invoice or retail price-list.

"Faithfully yours,
"HUGH MASSINGER.

As he rose from the desk, he glanced half involuntarily out of the study window. It pointed south. The moon was shining full on the water. That hateful poplar stared him straight in the face, as tall and gaunt and immovable as ever. On its roots, a woman in a white dress was standing, looking out over the angry sea, as Elsie had stood, for the twinkling of an eye, on that terrible evening when he lost her for ever. One second, the sight sent a shiver through his frame, then he laughed to himself, the next, for his groundless terror. How childish! How infantile! It was the gardener's wife, in her light print frock, looking out to sea for her boy's smack, over-due, no doubt—for Charlie was a fisherman.—But it was

intolerable that he, the Squire of Whitestrand, should be sub-
jected to such horrible turns as these.—He shook his fist angrily
at the offending tree. "You shall pay for it, my friend," he
muttered low but hoarse between his clenched teeth. "You
shan't have many more chances of frightening me!"

CHAPTER XXIX.

ACCIDENTS WILL HAPPEN.

DURING the whole of the next week, the Squire and a strange
artisan, whom he had specially imported by rail from London,
went much about together by day and night through the grounds
at Whitestrand. A certain air of mystery hung over their joint
proceedings. The strange artisan was a skilled workman in the
engineering line, he told the people at the Fisherman's Rest,
where he had taken a bed for his stay in the village; and indeed
sundry books in his kit bore out the statement—weird books of
a scientific and diagrammatic character, chockfull of formulæ in
Greek lettering, which seemed not unlikely to be connected with
hydrostatics, dynamics, trigonometry, and mechanics, or any
other equally abstruse and uncanny subject, not wholly alien to
 ecromancy and witchcraft. It was held at Whitestrand by
 hose best able to form an opinion in such dark questions, that
the new importation was "summat in the electric way;" and it
was certainly matter of plain fact, patent to all observers equally,
that he did in very truth fix up an elaborate lightning-conductor
of the latest pattern to the newly-thrown-out gable-end at what
had once been Elsie's window. It was Elsie's window still to
Hugh: let him twist it and turn it and alter it as he would, he
feared it would never, never cease to be Elsie's window.
But in the domain at large, the intelligent artisan with the
engineering air, who was surmised to be "summat in the electric
way," carefully examined, under Hugh's directions, many parts
of the grounds of Whitestrand. Squire was going to lay out the
garden and terrace afresh, the servants conjectured in their own
society: one or two of them, exceedingly modern in their views,
even opined in an off-hand fashion that he must be bent on
laying electric lights on. Conservative in most things to the
backbone, the servants bestowed the meed of their hearty
approval on the electric light: it saves so much in trimming
and cleaning. Lamps are the bug-bear of big country houses:
electricity, on the other hand, needs no tending. It was near
the poplar that Squire was going to put his installation, as they
call the arrangement in our latterday jargon; and he was going

to drive it, rumour remarked, by a tidal outfall. What a tidal
outfall might be, or how it could work in lighting the Hall,
nobody knew; but the intelligent artisan had let the words
drop casually in the course of conversation; and the Fisherman's
Rest snapped them up at once, and retailed them freely with
profound gusto to all after-comers.

Still, it was a curious fact in its own way that the installation
appeared to progress most easily when nobody happened to be
looking on, and that the skilled workman in the engineering
line generally stood with his hands in his pockets, surveying
his handicraft with languid interest, whenever anybody from
the village or the Hall lounged up by his side to inspect or
wonder at it.

More curious still was another small fact, known to nobody
but the skilled workman *in propriâ personâ*, that four small
casks of petroleum from a London store were stowed away, by
Hugh Massinger's orders, under the very roots of the big poplar;
and that by their side lay a queer apparatus, connected apparently in some remote way with electric lighting.

The Squire himself, however, made no secret of his own
personal and private intentions to the London workman. He
paid the man well, and he exacted silence. That was all. But
he explained precisely in plain terms what it was that he wanted
done. The tree was an eyesore to him, he said, with his usual
frankness—Hugh was always frank whenever possible—but his
wife, for sentimental reasons, had a special fancy for it. He
wanted to get rid of it, therefore, in the least obtrusive way he
could easily manage. This was the least obtrusive way. So
this was what he required done with it. The London workman
nodded his head, pocketed his pay, looked unconcerned, and
held his tongue with trained fidelity. It was none of his
business to pry into any employer's motives. Enough for him
to take his orders and to carry them out faithfully to the very
letter. The job was odd: an odd job is always interesting. He
hoped the experiment might prove successful.

The Whitestrand labourers, who passed by the poplar and
the London workman, time and again, with a jerky nod and
their pipes turned downward, never noticed a certain slender
unobtrusive copper wire which the strange artisan fastened one
evening, in the gray dusk, right up the stem and boles of the
big tree to a round knob on the very summit. The wire, however, as its fixer knew, ran down to a large deal box well buried
in the ground, which bore outside a green label, " Ruhmkorff
Induction Coil, Elliott's Patent." The wire and coil terminated
in a pile close to the four full petroleum barrels. When the
London workman had securely laid the entire apparatus,
undisturbed by loungers, he reported adversely, with great

solemnity, on the tidal outfall and electric light scheme to Hugh Massinger. No sufficient power for the purpose existed in the river. This adverse report was orally delivered in the front vestibule of Whitestrand Hall; and it was also delivered with sedulous care—as per orders received—in Mrs. Massinger's own presence. When the London workman went out again after making his carefully worded statement, he went out clinking a coin of the realm or two in his trousers' pocket, and with his tongue stuck, somewhat unbecomingly, in his right cheek, as who should pride himself on the successful outwitting of an innocent fellow-creature. He had done the work he was paid for, and he had done it well. But he thought to himself, as he went his way rejoicing, that the Squire of Whitestrand must be very well held in hand indeed by that small pale lady, if he had to take so many cunning precautions in secret beforehand when he wanted to get rid of a single tree that offended his eye in his own gardens.

The plot was all well laid now. Hugh had nothing further left to do but to possess his soul in patience against the next thunderstorm. He had not very long to wait. Before the month was out, a thunderstorm did indeed burst in full force over Whitestrand and its neighbourhood—one of those terrible and destructive east coast electric displays which invariably leave their broad mark behind them. For along the low, flat, monotonous East Anglian shore, where hills are unknown and big trees rare, the lightning almost inevitably singles out for its onslaught some aspiring piece of man's handiwork — some church steeple, some castle keep, the turrets on some tall and isolated manor-house, the vane above some ancient castellated gateway.

The reason for this is not far to seek. In hilly countries the hills and trees act as natural lightning-conductors, or rather as decoys to draw aside the fire from heaven from the towns or farmhouses that nestle far below among the glens and valleys. But in wide level plains, where all alike is flat and low-lying, human architecture forms for the most part the one salient point in the landscape for lightning to attack : every church or tower with its battlements and lanterns stands in the place of the polished knobs on an electric machine, and draws down upon itself with unerring certainty the destructive bolt from the overcharged clouds. Owing to this cause, the thunderstorms of East Anglia are the most appalling and destructive in their concrete results of any in England. The laden clouds, big with electric energy, hang low and dark above one's very head, and let loose their accumulated store of vivid flashes in the exact midst of towns and villages.

This particular thunderstorm, as chance would have it, came

late at night, after three sultry days of close weather, when big
black masses were just beginning to gather in vast battalions
over the German Ocean; and it let loose at last its fierce artillery
in terrible volleys right over the village and grounds of Whitestrand. Hugh Massinger was the first at the Hall to observe
from afar the distant flash, before the thunder had made itself
audible in their ears. A pale light to westward, in the direction
of Snade, attracted, as he read, his passing attention. "By
Jove!" he cried, rising with a yawn from his chair, and laying
down the manuscript of "A Life's Philosophy," which he was
languidly correcting in its later stanzas, "that's something like
lightning, Winifred! Over Snade way, apparently. I wonder
if it's going to drift towards us?—Whew—what a clap! It's
precious near. I expect we shall catch it ourselves shortly."

The clouds rolled up with extraordinary rapidity, and the
claps came fast and thick and nearer. Winifred cowered down
on the sofa in terror. She dreaded thunder; but she was too
proud to confess what she would nevertheless have given worlds
to do—hide her frightened little head with sobs and tears in its
old place upon Hugh's shoulder. "It's coming this way," she
cried nervously after a while. "That last flash must have been
awfully near us."

Even as she spoke, a terrific volley seemed to burst all at once
right over their heads and shake the house with its irresistible
majesty. Winifred buried her face deep in the cushions. "Oh,
Hugh," she cried in a terrified tone, "this is awful—awful!"

Much as he longed to look out of the window, Hugh could
not resist that unspoken appeal. He drew up the blind hastily
to its full height, so that he might see out to watch the success
of his deep-laid stratagem; then he hurried over with real
tenderness to Winifred's side. He drew his arm round her and
soothed her with his hand, and laid her poor-throbbing aching
head with a lover's caress upon his own broad bosom. Winifred
nestled close to him with a sigh of relief. The nearness of
danger, real or imagined, rouses all the most ingrained and profound of our virile feelings. The instinct of protection for the
woman and the child comes over even bad men at such moments
of doubt with irresistible might and majesty. Small differences
or tiffs are forgotten and forgiven: the woman clings naturally
in her feminine weakness to the strong man in his primary
aspect as comforter and protector. Between Hugh and Winifred
the estrangement as yet was but vague and unacknowledged.
Had it yawned far wider, had it sunk far deeper, the awe and
terror of that supreme moment would amply have sufficed to
bridge it over, at least while the orgy of the thunderstorm
lasted.

For next instant a sheet of liquid flame seemed to surround

and engulf the whole house at once in its white embrace.   The
world became for the twinkling of an eye one surging flood of
vivid fire, one roar and crash and sea of deafening tumult.
Winifred buried her face deeper than ever on Hugh's shoulder,
and put up both her small hands to her tingling ears, to crush if
possible the hideous roar out.   But the light and sound seemed
to penetrate everything: she was aware of them keenly through
her very bones and nerves and marrow; her entire being
appeared as if pervaded and overwhelmed with the horror of the
lightning.   In another moment all was over, and she was conscious only of an abiding awe, a deep-seated after-glow of alarm
and terror.   But Hugh had started up from the sofa now, both
his hands clasped hard in front of his breast, and was gazing
wildly out of the big bow-window, and lifting up his voice in a
paroxysm of excitement.   "It's hit the poplar!" he cried.   "It's
hit the poplar!   It must be terribly near, Winnie!   It's hit the
poplar!"

Winifred opened her eyes with an effort, and saw him standing
there, as if spellbound, by the window.   She dared not get up
and come any nearer the front of the room, but, raising her eyes,
she saw from where she sat, or rather crouched, that the poplar
stood out, one living mass of rampant flame, a flaring beacon,
from top to bottom.   The petroleum, ignited and raised to
flashing-point by the fire which the induction coil had drawn
`own from heaven, gave off its blazing vapour in huge rolling
 heets and forked tongues of flame, which licked up the crackling
 .ranches of the dry old tree from base to summit like so much
touchwood.   The poplar rose now one solid column of crimson
fire.   The red glow deepened and widened from moment to
moment.   Even the drenching rain that followed the thunder-
clap seemed powerless to check that frantic onslaught.   The fire
leaped and danced through the tall straight boughs with mad
exultation, hissing out its defiance to the big round drops which
burst off into tiny balls of steam before they could reach the
red-hot trunk and snapping branches.   Even left to itself, the
poplar, once ignited, would have burnt to the ground with
startling rapidity ; for its core was dry and light as tinder, its
wood was eaten through by innumerable worm-holes, and the
hollow centre of mouldering dry-rot, where children had loved
to play at hide-and-seek, acted now like a roaring chimney flue,
with a fierce draught that carried up the circling eddies of
smoke and flame in mad career to the topmost branches.   But
the fumes of the petroleum, rendered instantly gaseous by the
electric heat, made the work of destruction still more instan-
taneous, terrible, and complete than it would have proved if
left to unaided nature.   The very atmosphere resolved itself into
one rolling pillar of fluid flame.   The tree seemed enveloped in

a shroud of fire. All human effort must be powerless to resist it. The poplar dissolved almost as if by magic with a wild rapidity into its prime elements.

A man must be a man come what may. Hugh leaped towards the window and flung it open wildly. "I must go!" he cried. "Ring the bell for the servants." The savage glee in his voice was well repressed. His enemy was low, laid prone at his feet, but he would at least pretend to some spark of magnanimity. "We must get out the hose!" he exclaimed. "We must try to save it!" Winifred clung to his arm in horror. "Let it burn down, Hugh!" she cried. "Who cares for the poplar? I'd sooner ten thousand poplars burned to the ground than that you should venture out on such an evening!"

Her hand on his arm thrilled through him with horror. Her words stung him with a sense of his meanness. Something very like a touch of remorse came over his spirit. He stooped down and kissed her tenderly. The next flash struck over towards the sandhills. The thunder was rolling gradually seaward.

Hugh slept but little that eventful night ; his mind addressed itself with feverish eagerness to so many hard and doubtful questions. He tossed and turned and asked himself ten thousand times over—was the tree burnt through—burnt down to the ground? Were the roots and trunk consumed beyond hope—or rather beyond fear—of ultimate recovery? Was the hateful poplar really done for? Would any trace remain of the barrels that had held the tell-tale petroleum? any relic be left of the Ruhmkorff Induction Coil? What jot or tittle of the evidence of design would now survive to betray and convict him? What ground for reasonable suspicion would Winifred see that the fire was not wholly the result of accident?

But when next morning's light dawned and the sun arose upon the scene of conflagration, Hugh saw at a glance that all his fears had indeed been wholly and utterly groundless. The poplar was as though it had never existed. A bare black patch by the mouth of the Char, covered with ash and dust and cinder, alone marked the spot where the famous tree had once stood. The very roots were burned deep into the ground. The petroleum had done its duty bravely. Not a trace of design could be observed anywhere. The Ruhmkorff Induction Coil had melted into air. Nobody ever so much as dreamed that human handicraft had art or part in the burning of the celebrated Whitestrand poplar. The *Times* gave it a line of passing regret ; and the Trinity House deleted it with pains as a lost landmark from their sailing directions.

Hugh set his workmen instantly to stub up the roots. And Winifred, gazing mournfully next day at the ruins, observed

with a sigh : " You never liked the dear old tree, Hugh ; and it
seems as if fate had interposed in your favour to destroy it. I'm
sorry it's gone ; but I'd sacrifice a hundred such trees any day
to have you as kind to me as you were last evening."

The saying smote Hugh's heart sore. He played nervously
with the button of his coat. " I wish you could have kept it,
Winnie," he said not unkindly. " But it's not my fault.—And I
bear no malice. I'll even forgive you for telling me I'd never
make a poet ; though that, you'll admit, was a hard saying. I
think, my child, if you don't mind, I'll ask Hatherley down next
week to visit us.—There's nothing like adverse opinion to
improve one's work. Hatherley's opinion is more than adverse.
I'd like his criticism on ' A Life's Philosophy ' before I rush into
print at last with the greatest and deepest work of my lifetime."

That same evening, as it was growing dusk, Warren Relf and
Potts, navigating the *Mud-Turtle* around by sea from Yarmouth
Roads, put in for the night to the Char at Whitestrand. They
meant to lie by for a Sunday in the estuary, and walk across the
fields, if the day proved fine, to service at Snade. As they
approached the mouth they looked about in vain for the familiar
landmark. At first they could hardly believe their eyes : to men
who knew the east coast well, the disappearance of the Whitestrand poplar from the world seemed almost as incredible as the
sudden removal of the Bass Rock or the Pillars of Hercules.
Nobody would ever dream of cutting down that glory of Suffolk,
that time-honoured sea-mark. But as they strained their eyes
through the deepening gloom, the stern logic of facts left them
at last no further room for syllogistic reasoning or *à priori*
scepticism. The Whitestrand poplar was really gone. Not a
stump even remained as its relic or its monument.

They drove the yawl close under the shore. The current was
setting out stronger than ever, and eddying back against the
base of the roots with a fierce and eager swirling movement.
Warren Relf looked over the bank in doubt at the charred and
blackened soil beside it. He knew in a second exactly what had
happened. " Massinger has burned down the poplar, Potts," he
cried aloud. He did not add, " because it stood upon the very
spot where Elsie Challoner threw herself over." But he knew
it was so. They turned the yawl up stream once more. Then
Warren Relf murmured in a low voice, more than half to himself, but in solemn accents : " So much the worse in the end for
Whitestrand."

All the way up to the Fisherman's Rest he repeated again and
again below his breath : " So much the worse in the end for
Whitestrand."

CHAPTER XXX.

THE BARD IN HARNESS.

" I NEVER felt more astonished in my life," Hatherley remarked one day some weeks later to a chosen circle at the Cheyne Row Club, " than I felt on the very first morning of my visit to Whitestrand. Talk about being driven by a lady, indeed! Why, that frail little woman's got the Bard in harness, as right and as tight as if he were a respectable cheesemonger.—What on earth do you think happened? As the Divine Singer and I were starting out, stick in hand, for a peregrination of the estate—or what there is left of it—if that perky little atomy didn't poke her fuzzy, tow-bewigged head out of the dining-room window, and call out in the most matter-of-fact tone possible: ' Hugh, if you're going to the village to-day, mind you don't forget to bring me back three kippered herrings!'—' Three *what?* ' said I, scarcely believing my ears.—' Three kippered herrings,' that unblushing little minx repeated in an audible voice, wholly un- abashed at the absurdity of her request.—' Well,' said I, in a fever of surprise, ' it may be all right when you've got them well in hand, you know ; but you'll admit, Mrs. Massinger, that's not the use to which we generally put immortal minstrels!'— ' Oh, but this is such a very mild specimen of the genus, though!' Mrs. Massinger answered, laughing carelessly.—I looked at the Bard with tremulous awe, expecting to see the angry fire in his cold gray eye flashing forth like the leven bolt from heaven to scath and consume her. Not a bit of it. Nary scath! The Immortal Singer merely took out his tablets from his waistcoat pocket and made a note of the absurd commission. And when we came home again an hour afterwards, I solemnly assure you he was carrying those three identical kippered herrings, wrapped up in a sheet of dirty newspaper, in the very hand that wrote ' The Death of Alaric.'—It's too surprising. The Bard's done for. His life is finished. There the Man stops. The Husband and Father may drag out a wretched domestic existence yet for another twenty years. But the Man is dead, hopelessly dead. Julius Cæsar himself's not more utterly defunct. That girl has extinguished him."

" Are there any children, then ? " one of the chosen circle put in casually.

" Children! No. Bar twins, the plural would surely be premature, so far. There was a child born just after old Mrs. Meysey's death, I believe ; but it came to nothing—a mere abortive attempt at a son and heir—and left the mother a poor

wreck, her own miserable faded photograph. She was a nice
little girl enough, in her small way, when she was here in town;
amusing and sprightly; but the Bard has done for her, as she's
done for the Bard. It's a mutual annihilation society, like
Stevenson's Suicide Club on a more private platform.—He seems
to have crushed all the giddy girlishness out of her. The fact
is, this is a case of incompatibility of disposition—for which
cause I believe you can get a divorce in Illinois or some other
enlightened Far Western community. You can't stop three days
at Whitestrand without feeling there's a skeleton in the house
somewhere!"

The skeleton in the house, long carefully confined to its
native cupboard, had indeed begun to perambulate the Hall in
open daylight during the brief period of Hatherley's visit. He
reached the newly remodelled home just in time to dress for
dinner. When he descended to the ill-lighted drawing-room,
five minutes late—Whitestrand could boast no native gas-
supply, and candles are expensive—he gave his arm with a
sense of solemn obligation to poor dark-clad Winifred.
Mrs. Massinger was indeed altered—sadly altered. Three
painful losses in quick succession had told upon that slender
pale young wife. She showed her paleness in her deep black
dress: colours suited Winifred: in mourning, she was hardly
an pretty. The little "arrangement in pink and white" had
led almost into white alone: the pinkness had proved a
fleeting pigment: she was not warranted fast colours. But
Hatherley did his best with innate gallantry not to notice the
change. Fresh from town, crammed with the last good things
of the Cheyne Row and Mrs. Bouverie Barton's Wednesday
evenings, he tried hard with conscientious efforts to keep the
conversation from flagging visibly. At first he succeeded with
creditable skill; and Hugh, looking across at his wife with a
curious smile, said in a tone of genuine pleasure: "How delightful it is, after all, Winnie, to get a hold of somebody, direct from
the real live world of London, in the midst of our fossilized
antediluvian Whitestrand society!—I declare, Hatherley, it does
one's heart good, like champagne, to listen to you. A breath of
Bohemia blows across Suffolk the moment you arrive. Poor
drowsy, somnolent, petrified Suffolk! 'Silly Suffolk,' even the
aborigines themselves call it. It's catching, too. I'm almost
beginning to fall asleep myself, by force of example."
At the words, Winifred fired up in defence of her native
county. "I'm sure, Hugh," she said with some asperity, "I
don't know why you're always trying to run down Suffolk! If
you didn't like us, you should have avoided the shire; you
should have carried your respected presence elsewhere. Suffolk

never invited you to honour it with your suffrages. You came
and settled here of your own free will. And who could be nicer
or more cultivated, if it comes to that, than some of our Suffolk
aborigines, as you call them? Dear old Mrs. Walpole at the
vicarage, for example."

Hugh balanced an olive on the end of his fork. "An amiable
old Hecuba," he answered provokingly. "What's Hecuba to
me, or I to Hecuba? Her latest dates are about the period of
the siege of Troy, or, to be more precisely accurate, the year
1850. She's extremely well read, I grant you that, in Bulwer
Lytton and the poets of the Regency. She adores Cowper, and
considers Voltaire a most dangerous writer. She has even heard
of Bismarck and Bulgaria; and she understands that a young
.man named Swinburne has lately published some very objection-
able and unwholesome verses, not suited to the cheek of the
young person.—The idea of sticking *me* down with people like
that, who never read a line of Browning in their lives, and ask
if Mr. William Morris 'the upholsterer,' who furnished and
decorated our poor little drawing-room, is really a brother of
that eccentric and rather heterodox preacher!—My dear
Hatherley, when *you* come down, I feel like a man who has
breathed fresh air on some high mountain—stimulated and
invigorated. You palpitate with actuality. Down here, we
stagnate in the seventeenth century."

Winifred bit her lip with vexation, but said nothing. It was
evident the subject was an unpleasant one to her. But *she* at
least would not trot out the skeleton. Women are all for due
concealment of your dirty linen. It is men who insist on washing it in public.

Next morning—the morning of the kippered herring adventure—Hugh showed Hatherley round tho Whitestrand estate.
Hatherley himself was not, to say the truth, in the best of
humours. Mrs. Massinger was dull and not what she used to
be: she obviously resented his bright London gossip, as throwing into stronger and clearer relief the innate stupidity of her
ancestral Suffolk. The breakfast was bad; the coffee sloppy;
and the dishes suggested too obvious reminiscences of the
joints and *entrées* at last night's dinner. Clearly, the Massingers were struggling hard to keep up appearances on an insufficient income. They were stretching their means much too
thin. The Morris drawing-room was all very well in its way,
of course; but tulip-pattern curtains and De Morgan pottery
don't quite make up for a *réchauffé* of kidneys. Moreover, a
suspicion floated dimly through the air that to-morrow's dawn
would see those three kippered herrings as the sole alternative
to the curried drumsticks left behind as a legacy by this
evening's roast chicken. Hatherley was an epicure, like most

club-bred men, and his converse for the day took a colour from
the breakfast table for good or for evil. So he started out that
morning in a dormant ill-humour, prepared to tease and
"draw" Massinger, who had had the bad taste to desert
Bohemia for dull respectability and ill-paid Squiredom in the
wilds of Suffolk.

Hugh showed him first the region of the sandhills. The
sandhills were a decent bit to begin with. "Æolian sands!"
Hatherley murmured contemplatively as Hugh mentioned the
name. "How very pretty! How very poetical! You can
hardly regret it yourself, Massinger, this overwhelming of your
salt marshes by the shifting sands, when you reflect at leisure it
was really done by anything with so sweet an epithet as Æolian."

"I thought so once," Hugh answered dryly, with obvious
distaste, "when it was the property of my late respected father-
in-law. But circumstances alter cases, you know, as somebody
once remarked with luminous platitude; and since I came into
the estate myself, to tell you the truth, I can't forgive the
beastly sands, even though they happen to be called Æolian."

"Æolian sands," Hatherley repeated once more, half aloud,
with a tender reluctance. "Curious; there's hardly any word
in the language to rhyme with so simple a sound as Æolian.
Tmolian does it, of course; but Tmolian, you see, is scarcely
English, or if English at all, only by courtesy. There's a fellow
called Croll, I believe, who's invented a splendid theory of his
own about the Glacial Epoch; but I've never seen it anywhere
described in print as the Crollian hypothesis. One might coin
the adjective, of course, on the analogy of Darwinian and
Carlylese and Ruskinesque and Tennysonian; but it's scarcely
legitimate to coin a word for the sake of a rhyme. Æolian—
Crollian: the jingle would only go down, I'm afraid, in geological circles."

Hugh's lip curled contemptuously. He had passed through
all that: he knew its hollowness only too well—the merely
literary way of regarding things. Time was when he himself
had seen in everything but a chance for crisp and telling
epigrams, an opening for a particular rhyme or turn of phrase.
Nowadays, however, all that was changed: he knew better: he
was a practical man—a Spuire and a landlord. "My dear
fellow," he said, with some slight acerbity peeping through the
threadbare places in his friendly tone, "men talk like that
when they're hopelessly young. Contact with affairs makes a
man soon forget phrases. We deal in facts, not words, when
we finally arrive at years of discretion. I think now of the
reality of the blown sand—the depreciation and loss of rent—
not the mere prettiness of the sound Æolian."

"Yes, I know, my dear boy," Hatherley answered, in his

patronizing way, scarcely smearing his barb with delusive honey. "You've gone over to the enemy now: you've elected to dwell in the courts of Gath: you're no longer of Ours: you're an adopted Philistine. Deserters do well to fight in defence of their new side. You'd rather have your wretched fat salt marshes, with their prize oxen and their lean agues, than all these pretty little tumbled sandhills that make such a fairyland of mimic hillsides.—Don't say you wouldn't, for I know you would: you descend on stepping-stones of your dead self, the opposite way from Tennyson's people, to lower things —even to the nethermost abysses of Philistia."

Hugh swung his cane uneasily in his hand. He remembered only too well that summer afternoon when he himself—not yet a full-fledged squireen—had indulged in that self-same rhyme of "Æolian," "Tmolian," before the astonished face of old Mr. Meysey. He remembered the magnificent long-horned Highland cattle—"Bulls that walk the pastures in kingly-flashing coats," he had called them that day, after George Meredith. He knew now they were only old Grimes's black Ayrshires, fattened for market upon the rank salt-marsh vegetation. "Well, you see, Hatherley," he said, with a certain inward consciousness of appearing to his friend at an appalling disadvantage, "we must look at practical matters from a practical standpoint. Government's behaved scandalously to the landowners about the protection of the Suffolk foreshore. These sandhills tell upon a fellow's income. If the sand could only be turned into gold dust——"

Hatherley interrupted him with a happy thought. "'Where Afric's sunny fountains Roll down their golden sand,'" he cried with an attitude. "If the Char were only Pactolus, now, 'a fellow's income' would be still intact. There's the very rhyme for you. 'Æolian'—'Pactolian:' you can write a sonnet to it embodying that notion.—At least you could have written one, in the good old days, when you were still landless and still immortal. But in these latter times, as you say yourself, contact with affairs has certainly made you forget phrases.—You've come down from Olympus to be a Suffolk Squire. You'll admit it yourself, there's been a terrible falling off, of late, you know —one can't deny it—in your verses, Massinger."

"Bohemia is naturally intolerant of seceders," Hugh answered gloomily. "Each man sees in his neighbour's backsliding the premonition of his own proximate downfall.—You will marry in time, and migrate, even you yourself, to fixed quarters in Askelon.—Prague's a capital town to secure lodgings in for some weeks of one's youth, but it's not the precise place where a man would like to settle down for a whole lifetime."

They walked along in silence for a while, each absorbed in his own thoughts—Hatherley ruminating upon this melancholy spectacle of a degenerate son of dear old Cheyne Row gone wrong for ever: Massinger reflecting in his own mind upon the closer insight into the facts of life which property, with its cares and responsibilities, gives one—when he suddenly halted with a short sharp whistle at the turn of the path. " Whew ! " he cried; " why, what the dickens is this? The poplar's disappeared—at least, its place, I mean."

" Ah, yes! Mrs. Massinger told me all about that unlucky poplar when you were gone last night," Hatherley answered cheerfully. " The only good object in the view, she said—and I can easily believe her, to judge by the remainder. It got struck by lightning one stormy night, and disappeared then and there entirely ! "

" This is strange—very strange! " Hugh went on to himself, never heeding the babbling interruption. " The sand's clearly collected on this side of late. There's a distinct hummock here, like the ones at Grimes's.—I wonder what on earth these waves and mounds of sand can mean ?—The wind's not going to attack this side of the river, too, is it ? "

" Ah, Squoire," a man at work in the field put in, coming up to join them, and leaning upon his pitchfork—" ah'm glad yo've come to see it yourself, naow. That's jest what it be. The and's a-driftin'. Ah said to Tom, the night the thunderbolt ook th' owd poplar—ah said: ' Tom,' says ah, ' that there poplar were the only bar as stopped the river an' the sand from shifting. It's shifted all along till it's reached the poplar ; an' naow it'll shift an' shift an' shift till it gets to Lowestoft or mayhap to Norwich.'—An' if yo'll look, Squoire, yo'll see for yourself—the river's acshally runnin' zackly where the tree had used to stand ; an' the sand's a-driftin' an' a-driftin', same as it allays drift down yonner at Grimes's. An' it's my belief it'll never stop till it's swallowed up the Hall and the whole o' Whitestrand."

Hugh Massinger gazed in silence at the spot where the Whitestrand poplar had once stood with an utter feeling of sinking helplessness taking possession at once of his heart and bosom. A single glance told him beyond doubt the man was right. The poplar had stood as the one frail barrier to the winds and waves of the German Ocean. He had burnt it down, by wile and guile, of deliberate intent, that night of the thunderstorm, to get rid of the single mute witness to Elsie's suicide. And now, his Nemesis had worked itself out. The sea was advancing, inch by inch, with irresistible march, against doomed Whitestrand.,

Inch by inch! Nay, yard by yard. Gazing across to the

opposite bank, and roughly measuring the distance with his eye, Hugh saw the river had been diverted northward many feet since he last visited the site of the poplar. He always avoided that hateful spot: the very interval that had elapsed since his last visit enabled him all the better to gauge at sight the distance the river had advanced meanwhile in its silent invasion.

"I must get an engineer to come down and see to this," he said shortly. "We must put up a breakwater ourselves, I suppose, since a supine administration refuses to help us.—I wonder who's the proper man to go to for breakwaters? I'd wire to town to-night, if I knew whom to wire to, and check the thing before it runs any farther."

"What's that Swinburne says?" Hatherley asked musingly. "I forget the exact run of the particular lines, but they occur somewhere in the 'Hymn to Proserpine'—

'Will ye bridle the deep sea with reins? will ye chasten the high sea with
　　rods?
Will ye take her to chain her with chains who is older than all, ye gods?'

I don't expect, my dear boy, your engineer will do much for you. Man's but a pigmy before these natural powers. A breakwater's helpless against the ceaseless dashing of the eternal sea."

Hugh Massinger almost lost his temper—especially when he reflected with bitter self-abasement that those were the very lines he had quoted to Elsie—in his foolish pre-territorial days —about Mr. Meysey's sensible proposals for obtaining an injunction against the German Ocean. "Eternal sea! Eternal fiddlesticks!" he answered testily. "It's all very well for you to talk; but it's a matter of life and death to me, this checking the inroads of your eternal humbug. Eternal sea, indeed! What utter rubbish! It's the curse of the purely literary intellect that it never looks at Things at all, but only at Phrases.—We've got to built a breakwater, that's what it comes to. And a breakwater 'll run into a pot of money."

"Pity the old tree ever got burnt down, anyhow, to begin with," Hatherley murmured low, endeavouring, now he had fairly drawn his man, to assume a sympathetic expression of countenance.

"No!" Hugh thundered back savagely at last, unable to control himself. "Having to build a breakwater's bad enough; but I wouldn't have that hateful old tree back again there for all the gold that ever flowed in that Pactolus you chatter about. —Leave the tree alone, I say. Confound it! I hate it!"

They walked back slowly to the Hall in silence, passing through the village even so, out of pure habit, for the three

herrings. Hugh was evidently very much put out. Hatherley
considered him even rude and bearish. A man should restrain
himself before the faces of his guests. At the door, Hatherley
strolled off round the garden walks and lit a cigar. Hugh went
up to his own dressing-room.

The rest Hatherley never knew; he only knew that at
dinner that night Mrs. Massinger's eyes were red and sore with
crying. For when Hugh reached his own room—that pretty
little dressing-room with the pomegranate wall-paper and the
pale blue Lahore hangings—he found Winifred fiddling at his
private desk, a new tall black-walnut desk with endless drawers
and niches and pigeon-holes. A sudden something rose in his
throat as he saw her fumbling at the doors of the cabinet.
Where had she found that carefully guarded key?—Aha, he
knew! That fellow Hatherley!—Hatherley had taken a cigar
from his case as they went out for their stroll together that
luckless morning; and instead of returning the case to its owner,
had laid it down in his careless way on the study table. He
always kept the key concealed in the case.—Winifred must
accidentally have found it, and tried to worm out her husband's
secrets.—He hated such meanness in other people. How much,
he wondered, had she found out now after all for her trouble?

Ah!

They both cried out in one voice together; for Winifred had
)ened a pigeon-hole box with the special key, and was looking
tently with rigid eyes at—a small gold watch and a bundle of
letters.

With a wild dart forward, Hugh tore them from her grasp
and crunched them in his hand; but not before Winifred had
seen two things: first, that the watch was a counterpart of her
own—the very watch Hugh had given to Elsie Challoner;
second, that the letters were in a familiar hand—no other hand
than Elsie Challoner's.

She fronted him long with a pale cold face. Hugh took the
watch and letters before her very eyes, and locked them up again
in their pigeon-hole, angrily. "So this is how you play the spy
upon me!" he cried at last with supreme contempt in his voice
and manner.

But Winifred simply answered nothing. She burst into a
fierce wild flood of tears. "I knew it!" she moaned in an
agony of slighted affection. "I knew it! I knew it!"

So, after all, in spite of her flight and her pretended coolness,
Elsie was corresponding still with her husband! Cruel, cruel,
cruel Elsie! Yet why had she given him back his watch
again? That was more than Winifred could ever explain in
her simple philosophy. She could only cry and cry her eyes
out.

CHAPTER XXXI.

COMING ROUND.

WHEN Warren Relf steered back his barque to San Remo and Elsie that next autumn, he had not yet exactly been " boomed," as Edie had predicted; but his artistic or rather his business prospects had improved considerably through the intervening summer. Hatherley's persistent friendly notices of his work in the *Charing Cross Review*, and Mitchison's constant flow of rhapsodies about his "charming *morbidezza*" in West End drawing-rooms, had begun to bring his sea-pieces at last more prominently into notice. The skipper of the *Mud-Turtle* had gone up one. It was the mode to speak of him now in artistic coteries, no longer as a melancholy instance of well-meaning failure, but as a young man of rising though misunderstood talent. His knowledge of " values " was allowed to be profound. If you wished to lead the fore-front of opinion, indeed, you referred familiarly in a parenthetical side-sentence to "genius like Burne Jones's, or Relf's, or Watts's." To be sure, he didn't yet sell; but it was understood in astute buying circles that people who could pick up an early Relf dirt cheap and were prepared to hang on long enough to their purchase, would be sure in the end to see the colour of their money. It was even asserted by exceptionally knowing connoisseurs at the Burlington and the Savage that that colour would most probably have changed meanwhile, by the subtle alchemy of unearned increment, from silvery white to golden yellow. Warren Relf sat perched on the flowing tide of opportunism ; and all critics are abandoned opportunists by use and by nature. They invariably salute the rising sun; the coming man has their warmest suffrages.

That winter at San Remo was the happiest Warren had yet passed there ; for he began to perceive that Elsie was relenting. In a timid, tremulous, shamefaced, unacknowledged sort of way, she was learning little by little to love him. She would not confess it at first, even to herself. Elsie was too much of a woman to admit in the intimacy of her own heart, far less in the ear of any outside confidante, that having once loved Hugh she could now veer round and love Warren. The sense of personal consistency runs deep in women. They can't bear to turn their backs upon their dead selves, even though it be in order to rise to higher and ever higher planes of affection and devotion. Still, in spite of everything, Elsie Challoner grew by degrees dimly aware that she did actually love the quiet young marine painter. She had a hard struggle with herself, to be sure, before she could quite recognize the fact; but she recognized it at last, and in her own heart frankly admitted it. Warren was not indeed externally brilliant and vivid, like Hugh; he didn't sparkle with epigram and repartee; the soul that was in him let itself out more fully and freely on quiet canvas, in beautiful dreamy poetic imaginings, than in the feverish give-and-take of modern society. It let itself out more fully and freely, too, in the gentle repose of *tête-à-tête* talk than in the stimulating atmosphere of a big dining-room, or of Mrs. Bouverie Barton's celebrated Wednesday evening receptions. But while Hugh scintillated, Warren Relf's nature burned rather with a clear and steady flame. It was easy enough for anybody to admire Hugh; his strong points glittered in the eye of day: only those who dip a little below the surface ever reached the profounder depths of good and beauty that lay hid in such a mind as Warren's. Yet Elsie felt in her own soul it was a truer thing after all to love Warren than to love Hugh; a greater triumph to have won Warren's deep and earnest regard than to have impressed Hugh's fancy once with a selfish passion. She felt all that; but being a woman, of course she never acknowledged it. She went on fighting hard against her own heart, on behalf of the old dead worse love, and to the detriment of the new and living better one; and all the while she pretended to herself she was thereby displaying her profound affection and her noble consistency. She must never marry Warren, whom she truly loved, and who truly loved her, for the sake of that Hugh who had never loved her, and whom she herself could never have loved had she only known him as he really was in all his mean and selfish inner nature. That may be foolish, but it's intensely womanly. We must take women as they are. They were made so at first, and all our philosophy will never mend it.

She couldn't endure that any one should imagine she had forgotten her love and her sorrow for Hugh. She couldn't endure, after her experience with Hugh, that any man should take her, thus helpless and penniless. If she'd been an heiress like Winifred, now, things might perhaps have been a little different; if by marrying Warren she could have put him in a position to prosecute his art, as she would have wished him to prosecute it, without regard for the base and vulgar necessity of earning bread-and-cheese for himself and his family, she might possibly have consented in such a case to forego her own private and personal feelings, and to make him happy for art's sake and humanity's. But to burden his struggling life still further, when she knew how little his art brought him, and how much he longed to earn an income for his mother and Edie to retire upon—*that* she couldn't bear to face for a moment. She

would dismiss the subject; she would make him feel she could never be his; it was only tantalizing poor kind-hearted Warren to keep him dangling about any longer.

"Elsie," he said to her one day on the hills, as they strolled together, by olive and pinewood, among the asphodels and anemones, "I had another letter from London this morning. The market's looking up. Benson has sold the 'Rade de Villefranche.'"

"I'm so glad, Warren," Elsie answered warmly. "It's a sweet picture—one of your loveliest. Did you get a good price for i ?"

"Forty guineas. That's not so bad as prices go. So I'm going to buy Edie that new dinner dress you and I were talking about. I know you won't mind running over to Mentone and choosing some nice stuff at the draper's there for me. Things are looking up. There's no doubt I'm rising in the English market. My current quotations improve daily. Benson says he sold that bit to a rich American. Americans, if you can once manage to catch them, are capital customers—'patrons,' I suppose, one ought to say; but I decline to be patronized by a rich American. I think 'customer,' after all, a much truer and sincerer word— ten thousand times as manly and independent."

"So I think too. I hate patronage. It savours of flunkeydom; betrays the toadyism of fashionable art—the 'Portrait-of-a-Gentleman' style of painting.—But, oh, Warren, I'm so sorry the Rade's to be transported to America. It's such a graceful, delicate, dainty little picture. I quite loved it. To me that seems the most terrible part of all an artist's trials and troubles. There you toil and moil and slave and labour at one of your exquisite, poetical, self-absorbing pictures; you throw a part of your life, a share of your soul, a piece of your own inner spiritual being, on to your simple square of dead canvas; you make it live and breathe and feel almost; you work away at it, absorbed and entranced in it, living in it and dreaming of it, for days and weeks and months together; you give it a thousand last long loving touches; you alter and correct, and improve and modify; you wait till it all absolutely satisfies your own high and exacting critical standard; and then, after you've lavished on it your utmost care and skill and pains—after you've learned to know and to love it tenderly—after it's become to you something like your own child—an offspring of your inmost and deepest nature—you sell it away for prompt cash to a rich American, who'll hang it up in his brand-new drawing-room at St. Louis or Chicago between two horrid daubs by fashionable London or Paris painters, and who'll say to his friends with a smile after dinner: 'Yes, that's a pretty little thing enough in its way, that tiny sea-piece there. I gave forty guineas in Eng-

land for that: it's by Relf of London.—But observe this splendid
" Cleopatra " over here, just above the sideboard : she's a real
So-and-so '—torture itself will not induce the present chronicler
to name the particular painter of fashionable nudities whom
Elsie thus pilloried on the scaffold of her high disdain—' I
paid for that, sir, a cool twenty thousand dollars!'"

Warren smiled a smile of thrilling pleasure, and investigated
his boots with shy timidity. Such sympathy from her out-
weighed a round dozen of American purchasers. "Thank you,
Elsie," he said simply. " That's quite true. I've felt it myself.—
But still, in the end, all good work, if it's really good, will appeal
somehow, at some time, to somebody, somewhere. I confess I
often envy authors in that. Their finished work is impressed
upon a thousand copies, and scattered broadcast over all the
world. Sooner or later it's pretty sure to meet the eyes of most
among those who are capable of appreciating it.—But a painting
is a much more monopolist product. If the wrong man happens
at first to buy it and to carry it into the wholly wrong society,
the painter may feel for the moment his work is lost, and his
time thrown away, so far as any direct appreciation or loving
sympathy with his idea is concerned.—Still, Elsie, it gets its
reward in due time. When we're all dead and gone, some soul
will look upon the picture and be glad. And it's a great thing
to have sold the Rade, anyway, because of the dear old Mater
and Edie.—I'm able to do a great deal more for them now; I
hope I shall soon be in a position to keep them comfortably.—
And do you know, somehow, these last few years—I'm ashamed
to say it, but it's the fact none the less—I've begun to feel a
sort of nascent desire to be successful, Elsie."

Elsie dropped her voice a tone lower. "I'm sorry for that,
Warren," she answered shyly.

" Why so ? "

Elsie dissimulated. " Because one of the things I most admired
about you when I first knew you was your sturdy desire to do
good work for its own sake, and to leave success to take care of
itself in the dim background."

" But, Elsie, I've many more reasons now to wish for success.
—You know why—I've never told you, but I begin to hope—I've
ventured to hope the last few months—I know it's presumptuous
of me, but still I hope—that when I can earn enough to make a
wife happy—— "

Elsie stopped dead short at once on the narrow path that
wound in and out among the clambering pine-woods, and front-
ing him full, with her parasol planted firmly on the ground, cut
him off in a desperately resolute tone : " Warren, if I wouldn't
marry you unsuccessful, you may be quite sure success at any
rate would never, never induce me to marry you."

It was the first time in all her life she had said a single word about marriage before him, and Warren therefore at once accepted it, paradoxically but rightly, as a good omen. "Then you love me, Elsie?" he cried, all trembling.

Elsie's heart fluttered with painful tremors. "Don't ask me, Warren!" she murmured, thrilling. "Don't make me say so.— Don't worm it out of me!—Dear Warren, you know I like you dearly. I feel and have always felt towards you like a sister. After all I've suffered, don't torment me any more.—I can never, never, never marry you!"

"But you do love me, Elsie?"

Elsie's eyes fell irresolute to the ground. It was a hard fight between love and pride. But Warren's pleading face conquered in the end. "I do love you, Warren," she answered simply.

"Then I don't mind the rest," Warren cried with a joyous burst, seizing her hand in his. "If you love me, Elsie, I can wait for ever. Success or no success, marriage or no marriage, I can wait for ever. I only want to know you love me."

"You will have to wait for ever," Elsie answered low. "You have made me say the word, and in spite of myself I have said it. I love you, Warren, but I can never, never, never marry you!"

"And I say," Edie Relf remarked with much incisiveness, when Elsie told her bit by bit the whole story that same evening at the Villa Rossa, "that you treated him very shabbily indeed, and that Warren's a great deal too good and kind and sweet to you. Some girls don't know when they're well off. Warren's a brick—that's what I call him."

"That's what I call him too," Elsie answered, half tearful. "At least I would, if brick was a word I ever applied to anybody anywhere. But still—I can never, never, never marry him!"

"Thank goodness," Edie said, with a jerk of her head, "*I* wasn't born romantic and hysterical. Whenever any nice good fellow that I can really like swims into my ken and asks *me* to marry him—which unfortunately none of the nice good fellows of my acquaintance show the slightest inclination at present to do—I shall answer him promptly, 'Like a bird—Arthur,' or Thomas, or Guy, or Walter, or Reginald, or whatever else his nice good name may happen to be—Mr. Hatherley's is Arthur —and proceed at once to make him happy for ever. But some people seem to prefer tantalizing them. For my own part, my dear, I've a distinct preference for making men happy whenever possible. I was born to make a good man happy, and I'd make him happy with the greatest pleasure in life, if only the good man would recognize my abilities for the production of happi-

ness, and give me the desired opportunity for translating my
benevolent wishes towards him into actual practice. But good
men are painfully scarce nowadays. They don't swarm. They
retire bashfully. Very few of them seem to float by accident in
their gay shallops towards the port of San Remo."

CHAPTER XXXII.

ON TRIAL.

MATTERS at Whitestrand had been going, meanwhile, from bad
to worse. Winifred never spoke another word to Hugh about
Elsie's watch. Her pride prevented her. She would not stoop
to demand an explanation. And Hugh had no explanation of
his own to volunteer. No ready lie rose spontaneous to his
lips. He dropped the subject, then and for ever.

But the question of the encroachments could not be quite so
cavalierly dropped: it pressed itself insidiously and silently
upon Hugh's attention. An eminent engineer came down from
London to inspect the sand-drifts, shortly after Hatherley's
visit. By that time, the sand had risen high on the post of the
aggressive notice-board which informed the would-be tourist
explorer, with the usual churlishness and the usual ignorance
of English procedure, that Trespassers would be Prosecuted
with the Utmost Rigour of the Law. The ocean, however,
refused to be terrorized, and trespassed unabashed in the very
face of the alarming notice. Hugh took his new ally down to
inspect the threatened corner of the estate. The eminent
engineer stroked a reflective chin and remarked cheerfully with
a meditative smile that currents were very ticklish things to
deal with, on their own ground : that when you interfered with
the natural course of a current, you never could tell which way
it would go next; and that diverting it was much like taking a
leap in the dark, as far as probable consequences to the shore
were concerned. After which reassuring vaticinations, the
eminent engineer proceeded at once with perfect confidence to
erect an expensive and ingenious breakwater off the site of the
poplar, which strained the slender balloon of Hugh's remaining
credit to the very verge of its utmost bursting point. A year
passed by in the work of building and throwing out the breakwater : and as soon as it was finished, with much acclamation,
a scour set in just round its sides which ate away the grounds
behind even faster than ever. The eminent engineer, pocketing
his cheque, stroked his chin once more in placid contentment,

and observed with the complacency of a scientific looker-on:
"Just as I told you. It's impossible to calculate the exact
effect of these things beforehand. The scour will do more
harm than the sea did. We have the satisfaction of knowing,
however, that we've done our duty. Perhaps, now, the safest
thing for the estate would be to turn right round and pull it
all down again."

The estate, in fact, was simply doomed. Æolian, Pactolian,
indeed : ah me, the irony of it! Those Æolian sands were overwhelming Whitestrand. The poplar had formed its one frail
support. In destroying the poplar, Hugh had simply outwitted
himself. No earthly science could now repair that fatal step.
Physicians were in vain. Engineers and breakwaters were of
no avail. The cruel crawling sea had begun remorselessly to
claim its own, and day after day it claimed it piecemeal.

Nor was that all. Hugh's affairs were getting more and more
involved in other ways also. Those were the days of the
decline of Squiredom. Agricultural depression had told upon
the rents. Turnips were a failure. Mangolds were feeble.
Hessian fly had made waste straw of old Grimes's wheat crops.
Barley had never done so badly for years. Foot-and-mouth
disease and pleuro-pneumonia had combined with American
competition and Australian mutton to lower prices and to
starve landlords. Time was, indeed, when Hugh would have
laughed aloud at the bare idea of being seriously affected by
the fall in corn or taking a personal interest in the ridiculous
details of the diseases of cattle. Such loathsome things were
the business of the veterinaries. Now, however, he laughed on
the wrong side of his mouth : he complained bitterly of the
supineness of government in not stamping out the germs of
rinderpest, and in taking so little care of the soil of England.
Buff all his days till then, by political conviction, he began to
go over to the Blues out of sheer chagrin. He doubted the
wisdom of free trade, and coquetted openly with the local
apostles of retributive protection. But rents came in worse and
worse for all that, at each successive Whitestrand audit. The
interest on the mortgage was hard to raise, and the servants'
wages at the Hall, it was whispered about, had fallen into
arrears for a whole quarter. Clearly the young Squire must be
short of funds; and nothing was afloat to help his exchequer
into safer waters.

But drowning men cling to the proverbial straw. For his
own part, Hugh had high hopes at first of his " Life's Philosophy." He had trimmed his little bark most cunningly, he
thought, to tempt the stormy sea of popular approbation.
There was the big long poem for heavy ballast, and the songs
and occasional pieces in his lightest vein for cork belts to

redress the balance. Sooner or later, the world must surely
catch glimpses of the truth, that it still enclosed a great
unknown Poet! He waited for the storm of applause to begin;
the critics would doubtless soon get up their concerted pæan.
But one day, a few weeks after the volume was published, he
took up a copy of the *Bystander*, that most superior review—
the special organ of his own special clique—and read in it with
hushed breath   a hostile notice of his new and hopeful
volume. His heart sank as he read and read. Line after line,
the sickening sense of failure deepened upon him. It had not
been so in the old days. Then, the critics had hasted to bring
him butter in a lordly dish. But now, all that was utterly
changed. He read with a cheek flushed with indignation. At
last, the review touched bottom. "Mr. Massinger," said his
critic in concluding his notice, " has long since retired, we all
know, into Lowther Arcadia. There, among the mimic ranges
of the Suffolk sandhills—a doll's paradise of dale and mountain
—he has betaken himself with his pretty little pipe to the green
side of a pretty little knoll, and has tuned his throat to a pretty
little lay, all about a series of pretty little ladies, of the usual
insipid Lowther-Arcadian style of beauty. Now, these waxen-
faced damsels somehow fail to interest us. Their cheeks are
all most becomingly red; their eyes are all most liquidly blue;
their locks are all of the yellowest tow; and their philosophy is
 ⌐ cheap and ineffective mixture of the Elegant Extracts with
 he choicest old crusted English morals of immemorial pro-
 erbial wisdom. In short, they are unfortunately stuffed with
sawdust. The long poem which gives a title to the volume,
on the other hand, though molluscoid in its flabbiness, is as
ambitious as it is feeble, and as dull as it is involved. Here,
for example, selected from some five hundred equally inflated
stanzas, are the modest views Mr. Massinger now holds on his
own position in the material Cosmos. The scene, we ought to
explain, is laid in Oxford: the time, midnight or a little later:
and the Bard speaks *in propriâ personâ* :—

> "'The city lies below me wrapped in slumber;
>   Mute and unmoved in all her streets she lies :
> 'Mid rapid thoughts that throng me without number
>   Flashes the phantom of an old surmise.
> Her hopes and fears and griefs are all suspended :
>   Ten thousand souls throughout her precincts take
> Sleep, in whose bosom life and death are blended,
>   And I alone awake.

> "' Am I alone the solitary centre
>   Of all the seeming universe around,
> With mocking senses, through whose portals enter
>   Unmeaning phantasies of sight and sound?

C

> Are all the countless minds wherewith I people
> The empty forms that float before my eyes
> Vain as the cloud that girds the distant steeple
> With snowy canopies ?
>
> " 'Yet though the world be but myself unfolded—
> Soul bent again on soul in mystic play—
> No less each sense and thought and act is moulded
> By dead necessities I may not sway.
> Some mightier power against my will can move me ;
> Some potent nothing force and overawe :
> Though I be all that is, I feel above me
> The godhead of blind law ! '

" Seven or eight pages of this hysterical, cartilaginous, invertebrate nonsense have failed to convince us that Mr. Massinger is really, as he seems implicitly to believe, the hub of the universe, and the sole intelligent or sentient being within the entire circle of organic creation. Many other poets, indeed, have thought the same, but few have been so candid as to express their opinion. We are tempted, therefore, to conclude our notice of our Bard's singular views as to Mr. Massinger's Place in Nature with a small apologue, in his own best manner, which we will venture to entitle—

" 'MARINE PHILOSOPHY IN SILLY SUFFOLK.

> " ' A jellyfish swam an East Anglian sea,
> And he said, "This world, it consists of me.
> There's nothing above, and there's nothing below,
> That a jellyfish ever can possibly know—
> Since we've got no sight or hearing or smell—
> Beyond what our single sense can tell.
> Now all we can learn from the sense of touch
> Is the fact of our feelings, viewed as such ;
> But to think they have any external cause
> Is an inference clean against logical laws.
> Again, to suppose, as I've hitherto done,
> There are other jellyfish under the sun
> Is a pure assumption that can't be backed
> By one jot of proof or one single fact :
> And being a bit of a submarine poet,
> I've written some amateur lines to show it.
> In fact (like Hume) I distinctly doubt
> If there's anything else at all about :
> For the universe simply centres in me,
> And if I were not, why nothing would be ! "
>   Just then, a shark, who was passing by,
> Gobbled him down, in the twink of an eye :
> And he died, with a few convulsive twists :
> —But, somehow, the universe still exists.' "

Hugh laid down the *Bystander* on the table by his side with a burning sense of wrong and indignation. The measure he himself had often meted to others, therewithal had it been meted to him; and he realized now in his own person the bitterness of the stings he had often inflicted out of pure wantonness on endless young and anonymous authors. And how unjust, too, this sweeping condemnation, when he came to think of his splendid "Ode to Manetho," his touching "Lines on the Death of a Skye Terrier," his exquisitely humorous "Song of Fee-faw-fum!" He knew they were good, every verse and word of them. This was a crushing review, and from his own familiar friend as well; for he saw at once from that unmistakable style that it was Mitchison who had penned this cruel criticism. Cheyne Row had clearly cast off her recalcitrant son. He was to it now an outcast and a pariah, a wicked deserter to the camp of the Philistines.

At the same moment, Winifred, on the sofa opposite, coughing her dry little cough from time to time, was flushing painfully over some funny passage or other she was reading with much gusto in the *Charing Cross Review*. They seldom spoke unnecessarily to one another nowadays. They were leading a life of mutual avoidance, as far as possible, communicating only on strictly practical topics, when occasion demanded, and not even then in the most amicable spirit. But just at that moment, Winifred's flushed face filled Hugh with intense and profound suspicion. What could she be reading that made her blush so?

"Let me see it," he cried, as Winifred tried to smuggle away he paper unseen under a pile of magazines.

"No, no! There's nothing in it!" Winifred answered nervously.

"I *must* see," Hugh went on, and snatched it from her hand. Winifred fought hard to tear it or to destroy it. But Hugh was too strong for her. He caught it and opened it. A single phrase on a torn page caught his eye as he did so. "Verses addressed to Mr. Massinger of Whitestrand Hall, formerly a poet." He glanced at the end. They were signed "A. H."—It was Arthur Hatherley.

Bohemia had declared open war upon him. He saw why. Those tell-tale words, "Of Whitestrand Hall," struck the keynote of its virtuous indignation. And that fellow Relf, too, had poisoned the mind of Cheyne Row against him. Henceforth, he might expect no quarter thence. His own familiar friends had turned to rend him. No more could he hope to roll the cheerful log. His dream of literary glory was gone—clean gone—vanished for ever.

Winifred had lifted the paper which Hugh flung from him, and was skimming the *Bystander* review meanwhile. Her cheek flushed hotter and redder still. But she said never a word in any way about it. She wouldn't seem to have noticed the attack. "Shall I accept Lady Mortmayne's invitation?" she asked with a chilly heartsinking.

Bohemia had clearly turned against them; but Philistia at least, Philistia was left to console their bosoms. If one can't be a poet, one can at any rate be a snob. In the bitterness of his heart, Hugh answered: "Yes. Go anywhere on earth to a body with a handle." Then he tried to rouse himself, to put on a cheerful and unconcerned manner. "I like to patronize art," he went on with a hard smile, "and as a work of art I consider Lady Mortmayne almost perfect."

Winifred laid down her paper on the table. "What shall I say to her?" she asked glassily. She was a timid letter-writer. Even since their estrangement, Hugh most often dictated her society notes for her.

"Dear Lady Mortmayne, we shall have great pleasure—— " Hugh began with vigour.

"Isn't 'we have great pleasure' better English, Hugh?" Winifred asked quietly, as she examined her nib with close attention.

"No," Hugh blurted back, "certainly not. Shall have great pleasure's quite good enough for me, so I suppose it's good enough for you too—isn't it?"

"I don't know about that. Literary English and society English are two distinct dialects."

Hugh bit his lip with an angry look. He was getting positively cruel now. "If you can write so well," he muttered between his clenched teeth, "write it yourself. 'Great pleasure in accepting your kind invitation for Thursday next.'"

"Doesn't 'Thursday the 17th' sound rather more formal?" Winifred asked once more, looking up from her paper.

"Of course it does. That's just my reason for carefully avoiding it. Why on earth should you go out of your way to be so precious formal? Thursday next's what everybody says in conversation. Write exactly as you always speak. Formal, indeed! Such absurd rubbish with a next-door neighbour!"

"But she writes, 'Lady Mortmayne requests the pleasure.' I think I ought to answer her in the third person."

"That's because she was sending out ever so many invitations at once, all exactly alike. 'Lady Mortmayne requests the bother—I mean the pleasure—of Mr. and Mrs. So-and-so's company.' It's different when you're answering people you know intimately. You needn't be absolutely wooden then. Besides, you've got to make that long explanation about those dahlia roots you remember you promised her. No literary man in all England would trust himself to write so complicated a letter as the dahlia roots must make, in the third person. Our language isn't adapted to it; it can't be done. But fools rush

in where angels fear to tread, we all know perfectly. Write it,
if you choose, in the third person."

"I think I will. I'll begin all over again. Thanks very much
for calling me a fool. I won't return the compliment and call you
an angel. 'Mr. and Mrs. Massinger have great pleasure——'"

"*Will* have great pleasure!"

"Have great pleasure. I prefer it so, thank you. It's better
English. 'Have great pleasure in accepting Lady Mortmayne's
kind invitation for Thursday the 17th, and will bring the dahlias
she promised——'"

"Who promised? Lady Mortmayne?"

"Oh, bother! I mean 'the dahlias Mrs. Massinger promised,
which she would have brought before, but she was unfortunately
prevented by her gardener having quite inadvertently——'"

"For Heaven's sake, split it up into short sentences," Hugh
cried, on tenter-hooks. "I couldn't let such a note as that go
out of my house—I mean, our house, Winifred—if my life
depended upon it. A man of letters allow his wife to make
such an exhibition of impossible English! I won't dictate to
you in the third person—the thing's impossible: I'll be no
party to murdering our mother tongue—but you might at least
say, 'Mrs. Massinger will at the same time bring the dahlias she
promised Lady Mortmayne. They would have been sent before'
—and so forth, and so forth, in logical clauses. My English
tyle may not perhaps suit the exalted standard of our friends
1 the *Bystander*, but I can at least avoid running a whole letter
.uto one long tortuous snake-like sentence. I never lose myself
in the sands of rhetoric. My English will parse, if it won't
construe."

"I wish I was clever," Winifred said, growing red, "and then
I could write my own letters without you."

"'Be good, my child, and let who will be clever:' Charles
Kingsley," Hugh quoted provokingly. "'An honest man's the
noblest work of God:' Alexander Pope. (I think it was Pope:
or was it Sam Johnson?) A placid woman runs him close, ecod:
Hugh Massinger. Ecod's a powerful weak rhyme, I admit, but
what can you expect from a mere impromptu? I only wish all
women were placid. Well, the moral of these three immortal
lines, selected from the works of three poets in three different
ages born (Dryden), is simply this—you do very well as you are,
Winifred. Don't seek to be clever. It doesn't suit you. Take
my advice. Leave it alone.—For if you do, you'll find it in the
end a complete failure."

"Hugh! You insult me."

"Very well then, my dear. You will be able to exercise
Christian patience and resignation in pocketing the insult—as I
have to do from you very often."

Winifred shut down her writing-caso with a bang and burst, not into tears, but into an uncontrollable fit of violent coughing. She coughed and coughed till her face was purple and livid with the effort. Hugh watched her silently, as hard as adamant. She had often coughed this way of late. The habit was growing on her. Hugh thought she ought to cure herself of it.

"I shall go up next week again to consult Sir Anthony Wraxall," she said at last, when she recovered her breath, gasping and choking. "Will you go with me, Hugh?"

"We've no cash now to waste on junketing and gadding about in town," Hugh answered gloomily. "A pretty time to talk about riotous living, with the servants' wages all overdue, and duns bothering at the door for their wretched money. My presence could hardly give you any appreciable pleasure. You can stop at the dingy old lodgings in Albert Row, and Mrs. Bouverie Barton will help gad about with you. You can trapes together over half London."

Winifred bowed her poor head down in silence. Her heart was sick. It was full to bursting. This was all she had bought with the fee-simple of Whitestrand.

That moment the servant came in with a paper on a tray. "What is it?" Hugh asked, glancing listlessly towards it.

"It's the Queen's taxes, sir," the maid answered : the financial crisis had long since compelled them to discharge their last surviving footman.

"Tell the Queen she must call again," Hugh burst out savagely. "She can't have them. She may whistle for her money.—Queen's taxes indeed! The butcher and the baker'll be calling to get their bills paid next! But they won't succeed ; that's one comfort. You can't get blood out of a stone, thank goodness."

CHAPTER XXXIII.

AN ARTISTIC EVENT.

"Mr. WARREN RELF," said the daintily etched invitation card, "requests the pleasure of a visit from Mr. and Mrs. Bouverie Barton and friends to a Private View of his Paintings and Water-colour Sketches, on Saturday, October the 3rd, from 2.30 to 6 P.M., at 128, Bletchingley Road, South Kensington."

Such a graceful little invitation card never was seen, neatly designed by the artist himself, with a bold flight of sea-gulls engaged in winging their way across the upper left-hand corner; and a stretch of stormy waves bestridden by a fishing-smack in

full career before the brisk breeze occupying the larger part
of its broad face in very delicate and exquisite outline. When
Winifred Massinger saw it carelessly stuck aside among a heap
of others on Mrs. Bouverie Barton's occasional table in South
Audley Street, she took it up with a start and examined it
closely. "Mr. Warren Relf!" she cried, in a tone of some
surprise. "Then you know him, Mrs. Barton? I didn't remember he was one of your circle. But there, of course you
know everybody.—What a sweet little etching !"

"What ? Mr. Warren Relf?—Oh yes, I know him. Not, I'm
afraid, a very successful artist, as yet; but they say he has merit
—in his own way, merit. And he's rising now; a coming
man, I'm told, in his special line. Mr. Mitchison thinks his
delicacy of touch and purity of colour are something really quite
remarkable. I'm going to see these new pictures of his on
Saturday, if I can sandwich him in edgeways between the
Society for the Higher Education of Women and the Richter
concert or tea at the MacKinnons'. I've only five engagements
for Saturday. Quite an empty day.—Have you got a card for
the private view yourself, dear ? "

"No," Winifred answered with a slight blush. "My husband
knew Mr. Relf quite intimately once upon a time; but the fact
is, somehow, since our marriage, a coolness seems to have sprung
up between them—I don't know why; perhaps from the ordinary
human perversity. At any rate, Hugh won't even so much as
ee him now. Mr. Relf's been yachting down our way the last
wo or three summers, and Hugh positively wouldn't let me ask
him in to have a cup of afternoon tea with us in the garden at
Whitestrand.—But I should like to see his new pictures immensely.—I used to think his pieces awfully funny, I remember,
and quite meaningless, in the old days, down in dear old Suffolk;
but Mr. Hatherley tells me that was only my unregenerate
nature, and that they're really beautiful—a great deal too good
for me. He considers Mr. Relf a very great painter, and has
wonderful hopes about his artistic future. I wish I could find
out what I thought of them nowadays, after my taste's been
educated and turned topsy-turvy by contact with so much
æsthetic society."

"Well, then, would you like to go with us, dear ?" Mrs.
Bouverie Barton asked kindly.

Winifred turned over the card with a wistful look. "It says,
'Mr. and Mrs. Bouverie Barton *and friends,*'" she repeated with
emphasis. "So of course you can take whoever you like with
you, can't you, Mrs. Barton?—Saturday the 3rd, from 2.30 to 6
P.M.—I think I might.—I'll risk it anyhow.—That'd suit me
admirably. My appointment with Sir Anthony's for two
precisely."

" Your appointment with Sir Anthony ? " Mrs. Barton echoed in a grieved undertone.

Winifred coughed—such a nasty dry little hacking cough. " Why, yes, Sir Anthony Wraxall," she answered, checking herself with some difficulty from a brief paroxysm of her usual trouble. "I've come up this week, in fact, on purpose to consult him. Hugh made me come, my lungs have been so awfully odd lately. I've seen Sir Anthony twice already; and he's punched me and pummelled me and pulled me about till there's not much left of me whole anywhere; so on Saturday he means by summary process to get rid of the rest of me altogether. Would you mind calling for me at Sir Anthony's at three sharp? He gives me an hour, a whole hour; an unusual concession for a man whose time's money—worth a golden guinea every three minutes."

" My dear," Mrs. Bouverie Barton put in tenderly—everybody knows Mrs. Bouverie Barton, the most charming and sympathetic hostess in literary London—" you hardly seem fit to go running about town sight-seeing at present.—Does Mr. Massinger seriously realize how extremely weak and ill you are?—It scarcely seems to me you ought to be troubling your poor little head about private views or anything of the sort with a cough like that upon you."

" Oh, it isn't much, I assure you, dear Mrs. Barton," Winifred answered with a quiet sigh, the tears coming up into her eyes as she spoke at the touch of sympathy. " Hugh doesn't think it's at all serious. I've been a good deal troubled and worried of late, that's all.—Sir Anthony'll set me all right soon.—You see I've had a great deal of trouble." The tears stood brimming her poor dim eyes. Wife and mother as she had been already, she was still young, very, very young. Her face looked pale and sadly pathetic.

Mrs. Bouverie Barton raised the small white hand gently in her own. It was thin and delicate, with long and slender consumptive fingers. Mrs. Barton's mouth grew graver for a moment. That poor child had suffered much, she thought to herself, and she had probably much to suffer in future. How much, indeed, it was not in Winifred's cramped little nature to confide to any one.

At 128, Bletchingley Road, the ancestral home of all the Relfs – for one generation—a tiny eight-roomed London house in a side-street of intense South Kensington—all was bustle and flutter and feverish excitement. Edie Relf to-day was absolutely in her element. It was her joy in life, indeed, to compass the Impossible. And the Impossible now stared her frankly in the face in the concrete shape of a geometrical absurdity. She had undertaken to make the less contain the greater, all the axioms of Euclid to the contrary notwithstanding. What are space and time to a clever woman? Of no more importance in her scheme of things than to Emmanuel Kant or to Shadworth Hodgson. The Relfs had issued no fewer than three hundred and twenty separate invitation cards, each with that extensible india-rubber clause, "and friends," so capable of indefinite and incalculable expansion. Now, the little front drawing-room at Bletchingley Road could just be induced, when the furniture was abolished by Act of Parliament, and the piano removed upstairs to the back bedroom, to accommodate at a pinch some thirty-five persons, mostly chairless. Three hundred and twenty invited guests, plus an indefinite expansion under the casual category of desultory friends, cannot be reduced by any known process of arithmetic or mensuration into the limits of a space barely sufficient to supply standing-room for thirty-five. But that was just where Edie Relf's organizing genius knew itself in the presence of an emergency worthy of its steel. When an insoluble difficulty dawned serene upon her puzzled view, Edie Relf's spirits rose at once, Antæus-like, to the occasion, and soared beyond the narrow and hampering limitations of mundane geometry. "My dear Edie," Mrs. Relf cried in a voice of despair, "we can never, never, never pack them in anyhow."

"Herrings in a box would find themselves comparatively roomy and comfortable," Warren murmured, with a glance of slack despondency round the four scanty walls of the tiny drawing-room. "How on earth could you ever think of asking so many?"

"Nonsense, my dears!" Edie answered with a confident smile that presaged victory. "Leave that to me. It's my proper business. I see it all. The commanding officer should never be hampered by futile predictions of defeat and dishonour. Of course they won't come, the greater part of them. They never do rush, I regret to say, to inspect your immortal works, Warren. But still we must arrange, for all that, as if we expected the whole united British people—in case of a rush, don't you know, mother. Some day, I feel certain the rush will arrive; a Duke will invest his spare cash in 'Off the Nore; Morning,' and hang it up visibly to all beholders on the silver-gilt walls of his own dining-room. The picture-buying classes, with rolls of money jingling and clinking in their trousers' pockets, will see and admire that magnificent *chef-d'œuvre*—or at least, if they don't know how to admire, will determine to back a Duke's judgment—and will hurry down in their millions, with blank cheque-books protruding from their flaps, to crowd the studio and buy up the lot at a valuation. I confess even I should have some difficulty in seating and providing tea for the millions. But this lot's easy—a mere bagatelle. Let me see. We've only sent out cards, I think, for a poor trifle of three hundred and twenty."

"No," Warren corrected very gravely. "Three hundred and twenty cards, you mean, for six hundred and forty wives and husbands."

"Some of them are bachelors, my dear," Edie answered with a sagacious nod; "and some old maids, who never by any chance buy anything. As far as art's concerned, the old maid may be regarded as a mere cipher. But, for argument's sake, since you want to argufy, like the parson in the Black Country, we'll say six hundred. Now, what's six hundred human beings in a house like this—a mansion—a palace—a perfect Vatican— distributed over nearly four hours, and equally diffused throughout the entire establishment? Of course, my dear, you at once apply the doctrine of averages. That's scientific. Each party stops not longer than an hour at the very outside. You never have two hundred in the place at once. And what's two hundred? A mere trifle! I declare it affords no scope at all for a girl's ingenuity. Like our respected ancestor, Warren Hastings, I stand aghast at my own moderation.—I really wish, mother, now I come to think of it, we'd sent out invitations for a thousand."

"Six hundred's quite enough for me, I'm sure," Warren replied, glancing round the room once more in palpable doubt. "How do you mean to arrange for them, Edie?"

"Oh, easy enough. Nothing could be simpler. I'll tell you how. First of all, you throw open the folding-doors—or rather, to save the room at the sides, you lift them bodily off their hinges, and stick them out of the dining-room window into the back garden."

"They won't go through," Warren objected, measuring with his eye.

"Rubbish, my dear! Won't go through, indeed! You men have no imagination and no invention. You manufacture difficulties out of pure obstructiveness. If they won't go through whole, why, just take out the panels and unglue the wood-work, that's all.—Very well, then; that throws the draw- ing-room and dining-room into one good big reception-room, from which of course we remove all the furniture. Next, we range the chairs in a long row round the sides for the old ladies —the old ladies are very important; keep 'em downstairs, or else they'll prevent their husbands from buying—and let the men and the able-bodied girls stand up and group themselves in picturesque clusters here and there about the vacant centre. What could be easier, simpler, or more effective? A room treated so furnishes itself automatically with human properties. With tact and care, we could easily squeeze in some seventy or eighty."

"We could," Warren answered, after a mental calculation of square area.—"But how about the pictures?"

"Hear him, mother! Oh, but men are helpless! Where should the pictures be but up in the studio, stupid! We wouldn't take all the people up to see them at once, of course. You and I would go around, looking very affable, with a professional smile—so, you know—perpetually playing about the corners of our mouths, and carry off the men with the most purchasing faces in constant relays up to admire the immortal master-pieces. Meanwhile, mother and Mr. Hatherley, down below here, would do the polite to the old ladies and undertake the deportment business. Or perhaps Mr. Hatherley'd better be stationed on guard upstairs, to fire off some of his gushing critical remarks from time to time about the aërial perspective and the middle distances. Mr. Hatherley always knows just what to say to weigh down the balance for a hesitating purchaser."

"Edie," Warren cried, flinging himself down with a disgusted face upon the dining-room sofa, "I hate all this horrid advertising and touting, for all the world as if one were the catchpenny proprietor of a patent medicine, instead of an honest hard-working British artist!"

"I know you do, my dear boy," Edie answered imperturbably; "and that's all the more reason why those who have the charge of you should undertake to push you and tout for you against your will, till they positively make you achieve the success you yourself will never have the meanness to try for.— But, thank goodness, *I* don't mind puffing. I'm intriguer enough myself for the whole family. If it hadn't been for my egging you on, and pestering you and bullying you and keeping you up to it, we should never have got up this private view of your things at all.—And now, having started and arranged the entire show, I mean to work it my own way without interference. I'm the boss who runs this concern, I can tell you, Warren. Decidedly, Mr. Hatherley shall stop upstairs, with his hair down his back, and deliver wild panegyrics in an ecstatic voice on the aërial perspective and the middle distances. —I shall nudge him when a probable purchaser comes in, to make him turn on the aërial perspective.—I only wish with all my heart we had dear old Elsie over here to help us."

"But the tea, Edie? How about the tea, dear?" Mrs. Relf interposed with a doubtful countenance.

"And you too, Brutus!" her daughter cried, looking down on her with a despondent shake of the head, which implied a profound and melancholy shock of disappointment. "I thought, mother, I'd brought you up better than that!—The tea, my beloved, will be duly laid out in your own bedroom, which I mean to transform, for this occasion only, with entirely new scenery, decorations, and properties throughout, into a gorgeously furnished oriental lounge and enchanted coffee divan. There, Martha, attired as a Circassian slave—or at least in her best bib and tucker—shall serve out ices, sherbet, and spicèd dainties every one from silken Samarcand to cedared Lebanon. The door into my own bedroom will also be open, and in that spacious apartment we shall have a sort of grand supplementary tea and refreshment room, where the Jacksons' parlour-maid, borrowed for the occasion, as Circassian number two, and becomingly endued in a Liberty apron and a small red cap (price ninepence), shall dispense claret-cup, sponge-cake, and Hamburg grapes to the deserving persons who have earned their restoratives by the encouragement of art through a judicious purchase. The thing's as easy as ABC. I've not the least doubt it'll run me off my legs. I shall perish in the attempt—but I shall die victorious."

"In your own bedroom, dear!" Mrs. Relf cried aghast. "You'll have the tea in your own bedroom! But where on earth shall we sleep, Edie?"

Edie looked down at her once more with a solemn glance of high disdain. "Sleep!" she cried. "Did you say *sleep*, mother? The craven wretch who dreams of sleeping at such a crises is unworthy of being Warren Relf's progenitor.—Or ought it to be progenitrix in the feminine, I wonder?—We shall sleep, if at all, my dear (which I greatly doubt), on the floor in the box-room, already occupied by the iron legs of the three best bedsteads.—But don't be afraid. Leave it all to me, darling. Trust your daughter; and your daughter, as usual, will pull you through. If there's anything on earth I love, it's a jolly good muddle."

And jolly as the muddle undoubtedly was, Edie Relf did pull them through in the end with triumphant strategy. Saturday the 3rd was a brilliant success. Bletchingley Road, that mere suburban byway, had never before in its checkered career beheld so many real live carriages together. The six hundred, or at least a very fair proportion of them, boldly they drove and well, down that narrow side street. All the world wondered. The neighbours looked on and admired with vicarious pride. They felt themselves raised in the social scale by their close proximity to so fashionable a gathering. Number 128 itself was a changed character; it hardly knew its own ground-plan. In the drawing-room and dining-room, thrown wide into one, a goodly collection of artists and picture-buyers and that poor residuum the general public, streamed through incessantly in a constant tide on its way to the studio. The tearoom (late Mrs. Relf's bedroom) blazed out resplendent in borrowed plumes—oriental rugs, Japanese fans, and hanging parasols, arranged *à la* Liberty. Rout seats covered with eastern stuffs lined the walls and passages. The studio, in particular, proudly posed as a work of art of truly Whistleresque magnificence. Talk about tone! The effect was unique. Warren Relf himself, who for three nights previously had "had a bed out" at the lodgings next door, and swallowed down a hasty chop for luncheon at the Cheyne Row Club, had superintended in person the hanging of the wonderful sage-green cretonne and the pale maize silk that so admirably threw up the dainty colours of his delicate and fantastic sea-pieces. Elsewhere, Edie alone had reigned supreme. And as two of the clock chimed from Kensington church tower on that eventful afternoon, she murmured aside to her mother, with an enraptured gaze at the scarlet and green *kakemonos* on the wall of the staircase : "My dear, there's not a speck of dust in this house, nor a bone in my body that isn't aching."

When the hired man from the mews behind flung open the drawing-room door in his lordly way and announced in a very loud voice, "Mrs. Bouverie Barton and Mrs. Hugh Massinger," neither Warren nor Edie was in the front room to hear the startling announcement, which would certainly for the moment have taken their breath away. For communications between the houses of Relf and Massinger had longed since ceased. But Warren and Edie were both upstairs. So Winifred and her hostess passed idly in (just shaking hands by the doorway with good old Mrs. Relf, who never by any chance caught anybody's name) and mingled shortly with the mass of the visitors. Winifred was very glad indeed of that, for she wanted to escape observation. Sir Anthony's report had been far from reassuring. She preferred to remain as much in the background as possible that afternoon : all she wished was merely to observe and to listen.

As she stood there mingling with the general crowd and talking to some chance acquaintance of old London days, she happened to overhear two scraps of conversation going on behind her. The first was one that mentioned no names; and yet, by some strange feminine instinct, she was sure it was of herself the speakers were talking.

"Oh yes," one voice said in a low tone, with the intonation that betrays a furtive side-glance; "she's far from strong—in fact, very delicate. He married her for her money—of course : that's clear. She hadn't much else, poor little thing, except a certain short-lived *beauté du diable*, to recommend her. And

she has no go in her; she won't live long. You remember what
Galton remarks about heiresses? They're generally the last
decadent members, he says, of a moribund stock whose strength
is failing.   They bear no children, or if any, weaklings : most of
them break down with their first infant; and they die at last
prematurely of organic feebleness. Why, he just sold himself
outright for the poor girl's property; that's the plain English of
it; and now, I hear, with his extravagant habits, he's got himself after all into monetary difficulties."

"Agricultural depression?" the second voice inquired—an
older man's and louder.

"Worse than that, I fear; agricultural depression and an
encroaching sea. Besides which, he spends too freely.—But
excuse me, Dr. Moutrie," in a very low tone: "I'm afraid the
lady's rather near us."

Winifred strained her ears to the utmost to hear the rest;
but the voices had sunk too low now to catch a sound, and
the young man with whom she was supposed to be talking had
evidently got tired of the very perfunctory Yeses and Noes she
was dealing out to him right and left at irregular intervals with
charming irrelevance. She roused herself, and endeavoured
spasmodically to regain the lost thread of her proper conversation. But even as she did so, another voice, far more distinct,
from a lady in front, caught her attention with the name " Miss
Challoner."   Winifred pricked up her ears incontinently.
Could it be of her Elsie that those two were talking? Challoner's not such a *very* uncommon name, to be sure! And yet
—and yet, there are not so many Miss Challoners, either,
distributed up and down the surface of Europe, as to make
the coincidence particularly improbable. Challoners are not
so plentiful as blackberries. It might every bit as well be Elsie
as any other Miss Challoner unattached. Winifred strained her
ears once more to catch their talk with quickened interest.

"Oh yes," the second lady addressed made answer cheerfully;
"she was very well when we last saw her in April at San Remo.
We had the next villa to the Relfs on the hillside, you know.
But Miss Challoner doesn't come to England now; she was
going as usual to St. Martin Lantosque to spend the summer,
when we left the Riviera. She always goes there as soon as the
San Remo season's over."

"How did the Relfs first come to pick her up?" the other
speaker asked curiously.

"Oh, I fancy it was Mr. Warren Relf himself who made her
acquaintance somewhere unearthly down in Suffolk, where she
used to be a governess. He's always there, I believe, lying on
a mudbank, yachting and sketching."

Winifred could restrain her curiosity no longer. "I beg your pardon," she said, leaning forward eagerly, "but I think you mentioned a certain Miss Challoner. May I ask, does it happen by any chance to be Elsie Challoner, who was once at Girton? Because, if so, she was a governess of mine, and I haven't heard of her for a long time past. Governesses drop out of one's world so fast. I should be glad to know where she's living at present."

The lady nodded. "Her name's Elsie," she said with a quiet inclination, "and she was certainly a Girton girl; but I hardly think she can be the same you mention. I should imagine, indeed, she's a good deal too young a girl to have been your governess."

It was innocently said, but Winifred's face was one vivid flush of mingled shame and humiliation. Talk about *beauté du diable* indeed; she never knew before she had grown so very plain and ancient. "I'm not quite so old as I look, perhaps," she answered hastily. "I've had a great deal to break me down. But I'm glad to learn where Elsie is, anyhow. You said she was living at San Remo, I fancy?"

"At San Remo. Yes. She spends her winters there. For the summers, she always goes up to St. Martin."

"Thank you," Winifred answered with a throbbing heart. "I'm glad to have found out at last what's become of her.— Mrs. Barton, if you can tear yourself away from Dr. and Mrs. Tyacke, who are always so alluring, suppose we go upstairs now and look at the pictures."

In the studio, Warren Relf recognized her at once, and with much trepidation came up to speak to her. It would all be out now, he greatly feared; and Hugh would learn at last that Elsie was living. For Winifred's own sake—she looked so pale and ill—he would fain have kept the secret to himself a few months longer.

Winifred held out her hand frankly. She liked Warren; she had always liked him; and besides, Hugh had forbidden her to see him. Her lips trembled, but she was bold, and spoke. "Mr. Relf," she said with quiet earnestness, "I'm so glad to meet you here to-day again—glad on more than one account. You go to San Remo often, I believe. Can you tell me if Elsie Challoner is living there?"

Warren Relf looked back at her in undisguised astonishment. "She is," he answered. "Did my sister tell you so?"

"No," Winifred replied with bitter truthfulness. "I found it out." And with that one short incisive sentence, she moved on coldly, as if she would fain look at the pictures.

"Does—does Massinger know it?" Warren asked all aghast, taken aback by surprise, and unwittingly trampling on her tenderest feelings.

Winifred turned round upon him with an angry flash. This was more than she could bear. The tears were struggling hard to rise to her eyes; she kept them back with a supreme effort. "How should I know, pray?" she answered fiercely, but very low. "Does he make me the confidante of all his loves, do you suppose, Mr. Relf?—He said she was in Australia.—He told me a lie.—Everybody's combined and caballed to deceive me.—How should I know whether he knows or not? I know nothing. But one thing I know: from my mouth at least he shall never, never, never hear it."

She turned away, stern and hard as iron. Hugh had deceived her; Elsie had deceived her. The two souls she had loved the best on earth! From that moment forward, the joy of her life, whatever had been left of it, was all gone from her. She went forth from the room a crushed creature.

How varied in light and shade the world is! While Winifred was driving gloomily back to her own lodgings—solitary and heart-broken, in Mrs. Bouverie Barton's comfortable carriage—revolving in her own wounded soul this incredible conspiracy of Hugh's and Elsie's—Edie Relf and her mother and brother were joyfully discussing their great triumph in the now dismantled and empty front drawing-room at 128, Bletchingley Road, South Kensington.

"Have you totted up the total of the sales, Warren?" Edie Relf inquired with a bright light in her eye and a smile on her lips; for the private view—her own inception—had been more than successful from its very beginning.

Warren jotted down a series of figures on the back of an envelope and counted them up mentally with profound trepidation. "Mother," he cried, clasping her hand with a convulsive clutch in his, "I'm afraid to tell you; it's so positively grand. It seems really too much.—If this goes on, you need never take any pupils again.—Edie, we owe it all to you.—It can't be right, yet it comes out square. I've reckoned up twice and got each time the same total—Four hundred and fifty!"

"I thought so," Edie answered with a happy little laugh of complete triumph. "I hit upon such a capital dodge, Warren. I never told you beforehand what I was going to do, for I knew if I did, you'd never allow me to put it into execution; but I wrote the name and price of each picture in big letters and plain figures on the back of the frame. Then, whenever I took up a person with a good, coiny, solvent expression of countenance, and a picture-buying crease about the corners of the mouth, to inspect the studio, I waited for them casually to ask the name of any special piece they particularly admired. 'Let me see,' said I. 'What does Warren call that? I think it's on the back here.' So I turned round the frame, and there they'd see it, as large as life: 'By Stormy Seas—Ten Pounds;' or, 'The Haunt of the Sea-Swallows—Thirty Guineas.' That always fetched them, my dear. They couldn't resist it. It's a ticklish thing to inquire about prices. People don't like to ask, for fear they should offend you, or the figure should happen to be too stiff for their purses; and it makes them feel small to inquire the price and find it's ten times as much as they expected. But when they see the amount written down in black and white before their own eyes, at our astonishingly low cash quotations, what on earth can they do, being human, but buy them?—Warren, you may give me a kiss, if you like. I'll tell you what I've done: I've made your fortune."

Warren kissed her affectionately on the forehead, half abashed. "You're a bad girl, Edie," he said good-humouredly; "and if I'd only known it, I'd certainly have taken a great big cake of best ink-eraser and rubbed your plain figures all carefully out again.—But I don't care a pin in the end, after all, if I can make this dear mother and you comfortable."

"And marry Elsie," Edie put in mischievously.

Warren gave a quiet sigh of regret. "And marry Elsie," he added low. "But Elsie will never marry me."

"You goose!" said Edie, and laughed at him to his face. She knew women better than he did.

"That dear Mr. Hatherley managed quite half," she went on after a pause. "If you'd only heard him discussing textures, or listened to the high-flown nonsense he talked about 'delicate touch,' and 'crystalline purity,' and 'poetical undertones,' and 'keen insight into the profoundest recesses of nature,' you'd have blushed to learn what a great painter you are, Warren. Why, he made out that a wave to your artistic eyes shone like opal and beryl to the ignoble vulgar. He remarked that liquid sapphires simply strewed your summer seas, and mud in your hands became more gorgeous than marble to the common understanding. The dear good fellow! That's what I call something like a friend for you. Your artistic eye, indeed! I could just have thrown my arms around his neck and kissed him!"

"Edie!" her mother exclaimed reprovingly. The last generation deprecates such open expression of feminine approbation.

"I could, mother," Edie answered with a bounce, unabashed. "And what's more, I should have awfully liked to do it. I should love to kiss him; and I don't care twopence who hears me say so.—Goodness gracious, I do hope that isn't Mr. Hatherley out on the staircase there!"

But it was only Martha bringing back from the attics the strictly necessary in the way of furniture for the meal that was to serve them in lieu of dinner.

B

And all this while, poor lonely Winifred was rocking herself wildly backward and forward in Mrs. Bouverie Barton's comfortable carriage, and muttering to herself in a mad fever of despair: "I could have believed it of Hugh; but of Elsie, of Elsie—never, never!"

Elsie's ring gleamed bright on her finger—the ring, as she thought, that Elsie had sent her; the ring that Hugh had really enclosed in the forged letter. Hateful, treacherous, cruel souvenir! At Hyde Park Corner, where the crowd of carriages and riders was thickest, she tore it off and flung it with mad energy into the midst of the roadway. The horses might trample it under foot and destroy it. Elsie, too—Elsie—Elsie was a traitor! She flung it from her like some poisonous thing; and then she sank back exhausted on the cushions.

CHAPTER XXXIV.

THE STRANDS DRAW CLOSER.

"I FEEL it my duty to let you know," Sir Anthony Wraxall wrote to Hugh a day or two later—by the hand of his amanuensis—"that Mrs. Massinger's lungs are far more seriously and dangerously affected that I deemed it at all prudent to inform her in person last week, when she consulted me here on the subject. Galloping consumption, I regret to say, may supervene at any time. The phthisical tendency manifests itself in Mrs. Massinger's case in an advanced stage; and general tuberculosis may therefore on the shortest notice carry her off with startling rapidity. I would advise you, under these painful circumstances, to give her the benefit of a warmer winter climate; if not Egypt or Algeria, then at least Mentone, Catania, or Malaga. She should not on any account risk seeing another English Christmas. If she remains in Suffolk during the colder months of the present year, I dare not personally answer for the probable consequences."

Hugh laid down the letter with a sigh of despair. It was the last straw, and it broke his back with utter despondency. How to finance a visit to the south he knew not. Talk about Algeria, Catania, Malaga! he had hard enough work to make both ends meet anyhow at Whitestrand. During the time that had elapsed since Hatherley's visit, his dreams had fled, his acres had melted, and his exchequer had emptied itself with unexampled rapidity. The Whitestrand currency was already very much inflated indeed: half of it consisted frankly of unredeemed mortgage, and the other half of unconsolidated floating debt to the butcher and baker. He had trusted first of all to the breakwater to redeem everything : but the breakwater, that broken reed, had only pierced the hand that leaned upon it. The sea shifted and the sand drifted worse than ever. Then he had hoped the best from " A Life's Philosophy ; " but " A Life's Philosophy," published after long and fruitless negotiations, at his own risk—for no firm would so much as touch it as a business speculation—had never paid the long printer's bill, let alone recouping him for his lost time and trouble. Nobody wanted to read about his life or his philosophy. No epic poem could have fallen flatter. It went as dead as a blank-verse tragedy, waking laughter in indolent reviewers. He had in his desk at that very moment the first statement of accounts for the futile venture ; and it showed a balance on the debit side of some £54 7s. 11d. There was a fatal precision that was simply crushing about that odd item of 7s. 11d. He had dreamed of thousands, and he had this to pay ! Foiled—and by an accountant ! the melodramatist within him remarked angrily. Hugh groaned as he thought of his own high hopes, and their utter frustration by a numerical deficit of so base a sum as £54 7s. 11d. He would have endured the round hundred with far greater complacency. That was at least heroic. But 7s. 11d. ! The degradation sank deep into his poet's heart. To be balked of Parnassus by 7s. 11d. !

Of Winifred's health, Hugh thought far less than of the financial difficulty. He saw she was ill, decidedly ill, but not so ill as everybody else who saw her imagined. Wrapped up in his own selfish hopes and fears, never really fond of his poor small wife, and now estranged for months and months by her untimely discovery of Elsie's watch, which both he and she had entirely misinterpreted, Hugh Massinger had seen that frail young creature grow thinner and paler day by day without at any time realizing the profundity of the change or the actual seriousness of her failing condition. Even when those whom we devotedly love grow ill by degrees before our very eyes, we are apt long to overlook the gradual stages, if we see them constantly from day to day ; our standard varies too slowly for comparison : the stranger who comes at long intervals finds himself often far better able to mark and report upon the progress of disease than those who watch and observe the patient most anxiously. But with Hugh, complete indifference helped also to mask the insidious effect of a creeping illness ; he didn't care enough about Winifred's health to notice whether she was looking really feebler or otherwise. And even now, when Sir Anthony Wraxall wrote in such plain terms, the main thought in his own mind was merely that these doctors were always terrible alarmists. He would take Winifred away to the south, of course: a doctor's orders must be obeyed at all hazards. So much, conventional morality imposed upon him. But she wasn't half so ill, he felt certain, as Sir Anthony thought her. Most of it was just her nasty hysterical temperament. A winter with the swallows would soon bring her round. She'd be all right again with a short course of warmer weather.

He went out into the drawing-room to join Winifred. He found her lying lazily on the sofa, pretending to read the first volume of Besant's last new novel from Mudie's. "The wind's shifted," he began uneasily. "We shall get it warmer, I hope, soon, Winifred."

"Yes, the wind's shifted," Winifred answered gloomily, looking up in a hopeless and befogged way from the pages of her story. "It blew straight across from Siberia yesterday; to-day it blows straight across from Greenland. That's all the change we ever get, it seems to me, in the weather in England. One day the wind's easterly and cold; another day it's westerly and damp. Bronchitis on one side; rheumatism on the other. There's the whole difference."

"How would you like to go abroad for the winter, I wonder?" Hugh asked tentatively, with some faint attempt at his old kindliness of tone and manner.

His wife glanced over at him with a sudden and strangely suspicious smile. "To San Remo, I suppose?" she answered bitterly.

She meant the name to speak volumes to Hugh's conscience; but it fell upon his ears as flat and unimpressive as any other. "Not necessarily to San Remo," he replied, alll unconscious. "To Algeria, if you like—or Mentone, or Bordighera."

Winifred rose, and walked without one word of explanation, but with a resolute air, into the study, next door. When she came out again, she carried in her two arms Keith Johnston's big Imperial Atlas. It was a heavier book than she could easily lift in her present feeble condition of body, but Hugh never even offered to help her to carry it. The day of small politenesses and courtesies was long gone past. He only looked on in mute surprise, anxious to know whence came this sudden new-born interest in the neglected study of European geography.

Winifred laid the atlas down with a flop on the five o'clock tea-table, that staggered with its weight, and turned the pages with feverish haste till she came to the map of Northern Italy. "I thought so," she gasped out, as she scanned it close, a lurid red spot burning bright in her cheek. "Mentone and Bordighera are both of them almost next door to San Remo.—The nearest stations on the line along the coast.—You could run over there often by rail from either of them."

“ Run over—often—by rail—to San Remo ? ” Hugh repeated
with a genuinely puzzled expression of countenance.

“ Oh, you act admirably ! ” Winifred cried with a sneer.
“ What perfect bewilderment ! What childlike innocence !
I’ve always considered you an Irving wasted upon private life.
If you’d gone upon the stage, you’d have made your fortune ;
which you’ve scarcely succeeded in doing, it must be confessed,
at your various existing assorted professions.”

Hugh stared back at her in blank amazement. “ I don’t
know what you mean,” he answered shortly.

“ Capital ! capital ! ” Winifred went on in her bitter mood,
endeavouring to assume a playful tone of unconcerned irony.
“ I never saw you act better in all my life—not even when you
were pretending to fall in love with me. It’s your most successful part—the injured innocent :—much better than the part
of the devoted husband. If I were you, I should always stick
to it. It suits your features.—Well, well, we may as well go to
San Remo itself, I suppose, as anywhere else in the immediate
neighbourhood. I’d rather be on the spot and see the whole
play with my own eyes, than guess at it blindly from a distance,
at Mentone or Bordighera. You may do your Romeo before an
admiring audience. San Remo it shall be, since you’ve set
your heart upon it.—But it’s very abrupt, this sudden conver-
sion of yours to the charms of the Riviera.”

“ Winifred,” Hugh cried, with transparent conviction in
every note of his voice, “ I see you’re labouring under some
distressing misapprehension ; but I give you my solemn word
of honour I don’t in the least know what it is you’re driving at.
You’re talking about somebody or something unknown that I
don’t understand. I wish you’d explain. I can’t follow you.”

But he had acted too often and too successfully to be believed
now for all his earnestness. “ Your solemn word of honour ! ”
Winifred burst out angrily, with intense contempt. “ Your
solemn word of honour, indeed ! And pray, who do you think
believes now in your precious word or your honour either ?—
You can’t deceive me any longer, thank goodness, Hugh. I
know you want to go to San Remo ; and I know for whose sake
you want to go there. This solicitude for my health’s all a
pure fiction. Little you cared for my health a month ago ! Oh
no, I see through it all distinctly. You’ve found out there’s a
reason for going to San Remo, and you want to go for your own
pleasure accordingly.”

“ I don’t want to go to San Remo at all,” Hugh cried, getting
angry. “ I never said a word myself about San Remo ; I never
proposed or thought of San Remo. It was you yourself who
first suggested the very name. I’ve nothing to do with it ; and
what’s more, I won’t go there.”

"Oh yes, I know," Winifred answered provokingly, with another of her frequent sharp fits of coughing. "You didn't mention it. Of course I noticed that. You're a great deal too sharp to commit yourself so. You carefully avoided naming San Remo, for fear you should happen to rouse my intuitive suspicions. You proposed we should go to Mentone or Bordighera instead, where you could easily run across whenever you liked to your dear San Remo, and where I should be perhaps a little less likely to find out the reason you wanted to go there for.—But I see through your plans. I checkmate your designs. I won't give in to them. Whatever comes, you may count at least upon finding me always ready to thwart you. I shall go to San Remo, if I go away at all, and to nowhere else on the whole Riviera. I prefer to face the worst at once, thank you. I shall know everything, if there's anything to know. And I won't be shuffled off upon your Mentone or your Bordighera, while you're rehearsing your balcony scenes at San Remo alone; so that's flat for you."

An idea flashed sudden across Hugh's mind. "I think, Winifred," he said calmly, "you're labouring under a mistake about the place you're speaking of. The gaming tables are not at San Remo, as you suppose, but at Monte Carlo, just beyond Mentone. And if you thought I wanted to go to the Riviera for the sake of repairing our ruined estate at Monte Carlo, you're very much mistaken. I wanted to go, I solemnly declare, for your health only."

Winifred rose, and faced him now like an angry tigress. Her sunken white cheeks were flushed and fiery indeed with suppressed wrath, and a bright light blazed in her dilated pupils. The full force of a burning indignation possessed her soul. "Hugh Massinger," she said, repelling him haughtily with her thin left hand, "you've lied to me for years, and you're lying to me now as you've always lied to me. You know you've lied to me, and you know you're lying to me. This pretence about my health's a transparent falsehood. These prevarications about the gambling tables are a tissue of fictions. You can't deceive me. I *know* why you want to go to San Remo!" And she pushed him away in disgust with her angry fingers.

The action and the insult were too much for Hugh. He could no longer restrain himself. Sir Anthony's letter trembled in his hands; he was clutching it tight in his waistcoat pocket. To show it to Winifred would have been cruel, perhaps, under any other circumstances; but in face of such an accusation as that, yet wholly misunderstood, flesh and blood—at least Hugh Massinger's—could not further resist the temptation of producing it. "Read that," he cried, handing her over the letter coldly; "you'll see from it why it is I want to go; why, in spite of all we've lost and are losing, I'm still prepared to submit to this extra expenditure."

"Out of *my* money," Winifred answered scornfully, as she took the paper with an inclination of mock-courtesy from his tremulous hands. "How very generous! And how very kind of you!"

She read the letter through without a single word; then she yielded at last, in spite of herself, to her womanly tears. "I see it all, Hugh," she cried, flinging herself down once more in despair upon the sofa. "You fancy I'm going to die now; and it will be *so* convenient, so very convenient for you, to be near her there next door at San Remo!"

Hugh gazed at her again in mute surprise. At last he saw it—he saw it in all its naked hideousness. A light began gradually to dawn upon his mind. It was awful—it was horrible in its cruel Nemesis upon his unspoken crime. To think she should be jealous—of his murdered Elsie! He could hardly speak of it; but he must, he must. "Winnie," he cried, almost softened by his pity for what he took to be her deadly and terrible mistake, "I understand you, I think, after all. I know what you mean.—You believe—that Elsie—is at San Remo."

Winifred looked up at him through her tears with a withering glance. "You have said it!" she cried in a haughty voice, and relapsed into a silent fit of sobbing and suppressed cough, with her poor wan face buried deep once more like a wounded child's in the cushions of the sofa.

What would not Hugh have given if only he could have explained to her there that moment that Elsie was lying dead, for three years past and more, in her nameless grave at Orfordness! But he could not. He dared not. His own past lies rose up in judgment at last against him. He bowed his head, unable even to weep. Jealous of Elsie! of poor dead Elsie! That was what she meant, then, by the talk about his balcony scene! But Elsie would never play Juliet to his Romeo again. Elsie was dead, and Winifred, alas, would never now believe it. Truly, his punishment was greater than he could bear. He bowed his head in silent shame. The penalty of his sin was bitter upon him.

One only way now lay open before him. He would take her to San Remo, and let her see for herself how utterly groundless, and futile, and unjust were her base suspicions. He would show her that Elsie was not at San Remo.

CHAPTER XXXV.

RETRIBUTION.

OH the horror and drudgery of those next few weeks, while
Hugh, in a fever of shame and disgust, was anxiously and
wearily making difficult arrangements, financial or otherwise,
for that hopeless flitting to the sunny South, that loomed ahead
so full of gloom and wretchedness for himself and Winifred!
The speechless agony of running about, with a smile on his
lips and that nameless weight on his crushed heart, driving
horrid, sordid, cheese-paring bargains with the family attorney
and the London money-lenders for still further advances on
those squalid worthless pieces of stamped paper! The ignominious discussions of percentage and discount, the undignified
surrender of documents and title-deeds, the disgusting counter-
checks and collateral securities, the insulting whispers of doubt
and uncertainty as to his own final financial solvency! All
these indignities would in themselves have been quite excruciating enough to torture a proud man of Hugh Massinger's
haughty and sensitive temperament. But to suffer all these,
with the superadded wretchedness of Winifred's growing illness
and Winifred's gathering cloud of suspicion about his own
conduct, was simply unendurable. Above all, to know in his
own soul that Winifred was jealous of poor dead Elsie! If only
he could have made a clean breast of it all! If only he could
have said to her in one single outburst, "Elsie is dead!" it
might perhaps have been easier. But after all his own clever
machinations and deceptions, after all his long course of
confirmatory circumstantial evidence—the letters, the ring, the
messages, the details—how on earth could Winifred ever believe
him? His cunning recoiled with fatal precision upon his own
head. The bolt he had shot turned back upon his breast. The
pit that he digged he himself had fallen therein.

So there was nothing for it left now but to face the unspeakable, to endure the unendurable. He must go through with it
all, let it cost what it might. For at least in the end he had
one comfort. At San Remo, Winifred would find out she was
mistaken; there was no Elsie at all, there or elsewhere.

What had led her astray into this serious and singular error,
he wondered. That problem exercised his weary mind not a
little in the night-watches. Morning after morning, as the
small hours clanged solemnly from the Whitestrand church
tower, Hugh lay awake and turned it over in anxious debate

with his own wild thoughts. Could somebody have told her they had met some Miss Challoner or other accidentally at San Remo? Could Warren Relf, vile wretch that he was, industriously have circulated some baseless rumour as to Elsie's whereabouts on purpose to entrap him? Or could Winifred herself intuitively have arrived at her own idea, woman-like, by some false interference—some stupid mistake as to postmark or envelope or name or handwriting? It was all an insoluble mystery to him; and Winifred would do nothing towards clearing it up. Whenever he tried by devious routes to approach the subject from a fresh side, Winifred turned round upon him at once with fierce indignation in her pale blue eyes and answered always: "You know it all. Don't try to deceive me. It's no good any longer. I see through you at last. Why go on lying to me?"

The more he protested, the more scornful and caustic Winifred grew. The more genuinely and sincerely he declared his bewilderment, the more convinced she felt in her own mind that he acted a part with marvellous skill and with consummate heartlessness.

It was terrible not to be trusted when he told the plain truth; but it was his own fault. He could not deny it. And that it was his own fault made it all the bitterer for him. He hadn't even the solace of a righteous indignation to comfort his oul in this last depth of contumely.

When you know that troubles come undeserved, you have the easy resource of conscious rectitude at any rate to support you. The just man in adversity is least to be pitied. It is the sinner who feels the whip smart. Hugh had to swallow it all manfully, and to eat humble-pie at his private table into the bargain. It was his own fault; he had unhappily no one but himself to blame for it.

Meanwhile, Winifred grew rapidly worse, so ill, that even Hugh began to perceive it, and despaired of being able to carry her in safety to San Remo. The shock at the Relfs' had told seriously upon her weak and shattered constitution: the constant friction of her relations with Hugh continued to tell upon it every day that passed over her. The motherless girl and childless mother brooded in secret over her great grief; she had no one, absolutely no one on earth who could sympathize with her in her terrible trouble. She longed to fling herself upon Elsie's bosom—the dear old Elsie that had once been, the Elsie that perhaps could still understand her—and to cry aloud to her for pity, for sympathy. When she got to San Remo, she sometimes thought, she would tell all—every word—to Elsie; and Elsie at least must be very much changed if in spite of all she could not feel for her.

Proud as she was, she would throw herself on Elsie's mercy.
Elsie had wronged her, and she would tell all to Elsie. But
not to Hugh. Hugh was hard and cold and unyielding as
steel. It would not be for long. She would soon be released.
And then Hugh—— She shrank from thinking it.

Money was cheap, the lawyers said; but Hugh found he had
to pay dear for it. Money was plentiful, the newspapers reported; but Hugh found it as scarce as charity. He took a
long time to conclude his arrangements; and when he con-
cluded them, the terms were ruinous. Never mind; Winifred
wouldn't last long; he had only himself to think about in
future.

At last the day came for their journey South. They were
going alone, without even a maid; glad to have paid the servants their arrears and escape alive from the clutches of the
butchers and bakers. November fogs shrouded the world.
Hugh had completed those vile transactions of his with the
attorneys and the money-lenders, and felt faintly cheered by
the actual metallic chink of gold for the journey rattling and
jingling in his trousers' pocket. But Winifred sat very weak
and ill in the far corner of the first-class carriage that bore
them away from Charing Cross Station. They had come up the
day before from Almundham to town, and spent the night luxu-
riously in the rooms of the Métropole. You must make a dying
woman comfortable. And Hugh had dropped round with defiant
pride into the Cheyne Row Club, assuming in vain the old jaunty
languid poetical air—" of the days before he had degenerated
into landowning," Hatherley said afterwards—just to let recalcitrant Bohemia see for itself it hadn't entirely crushed him by its
jingling jibes and its scathing critiques of " A Life's Philosophy."
But the protest fell flat; it was indeed a feeble one : heedless
Bohemia, engrossed after its wont with its last new favourite,
the rising author of " Lays of the African Lakeland," held out to
Hugh Massinger of Whitestrand Hall its flabbiest right hand of
lukewarm welcome. And this was the Bohemia that once had
grasped his landless fingers with fraternal fervour of sympathetic
devotion! The chilliness of his reception in the scene of his
ancient popularity stung the Bard to the quick. No more for
him the tabour, the cymbals, and the oaten pipe; no more the
blushful Cheyne Row Hippocrene. He felt himself *démodé.*
The rapid stream of London society and London thought had
swept eddying past and left him stranded. As the train rolled
on upon its way to Dover, Hugh Massinger of Whitestrand Hall
—and its adjacent sandhills—leaned back disconsolate upon the
padded cushions of his leather-lined carriage and thought with
a sigh to himself of the days without name, without number,

when, proud as a lord, he had travelled third in a bare pen on the honest earnings of his own right hand, and had heard of mortgages, in some dim remote impersonal way, only as a foolish and expensive aristocratic indulgence. A mortgage was nowadays a too palpable reality, with the glamour of romance well worn off it. He wished its too, too solid sheepskin would melt, and reduce him once more to wooden seats and happiness. Oh, for some enchanted carpet of the Arabian Nights, to transport him back with a bound from his present self to those good old days of Thirds and Elsie!

But enchanted carpets are now unhappily out of date, and Channel steamers have quite superseded the magical shallops of good Haroun-al-Raschid. In plain prose, the Straits were rough, and Winifred suffered severely from the tossing. At Calais, they took the through train for Marseilles, having secured a *coupé-lit* at Charing Cross beforehand.

That was a terrible night, that night spent in the *coupé-lit* with Winifred: the most terrible Hugh had ever endured since the memorable evening when Elsie drowned herself.

They had passed round Paris at gray dusk, in their comfortable through-carriage, by the Chemin de Fer de Ceinture to the Gare de Lyon, and were whirling along on their way to Fontainebleau through the shades of evening, when Winifred first broke the ominous silence she had preserved ever since they topped at St. Denis. "It won't be for long now," she said lryly, "and it will be so convenient for you to be at San Remo."

Hugh's heart sank once more within him. It was quite clear that Winifred thought Elsie was there. He wished to heaven she was, and that he was no murderer. Oh, the weight that would have been lifted off his weary soul if only he could think it so! The three years' misery that would rise like a mist from his uncertain path, if only he did not know to a certainty that Elsie lay buried at Orfordness in the shipwrecked sailors' graveyard by the Low Lighthouse. He looked across at Winifred as she sat in her place. She was pale and frail; her wasted cheeks showed white and hollow. As she leaned back there, with a cold light gleaming hard and chilly from her sunken blue eyes —those light blue eyes that he had never loved—those cruel blue eyes that he had learned at last to avoid with an instinctive shrinking, as they gazed through and through him with their flabby persistence—he said to himself with a sigh of relief: "She can't last long. Better tell her all, and let her know the truth. It could do no harm. She might die the happier. Dare I risk it, I wonder? Or is it too dangerous?"

"Well?" Winifred asked in an icy tone, interpreting aright the little click in his throat and the doubtful gleam in his shifty eyes as implying some hesitating desire to speak to her.

" What lie are you going to tell me next ? Speak it out boldly ! don't be afraid. It's no novelty. You know I'm not easily disconcerted."

He looked back at her nervously with bent brows. That fragile small creature ! He positively feared her. Dare he tell her the truth ? And would she believe it ? Those blue eyes were so coldly glassy. Yet, with a sudden impulse, he resolved to be frank; he resolved to unburden his guilty soul of all its weight of care to Winifred.

" No lie, Winifred, but the solemn truth," he blurted out slowly, in a voice that of itself might have well produced complete conviction—on any one less incredulous than the wife he had cajoled and deceived so often. " You think Elsie's at San Remo, I know.—You're wrong there; you're quite mistaken. —She's not in San Remo, nor in Australia either. That was a lie.—Elsie's dead—dead three years ago—before we were married.—Dead and buried at Orfordness. And I've seen her grave, and cried over it like a child, too."

He spoke with solemn intensity of earnestness; but he spoke in vain. Winifred thought, herself, till that very moment, she had long since reached the lowest possible depth of contempt and scorn for the husband on whom she had thrown herself away; but as he met her then with that incredible falsehood— as she must needs think it—on his lying lips, with so grave a face and so profound an air of frank confession, her lofty disdain rose at once to a yet sublimer height of disgust and loathing of which till that night she could never even have conceived herself capable. " You hateful Thing !" she cried, rising from her seat to the centre of the carriage, and looking down upon him physically from her point of vantage as he cowered and slank like a cur in his corner. " Don't dare to address me again, I say, with lies like that. If you can't find one word of truth to tell me, have the goodness at least, since I don't desire your further conversation, to leave me the repose of your polite silence."

" But, Winifred," Hugh cried, clasping his hands together in impotent despair, " this *is* the truth, the very, very truth, the whole truth, that I'm now telling you. I've hidden it from you so long by deceit and treachery. I acknowledge all that: I admit I deceived you. But I want to tell you the whole truth now; and you won't listen to me ! Oh, heaven, Winifred, you won't listen to me ! "

On any one else, his agonized voice and pleading face would have produced their just and due effect; but on Winifred— impossible. She *knew* he was lying to her even when he spoke the truth ; and the very intensity and fervour of his horror only added to her sense of utter repulsion from his ingrained falseness and his native duplicity. To pretend to her face, with agonies of mock remorse, that Elsie was dead, when she knew he was going to San Remo to see her! And taking his own wedded wife to die there! The man who could act so realistically as that, and tell lies so glibly at such a moment, must be falser to the core than her heart had ever dreamed or conceived of.

"Go on," she murmured, relapsing into her corner. "Continue your monologue. It's supreme in its way—no actor could beat it. But be so good as to consider my part in the piece left out altogether. I shall answer you no more. I should be sorry to interrupt so finished an artist!"

Her scathing contempt wrought up in Hugh a perfect fury of helpless indignation. That he should wish to confess, to humble himself before her, to make reparation! and that Winifred should spurn his best attempt, should refuse so much as to listen to his avowal! It was too ignominious. "For heaven's sake," he cried, with his hands clasped hard, "at least let me speak. Let me have my say out. You're all wrong. You're wronging me utterly. I've behaved most wickedly, most cruelly, I know: I confess it all. I abase myself at your feet. If you want me to be abject, I'll grovel before you! I admit my crime, my sin, my transgression.—I won't pretend to justify myself at all.—I've lied to you, forged to you, deceived you, misled you!" (At each clause and phrase of passionate self-condemnation, Winifred nodded a separate sardonic acquiescence.) "But you're wrong about this. You mistake me wholly.—I swear to you, my child, Elsie's not alive. You're jealous of a woman who's been dead for years. For my sin and shame I say it, she's dead long ago!"

He might as well have tried to convince the door-handle. Winifred's loathing found no overt vent in angry words; she repressed her speech, her very breath almost, with a spasmodic effort. But she stretched out both her hands, the palms turned outward, with a gesture of horror, contempt, and repulsion; and she averted her face with a little cry of supreme disgust, checked deep down in her rising throat, as one averts one's face instinctively from a loathsome sore or a venomous reptile. Such hideous duplicity to a dying woman was more than she could brook without some outer expression of her outraged sense of social decency.

But Hugh could no longer restrain himself now; he had begun his tale, and he must run right through with it. The fever of the confessional had seized upon his soul; remorse and despair were goading him on. He must have relief for his pent-up feelings. Three years of silence were more than enough. Winifred's very incredulity compelled him to continue. He must tell her all—all, all, utterly. He must make her understand to the uttermost jot, willy, nilly, that he was not deceiving her!

He opened the floodgates of his speech at once, and flowed on in a headlong torrent of confession. Winifred sat there, cowering and crouching as far from him as possible in the opposite corner, drinking in his strange tale with an evident interest and a horrible placidity. Not that she ever moved or stirred a muscle; she heard it all out with a cold set smile playing around the corners of her wasted mouth, that was more exasperating by far to behold than any amount of contradiction would have been to listen to. It goaded Hugh into a perfect delirium of feverish self-revelation. He would not submit to be thus openly defied; he must tell her all—all—all, till she believed him.

With eager lips, he began his story from the very beginning, recapitulating point by point his interview with Elsie in the Hall grounds, her rushing away from him to the roots of the poplar, her mad leap into the swirling black water, his attempt to rescue her, his unconsciousness, and his failure. He told it all with dramatic completeness. Winifred saw and heard every scene and tone and emotion as he reproduced it. Then he went on to tell her how he came to himself again on the bank of the dike, and how in cold and darkness he formed his Plan, that fatal, horrible, successful Plan, which he had ever since been engaged in carrying out and in detesting. He described how he returned to the inn, unobserved and untracked; how he forged the first compromising letter from Elsie; and how, once embarked upon that career of deceit, there was no drawing back for him in crime after crime till the present moment. He despised himself for it; but still he told it. Next came the episode of Elsie's bedroom: the theft of the ring and the other belongings; the hasty flight, the fall from the creeper; and his subsequent horror of the physical surroundings connected with that hateful night adventure. In his agony of self-accusation he spared her no circumstance, no petty detail: bit by bit he retold the whole story in all its hideous inhuman ghastliness— the walk to Orfordness, the finding of the watch, the furtive visit to Elsie's grave, his horror of Winifred's proposed picnic to that very spot a year later. He ran, unabashed, in an ecstasy of humiliation, through the entire tale of his forgeries and his deceptions: the sending of the ring; the audacious fiction of Elsie's departure to a new home in Australia: the long sequence of occasional letters; the living lie he had daily and hourly acted before her. And all the while, as he truly said, with slow tears rolling one by one down his dark cheeks, he knew himself a murderer: he felt himself a murderer; and all the while, poor Elsie was lying, dishonoured and unknown, a nameless corpse, in her pauper grave upon that stormy sand-pit.

Oh, the joy and relief of that tardy confession! the gush and flow of those pent-up feelings! For three long years and more, he had locked it all up in his inmost soul, chafing and seething with the awful secret; and now at last he had let it all out, in one burst of confidence, to the uttermost item.

As for Winifred, she heard him out in solemn silence to the bitter end, with ever growing contempt and shame and hatred. She could not lift her eyes to his face, so much his very earnestness horrified and appalled her. The man's aptitude for lying struck her positively dumb. The hideous ingenuity with which he accounted for everything—the diabolically clever way in which he had woven in, one after the other, the ring, the watch, the letters, the picnic, the lonely tramp to Orfordness—smote her to the heart with a horrible loathing for the vile wretch she had consented to marry. That she had endured so long such a miserable creature's bought caresses filled her inmost soul with a sickening sense of disgust and horror. She cowered and crouched closer and closer in her remote corner: she felt that his presence there actually polluted the carriage she occupied; she longed for Marseilles, for San Remo, for release, that she might get at least farther and farther away from him. She could almost have opened the door in her access of horror and jumped from the train while still in motion, so intense was her burning and goading desire to escape for ever from his poisonous neighbourhood.

At last, as Hugh with flushed face and eager eyes calmed down a little from his paroxysm of self-abasement and self-revelation, Winifred raised her eyes once more from the ground and met her husband's—ah, heaven!—that she should have to call that thing her husband! His acting chilled her; his pretended tears turned her cold with scorn. "Is that all?" she asked in an icy voice. "Is your romance finished?"

"That's all!" Hugh cried, burying his face in his hands and bending down his body to the level of his knees in utter and abject self-humiliation. "Winifred! Winifred! it's no romance. Won't you, even now, even now believe me?"

"It's clever—clever—extremely clever!" Winifred answered in a tone of unnatural calmness. "I don't deny it shows great talent. If you'd turned your attention seriously to novel-writing, which is your proper *métier*, instead of to the law, for which you've too exuberant an imagination, you'd have succeeded ten thousand times better there than you could ever do at what you're pleased to consider your divine poetry. Your story, I allow, hangs together in every part with remarkable skill. It's a pity I should happen to know it all from beginning to end for a tissue of falsehoods.—Hugh, you're the profoundest and most eminent of liars.—I've known people before who would tell a lie to serve their own ends, when there was anything to gain by it.—I've known people before who, when a lie or the truth would either of them suit their purpose equally, told the lie by preference out of pure love of it.—But I've never till to-night met anybody on earth who would tell a lie for the mere lie's sake, to make himself look even more utterly mean and despicable and small than he is by nature.—You've done that. You've reached that unsurpassed depth of duplicity. You've deliberately invented a clever tissue of concerted lies—even *you* yourself couldn't fit them all in so neat and pat on the spur of the moment—you must have worked your romance up by careful stages in your own mind beforehand—and all for what? To prove yourself innocent? Oh no; not at all! but to make yourself out even worse than you are—a liar, a forger, and all but a murderer.—I loathe you; I despise you.—For all your acting, you know you're lying to me even now, this minute. You know that Elsie Challoner, whom you pretend to be dead, is awaiting your own arrival to-night by arrangement at San Remo."

Hugh flung himself back in the final extremity of utter despair on the padded cushions. He had played his last card with Winifred, and lost. His very remorse availed him nothing. His very confession was held to increase his sin. What could he do? Whither turn? He knew no answer. He rocked himself up and down on his seat in hopeless misery. The worst had come. He had blurted out all. And Winifred, Winifred would not believe him.

"I wish it was true!" he cried; "I wish it was true, Winnie! I wish she was there. But it isn't; it isn't! She's dead! I killed her! and her blood has weighed upon my head ever since! I pay for it now! I killed her! I killed her!"

"Listen!"

Winifred had risen to her full height in the *coupé* once more, and was standing, gaunt and haggard and deadly wan like a shrunken little tragedy queen above him. Her pale white face showed paler and whiter and more death-like still by the feeble light of the struggling oil-lamp; and her bloodless lips trembled and quivered visibly with inner passion as she tried to repress her overpowering indignation with one masterful effort. "Listen!" she said, with fierce intensity. "What you say is false. I know you're lying to me. Warren Relf told me himself the other day in London that Elsie Challoner was still alive, and living, where you know she lives, over there at San Remo."

Warren Relf! That serpent! That reptile! That eaves-dropper! Then *this* was the creature's mean revenge! He had lied that despicable lie to Winifred! Hugh hated him in his soul more fiercely than ever. He was baffled once more; and always by that same malignant intriguer!

"Where did you see Relf?" he burst out angrily. His indignation, flaring up to white-heat afresh at this latest machination of his ancient enemy, gave new strength to his words and new point to his hatred. "I thought I told you long since at Whitestrand to hold no further communication with that wretched being!"

But Winifred by this time, worn out with excitement, had fallen back speechless and helpless on the cushions. Her feeble strength was fairly exhausted. The fatigue of the preparations, the stormy passage, the long spell of travelling, the night journey, and, added to it all, this terrible interview with the man she had once loved, but now despised and hated, had proved too much in the end for her weakened constitution. A fit of wild incoherence had overtaken her; she babbled idly on her seat in broken sentences. Her muttered words were full of "mother" and "home" and "Elsie." Hugh felt her pulse. He knew it was delirium. His one thought now was to reach San Remo as quickly as possible. If only she could live to know Warren Relf had told her a lie, and that Elsie was dead —dead—dead and buried!

Perhaps even this story about Warren Relf and what he had told her was itself but a product of the fever and delirium! But more probably not. The man who could open other people's etters, the man who could plot and plan and intrigue in secret to set another man's wife against her own husband, was capable of telling any lie that came uppermost to hurt his enemy and to serve his purpose. He knew that lie would distress and torture Winifred, and he had struck at Hugh, like a coward that he was, through a weak, hysterical, dying woman! He had played on the mean chord of feminine jealousy. Hugh hated him as he had never hated him before. He should pay for this soundly—the cur, the scoundrel!

CHAPTER XXXVI.

THE OTHER SIDE OF THE SHIELD.

THAT self-same night, another English passenger of our acquaintance was speeding in hot haste due southward to San Remo, not indeed by the Calais and Marseilles express, but by the rival route *viâ* Boulogne, the Mont Cenis, Turin, and Savona. Warren Relf had chosen the alternative road by deliberate design, lest

Hugh Massinger and he should happen to clash by the way, and a needless and unseemly scene should perhaps take place before Winifred's very eyes at some intermediate station.

It was by the merest accident in the world, indeed, that Warren had heard, in the nick of opportunity, of the Massingers' projected visit to San Remo. For some weeks before, busy with the "boom," he had hardly ever dropped in for a gossip at his club in Piccadilly. Already he had sent off his mother and sister to the Riviera—this time, too, much to his pride and delight, minus the wonted dead-weight cargo of consumptive pupils—and being thus left entirely to his own devices at 128, Bletchingley Road, he had occupied every moment of his crowded day with some good hard work in finishing sketches and touching up pictures commissioned in advance from his summer studies, before setting out himself for winter quarters. But on the particular night when Hugh Massinger came up to town *en route* for the sunny South with Winifred, Warren Relf, having completed a fair day's work for a fair day's wage in his own studio—he was fufilling an engagement to enlarge a sketch of the Martellos at Aldeburgh for some Sheffield cutlery-duke or some Manchester cotten-marquis—strolled round in the evening for a cigar and a chat on the comfortable lounges of the Mother of Genius.

In the cosy smoking-room at the Cheyne Row Club, he found Hatherley already installed in a big armchair, discussing coffee and the last new number of the *Nineteenth Century.*

"Hullo, Relf! The remains of the Bard were in here just now," Hatherley exclaimed as he entered. "You've barely missed him. If you'd dropped in only ten minutes earlier, you might have inspected the interesting relics. But he's gone back to his hotel by this time, I fancy. The atmosphere of Cheyne Row seems somewhat too redolent of vulgar Cavendish for his refined taste. He smokes nothing nowadays himself but the best regalias!"

"What, Massinger?" Relf cried in some slight surprise. "How was he, Hatherley, and what was he doing in town at this time of year? All good squires ought surely to be down in the country now at their hereditary work of supplying the market with a due proportion of hares and partridges."

"Oh, he's a poor wreck," Hatherley answered lightly. "You've hit it off exactly—sunk to the level of the landed aristocracy. He exhales an aroma of vested interests. Real estate's his Moloch at present, and he bows the knee to solidified sea-mud in the temple of Rimmon. He has no views on anything in particular, I believe, but riparian proprietorship: complains still of the German Ocean for disregarding the sacred rights of property; and holds that the sole business of an enlightened British legislature is to keep the sand from blowing in at his own inviolable dining-room windows. Poor company, in fact, since he descended to the Squirearchy. He's never forgiven me that playful little bantering ballade of mine, either, that I sent to the *Charing Cross Review*, you remember, chaffing him about his 'Life's Tomfoolery,' or whatever else he called the precious nonsense. For my part, I hate such vapid narrowness. A man should be able to bear chaff with good-humour. Talk about the *genus irritabile*, indeed: your poet should feel himself superior to vindictiveness —' Dowered with the love of love, the hate of hate, the scorn of scorn,' as a distinguished peer admirably words it."

"How long's he going to stop in town—do you know?" Relf asked curiously.

"Thank goodness, he's not going to stop at all, my dear fellow. If he were, I'd run down to Brighton for the interval. A month of Massinger at the Cheyne Row would be a perfect harvest for the seaside lodgings. But I'm happy to tell you he's going to remove his mortal remains—for the soul of him's dead —dead and buried, long ago, in the Whitestrand sandhills—to San Remo to-morrow. Poor little Mrs. Massinger's seriously ill, I'm sorry to say. Too much Bard has told at last upon her. Bard for breakfast, Bard for lunch, and Bard for dinner would undermine in time the soundest constitution. Sir Anthony finds it's produced in her case suppressed gout, or tubercular diathe-is, or softening of the brain, or something lingering and humor-us of that sort; and he's ordered her off, post haste, by the first express, to the Mediterranean. Massinger objected at first to San Remo, he tells me, probably because, with his usual bad taste, he didn't desire to enjoy your agreeable society; but that skimpy little woman, gout or no gout, has a will of her own, I can tell you; San Remo she insists upon, and to San Remo the Bard must go accordingly. You should have seen him chafing with an internal fire as he let it all out to us, hint by hint, in the billiard-room this evening. Poor skimpy little woman, though, I'm awfully sorry for her. It's hard lines on her. She had the makings of a nice small hostess in her once; but the Bard's ruined her—sucked her dry and chucked her away—and she's dying of him now, from what he tells me."

Warren Relf looked back with a start of astonishment. "To San Remo?" he cried. "You're sure, Hatherley, he said San Remo?"

"Perfectly certain. San Remo it is. Observe, hi presto, there's no deception. He gave me this card in case of error: 'Hugh Massinger, for the present, Poste Restante, San Remo.' No other address forthcoming as yet. He expects to settle down at a villa when he gets there."

Relf made up his mind with a single plunge as he knocked

his ash off. "I shall go by to-morrow's express to the Riviera," he said shortly.

"To pursue the Bard? I wouldn't, if I were you. To tell you the truth, I know he doesn't love you."

"He has reason, I believe. The feeling is to some extent mutual. No, not to pursue him—to prevent mischief.—Hand me over the Continental Bradshaw, will you?—Thanks. That'll do. Do you know which line? Marseilles, I suppose? Did he happen to mention it?"

"He told me he was going by Dijon and Lyons."

"All right. That's it. The Marseilles route. Arrive at San Remo at 4.30. I'll go round the other way by Turin and intercept him. Trains arrive within five minutes of one another, I see. That'll be just in time to prevent any *contretemps.*"

"Your people are at San Remo already, I believe?"

"My people—yes. But how did you know? They were at Mentone for a while, and they only went on home to the Villa Rossa the day before yesterday."

"So I heard from Miss Relf," Hatherley answered with a slight cough. "She happened to be writing to me—about a literary matter—a mere question of current art-criticism—on Wednesday morning."

Warren hardly noticed the slight hesitation : and there was nothing odd in Edie's writing to Hatherley : that best of sisters was always jogging the memory of inattentive critics. While Edie lived, indeed, her brother's name was never likely to be forgotten in the weekly organs of artistic opinion. She insured it, if anything, an undue prominence. For her much importunity, the sternest of them all, like the unjust judge, was compelled in time to notice every one of her brother's performances.

So Warren hurried off by himself at all speed to San Remo, and reached it at almost the same moment as Massinger. If Hugh and Elsie were to meet unexpectedly, Warren felt the shock might be positively dangerous.

As he emerged from the station, he hired a close carriage, and ordered the *vetturino* to draw up on the far side of the road and wait a few minutes till he was prepared for starting. Then he leaned back in his seat in the shade of the hood, and held himself in readiness for the arrival of the Paris train from Ventimiglia.

He had waited only a quarter of an hour when Hugh Massinger came out hastily and called a cab. Two porters helped him to carry out Winifred, now seriously ill, and muttering inarticulately as they placed her in the carriage. Hugh gave an inaudible order to the driver, who drove off at once with a nod and a smile and a cheery "Si, signor."

"Follow that carriage!" Warren said in Italian to his own

cabman. The driver nodded and followed closely. They drove up through the narrow crowded little streets of the old quarter, and stopped at last opposite a large and dingy yellow-washed *pension*, in the modern part of the town, about the middle of the Avenue Vittorio-Emmanuele. The house was new, but congenitally shabby. Hugh's carriage blocked the way already. Warren waited outside for some ten minutes without showing his face, till he thought the Massingers would have engaged rooms: then he entered the hall boldly and inquired if he could have lodgings.

"On what floor has the gentleman who has just arrived placed himself?" he asked of the landlord, a portly Piedmontese, of august dimensions.

"On the second story, signor."

"Then I will go on the third," Warren Relf answered with short decision. And they found him a room forthwith without further parley.

The *pension* was one of those large and massive solid buildings, so common on the Riviera, let out in flats or in single apartments, and with a deep well of a square staircase occupying the entire centre of the block like a covered courtyard. As Warren Relf mounted to his room on the third floor, with the chatty Swiss waiter from the canton Ticino, who carried his bag, he asked quietly if the lady on the *segondo* who seemed so ill was n any immediate or pressing danger.

"Danger, signor? She is ill, certainly; they carried her upstairs: she couldn't have walked it. Ill—but ill." He expanded his hands and pursed his lips up.—"But what of that? The house expects it. They come here to die, many of these English. The signora no doubt will die soon. She's a very bad case. She has hardly any life in her."

Little reassured by this cold comfort, Warren sat down at the table at once, as soon as he had washed away the dust of travel, and scribbled off a hasty note to Edie—

"Dearest E.,

"Just arrived. Hope you received my telegram from Paris. For heaven's sake, don't let Elsie stir out of the house till I have seen you. This is most imperative. Massinger and Mrs. Massinger are here at this *pension*. He has brought her South for her health's sake. She's dying rapidly. I wouldn't for worlds let Elsie see either of them in their present condition: above all, she mustn't run up against them unexpectedly. I may not be able to sneak round to-night, but at at all hazards keep Elsie in till I can get to the Villa Rossa to consult with you. Elsie must of course return to England at once, now Massinger's come here. We have to face a very serious crisis. I won't write further, preferring to come and arrange in person. Meanwhile, say nothing to Elsie just yet; I'll break it to her myself.

> "In breathless haste,
>> "Yours ever, very affectionately,
>>> "WARREN."

He sent the note round with many warnings by the Swiss waiter to his mother's house. When Edie got it, she could have cried with chagrin. Could anything on earth have been more unfortunate? To think that Elsie should just have gone out shopping before the note arrived—and should be going to call at the Grand Hotel Royal in that very Avenue Vittorio-Emmanuele!

If Warren had only known that fact, he would have gone out at all risks to intercept and prevent her. But as things stood, he preferred to lurk unseen on his third floor. till night came on. He wanted to keep as quiet as possible. He didn't wish Massinger to know, for the present at least, of his arrival in San Remo. Later on, perhaps, when Elsie had safely started for England, he might see whether he could be of any service to Winifred.

And to Hugh too; for in spite of all, though he had told Hatherley their dislike was mutual, he pitied Massinger too profoundly now not to forget his righteous resentment at such a moment. If Warren's experience and connection at San Remo were of any avail, he would gladly place them at Massinger's disposal. Too manly himself to harbour a grudge, he scarcely recognized the existence of vindictive feeling in others.

Warren Relf! That serpent! That reptile! That eavesdropper! How strangely each of us looks to each! How grotesquely our perverted inner mirror, with its twists and curves, distorts and warps the lineaments of our fellows! Warren Relf! That implacable malignant enemy, for ever plotting and planning and caballing against him! Why, Warren Relf, whom Hugh so imaged himself in his angry mind, was sitting that moment with his head bent down to the bare table, and muttering half aloud through his teeth to himself: "Poor, poor Massinger! How hard for him to bear! Alone with that unhappy little dying soul! Without one friend to share his trouble! I wish I could do anything on earth to help him!"

CHAPTER XXXVII.

PROVING HIS CASE.

At the *pension*, Hugh had engaged in haste a dull private sitting-room on the second floor, with bedroom and dressing-room adjoining at the side; and here he laid Winifred down on the horse-hair sofa, wearied out with her long journey and her fit of delirium, but now restored for the time being by rest and food, in one of those marvellous momentary rallies which so often tempt consumptive patients to use up in a single dying flicker their small remaining reserve of vital energy. The house itself was dingy, stingy, bare, and second-rate; but the soft Italian air and the full sunshine that flooded the room through the open windows had a certain false exhilarating effect, like a glass of champagne; and under their stimulating influence Winifred felt a temporary strength to which she had long been quite unaccustomed. The waiter had brought her up refreshments on a tray, soup and sweetbreads and country wine —the plain sound generous Ligurian claret—and she had eaten and drunk with an apparent avidity which fairly took her 'iusband's breath away. The food supplied her with a sudden .ccess of hectic energy. "Wheel me over to the window," she ried in a stronger voice to Hugh. And Hugh wheeled the sofa over as he was bid to a point where she could see the town and the hills and the villas and the lemon-gardens, and the tall date-palms with their feathery foliage on the piazza opposite, to the cobalt-blue sea, and the gracious bays, and the endless ranges of the Maritime Alps on either side, towards Bordighera one way and Taggia the other.

It was beautiful, beautiful, very beautiful. For the moment, the sight soothed Winifred. She was content now to die where she lay. Her wounded heart asked nothing further from unkind fortune. She looked up at her husband with a stony gaze. "Hugh," she said, in firm but grimly resolute tones, with no trace of tenderness or softening in her voice, "bury me here. I like the place. Don't try to take me home in a box to Whitestrand."

Her very callousness, if callousness it were, cut him to the heart. That so young and frail and delicate a girl should talk of her own death with such seeming insensibility was indeed terrible. The proud hard man was broken at last. Shame and remorse touched his soul. He burst into tears, and kneeling by her side, tried to take her hand with some passing show of affection in his. Winifred withdrew it, coldly and silently, as his own approached it. "Winnie," he cried, bending over her face, "I don't ask you to forgive me. You can't forgive me. You could never forgive me for the wrong I've done you. But I do ask you, from my soul I do ask you, in this last extremity, to believe me and to listen to me. I did not lie to you last night. It was all true, what I told you in the *coupé.* I've never intrigued against you in the way you believe. I've never deceived you for the purpose you suppose. I've treated you cruelly, heartlessly, wickedly—I acknowledge that; but oh, Winnie, Winnie, I can't bear you to die as you will, believing what you do believe about me.—This is the hardest part of all my punishment. Don't leave me so! My wife, my wife, don't kill me with this coldness!"

Winifred looked over at him more stonily than ever. "Hugh," she said with a very slow and distinct utterance, "every word you say to me in this hateful strain only increases and deepens my loathing and contempt for you.—You see I'm dying—you know I'm dying. In your way, I really and truly believe you feel some tiny twinge of compunction, some faint sort of pity and regret and sympathy for me. You know you've killed me, broken my heart; and in a careless fashion, you're rather sorry for it. If you knew how, you'd like, without bothering yourself much, to console me. And yet, to lie is so ingrained in the very warp and woof of your nature, that even so, you can't help lying to me! You can't help lying to your own wife, at death's door, in her last extremity—your own wife, whom you've slowly ground down and worn out with your treachery—your own wife, whom you've betrayed and tortured and killed at last for that other woman!—Don't I know it all, so that you can't deceive me? Don't I know every thought and wish of your heart? Don't I know how you've kept her letters and her watch? Don't I know how you've brooded and moaned and whispered about her? Don't I know how you've brought me to San Remo to-day, dying as I am, to be near her and to caress her when I'm dead and buried?—You've tried to hound me and to drive me to my grave, that you might marry Elsie.— You've tried to murder me by slow degrees, that you might marry Elsie.—Well, you've carried your point: you've succeeded at last.—You've killed me now, or as good as killed me; and when I'm dead and gone, you can marry Elsie.—I don't mind that. Marry her and be done with it.—But if ever you dare to tell me again that lying story you concocted last night so glibly in the *coupé,*—Hugh Massinger, I'll tell you in earnest what I'll do: I'll jump out of that window before your very face and dash myself to pieces on the ground in front of you."

She spoke with feverish and lurid energy. Hugh Massinger

bent his head to his knees in abject wretchedness as she flung that threat from her clenched teeth at him. His very remorse availed him nothing. The girl was adamantine, inexorable, impervious to evidence. Nothing on earth that he could say or do would possibly move her. He felt himself unjustly treated now; and he pitied Winifred.

"Winifred, Winifred, my poor wronged and injured Winifred," he cried at last, in another wild outburst, "I can do or say nothing, I know, to convince you. But one thing perhaps will make you hesitate to disbelieve me. Look here, Winifred; watch me closely!"

A happy inspiration had come to his aid. He brought over the little round table from the corner of the room and planted it full in front of the sofa where Winifred was lying. Then he set a chair close by the side, and selecting a pen from his writing-case, began to produce on a sheet of note-paper, under Winifred's very eyes, some lines of manuscript—in Elsie's hand-writing. Slowly and carefully he framed each letter in poor dead Elsie's bold and large-limbed angular character. He didn't need now any copy to go by; long practice had taught him to absolute perfection each twist and curl and flourish of her pen—the very tails of her *g*s, the black downstroke of her *f*s, the peculiar unsteadiness of her *s*s and her *w*s. Winifred, sitting by in haughty disdain, pretended not even to notice his strange proceeding. But as the tell-tale letter grew on apace beneath his practised pen—Elsie all over, past human conceiving—she condescended at last, by an occasional hasty glimpse or side-glance, to manifest her interest in this singular pantomime. Hugh persevered to the end in solemn silence, and when he had finished the whole short letter, he handed it to her in a sort of subdued triumph. She took it with a gesture of supreme unconcern. "Did any man ever take such pains before," she cried ironically, as she glanced at it with an assumption of profound indifference, "to make himself out to his wife a liar, a forger, and perhaps a murderer!"

Hugh bit his lip with mortification, and watched her closely. The tables were turned. How strange that he should now be all eager anxiety for her to learn the truth he had tried so long and so successfully with all his might to conceal from her keenest and most prying scrutiny!

Winifred scanned the forged letter for a minute with apparent carelessness. But as she read and re-read it, in a mere haze of perception, some shadow of doubt for the first time obtruded itself faintly one moment upon her uncertain soul. For Hugh had indeed chosen his specimen letter cleverly—ah, that hateful cleverness of his! how even now it told with full force against him! When you have to deal with so cunning a rogue, you can never be sure. The more certain things seem, the more cause for distrusting them. He had written over again from memory the single note of Elsie's—or rather of his own in Elsie's hand—that Winifred had never happened at all to show him—the second note of the series, the one he despatched on the day of her father's death. It had reached her at Invertanar Castle, redirected from Whitestrand, two mornings later. Winifred had read the few lines as soon as they arrived, and then burnt the page in haste, in the heat and flurry of that tearful time. But now, as the letter lay before her in fac-simile once more, the very words and phrases came back to her memory, as they had come back to Hugh's, with all the abnormal vividness and distinctness of such morbid moments. Ill as she was—nay, rather dying—he had fairly aroused her feminine curiosity. "How did you ever come to know what Elsie wrote me that day?" she asked coldly.

"Because I wrote it myself," Hugh answered with an eager forward movement.

For half a minute, Winifred's soul was staggered. It looked plausible enough; he might have forged it. He could forge anything. Then with a sudden deep-drawn "Ah!" a fresh solution forced itself upon her mind. "You wretch!" she cried, holding her head with her hands; "I see it all now! How dare you lie to me? This is worse than I ever dreamt or conceived. Elsie spent that week with you in London!"

With a loud groan, Hugh flung himself back on his vacant chair. His very cleverness had recoiled upon him with deadly force again. The inference was obvious!—too, too, too obvious! What other interpretation could Winifred possibly put upon the facts? He wondered in his heart he could have missed that easy solution himself. "She wasn't!" he cried out with an agonized cry. "She was dead—dead—dead, I tell you—drowned and buried at Orfordness!"

Winifred looked hard at him, half doubtful still. Could any man be quite so false and heartless? Admirably as he acted, could he act like this? What tragedian had ever such command of his countenance? Might not that strange story of his, so pat and straight, so consonant with the facts, so neatly adapted in every detail to the known circumstances, perhaps after all be actually true? Could Elsie be really and truly dead? Could ring and letters and circumstantial evidence have fallen out, not as she conceived, but as Hugh pretended?

She hardly knew which thing would make her hate and despise him most—the forgery or the lie: that long deception, or that secret intrigue: his silent mourning over a dead love, or his clandestine correspondence with a living lover. Whichever was worst, she would choose to believe: for the wickedest course was likeliest to be the true one. It was a question merely when he had lied the most—now or then? to his dying wife or to his betrothed lover? Winifred gazed on at him, scorning and loathing him. "I can't make my mind up," she muttered slowly. "It's hard to believe that Elsie's dead. But for Elsie's sake, I hope so! I hope so!—That *you* have deceived me, I know and am sure. That Elsie's deceived me, I should be sorry to think, though I've often thought it. Your story, incredible as it may be, brings home all the baseness and cruelty to yourself. It exculpates Elsie. And I wish I could believe Elsie was innocent. I could endure your wickedness if only I knew Elsie didn't share it!"

Hugh leaped from his chair with his hands clasped. "Believe what you will about *me*," he cried. "I deserve it all. I deserve everything. But not of *her*—not of *her*, I beg of you. Believe no ill of poor dead Elsie!"

Winifred smiled a coldly satirical smile. "So much devotion does you honour indeed," she said in a scathing voice. "Your consideration for dead Elsie's reputation is truly touching.—I only see one flaw in the case. If Elsie's dead, how did Mr. Relf come to tell me, I should like to know, she was living at San Remo?"

"Relf!" Hugh cried, taken aback once more. "Relf! Always that serpent! That wriggling, insinuating, back-stairs in-riguer! I hate the wretch. If I had him here now, I'd wring is wry neck for him with the greatest pleasure.—He's at the bottom of everything that turns up against me. He told you a lie, that's the plain explanation, and he told it to baffle me. He hates me, the cur, and he wanted to make my game harder. He knew it would sow distrust between you and me if he told you that lie; and he had no pity, like an unmanly sneak that he is, even on a poor weak helpless woman."

"I see," Winifred murmured with exasperating calmness. "He told me the truth. It's his habit to tell it. And the truth happens to be very disconcerting to you, by making what you're frank enough to describe as your game a little harder. The word's sufficient. You can never do anything but play a game. That's very clear. I understand now. I prefer Mr. Relf's assurance to yours, thank you!"

"Winifred," Hugh cried, in an agony of despair, "let me tell you the whole story again, bit by bit, act by act, scene by scene"—Winifred smiled derisively at the theatrical phrase—"and you may question me out on every part of it. Cross-examine me, please, like a hostile lawyer, to the minutest detail.—Oh, Winnie, I want you to know the truth now. I wish you'd believe me. I can't endure to think that you should die mistaking me."

His imploring look and his evident earnestness shook Winifred's wavering mind again. Even the worst of men has his truthful moments. Her resolution faltered. She began, as he suggested, cross-questioning him at full. Hugh answered every one of her questions at once with prompt simplicity. Those answers had the plain ring of reality about them. A clever man can lie ingeniously, but he can't lie on the spur of the moment for long together. Winifred left no test untried. She asked him as to the arrangement of Elsie's room; as to the things he had purloined from the drawers and dressing-table; as to her letters to the supposed Elsie in Australia, all of which Hugh had of course intercepted and opened. Nowhere for one moment did she catch him tripping. He gave his replies plainly and straightforwardly. The fever of confession had seized hold of him once more. The pent-up secret had burst its bounds. He revealed his inmost soul to Winifred—he even admitted, with shame and agony, his abiding love and remorse for Elsie.

Overcome by her feelings, Winifred leaned back on the sofa and cried. Thank Heaven, thank Heaven, she could cry now. He was glad of that. She could cry, after all. That poor little cramped and cabined nature, turned in upon itself so long for lack of an outlet, found vent at last. Hugh cried himself, and held her hand. In her momentary impulse of womanly softening, she allowed him to hold it. Her wan small face pleaded piteously with his heart. "Dare I, Winnie?" he asked with a faint tremor, and leaning forward, he kissed her forehead. She did not withdraw it. He thrilled at the concession. Then he thought with a pang how cruelly he had worn her young life out. She never reproached him; her feelings went far too deep for reproach. But she cried silently, silently, silently.

At length she spoke. "When I'm gone," she said in a fainter voice now, "you must put up a stone by Elsie's grave. I'm glad Elsie at least was true to me!"

Hugh's heart gave a bound. Then she wavered at last! She accepted his account! She knew that Elsie was dead and buried! He had carried his point. She believed him!—she believed him!

Winifred rose, and staggered feebly to her feet. "I shall go to bed now," she said in husky accents. "You may send for a doctor. I shan't last long. But on the whole, I feel better so. I wanted Elsie to be alive indeed, because I hunger and thirst for sympathy, and Elsie would give it me. But I'm glad at least Elsie didn't deceive me!" She paused for a moment and wiped her eyes; then she steadied herself by the bar of the window—the air blew in so warm and fresh. She looked out at the palms and the blue, blue sea. It seemed to calm her, the beautiful South. She gazed long and wearily at the glassy

water. But her dream didn't last undisturbed for many
minutes. Of a sudden, a shade came over her face. Something
below seemed to sting and appal her. She started back, tottering, from the open window. "Hugh, Hugh!" she cried, ghastly
pale and quivering, "you said she was dead!—you said she was
dead! You lie to me still. Oh, Heaven, how terrible!"

"So she is," Hugh groaned out, half catching her in his arms
for fear she should fall. "Dead and buried, on my honour, at
Orfordness, Winifred!"

"Hugh, Hugh! can you *never* tell me the truth?" And she
stretched out one thin white bony forefinger towards the street
beyond. One second she gasped a terrible gasp; then she flung
out the words with a last wild effort: "That's she!—that's
Elsie!"

CHAPTER XXXVIII.

GHOST OR WOMAN?

WINIFRED spoke with such concentrated force of inner conviction that, absurd and incredible as he knew it to be—for had he
not seen Elsie's own grave that day at Orfordness?—Hugh
rushed over to the window in a fever of sudden suspense and
anxiety, and gazed across the street to the exact spot where
Vinifred's ghost-like finger pointed eagerly to some person or
hing on the pavement opposite. He was almost too late, however, to prove her wrong. As he neared the window, he caught
but a glimpse of a graceful figure in light half-mourning—like
Elsie's, to be sure, in general outline, though distinctly a trifle
older and fuller—disappearing in haste round the corner by the
pharmacy.

The figure gave him none the less a shock of surprise. It
was certainly a very strange and awkward coincidence. He
hadn't been in time to catch the face, indeed, as Winifred had
done; but the figure alone, the figure recalled every trait of
Elsie's. How singular, after Winifred had come to San Remo
with this profound belief in Elsie's living there, that on the
very first day of their stay in the town they should happen to
light by pure accident upon a person so closely recalling Elsie!
Surely, surely the stars in their courses were fighting against
him. Warren Relf could not be blamed for this. It was
destiny, sheer adverse destiny. Accidental resemblances and
horrid coincidences were falling together blindly with unconscious cunning, on purpose, as it were, to spite and disconcert
him. The laws of chance were setting themselves by the ears
for his special discomfiture. No ordinary calculation could

account for this. It had in it something almost supernatural.
He glanced at Winifred. She stood triumphant there—
triumphant but heart-broken—exulting over his defeat with
one dying "I told you so," and chuckling out inarticulately in
her thin small voice, with womanish persistence: "That's she!—
that's Elsie!"

"It's very like her!" he moaned in his agony.

"Very like her!" Winifred cried with a fresh burst of unnatural strength. "Very like her!—Oh, Hugh, I despise you!
I tell you I saw her face to face! It's Elsie—it's Elsie!"

A picture sometimes darts across one's eye for a brief moment,
and remains vaguely photographed for a space on the retina,
but uninterpreted by the brain, till it grows, as we dwell upon
it mentally afterwards, ever clearer and clearer, and at last with
a burst flashes its real significance fully home to us in a flood of
conviction. As Hugh stood there, absorbed, by the half-open
window, the picture he had caught of that slight lithe figure
sweeping round the corner with Elsie's well-known gait came
home to him thus with a sudden rush of indubitable certainty.
He no longer hesitated. He saw it was so. He knew her now!
It was Elsie, Elsie!

His brain reeled and whirled with the unexpected shock; the
universe turned round on him as on a pivot. "Winifred," he
cried, "you're right! you're right! There can't be anybody
else on earth so like her! I don't know how she's come back to
life! She's dead and buried at Orfordness! It's a miracle! a
miracle! But that's she that we saw! I can't deny it. That's
she!—that's Elsie!"

His hat lay thrown down on the table by his side. He
snatched it up in his eager haste to follow and track down this
mysterious resemblance. He couldn't let Elsie's double, her
bodily simulacrum, walk down the street unnoticed and un-
questioned. A profound horror possessed his soul. A doubter
by nature, he seemed to feel the solid earth failing beneath his
feet. He had never before in all his life drawn so perilously
close to the very verge and margin of the unseen universe. It
was Elsie herself, or else—the grave had yielded up its shadowy
occupant.

He rushed to the door, on fire with his sense of mystery and
astonishment. A loud laugh by his side held him back as he
went. He turned round. It was Winifred, laughing, choking,
exultant, hysterical. She had flung herself down on the sofa
now, and was catching her breath in spasmodic bursts with
unnatural merriment. That was the awful kind of laughter
that bodes no good to those who laugh it—hollow, horrible,
mocking, delusive. Hugh saw at a glance she was dangerously
ill. Her mirth was the mirth of mania, and worse. With a

burning soul and a chafing heart, he turned back, as in duty bound, to her side again. He must leave Elsie's wraith to walk by itself, unexplained and uninvestigated, its ghostly way down the streets of San Remo. He had more than enough to do at home. Winifred was dying!—dying of laughter.

And yet her laugh seemed almost hilarious. In spite of all, it had a ghastly ring of victory and boisterous joy in it. "Oh, Hugh," she cried, with little choking chuckles, in the brief intervals of her spasmodic peals, "you're *too* absurd! You'll kill me! you'll kill me!—I can't help laughing; it's *so* ridiculous. —You tell me one minute, with solemn oaths and ingenious lies, you've seen her grave—you know she's dead and buried: you pull long faces till you almost force me to believe you—you positively cry and moan and groan over her—and then the next second, when she passes the window before my very eyes, alive and well, and in her right mind, you seize your hat, you want to rush out and find her and embrace her—here, this moment, right under my face—and leave me alone to die by myself, without one soul on earth to wait upon me or help me!" Her emotion supplied her with words and images above her own level.—"It's just grotesque," she went on after a pause. "It's inhuman in its absurdity. Wicked as you are, and shameless as you are, it's impossible for any one to take you seriously.— You're the living embodiment of a little, inconsequent, meddling, muddling, mischief-making medieval demon. You're a burlesque Mephistophiles. You've got no soul, and you've got no feelings. But you make me laugh! Oh, you make me laugh! You've broken my heart; but you'll be the death of me.—Puck and Don Juan rolled into one!—'Elsie's dead!—Why, there's dear Elsie!'—It's too incongruous; it's too ridiculous." And she exploded once more in a hideous semblance of laughter.

Hugh gazed at her blankly, sobered with alarm. Was she going mad? or was he mad himself?—that he should see visions, and meet dead Elsie! Could it really be Elsie? He had heard strange stories of appearances and second-sight, such as mystics among us love to dwell upon; and in all of them the appearances were closely connected with death-bed scenes. Could any truth lurk, after all, in those discredited tales of wraiths and visions? Could Elsie's ghost have come from the grave to prepare him betimes for Winifred's funeral? Or did Winifred's dying mind, by some strange alchemy, project, as it were, an image of Elsie, who filled her soul, on to his own eye and brain, as he sat there beside her?

He brushed away these metaphysical cobwebs with a dash of his hand. Fool that he was to be led away thus by a mere accidental coincidence or resemblance! He was tired with sleeplessness; emotion had unmanned him.

Winifred's laugh dissolved itself into tears. She broke down now, hysterically, utterly. She sobbed and moaned in agony on the sofa. Deep sighs and loud laughter alternated horribly in her storm of emotion. The worst had come. She was dangerously ill. Hugh feared in his heart she was on the point of dying.

"Go!" she burst out, in one spasmodic effort, thrusting him away from her side with the palm of her open hand. "I don't want you here. Go—go—to Elsie! I can die now. I've found you all out. You're both of you alike; you've both of you deceived me."

Hugh rang the bell wildly for the Swiss waiter. "Send the chambermaid!" he cried in his broken Italian. "The patroness! A lady! The signora is ill. No time to be lost. I must run at once and find the English doctor."

When Winifred looked around her again, she found two or three strange faces crowded beside the bed on which they had laid her, and a fresh young Italian girl, the landlady's daughter, holding her head and bathing her brows with that universal specific, orange-flower water. The faint perfume revived her a little. The landlady's daughter was a comely girl, with sympathetic eyes, and she smiled the winsome Italian smile as the poor pale child opened her lids and looked vaguely up at her. "Don't cry, signorina," she said soothingly. Then her glance fell, woman-like, upon the plain gold ring on Winifred's thin and wasted fourth finger, and she corrected herself half unconsciously: "Don't cry, signora. Your husband will soon be back by your side : he's gone to fetch the English doctor."

"I don't want him," Winifred cried, with intense yearning, in her boarding-school French, for she knew barely enough Italian to understand her new little friend. "I don't want my husband; I want Elsie. Keep him away from me—keep him away, I pray.—Hold my hand yourself, and send away my husband! Je ne l'aime pas, cet hommelà!" And she burst once more into a discordant peal of hysterical laughter.

"The poor signora!" the girl murmured, with wide open eyes, to the others around. "Her husband is cruel. Ah, wicked wretch! Hear what she says! She says she doesn't want any more to see him. She wants her sister!"

As she spoke, a white face appeared suddenly at the door— a bearded man's face, silent and sympathetic. Warren Relf had heard the commotion downstairs, from his room above, and had seen Massinger run in hot haste for the doctor. He had come down now with eager inquiry for poor wasted Winifred, whose face and figure had impressed him much as he saw her borne out by the porters at the railway station.

"Is the signora very ill?" he asked in a low voice of the

nearest woman. "She speaks no Italian, I fear. Can I be of any use to her?"

"Ecco! 'tis Signor Relf, the English artist!" the woman cried, in surprise; for all San Remo knew Warren well as an old inhabitant.—"Come in, signor," she continued, with Italian frankness—for bedrooms in Italy are less sacred than in England. "You know the signora? She is ill—very ill: she is faint—she is dying."

At the name, Winifred turned her eyes languidly to the door, and raised herself, still dressed in her travelling dress, on her elbows on the bed. She yearned for sympathy. If only she could fling herself on Elsie's shoulder! Elsie, who had wronged her, would at least pity her. "Mr. Relf," she cried, too weak to be surprised, but glad to welcome a fellow-countryman and acquaintance among so many strangers—and with Hugh himself worse than a stranger—"I'm going to die. But I want to speak to you. You know the truth. Tell me about Elsie. Why did Elsie Challoner deceive me?"

"Deceive you!" Warren answered, drawing nearer in his horror. "She didn't deceive you. She couldn't deceive you. She only wished to spare your heart from suffering all her own heart had suffered. Elsie could never deceive any one."

"But why did she write to say she was in Australia, when he was really living here in San Remo?" Winifred asked piteously. "And why did she keep up a correspondence with my husband?"

"Write she was in Australia! She never **wrote**," Warren cried in haste, seizing the poor dying girl's thin hand in his.—"Mrs. Massinger, this is no time to conceal anything. I dare not speak to you against your husband, but still——"

"I hate him!" Winifred gasped out, with concentrated loathing. "He has done nothing since I knew him but lie to me and deceive me. Don't mind speaking ill of him; I don't object to that. What kills me is that Elsie has helped him! Elsie has helped him!"

"Elsie has not," Warren answered, lifting up her white little hand to his lips and kissing it respectfully. "Elsie and I are very close friends. Elsie has always loved you dearly. If she's hidden anything from you, she hid it for your own sake alone.—It was Hugh Massinger who forged those letters.—I can't let you die thinking ill of Elsie. Elsie has never, never written to him.—I know it all.—I'll tell you the truth. Your husband thought she was drowned at Whitestrand!"

"Then Hugh doesn't know she's living here?" Winifred cried eagerly.

Warren Relf hardly knew how to answer her in this unexpected crisis. It was a terrible moment. He couldn't expose

Elsie to the chance of meeting Hugh face to face. The shock and strain, he knew, would be hard for her to bear. But, on the other hand, he couldn't let that poor broken-hearted little woman die with this fearful load of misery unlightened on her bosom. The truth was best. The truth is always safest. "Hugh doesn't know she's living here," he answered slowly. "But if I could only be sure that Hugh and she would not meet, I'd bring her round, before she leaves San Remo, this very day, and let you hear from her own lips, beyond dispute, her true story."

Winifred clenched her thin hands hard and tight. "He shall never enter this room again," she whispered hoarsely, " till he enters it to see me laid out for burial."

Warren Relf drew back, horrified at her unnatural sternness. "Oh no," he cried. "Mrs. Massinger—you don't mean that: remember, he's your husband."

" He never was *my* husband," Winifred answered with a fresh burst of her feverish energy. "He was Elsie's husband—Elsie's at heart. He loved Elsie. He never married *me* myself at all; he married only the manor of Whitestrand.—He shall never come near me again while I live.—I shall hold him off. I'm a weak woman ; but I've strength enough and will enough left for that.—I shall keep him at arm's-length as long as I live. —Don't be afraid. Bring Elsie here; I want to see her. I should die happy if only I knew that Elsie hadn't helped that man to deceive me."

Meanwhile, Hugh Massinger was hurrying along on his way to the English doctor's, saying to himself a thousand times over: "I don't care how much she thinks ill of *me* ; but I can't endure she should die thinking ill of poor dead Elsie. If only I could make her believe me in that. If only she knew that Elsie was true to her, that poor dead Elsie had never deceived her!" He had so much of chivalry, so much of earnestness, so much of devotion, still left in him. But he thought most of poor dead Elsie, not at all of poor deceived and dying Winifred. For he no longer believed it was really Elsie he had seen in the street: the delusion had come and gone in a flash. How could it be Elsie? Such sights are impossible. He was no dreamer of dreams or seer of visions. Elsie was dead and buried at Orfordness, and this other figure—was only, after all, very, very like her.

CHAPTER XXXIX.

AFTER LONG GRIEF AND PAIN.

THE time to stand upon trifles was past. Let him run the risk of meeting Massinger by the way or not, Warren Relf must needs go round and fetch Elsie to comfort and console poor dying Winifred. He hastened away at the top of his speed to the Villa Rossa. At the door, both girls together met him. Elsie had just returned, basket in hand, from the Avenue Vittorio-Emmanuele, and had learnt from Edie so much of the contents of Warren's hasty letter as had been intended from the first for her edification.

Warren hadn't meant to let Elsie know that Hugh and Winifred had come to San Remo; or, at any rate, not immediately. He wished rather to break it by gradual stages, and to prepare her mind as quietly as possible for a hasty return home to England. But the sight of poor Winifred's dying misery and distress had put all that on a different footing. Even though it cost Elsie a bitter wrench, he must take her round at all costs to see Winifred. He kissed his sister, a mechanical kiss; then h rned round, and, half by accident, half by design, for the fi ime in his life he kissed Elsie too, like one who hardly k.... s he does it. Elsie drew back, a trifle surprised, but did not resent the unexpected freedom. After all, one may always kiss one's brother; and she and Warren were brother and sister.— Did it run in the family, peradventure, that false logic of love? Was Elsie now deceiving herself with the self-same plea as that with which Hugh had once in his turn deceived her?

Warren drew her aside gently into the tiny salon, and motioned to Edie not to follow them. Elsie's heart beat high with wonder. She was aware how much it made her pulse quicken to see Warren again—with something more than the mere fraternal greeting she pretended. Her little self-deception broke down at last : she knew she loved him—in an unpractical way; and she was almost sorry she could never, never make him happy.

But Warren's grave face bade her heart stand still for a beat or two next moment. He had clearly something most serious to communicate—something that he knew would profoundly distress her. A womanly alarm came over her with a vague surmise. Could Warren be going to tell her——? Oh no! Impossible. She knew dear Warren too well for that! he at least could never be cruel.

If Warren was going to tell her *that*, her faith in her kind would die out for ever. And then, she almost smiled to herself at her own frank and feminine inconsistency. She, who could never love again!—she, who had always scrupulously told him she cared for him only as a sister for a brother!—she, who wanted him to marry "some nice girl, who would make him happy." She recognized now that if that "nice girl" had in reality floated across Warren Relf's spiritual horizon, her life would again be left unto her desolate. It flashed across her mind with vivid distinctness, in that moment of painful doubt and uncertainty, that after all she really loved him!—beyond shadow of question, she really loved him!

"Well, Warren?" she asked with tremulous eagerness, drawing closer up to him in her sweet womanly confidence, and gazing into his eyes, half afraid, half affectionate. How could she ever have doubted him, were it only for a second?

"Elsie," Warren cried, laying his hand with unspoken tenderness on her shapely shoulder, "I want you to come round at once to the *pension* on the piazza.—It's better to tell it all out at once. Winifred Massinger's come to San Remo, very ill—dying, I fear. She knows you're here, and she's asked to see you."

Elsie's face grew red and then white for a moment, and she trembled visibly. "Is *he* there?" she asked, after a short pause. Then, with a sudden burst of uncontrollable tears, she buried her face in her hands on the table.

Warren soothed her with his hand tenderly, and, leaning over her, told her, in haste and in a very low voice, the whole sad story. "I don't think he'll be there," he added at the end. "Mrs. Massinger said she wouldn't allow him to enter the room. But in any case—for that poor girl's sake—you won't refuse to go to her now, will you, Elsie?"

"No," Elsie answered, rising calmly with womanly dignity, to face it all out. "I *must* go. It would be cruel and wicked of course to shirk it. For Winifred's sake, I'll go in any case —But, Warren, before I dare to go——" She broke off sud·denly, and with a woman's impulse held up her pale face to him in mute submission.

A thrill coursed through Warren Relf's nerves; he stooped down and pressed his lips fervently to hers. "Before you go, you are mine then, Elsie!" he cried eagerly.

Elsie pressed his hand faintly in reply. "I am yours, Warren," she answered at last very low, after a short pause. "But I can't be yours as you wish it for a long time yet. No matter why. I shall be yours in heart.—I couldn't have gone on any other terms. And with that, I think, I can go and face it."

At the *pension*, Hugh had already brought the English doctor, who went in alone to look after Winifred. Hugh had tried to accompany him into the bedroom! but Winifred, true to her terrible threat, lifted one stern forefinger before his swimming eyes and cried out "Never!" in a voice so doggedly determined that Hugh slank away abashed into the anteroom.

The English doctor stopped for several minutes in consultation, and Winifred spoke to him, simply and unreservedly about her husband. "Send that man away!" she cried, pointing to Hugh, as he stood still peering across from the gloom of the doorway. "I won't have him in here to see me die! I won't have him in here! It makes me worse to see him about the place. I hate him!—I hate him!"

"You'd better go," the doctor whispered softly, looking him hard in the face with his inquiring eyes. "She's in a very excited, hysterical condition. She's best alone, with only the women. —A husband's presence often does more harm than good in such nervous crises. Nobody should be near to increase her excitement.—Have the kindness to shut the door, if you please. You needn't come back for the present, thank you."

And then Winifred unburdened once more her poor laden soul in convulsive sobs. "I want to see Elsie! I want to see Elsie!"

"Miss Challoner?" the doctor asked suggestively. He knew her well as the tenderest and best of amateur nurses.

Winifred explained to him with broken little cries and eager words that she wished to see Elsie in Hugh's absence.

At the end of five minutes' soothing talk, the doctor read it all to the very bottom with professional acuteness. The poor girl was dying. Her husband and she had never got on. She hungered and thirsted for human sympathy. Why not gratify her yearning little soul? He stepped back into the bare and dingily lighted sitting-room. "I think," he said persuasively to Hugh, with authoritative suggestion, "your wife would be all the better in the end if she were left entirely alone with the womenkind for a little. Your presence here evidently disturbs and excites her. Her condition's critical, distinctly critical. I won't conceal it from you. She's over-fatigued with the journey and with mental exhaustion. The slightest aggravation of the hysterical symptoms might carry her off at any moment. If I were you, I'd stroll out for an hour. Lounge along by the shore or up the hills a bit. I'll stop and look after her. She's quieter now. You needn't come back for at least an hour."

Hugh knew in his heart it was best so. Winifred hated him, not without cause. He took up his hat, crushed it fiercely on his head, and, strolling down by himself to the water's edge, sat in the listless calm of utter despair on a bare bench in the cool fresh air of an Italian evening. He thought in a hopeless, helpless, irresponsible way about poor dead Elsie and poor dying Winifred.

Five minutes after Hugh had left the *pension*, Warren Relf and Elsie mounted the big centre staircase and knocked at the door of Winifred's bare and dingy salon. The *patron* had already informed them that the signor was gone out, and that the signora was up in her room alone with the women of the hotel and the English doctor.

Warren Relf remained by himself in the ante-room. Elsie went in unannounced to Winifred.

Oh, the joy and relief of that final meeting! The poor dying girl rose up on the bed with a bound to greet her. A sudden flush crimsoned her sunken cheeks. As her eyes rested once more upon Elsie's face—that earnest, serious, beautiful face she had loved and trusted—every shadow of fear and misery faded from her look, and she cried aloud in a fever of delight: "Oh, Elsie, Elsie, I'm glad you've come. I'm glad to hold your hand in mine again; now I can die happy!"

Elsie saw at a glance that she spoke the truth. That bright red spot in the centre of each wan and pallid cheek told its own sad tale with unmistakable eloquence. She flung her arms fervently round her feeble little friend. "Winnie, Winnie!" she cried—"my own sweet Winnie! Why didn't you let me know before? If I'd thought you were like this, I'd have come to you long ago!"

"Then you love me still?" Winifred murmured low, clinging tight and hard to her recovered friend with a feverish longing.

"I've always loved you; I shall always love you," Elsie answered slowly. "My love doesn't come and go, Winnie. If I hadn't loved you more than I can say, I'd have come long since. It was for your own sake I kept so long away from you."

The English doctor rose with a sign from the chair by the bedside and motioned the women out of the room.—"We'll leave you alone," he said in a quiet voice to Elsie.—"Don't excite her too much, if you please, Miss Challoner. But I know I can trust you. I leave her in the very best of hands. You can only be soothing and restful anywhere."

The doctor's confidence was perhaps ill-advised. As soon as those two were left by themselves—the two women who had loved Hugh Massinger best in the world, and whom Hugh Massinger had so deeply wronged and so cruelly injured, they fell upon one another's necks with a great cry, and wept, and caressed one another long in silence. Then Winifred,

leaning back in fatigue, said with a sudden burst: "Oh, Elsie,
Elsie! I can't die now without confessing it, all, every word to
you: once, do you know—more than once I distrusted you!"

"I know, my darling," Elsie answered with a tearful smile,
kissing her pale white fingers many times tenderly. "I know,
I understand. You couldn't help it. You needn't explain. It
was no wonder."

Winifred gazed at her transparent eyes and truthful face. No
one who saw them could ever distrust them, at least while he
looked at them. "Elsie," she said, gripping her tight in her
grasp—the one being on earth who could truly sympathize with
her—"I'll tell you why: he kept your letters all in a box—
your letters and the little gold watch he gave you."

"No, not the watch, darling," Elsie answered, starting back.
—"Winnie, I'll tell you what I did with that watch: I threw
it into the sea off the pier at Lowestoft."

A light broke suddenly over Winifred's mind; she knew now
Hugh had told her the truth for once. "He picked it up at
Orfordness," she mused simply. "It was carried there by the
tide with a woman's body—a body that he took for yours,
Elsie."

"He doesn't know I'm alive even now, dearest," Elsie whispered by her side. "I hope while I live he may never know
it; though I don't know now how we're to keep it from him, I
confess, much longer."

Then Winifred, emboldened by Elsie's hand, poured out her
ull grief in her friend's ear, and told Elsie the tale of her long,
.ong sorrow. Elsie listened with a burning cheek. "If only I'd
known!" she cried at last. "If only I'd known all this ever so
much sooner! But I didn't want to come between you two. I
thought perhaps I would spoil all: I fancied you were happy
with one another."

"And after I'm dead, Elsie, will you—see him?"

Elsie started. "Never, darling," she cried. "Never, never!"

"Then you don't love him any longer, dear?"

"Love him? Oh no! That's all dead and buried long ago.
I mourned too many months for my dead love, Winifred; but
after the way Hugh's treated you—how could I love him? how
could I help feeling harshly towards him?"

Winifred pressed her friend in her arms harder than ever.
"Oh, Elsie!" she cried, "I love you better than anybody else in
the whole world. I wish I'd had you always with me. If you'd
been near, I might have been happier. How on earth could I
ever have ventured to mistrust you!"

They talked long and low in their confidences to one another,
each pouring out her whole arrears of time, and each understanding for the first moment many things that had long been

strangely obscure to them. At last Winifred repeated the tale of her two or three late stormy interviews with her husband. She told them truthfully, just as they occurred—extenuating nothing on either side—down to the very words she had used to Hugh: "You've tried to murder me by slow torture, that you might marry Elsie:" and that other terrible sentence she had spoken out that very evening to Warren: "He shall not enter this room again till he enters it to see me laid out for burial."

Elsie shuddered with unspeakable awe and horror when that frail young girl, so delicate of mould and so graceful of feature even still, uttered those awful words of vindictive rancour against the man she had pledged her troth to love and to honour. "Oh, Winifred!" she cried, looking down at her with mingled pity and terror traced in every line of her compassion-ate face, "you didn't say that! You could never have meant it!"

Winifred clenched her white hands yet harder once more. "Yes, I did," she cried. "I meant it, and I mean it. He's hounded me to death; and now that I'm dying, he shan't gloat over me!"

"Winnie, Winnie, he's your husband, your husband! Remember what you promised to do when you married him."

"That's just what Mr. Relf said to me this afternoon," Winifred cried excitedly. "And I answered him back: 'He never was a husband of mine at all. He was Elsie's husband. He loved Elsie. He never married *me:* he only married the manor of Whitestrand. He shan't come near me again while I live. I only want to know before I die that Elsie never helped that wretch to deceive me!'"

"And you know that now, darling!"

"Elsie, Elsie, I know it! Forgive me." She stretched out her arms with an appealing glance.

Elsie stooped down and kissed her once more. "Winnie," she pleaded in a low soft voice, "he's your husband, after all. Don't feel so bitterly to him. I know he's wronged you; I know he's blighted your dear life for you; I can see how he's crushed your very soul out by his coldness and his cruelty, and his pride and his sternness. But for all that, I can't bear to hear you say you'll die in anger—die, and leave him behind unforgiven. Oh, for my sake, and for your own sake, Winnie, if not for his—do see him and speak to him, just once, forgivingly."

"Never!" Winifred answered, starting up on the bed once more with a ghastly energy. "He's driven me to the grave: let him have his punishment!"

Elsie drew back, more horrified than ever. Her face spoke better than her words to Winifred. "My darling," she cried,

"you *must* see him. You must never die and leave him so."
Then in a gentler voice she added imploringly: ".Forgive us
our trespasses, as we forgive them that trespass against us."

Winifred buried her face wildly in her bloodless hands. "I
can't," she moaned out; "I haven't the power. It's too late
now.   He's been too cruel to me."

For many minutes together, Elsie bent tenderly over her,
whispering words of consolation and comfort in her ears, while
Winifred listened and cried silently. At last, after Elsie had
soothed her long, and wept over her much with soft loving
touches, Winifred looked up in her face with a wistful gaze.
"I think, Elsie," she said slowly, "I could bear to see him, if
you would stop with me here and help me."

Elsie shrank into herself with a sudden horror. That would
be a crucial trial, indeed, of her own forgiveness for the man
who had wronged her, and her own affection for poor dying
Winifred. Meet Hugh again, so painfully, so unexpectedly!
Come back to him at once, from the tomb, as it were, to remind
him of his crime, and before Winifred's eyes—poor dying
Winifred's!   The very idea made her shudder with alarm.
"Oh, Winnie,"she cried, looking down upon her friend with her
great gray eyes, "I couldn't face him. I thought I should
never see him again. I daren't do it. You mustn't ask me."

"Then you haven't forgiven him yourself!" Winifred burst
out eagerly. "You love him still! You love him—and you
hate him!—Elsie, that's just the same as me. I hate him—but
  love him; oh! how I do love him!"

She spoke no more than the simple truth. She was judging
Elsie by her own heart. With that strange womanly paradox
we so often see, she loved her husband even now, much as she
hated him. It was that indeed that made her hate him so
much: her love gave point to her hatred and her jealousy.

"No, darling," Elsie answered, bending over her closer and
speaking lower in her ear than she had yet spoken. "I don't
love him; and I don't hate him. I forgive him all! I've
forgiven him long ago.—Winnie, I love some one else now.
I've given my heart away at last, and I've given it to a better
man than Hugh Massinger."

"Then why won't you wait and help me to see him?" Winifred cried once more in her fiery energy.

"Because—I'm ashamed. I can't look him in the face;
that's all, Winnie."

Winifred clung to her like a frightened child to its mother's
skirts. "Elsie," she burst out, with childish vehemence,
"stop with me now to the end! Don't ever leave me!"

Elsie's heart sank deep into her bosom. A horrible dread
possessed her soul. She saw one ghastly possibility looming

before them that Winifred never seemed to recognize. Hugh
kept her letters, her watch, her relics. Suppose he should come
and—recognizing her at once, betray his surviving passion for
herself before poor dying Winifred! She dared hardly face so
hideous a chance. And yet, she couldn't bear to untwine herself from Winifred's arms, that clung so tight and so tenderly
around her. There was no time to lose, however: she must
make up her mind. "Winifred," she murmured, laying her
head close down by the dying girl's, "I'll do as you say. I'll
stop here still. I'll see Hugh. As long as you live, I'll never
leave you!"

Winifred loosed her arms one moment again, and then flung
them in a fresh access of feverish fervour round her recovered
friend—her dear beautiful Elsie. "You'll stop here," she cried
through her sobs and tears; "you'll help me to tell Hugh I
forgive him."

"I'll stop here," Elsie answered low, "and I'll help you to
forgive him."

CHAPTER XL.

AT REST AT LAST.

WINIFRED fell back on the pillows wearily. "I love him," she
whispered once more. "He hates me, Elsie; but in spite of all,
I love him, I love him."

For years she had locked up that secret in her own soul.
She had told it to no one, least of all to her husband. But,
confined to the narrow space of her poor small heart, and
battling there with her contempt and scorn, it had slowly eaten
her very life out. Hating and despising him for his crooked
ways, she loved him still, for her old love's sake: with a
woman's singleness of heart and purpose, she throned him in
her love, supreme and solitary. And the secret at last had
framed itself into words and confided itself almost against her
will to Elsie.

Her face was growing very pale now. After all this excitement, she needed rest. The inevitable reaction was beginning
to set in. She fumbled with her fingers on the bedclothes
nervously; her face twitched with a painful twitching. The
symptoms alarmed and frightened Elsie; she opened the door
of the little *salon* and signalled to the English doctor to return
to the bedroom. He came in, and cast a keen glance at the
bed. Elsie looked up at him with inquiring eyes. The doctor
nodded gravely and drew his long beard through his closed

hand. "A mere question of hours," he whispered in her ear. "It may be delayed; it may come at any time. She's over-taxed her strength. Hysteria, followed by proportionate pros-tration. Her heart may fail from moment to moment."

"Where's her husband?" Elsie cried in a fever of dismay. Her one wish now was for Hugh to present himself. She forgot at once her own terror and false shame; she remembered no more her feminine shrinking; self had vanished from her mind altogether; she thought only of poor dying Winifred. And of Hugh too. For she couldn't bear to believe, even after all she had heard and known of his life, that the Hugh she had once loved and trusted could let his wife thus die in his absence—could let her die, himself unforgiven.

"I've sent him off about his business for an hour's stroll," the doctor answered with professional calmness. "She's evi-dently in a highly hysterical condition, and the sight of him only increases her excitement. It's a sad case, but a painfully common one. A husband's presence is often the very worst thing on earth for a patient so affected. I thought it would do her far more good to have you alone with her—you're always so gentle and so soothing, Miss Challoner."

Elsie glanced back at him with swimming eyes. "But sup-pose she were to die while he's gone," she murmured low with profound emotion.

The doctor pursed up his lips philosophically. "It can't be elped," he answered with a faint shrug. "That's just what'll appen, I'm very much afraid. We can only do the best we .an. This crisis has evidently been too severe for her."

As he spoke, Winifred turned up from the bed an appealing face, and beckoned Elsie to bend down closer to her. "Elsie," she whispered, in a low hoarse voice, "send out for Hugh. I want him now.—I should like to kiss him before I die. I think I'm going. I won't last much longer."

Elsie hurried out to Warren in the anteroom. "Go," she cried eagerly, through her blinding tears—"go and find Hugh. Winifred wants him; she wants to kiss him before she dies. Look for him through all the streets till you find him, and send him home. She wants to forgive him."

Warren gazed close at her with reverent eyes. "She wants to forgive him, Elsie?" he cried half incredulous. "She wants to forgive him, that hard little woman! You've brought her round to that already?"

"Yes," Elsie answered.—"Go quick and find him. She isn't hard; she's tender as a child. She's dying now—dying of cramped and thwarted affection. In another half-hour, it may be too late. Go at once, I beg of you."

Warren answered her never a single word, but, nodding

acquiescence, rushed down by himself to the esplanade and the shore in search of his enemy. Poor baffled enemy, how his heart ached for him! At such a moment, who could help pitying him?

"Is he coming?" Winifred asked from the bed feebly.

"Not yet, darling," Elsie answered in a hushed voice; "but Warren's gone out to try and find him. He'll be here soon. Lie still and wait for him."

Winifred lay quite still for some minutes more, breathing hard and loud on the bed where they had laid her. The moments appeared to spread themselves over hours. But no Hugh came. At last she beckoned Elsie nearer again, with a frail hand that seemed almost to have lost all power of motion. Elsie leant over her with her ear laid close to Winifred's lips. The poor girl's voice sounded very weak and all but inaudible now. "I can't last till he comes, Elsie," she murmured low. "But tell him I forgave him. Tell him I asked him to forgive me in turn. Tell him I wanted to kiss him good-bye. But even that last wish was denied me. And Elsie"—her fingers clutched her friend's convulsively—"tell him all along I've always loved him. I loved him from the very depths of my soul. I never loved any one as I loved that man. When I hated him most, I loved him dearly. It was my very love that made me so hate him. He starved my heart; and now it's broken."

Elsie stooped down and kissed her forehead. A smile played lambent over Winifred's face at the gentle kiss. The doctor lifted his open hand in warning. Elsie bent over her with gathered brows and strained her eyes for a sign of breath for a moment. "Gone?" she asked at last with mute lips of the doctor.

"Gone," the calmer observer answered with a grave inclination of his head toward Elsie. "Rapid collapse. A singular case. She suffered no pain at the last, poor lady."

Elsie flung herself wildly into an easy-chair and burst into tears more burning than ever.

A touch on her shoulder. She looked up with a start. Could this be Hugh? Thank Heaven, no! It was Warren who touched her shoulder lightly. Half an hour had passed, and he had now come back again. But, alas, too late. "No need to stop here any longer," he said reverently. "Hugh's downstairs, and they're breaking the news to him. He doesn't know yet you're here at all. I didn't speak to him. I thought some other person would move him more. I saw him on the quay, and I sent an Italian I met on the beach to tell him he was wanted, and his wife was dying.—Come up to my room on the

floor above. Hugh needn't know even now, perhaps, that you're
here at San Remo."

Too full to speak, Elsie followed him blindly from the chamber
of death, and stumbled somehow up the broad flight of stairs to
Warren's apartments on the next story. As she reached the
top of the open flight, she heard a voice—a familiar voice, that
would once have thrilled her to the very heart—on the landing
below, by Winifred's bedroom. Shame and fascination drew
her different ways. Fascination won. She couldn't resist the
dangerous temptation to look over the edge of the banisters for
a second. Hugh had just mounted the stairs from the big
entrance hall, and was talking by the door in measured tones
with the English doctor.

"Very well," he said in his cold stern voice, the voice he had
always used to Winifred—a little lowered by conventional respect, indeed, but scarcely so subdued as the doctor's own.
"I'm prepared for the worst. If she's dead, say so. You
needn't be afraid of shocking my feelings; I expected it shortly."

She could see his face distinctly from the spot where she
stood, and she shrank back aghast at once from the sight with
surprise and horror. It was Hugh to be sure, but oh, what a
Hugh! How changed and altered from that light and bright
young dilettante poet she had loved and worshipped in the old
days at Whitestrand! His very form and features, and limbs
and figure were no longer the same; all were unlike, and the
difference was all to their disadvantage. The man had not only
grown sterner and harder; he was coarser and commoner and
less striking than formerly. His very style had suffered visible
degeneration. No more of the jaunty old poetical air; turnips
and foot-and-mouth disease, the arrears of rent and the struggle
against reduction, the shifting sands and the weight of the
riparian proprietors' question, had all left their mark stamped
deep in ugly lines upon his face and figure. He was handsome
still, but in a less refined and delicate type of manly beauty.
The long smouldering war between himself and Winifred had
changed his expression to a dogged ill-humour. His eyes had
grown dull and sordid and selfish, his lips had assumed a sullen
set, and a ragged beard with unkempt ends had disfigured that
clear-cut and dainty chin that was once so eloquent of poetry
and culture. Altogether, it was but a pale and flabby version
of the old, old Hugh—a replica from whose head the halo had
faded. Elsie looked down on him from her height of vantage
with a thrill of utter and hopeless disillusionment. Then she
turned with a pang of remorse to Warren. Was it really possible? Was there once a time when she thought in her heart
that self-centred, hard-hearted, cold-featured creature more
than a match for such a man as Warren?

"She *is* dead," the doctor answered with professional respect. "She died half an hour ago, quite happy. Her one regret seemed to bo for your absence. She was anxiously expecting you to come back and see her."

Hugh only answered: "I thought so. Poor child." But the very way he said it—the half-unconcerned tone, the lack of any real depth of emotion, nay, even of the decent pretence of tears, shocked and appalled Elsie beyond measure. She rushed away into Warren's room, and gave vent once more to her torrent of emotion. The painter laid his hand gently on her beautiful hair. "Oh, Warren," she cried, looking up at him half doubtful, "it makes me ashamed——" And she checked herself suddenly.

"Ashamed of what?" Warren asked her low.

In the fever of her overwrought feelings, she flung herself passionately into his circling arms. "Ashamed to think," she answered with a sob of distress, "that I once loved him!"

CHAPTER XLI.

REDIVIVA!

HUGH sat that evening, that crowded evening, alone in his dingy, stingy rooms with his dead Winifred. Alone with his weary, dreary thoughts—his thoughts, and a corpse, and a ghostly presence! Two women had loved him dearly in their time, and he had killed 'them both—Elsie and Winifred. That was the burden of his moody brooding. What curse, he asked himself, lay upon his head? And his own heart told him, in fitful moments of remorse, the curse of utter and ingrained selfishness. He pretended not to listen to it or to believe its witness; but he knew it spoke true, true and clear in spite of itself.

He sat there bitterly, late into the night, with two candles burning dim on the bare table by his side, and his head buried between his feverish hands in gloomy misery. It was a hateful night—hateful and ghastly; for in the bedroom at the side, the attendants of death, despatched by the doctor, were already busy at their gruesome work, performing the last duties for poor martyred Winifred.

He had offered her up on the altar of his selfish remorse and regret for poor martyred Elsie. The last victim had fallen on the grave of the first. She, too, was dead. And now his house was indeed left unto him desolate.

Somehow, as he sat there, with whirling brain and heated

brow, on fire in soul, he thought of Elsie far more than of Winifred. The new bereavement, such as it was, seemed to quicken and accentuate the sense of the old one. Was it that Winifred's wild belief in her recognition of Elsie that day in the street had roused once more the picture of his lost love's face and form so vividly in his mind? Or was it that the girl whom Winifred had pointed out to him did really to some slight extent resemble Elsie? and so recall her more definitely before him? He hardly knew; but of one thing he was certain—Elsie that night monopolized his consciousness. His three-year-old grief was still fresh and green. He thought much of Elsie, and little of Winifred.

It was a fixed idea with poor Winifred, he knew, that Elsie was alive and settled at San Remo. How the idea first came into her poor little head, he really knew not. He thought now the story about Warren Relf having given her the notion was itself a mere piece of her dying hysterical delirium. So was her confident immediate identification of the girl in the street as the actual Elsie. No trusting, of course, to a dying woman's impressions. Still, it was strange that Winifred should have died with Elsie, Elsie, Elsie, floating ever in her mind's eye before her. Strange, too, that the second victim of his selfish love should have died with her soul so fiercely intent upon the fixed and permanent image of the first one. Strange, furthermore, that a girl seen casually in the street should as a matter of fact, even in his own unprejudiced eyes, have so closely and curiously resembled Elsie. It was all odd. It all fitted in to a nicety with the familiar patness of that curious fate that seemed through life to dog him so persistently. Coincidence jostled against coincidence to confound him: opportunity ran cheek by jowl with occasion to work him ill. And yet, had he but known the whole truth as it really was, he would have seen there was never a genuine coincidence anywhere in it all—that everything had come pat by deliberate design: that Winifred had fixed upon San Remo on purpose, because she actually knew Elsie to be living there: and that the girl they had seen in the street that afternoon was none other than Elsie herself—his very Elsie in flesh and blood, not any vain or deceptive delusion.

Late at night, the well-favoured landlady came up, courteous and Italian, all respectful sympathy, in a black gown and a mourning head-dress, hastily donned, as becomes those who pay visits of condolence in whatever capacity to the recently bereaved. As for Hugh himself, he wore still his rough travelling suit of gray homespun, and the dust of his journey lay thick upon him. But he roused himself listlessly at the landlady's approach. She was bland, but sympathetic. Where

would Monsieur sleep? the amiable proprietress inquired in
lisping French. Hugh started at the inquiry. He had never
thought at all of that. Anywhere, he answered, in a careless
voice: it was all the same to him: *sous les toits*, if necessary.

The landlady bowed a respectful deprecation. She could offer
him a small room, a most diminutive room, unfit for Monsieur,
in his present condition, but still a *chambre de maître*, just above
Madame. She regretted she was unable to afford a better; but
the house was full, or, in a word, crowded. The world, you see,
was beginning to arrive at San Remo for the season. Proprietors
in a health-resort naturally resent a death on the premises,
especially at the very outset of the winter: they regard it as
a slight on the sanitary reputation of the place, and incline to
be rude to the deceased and his family. Yet nothing could be
more charming than the landlady's manner; she swallowed her
natural internal chagrin at so untoward an event in her own
house and at such an untimely crisis, with commendable politeness. One would have said that a death rather advertised the
condition of the house than otherwise. Hugh nodded his head
in blind acquiescence "Où vous voulez, Madame," he answered
wearily. "Upstairs, if you wish. I'll go now.—I'm sorry to
have caused you so much inconvenience; but we never know
when these unfortunate affairs are likely to happen."

The landlady considered in her own mind that the gentleman's
tone was of the most distinguished. Such sweet manners! So
thoughtful—so considerate—so kindly respectful for the house's
injured feelings! She was conscious that his courtesy called
for some slight return. "You have eaten nothing, Monsieur,"
she went on, compassionately. "In effect, our sorrow makes us
forget these details of everyday life. You do not derange us at
all; but you must let me send you up some little refreshment."

Hugh nodded again.

She sent him up some cake and red wine of the country by
the Swiss waiter, and Hugh ate it mechanically, for he was not
hungry. Excitement and fatigue had worn him out. His game
was played. He followed the waiter up to the floor above, and
was shown—into the next room to Warren's.

He undressed in a stupid, half dead-alive way, and lay down
on the bed with his candle still burning. But he didn't sleep.
Weariness and remorse kept him wide awake, worn out as he
was, tossing and turning through the long slow hours in silent
agony. He had time to sound the whole gamut of possible
human passion. He thought of Elsie, the weary night through:
of dead Elsie, and at times, more rarely, of dead Winifred too,
alone in the chamber of death beneath him. Elsie, in her
nameless grave away at Orfordness: Winifred, unburied below,
here at San Remo. A wild unrest possessed his fevered limbs

He murmured Elsie's name to himself, in audible tones, a hundred times over.

Strange to say, the sense of freedom was the strongest of all the feelings that crowded in upon him. Now that Winifred was dead, he could do as he chose with his own. He was no longer tied to her will and her criticisms. When he got back to England—as he would get back, of course, the moment he had decently buried Winifred—he meant to put up a fitting gravestone at Orfordness, if he sold the wretched remainder of Whitestrand to do it. A granite cross should mark that sacred spot. Dead Elsie's grave should no longer be nameless. So much, at least, his remorse could effect for him.

For Winifred was dead, and Whitestrand was his own. At the price of that miserable manor of blown sand he had sold his own soul and Elsie's life; and now he would gladly get rid of it all, if only he could raise out of its shrunken relics a monument at Orfordness to Elsie. For three long years, that untended grave had silently accused the remnants of his conscience: he determined it should accuse his soul no longer.

He would have to begin life all over again, of course. This first throw had turned out a fatal error. He had staked everything upon winning Whitestrand; and with what result? Elsie lost, and Whitestrand, and Winifred! Loss all round: loss and confusion. In the end, he found himself far worse off han he had ever been at the very outset, when the world was still before him where to choose. No new career now opened its doors to him. The bar was closed: he had had his chance there, and missed it squarely. Bohemia was estranged; small room for him now in literature or journalism. Whitestrand had spoilt his whole scheme of life for him. He was wrecked in port. And he could never meet with another Elsie.

The big clock on the landing ticked monotonously. Each swing of the pendulum tortured him afresh; for it called aloud to his heart in measured tones. It cried as plain as words could say: "Elsie, Elsie, Elsie, Elsie!"

Ah, yes! He was young enough to begin life afresh, if that were all. To begin all over again is less than nothing to a brave man. But for whom or for what? Selfish as he was, Hugh Massinger couldn't stand up and face the horrid idea of beginning afresh for himself alone. He must have some one to love, or go under for ever.

And still the clock ticked and ticked on: and still it cried in the silence of the night: "Elsie, Elsie, Elsie, Elsie!"

At last day dawned, and the morning broke. Pale sunlight streamed in at the one south window. The room was bare—a mere servant's attic. Hugh lay still and looked at the gaping cracks that diversified the gaudily painted Italian ceiling. All night through, he had fervently longed for the morning, and thought when it came he would seize the first chance to rise and dress himself. Now it had really come, he lay there unmoved, too tired and too feeble to think of stirring.

Five—six—half-past six—seven. He almost dozed out of pure weariness.

Suddenly, he woke with a quick start. A knock at the door! —a timid knock. Somebody come with a message, apparently. Hugh rose in haste, and held the door just a little ajar to ask in his bad Italian, "What is it?"

A boy's hand thrust a letter sideways through the narrow opening. "Is it for you, signor?" he asked, peering with black eyes through the chink at the Englishman.

Hugh glanced at the letter in profound astonishment. Oh, Heavens, what was this? How incredible—how mysterious! For a moment the room swam wildly around him; he hardly knew how to believe his eyes. Was it part of the general bewilderment of things that seemed to conspire by constant shocks against his perfect sanity? Was he going mad, or was some enemy trying to confuse and confound him? Had some wretch been dabbling in hideous forgeries? For the envelope was addressed—Oh, horror of horrors!—in dead Elsie's hand; and it bore in those well-known angular characters the simple inscription, "WARREN RELF, Esq., Villa della Fontana (Piano 3°), Avenue Vittorio Emmanuele, San Remo."

He recognized this voice from the grave at once. Dead Elsie! To Warren Relf! His fingers clutched it with a fierce mad grip. He could never give it up. To Warren Relf! And from dead Elsie!

"Is it for you, signor?" the boy asked once more, as he let it go with reluctance from his olive-brown fingers.

"For me?—Yes," Hugh answered, still clutching it eagerly. "For me!—Who sends it?"

"The signorina at the Villa Rossa—Signorina Cialoner," the boy replied, getting as near as his Italian lips could manage to the sound of Challoner. "She told me most stringently to deliver it up to yourself, signor, into your proper fingers, and on no account to let it fall into the hands of the English gentleman on the second story."

"Good," Hugh answered, closing the door softly. "That's quite right. Tell her you gave it me." Then he added in English with a cry of triumph: "Good morning, jackanapes!" After which he flung himself down on the bed once more in a perfect frenzy of indecision and astonishment.

For two minutes he couldn't make up his mind to break open that mysterious missive from the world of the dead, so strangely

delivered by an unknown hand at his own door on the very
morrow of Winifred's sudden death, and addressed in buried
Elsie's hand, as clear as of old, to his dearest enemy. What a
horrible concatenation of significant circumstances! He turned
it over and over again, unopened, in his awe; and all the time
that morose clock outside still ticked in his ear, less loudly than
before: "Elsie, Elsie, Elsie, Elsie!"

At last, making up his mind with a start, he opened it, half
overcome with a pervading sense of mystery. And this was
what he read in it, beyond shadow of doubt, in dead Elsie's
very own handwriting:

"Villa Rossa, Thursday, 7.30, morning.

"DEAREST WARREN,

"I will be ready, as you suggest, by the 9.40. But
you mustn't go with me farther than Paris. That will allow
you to get back to Edie and the Motherkin by the 6.39 on
Saturday evening.—I wish I could have waited here in San
Remo till after dear Winifred's funeral was over; but I quite
see with you how dangerous such a course might prove. Every
moment I stop exposes me to the chance of an unexpected
meeting. You must call on Hugh when you get back from
Paris, and give him poor Winifred's last forgiving message.
Some day—*you* know when, dearest—I may face seeing him
myself, perhaps; and then I can fulfil my promise to her in
person. But not till then. And that may be never. I hardly
know what I'm writing, I feel so dazed; but I'll meet you at
the station at the hour you mention.—No time for more. In
great haste—my hand shakes with the shock still—
"Yours ever lovingly and devotedly,

"ELSIE."

The revulsion was awful. For a minute or two Hugh failed
to take it all in. You cannot unthink past years at a jump.
The belief that Elsie was dead and buried at Orfordness had
grown so ingrained in the fabric of his brain that at first he
suspected deliberate treachery. Such things have been. He
had forged himself: might not Warren Relf, that incarnate
fiend, be turning his own weapon—meanly—against him?

But as he gazed and gazed at dead Elsie's hand—dead Elsie's
own hand—unmistakably hers—no forger on earth (not even
himself) was ever half so clever—the truth grew gradually
clearer and clearer. Dead Elsie was Elsie dead no longer; she
had escaped on that awful evening at Whitestrand. It wasn't
Elsie at all that was buried in the nameless grave at Orfordness. The past was a lie. The present alone—the present was
true. Elsie was here, to-day, at San Remo!

With a great thrill of joy, that fact at last came clearly home to him. The world whirled back through the ages again. Then Elsie, his Elsie, was still living! He hadn't killed her. He was no murderer. It was all a hideous, hideous mistake. The weight, the weight was lifted from his soul. A mad delight usurped its place. His heart throbbed with a wild pulsation. The clock on the staircase ticked loud for joy: " Elsie, Elsie, Elsie, Elsie ! "

He buried his face in his hands and wept—wept as he never had wept for Winifred—wept as he never had wept in his life before—wept with frantic gladness for Elsie recovered.

Slowly his conceptions framed themselves anew. His mind could only take it all in piecemeal. Bit by bit he set himself to the task—no less a task than to reconstruct the universe.— Winifred must have known Elsie was here. It was Elsie herself that Winifred and he had seen yesterday.

Fresh thoughts poured in upon him in a bewildering flood. He was dazzled, dazed, dumfounded with their number. Elsie was alive, and he had something left, therefore, to live for. Yesterday morning that knowledge would have been less than nothing worth to him while Winifred lived. To-day, thank Heaven—for Winifred was dead—it meant more to him than all the wealth of Crœsus.

He saw through that miserable money-grubbing now. Gold, indeed! what better was gold than any other chemical element? Next time—next time, he would choose more wisely. Wisdom in life, he thought to himself with a flash of philosophy, means just this—to know what things will bring you most happiness.

How opportunely Winifred had disappeared from the scene! In the nick of time—on the very stroke and crisis of his fate! At the turn of the tide that leads on to fortune! *Felix opportunitate mortis*, indeed! He had no regret, no remorse now, for poor betrayed and martyred Winifred.

Winifred! What was Winifred to him, or he to Winifred, in a world that still held his own beloved Elsie ?

How vividly those words came back to him now: " Don't I know how you've brought me to San Remo, dying as I am, to be near her and to see her when I'm dead and buried! You've tried to murder me by slow degrees, to marry Elsie !—Well, you've carried your point: you've killed me at last; and when I'm dead and gone, you can marry Elsie."

He hadn't meant it; he had never dreamt of it. But how neat and exact it had all come out! How fortune, whom he reviled, had been playing his game! His sorrow was turned at once into wild rejoicing. Winifred dead and Elsie living! What fairy tale ever ended so pat? He repeated it over and over again to himself: "They were both married and lived happily ever after."

All's well that ends well. The Winifred episode had come and gone. But Elsie remained as permanent background.

And how strangely Winifred herself, in her mad desire, had contributed to this very *dénouement* of his troubles. "I shall go to San Remo, if I go at all, and to nowhere else on the whole Riviera. I prefer to face the worst, thank you!" The words flashed back with fresh meaning on his soul. If she hadn't so set her whole heart on San Remo, he himself would never have thought of going there. And then, he would never have known about Elsie. For that, at least, he had to thank Winifred.

"When I'm dead and gone, you can marry Elsie!"

But what was this discordant note in the letter—Elsie's letter—to Warren Relf—Warren Relf, his dearest enemy? Was Warren Relf at the *pension*, then? Had Warren Relf been conspiring against him? In another flash, it all came back to him—the two scenes at the Cheyne Row Club—Warren's conversation with his friend Potts—the mistakes and errors of his hasty preconceptions. How one fundamental primordial blunder had coloured and distorted all his views of the case! He felt sure now, morally sure, that Warren Relf had rescued Elsie—the sneak, the eavesdropper, in his miserable mud-boat! And yet—if Warren Relf hadn't done so, there would be no Elsie at all for him now to live for. He recognized the fact; and he hated him for it. That he should owe his Elsie to that cur, that serpent!

And all these years Warren Relf—insidious creature—had kept her in hiding, for his own base objects, and had tried to wriggle himself, with snake-like and lizard-like contortions and twistings, into Hugh's own rightful place in Elsie's affections! The mean, mean reptile! to worm his way in secret into the sacred love of another man's maiden! Hugh loathed and hated him!

Discordant note! Why, yes—see this: "Some day—*you* know when, dearest—I may face seeing him myself, perhaps."—Then surely Elsie must have consented to fling herself away upon Relf, as he, Hugh, had flung himself away upon Winifred. But that was before Winifred died. He was free now—free, free as the wind, to marry Elsie. And Elsie would marry him: he was sure of that. Elsie's heart would come back to roost like his own, on the old perch. Elsie would never belie her love! Elsie would love him; Elsie would marry him.

What! Accept that creature Relf in his own place? Hyperion to a Satyr! Impossible! Incredible! Past all conception! No Eve would listen to such a serpent nowadays. Especially not when he, Hugh Massinger, was eager and keen to woo and wed her. "The crane," he thought, with his old knack of seeing everything through a haze of poetry—"the crane may chatter idly of the crane, The dove may murmur of the dove, but I—An eagle—clang an eagle to the sphere." When once he appeared in his panoply before her eyes as Elsie's suitor, your Warren Relfs and your lesser creatures would be forgotten and forsaken, and he would say to Elsie, like the Prince to Ida: "Lay thy sweet hands in mine and trust to me."

And Elsie, Elsie herself felt it; felt it already—of that he was certain. Felt this Relf creature was not worthy of her; felt she must answer to her truer instincts; felt her old love must soon return. For did she not say in this very letter, "But not till then. And that may be never"?

That may be never! Oh, precious words! She was leaving the door half-open, then, for her poet.

Poet! His heart leaped up at the thought. New vistas—old vistas long since closed—opened out afresh in long perspective before him. Ay, with such a fount of inspiration as that, to what heights of poetry might he not yet attain! What peaks of Parnassus might he not yet scale! On what pinnacles of glory might he not yet poise himself! Elsie, Elsie, Elsie, Elsie! That was a talisman to crush all opposition, an "Open Sesame" to prise all doors. With Elsie's love, what would be impossible to him?

Life floated in new colours before his eager eyes. He dreamed dreams and saw visions, as he lay on his bed in those golden moments. Earth was dearer, fairer, than he ever deemed it. The fever of love and ambition and hate was upon him now in full force. He reeled and revelled in the plenitude of his own wild and hectic imagination. He could do anything, everything, anything. He could move mountains in his fervent access of faith; he could win worlds in his mad delight; he could fight wild beasts in his sudden glory of heroic temper.

And all the while, poor dead Winifred lay cold and white in the bedroom below. And Elsie was off—off to England—with Warren Relf—that wretch! that serpent! by the 9.40.

CHAPTER XLII.

FACE TO FACE.

THAT hint sobered him. He roused himself to actual action at last. It was now eight, and Elsie was off by the 9.40! Too many thoughts had crowded him too fast. That single hour enclosed for Hugh Massinger a whole eternity. Earth had become another world for him since the stroke of seven. The sun had gone back upon the dial of his life, and left him once more at the same point where he had stood before he ever met Winifred. At the same point, but oh, how differently circumstanced! He had gained experience and wisdom since then: he had learned the lessons of A Life's Philosophy. All was not gold that glittered, he knew nowadays. The life was more than food, the body than raiment, love than Whitestrand, Elsie than Winifred. He would never go astray after the root of all evil, as long as he lived and loved, again. He would be the Demas of no delusive silver mine. On his voyage of discovery, he had found out his own soul—for he had a soul, a soul capable of appreciating Elsie; and he would not fling it away a second time for filthy lucre, common dross, the deceitfulness of riches, the mammon of unrighteousness. He had a soul capable of appreciating Elsie: he repeated to himself with the minor poet's intense delight in the ring and flow of his own verses, those two lines, the refrain of a *villanelle* he had once—years and years ago—sent her: "So low! She loves me! Can I be so low? So base! I love her! Can I be so base?" He loved Elsie. And Elsie was off by the 9.40.

There was the key to the immediate future. He rose and dressed himself with all expedition, remembering—though by an afterthought—for decency's sake to put on his black cutaway coat and his darkest trousers—he had with him none black save hose of his evening suit—and to approach as near to a mourning tie as the narrow resources of his wardrobe permitted. But it was all a hollow, hollow mockery, a transparent farce, a mere outer semblance: his coat might be black, but his heart was blithe as a lark's on a bright May morning.

He drew up the blind: the sun was flooding the bay and the hillsides with Italian lavishness. Flowers were gay on the parterres of the public garden. Who could pretend to be sad at soul on a day like this, worthy of whitest chalk, when the sun shone and flowers bloomed and Elsie was alive again? Let the dead bury their dead. For him, Elsie! for Elsie was alive again.

He lived once more a fresh life. What need to play the hypocrite, here, alone, in his own hired house, in the privacy of his lonely widowed bedchamber? He smiled to himself in the narrow looking-glass fastened against the wall. He laughed hilariously. He showed his even white teeth in his joy: they shone like pearl. He trimmed his beard with unwonted care; for now he must make himself worthy of Elsie. "If I be dear to some one else," he murmured, with the lover in *Maud*, "then I should be to myself more dear." And that he was dear to

Elsie, he was quite certain. Her love had suffered eclipse, no doubt: Warren Relf, like a shadow, had flitted for a moment in between them; but when once he, Hugh, burst forth like the sun upon her eyes once more, Warren Relf, paled and ineffectual, would hide his diminished head and vanish into vacancy.

"Warren Relf! That reptile—that vermin! Ha, ha! I have you now at my feet—my heel on your neck, you sneaking traitor. Hiding my Elsie so long from my sight! But I nick you now, on the eve of your victory. You think you have her safe in the hollow of your hand. You'll carry her off away from me to England! Fool! Idiot! Imbecile! Fatuous! You reckon this time without your hostess. There's many a slip 'twixt the cup and the lip. I'll dash away this cup, my fine fellow, from yours. Your lip shall never touch my Elsie's. Nectar is for gods, and not for mudlarks. I'll bring you down on your marrow-bones before me. You tried to outwit me. Two can play at that game, my friend."—He seized the bolster from the bed, and flinging it with a dash on the carpetless floor, trampled it in an access of frenzy underfoot, for Warren in effigy. The relief from his strain had come too quick. He was beside himself now with love and rage, mad with excitement, drunk with hatred and joy and jealousy. That creature marry his Elsie, forsooth! He danced in a fever of prospective triumph over the prostrate body of his fallen enemy.

Warren Relf, meanwhile, by himself next door, was saying to himself, as he dressed and packed, in sober sincerity: "Poor Massinger! What a terrible time he must be having, down there alone with his dead wife and his accusing conscience! Ought I to go down and lighten his burden for him, I wonder? Such remorse as his must be too heavy to bear. Ought I to tell him that Elsie's alive?—that that death at least doesn't lie at his door?—that he has only to answer for poor Mrs. Massinger? —No. It would be useless for *me* to tell him. He hates me too much. He wouldn't listen to me. Elsie shall break it to him in her own good time. But my heart aches for him, for all that, in spite of his cruelty. His worst enemy could wish him no harm now. He must be suffering agonies of regret and repentance. Perhaps at such a moment he might accept consolation even from me. But probably not. I wish I could do anything to lessen this misery for him."

Why did no answer come from Elsie? That puzzled and surprised Warren not a little. He had begged her to let him know first thing in the morning whether she could get away by the 9.40. He wondered Elsie could be so neglectful—she, who was generally so thoughtful and so trustworthy. Moment after moment he watched and waited: a letter must surely come from Elsie.

After a while, Hugh's access of mania—for it was little less—cooled down somewhat. He began to face the position like a man. He must be calm; he must be sane; he must deliberate sensibly.

Elsie was going by the 9.40; and Warren Relf would be there to join her. "I'll meet you at the station at the hour you mention." But not unless Relf received that letter. Should he ever receive it? That was the question.

He glanced once more at the envelope—torn hastily open: "WARREN RELF, Esq., Villa della Fontana (Piano 3°)." Then Warren Relf was here, in this selfsame house—on this very floor—next door, possibly! He would like to go in and wring the creature's neck for him!—But that would be rash, unadvisable—premature, at any rate. The wise man dissembles his hate—for a while—till occasion offers. Some other time. With better means and more premeditation.

If he wrung the creature's neck now, a foolish prejudice would hang him for it, under all the forms and pretences of law. And that would be inconvenient—for then he could never marry Elsie!

How inconsistent! that one should be permitted to crush underfoot a lizard or an adder, but be hanged, by a wretched travesty of justice, for wringing the neck of that noxious vermin! He stamped with all his might upon the bolster (vice Warren Relf, not then producible) and gnashed his teeth in the fury of his hatred. "Some day, my fine fellow, it'll be your own turn," he muttered to himself, " to get really danced upon. And when your turn comes, you shall find no mercy."

Curses, says the proverb, come home to roost.

Again he sobered himself with a violent effort. It was hard to be calm with Elsie alive, and Warren Relf, as yet unchoked, separated from him perhaps by no more than a thin lath-and-plaster partition. But the circumstances absolutely demanded calmness. He *would* restrain himself; he *would* be judicial. What ought he to do *in re* this letter? Destroy it at once, or serve it upon the person for whom it was intended?

Happy thought! If he let things take their own course, Relf would probably never go down to the station at all, waiting like a fool to hear from Elsie; and then—why, then, he might go himself and—well—why not?—run away with her himself offhand to England!

There, now, would be a dramatic triumph indeed for you! At the very moment when the reptile was waiting in his lair for the heroine, to snatch her by one bold stroke from his slimy grasp, and leave him, disconsolate, to seek her in vain in an empty waiting-room! It was splendid!—it was magnificent! The humour of it made his mouth water.

But no! The scandal—the gossip—the indecency! With Winifred dead in the room below! He must shield Elsie from so grave an imputation. He must bide his time. He must simulate grief. He must let a proper conventional interval elapse. Elsie was his, and he must guard her from evil tongues and eyes. He must do nothing to compromise Elsie.

Still, he might just go to the station to meet her. To satisfy his eyes. No harm in that. Why give the note at all to the reptile?

But looking at it impartially, the straight road is always the safest. The proverb is right. Honesty appears to be on the whole the best policy. He had tried the crooked path already, and found it wanting. Lying too often incurs failure. Henceforth, he would be—reasonably and moderately —honest.

Excess is bad in any direction. The wise man will therefore avoid excess, be it either on the side of vice or of virtue. A middle course of external decorum will be found by average minds the most prudent. On this, O British ratepayer, address yourself!

Hugh took from his portmanteau an envelope and his writing-case. With Elsie's torn envelope laid before him for a model, he exercised yet once more his accustomed skill in imitating to the letter—to the very stroke, even—the turns and twists of that sacred handwriting. But oh, with what different feelings now! No longer dead Elsie's, but his living love's. She wrote it herself, that very morning. Addressed as it was to Warren Relf, he pressed it to his lips in a fervour of delight, and kissed it tenderly—for was it not Elsie's?

His beautiful, pure, noble-hearted Elsie! To write to that reptile! And "Dearest Warren," too! What madness! What desecration! Pah! It sickened him.

But it was not for long. The sun had risen. Before its rays the lesser Lucifers would soon efface themselves.

He rang the bell, and after the usual aristocratic Italian interval, a servant presented himself. Your Italian never shows a vulgar haste in answering bells. Hugh handed him the letter, readdressed to Warren in a forged imitation of Elsie's handwriting, and asked simply: "This gentleman is in the *pension*, is he?"

Luigi bowed and smiled profusely. "On the same floor; next door, signor," he answered, indicating the room with a jerk of his elbow. The Italian waiter lacks polish. Hugh noted the gesture with British disapproval. His tastes were fine: he disliked familiarity.

On the same floor—as yet unchoked! And he couldn't get at him. Horrible! horrible!

Hugh dared not stop at the *pension* for breakfast. He was afraid of meeting Relf face to face, and till his plan was carried into execution—for he had indeed once more a plan—he thought it wisest and safest for the present to avoid him studiously. He wanted to make sure with his own two eyes that Elsie was in very truth alive. The legal side of him craved evidence. When a woman has been dead, undoubtedly dead, for three long years, only ocular demonstration *in propriâ personâ* can fully convince a reasonable man she is quite resuscitated. The age of miracles is now past: the age of scepticism is here upon us. Hugh knew too well, from his own private experience, that documentary evidence may be but a fallible guide to the facts of history. Some brute might perhaps have meanly stooped to the caddish device of forgery to confound him. He wouldn't have forged for such a purpose himself: he would use that doubtful weapon in self-defence only. Let Relf go down to the station by all means: he would follow after, at a safe distance, or go before, if that seemed better, and on the unimpeachable authority of his own retina and his own discriminative optic nerves make perfectly certain he saw Elsie. Unseen, of course; for at present he meant to keep quite dark. Elsie perhaps would hardly like to know he had stolen away at such a moment—even to see *her*—from dead Winifred.

For Elsie's sake he must assume some regret for dead Winifred.

So he told the landlady with a sigh of sensibility he had no heart that morning to taste his breakfast. He would go and stroll by the sea-shore alone. Everything had been arranged about the poor signora. "What grief?" said the landlady. "Look you, Luigi, he can eat nothing."

At a shabby *trattoria* in the main street, he took his breakfast—a sloppy breakfast; but the coffee was good, with the exquisite aroma of the newly roasted berry, and the fresh fruit was really delicious. On the Mediterranean slope, coffee and fresh fruit cover a multitude of sins. What could you have nicer, now, than these green figs, so daintily purpled on the sunny side, and these small white grapes from the local vineyards with their faint undertone of musky flavour? The olives, too, smack of the basking soil; "the luscious glebe of vine-clad lands," he had called it himself in that pretty song in "A Life's Philosophy."—He repeated the lines for his own pleasure, rolling them on his palate with vast satisfaction, as a connoisseur rolls good old Madeira:

> " My thirsty bosom pants for sunlit waters,
>   And luscious glebe of vine clad-lands,
>   And chanted psalms of freedom's bronze-cheeked daughters,
>   And sacred grasp of brotherly hands."

That was written before he knew Winifred! His spirits were high. He enjoyed his breakfast. A quarter to nine by the big church clock; and Elsie goes at 9.40.

He strolled down at his leisure to the station with his hands in his pockets. Fresh air and sunshine smiled at his humour. He would have liked to hide himself somewhere, and "see unseen," like Paris with the goddesses in the dells of Ida; but stern fact intervened, in the shape of that rigid continental red-tape railway system which admits nobody to the waiting-rooms without the passport of a ticket. He must buy a ticket for form's sake, then, and go a little way on the same line with them; just for a station or two—say to Monte Carlo.—He presented himself at the wicket accordingly, and took a first single as far as the Casino.

In the waiting-room he lurked in a dark corner, behind the bookstall with the paper-covered novels. Elsie and Relf would have plenty to do, he shrewdly suspected, in looking after their own luggage without troubling their heads about casual strangers. So he lurked and waited. The situation was a strange one. Would Elsie turn up? His heart stood still. After so many years, after so much misery, to think he was waiting again for Elsie!

As each new-comer entered the waiting-room, his pulse leaped again with a burst of expectation. The time went slowly: 9.30, 9.35, 9.36, 9.37—would Elsie come in time for the 9.40?

A throb! a jump!—alive! alive! It was Elsie, Elsie, Elsie, Elsie!

She never turned; she never saw. She walked on hastily, side by side with Warren, the serpent, the reptile. Hugh let her pass out on to the platform and choose her carriage. His flood of emotion fairly overpowered him. Then he sneaked out with a hangdog air, and selected another compartment for himself, a long way behind Elsie's. But when once he was seated in his place, at his ease, he let his pent-up feelings have free play. He sat in his corner, and cried for joy. The tears followed one another unchecked down his cheeks. Elsie was alive! He had seen Elsie!

The train rattled on upon its way to the frontier. Bordighera, Ventimiglia, the Roya, the Nervia, were soon passed. They entered France at the Pont St. Louis.

Elsie was crying in her carriage too—crying for poor tortured, heart-broken Winifred. And not without certain pangs of regret for Hugh as well. She had loved him once, and he was her own cousin. "Oh, Warren," she cried, for they had no others with them in their through-carriage—it was the season when hardly anybody travels northward—" how terribly he must feel it, all alone by himself in a strange land, with that poor dead girl that he hounded to death for his only company! I ran't bear to think how much he must be suffering. Perhaps at Marseilles you'd better telegraph to him your profound sympathy, and tell him that Winifred said before she died—said earnestly she loved him and forgave him."

"I will," Warren answered. "I thought of him myself not without some qualms at the *pension* this morning. Perhaps at times, for your sake, knowing what you suffered, I've been too harsh towards him.—Elsie, he's a very heartless man, we both know; but even *he* must surely feel this last blow, and his own guilt for it. We've never spoken of him together before; let's never speak of him together again. This word's enough. The telegram shall be sent, and I hope and trust it will save him something of his self-imposed misery."

And all the time Hugh Massinger, in his own carriage, was thinking—not of poor dead Winifred; not of remorse, or regret, or penitence; not of his sin and the mischief it had wrought—but of Elsie. The bay of Mentone smiled lovely to his eyes. The crags of the steep seaward scarp on the Cap Martin side glistened and shone in the morning sunlight. The rock of Monaco rose ⌐heer like a painter's dream from the sea in front of him. And s he stepped from the carriage at Monte Carlo station, with the ʌountains above and the gardens below, flooded by the rich Mediterranean sunlight, he looked about him at the scene in pure æsthetic delight, saying to himself in his throbbing heart that the world after all was very beautiful, and that he might still be happy at last with Elsie.

CHAPTER XLIII.

AT MONTE CARLO.

HUGH had not had the carriage entirely to himself all the way; a stranger got in with him at Mentone station. But so absorbed was Hugh in his own thoughts that he hardly noticed the new comer's presence. Full of Elsie and drunk with joy, he had utterly forgotten the man's very existence more than once. Crying and laughing by turns as he went, he must have impressed the stranger almost like a madman. He had smiled and frowned and chuckled to himself, exactly as if he had been

quite alone; and though he saw occasionally, with a careless
glee, that the stranger leaned back nervously in his seat and
seemed to shrink away from him, as if in bodily fear, he scarcely
troubled his head at all about so insignificant and unimportant
a person. His soul was all engrossed with Elsie. What was a
casual foreigner to him, with Elsie, Elsie, Elsie, recovered?

The Casino gardens were already filled with loungers and
children—gamblers' children, in gay Parisian dresses—but the
gaming-rooms themselves were not yet open. Hugh, who had
come there half by accident, for want of somewhere better to go,
and who meant to return to San Remo by the first train, strolled
casually without any thought to a seat on the terrace. Preoccupied as he was, the loveliness of the place nevertheless took
him fairly by surprise. His poet's soul lay open to its beauty.
He had never visited Monte Carlo before; and even now he had
merely mentioned the name at random as the first that occurred
to him when he went to take his ticket at the San Remo
booking-office. He had stumbled upon it wholly by chance.
But he was glad he had come; it was all so lovely. The smiling
aspect of the spot took his breath away with wonder. And the
peaceful air of all that blue bay soothed somewhat his feverish
excitement at the momentous discovery that Elsie, his Elsie, was
still living.

He gazed around him with serene delight. This was indeed
a day of joyful surprises. The whole place looked more like a
scene in fairyland in full pantomime time than like a prosaic
bit of this workaday world of ours. In front lay the cobalt-
blue Mediterranean, broken on every side into a hundred tiny
sapphire inlets. Behind him in serried rank rose tier after tier
of Maritime Alps, their solemn summits mysteriously clouded
in a fleecy haze. To the left, on the white rock that stretched
upon the bay as some vast Miltonic monster suns his huge
length on the broad Atlantic,

> How like a gem the sea-girt city
> Of little Monaco basking glowed!

He had never before fully understood the depth and beauty of
those lines of Tennyson's: he repeated them over now musingly
to himself, and drank in their truthfulness with a poet's appreciation. To the right, the green Italian shore faded away by
degrees into the purple mountains which guard like sentinels
the open mouth of the Gulf of Genoa. Lovely by nature, that
exquisite spot—the fairest, perhaps, in all Europe—has been
made still lovelier by all the resources of human art. From
the water's edge, terraces of luscious tropical vegetation rise
one after another in successive steps towards the grand façade
of the gleaming Casino, divided from one another by parapets

of marble balustrades, and connected together from place to place by broad flights of Florentine staircases. Fantastic clusters of palms and aloes, their base girt round with rare exotic flowers, thrust themselves cunningly into the foreground of every beautiful view, so that the visitor looks out upon the bay and the mountains through artistic vistas deftly arranged in the very spot where a Tuscan painter's exuberant fancy would have wished to set them for scenic effect. To Warren Relf, to be sure, Monte Carlo seemed always too meretriciously obtrusive to deserve his pencil; but to Hugh 'Massinger's more gorgeous oriental taste it revealed itself at once in brilliant colours as a dream of beauty and a glimpse of Paradise.

From the bench where he sat, he gazed across to Monaco past a feathery knot of drooping date branches : he caught a glimpse of Bordighera on the other side through a graceful framework of spreading dracænas and quaint symmetrical rosettes of fan-palms. The rock itself delighted and rejoiced his poet's soul: his fancy, quickened by that day's adventures, saw in it a thousand strange similitudes. Now it was a huge petrified whale, his back rising two hundred feet or more above the water's edge : and now it was some gigantic extinct saurian, his head turned toward the open sea, and his tail just lashing the last swell of the mainland at the narrow isthmus where it joined the mountains. Perched on its summit stood the tiny town, with its red-tiled houses and clambering streets, and the mediæval bastions of its petty Prince's disproportioned palace. Through that clear Italian air he could see it all with the utmost distinctness—the tall gray tower with its Mauresque battlements, the long white façade with its marble pillars, the tiny Place d'Armes with its rows of plane-trees, its dozen brass cannon, and its military forces engaged that moment before his very eyes in duly performing their autumn manœuvres. For the entire strength of the Monegasque army was deploying just then before his languidly attentive vision : anything more grotesque than its petty evolutions he had never before beheld— outside an opéra bouffe of Offenbach's. Twenty fantastically dressed soldiers, of various sizes, about one-half of whom were apparently officers, composed the entire princely service; and they went through their mock-drill with a mixture of gravity and casual nonchalance which made Hugh, who observed them from a distance through his pocket field-glass, smile in spite of himself at the ridiculous ceremonial—it recalled so absurdly the "Grand Duchess of Gérolstein." He laughed a soft little laugh below his breath: he was blithe to-day, for Winifred was dead, and he had seen Elsie.

He looked away next to the nearer foreground. The dream-land of Monte Carlo floated in morning lights before his enchanted eyes. The great and splendid turreted Casino, the exquisite green lawns and gardens, the brilliant rows of shops and cafés, the picturesque villas dotted up and down the smooth and English-looking sward, the Italian terraces with their marble steps, the glorious luxuriance of waving palm-trees, massive agaves, thick clustering yucca blossoms, and heavy breadths of tropical foliage—all alike fired and delighted his poetical nature. The bright blue of Mediterranean seas, the dazzling white of Mediterranean sunshine, the brilliant russet of Mediterranean roofs, soothed and charmed his too exalted mood. He needed repose, beauty, and nature. He looked at his watch and consulted the little local time-table he had bought at San Remo.—After all, why return to that lonely *pension* and to dead Winifred so very soon? It was better to be here—here, where all was bright and gay and lively. He might sit in the gardens all day long and return by the last train to-night to Winifred. No need to report himself now any longer. He was free, free: he would stop at Monte Carlo.

Why leave, indeed, that glorious spot, the loveliest and deadliest siren of our civilization? He felt his spirit easier here, with those great gray crags frowning down upon him from above, and those exquisite bays smiling up at him from below. Nature and art had here combined to woo and charm him. It seemed like a poet's midsummer dream, crystallized into lasting and solid reality by some gracious wave of Titania's wand.

He murmured to himself those lines from the " Daisy "—

> Nor knew we well what pleased us most;
> Not the clipt palm of which they boast;
> 　　But distant colour, happy hamlet,
> A moulder'd citadel on the coast;
>
> Or tower, or high hill-convent, seen
> A light amid its olives green;
> 　　Or olive-hoary cape in ocean;
> Or rosy blossom in hot ravine.

Exquisite lines! He looked across to Cap Martin and understood them all. Then his own verses on his first Italian tour came back with a burst of similarity to his memory. In his exultation and unnatural excitement he had the audacity to compare them with Tennyson's own. Why might not he, too, build at last that mansion he had talked about long, long ago, on the summit of Parnassus?

> I found it not, where solemn Alps and gray
> Draw purple glories from the new-born day;
> 　　Nor where huge sombre pines loom overhanging
> Niagara's rainbow spray.

> Nor in loud psalms whose palpitating strain
> Thrills the vast dome of Buonarotti's fane:
>   On canvas quick with Guido's earnest passion,
> Or Titian's statelier vein.

Tennyson indeed! Who prates about Tennyson? Were not his own sonorous round-mouthed verses worth every bit as much as many Tennysons? He repeated them over lovingly to himself. The familiar ring intoxicated his soul. He was a poet too. He would yet make a fortune, for himself and for Elsie!

Echoes, echoes, mere echoes all of them! But to Hugh Massinger, in his parental blindness, quite as good and true as their inspired originals. So the minor poet for ever deceives himself.

Guido, to be sure, he now knew to be feeble. He'd outlived Guido, and reached Botticelli. Not that the one preference was any profounder or truer at bottom than the other; but fashion had changed, and he himself had changed with it. He wrote those verses long, long ago. In those days Guido was not yet exploded. He wished he could find now some good dissyllabic early Italian name (with the accent on the first) that would suit modern taste and take the place in the verse of that too tell-tale Guido.

For Elsie was alive, and he must be a poet still. He must build up a fortune for himself and for Elsie.

Somebody touched his elbow as he sat there. He looked up, not without some passing tinge of annoyance. What a bore to be discovered! He didn't want to be disturbed or recognized just then—at Monte Carlo—and with Winifred lying dead on her bed at San Remo!

It was a desultory London club acquaintance—a member of the Savage—and with him was the man who had come with Hugh in the train from Mentone.

"Hullo, Massinger," the desultory Savage observed complacently: "who'd have ever thought of meeting you here. Down in the South for the winter, or on a visit? Come for pleasure, or is your wife with you? Whitestrand too much for you in a foggy English November, eh?"

Hugh made up his mind at once to his course of action: he would say not a single word about Winifred. "On a visit," he answered, with some slight embarrassment. "I expect to stop only a week or two." As a matter of fact, it was not his intention to remain very long after Winifred's funeral. He was in haste, as things stood, to return to England—and Elsie.— "I came over with your friend from Mentone this morning, Lock."

x

"And he took you for a maniac, my dear boy," the other answered with a quiet smile. "I've duly explained to him that you are not mad, most noble Massinger; you're only a poet. The terms, though nearly, are not quite synonymous." Then he added in French: "Let me introduce you now to one another. M. le Lieutenant Fédor Raffalevsky, of the Russian navy."

M. Raffalevsky bowed politely. "I fear, Monsieur," he said, with a courtly air, "I caused you some slight surprise and discomfort by my peculiar demeanour in the train this morning.— To tell you the truth, your attitude discomposed me. I was coming to Monte Carlo to join in the play, and I carried no less a sum for the purpose than three hundred thousand francs about my body. Not knowing I had to deal with a person of honour, I felt somewhat nervous, you may readily conceive, as to your muttered remarks and apparent abstraction. Figure to yourself my situation. So much money makes one naturally fanciful! Monsieur, I trust, will have the goodness to forgive me."

"To say the truth," Hugh answered frankly, "I was so much absorbed in my own thoughts that I scarcely noticed any little hesitation you may have happened to express in your looks and manner. Three hundred thousand francs is no doubt a very large sum. Why, it's twelve thousand pounds sterling—isn't it, Lock?—You mean to try your luck, then, *en gros*, Monsieur?"

The Russian smiled. "For once," he answered, nodding his head good-humouredly. "I have a system, I believe: an infallible system. I'm a mathematician myself by taste and habit. I've invented a plan for tricking fortune—the only safe one ever yet discovered."

Hugh shook his head almost mechanically. "All systems alike are equally bad," he replied in a politely careless tone. Gambler as he had always been by nature, he had too much common-sense to believe in martingales. "The bank's bound to beat you in the long run, you know. It has the deepest purse, and must win in the end, if you go on long enough."

The Russian's face wore a calm expression of superior wisdom. "*I* know better," he answered quietly. "I've worked for years at the doctrine of chances. I've calculated the odds to ten places of decimals. If I hadn't, do you think I'd risk three hundred thousand francs on the mere turn of a wretched roulette table?"

The doors of the Casino were now open, and players were beginning to crowd the gambling rooms. "Let's go in and watch him," Lock suggested in English. "There can be no particular harm in looking on. I'm not a player myself, like you, Massinger; but I want to see whether this fellow really wins or loses. He believes in his own system most profoundly,

I observe. He's a very nice chap, the Paymaster of the Russian Mediterranean squadron. I picked him up at the Cercle Nautique at Nice last week; and he and I have been going everywhere in my yacht ever since together."

"All right," Hugh answered, with the horrible new-born careless glee of his recent emancipation. "I don't mind twopence what I do to-day. Vogue la galère! I'm game for anything, from pitch-and-toss to manslaughter." He never suspected himself how true those casual words of the stock slang expression were soon to become. Pitch-and-toss first, and afterwards manslaughter.

They strolled round together to the front of the Casino, that stately building in the gaudiest Hausmannized Parisian style, planted plump down with grotesque incongruity beneath the lofty crags of the Maritime Alps. The palace of sin faces a large and handsome open square, with greensward and fountains and parterres of flowers; and all around stand coquettish shops, laid temptingly out with bonnets and jewelry and æsthetic products, for people who win largely disburse freely, and many ladies hover about the grounds, with fashionable dresses and shady antecedents, by no means slow to share the good fortune of the lucky and all too generous hero of the day. Hugh mounted the entrance staircase with the rest of the crowd, and pushed through the swinging glass doors of the Casino. Within, they came upon the large and spacious vestibule, its roof supported by solid marble and porphyry pillars. Presentation of heir cards secured them the right of entry to the *salles de jeu,* for everything is free at Monte Carlo—except the tables. You may go in and out of the rooms as you please, and enjoy for nothing—so long as you are not fool enough to play—the use of two hundred European newspapers, and the music of a theatre, where a splendid band discourses hourly to all comers the enlivening strains of Strauss and of Gungl. But all that is the merest prelude. The play itself, which forms the solid core of the entire entertainment, takes place in the gambling saloons on the left of the Casino.

Furnished with their indispensable little ticket of introduction, the three new-comers entered the rooms, and took their place tentatively by one of the tables. The Russian, selecting a seat at once, addressed himself to the task like one well accustomed to systematic gambling. Hugh and his acquaintance Lock stood idly behind, to watch the outcome of his infallible method.

And all the time, alone at San Remo, Winifred's body lay on the solitary bed of death, attended only at long intervals by the waiting-women and landlady of the shabby *pension.*

CHAPTER XLIV.

"LADIES AND GENTLEMEN, MAKE YOUR GAME!"

THOUGH play had only just begun when Hugh and his companions entered the saloon, the rooms were already pretty well crowded with regular visitors, who came early to secure their accustomed seats, and who leant forward with big rolls of gold piled high in columns on the table before them, marking down with a dot on their tablets the winning numbers, and staking their twenty or thirty napoleons with mechanical calmness on every turn of that fallacious whirligig. Hugh had often heard or read sensational descriptions of the eagerness depicted upon every face, the anxious gaze, the rapt attention, the obvious fascination of the game for its votaries; but what struck him rather on the first blush of it all was the exact opposite: the stolid indifference with which men and women alike, inured to the varying chances of the board, lost or won a couple of dozen pounds or so on each jump of the pea, as though it were a matter of the supremest unconcern to them in their capacity of gamblers whether they or the bank happened to take up each particular little heap of money. They seemed, indeed, to be mostly rich and *blasé* people, suffering from a chronic plethora of the purse, who could afford to throw away their gold like water, and who threw it away carelessly out of pure wantonness, for the sake of the small modicum of passing excitement yielded by the uncertainty to their jaded palates.

One player in particular Hugh watched closely—an austere-looking man with the air and carriage of a rural dean—to detect if possible some trace of emotion in his eyes or muscles. He could observe none; the man's features were rigid as if carved in stone. A slight twitching of the fingers from time to time perhaps faintly betrayed internal excitement; but that was all. The clear-cut face and thin lips moved no more than the busts of those Elizabethan Meyseys, hewn in marble or carved in wood, in the cold chancel at sand-swept Whitestrand.

Nevertheless, he remarked with surprise from the very first moment that even at that early hour of the morning, when the day's work had hardly yet got well under weigh, the rooms, though large and lofty, were past all belief hot and close, doubtless from the strange number of feverish human hearts and lungs, all throbbing and panting their suppressed excitement, in that single Casino, and warming the air with their internal fires. He raised his eyes and glanced for a moment around the saloon. It was spacious and handsome, after its own gaudy fashion, richly decorated in the Mauresque style of the Spanish Alhambra, though with far less taste and harmony of colour than in the restorations to which his eye had been long familiarized in London and Sydenham. At Monte Carlo, to say the truth, a certain subdued tinge of vulgar garishness just mars the native purity of the style into perfect accord with the nature and purposes of that temple of Mammon in his vilest avatar.

Hugh, however, for his part had no scruples in the matter of gambling. He gazed up and down at the ten or twelve roulette tables that crowded the *salles de jeu*, with the utmost complacency. He liked play, and it diverted him to watch it, especially when the man he meant to observe was the propounder of a new and infallible system. Infallible systems are always interesting: they collapse with a crash—amusing to everybody except their propounder. He bent his eyes closely upon the hands of the Russian, who had now pulled out his roll of gold and silver, and was eagerly beginning to back his chosen numbers, doubtless with the blind and stupid confidence of the infatuated system-monger.

Raffalevsky, however, played a cautious opening. He started modestly with four five-franc pieces, distributed about on a distinct plan, and each of them staked on a separate number. The five-franc piece, in fact, is the minimum coin permitted to how its face on those aristocratic tables ; and six thousand francs s the maximum sum which the bank allows any one player to hazard on a single twist of the roulette : between these extreme limits, all possible systems must needs confine themselves, so that the common martingale of doubling the stakes at each unsuccessful throw becomes here practically impossible. Raffalevsky's play had been carefully calculated. Hugh, who was already well versed in the mysteries of roulette, could see at a glance that the Russian had really a method in his madness. He was working on strict mathematical principles. Sometimes he divided or decreased his stake; sometimes, at a bound, he trebled or quadrupled it. Sometimes he plunged on a single number ; sometimes for several turns together he steadily backed either red or black, *pair* or *impair*. But on the whole, by hap or cunning, he really seemed to be winning rapidly. His sustained success made Hugh more anxious than ever to watch his play. It was clear he had invented a genuine system. Might it be after all, as he said, an infallible one?

If only Hugh could find it out! He must, he would marr" Elsie. How grand to marry her, a rich man ! He would love to lay at Elsie's feet a fortune worthy of his beautiful Elsie.

Things were all changed now. He had something to live, to

work, to gamble for! If only he could say to his recovered Elsie: "Take me, rich, famous, great—take me, and White-strand, no longer sand-swept. I lay it all in your lap for your gracious acceptance—these piles of gold—these heaps of coins!" But he had nothing, nothing, save the few napoleons he carried about him. If he had but the Russian's twelve thousand pounds now! he would play and win—win a fortune at a stroke for his darling Elsie.

Fired with the thought, he watched Raffalevsky more closely than ever. In time, he began to perceive by degrees upon what principle the money was so regularly lost and won. It was a good principle, mathematically correct. Hugh worked it out hastily on the back of an envelope. Yes, in one hundred and twenty chances out of one hundred and thirty-seven, a man ought to win ten louis a turn, against seven lost, on an average reckoning. At last, Raffalevsky, after several good hazards, laid down five louis boldly upon 24. Hugh touched his shoulder with a gentle hand. "Wrong," he murmured in French. "You make a mistake there. You abandon your principle. You ought to have backed 27 this time."

The Russian looked back at him with an angry smile; so slight a scratch at once brought out the Tartar. "Back it your-self, then, Monsieur," he said sullenly. "I make my own game. —Pray, don't interrupt me. If your calculations go so very deep, put your own money down, and try your luck against me. My principles, when I first discovered them, were not worked out on the back of an envelope."

The gibe offended Hugh. In a second he saw that the fellow was wrong: he was misinterpreting the nature of his own discovery. He had neglected one obvious element of the problem. The error was mathematical: Hugh snapped at it mentally with his keen perception—he had taken a first in mathematics at Oxford —and noted at once that if the Russian pursued his present course for many turns together he was certain before long to go under hopelessly. For the space of one deep breath he hesitated and held back. What was the use of gambling with no capital to go upon? Then, more for the sake of proving himself right than of winning money, he dived into his pocket with a sudden resolution, and drawing forth five napoleons from his scanty purse, laid them without a word on 27, and awaited patiently the result of his action.

"The game is made," the croupier called out as Hugh with-drew his hand. After that warning signal, no stakes can be further received or altered. Whir-r-r went the roulette. The pea span round with whizzing speed. Hugh looked on, all eager, in a fever of suspense. He half regretted he had backed 27. He was sure to lose. The chances, after all, were so enor-

mous against him. Thirty-six to one! If you win, it's a fluke.
What a fool he had been to run the risk of making himself look
small in this gratuitous way before the cold eyes of that unfeeling Russian!

He knew he was right, of course: 27 was the system. But a
sensible system never hangs upon a single throw. It depends
upon a long calculation of chances. You must let one risk
balance another. Raffalevsky had twelve thousand pounds to
fall back upon. If he failed once, to him that didn't matter: he
could go on still and recoup himself in the end by means of the
system. Only under such circumstances of a full purse can any
method of gambling ever by any possibility be worth anything.
Broken reeds at the best, even for a Rothschild, they must
almost necessarily pierce the hand that leans upon them if it
ventures to try them on a petty scrap of pocket capital. And
Hugh's capital was grotesquely scrappy for such a large venture
—he had only some seventy-five pounds about him.

How swift is thought, and how long a time it seemed before
the pea jumped! He had reasoned out all this, and a thousand-
fold more, in his own mind with lightning speed while that
foolish wheel was still whirling and spinning. If he won at all,
it could only be by a rare stroke of fickle fortune. Thirty-six
to one were the odds against him! And if he lost, he must
either leave off at once, or else, in accordance with the terms of
the system, stake ten louis next turn on 14, or nine louis on odd
r even. At that rate, his poor little capital would soon be
xhausted. How he longed for Raffalevsky's twelve thousand
o draw upon! He would feel so small if 27 lost. And if there
was anything on earth that Hugh Massinger hated it was feeling
small: the sense of ignominy, and its opposite the feeling of
personal dignity, were deeply rooted in the very base and core
of his selfish nature.

At last the pea jumped. A breathless second! The croupier
looked over at it and watched its fall. "Vingt-sept," he cried
in his stereotyped tone. Hugh's heart leapt up with a sudden
wild bound. The fever of play had seized on him now. He
had won at a stroke—a hundred and seventy-five louis.

Here was a capital indeed upon which to begin. He would
back his own system with this against Raffalevsky's. Or rather,
he would back Raffalevsky's discovery, as rightly apprehended
and worked out by himself, against Raffalevsky's discovery as
wrongly applied and distorted through an essential error of
detail by its original inventor.

It was system pitted against system now. The croupier
raked in the scattered gold heaped on the various cabalistic
numbers, squares, and diamonds—and amongst them, Raffalevsky's five napoleons upon 24. Then he paid the lucky

players their gains; counting out three thousand five hundred francs with practised ease, and handing them to Hugh, who was one among the principal winners by that particular turn. In two minutes more, the board was cleared; the wooden cue had hauled in all the bank's receipts; the fortunate players had added their winnings to the heap before them; and all was ready for a further venture. "Messieurs et mesdames, faites le jeu," the harsh voice of the croupier cried mechanically. The players laid down their stakes once more; the croupier waited the accustomed interval. "Le jeu est fait, rien ne va plus," he cried at last; and the pea again went buzzing and whizzing. Hugh was backing his system this time on the regular rule: three louis on the left-hand row of numbers.

He lost. That was but a small matter, of course. He had won to begin with; and a stroke of luck at the first outset is responsible for the greater part of the most reckless playing. Time after time he staked and played—staked and played—staked and played again, sometimes losing, sometimes winning; but on the whole, the system, as he had anticipated, proved fairly trustworthy. The delirium of play had taken full possession of him, body and soul, by this time. He was piling up gold; piling it fast; how fast, he never stopped to think or count: enough for him that the system won; as long as it won, what waste of time at a critical moment to stop and reckon the extent of his fortune.

He only knew that every now and then he thrust a fresh handful of gold or notes into his pocket—for Elsie—and went on playing with feverish eagerness with the residue of his winnings left upon the table.

By two o'clock, however, he began to get hungry. This sort of excitement takes it rapidly out of a man. Lock had disappeared from the scene long since. He wanted somebody to go and feed with. So he leaned over and whispered casually to Raffalevsky: "Shall we turn out now and take a mouthful or two of lunch together?"

Raffalevsky looked back at him with a pale face. "As you will," he said wearily. "I'm tired of this play. Losses, losses all along the line. The system breaks down here and there, I find, in actual practice."

So Hugh had observed with a placid smile for the last hour or two.

They left the tables, and strolled across the square to the stately portals of the Hotel de Paris. Hugh was in excellent spirits indeed. "Permit me to constitute myself the host, Monsieur," he said with his courtliest air to Raffalevsky. He had won heavily now, and was in a humour on all grounds to spend his winnings with princely magnificence.

The Russian bowed. "You are very kind, monsieur," he answered with a smile. Then he added, half apologetically, at the end of a pause: "And after all, it was my own system."

The carte was tempting, and money was cheap—cheaper than in London. Hugh ordered the most sumptuous and *recherché* of luncheons, with wine to match, on a millionaire scale, and they sat down together at the luxurious tables of that lordly restaurant. While they waited for their red mullet, Hugh pulled out a stray handful of notes and gold and began to count up the extent of his winnings. He trembled himself when he saw to how very large a sum the total amounted. He had pocketed no less in that short time than fourteen hundred louis! Fools that plod and toil and moil in London for a long, long year upon half that pittance! How he pitied and despised them! In three brief hours, by the aid of a system, he had won offhand fourteen hundred louis!

He mentioned the sum of his winnings with bated breath to the unsympathetic Russian. Raffalevsky bit his lip with undisguised jealousy. "And I," he said curtly, in a cold voice, "have dropped sixteen hundred."

It's wonderful with what placid depths of heroism the winners can endure the losses of the losers. "Never mind, my friend," Hugh answered back cheerily. "Fortune always takes a turn in the long run. Her wheel will alter. You'll win soon. And besides, you know, you have an infallible system."

"It's the cursed system that seems to have betrayed me," the Russian blurted back with a savage outburst of unchecked temper. "It worked out so well on paper, somehow; but on these precious tables, with their turns and their evolutions, something unexpected is always bobbing up to spoil and prevent my legitimate triumph. Would you believe it, now, last turn but one, and the turn before it, I had calculated seven hundred and twenty-two distinct chances all in my favour to a miserable solitary one against me: and not one of the seven hundred and twenty-two good combinations ever turned up at all, but just the one beastly unlucky conjunction that made against me and ruined my speculations. You might play for seven hundred and twenty-two turns on an average again without that ever happening a second time to confound you."

At the table behind them, a philosophically minded Frenchman of the *doctrinaire* type—a close-shaven old gentleman with an official face, white hair, and an unimpeachable necktie—was discoursing aloud to a friend beside him of the folly of gambling. "I'm not going to moralize," he remarked aloud, in that very clear and audible tone which the *doctrinaire* Frenchmen generally adopts when he desires to air his own private opinions; "for Monte Carlo's hardly the place, let us admit, for a deliberate conférence. But on the whole, viewed merely as betting, it's a peculiarly bad way of risking your money. Imagine, for example, that you want to gamble; there are many other much better and fairer methods of gambling than this. Figure to yourself, first, that you and I play *rouge et noir* by a turn of the cards at a louis a cut: *eh bien*, we stand to lose or win on an absolute equality one with the other. That is just, so. We back our luck at no special disadvantage. But figure to yourself, on the contrary, that we play against a bank which gives itself one extra chance in its own favour out of every thirty-seven, and, understand well, we are backing our luck against unequal odds, so that in the long run the bank *must* win from us. You have only to play so many times running on an average in order to contribute with almost unerring certainty one napoleon towards the private income of the Prince of Monaco. For me, I do not care for his Serenity: I prefer to spend my napoleon on a good dinner, and to let the fools who frequent the Casino keep up the music and the gardens and the theatre for my private amusement."

From his seat in front, Hugh thoroughly despised that close-shaven Frenchman to the bottom of his soul. Mean wretch, who could thus coldly calculate the chances of loss, when he himself had just won at one glorious sitting fourteen hundred golden louis! He turned round in his chair, flushed red with success, and flung the fact, as it were, full in front of the Frenchman's *doctrinaire* folding eye-glasses.

The philosopher smiled. "Monsieur," he answered with perfect good-humour, and an olive poised on the tip of his fork, "you are one of the few whose special good fortune, occasionally realized, alone attracts the thousands of unfortunate pigeons. Every now and then, in effect, one hears at Monte Carlo of people who at a few strokes of the wheel have won for themselves prodigious fortunes. But then, one must remember that the chances are always rather against you than for you, and above all that the longest purse has always the advantage. A few people win very large sums; a few more win moderate sums; a good many win a little; and by far the most part— say two out of three—lose, and often lose heavily. Voilà tout! We have there the Iliad of gambling in a nutshell. You have been lucky enough yourself to win; that is well.—And Monsieur your friend there—pray, what has he done also?"

"Lost sixteen hundred," the Russian burst out with a sulky nod.

The close-shaven gentleman smiled pleasantly. "So the bank gains two hundred on the pair, it seems," he murmured with a faint shrug.—"Thank you, Monsieur: you prove my point. If ever I should be seized with a desire for gambling, which

Heaven forbid, I shall gamble where the chances that make for
me are at least as good as the chances that tell against me.
I dislike a game where I *must* lose if I keep on long enough. I
have no desire to increase the revenues of that amiable crowned
head, the Prince of Monaco."

Hugh's contempt for that man knew no bounds. A mere
wretched purblind political economist, no doubt, reasoning and
calculating on a matter like that, when he, Hugh, with his successful boldness, had a thousand pounds neatly tucked away in
gold and notes in his own trousers pockets! Thus do fools fling
away fortune! He laughed to scorn those London lawyers and
money-lenders. Here was the true Eldorado indeed : here a
genuine Pactolus flowed full and free through a Tom Tiddler's
ground of unimaginable wealth, unchecked in its course by
seven per cent. or by mean barriers of collateral security. He
would soon be rich—rich, rich, for Elsie.

CHAPTER XLV.

PACTOLUS INDEED!

AFTER a sumptuous lunch, they returned to the rooms. To
the rooms!—say rather to the treasure-house of Crœsus! On
the steps, they passed a young English lad, who looked barely
twenty. "Don't tell mamma I played," he was saying to a
companion ruefully as they passed him. "She'd break her
heart over it, if she ever knew it." But Hugh had no time
to notice in passing the pathos of the remark. Who could
bother his head about trifles like that, forsooth, when he's
coining his hundreds on the turn of a roulette table?

He meant to win hundreds—thousands—now. He meant to
build up a colossal fortune—for Elsie, for Elsie.

These years had taught him a certain sort of selfish unselfish-
ness. It was no longer for his own use that he wanted money ;
he longed to lay it all down at Elsie's feet. She was his Queen :
he would do her homage.

The tables had filled up three files deep with players by this
time. Hugh had hard work to edge his way dexterously in
between them : the Russian followed with equal difficulty.
But a croupier, recognizing them, motioned both with a courteous wave of his hand to two vacant chairs he had kept on
purpose. Men who win—or lose—large sums command respect
instinctively at Monte Carlo. Hugh and the Russian had each
qualified, on one or other of these opposite grounds, for a seat at
the table. Hugh's turn by the system, however, had not yet

come on : he had to wait, according to his self-imposed law, till
one of the four middle numbers should happen to turn up
before he again began staking. So he gazed around with placid
interest for some minutes at his crowded fellow-players. Success
excites some nervous heads; it always made Hugh Massinger
placid. There they sat and stood, not less, he thought, than five
hundred busy men and women, fifty or sixty jostling one another
round each separate board, playing away as if for dear life, and
risking fortunes giddily on the jump of a pea in that meaningless
little whirligig of a spinning roulette wheel. She was a German,
he conjectured, that flat-faced impassive lady opposite, gambling
cautiously but very high, and laden on her neck and arms and
ears with an atrocious dead-weight of vulgarly expensive jewelry.
Then the bold but handsome young girl at her side, with the exquisite bonnet and well-cut mantle, and the remarkably full-blown
Pennsylvanian twang, must surely by her voice be an American
citizen. By her voice and by her play; for she risked her broad
gold hundred-franc pieces with true-born American recklessness
of consequence. And there, a little way off, stands a newly
married Englishman, with his pretty small bride nestling close
up to him in wifely expostulation. Hugh could even catch
snatches of their whispered colloquy : "Don't, George, don't."—
"Just this once, Nellie: a napoleon on red."—Black wins: he
loses.—"H'm, the chances there are only even. If I win next
time, I get nothing but my own old napoleon back again. I'll
go it one better now : a nap on a column. Then if I win, you
see, I get four times my stake, Nellie."—Lost again! How fast
they rake it in!—"Well, then, I'll back a number this time."—
"Oh, but, George dear, you know you really can't afford it."—
George, unabashed by her wifely reproof, plumps down his
napoleon on 32. Whirr goes the roulette.—"Dix-huit," cries the
croupier, and sweeps in the gold with a careless curve of his
greedy hand-rake. Poor souls! In his heart, Hugh Massinger
was genuinely sorry for them. If only they had known his
infallible system!

But even as he thought it, he roused himself with a start.
Eighteen was one of the very numbers he had just been waiting
for. No time for otiose reflections now; no time for foolish waste
of sympathy: the moment had arrived for vigorous action.
With a sharp decisive air, he plunged down a hundred louis
on white. Bystanders stared and whispered and nudged one
another. White won, and he took up his winnings with the
utmost complacency. How quickly one accustoms one's self to
these big figures! A hundred louis seemed nothing now, in pur-
suance of the system. Then he glanced across at George, poor
luckless George, with a mute inquiry. How that smooth-faced
young Englishman envied him his success; for George, poor

George, had lost again. "Madame," Hugh said, addressing himself with an apologetic smile to the pretty young wife, "allow
me to venture ten louis for you."—The blushing girl shrank
back timidly. Hugh laid down ten pieces of gold on a number
again, backing his own luck separately by the regular rule on a
column of figures. Chance seemed to favour him: he was "in
the vein," as gamblers say in their hateful dialect. The number
won for poor shrinking little Mrs. Nellie, and the column also
won as well for Hugh himself. He pulled in his own pile of
gold carelessly, and handed the other to the pretty young
Englishwoman. "It isn't ours," she murmured with a shy look.
"You mustn't ask me; I really couldn't take it."

Hugh laughed, and pressed it on the anxious husband, who
cast a sidelong glance at the heap of gold, and finally in some
vague half-hearted way decided upon accepting it. "Now go,"
Hugh said with a fatherly air. "You don't understand this sort
of thing, you know. You belong to the class predestined to be
cheated. The sooner you leave this place the better. Let nothing
induce you ever to risk another penny as long as you live at
these precious tables." We can all be so wise and prudent for
others.

"But it's really yours," the young Englishman went on,
glancing down at it sheepishly. "You risked your own money,
you see, to win it."

"Not at all," Hugh answered with his pleasantest smile; he
'knew how to do a gracious act graciously. "I've taken back
my own ten louis out of it for myself. The rest is your wife's. I
staked it in her name. It was her good luck alone that won for
both of us. If you compel me to keep it, you spoil my break.
A burst of fortune must end somewhere. Don't stand in my
way, please, for such a mere trifle."

The Englishman's hand closed, half reluctantly, over the ill-
gotten money, and Hugh, undisturbed, turned back again with
a nod to his own gambling. The episode warmed him up to his
work. A pleasant sense of a generous action prettily performed
inspired and invigorated his play from that moment. He went
on with his game with an approving conscience. Some people's
consciences approve so blandly. The other players, too, observed
and applauded. Gamblers overflow with petty superstitions.
One of their profoundest is the rooted belief that meanness and
generosity bring each its due reward: whoever gambles in a
lavish, free-hearted, open-handed way is sure, they think, to
become the favourite of fortune.

The Russian, on the other hand, kept on losing steadily.
Now and again, indeed, he won for awhile on some great *coup*,
raking in his fifty or a hundred louis; but that was by exception: for the most part, he frittered away his winnings time

after time, and had recourse with alarming frequency of iteration to his bundle of notes, from which he changed a thousand
francs every half-hour or so with persistent ill-fortune. Turn
upon turn, he saw his money ruthlessly swept in by the relent-
less bank with unvarying regularity. Now it was zero that
turned up, to confound his reckoning, and the croupier with
his bow made a clean sweep, offhand, of the entire table: now
it was a long succession of left-hand numbers that won with
a rush, while he had staked his gold with unvarying mishap
upon the right-hand column. It was agonizing each time to
him to see the bank carelessly ladling out large sums to Hugh,
while he himself went on losing and losing. But at all hazards,
he would follow his calculations to the bitter end. Luck must
have a turn somewhere; and at any rate, plunging would never
improve matters. Hugh pitied him from his heart, poor ignorant devil. Why couldn't he find out with an exercise of reason
that obvious flaw in his own system?

A thousand francs on seven! The table stares, gapes, and
whispers. Heavy for a number! Who puts it on? This Monsieur on the seat here—pointing to Hugh. The croupier shrugs
his shoulder and spins. Out jumps the pea. Fourteen wins.—
Monsieur was very nearly right again, voyez-vous ?—Fourteen,
my friend, is just the precise double of seven. Monsieur's luck
is something truly miraculous.—He goes a thousand francs once
more, still on seven. *Ciel!* but he has the courage of his con-
victions, *mon ami!* Twenty-three wins.—Wrong again! He
drops on that a second thousand. But with what grace! A
thousand francs is nothing to these milords. Hugh smiles
imperturbably and stakes a third. On seven again! The man
is wonderful. What wins this time?—"Sept gagne," cries
everybody in hushed admiration; and Hugh, more sphinx-like
in his smile than ever, but conscious of a dozen admiring eyes
fixed full upon him, takes coolly up his thirty-five thousand.
Thirty-five thousand francs is not to be sneezed at. Fourteen
hundred pounds sterling! The biggest haul yet, but nothing
when you're accustomed to it. What a run of luck! Monsieur
was in the vein indeed. He played on and on, more elated than
ever. At this rate, he would soon earn a fortune for Elsie.

Elsie, Elsie, Elsie, Elsie! Through the din and noise of that
crowded gambling-hell, one sacred name still rang distinct and
clear in his ears. It was all for Elsie, for Elsie, for Elsie! He
must make himself rich, to marry Elsie.

He played on still with careless eagerness till the tables closed
—played with a continuous run of luck, often varying, of course
—for who minds a few hundreds to the bad now and then when
he's winning one time with another his thousands?—but on the
whole a run of luck persistently favourable. Raffalevsky, mean-

while, had played and lost. At the end of the day, as the
lackeys came in to bow the world out with polite smiles, they
both rose and left the rooms together. Then a sudden thought
flashed across his soul. Too late to return to San Remo now!
Awkward as it was, he must stop the night out at Monte Carlo.
Full of himself—of play and of Elsie—he had actually forgotten
all about Winifred!

They wa'ked across side by side to the Hotel de Paris. Hugh
was far too feverishly excited now with his day's play to care
in the least about the slight and the insult to that poor dead
girl. The mere indecency of it was all that he minded. A
cynical hardness possessed him at last. Nobody need know.
He strolled to the telegraph office and boldly sent off a message
to the *pension :*

"Detained at Mentone with sympathizing friends. Return
to-morrow. Make all arrangements on my account.—MAS-
SINGER."

Then he presented himself at the bureau of the Hotel de Paris.
Monsieur had no luggage; but no matter for that : the hotel
made haste to accommodate him at once with the best of rooms,
not even requiring a deposit beforehand. All Monte Carlo knew
well, indeed, that Monsieur had been winning. His name and
fame had been noised abroad by many-headed trumpeters. His
pockets were literally stuffed with gold. He was the hero of
the day. He had carried everything at the Casino before him.
Attentive servants awaited his merest beck or nod; everybody
was pleased; the world smiled on him. Alphonse, Marie, look
well after Monsieur! Monsieur has had the very best of
fortune.

He supped with Raffalevsky in a beautifully decorated *salle-
à-manger.* They recounted to one another, gleefully, gloomily,
their winnings and losses. The totals were heavy. They totted
them up with varying emotions. Hugh had won three thousand
four hundred pounds. Raffalevsky had made a hole in his
larger capital to the tune of something like two thousand seven
hundred. At the announcement, Hugh smiled his most benevolent and philosophical smile. "After all," he said, as he scanned
the wine-card, toothpick in hand, in search of a perfectly sound
Burgundy, "if one man wins, another *must* lose. You have
there the initial weak point of gambling. It's at bottom a
truly anti-social amusement. But these things equalize themselves in the long run ; they equalize themselves by the doctrine
of averages. Taken collectively, we're better off than we were
at lunch at any rate. Then, his Serenity of Monaco had pocketed
a couple of hundred louis out of the pair of us, viewed in the
lump. This evening, on the contrary, we're seven hundred
pounds to the good, as a firm, against him.—I like to best these

hereditary plunderers. It's a comfort to think that, in spite
of everything, we're more than even with him on the day's
transactions!"

Raffalevsky, however, strange to say, appeared to derive but
scanty consolation from this very vicarious joint-stock triumph;
he didn't see things in the proper light. The man was sullen,
positively sullen. Apparently, a person of morose disposition!
People oughtn't to let a little reverse of fortune produce such
obviously damping effects upon their minds and spirits. At all
hazards, they should at least be polite in general society. "If
you'd lost fifty or sixty thousand francs yourself, Monsieur," the
Russian cried petulantly, "you wouldn't talk in quite so airy
and easy a way about our joint position."

"Possibly not," Hugh answered, with perfect good-humour,
showing his even row of pearl-white teeth in a pleasant smile,
and toying with the pickle-fork. Fortune had favoured him.
He would bear it gracefully. No meanness for him! He would
do things on the proper scale now. He'd stand Raffalevsky a
splendid supper. He summoned the waiter with a lordly wave
of his languid hand and ordered a bottle of the very finest white
Hermitage.

CHAPTER XLVI.

THE TURN OF THE TIDE.

AT Paris, Warren Relf parted with Elsie. He saw her safely
to the Northern Railway Station, put her into the first night-
train for Calais, and then wriggled back himself to his temporary
lair, a quiet hotel on the Cours-la-Reine, just behind the Palais
de l'Industrie. He went back to bed, but not to sleep. It was
a gusty night, that night in Paris. The wind shook and rattled
the loose panes in the big French windows that opened on to
the balcony; the rain beat wildly in sudden rushes against the
rattling glass; the chimney-pots on all the neighbouring roofs
moaned and howled and shivered in concert. Warren Relf
reproached himself bitterly, as he listened to its sound, that
he hadn't decided on escorting Elsie the whole of her way across
to England. Mrs. Grundy would no doubt have disapproved,
to be sure; but what did he care in his heart, after all, for that
strange apotheosis of censorious matronhood? It would have
been better to have seen Elsie safe across the Channel, Mrs.
Grundy to the contrary notwithstanding, and installed her
comfortably in London lodgings. He wished he had done it,
now he heard how the wind was roaring and tearing; a north-

east wind, yet damp and rain-laden. Warren Relf knew its ways and its manners full well. It must be blowing great-guns across the North Sea now, he felt only too sure, and forcing whole squadrons of angry waves through the narrow funnel of the Straits of Dover.

As the night wore on, however, the wind rose steadily, till it reached at last the full dignity of a regular tempest. Warren Relf couldn't sleep in his bed for distress. He rose often, and looked out on the gusty street for cold comfort. The gas was flaring and flickering in the lamps; the wind was sweeping fiercely down the Cours-la-Reine; and the few belated souls who still kept the pavement were cowering and running before the beating rain with heads bent down and cloaks or overcoats wrapped tight around them. It must indeed be an awful night on the English Channel; Warren stood aghast to think to himself how awful. What on earth could ever have possessed him, he wondered now, to let Elsie make her way alone, on such a terrible evening as this, without him by her side, across the stormy water!

He would receive a telegram, thank Heaven, first thing in the morning. Till then, his suspense would be really painful.

As for Elsie, she sped all unconscious on her way to Calais, comfortably ensconced in her first-class compartment "pour dames seules," of which she had fortunately the sole monopoly. The rain beat hard against the windows, to be sure; and the l shook the door with its gusts more than once, or made feeble oil-lamp in the roof of the carriage flicker fitfully; but Elsie, absorbed in deeper affairs, hardly thought of it at all in her own mind till she reached the stretch of open coast that abuts on the mouth of the Somme near Abbeville. There the fact began at last to force itself upon her languid attention that the Channel crossing would be distinctly rough. Still, even then, she hardly realized its full meaning, for the wind was off-shore along the Picardy coast; and it was not till the train drew up with a dash on the quay at Calais that she fully under-stood the serious gravity of the situation. The waves were breaking fiercely over the mouth of the harbour, and the sea was rising so high outside that passengers were met with stern resolve at the terminus wall by the curt notice:

"Owing to the rough weather prevailing to-night, the Dover boat will not sail till morning."

"A cause du mauvais temps." Cause enough, to be sure, with such a sea running! Elsie saw at a glance that to cross through such a mountain of waves would have been quite impossible. Did the Boulogne boat intend to start? she asked helplessly.— No, madame; the service all along the coast was interrupted to-night, by stress of weather. There would be no steamer till

the wind moderated. To-morrow morning, perhaps, or to-
morrow evening.

So Elsie went perforce to an hotel in the town and waited
patiently for the sea to calm itself. But she, too, got no sleep;
she lay awake all night, and thought of Winifred.

Away at Monte Carlo, no wind blew. Hugh Massinger went
to rest there at his ease at the Hotel de Paris, and slept his sleep
out with perfect complacency. No qualms of conscience, no
thoughts of Winifred, disturbed his slumber. He had taken
the precaution to doubly lock and bolt his door, and to lay
his winnings between the bolster and the mattress; so he had
nothing to trouble about. He had also been careful to purchase
a good six-chambered revolver at one of the numerous shops
that line the Casino gardens. It isn't safe, indeed, at Monte
Carlo, they say, for a successful player, recognized as such, to
go about with too much money as hard cash actually in his
possession. Raffalevsky, in fact, had told him, with most unnecessary details, some very unpleasant stories, before he retired
to rest, about robberies committed at Monte Carlo upon the
helpless bodies of heavy winners. Raffalevsky was clearly in
a savage ill-temper that evening at having dropped a few
thousand pounds at the tables — strange, that men should
permit themselves to be so deeply affected by mere transient
trifling monetary reverses—and he took it out by repeating or
inventing truculent tales, evidently intended to poison the calm
rest of Hugh Massinger's innocent slumbers. There was that
ugly anecdote, for example, about the lucky *boulevardier* in the
high financial line who won three hundred thousand francs at
a couple of sittings—and was murdered in a first-class carriage
on his way back to Nice by an unknown assailant, never again
recognized or brought to justice. There was that alarming
incident of the fat Lyons silk-merchant with the cast in his
eye who deposited his gains, like a prudent bourgeois that he
was, with a banker at Monaco, but was nevertheless set upon
by an organized band of three well-dressed but ill-informed
ruffians, who positively searched him from head to foot, stripped
him, and then threw him out upon the four-foot way, a helpless
mass, in the Mont Boron Tunnel, happy to escape with bare life
and a broken leg from the merciless clutches of the gang of
miscreants. And there was that dramatic incident of the
Nevada heiress who, coming to Monte Carlo with the gold of
California visibly bulging her capacious pockets, had to fight
for her life in her own bedroom at this very hotel, and defend
her property from unholy hands by the summary process of
shooting down with her own domestic revolver two of her
cowardly midnight visitors. She was complimented by the
authorities on her gallant defence, and replied with spirit that,

for the matter of that, this sort of thing was really no novelty to her; for she'd shot down more than one importunate suitor for her hand and heart already in Nevada.

Then Raffalevsky had grown more lugubrious in his converse still, and descended to tales of the recurrent suicides that diversify the monotony of the Monegasque world. He estimated that twelve persons at least per annum, on a moderate average, blew their brains out in the Casino and grounds, after risking and losing their last napoleon at the roulette tables. To kill yourself in the actual saloons themselves, he admitted with a sigh, was indeed considered by gentlemanly players as a boorish solecism: persons of breeding, intent on an exit from this vale of tears, usually retired for the purpose of shooting themselves to a remote and sequestered spot in the Casino gardens, behind a convenient clump of picturesque date-palms. This spot was known to habitual frequenters of Monte Carlo as the Place Hari-kiri, or Happy Despatch Point. But if, by hazard, any inconsiderate person was moved to shoot himself in the *salles de jeu*, a rapid contingent of trained lackeys stood ever at hand ready to rush in at a moment's notice to drag away the offender's body or wipe up the mess; and play proceeded at once the same as usual.

Raffalevsky dilated upon all the particulars of the various murders, suicides, and robberies, with a wealth of diction and a fertile exuberance of sanguinary detail that would certainly ave done honour in its proper place to M. Zola or a penny readful. It shocked Hugh's fine sense of the becoming in language—his keen feeling for reserve in literature—to listen to so many revolting and sickening items. But the Russian was clearly in a humour that evening for blood and wounds. He spared no strong point in his catalogue of horrors. He revelled in gore. He insisted on the minutest accuracy of anatomical description. He robbed and murdered like one who loved it. He even strained the resources of the French language, sufficiently rich, for the rest, in terms of awe, as he rang the changes and piled up the agonies in his vivid recital of crimes and catastrophies.

Nevertheless, Hugh slept soundly in spite of it all in his bed till morning, and when he woke, found his goodly pile of gold and notes intact as ever between bolster and mattress. He had never slept so well since he went to Whitestrand.

But at Whitestrand itself that night things were quite otherwise. Such a storm was hardly remembered on the German Ocean within the memory of the oldest sailors. Early in the evening, the coastguardman at the shelter just beyond the Hall grounds, warned by telegram from the Meteorological Office, had raised the cone for heavy weather from the north-east. By nine o'clock, the surf was seething and boiling on the bar, and the waves were dashing themselves in huge sheets of foam against Hugh Massinger's ineffectual breakwater. The sand flew free before the angry gusts: it blinded the eyes and filled the lungs of all who tried to face the storm on the sea-front: even up the river and at the Hall itself it pervaded the air with a perfect bombardment of tiny grains. It was only possible to remain outdoors by turning one's back upon the fierce blast, or by covering one's face, not with a veil, but with a silk pocket-handkerchief. The very coastguardmen, accustomed by long use to good doses of solid silica in the lungs, shrank back with alarm from the idea of facing that running fire of driven sand-particles. As for the smacks and boats at large on the sea, they were left to their fate—nothing could be done by human hands to help or save them.

By midnight, tide was well at its full, and, the beach being covered, the bombardment of sand slowly intermitted a little. But sheets of foam and spray still drove on before the wind, and fishermen, clad in waterproof suits from head to foot, stood facing them upon the shore to watch the fate of Hugh Massinger's poor helpless breakwater. The sea was roaring and raving round its sides now like a horde of savages, and the scour was setting in fiercer than ever to wash away whatever remained of Whitestrand.

"Will it stand, Bill?" the farm-bailiff asked in anxious tones of Stannaway the innkeeper, as they strained their eyes through the gloom and spray to catch sight of the frail barrier that alone protected them—the stone breakwater which had taken the place of the old historical Whitestrand poplar.

Stannaway shook his head despondently. "Sea like that's bound to wash it away," he answered hard through the teeth of the wind. "It'd wash away anything. An' when it goes, it's all up with Whitestrand."

The whole village, indeed, men, women, and children alike, had collected by this time at the point by the river, to watch the progress of the common enemy. There was a fearful interest for every one of them in seeing the waves assail and beat down that final barrier of their hearths and homes. If the breakwater went, Whitestrand must surely follow it, now or later, bit by bit, in piecemeal destruction. The sea would swallow it up wholesale, as it swallowed up Dunwich and Thorpe and Slaughden. Those domestic examples gave point to their terror. To the Suffolk coast-dwellers, the sea indeed envisages itself ever, not as a mere natural expanse of water, but as a slow and patient yet implacable assailant.

By two in the morning, a fresh excitement supervened to keep up the interest: a collier hull, deserted and waterlogged, came drifting in by slow stages before the driving gale across the broad sand-flats. She was a dismasted hulk, rackety and unseaworthy, abandoned by all who had tried to sail her; and she drifted slowly, slowly, slowly on, driven before the waves, foot by foot, a bit at a time, over the wet sands, till at last, with one supreme effort of force, the breakers cast her up, a huge burden, between the shore and the breakwater, blocking with her broadside one entire end of the channel created by the scour behind the spot once occupied by the famous poplar. The waves, in fact, dashed her full against the further end of the breakwater, and jammed her up with prodigious force between shore and wall, a temporary barrier against their own advances. Then retiring for a moment to recruit their rage, they broke in sheets of helpless foam against the wooden bulwark they had raised themselves in the direct line of their own progress.

What followed next, followed so fast that even the sturdy Whitestranders themselves, accustomed as they were to heavy seas and shifting sands and natural changes of marvellous rapidity, stood aghast at its suddenness and its awful energy. In a few minutes, before their very eyes, the sea had carried huge masses and shoals of flying sand over the top of the wall and the stranded ship, and lodged them deep in the hollow below that the scour had created in the rear of the breakwater. The wall was joined as if by some sudden stroke of a conjurer's wand to the mainland beyond; and the sea, still dashing madly against the masonry and the ship, set to work once more to erect fresh outworks in front against its own assaults by piling up sand with incredible speed in dunes and mounds upon their outer faces. Even as they looked, the breakwater was rapidly lost to view in a mountain of beach: the broken stump of mast on the wrecked collier hardly showed above the level of the mushroom hillock that covered and overwhelmed with its hasty débris the buried hull of the unknown vessel. Hummock after hummock grew apace outside with startling rapidity in successive lines along the shore to seaward. New land was forming at each crash of the waves. The Æolian sand was doing its work bravely. By five in the morning, men walked secure where the sea had roared but six hours before. It had left the buried breakwater now a quarter of a mile inland at least, and was still engaged with mad eagerness in its rapid task of piling up fresh mounds and heaps in endless rows, to seaward and to seaward and ever to seaward.

Whitestrand was saved. Nay, more than that: it was gaining once more in a single night all that it had lost in twenty years to the devouring ocean.

When morning broke, the astonished Whitestranders could

hardly recognize their own beach, their own shore, their own salt marshes, their own river. Everything was changed as if by magic. The estuary was gone, and in its place stretched a wide expanse of undulating sandhills. The Char had turned its course visibly southward, bursting the dikes on the Yondstream farms, and flowing to the sea by the old channel from which Oliver's engineers had long since diverted it. The Hall stood half a mile farther from the water's edge than it had done of old, and a belt of bare and open dune-land lay tossed between its grounds and the new high-tide mark. The farm-bailiff examined them in the gray dawn with a practical eye. "If we plant them hills all over with maramgrass and tamarisk," he said reflectively, "they'll mat like the other ones, and Squire'll have as many acres of new pasture-land north o' Char as ever he lost o' salt marsh and meadow south of the old river."

If Hugh Massinger had only known it, indeed, the storm and the strange chances of tempest had done far more for him that single night while he slept at Monte Carlo than luck at roulette had managed to do for him the day before in that hot and crowded sink of iniquity in the rooms of the Casino.

For from that day forth Whitestrand was safe. It was more than safe; it began to grow again. The blown sand ceased to molest it: the sea and the tide ceased to eat it away: the breakwater had done its work well, after all; and a new barrier of increasing sandhills had sprung up spontaneously by the river's mouth to guard its seaward half from future encroachment. If Hugh could only have known and believed it, the estate was worth every bit as much that wild morning as ever it had been in the palmiest days of the Elizabethan Meyseys. And the family solicitor, examining the mortgages in his own office, remarked to himself with a pensive glance that the Squire might have raised that little sum, if only he'd waited, at scarcely more than half the interest, on his own security and his improved property. For Whitestrand now would fetch money.

CHAPTER XLVII.

FORTUNE OF WAR.

At Monte Carlo, on the other hand, day dawned serene and calm and cloudless. Hugh Massinger rose, unmindful of his far-away Suffolk sandhills, and gazed with a pleasant dreamy feeling out of the window of his luxurious first-floor bedroom. It was a strange outlook. On one side, the ornate and over-

loaded Parisian architecture of that palace of Circe, plumped
down so grotesquely, with its meretricious town-bred airs and
graces, among the rugged scenery of the Maritime Alps : on the
other side, the inaccessible crags and pinnacles of the Tête-de-
Chien, gray and lonely as any mountain side in Scotland or
Savoy—the actual terminus of the main range of snow-clad
Alps, whose bald peaks topple over sheer three thousand feet
into the blue expanse of the Mediterranean, that washes the
base of their precipitous bluffs. The contrast was almost ludicrous in its quaint extremes. If wit be rightly defined as the
juxtaposition of the incongruous, then is Monte Carlo indeed a
grand embodiment of the practically witty. The spot would be
a Paradise if it were not a Hell. The Casino stands on its ledge
of terrace like a fragment of Paris in its worst phase, dropped
down from the clouds by some Merlin's art amid the wildest
and most exquisite rocky scenery on the whole glorious stretch
of enchanted coast that spreads its long and fantastic panorama
in unbroken succession of hill and mountain from the quays of
Marseilles to the palaces of Genoa.

He did not wholly approve the desecration. Hugh Massinger's tastes were not all distorted. Dissipation to him was
but a small part and fraction of existence. He took it only as
the mustard of life—an agreeable condiment to be sparingly
partaken of.—The poet's instinct within him had kept alive and
'resh his healthy interest in simpler things, in hill and dale, in
:alm and peaceful country pleasures. After that feverish day
)f gambling at Monte Carlo, he would dearly have loved to rise
early and saunter out alone for a morning walk ; to scale before
breakfast the ramping cliffs of the Tête-de-Chien, and to reach
the mouldering Roman tower of Turbia, that long mounted
guard on the narrow path where Gaul and Italy marched
together. But that hateful pile of gold and notes between the
pillow and the mattress restrained his desire. It would be
dangerous to wander among the lonely mountains with so large
a sum as that concealed about his person ; dangerous to leave
it unguarded at the hotel, or to entrust it to the keeping
of any casual stranger. "Cantabit vacuus coram latrone
viator," he murmured to himself half aloud with a sigh of
regret, as he turned away his eyes from that glorious semicircle
of jagged peaks that bounded his horizon. He must stop at
home and take care of his money-bags, like any vulgar cheese-
mongering millionaire of them all. Down, poet's heart, with
your unreasonable aspirations for the lonely mountain heights !
Amaryllis and asphodel are not for you. Shoulder your muck-
rake with a manful smile, and betake you to the Casino where
Circe calls, as soon as the great gate swings once more on its
grating hinges. You cannot serve two masters. You have

chosen Mammon to-day, and him you must worship. No
mountain air for your lungs this morning; but the close and
crowded atmosphere of the roulette tables. Keep true to your
creed for a little while longer: it is all for Elsie's sake!—For
Elsie! For Elsie!—He withdrew his head from the window
with a faint flush of shame. Ah, heaven, to think he should
think of Elsie in such a connection and at such a moment!

He had the grace himself to be heartily disgusted at it.
Gambling was indeed a hateful trade. When once he had won
a fortune for Elsie, he would never again touch card or dice,
never let her learn whence that fortune had been gathered. He
would even try to keep her out of his mind, for her purity's
sake, while he remained at Monte Carlo. He loved her too well
to drag her into that horrid Casino, were it but in memory. A
man is himself, one and indivisible; but still he must hold the
various parts of his complex nature at arm's-length, sometimes:
he must prevent them from clashing: he must refrain from
mixing up what is purest and truest and profoundest in his
heart with all that is vilest and lowest and ugliest and most
money-grubbing. Hugh had an unsullied shrine left vacant
for Elsie still: he would not profane that inmost niche of his
better soul with the poisonous air of the gambling hells of
Monaco. Let him sink where he would, he was yet a poet.

He dressed himself slowly and went down to breakfast.
Attentive waiters, expectant of a duly commensurate tip,
sniffing *pour-boire* from afar, crowded round for the honour of
his distinguished orders. Raffalevsky joined him in the *salle-à-
manger* shortly. The Russian was haggard and pale from sleeplessness: dark rings surrounded his glassy black eyes: his face
was the face of a boiled codfish. No waiter hurried to receive
his commands: all Monte Carlo knew him well already for a
heavy loser. Your loser seldom overflows into generous tipping.
Hugh beckoned him over to his own table: he would extend to
the Russian the easy favour of his profuse hospitality. Raffalevsky seated himself in a sulky humour by the winner's side.
He meant to play it out still, he said, to the bitter end. He
couldn't afford to lose and leave off; that game was for capi-
talists. For himself, he speculated—well—on borrowed funds.
He must win all back or lose all utterly. In the latter case—a
significant gesture completed the sentence. He put up his
hand playfully to his right ear and clicked with his tongue,
like the click of a revolver barrel. Hugh smiled responsive his
most meaning smile. "Espérons toujours," he murmured
philosophically in his musical voice and perfect accent. No
man on earth could ever bear with more philosophical composure than Hugh Massinger the misfortunes of others.

Before he left the breakfast-table that morning, a waiter

presented the bill, all deferential politeness. "I sleep here to-
night again," Hugh observed with a yawn, as he noted atten-
tively the lordly conception of its various items. The waiter
bowed a profound bow.—"At Monte Carlo, Monsieur," he said
significantly, "one pays daily."—Hugh drew out a handful of
gold from his pocket with a laugh and paid at once. But the
omen disquieted him. Who wins to-day may lose to-morrow.
Clearly the hotel at least had thoroughly learnt that simple
lesson.

They filed in among the first at the doors of the Casino.
Once started, Hugh played, with scarcely an intermission for
food, till the tables closed again. He kept himself up with
champagne and sandwiches. That was indeed a glorious day!
A wild success attended his hazards. He staked and won;
staked and lost; staked and won; staked and lost again. But
the winnings by far outbalanced the losses. It went the round
of the tables, in frequent whispers, that a young Englishman, a
poet by feature, was breaking the bank with his audacious
plunging. He plunged again, and again successfully. People
crowded up from their own game at neighbouring boards to
watch and imitate the too lucky Englishman. "Give him his
head! He's in the vein!" they said. "A man in the vein
should always keep playing." The young lady with the fine
Pennsylvanian twang remarked with occidental plainness of
speech that she "wouldn't object to running a partnership."
Hugh laughed and demurred.—"You might dilute the luck,
you know," he answered good-humouredly. "But if you'll
hand me over a hundred louis, I don't mind putting them on
31 for you." He did, and they won. The crowd of gamblers
applauded, all hushed, with their usual superstitious awe and
veneration. "He has the run of the numbers," they said in
concert. To gamblers generally, fate is a goddess, a living
reality, with capricious likes and dislikes of her own. They are
ever ready to back her favourite for the time being; they look
upon play as a predestined certainty.

Raffalevsky meanwhile lost and lost with equal persistence.
He drank as much champagne as Hugh; but the wine inspired
no lucky guesses. When they came to count up their gains
and losses at the end of the day, they found it was still a neck-
and-neck race, in opposite ways, between them. Hugh had
won altogether close on nine thousand pounds. Raffalevsky
had lost rather more than eight thousand five hundred.

"Never mind," Hugh remarked with his inexhaustible buoy-
ancy. "We're still to the good against his Monegasque High-
ness. There's a balance of something like five hundred pounds
in our joint favour."

"In other words," Raffalevsky answered with a grim smile,

"you've won all my money and some other fellow's too. You're
the sponge that sucks up all my lifeblood. I've got barely
three thousand five hundred left. When that goes —— " And
he repeated once more the same expressive suicidal pantomime.

That night, Hugh slept at Monte Carlo once more. He had
lost all sense of shame and decency now. He sent off a note for
two thousand francs to the people at the *pension*, just as a
guarantee of good faith—as the newspapers say—and to let
them know he was really returning. But he had formed a
shadowy plan of his own by this time. He would wait another
day at the Casino and go home to San Remo with Warren Relf
by the train that reached there at 6.39—the train by which
Elsie had said in her note he would be returning.

Why he wished to do so, he hardly with distinctness knew
himself. Certainly he did not mean to pick a quarrel; he only
knew in a vague sort of way he was going by that train; and
until it started, he would keep on playing.

And lose every penny he'd won, perhaps! Why not leave off
at once, secure of his eight thousand? Bah! what was eight
thousand now to him? He'd win a round twenty before he left
off—for Elsie.

So he played next day from morning till night; played, and
drank champagne feverishly. Such luck had never been known
at the tables. Old players stood by with observant faces and
admired his vein. Was ever a system seen like his? Such
judgment, they said; such restraint; such coolness!

But inwardly, Hugh was consumed all day by a devouring
fire. His excitement at last knew no bounds. He drank champagne by the glassful to keep his nerve up. He had won before
nightfall, all told, no less a sum than eleven thousand pounds
sterling. What was the miserable remnant of Whitestrand,
now, to him! Let Whitestrand sink in the sea for all he cared
for it! He had here a veritable mine of wealth. He would go
back to San Remo to bury Winifred—and return to heap up a
gigantic fortune.

Eleven thousand pounds! A mere bagatelle. At five per
cent. five hundred and fifty a year only!

His train was due to start at five. About four o'clock, Raffalevsky came up to him from another table. The Russian's face
was white as death. "I've lost all," he murmured hoarsely,
drawing Hugh aside. "The whole, the whole, my three hundred thousand francs of borrowed capital!—And what's worse
still, I borrowed it from the chest—government money—the
treasury of the squadron! If I go back alive, I shall be court-
martialed.—For Heaven's sake, my friend, lend me at least a few
hundred francs to retrieve my luck with!"

Hugh put his hand to his pile and drew out three notes of a

thousand francs each—a hundred and twenty pounds sterling in all. It was nothing, nothing. "Good luck go with them," he cried good-humouredly. "When those are gone, my dear fellow, come back for more. I'm not the man, I hope and trust, to turn my back upon a comrade in misfortune."

The Russian snapped at them with a grateful gesture, but without hesitation or spoken thanks, and returned in hot haste to his own table. Gamblers have little time for needless talking.

At a quarter to five, after a last hasty draught of champagne at the buffet, Hugh turned to go out, with his cash in his pocket. In front of him he saw just an apparition of Raffalevsky, rushing wildly away with one hand upon his forehead. The man's face was awful to behold. Hugh felt sure the Russian had lost all once more, and been too much ashamed even to renew his application.

The great door swung slow upon its hinges, and Raffalevsky burst into the outer corridor, bowed from the room with great dignity, in spite of his frantic haste, by a well-liveried attendant. There is plenty of obsequiousness at Monte Carlo for every player, even if he has lost his last louis.

They emerged once more upon the beautiful terrace, the glorious view, the pencilled palm-trees. All around, the sinking Italian sun lit up that fairy coast with pink and purple. Bay and rock and mountain-side showed all the more exquisite fter the fetid air of those crowded gaming saloons. High up n the shoulders of the inaccessible Alps the great square Roman keep of Turbia gazed down majestically with mute contempt on the feverish throng of miserable idlers who poured in and out through the gaudy portals of the garish Casino. A serene delight pervaded Hugh Massinger's placid soul; he felt himself vastly superior to these human butterflies; he knew his own worth as he turned entranced from the marble steps to the beautiful prospect that spread everywhere unrolled like a picture around him. Poet as he was, he despised mere gamblers; and he carried eleven thousand pounds odd of winnings in notes in his pocket.

R'r'r! A sharp report! A cry! A concourse! Something uncanny had surely happened. People were running up where the pistol went off. Hugh Massinger turned with a shudder of disgust. How discomposing! The usual ugly Monte Carlo incident! Raffalevsky had shot himself behind the shade of the palm-trees.

The man was lying, a hideous mass, in a crimson pool of his own blood, prone on the ground—hit through the temple with a well-directed bullet. It was a horrid sight, and Hugh's nerves were sensitive. If it hadn't been for the champagne, he would really have fainted. Besides, the train was nearly due. If

you hover about where men have killed themselves, you're liable
to be let in for whatever may happen to the Monegasque equiva-
lent for that time-honoured institution, our own beloved British
coroner's inquest. He might be hailed as a witness. Is that
law ? Ay, marry, is it? Crowner's quest law! Better give it
all a wide berth at once. The bell was ringing for the train below.
With a sudden shudder, Hugh hurried away from the ghastly
object. After all, he had done his best to save him—lent him
or given him three thousand francs to retrieve his losses. It
was none of his fault. If one man wins, another man loses!
Luck, luck, the mere incalculable chances of the table! If their
places had been reversed, would that morose, unsociable, ill-
tempered Russian have volunteered to give him three thousand
francs to throw away, he wondered? Never, never: 'twas all
for the best. The Russian had lost, and he had won—eleven
thousand pounds odd, for Elsie.

He rushed away and dashed headlong into the station. His
own revolver was safe in his pocket. He carried eleven thousand
pounds odd about him. No man should rob him without a fight
between here and San Remo.

CHAPTER XLVIII.

AT BAY.

HONEST folk give lucky winners a wide berth at the Casino
railway station, lest they should be suspected of possible evil
designs upon their newly got money. Hugh found, therefore,
he could pick his own seat quite at will, for nobody seemed
anxious to claim the dubious honour of riding alone with him.
So he strolled along the train, humming a gay tune, and in-
specting the carriages with an attentive eye, till he reached
a certain first-class compartment not far from the front, where
a single passenger was quietly seated. The single passenger
made his heart throb; for it was Warren Relf—alone and
unprotected.

He hardly knew why, but, flushed with wine and continued
good fortune, he meant to ride back in that very carriage, face
to face with the baffled and defeated serpent ; for Hugh had
already discounted his prospective victory. Warren was looking
the opposite way, and did not perceive him. Hugh waited,
therefore, till the train was just about to start from the station,
and then he jumped in—too late for Warren, if he would, to
change his carriage.

In a second, the painter turned round and recognized his

companion. He gave a sudden start. At last the two men had met in earnest. A baleful light beamed in Hugh's dark eye. His blood was up. He had run too fast through the whole diapason of passion. Roulette and champagne, love and jealousy, hatred and vindictiveness, had joined together to fire and inflame his heart. He was at white-heat of exultation and excitement now. He could hardly contain his savage joy. "Have I found thee, O my enemy?" he cried out, half aloud. Another time, it was just the opposite way. "Hast thou found me, O my enemy?" he had cried to Warren with an agonized cry at their last meeting in the club in London.

Warren Relf, gazing up in surprise, answered him back never a word; he only thought to himself silently that he was not and had never been Hugh Massinger's enemy. From the bottom of his heart, the painter pitied him : he pitied him ten thousand times more than he despised him.

They stood at gaze for a few seconds. Then, "Where have you been?" Hugh asked at last insolently. The champagne had put him almost beside himself. Drunk with wine, drunk with good fortune, he allowed his true nature to peep forth for once a little too obviously. He would make this fellow Relf know his proper place before gentlemen at last—a mere ignorant upstart, half way between a painter and a common sailor.

"To Paris," Warren answered with curt decision. He was in no humour for a hasty quarrel to-day with this half-drunken madman.

"What for?" Hugh continued, as rudely as before. Then added with a loud and ugly laugh: "You need tell me no lies. I know already. I've found you out.—To see my cousin Elsie across to England."

At the word, Warren's face fell somewhat ominously. He leaned back, half irresolute, in the corner of the carriage and played with twitching fingers at the leather window-strop. "You are right," he answered low, in a short sharp voice. "I never lie. I went to escort Miss Challoner from you and San Remo."

Hugh flung himself into an attitude of careless ease. This colloquy delighted him. He had the fellow at bay. He began to talk, as if to himself, in a low monologue. "Heine says somewhere," he observed with a sardonic smile, directing his observation into blank space, as if to some invisible third person, "that he would wish to spend the evening of his days in a cottage by the sea, within sound of the waves, with his wife and children seated around him—and a large tree growing just outside his grounds, from whose branches might dangle the body of his enemy."

Warren Relf sat still in constrained silence. For Elsie's sake, he would allow no quarrel to arise with this madman, flown with insolence and wine. He saw at once what had happened: Massinger was drunk with luck and champagne. But he would avoid the consequences. He would change carriages when they stopped on the frontier at Ventimiglia.

The bid for an angry repartee had failed. So Hugh tried again; for he *would* quarrel. "A great many murders take place on this line," he remarked casually, once more in the air. "It's a dangerous thing, they tell me, for a winner at Monte Carlo to go home alone in a carriage by himself with one other passenger."

Still Warren Relf held his peace, undrawn.

Hugh tried a third time. He went on to himself in a musing monologue. "Any man who travels anywhere by train with a large sum of money about his person is naturally exposed to very great peril," he said slowly. "I've been to Monte Carlo, playing, to-day, and I've won eleven thousand pounds; eleven—thousand—pounds—sterling. I've got the money now about me. There it is, you see, in French banknotes. A very large sum. Eleven—thousand—pounds—sterling."

Still Warren said nothing, biting his lip hard, but with an abstracted air looked out of the window. Hugh was working himself up into a state of frantic excitement now, though well suppressed. Fate had delivered his enemy plump into his hands, and he meant to make the very best use of his splendid opportunit.

"A fool in Paris once called in a barber," he went on quietly, with a studious outer air of calm determination, "and ordered him, for a joke, to shave him at once, with a pistol lying before him on the dressing-table. 'If your hand slips and you cut my skin,' the fool said, 'I'll blow your brains out.' To his surprise, the barber began without a word of reply, and shaved him clean with the utmost coolness. When he'd finished, the patient paid down ten pounds, and asked the fellow how he'd managed to keep his hand from trembling. 'Oh,' said the barber, 'easy enough: it didn't matter the least in the world to me. I thought you were mad. If my hand had slipped, I knew what to do: I'd have cut your throat without one moment's hesitation, before you had time to reach out for your pistol. I'd say it was an accident; and any jury in all Paris would without a doubt at once have acquitted me.'—The story's illustrative. I hope, Mr. Relf, you see its applicability?"

"I do not," Warren answered, surprised at last into answering back, and with an uneasy feeling that Massinger was developing dangerous lunacy. "But I must beg you will have the goodness not to address your conversation to me any further."

“The application of my remark,” Hugh went on to himself,
groping with his hand in his pocket for his revolver, and with-
drawing it again as soon as he felt quite reassured that the
deadly weapon was safely there, “ought at once to be obvious
to the meanest understanding. There are some occasions where
homicide is so natural that everybody jumps at once to a particular conclusion.—Observe my argument. It concerns you
closely.—Many murders have taken place on this line—murders
of heavy winners at Monte Carlo. Many travellers have committed murderous assaults on the persons of winners with large
sums of money about them.—Now follow me closely. I give
you fair warning.—If a winner with eleven thousand pounds in
his pocket were to get by accident into a carriage with one other
person, and a quarrel were by chance to arise between them,
and the winner in self-defence were to fire at and kill that other
person—do you think any jury in all the world would convict
him for protecting his life from the aggressor? No, indeed,
my good sir! In such a case, the other person’s life would be
wholly at the offended winner’s mercy.—Do you follow my
thought? Do you understand me now?—Aha, I expected so!
Warren Relf, I’ve got you in my power. I can shoot you like
a dog; I can do as I like with you.”

With a sudden start, Warren Relf woke up all at once to a
consciousness of the real and near danger that thus unexpectedly
and closely confronted him. It was all true; and all possible!
igh was mad—or maddened at least with play and drink: he
liberately meant to take his enemy’s life, and trust to the
thorities accepting his plausible story that he was forced to
do so in self-defence or in defence of his money.

“You blackguard!” the painter cried as the truth came home
to him in all its naked ugliness, facing Hugh in his righteous
indignation like a lion. “How dare you venture on such a
cowardly scheme? How dare you concoct such a vile plot?
How dare you confess to me you mean to put it into execution?”

“I’m a gentleman,” Hugh answered, smiling across at him
still with a hideous smile of pure drunken devilry, and finger-
ing once more the revolver in his pocket. “I’ll shoot no man
without due explanation and reason given. I’ll tell you why.
You’ve tried to keep Elsie out of my way all these long years
for your own vile and designing purposes—to beguile and entrap
that innocent girl into marrying *you*—such a creature as *you* are;
and by your base machinations you’ve succeeded at last in gaining her consent to your wretched advances. How she was so
lost to all sense of shame and self-respect—she, a Massinger on
her mother’s side—as to give her consent to such a degrading
engagement, I can’t imagine. But you extorted it somehow—
by alternate threats and cringing, I suppose—by scolding her

and cajoling her—by lies and by slanders—by frightening *her* and libelling *me*—till the poor terrified girl, tortured out ot her wits, decided to accept you, at last, out of pure weariness. A Man would be ashamed, I say, to act as you have done; but a Thing like you—pah—there—it revolts me even to talk to you!"

Warren Relf's face was livid crimson with fiery indignation; but he would not do this drunken madman the honour of contradicting or arguing with him. Elsie to him was far too sacred and holy a subject to brawl over with a half-tipsy fool in a public conveyance. He clutched his hands hard and kept his temper; he preferred to sit still and take no outer notice.

Hugh mistook his enforced calm for cowardice and panic. "Aha!" he cried again, "so you see, my fine friend, you've been found out! You've been exposed and discredited. You've got no defence for your mean secretiveness. Going and hiding away a poor terrified, friendless, homeless girl from her only relations and natural protectors—working upon her feelings by your base vile tricks—setting your own wretched womankind to bully and badger her by day and by night, till she gives her consent at last—out of pure disgust and weariness, no doubt—to your miserable proposals. The sin and the shame of it! But you forgot you had a Man to deal with as well! You're brought to book now. I've found you out in the nick of time, and I mean to take the natural and proper advantage of my fortunate discovery. Listen here to me, now, you infernal sneak: before I shoot you, I propose to make you know my plans. I shall have my legitimate triumph out of you first. I shall tell you all; and then, you coward—I'll shoot you like a dog, and nobody on earth will ever be one penny the wiser."

Warren saw the man had fairly reached the final stage of dangerous lunacy. He was simply raving with success and excitement. His blood was up, and he meant murder. But the painter fortunately kept his head cool. He didn't attempt to disarm or disable him as yet; he waited to see whether Hugh had or had not a pistol in his pocket. Perhaps Hugh, with still deeper cunning, was only trying to egg him on into a vain quarrel, that he might disgrace him in the end by a horribly plausible and vindictive charge of attempted robbery.

"I've won eleven thousand pounds," Hugh went on distinctly, with marked emphasis, in short sharp sentences. "My wife's dead, and I've inherited Whitestrand. I mean to marry Elsie Challoner. I can keep her now as she ought to be kept; I can make her the wife of a man of property. You alone stand in my way. And I mean to shoot you, just to get rid, of you offhand.—Sit still there and listen: don't budge an inch or, by Heaven, I'll fire at once and blow your brains out. Lift

hand or foot and you're a dead man.—Warren Relf, I mean
to shoot you. No good praying and cringing for your life, like
the coward that you are, for I won't listen. Even if you were
to renounce your miserable claim to my Elsie this moment, I
wouldn't spare you ; I'd shoot you still. You shall be punished
for your presumption—a creature like you ; and when you're
dead and buried, I shall marry Elsie.—Think of me, you cringing miserable cur—when you're dead and gone, enjoying myself
for ever with Elsie.—Yes, I mean to make you drink it, down to
the very dregs. Hear me out. You shall die like a dog ; and
I shall marry Elsie."

Warren Relf's eye was fixed upon him hard, watching him
close, as a cat watches, ready to spring, by an open mouse-
hole. This dangerous madman must be disarmed at all hazards,
the moment he showed his deadly weapon. For Elsie's sake, he
would gladly have spared him that final exposure. But the man,
in his insolent drunken bravado, made parley useless and mercy
impossible. It was a life-and-death struggle between them now.
Warren must disarm him ; nothing else was feasible.

As he watched and waited, Hugh dived with his hand into his
pocket for his revolver, and drew it forth, exultant, with maniac
eagerness. For a single second, he brandished it, loaded, in
Warren's face, laughing aloud in his drunken joy; then he
pointed it straight with deadly resolve at the painter's forehead.

CHAPTER XLIX.

THE UNFORESEEN.

QUICK as lightning, Relf leaped upon his frantic assailant, and
with one powerful arm, stiffened like an iron bar, dashed down
the upraised hand, and the revolver in its grasp, with all his
might, toward the floor of the carriage. A desperate struggle
ensued in that narrow compartment. The two men, indeed,
were just evenly matched. Warren Relf, strong from his
yachting experience, with sinewy limbs much exercised by
constant outdoor occupation, fought hard in sheer force of
thew and muscle, with the consciousness that therein lay his
one chance of saving Elsie from still further misery. Hugh
Massinger, on the other hand, well knit and wiry, now mad
with mingled excitement and drink, grappled wildly with his
adversary in the fierce strength of pure adventitious nervous
energy. The man's whole being seemed to pour itself forth
with a rush in one frantic outburst of insane vigour. He
gripped the revolver with his utmost force, and endeavoured

to wrench it, in spite of Warren's strong hand, from his enemy's
grasp, and to turn it by sheer power of wrist and arm once more
upon Elsie's new lover. "Blackguard!" he cried, through his
clenched teeth, as he fought tooth and nail with frenzied
struggles against his powerful opponent. "You shan't get off.
You shall never have her. If I hang for you now, I'll kill you
where you stand. I've always hated you. And in the end I
mean to do for you."

With a terrible effort, Warren wrested the loaded revolver at
last from his trembling hands. Hugh battled for it savagely
like a wild beast in a life-and-death struggle. Every chamber
had a cartridge jammed home in its recess. To fight for the
deadly weapon would be downright madness. If it went off by
accident somebody would be wounded; the ball might even go
through the woodwork into the adjoining compartments. Without one moment's hesitation Warren raised the fatal thing aloft
in his hand high above his head. The window on the seaward
side was luckily open. As he swung it, Hugh leaped up once
more and tried to snatch the loaded pistol afresh from his
opponent's fingers; but the painter was too quick for him;
before he could drag down that uplifted arm with his whole
weight flung upon the iron biceps, Warren Relf had whirled the
disputed prize round his head and flung it in an arch far out to
sea through the open window. The railway runs on a ledge of
rock overhanging the bay. It fell with a splash into the deep
blue water. Hugh Massinger, thus helplessly balked for the
moment of his expected revenge, sprang madly on his foe in a
wild assault, with teeth and nails and throttling fingers, as a
wounded tiger springs in its vindictive death-throes on the
broad flanks of an infuriated elephant.

Next instant, they were plunged in the deep arch of a tunnel,
and continued their horrible hand-to-hand battle for several
minutes in utter darkness. Rolling and grappling in the
gloom together, they rose and fell, now one man on top and
now the other, round after round, like a couple of angry
wrestlers. The train rushed out into the light once more and
plunged a second time into a still blacker tunnel. But still
they fought and tore one another fiercely. All the way from
Monte Carlo to the frontier, indeed, the line alternates between
bold ledges that just overhang the deep blue bays and tunnels
that pierce with their dark archways the intervening headlands.
When they emerged a second time upon the light of day, Hugh
Massinger had his hands tight pressed in a convulsive grasp
upon Warren Relf's throat; and Warren Relf, purple and black
in the face, was tearing them away with horrible contortions of
arms and legs, and striving to defend himself by brute force
from the would-be murderer's close-gripped clutches.

"Aha!" Hugh cried, as he held his enemy down on the seat with a gurgle in his throat, "I have you now! I've got you; I've done for you. You shall choke for your insolence! You shall choke—you shall choke for it."

With an awful rally for dear life, Warren Relf leaped up and turned the tables once more upon his overspent opponent. Seizing Hugh round the waist in his powerful arms, in an access of despair, he flung him from him as one might fling a child, with all his store of gathered energy. If only he could hold the man at bay till they reached Mentone, help would come —the porters would see and would try to secure him. He had no time to think in the hurry of the moment that even so all the world would believe he himself was the aggressor, and Hugh Massinger, with that great roll of notes stowed away in his pocket, was the injured innocent. Fighting instinctively for life alone, he flung his mad assailant right across the carriage with his utmost force. Hugh, staggered and fell against the door of the compartment; his head struck sharp against the inner brass handle. With a loud cry, the would-be murderer dropped helpless on the floor. Warren saw his temple was bleeding profusely. He seemed quite stunned—stunned or dead? His face, which but a moment before had glowed livid red, grew pale as death with a horrible suddenness. Warren leaned over him, flushed with excitement, and hot with that ible wild-beast-like struggle. Was the man feigning, or he really killed?—O heavens, would they say he, Warren, murdered him?

In a moment the full horror of the situation came over him.

He felt Hugh's pulse: it was scarcely beating. He peered into his eyes: they were glazed and senseless. He couldn't tell if the man were dead or alive; but he stood aghast now with equal awe at either horrible and unspeakable predicament. Only four minutes or so more till Mentone! What time to decide how to act in the interval? O dear heaven, those accusing, tell-tale bank-notes! Those lying bank-notes, with their mute false witness against his real intentions! If Hugh was dead, who would ever believe he had not tried to rob and murder him? Whatever came of it, he must try to recover Hugh from his dead-faint at all hazards. Water, water! Oh, what would he not give for one glass of water! He essayed to bind up the wound on the head with his own handkerchief. It was all of no avail: the wound went bleeding steadily on. It went bleeding on; that looked as though Hugh were still alive. For if Hugh was dead, they would take him for a murderer!

Four minutes only till they reached Mentone; but oh, what an eternity of doubt and terror! In one single vivid panoramic picture, the whole awfulness of his situation burst full upon him. He saw it all—all, just as it would happen. What other interpretation could the outside world by any possibility set upon the circumstances? A winner at Monte Carlo, returning home to San Remo with a vast sum in bank-notes concealed about his person, gets into a carriage alone with a fellow-countryman of his acquaintance, to whom he would naturally at once confide the fact of his luck and his large winnings. He is found dead or dying in the train at the next station, his coat torn after a frantic struggle, and the carriage bearing every possible sign of a desperate fight for life between aggressor and defender. His revolver gone, his head broken, his arms black with numerous bruises, who could doubt that he had fought hard for his life and his money, and succumbed at last by slow degrees to the most brutal violence? Who would ever believe the cock-and-bull story which alone Warren Relf could set up in self-justification? How absurd to pretend that the man with the money was the real aggressor, and that the man with none acted only in pure self-defence, without the slightest intention of seriously injuring his wild assailant! An accident, indeed! No jury on earth would accept such an incredible line of defence. It was palpably past all reasonable belief—to any one but himself and Hugh Massinger—on the very face of it.

And then, a still more ghastly scene rose clear before his eyes, with the vividness and rapidity of a great crisis. At such supreme moments, indeed, we do not think in words or logical phrases at all; we see things unrolled in vast perspective as a living tableau of events before us; we feel and realize past, present, and future in incredible lightning-like flashes and whirls of some internal sense: our consciousness ceases to be bound and cabined by the narrow limits of space and time: a single second suffices for us to know and recognize at a glance what in other phases it would take us a whole hour deliberately to represent by analytic stages to our mental vision. Warren Relf, alone in that cramped compartment with Hugh Massinger, or Hugh Massinger's corpse—he knew not which—beheld in his mind's eye in a graphic picture a court of justice, installed and inaugurated: advocates pleading his case in vain: a *juge d'instruction* cross-questioning him mercilessly with French persistence on every detail of the supposed assault: a jury of stolid *bourgeois* listening with saturnine incredulity in every line of their faces to his improbable explanations—a delay—a verdict—a sentence of death: and behind all—Elsie, Elsie, Elsie, Elsie.

Therein lay the bitterest sting of the whole tragedy. That Elsie should ever come to know he had been forced by circumstances, however imperious, into laying violent hands on Hugh

Massinger, was in itself more than his native equanimity could possibly endure. What would Elsie say? That was his one distinct personal thought. How could he ever bring himself even to explain the simple truth to her? He shrank from the idea with a deadly loathing. She must never know Hugh had tried to murder him—and for her as the prize. She must never know he had been compelled in self-defence to fling Hugh from his throat, and unwillingly to inflict that awful wound—for death or otherwise—upon his bleeding forehead.

Three minutes, perhaps, to Mentone still. On those three minutes hung all his future—and Elsie's happiness.

In the midst of the confused sea of images that surged up in endless waves upon his mind, one definite thought alone now plainly shaped itself in clear-cut mental outline before him. He must save Elsie—he must save Elsie: at all hazards, no matter how great—let him live or die—he must save Elsie. Through the mist of horror and agony and despair that dimmed his sight, that thought alone loomed clear and certain. Save Elsie the anguish of that awful discovery: save Elsie the inexpressible pain of knowing that the man she now loved and the man who once pretended to love her, had closed together in deadly conflict, and that Warren had only preserved Hugh from a murderer's guilt by himself becoming, in a moment of despair, perhaps Hugh's unwilling and unwitting executioner.

He glanced once more at the senseless mass that lay huddled in blood upon the floor of the carriage. Alive or dead? What hope of recovery? What chance of restitution? What room for repentance? If Hugh lived, would he clear Warren? or would he die in some hospital with a lie on his lips, condemning his enemy for the very assault he had himself so madly yet deliberately committed? What matter to Warren? Whichever way things happened to turn, the pain would be almost the same for Elsie. Concealment was now the only possible plan. He must conceal it all—all, all, from Elsie.

The train was slowing round a dangerous curve—a curve where the line makes a sharp angle round a projecting point—a triumph of engineering, experts consider it—with the sheer rock, rising straight above, and the blue sea dimpling itself into ripples below. He moved to the door, and gazed anxiously out. No room to jump just there; the rock and sea hemmed him in too closely. But beyond, by the torrent, a loose bank of earth on the further side might break his fall, if he chose to risk it. Madness, no doubt, ay, almost suicide; but with only two minutes more to Mentone, he had no time to think if it were madness or wisdom: time only to act, to act for the best, on the spur of the moment, while action of some sort still was possible. At such times, indeed, men do not reason: they follow only the strongest and deepest impulse. Warren Relf did not wait to argue out the results of his conduct with himself. If he leaped from the train, he must almost certainly be stunned or maimed, perhaps even killed outright by the concussion. At best, he must soon be taken by the myrmidons of justice and accused of the murder. To get away unperceived, along that single track of open coast, backed up in the rear by high mountains, was simply impossible. Had he stopped to reason, he might have remained where he was—and lost all. But he did not stop to reason; he only felt, and felt profoundly. His instincts urged him to leap while there was still time. He opened the door as he reached the torrent, and looking out upon the bank with cautious deliberation, prepared to jump for it at the proper moment.

The train was slowing much more distinctly now. He thought the brake must be put on hard. He could surely jump as he reached the corner without serious danger. He stepped with one foot on to the open footboard. It wasn't much to risk for Elsie. A single plunge, and all would be settled.

CHAPTER L.

THE CAP MARTIN CATASTROPHE.

As he paused there one second, before he jumped, he was dimly aware of a curious fact that caught his attention, sideways, even at that special moment of doubt and danger: many other doors on the landward side of the train stood also open, and other passengers beside himself, with fear and surprise depicted visibly on their pale faces, were stepping out, irresolute, just as he himself had done, upon the narrow footboard. Could they have heard the struggle? he wondered vaguely to himself. Could they have gained some hasty inkling of the tragic event that had taken place, so secretly, all unknown as he supposed, in his own compartment? Had some neighbouring traveller caught faintly the muffled sounds of a desperate fight? Had he suspected an attack upon some innocent passenger? Had he signalled the guard to stop the train? for it was slowing still, slowing yet more sensibly and certainly each moment. More and more pale faces now appeared at the doors; and a Frenchman standing on the footboard of the next compartment, a burly person of military appearance, with an authoritative air, cried aloud in a voice of quick command, "Sautez, donc! Sautez!" At the word, Warren leaped, he knew not why, from the doomed carriage.

The Frenchman leaped at the self-same moment. All down the train, a dozen or two of passengers followed suit as if by a concerted order. Warren had no idea in his own mind what was really happening, but he knew the train had slackened speed immensely, and that he had landed on his feet and hands on the rubbly bank with no more result, so far as he himself could see just then, than a sprained ankle and some few bleeding wounds on his knees and elbows.

Next instant a horrible crash resounded through the air, and bellowed and echoed with loud reverberation from the rocky walls of those sheer precipices. Thud, thud, thud followed close on the crash, as carriage after carriage shocked fiercely against the engine and the compartments in front of it. Then a terrible sight met his eyes. The train had just reached the ledge of cliff beyond, and with a wild rocking disappeared all at once over the steep side into the sea below. Nothing in life is more awful in its unexpectedness than a great railway accident. Before Warren had even time to know what was taking place by his side, it was all over. The train had fallen in one huge mass over the edge of the cliff, and Hugh Massinger, with his eleven thousand pounds safe in his pocket, was hurried away without warning or reprieve into ten fathoms deep of blue Mediterranean.

Everybody remembers the main features of that terrific accident, famous in the history of French railway disasters as the Cap Martin catastrophe. Shortly after passing Roquebruno ation (where the through-trains do not stop), one of the engine-heels became loosened by a violent shock against a badly-laid ...eeper, and, thus acting as a natural brake, brought the train almost to a stand-still for a few seconds, just opposite the very dangerous ledge known locally as the Borrigo escarpment. The engine there left the rails with a jerk, and many of the passengers, seeing something serious was likely to take place, seized the opportunity, just before the crash, of opening the doors on the landward side, and leaping from the train while it had reached its slowest rate of motion, on the very eve of its final disaster. One instant later, the engine oscillated violently and stopped altogether; the other carriages telescoped against it; and the entire train, thrown off its balance with a terrible wrench, toppled over the sheer precipice at the side into the deep water that skirts the foot of the neighbouring mountains. That was the whole familiar story as the public at large came, bit by bit, to learn it afterwards. But for the moment, the stunned and horrified passengers on the bank of the torrent only knew that a frightful accident had taken place with incredible rapidity, and that the train itself, with many of their fellow-travellers seated within, had sunk like lead in the twinkling of an eye to the bottom of the bay, leaving the few survivors there on dry land aghast at the inexpressible suddenness and awfulness of this appalling calamity.

As for Warren Relf, amid the horror of his absorbing life-and-death struggle with Hugh Massinger, and the abiding awe of its terrible consummation, he had never even noticed the angry jerking of the loosened wheel, the whirr that jarred through the shaken carriages, the growing oscillation from side to side, the evident imminence of some alarming accident. Sudden as the catastrophe was to all, to him it was more sudden and unexpected than to any one. Till the actual crash itself came, indeed, he did not realize why the other passengers were hanging on so strangely to the narrow footboard. The whole episode happened in so short a space of time—thirty seconds at best— that he had no opportunity to collect and recover his scattered senses. He merely recognized at first in some stunned and shattered fashion that he was well out of the fatal train, and that a dozen sufferers lay stretched in evident pain and danger on the low bank of earth beside him.

For all the passengers had not fared so well in their escape as he himself had done. Many of them had suffered serious hurt in their mad jump from the open doorway, alighting on jagged points of broken stone, or rolling down the sides of the steep ravine into the dry bed of the winter torrent. The least injured turned with one accord to help and tend their wounded companions. But as for the train itself, it had simply disappeared. It was as though it had never been. Scarcely a sign of it showed on the unruffled water. Falling sheer from the edge of that precipitous crag into the deep bay, it had sunk like a stone at once to the very bottom. Only a few fragments of broken wreckage appeared here and there floating loose upon the surface. Hardly a token remained beside to show the outer world where that whole long line of laden carriages had toppled over bodily into the profound green depths that still smiled so sweetly between Roquebrune and Mentone.

For a while, distracted by this fresh horror, Warren could only think of the dead and wounded. His own torn and blood-stained condition excited no more attention or curiosity now on the part of bystanders than that of many others among his less fortunate fellow-passengers. Nor did he even reflect with any serious realization that Elsie was saved and his own character practically vindicated. The new shock had deadened the sense and vividness of the old one. In the face of so awful and general a calamity as this, his own private fears and doubts and anxieties seemed to shrink for the moment into absolute insignificance.

In time, however, it began slowly to dawn upon his bewildered mind that other trains might come up from Monaco or Mentone and dash madly among the broken *débris* of the shattered carriages. Whatever caused their own accident might cause accidents also to approaching engines. Moreover, the wounded lay scattered about on all sides upon the track, some of them in a condition in which it might indeed be difficult or even dangerous to remove them. Somebody must certainly go forward to Mentone to warn the *chef de gare* and to fetch up assistance. After a hurried consultation with his nearest neighbours, Warren took upon himself the task of messenger. He started off at once on this needful errand, and plunged with a heart now strangely aroused into the deep darkness of the last remaining tunnel.

His sprained ankle caused him terrible pain at every step; but the pain itself, joined with the consciousness of performing an imperative duty, kept his mind from dwelling too much for the moment on his own altered yet perilous situation. As he dragged one foot wearily after the other through that long tunnel, his thoughts concentrated themselves for the time being on but one object—to reach Mentone and prevent any further serious accident.

When he had arrived at the station, however, and despatched help along the line to the other sufferers from the terrible disaster, he had time to reflect in peace for a while upon the sudden change this great public calamity had wrought in his own private position. The danger of misapprehension had been removed by the accident as if by magic. Unless he himself chose to reveal the facts, no soul on earth need ever know a word of that desperate struggle with mad Hugh Massinger in the wrecked railway carriage. Even supposing the bodies were ultimately dredged up or recovered by divers, no suspicion could now possibly attach to his own conduct. The wound on Hugh's head would doubtless be attributed to the fall alone; though the chance of the body being recognizable at all after so horrible a catastrophe would indeed be slight, considering the way the carriages had doubled up like so much trestle-work upon one another before finally falling. Elsie was saved; that much at least was now secured. She need know nothing. Unless he himself were ever tempted to tell her the ghastly truth, that terrible episode of the death-struggle in the doomed train might remain for ever a sealed book to the woman for whose sake it had all been enacted.

Warren's mind, therefore, was made up at once. All things considered, it had become a sacred duty for him now to hold his tongue for ever and ever about the entire incident. No man is bound to criminate himself; above all, no man is bound to expose himself when innocent to an unjust yet overwhelming suspicion of murder. But that was not all. Elsie's happiness depended entirely upon his rigorous silence. To tell the whole truth, even to her, would be to expose her shrinking and delicate nature to a painful shock, as profound as it was unnecessary, and as lasting as it was cruel. The more he thought upon it, the more plain and clear did his duty shine forth before him. Chance had supplied him with a strange means of honourable escape from what had seemed at first sight an insoluble dilemma. It would be folly and worse, under his present conditions, for him to refuse to profit by its unconscious suggestion.

Yet more: he must decide at once without delay upon his line of action. News of the catastrophe would be telegraphed, of course, immediately to England. Elsie would most likely learn the whole awful episode that very evening at her hotel in London: he could hear the very cries of the street boys ringing in his ears: "Speshul Edition. Appalling Railway Accident on the Riviayrer! Great Loss of Life! A Train precipitated into the Mediterranean!" If not, she would at any rate read the alarming news in an agony of terror in the morning papers. She knew Warren himself was returning to San Remo by that very train. She did not know that Hugh was likely to be one of his fellow-passengers. She must not hear of the accident for the first time from the columns of the *Times* or the *Pall Mall Gazette.* He must telegraph over at once and relieve beforehand her natural anxiety for her future husband's safety. But Hugh's name and fate need not be mentioned, at least for the present; he could reserve that revelation for a more convenient season. To publish it, indeed, would be in part to incriminate himself, or at least to arouse unjust suspicion.

He drove to the telegraph office, worn out as he was with pain and excitement, and despatched a hasty message that moment to Elsie: "There has been a terrible accident to the train near Mentone, but I am not hurt, at least to speak of—only a few slight sprains and bruises. Particulars in papers. Affectionately, WARREN." And then he drove back to the scene of the catastrophe.

It was a week before all the bodies were dredged up by relays of divers from the wreck of that ill-fated and submerged train. Hugh Massinger's was one of the last to be recovered. It was found, minus a large part of the clothing. The sea had torn off his coat and shirt. The eleven thousand pounds in French bank-notes never turned up at all again. His money indeed had perished with him.

They buried all that remained of that volcanic life on the sweet and laughing hillside at Mentone. A plain marble cross marks the spot where he rests. On the plinth stand graven those prophetic lines from the plaintive proem to "A Life's Philosophy"—

> " Here, by the haven with the hoary trees,
>   O fiery poet's heart, lie still :
> No longer strive amid tempestuous seas
>   To curb wild waters to thy lurid will.
>   Above thy grave
>   Wan olives wave,
> And oleanders court deep-laden bees."

That nought of fulfilment might be wanting to his prayer, Warren Relf with his own hand planted a blushing oleander above the mound where that fiery poet's heart lay still for ever. He had nothing but pity in his soul for Hugh's wasted powers. A splendid life, marred in the making by its own headstrong folly. And Winifred, who loved him, and whose heart he broke, lay silent in the self-same grave beside him.

CHAPTER LI.

NEXT OF KIN WANTED.

THE recovery of Hugh's body from the shattered train gave Warren Relf one needful grain of internal comfort. He identi-fied that pale and wounded corpse with reverent care, and waited in solemn suspense and unspoken anxiety for the result of the customary *post-mortem* examination. The doctors' report reassured his soul. Death had resulted, so the medical evidence conclusively proved, not from the violent injuries observed on the skull, and apparently produced, they said, by a blow against the carriage door, but from asphyxiation, due to drowning. Hugh was still alive, then, when the train went over ! His heart still beat and his breath still came and went feebly till the actual moment of the final catastrophe. It was the accident, not Warren's hand, that killed him. Innocent as Warren knew himself to be, he was glad to learn from this authoritative source that even unintentionally he had not made himself Hugh Mas-singer's accidental executioner.

But in any case they must break the news gently to Elsie. Warren's presence was needed in the south for the time being, to see after Winifred's funeral and other necessary domestic arrangements. So Edie went over to England on the very first day after the fact of Hugh's disappearance in the missing train had become generally known to the little world of San Remo, to soften the shock for her with sisterly tenderness. By a piece of rare good fortune, Hugh Massinger's name was not mentioned at all in the earlier telegrams, even after it was fairly well known at Mentone and Monte Carlo that the lucky winner, whose success was in everybody's mouth just then, had perished in one of the

lost carriages. The despatches only spoke in vague terms of
"an English gentleman lately arrived on the Riviera, who had
all but succeeded in breaking the bank that day at Monte Carlo,
and was returning to San Remo, elated by success, with eleven
thousand pounds of winnings in his pocket." It was not in the
least likely that Elsie would dream of recognizing her newly
bereaved cousin under this highly improbable and generalized
description—especially when Winifred, as she well knew, was
lying dead meanwhile, the victim of his cold and selfish cruelty,
at the *pension* at San Remo. Edie would be the first to bring her
the strange and terrible news of Hugh's sudden death. Warren
himself stopped behind at Mentone, as in duty bound, to identify
the body formally at the legal inquiry.

He had another reason, too, for wishing to break the news to
Elsie through Edie's mouth rather than personally. For Edie
knew nothing, of course, of the deadly struggle in the doomed
train, of that hand-to-hand battle for life and honour; and she
could therefore with truth unfold the whole story exactly as
Warren wished Elsie first to learn it. For her, there was
nothing more to tell than that Hugh, with incredible levity
and brutal want of feeling, had gone over to Monte Carlo to
gamble openly at the public tables, on the very days while his
poor young wife, killed inch by inch by his settled neglect, lay
dead in her lonely lodging at San Remo : that he had returned
a couple of evenings later with his ill-gotten gains upon the
fated train : and that, falling over into the sea with the carriages
from which Warren just barely escaped with dear life, he was
drowned in his place in one of the shattered and sunken compartments. That was all ; and that was bad enough in all conscience.
What need to burden Elsie's gentle soul any further with the
more hideous concomitants of that unspeakable tragedy ?

Elsie bore the news with far greater fortitude than Edie in
her most sanguine mood could have expected. Winifred's death
had sunk so deep into the fibres of her soul that Hugh's seemed
to affect her far less by comparison. She had learnt to know
him now in all his baseness. It was the recognition of the man's
own inmost nature that had cost her dearest. "Let us never
speak of him again, dear Warren," she wrote to her betrothed,
a few days later. "Let him be to us as though he had never
existed. Let his name be not so much as mentioned between us.
It pains and grieves me ten thousand times more, Warren, to
think that for such a man's sake as he was, I should so long
have refused to accept the love of such a man as I now know
you to be."

Those are the hardest words a woman can utter. To unsay
their love is to women unendurable. But Elsie no longer
shrank from unsaying it. Shame and remorse for her shattered

ideal possessed her soul. She knew she had done the true man wrong by so long rejecting him for the sake of the false one.

At sand-girt Whitestrand, meanwhile, all was turmoil and confusion. The news of the young Squire's tragic death, following so close at the heel of his frail little wife's, spread horror and shame through the whole community. The vicar's wife was all agog with excitement. The reticule trembled on her palpitating wrist as she went the round of her neighbours with the surprising intelligence. Nobody knew what might happen next, now the last of the Meyseys was dead and gone, while the sandbanks were spreading half a mile to seaward, and the very river was turned from its course by encroaching hummocks into a new-cut channel. The mortgagees, to be sure, were safe with their money. Not only was the property now worth on a rough computation almost as much as it had ever been, but Winifred's life had been heavily insured, and the late Mr. Massinger's estate, the family attorney remarked with a cheerful smile, was far more than solvent—in fact, it would prove a capital inheritance for some person or persons unknown, the heirs-at-law and next-of-kin of the last possessor. But good business lay in store, no doubt, for the profession still. Deceased had probably died intestate. Endless questions would thus be opened out in delicious vistas before the entranced legal vision. The marriage being subsequent to the late Married Woman's Property Act, Mrs. Massinger's will, if any, must be found and proved. The next-of-kin and heir-at-law must be hunted up. Protracted litigation would probably ensue; rewards would be offered for certificates of birth; records of impossible marriages would be freely advertised for, with tempting suggestions of pecuniary recompense to the lucky discoverer. Research would be stimulated in parish clerks; affidavits would be sworn to with charming recklessness; rival claimants would commit unblushing alternative perjuries on their own account, with frank disregard of common probability. It would rain fees. The estate would dissolve itself bodily by slow degrees in a quagmire of expenses. And all for the benefit of the good attorneys! The family lawyer, in the character of Danaë—for this occasion only, and without prejudice—would hold out his hands to catch the golden shower. A learned profession would no doubt profit in the end to a distinct amount by the late Mr. Massinger's touching disregard of testamentary provision for his unknown relations.

Alas for the prospects of the learned gentlemen! The question of inheritance proved itself in the end far easier and less complex than the family attorney in his professional zeal had at first anticipated. Everything unravelled itself with disgusting simplicity. The estate might almost as well have been unencumbered. The late Mrs. Massinger had left no will, and the property had therefore devolved direct by common law upon her surviving husband. This was awkward. If only now, any grain of doubt had existed in any way as to the fact that the late Mrs. Massinger had predeceased her unfortunate husband, legal acumen might doubtless have suggested innumerable grounds of action for impossible claimants on either side of the two families. But unhappily for the exercise of legal acumen, the case as it stood was all most horribly plain sailing. Hugh Massinger, Esquire, having inherited in due course from his deceased wife, the estate must go in the first place to Hugh Massinger himself, in person. And Hugh Massinger himself having died intestate, it must go in the next place to Hugh Massinger's nearest representative. True, there still remained the agreeable and exciting research for the missing heir-at-law; but the pursuit of hunting up the heir-at-law to a given known indisputable possessor is as nothing in the eyes of a keen sportsman compared with the Homeric joy of battle involved in the act of setting the representatives of two rival and uncertain claims to fight it out, tooth and nail together, on the free and open arena of the Court of Probate. It was with a sigh of regret, therefore, that the family attorney, good easy man, drew up the advertisement which closed for ever his vain hopes of a disputed succession between the moribund houses of Massinger and Meysey, and confined his possibilities of lucrative litigation to exploiting the house of Massinger alone, for his own use, enjoyment, and fruition.

It was some two or three weeks after Hugh Massinger's tragic death that Edie Relf chanced to observe in the Agony Column of that morning's *Times* a notice couched in the following precise and poetical language :—

"Hugh Massinger, Esquire, deceased, late of Whitestrand Hall, in the County of Suffolk.—Any person or persons claiming to represent the heir or heirs-at-law and next of kin of the above-named gentleman (who died at Mentone, in the Department of the Alpes Maritimes, in the French Republic, on or about the 17th day of November last past) are hereby requested to apply immediately to Alfred Heberden, Esq., Whitestrand, Suffolk, solicitor to the said Hugh Massinger."

Edie mentioned the matter at once to Warren, who had come over from France as soon as he had completed the necessary arrangements at San Remo and Mentone; but Warren heard it all with extreme disinclination. He couldn't bear even to allude to the fact in speaking to Elsie. Directly or indirectly, he could never inherit the estate of the man whose life he had been so nearly instrumental in shortening. And if Elsie was soon, as he hoped, to become his wife, he would necessarily participate in whatever benefit Elsie might derive from inheriting the relics of Hugh Massinger's ill-won Whitestrand property.

"No, no," he said. "The estate was simply the price of blood. He married that poor little woman for nothing else but for the sake of Whitestrand. He killed her by slow degrees through his neglect and cruelty. If he hadn't married her, he would never have been master of that wretched place : if he hadn't married her, he would have had nothing of his own to leave to Elsie. I can't touch it, and I won't touch it. So that's flat, Edie. It's the price of blood. Let it, too, perish with him."

"But oughtn't you at least to mention it to Elsie?" Edie asked, with her plain straightforward English common-sense. "It's her business more than it's yours, you know, Warren. Oughtn't you at least to give her the option of accepting or refusing her own property?—It's very kind of you, of course, to decide for her beforehand so cavalierly.—Perhaps, you see, when she learns she's an heiress, she may be inclined to transfer her affections elsewhere."

Warren smiled. That was a point of view that had never occurred to him. Your male lover makes so sure of his prey : he hardly allows in his own mind the possibility of rejection. But still he prevaricated. "I wouldn't tell her about it, just yet at least," he answered hesitatingly. "We don't know, after all, that Elsie's really the heir-at-law at all, if it comes to that. Let's wait and see. Perhaps some other claimant may turn up for the property."

"Perhaps," Edie replied, with her oracular brevity. "And perhaps not. There's nothing on earth more elastic in its own way than a good perhaps. India-rubber bands are just mere child's play to it.—Suppose, then, we pin it down to a precise limit of time, so as to know exactly where we stand, and say that if the estate isn't otherwise claimed within six weeks, we'll break it to Elsie, and allow her to decide for herself in the matter ? "

"But how shall we know whether it's claimed or not?" Warren asked dubiously.

"My dear, there exists in this realm of England a useful institution known to science as a penny post, by means of which a letter may be safely and inexpensively conveyed even to so remote and undistinguished a personage as Alfred Heberden, Esquire, solicitor to the deceased, Whitestrand, Suffolk.—I propose, in fact, to write and ask him."

Warren groaned. It was an awkward fix. He wished he could shirk the whole horrid business. To be saddled against your will with a landed estate that you don't want is a predicament that seldom disturbs a modest gentleman's peace of mind anywhere. But he saw no possible way out of the odd dilemma. Edie was right, after all, no doubt. As yet, at least, he had no authority to answer in any way for Elsie's wishes. If she wanted Whitestrand, it was hers to take or reject as she wished, and hers only. Still, he salved his conscience with the consolatory idea that it was not actually compulsory upon him to show Elsie any legal advertisement, inquiry, or suggestion which might happen to emanate from the solicitors to the estate of the late Hugh Massinger. So far as he had any official cognizance of the facts, indeed, the heirs, executors, and assigns of the deceased had nothing on earth to do in any way with Elsie Challoner, of San Remo, Italy. Second cousinhood is at best a very vague and uncertain form of relationship. He decided, therefore, not without some internal qualms, to accept Edie's suggested compromise for the present, and to wait patiently for the matter in hand to settle itself by spontaneous arrangement.

But Alfred Heberden, Esquire, solicitor to the deceased, acted otherwise. He had failed to draw any satisfactory communications in answer to his advertisement save one from a bogus firm of so-called Property Agents, the proprietors of a fallacious list of Next of Kin Wanted, and one from a third-rate pawnbroker in the Borough Road whose wife's aunt had once married a broken-down railway porter of the name of Messenger, from Weem in Shropshire, and who considered himself, accordingly, the obvious representative and heir-at-law of the late Hugh Massinger of the Utter Bar, and of Whitestrand Hall, in Suffolk, Esquire, deceased without issue. Neither of these applications, however, proving of sufficient importance to engage the attention of Mr. Alfred Heberden's legal mind, that astute gentleman proceeded entirely on his own account to investigate the genealogy and other antecedents of Hugh Massinger, with a single eye to the discovery of the missing inheritor of the estate, envisaged as a person from whom natural gratitude would probably wring a substantial solatium to the good attorney who had proved his title. And the result of his inquiries into the Massinger pedigree took tangible shape at last, a week or two later, in a second advertisement of a more exact sort, which Edie Relf, that diligent and careful student of the second column, the most interesting portion of the whole newspaper to Eve's like-minded daughters, discovered and pondered over one foggy morning in the blissful repose of 128, Bletchingley Road, South Kensington.

"CHALLONER: Heir-at-law and Next of Kin Wanted. Estate of HUGH MASSINGER, Esquire, deceased, intestate.—If this should meet the eye of ELSIE, daughter of the late Rev. H.

Challoner, and Eleanor Jane his wife, formerly Eleanor Jane Massinger, of Chudleigh, Devonshire, she is requested to put herself into communication with ALFRED HEBERDEN, Esq., Whitestrand, Suffolk, when she may hear of something greatly to her advantage."

Edie took the paper up at once to Warren. "For 'may' read 'will,'" she said pointedly. "Lawyers don't advertise unless they know. I always understood Mr. Massinger had no living relations except Elsie. This question has reached boiling-point now. You'll have to speak to her after that about the matter."

CHAPTER LII.

THE TANGLE RESOLVES ITSELF.

"You must never, never take it, Elsie," Warren said earnestly, as Elsie laid down the paper once more and wiped a tear from her eye nervously. "It came to him through that poor broken-hearted little woman, you know. He should never have married her; he should never have owned it. It was never truly or honestly his, and therefore it isn't yours by right. I couldn't bear, myself, to touch a single penny of it."

Elsie looked up at him with a twitching face. "Do you make hat a condition, Warren?" she asked, all tremulous.

Warren paused and hesitated, irresolute, for a moment. "Do 1 make it a condition?" he answered slowly. "My darling, how can I possibly talk of making conditions or bargains with you? But I could never bear to think that wife of mine would touch one penny of that ill-gotten money."

"Warren," Elsie said, in a very soft voice—they were alone in the room and they talked like lovers—"I said to myself more than once in the old, old days—after all *that* was past and done for ever, you know, dear—I said to myself: 'I would never marry any man now, not even if I loved him—loved him truly —unless I had money of my own to bring him.' And when I began to know I was getting to love you—when I couldn't any longer conceal from myself the truth that your tenderness and your devotion had made me love you against my will—I said to myself again, more firmly than ever: 'I will never let him take me thus penniless. I will never burden him with one more mouth to feed, one more person to house and clothe and supply, one more life to toil and moil and slave for. Even as it is, he can't pursue his art as he ought to pursue it; he can't give free play to his genius as his genius demands, because he has to turn aside from his own noble and exquisite ideals to suit the market and to earn money. I won't any further shackle his arm. I won't any further cramp his hand—his hand that should be free as the air to pursue unhampered his own grand and beautiful calling. I will never marry him unless I can bring him at least enough to support myself upon.'—And just the other day, you remember, Warren—that day at San Remo when I admitted at last what I had known so long without ever admitting it, that I loved you better than life itself—I said to you still : 'I am yours, at heart. But I can't be yours really for a long time yet. No matter why. I shall be yours still in myself, for all that.'—Well, I'll tell you now why I said those words.—Even then, darling, I felt I could never marry you penniless."

She paused, and looked up at him with an earnest look in her true gray eyes, those exquisite eyes of hers that no lover could see without an intense thrill through his inmost being. Warren thrilled in response, and wondered what could next be coming. "And you're going to tell me, Elsie," he said, with a sigh, "that you can't marry me unless you feel free to accept White-strand ?"

Elsie laid her head with womanly confidence on his strong shoulder. "I'm going to tell you, darling," she answered, with a sudden outburst of unchecked emotion, "that I'll marry you now, Whitestrand or no Whitestrand. I'll do as you wish in this and in everything. I love you so dearly to-day, Warren, that I can even burden you with myself, if you wish it : I can throw myself upon you without reserve : I can take back all I ever thought or said, and be happy anywhere, if only you'll have me, and make me your wife, and love me always as I myself love you. I want nothing that ever was his; I only want to be yours, Warren."

Nevertheless, Mr. Alfred Heberden did within one week of that date duly proceed in proper form to prove the claim of Elsie Challoner, of 128, Bletchingley Road, in the parish of Kensington, spinster, of no occupation, to the intestate estate of Hugh Massinger, Esquire, deceased, of Whitestrand Hall, in the county of Suffolk.

The fact is, an estate, however acquired, must needs belong to somebody somewhere ; and since either Elsie must take it herself, or let some other person with a worse claim endeavour to obtain it, Warren and she decided, upon further consideration, that it would be better for her to dispense the revenues of Whitestrand for the public good, than to let them fall by default into the greedy clutches of the enterprising pawnbroker in the Borough Road, or be swallowed up for his own advantage by any similar absorbent medium elsewhere. From the very first indeed, they were both firmly determined never to spend one shilling of the estate upon their own pleasures or their own necessities. But if wealth is to be dispensed in doing good at all, it is best that intelligent and single-hearted people should so dispense it, rather than leave it to the tender mercies of that amiable but somewhat indefinite institution, the Court of Chancery. Warren and Elsie decided, therefore, at last to prosecute their legal claim, regarding themselves as trustees for the needy or helpless of Great Britain generally, and to sell the estate, when once obtained, for the first cash price offered, investing the sum in consols in their own names, as a virtual trust-fund, to be employed by themselves for such special purposes as seemed best to both in the free exercise of their own full and unfettered discretion. So Mr. Alfred Heberden's advertisement bore good fruit in due season; and Elsie did at last, in name at least, inherit the manor and estate of Whitestrand.

But neither of them touched one penny of the blood-money. They kept it all apart as a sacred fund, to be used only in the best way they knew for the objects that Winifred in her highest moods might most have approved of.

And this, as Elsie justly remarked, was really the very best possible arrangement. To be sure, she no longer felt that shy old feeling against coming to Warren unprovided and penniless. She was content now, as a wife should be, to trust herself implicitly and entirely to her husband's hands. Warren's art of late had every day been more sought after by those who hold in their laps the absolute disposal of the world's wealth, and there was far less fear than formerly that the cares of a house-hold would entail on him the miserable and degrading necessity for lowering his own artistic standard to meet the inferior wishes and tastes of possible purchasers, with their vulgar ideals. But it was also something for each of them to feel that the other had thus been seriously tried by the final test of this world's gold—tried in actual practice and not found wanting. Few pass through that sordid crucible unscathed: those that do are of the purest metal.

On the very day when Warren and Elsie finally fixed the date for their approaching wedding, the calm and happy little bride-elect came in with first tidings of the accomplished arrangement, all tremors and blushes, to her faithful Edie. To her great chagrin, however, her future sister-in-law received the news of this proximate family event with an absolute minimum of surprise or excitement. "You don't seem to be in the least astonished, dear," Elsie cried, somewhat piqued at her cool reception. "Why anybody'd say, to see the way you take it, you'd known it all a clear twelvemonth ago!"

"So I did, my child—all except the mere trifling detail of the date," Edie answered at once with prompt common-sense, and an arch look from under her dark eyebrows. "In fact I arranged it all myself most satisfactorily beforehand. But what I was really thinking of just now was simply this—why shouldn't one cake do duty for both at once, Elsie?"

"For both at once, Edie? For me and Warren? Why, of course, one cake always does do for the bride and bridegroom together, doesn't it? I never heard of anybody having a couple, darling."

"What a sweet little silly you are, you dear old goose, you! Are you two the only marriageable people in the universe, then? I didn't mean for you and Warren at all, of course; I meant for you and myself, stupid."

"You and myself!" Elsie echoed, bewildered. "You and myself, did you say, Edie?"

"Why, yes, you dear old blind bat, you," Edie went on placidly, with an abstracted air; "we might get them both over the same day, I think seriously: kill two weddings, so to speak, with one parson. They're such a terrible nuisance in a house always."

"Two weddings, my dear Edie?" Elsie cried in surprise. "Why, what on earth are you ever talking about? I don't understand you."

"Well, Mr. Hatherley's a very good critic," Edie answered, with a twinkle: "he's generally admitted to have excellent taste; and he ventured the other day on a critical opinion in my presence which did honour at once to the acuteness of his perceptions and the soundness and depth of his æsthetic judgment. He told me to my face, with the utmost gravity, I was the very sweetest and prettiest girl in all England."

"And what did you say to that, Edie?" Elsie asked, amused, with some dawning perception of the real meaning of this queer badinage.

"I told him, my dear, I'd always considered him the ablest and best of living authorities on artistic matters, and that it would ill become my native modesty to differ from his opinion on such an important question, in which, perhaps, that native modesty itself might unduly bias me to an incorrect judgment in the opposite direction. So then he enforced his critical view in a practical way by promptly kissing me."

"And you didn't object?"

"On the contrary, my child, I rather liked it than otherwise."

"After which?"

"After which he proceeded to review his own character and

prospects in a depreciatory way, that led me gravely to doubt the accuracy of his judgment in that respect; and he finished up at last by laying those very objects he had just been depreciating, his hand and heart, at the foot of the throne, metaphorically speaking, for the sweetest girl in all England to do as she liked—accept or reject them."

"And the sweetest girl in all England?"——Elsie asked, smiling.

"Unconditionally accepted with the most pleasing promptitude.—You see, my dear, it'll be such a splendid thing for Warren, when he sets up house, to have an influential art-critic bound over, as it were, not to speak evil against him, by being converted beforehand into his own brother-in-law.—Besides which, you know, I happen, Elsie, to be ever so much in love with him."

"That's a good thing, Edie."

"My child, I consider it such an extremely good thing that I ran upstairs at once and had a regular jolly old-fashioned cry over it.—Elsie, Arthur's a dear good fellow.—And you and I can be married together. We've always been sisters, ever since we've known each other. And now we'll be sisters even more than ever."

THE END.

PRINTED BY WILLIAM CLOWES AND SONS, LIMITED, LONDON AND BECCLES.

"Give sorrow words: the grief that doth not speak
and bids it break."—*Shakespeare*.

LIST OF BOOKS PUBLISHED BY
CHATTO & WINDUS
111 ST. MARTIN'S LANE, CHARING CROSS, LONDON, W.C.

About (Edmond).—The Fellah: An Egyptian Novel. Translated by Sir RANDAL ROBERTS. Post 8vo, illustrated boards, *2s.*

Adams (W. Davenport), Works by.
A Dictionary of the Drama: being a comprehensive Guide to the Plays, Playwrights, Players, and Playhouses of the United Kingdom and America, from the Earliest Times to the Present Day. Crown 8vo, half-bound, *12s. 6d.* *[Preparing.*
Quips and Quiddities. Selected by W. DAVENPORT ADAMS. Post 8vo, cloth limp, *2s. 6d.*

Agony Column (The) of 'The Times,' from 1800 to 1870. Edited with an Introduction, by ALICE CLAY. Post 8vo, cloth limp, *2s. 6d.*

Aidé (Hamilton), Novels by. Post 8vo, illustrated boards, *2s.* each.
Carr of Carrlyon. | Confidences.

Albert (Mary).—Brooke Finchley's Daughter. Post 8vo, picture boards, *2s.*; cloth limp, *2s. 6d.*

Alden (W. L.).—A Lost Soul: Being the Confession and Defence of Charles Lindsay. Fcap. 8vo, cloth boards, *1s. 6d.*

Alexander (Mrs.), Novels by. Post 8vo, illustrated boards, *2s.* each.
Maid, Wife, or Widow? | Valerie's Fate. | Blind Fate.

Crown 8vo, cloth, *3s. 6d.* each.
A Life Interest. | Mona's Choice. | By Woman's Wit.

Allen (F. M.).—Green as Grass. With a Frontispiece. Crown 8vo, cloth, *3s. 6d.*

Allen (Grant), Works by.
The Evolutionist at Large. Crown 8vo, cloth extra, *6s.*
Post-Prandial Philosophy. Crown 8vo, art linen, *3s. 6d.*
Moorland Idylls. Crown 8vo, cloth decorated, *6s.*

Crown 8vo, cloth extra, *3s. 6d.* each; post 8vo, illustrated boards, *2s.* each.

Babylon. 12 Illustrations.	The Devil's Die.	The Duchess of Powysland.
Strange Stories. Frontis.	This Mortal Coil.	Blood Royal.
The Beckoning Hand.	The Tents of Shem. Frontis.	Ivan Greet's Masterpiece.
For Maimie's Sake.	The Great Taboo.	The Scallywag. 24 Illusts.
Philistia. | In all Shades	Dumaresq's Daughter.	At Market Value.

Under Sealed Orders. Crown 8vo, cloth extra, *3s. 6d.*
Dr. Palliser's Patient. Fcap. 8vo, cloth boards, *1s. 6d.*

Anderson (Mary).—Othello's Occupation: A Novel. Crown 8vo, cloth, *3s. 6d.*

Arnold (Edwin Lester), Stories by.
The Wonderful Adventures of Phra the Phœnician. Crown 8vo, cloth extra, with 12 Illustrations by H. M. PAGET, *3s. 6d.*; post 8vo, illustrated boards, *2s.*
The Constable of St. Nicholas. With Frontispiece by S. L. WOOD. Crown 8vo, cloth, *3s. 6d.*

Artemus Ward's Works. With Portrait and Facsimile. Crown 8vo, *3s. 6d.*

Ashton (John), Works by. Crown 8vo, cloth extra, 7s. 6d. each.
History of the Chap-Books of the 18th Century. With 334 Illustrations.
Social Life in the Reign of Queen Anne. With 85 Illustrations.
Humour, Wit, and Satire of the Seventeenth Century. With 82 Illustrations.
English Caricature and Satire on Napoleon the First. With 115 Illustrations.
Modern Street Ballads. With 57 Illustrations.

Bacteria, Yeast Fungi, and Allied Species, A Synopsis of. By
W. B. GROVE, B.A. With 87 Illustrations. Crown 8vo, cloth extra, 3s. 6d.

Bardsley (Rev. C. Wareing, M.A.), Works by.
English Surnames: Their Sources and Significations. FIFTH EDITION, with a New Preface.
Crown 8vo, cloth, 7s. 6d.
Curiosities of Puritan Nomenclature. Crown 8vo, cloth extra, 6s.

Baring Gould (Sabine, Author of 'John Herring,' &c.), Novels by.
Crown 8vo, cloth extra, 3s. 6d. each; post 8vo, illustrated boards, 2s. each.
Red Spider. | Eve.

Barr (Robert: Luke Sharp), Stories by. Cr. 8vo, cl., 3s. 6d. each
In a Steamer Chair. With Frontispiece and Vignette by DEMAIN HAMMOND.
From Whose Bourne, &c. With 47 Illustrations by HAL HURST and others.
A Woman Intervenes. With 8 Illustrations by HAL HURST. Crown 8vo, cloth extra, 6s.
Revenge! With 12 Illustrations by LANCELOT SPEED, &c. Crown 8vo, cloth, 6s.

Barrett (Frank), Novels by.
Post 8vo, illustrated boards, 2s. each; cloth, 2s. 6d. each.

Fettered for Life.	A Prodigal's Progress.
The Sin of Olga Zassoulich.	John Ford; and His Helpmate.
Between Life and Death.	A Recoiling Vengeance.
Folly Morrison. | Honest Davie.	Lieut. Barnabas. | Found Guilty.
Little Lady Linton.	For Love and Honour.

The Woman of the Iron Bracelets. Cr. 8vo, cloth, 3s. 6d.; post 8vo, boards, 2s.; cl. limp, 2s. 6d.
Crown 8vo, cloth extra, 3s. 6d. each.
The Harding Scandal. | A Missing Witness. With 8 Illustrations by W. H. MARGETSON.

Barrett (Joan).—Monte Carlo Stories. Fcap. 8vo, cloth, 1s. 6d.

Beaconsfield, Lord. By T. P. O'CONNOR, M.P. Cr. 8vo, cloth, 5s.

Beauchamp (Shelsley).—Grantley Grange. Post 8vo, boards, 2s.

Beautiful Pictures by British Artists: A Gathering of Favourites
from the Picture Galleries, engraved on Steel. Imperial 4to, cloth extra, gilt edges, 21s.

Besant (Sir Walter) and James Rice, Novels by.
Crown 8vo, cloth extra, 3s. 6d. each; post 8vo, illustrated boards, 2s. each; cloth limp, 2s. 6d. each.

Ready-Money Mortiboy.	By Celia's Arbour.
My Little Girl.	The Chaplain of the Fleet.
With Harp and Crown.	The Seamy Side.
This Son of Vulcan.	The Case of Mr. Lucraft, &c.
The Golden Butterfly.	'Twas in Trafalgar's Bay, &c.
The Monks of Thelema.	The Ten Years' Tenant, &c.

. There is also a LIBRARY EDITION of the above Twelve Volumes, handsomely set in new type on a
large crown 8vo page, and bound in cloth extra, 6s. each; and a POPULAR EDITION of The Golden
Butterfly, medium 8vo, 6d.; cloth, 1s.—NEW EDITIONS, printed in large type on crown 8vo laid paper,
bound in figured cloth, 3s. 6d. each, are also in course of publication.

Besant (Sir Walter), Novels by.
Crown 8vo, cloth extra, 3s. 6d. each; post 8vo, illustrated boards, 2s. each; cloth limp, 2s. 6d. each.
All Sorts and Conditions of Men. With 12 Illustrations by FRED. BARNARD.
The Captains' Room, &c. With Frontispiece by E. J. WHEELER.
All in a Garden Fair. With 6 Illustrations by HARRY FURNISS.
Dorothy Forster. With Frontispiece by CHARLES GREEN.
Uncle Jack, and other Stories. | Children of Gibeon.
The World Went Very Well Then. With 12 Illustrations by A. FORESTIER.
Herr Paulus: His Rise, his Greatness, and his Fall. | The Bell of St. Paul's.
For Faith and Freedom. With Illustrations by A. FORESTIER and F. WADDY.
To Call Her Mine, &c. With 9 Illustrations by A. FORESTIER.
The Holy Rose, &c. With Frontispiece by F. BARNARD.
Armorel of Lyonesse: A Romance of To-day. With 12 Illustrations by F. BARNARD.
St. Katherine's by the Tower. With 12 Illustrations by C. GREEN.
Verbena Camellia Stephanotis, &c. With a Frontispiece by GORDON BROWNE.
The Ivory Gate. | The Rebel Queen.
Beyond the Dreams of Avarice. With 12 Illustrations by W. H. HYDE.
Crown 8vo, cloth extra, 3s. 6d. each.
In Deacon's Orders, &c. With Frontispiece by A. FORESTIER.
The Revolt of Man. | The Master Craftsman.
A Fountain Sealed. With Frontispiece by H. G. BURGESS. Crown 8vo, cloth, 6s.
The City of Refuge. 3 vols., crown 8vo, 15s. net.
The Charm, and other Drawing-room Plays. By Sir WALTER BESANT and WALTER H. POLLOCK.
With 50 Illustrations by CHRIS HAMMOND and JULE GOODMAN. Crown 8vo, cloth, gilt edges, 6s.
Fifty Years Ago. With 144 Plates and Woodcuts. Crown 8vo, cloth extra, 5s.
The Eulogy of Richard Jefferies. With Portrait. Crown 8vo, cloth extra, 6s.
London. With 125 Illustrations. Demy 8vo, cloth extra, 7s. 6d.
Westminster. With Etched Frontispiece by F. S. WALKER, R.P.E., and 130 Illustrations by
WILLIAM PATTEN and others. Demy 8vo, cloth 18s.
Sir Richard Whittington. With Frontispiece. Crown — . ..
Gaspard de Coligny. W

Bechstein (Ludwig).—As Pretty as Seven, and other German Stories. With Additional Tales by the Brothers GRIMM, and 98 Illustrations by RICHTER. Square 8vo, cloth extra, 6s. 6d.; gilt edges, 7s. 6d.

Bellew (Frank).—The Art of Amusing: A Collection of Graceful Arts, Games, Tricks, Puzzles, and Charades. With 300 Illustrations. Crown 8vo, cloth extra, 4s. 6d.

Bennett (W. C., LL.D.).—Songs for Sailors. Post 8vo, cl. limp, 2s.

Bewick (Thomas) and his Pupils. By AUSTIN DOBSON. With 95 Illustrations. Square 8vo, cloth extra, 6s.

Bierce (Ambrose).—In the Midst of Life: Tales of Soldiers and Civilians. Crown 8vo, cloth extra, 6s.; post 8vo, illustrated boards, 2s.

Bill Nye's History of the United States. With 146 Illustrations by F. OPPER. Crown 8vo, cloth extra, 3s. 6d.

Biré (Edmond). — Diary of a Citizen of Paris during 'The Terror.' Translated and Edited by JOHN DE VILLIERS. With 2 Photogravure Portraits. Two Vols., demy 8vo, cloth, 21s.

Blackburn's (Henry) Art Handbooks.

Academy Notes, 1897. 1s.
Academy Notes, 1875-79. Complete in One Vol., with 600 Illustrations. Cloth, 6s.
Academy Notes, 1880-84. Complete in One Vol., with 700 Illustrations. Cloth, 6s.
Academy Notes, 1890-94. Complete in One Vol., with 800 Illustrations. Cloth, 7s. 6d.
Grosvenor Notes, Vol. I., 1877-82. With 300 Illustrations. Demy 8vo, cloth 6s.
Grosvenor Notes, Vol. II., 1883-87. With 300 Illustrations. Demy 8vo, cloth, 6s.

Grosvenor Notes, Vol. III., 1888-90. With 230 Illustrations. Demy 8vo cloth, 3s. 6d.
The New Gallery, 1888-1892. With 250 Illustrations. Demy 8vo, cloth, 6s.
English Pictures at the National Gallery. With 114 Illustrations. 1s.
Old Masters at the National Gallery. With 128 Illustrations. 1s. 6d.
Illustrated Catalogue to the National Gallery. With 242 Illusts. Demy 8vo, cloth, 3s.

The Illustrated Catalogue of the Paris Salon, 1897. With 300 Sketches. 3s.

Blind (Mathilde), Poems by.
The Ascent of Man. Crown 8vo, cloth, 5s.
Dramas in Miniature. With a Frontispiece by F. MADOX BROWN. Crown 8vo, cloth, 5s.
Songs and Sonnets. Fcap. 8vo, vellum and gold, 5s.
Winds of Passage: Songs of the Orient and Occident. Second Edition. Crown 8vo linen, 6s. net.

Bourget (Paul).—A Living Lie. Translated by JOHN DE VILLIERS. With special Preface for the English Edition. Crown 8vo, cloth, 3s. 6d.

Bourne (H. R. Fox), Books by.
English Merchants: Memoirs in Illustration of the Progress of British Commerce. With numerous Illustrations. Crown 8vo, cloth extra, 7s. 6d.
English Newspapers: Chapters in the History of Journalism. Two Vols., demy 8vo, cloth, 25s.
The Other Side of the Emin Pasha Relief Expedition. Crown 8vo, cloth, 6s.

Bowers (George).—Leaves from a Hunting Journal. Coloured Plates. Oblong folio, half-bound, 21s.

Boyle (Frederick), Works by. Post 8vo, illustrated bds., 2s. each.
Chronicles of No-Man's Land. | Camp Notes. | Savage Life.

Brand (John).—Observations on Popular Antiquities; chiefly Illustrating the Origin of our Vulgar Customs, Ceremonies, and Superstitions. With the Additions of Sir HENRY ELLIS, and numerous Illustrations. Crown 8vo, cloth extra, 7s. 6d.

Brewer (Rev. Dr.), Works by.
The Reader's Handbook of Allusions, References, Plots, and Stories. Eighteenth Thousand. Crown 8vo, cloth extra, 7s. 6d.
Authors and their Works, with the Dates: Being the Appendices to 'The Reader's Handbook,' separately printed. Crown 8vo, cloth limp, 2s.
A Dictionary of Miracles. Crown 8vo, cloth extra, 7s. 6d.

Brewster (Sir David), Works by. Post 8vo, cloth, 4s. 6d. each.
More Worlds than One: Creed of the Philosopher and Hope of the Christian. With Plates.
The Martyrs of Science: GALILEO, TYCHO BRAHE, and KEPLER. With Portraits.
Letters on Natural Magic. With numerous Illustrations.

Brillat-Savarin.—Gastronomy as a Fine Art. Translated by R. E. ANDERSON, M.A. Post 8vo, half-bound, 2s.

Brydges (Harold).—Uncle Sam at Home. With 91 Illustrations. Post 8vo, illustrated boards, 2s.; cloth limp, 2s. 6d.

Buchanan (Robert), Novels, &c., by.

Crown 8vo, cloth extra, 3s. 6d. each; post 8vo, illustrated boards, 2s. each.

The Shadow of the Sword.
A Child of Nature. With Frontispiece.
God and the Man. With 11 Illustrations by FRED. BARNARD.
The Martyrdom of Madeline. With Frontispiece by A. W. COOPER.

Love Me for Ever. With Frontispiece.
Annan Water. | **Foxglove Manor.**
The New Abelard. | **Rachel Dene.**
Matt: A Story of a Caravan. With Frontispiece.
The Master of the Mine. With Frontispiece.
The Heir of Linne. | **Woman and the Man.**

Crown 8vo, cloth extra, 3s. 6d. each.

Red and White Heather. | **Lady Kilpatrick.**

The Wandering Jew: a Christmas Carol. Crown 8vo, cloth, 6s.

The Charlatan. By ROBERT BUCHANAN and HENRY MURRAY. Crown 8vo, cloth, with a Frontispiece by T. H. ROBINSON, 3s. 6d.; post 8vo, picture boards, 2s.

Burton (Richard F.).—The Book of the Sword. With over 400

Illustrations. Demy 4to, cloth extra, 32s.

Burton (Robert).—The Anatomy of Melancholy. With Transla-

tions of the Quotations. Demy 8vo, cloth extra, 7s. 6d.

Melancholy Anatomised: An Abridgment of BURTON'S ANATOMY. Post 8vo, half-bd., 2s. 6d.

Caine (T. Hall), Novels by. Crown 8vo, cloth extra, 3s. 6d. each.;

post 8vo, illustrated boards, 2s. each; cloth limp, 2s. 6d. each.

The Shadow of a Crime. | **A Son of Hagar.** | **The Deemster.**

Also a LIBRARY EDITION of **The Deemster**, set in new type, crown 8vo, cloth decorated, 6s.

Cameron (Commander V. Lovett).—The Cruise of the 'Black

Prince' Privateer. Post 8vo, picture boards, 2s.

Cameron (Mrs. H. Lovett), Novels by. Post 8vo, illust. bds. 2s. ea.

Juliet's Guardian. | **Deceivers Ever.**

Captain Coignet, Soldier of the Empire: An Autobiography.

Edited by LOREDAN LARCHEY. Translated by Mrs. CAREY. With 100 Illustrations. Crown 8vo, cloth, 3s. 6d.

Carlyle (Jane Welsh), Life of. By Mrs. ALEXANDER IRELAND. With

Portrait and Facsimile Letter. Small demy 8vo, cloth extra, 7s. 6d.

Carlyle (Thomas).—On the Choice of Books. Post 8vo, cl., 1s. 6d.

Correspondence of Thomas Carlyle and R. W. Emerson, 1834-1872. Edited by C. E. NORTON. With Portraits. Two Vols., crown 8vo, cloth, 24s.

Carruth (Hayden).—The Adventures of Jones. With 17 Illustra-

tions. Fcap. 8vo, cloth, 2s.

Chambers (Robert W.), Stories of Paris Life by. Long fcap. 8vo,

cloth, 2s. 6d. each.

The King in Yellow. | **In the Quarter.**

Chapman's (George), Works. Vol. I., Plays Complete, including the

Doubtful Ones.—Vol. II., Poems and Minor Translations, with Essay by A. C. SWINBURNE.—Vol. III., Translations of the Iliad and Odyssey. Three Vols., crown 8vo, cloth, 3s. 6d. each.

Chapple (J. Mitchell).—The Minor Chord: The Story of a Prima

Donna. Crown 8vo, cloth, 3s. 6d.

Chatto (W. A.) and J. Jackson.—A Treatise on Wood Engraving,

Historical and Practical. With Chapter by H. G. BOHN, and 450 fine Illusts. Large 4to, half-leather, 28s.

Chaucer for Children: A Golden Key. By Mrs. H. R. HAWEIS. With

8 Coloured Plates and 30 Woodcuts. Crown 4to, cloth extra, 3s. 6d.

Chaucer for Schools. By Mrs. H. R. HAWEIS. Demy 8vo, cloth limp, 2s. 6d.

Chess, The Laws and Practice of. With an Analysis of the Open-

ings. By HOWARD STAUNTON. Edited by R. B. WORMALD. Crown 8vo, cloth, 5s.

The Minor Tactics of Chess: A Treatise on the Deployment of the Forces in obedience to Strategic Principle. By F. K. YOUNG and E. C. HOWELL. Long fcap. 8vo, cloth, 2s. 6d.

The Hastings Chess Tournament. Containing the Authorised Account of the 230 Games played Aug.-Sept., 1895. With Annotations by PILLSBURY, LASKER, TARRASCH, STEINITZ, SCHIFFERS, TEICHMANN, BARDELEBEN, BLACKBURNE, GUNSBERG, TINSLEY, MASON, and ALBIN; Biographical Sketches of the Chess Masters, and 22 Portraits. Edited by H. F. CHESHIRE. Crown 8vo, cloth, 7s. 6d.

Clare (Austin).—For the Love of a Lass. Post 8vo 2s. cl 2s. 6d.

Clive (Mrs. Archer), Novels by. Post 8vo, illust. boards, 2s. each.
Paul Ferroll. | Why Paul Ferroll Killed his Wife.

Clodd (Edward, F.R.A.S.).—Myths and Dreams. Cr. 8vo, 3s. 6d.

Coates (Anne).—Rie's Diary. Crown 8vo, cloth, 3s. 6d.

Cobban (J. Maclaren), Novels by.
The Cure of Souls. Post 8vo, Illustrated boards, 2s.
The Red Sultan. Crown 8vo, cloth extra, 3s. 6d. ; post 8vo, illustrated boards, 2s.
The Burden of Isabel. Crown 8vo, cloth extra, 3s. 6d.

Coleman (John).—Curly: An Actor's Story. With 21 Illustrations
by J. C. DOLLMAN. Crown 8vo, picture cover, 1s.

Coleridge (M. E.).—The Seven Sleepers of Ephesus. Cloth, 1s. 6d.

Collins (C. Allston).—The Bar Sinister. Post 8vo, boards, 2s.

Collins (John Churton, M.A.), Books by.
Illustrations of Tennyson. Crown 8vo, cloth extra, 6s.
Jonathan Swift: A Biographical and Critical Study. Crown 8vo, cloth extra, 8s.

Collins (Mortimer and Frances), Novels by.
Crown 8vo, cloth extra, 3s. 6d. each ; post 8vo, illustrated boards, 2s. each.
From Midnight to Midnight. | Blacksmith and Scholar.
Transmigration. | You Play me False. | The Village Comedy.

Post 8vo, illustrated boards, 2s. each.
Sweet Anne Page. | A Fight with Fortune. | Sweet and Twenty. | Frances.

Collins (Wilkie), Novels by.
Crown 8vo, cloth extra, many Illustrated, 3s. 6d. each ; post 8vo, picture boards, 2s. each ;
cloth limp, 2s. 6d. each.

*Antonina.	Armadale.	Jezebel's Daughter.
*Basil.	Man and Wife.	The Black Robe.
*Hide and Seek.	Poor Miss Finch.	Heart and Science.
*The Woman in White.	Miss or Mrs.?	'I Say No.'
*The Moonstone.	The New Magdalen.	A Rogue's Life.
After Dark.	The Frozen Deep.	The Evil Genius.
The Dead Secret.	The Law and the Lady.	Little Novels.
The Queen of Hearts.	The Two Destinies.	The Legacy of Cain.
No Name.	The Haunted Hotel.	Blind Love.
' Miscellanies.	The Fallen Leaves.	

Marked * are the NEW LIBRARY EDITION at 3s. 6d., entirely reset and bound in new style.

POPULAR EDITIONS. Medium 8vo, 6d. each; cloth, 1s. each.
The Woman in White. | The Moonstone. | Antonina.

The Woman in White and The Moonstone in One Volume, medium 8vo, cloth, 2s.

Colman's (George) Humorous Works: 'Broad Grins,' 'My Night-
gown and Slippers,' &c. With Life and Frontispiece. Crown 8vo, cloth extra, 7s. 6d.

Colquhoun (M. J.).—Every Inch a Soldier. Post 8vo, boards, 2s.

Colt-breaking, Hints on. By W. M. HUTCHISON. Cr. 8vo. cl., 3s. 6d.

Convalescent Cookery. By CATHERINE RYAN. Cr. 8vo, 1s. ; cl., 1s. 6d.

Conway (Moncure D.), Works by.
Demonology and Devil-Lore. With 65 Illustrations. Two Vols., demy 8vo, cloth, 28s.
George Washington's Rules of Civility. Fcap. 8vo, Japanese vellum, 2s. 6d.

Cook (Dutton), Novels by.
Post 8vo, illustrated boards, 2s. each.
Leo. | Paul Foster's Daughter.

Cooper (Edward H.).—Geoffory Hamilton. Cr. 8vo, cloth, 3s. 6d.

Cornwall.—Popular Romances of the West of England; or, The
Drolls, Traditions, and Superstitions of Old Cornwall. Collected by ROBERT HUNT, F.R.S. With
two Steel Plates by GEORGE CRUIKSHANK. Crown 8vo, cloth, 7s. 6d.

Cotes (V. Cecil).—Two Girls on a Barge. With 44 Illustrations by
F. H. TOWNSEND. Post 8vo, cloth, 2s. 6d.

Craddock (C. Egbert), Stories by.
The Prophet of the Great Smoky Mountains. Post 8vo, Illustrated boards, 2s.
His Vanished Star. Crown 8vo, cloth extra, 3s. 6d.

Cram (Ralph Adams).—Black Spirits and White. Fcap. 8vo,
cloth, 1s. 6d.

Crellin (H. N.), Books by.
Romances of the Old Seraglio. With 28 Illustrations by S. L. WOOD. Crown 8vo, cloth, 3s. 6d.
Tales of the Caliph. Crown 8vo, cloth, 2s.
The Nazarenes: A Drama. Crown 8vo, 1s.

Crim (Matt.).—Adventures of a Fair Rebel. Crown 8vo, cloth
extra, with a Frontispiece by DAN. BEARD, 3s. 6d.; post 8vo, illustrated boards, 2s.

Crockett (S. R.) and others. — Tales of Our Coast. By S. R.
CROCKETT, GILBERT PARKER, HAROLD FREDERIC, 'Q.,' and W CLARK RUSSELL. With 12
Illustrations by FRANK BRANGWYN. Crown 8vo, cloth, 3s. 6d.

Croker (Mrs. B. M.), Novels by. Crown 8vo, cloth extra, 3s. 6d.
each; post 8vo, illustrated boards, 2s. each; cloth limp, 2s. 6d. each.

Pretty Miss Neville.	Diana Barrington.	A Family Likeness.
A Bird of Passage.	Proper Pride.	'To Let.'
Village Tales and Jungle Tragedies.	Two Masters.	Mr. Jervis.

Crown 8vo, cloth extra, 3s. 6d. each.

Married or Single?	In the Kingdom of Kerry.
The Real Lady Hilda.	

Beyond the Pale. Crown 8vo, buckram, 6s.

Cruikshank's Comic Almanack. Complete in Two SERIES: The
FIRST, from 1835 to 1843; the SECOND, from 1844 to 1853. A Gathering of the Best Humour of
THACKERAY, HOOD, MAYHEW, ALBERT SMITH. A'BECKETT, ROBERT BROUGH, &c. With
numerous Steel Engravings and Woodcuts by GEORGE CRUIKSHANK, HINE, LANDELLS, &c.
Two Vols., crown 8vo, cloth gilt, 7s. 6d. each.
The Life of George Cruikshank. By BLANCHARD JERROLD. With 84 Illustrations and a
Bibliography. Crown 8vo, cloth extra, 6s.

Cumming (C. F. Gordon), Works by. Demy 8vo, cl. ex., 8s. 6d. ea.
In the Hebrides. With an Autotype Frontispiece and 23 Illustrations.
In the Himalayas and on the Indian Plains. With 42 Illustrations.
Two Happy Years in Ceylon. With 28 Illustrations.

Via Cornwall to Egypt. With a Photogravure Frontispiece. Demy 8vo, cloth, 7s. 6d.

Cussans (John E.).—A Handbook of Heraldry; with Instructions
for Tracing Pedigrees and Deciphering Ancient MSS., &c. Fourth Edition, revised, with 408 Woodcuts
and 2 Coloured Plates. Crown 8vo, cloth extra, 6s.

Cyples (W.).—Hearts of Gold. Cr. 8vo, cl., 3s. 6d.; post 8vo, bds., 2s.

Daudet (Alphonse).—The Evangelist; or, Port Salvation. Crown
8vo, cloth extra, 3s. 6d.; post 8vo, illustrated boards, 2s.

Davenant (Francis, M.A.).—Hints for Parents on the Choice of
a Profession for their Sons when Starting in Life. Crown 8vo, cloth, 1s. 6d.

Davidson (Hugh Coleman).—Mr. Sadler's Daughters. With a
Frontispiece by STANLEY WOOD. Crown 8vo, cloth extra, 3s. 6d.

Davies (Dr. N. E. Yorke-), Works by. Cr. 8vo, 1s. ea.; cl., 1s. 6d. ea.
One Thousand Medical Maxims and Surgical Hints.
Nursery Hints: A Mother's Guide in Health and Disease.
Foods for the Fat: A Treatise on Corpulency, and a Dietary for its Cure.

Aids to Long Life. Crown 8vo, 2s.; cloth limp, 2s. 6d.

Davies' (Sir John) Complete Poetical Works. Collected and Edited,
with Introduction and Notes, by Rev. A. B. GROSART, D.D. Two Vols., crown 8vo, cloth, 3s. 6d. each.

Dawson (Erasmus, M.B.).—The Fountain of Youth. Crown 8vo,
cloth extra, with Two Illustrations by HUME NISBET, 3s. 6d.; post 8vo, illustrated boards, 2s.

De Guerin (Maurice), The Journal of. Edited by G. S. TREBUTIEN,
With a Memoir by SAINTE-BEUVE. Translated from the 20th French Edition by JESSIE P. FROTH-
INGHAM. Fcap. 8vo, half-bound, 2s. 6d.

De Maistre (Xavier).—A Journey Round my Room. Translated
by Sir HENRY ATTWELL. Post 8vo, cloth limp, 2s. 6d.

De Mille (James).—A Castle in Spain. Crown 8vo, cloth extra, with
a Frontispiece, 3s. 6d.; post 8vo, illustrated boards, 2s.

Derby (The): The Blue Ribbon of the Turf. With Brief Accounts
of THE OAKS. By LOUIS HENRY CURZON. Crown 8vo, cloth limp, 2s. 6d.

Derwent (Leith), Novels by. Cr. 8vo, cl., 3s. 6d. ea.; post 8vo, 2s. ea.
Our Lady of Tears. | Circe's Lovers.

Dewar (T. R.).—A Ramble Round the Globe. With 220 Illustrations. Crown 8vo, cloth extra, 7s. 6d.

Dickens (Charles).—Sketches by Boz. Post 8vo, illust. boards, 2s.

About England with Dickens. By ALFRED RIMMER. With 57 Illustrations by C. A. VANDER HOOF, ALFRED RIMMER, and others. Square 8vo, cloth extra, 7s. 6d.

Dictionaries.
A Dictionary of Miracles: Imitative, Realistic, and Dogmatic. By the Rev. E. C. BREWER, L.L.D. Crown 8vo, cloth extra, 7s. 6d.
The Reader's Handbook of Allusions, References, Plots, and Stories. By the Rev. E. C. BREWER, LL.D. With an ENGLISH BIBLIOGRAPHY. Crown 8vo, cloth extra, 7s. 6d.
Authors and their Works, with the Dates. Crown 8vo, cloth limp, 2s.
Familiar Short Sayings of Great Men. With Historical and Explanatory Notes by SAMUEL A. BENT, A.M. Crown 8vo, cloth extra, 7s. 6d.
The Slang Dictionary: Etymological, Historical, and Anecdotal. Crown 8vo, cloth, 6s. 6d.
Words, Facts, and Phrases: A Dictionary of Curious, Quaint, and Out-of-the-Way Matters. By ELIEZER EDWARDS. Crown 8vo, cloth extra, 3s. 6d.

Diderot.—The Paradox of Acting. Translated, with Notes, by WALTER HERRIES POLLOCK. With Preface by Sir HENRY IRVING. Crown 8vo, parchment, 4s. 6d.

Dobson (Austin), Works by.
Thomas Bewick and his Pupils. With 95 Illustrations. Square 8vo, cloth, 6s.
Four Frenchwomen. With Four Portraits. Crown 8vo, buckram, gilt top, 6s.
Eighteenth Century Vignettes. IN THREE SERIES. Crown 8vo, buckram, 6s. each.

Dobson (W. T.).—Poetical Ingenuities and Eccentricities. Post 8vo, cloth limp, 2s. 6d.

Donovan (Dick), Detective Stories by.
Post 8vo, illustrated boards, 2s. each; cloth limp, 2s. 6d. each.

The Man-Hunter. | Wanted! | A Detective's Triumphs.
Caught at Last. | In the Grip of the Law.
Tracked and Taken. | From Information Received.
Who Poisoned Hetty Duncan? | Link by Link. | Dark Deeds.
Suspicion Aroused. | Riddles Read.

Crown 8vo, cloth extra, 3s. 6d. each; post 8vo, illustrated boards, 2s. each; cloth, 2s. 6d. each.
The Man from Manchester. With 23 Illustrations.
Tracked to Doom. With Six full-page Illustrations by GORDON BROWNE.
The Mystery of Jamaica Terrace.

The Chronicles of Michael Danevitch, of the Russian Secret Service. Crown 8vo, cloth, 3s. 6d.

Dowling (Richard).—Old Corcoran's Money. Crown 8vo, cl., 3s. 6d.

Doyle (A. Conan).—The Firm of Girdlestone. Cr. 8vo, cl., 3s. 6d.

Dramatists, The Old. Cr. 8vo, cl. ex., with Portraits, 3s. 6d. per Vol.
Ben Jonson's Works. With Notes, Critical and Explanatory, and a Biographical Memoir by WILLIAM GIFFORD. Edited by Colonel CUNNINGHAM. Three Vols.
Chapman's Works. Three Vols. Vol. I. contains the Plays complete; Vol. II., Poems and Minor Translations, with an Essay by A. C. SWINBURNE; Vol. III., Translations of the Iliad and Odyssey.
Marlowe's Works. Edited, with Notes, by Colonel CUNNINGHAM. One Vol.
Massinger's Plays. From GIFFORD'S Text. Edited by Colonel CUNNINGHAM. One Vol.

Duncan (Sara Jeannette: Mrs. EVERARD COTES), Works by.
Crown 8vo, cloth extra, 7s. 6d. each.

A Social Departure. With 111 Illustrations by F. H. TOWNSEND.
An American Girl in London. With 80 Illustrations by F. H. TOWNSEND.
The Simple Adventures of a Memsahib. With 37 Illustrations by F. H. TOWNSEND.

Crown 8vo, cloth extra, 3s. 6d. each.

A Daughter of To-Day. | Vernon's Aunt. With 47 Illustrations by HAL HURST.

Dyer (T. F. Thiselton).—The Folk-Lore of Plants. Cr. 8vo, cl., 6s.

Early English Poets. Edited, with Introductions and Annotations, by Rev. A. B. GROSART, D.D. Crown 8vo, cloth boards, 3s. 6d. per Volume.
Fletcher's (Giles) Complete Poems. One Vol.
Davies' (Sir John) Complete Poetical Works. Two Vols.
Herrick's (Robert) Complete Collected Poems. Three Vols.
Sidney's (Sir Philip) Complete Poetical Works. Three Vols.

Edgcumbe (Sir E. R. Pearce). Zephyrus: A Holiday in Brazil

Edwardes (Mrs. Annie), Novels by.
Post 8vo, illustrated boards, 2s. each.
Archie Lovell. | A Point of Honour.

Edwards (Eliezer).—Words, Facts, and Phrases: A Dictionary of Curious, Quaint, and Out-of-the-Way Matters. Cheaper Edition. Crown 8vo, cloth, 3s. 6d.

Edwards (M. Betham-), Novels by.
Kitty. Post 8vo, boards, 2s.; cloth, 2s. 6d. | Felicia. Post 8vo, illustrated boards, 2s.

Egerton (Rev. J. C., M.A.).— Sussex Folk and Sussex Ways.
With Introduction by Rev. Dr. H. WACE, and Four Illustrations. Crown 8vo, cloth extra, 5s.

Eggleston (Edward).—Roxy: A Novel. Post 8vo, illust. boards, 2s.

Englishman's House, The: A Practical Guide for Selecting or Building a House. By C. J. RICHARDSON. Coloured Frontispiece and 534 Illusts. Cr. 8vo, cloth, 7s. 6d.

Ewald (Alex. Charles, F.S.A.), Works by.
The Life and Times of Prince Charles Stuart, Count of Albany (THE YOUNG PRETENDER. With a Portrait. Crown 8vo, cloth extra, 7s. 6d.
Stories from the State Papers. With Autotype Frontispiece. Crown 8vo, cloth, 6s.

Eyes, Our: How to Preserve Them. By JOHN BROWNING. Cr. 8vo, 1s.

Familiar Short Sayings of Great Men. By SAMUEL ARTHUR BENT, A.M. Fifth Edition, Revised and Enlarged. Crown 8vo, cloth extra, 7s. 6d.

Faraday (Michael), Works by. Post 8vo, cloth extra, 4s. 6d. each.
The Chemical History of a Candle: Lectures delivered before a Juvenile Audience. Edited by WILLIAM CROOKES, F.C.S. With numerous Illustrations.
On the Various Forces of Nature, and their Relations to each other. Edited by WILLIAM CROOKES, F.C.S. With Illustrations.

Farrer (J. Anson), Works by.
Military Manners and Customs. Crown 8vo, cloth extra, 6s.
War: Three Essays, reprinted from 'Military Manners and Customs.' Crown 8vo, 1s.; cloth, 1s. 6d.

Fenn (G. Manville), Novels by.
Crown 8vo, cloth extra, 3s. 6d. each; post 8vo, illustrated boards, 2s. each.
The New Mistress. | Witness to the Deed. | The Tiger Lily. | The White Virgin.

Fin-Bec.—The Cupboard Papers: Observations on the Art of Living and Dining. Post 8vo, cloth limp, 2s. 6d.

Fireworks, The Complete Art of Making; or, The Pyrotechnist's Treasury. By THOMAS KENTISH. With 267 Illustrations. Crown 8vo, cloth, 5s.

First Book, My. By WALTER BESANT, JAMES PAYN, W. CLARK RUSSELL, GRANT ALLEN, HALL CAINE, GEORGE R. SIMS, RUDYARD KIPLING, A. CONAN DOYLE, M. E. BRADDON, F. W. ROBINSON, H. RIDER HAGGARD, R. M. BALLANTYNE, I. ZANGWILL, MORLEY ROBERTS, D. CHRISTIE MURRAY, MARY CORELLI, J. K. JEROME, JOHN STRANGE WINTER, BRET HARTE, 'Q.,' ROBERT BUCHANAN, and R. L. STEVENSON. With a Prefatory Story by JEROME K. JEROME, and 185 Illustrations. A New Edition. Small demy 8vo, art linen, 3s. 6d.

Fitzgerald (Percy), Works by.
Little Essays: Passages from the Letters of CHARLES LAMB. Post 8vo, cloth, 2s. 6d.
Fatal Zero. Crown 8vo, cloth extra, 3s. 6d.; post 8vo, illustrated boards, 2s.

Post 8vo, illustrated boards, 2s. each.

Bella Donna.	The Lady of Brantome.	The Second Mrs. Tillotson.
Polly.	Never Forgotten.	Seventy-five Brooke Street.

The Life of James Boswell (of Auchinleck). With Illusts. Two Vols., demy 8vo, cloth, 24s.
The Savoy Opera. With 60 Illustrations and Portraits. Crown 8vo, cloth, 3s. 6d.
Sir Henry Irving: Twenty Years at the Lyceum. With Portrait. Crown 8vo, 1s.; cloth, 1s. 6d.

Flammarion (Camille), Works by.
Popular Astronomy: A General Description of the Heavens. Translated by J. ELLARD GORE, F.R.A.S. With Three Plates and 288 Illustrations. Medium 8vo, cloth, 16s.
Urania: A Romance. With 87 Illustrations. Crown 8vo, cloth extra, 5s.

Fletcher's (Giles, B.D.) Complete Poems: Christ's Victorie in Heaven, Christ's Victorie on Earth, Christ's Triumph over Death, and Minor Poems. With Notes by Rev. A. B. GROSART, D.D. Crown 8vo, cloth boards, 3s. 6d.

Fonblanque (Albany).—Filthy Lucre. Post 8vo, illust. boards, 2s.

Francillon (R. E.), Novels by
Crown 8vo, cloth extra, 3s. 6d. each; post 8vo, illustrated boards, 2s. each.

One by One. | A Real Queen. | A Dog and his Shadow.
Ropes of Sand. Illustrated.

Post 8vo, illustrated boards, 2s. each.
Queen Cophetua. | Olympia. | Romances of the Law. | King or Knave?
Jack Doyle's Daughter. Crown 8vo, cloth, 3s. 6d.

Frederic (Harold), Novels by. Post 8vo, illust. boards, 2s. each.
Seth's Brother's Wife. | The Lawton Girl.

French Literature, A History of. By HENRY VAN LAUN. Three Vols., demy 8vo, cloth boards, 7s. 6d. each.

Friswell (Hain).—One of Two: A Novel. Post 8vo, illust. bds., 2s.

Fry's (Herbert) Royal Guide to the London Charities. Edited by JOHN LANE. Published Annually. Crown 8vo, cloth, 1s. 6d.

Gardening Books. Post 8vo, 1s. each; cloth limp. 1s. 6d. each.
A Year's Work in Garden and Greenhouse. By GEORGE GLENNY.
Household Horticulture. By TOM and JANE JERROLD. Illustrated.
The Garden that Paid the Rent. By TOM JERROLD.

My Garden Wild. By FRANCIS G. HEATH. Crown 8vo, cloth extra, 6s.

Gardner (Mrs. Alan).—Rifle and Spear with the Rajpoots: Being the Narrative of a Winter's Travel and Sport in Northern India. With numerous Illustrations by the Author and F. H. TOWNSEND. Demy 4to, half-bound, 21s.

Garrett (Edward).—The Capel Girls: A Novel. Crown 8vo, cloth extra, with two Illustrations, 3s. 6d. ; post 8vo, illustrated boards, 2s.

Gaulot (Paul).—The Red Shirts: A Story of the Revolution. Translated by JOHN DE VILLIERS. With a Frontispiece by STANLEY WOOD. Crown 8vo, cloth, 3s. 6d.

Gentleman's Magazine, The. 1s. Monthly. Contains Stories, Articles upon Literature, Science, Biography, and Art, and 'Table Talk' by SYLVANUS URBAN.
₊ Bound Volumes for recent years kept in stock, 8s. 6d. each. Cases for binding, 2s. each.

Gentleman's Annual, The. Published Annually in November. 1s.

German Popular Stories. Collected by the Brothers GRIMM and Translated by EDGAR TAYLOR. With Introduction by JOHN RUSKIN, and 22 Steel Plates after GEORGE CRUIKSHANK. Square 8vo, cloth, 6s. 6d. ; gilt edges, 7s. 6d.

Gibbon (Chas.), Novels by. Cr. 8vo, cl., 3s. 6d. ea.; post 8vo, bds., 2s. ea.
Robin Gray. With Frontispiece. | Loving a Dream.
The Golden Shaft. With Frontispiece. | Of High Degree.

Post 8vo, illustrated boards, 2s. each.
The Flower of the Forest. | In Love and War.
The Dead Heart. | A Heart's Problem.
For Lack of Gold. | By Mead and Stream.
What Will the World Say? | The Braes of Yarrow.
For the King. | A Hard Knot. | Fancy Free.
Queen of the Meadow. | In Honour Bound.
In Pastures Green. | Heart's Delight. | Blood-Money.

Gibney (Somerville).—Sentenced! Crown 8vo, cloth, 1s. 6d.

Gilbert (W. S.), Original Plays by. In Three Series, 2s. 6d. each.
The FIRST SERIES contains: The Wicked World—Pygmalion and Galatea—Charity—The Princess—The Palace of Truth—Trial by Jury.
The SECOND SERIES: Broken Hearts—Engaged—Sweethearts—Gretchen—Dan'l Druce—Tom Cobb—H.M.S. 'Pinafore'—The Sorcerer—The Pirates of Penzance.
The THIRD SERIES: Comedy and Tragedy—Foggerty's Fairy—Rosencrantz and Guildenstern—Patience—Princess Ida—The Mikado—Ruddigore—The Yeomen of the Guard—The Gondoliers—The Mountebanks—Utopia.

Eight Original Comic Operas written by W. S. GILBERT. In Two Series. Demy 8vo, cloth, 2s. 6d. each. The FIRST containing: The Sorcerer—H.M.S. 'Pinafore'—The Pirates of Penzance—Iolanthe—Patience—Princess Ida—The Mikado—Trial by Jury.

The SECOND SERIES containing: The Gondoliers—The Grand Duke—The Yeomen of the Guard—His Excellency—Utopia, Limited—Ruddigore—The Mountebanks—Haste to the Wedding.

The Gilbert and Sullivan Birthday Book: Quotations for Every Day in the Year, selected from Plays by W. S. GILBERT set to Music by Sir A. SULLIVAN. Compiled by ALEX. WATSON.

Gilbert (William), Novels by. Post 8vo, illustrated bds., 2*s.* each.
Dr. Austin's Guests. | James Duke, Costermonger.
The Wizard of the Mountain.

Glanville (Ernest), Novels by.
Crown 8vo, cloth extra, 3*s.* 6*d.* each ; post 8vo, illustrated boards, 2*s.* each.
The **Lost Heiress** : A Tale of Love, Battle, and Adventure. With Two Illustrations by H. NISBET.
The **Fossicker** : A Romance of Mashonaland. With Two Illustrations by HUME NISBET.
A Fair Colonist. With a Frontispiece by STANLEY WOOD.

The **Golden Rock.** With a Frontispiece by STANLEY WOOD. Crown 8vo, cloth extra, 3*s.* 6*d.*
Kloof Yarns. Crown 8vo, picture cover, 1*s.* ; cloth, 1*s.* 6*d.*

Glenny (George).—A Year's Work in Garden and Greenhouse :
Practical Advice as to the Management of the Flower, Fruit, and Frame Garden. Post 8vo, 1*s.* ; cloth, 1*s.* 6*d.*

Godwin (William).—Lives of the Necromancers. Post 8vo, cl., 2*s.*

Golden Treasury of Thought, The : An Encyclopædia of QUOTA-
TIONS. Edited by THEODORE TAYLOR. Crown 8vo, cloth gilt, 7*s.* 6*d.*

Gontaut, Memoirs of the Duchesse de (Gouvernante to the Chil-
dren of France), 1773-1836. With Two Photogravures. Two Vols., demy 8vo, cloth extra, 21*s.*

Goodman (E. J.).—The Fate of Herbert Wayne. Cr. 8vo, 3*s.* 6*d.*

Greeks and Romans, The Life of the, described from Antique
Monuments. By ERNST GUHL and W. KONER. Edited by Dr. F. HUEFFER. With 545 Illustrations. Large crown 8vo, cloth extra, 7*s.* 6*d.*

Greville (Henry), Novels by.
Post 8vo, illustrated boards, 2*s.* each.
Nikanor. Translated by ELIZA E. CHASE.
A Noble Woman. Translated by ALBERT D. VANDAM.

Griffith (Cecil).—Corinthia Marazion : A Novel. Crown 8vo, cloth
extra, 3*s.* 6*d.* ; post 8vo, illustrated boards, 2*s.*

Grundy (Sydney).—The Days of his Vanity : A Passage in the
Life of a Young Man. Crown 8vo, cloth extra, 3*s.* 6*d.* ; post 8vo, illustrated boards, 2*s.*

Habberton (John, Author of ' Helen's Babies '), Novels by.
Post 8vo, illustrated boards, 2*s.* each ; cloth limp, 2*s.* 6*d.* each.
Brueton's Bayou. | **Country Luck.**

Hair, The : Its Treatment in Health, Weakness, and Disease. Translated from the German of Dr. J. PINCUS. Crown 8vo, 1*s.* ; cloth, 1*s.* 6*d.*

Hake (Dr. Thomas Gordon), Poems by. Cr. 8vo, cl. ex., 6*s.* each.
New Symbols. | Legends of the Morrow. | The Serpent Play.
Maiden Ecstasy. Small 4to, cloth extra, 8*s.*

Halifax (C.).—Dr. Rumsey's Patient. By Mrs. L. T. MEADE and
CLIFFORD HALIFAX, M.D. Crown 8vo, cloth, 6*s.*

Hall (Mrs. S. C.).—Sketches of Irish Character. With numerous
Illustrations on Steel and Wood by MACLISE, GILBERT, HARVEY, and GEORGE CRUIKSHANK.
Small demy 8vo, cloth extra, 7*s.* 6*d.*

Hall (Owen).—The Track of a Storm. Crown 8vo, cloth, 6*s.*

Halliday (Andrew).—Every-day Papers. Post 8vo, boards, 2*s.*

Handwriting, The Philosophy of. With over 100 Facsimiles and
Explanatory Text. By DON FELIX DE SALAMANCA. Post 8vo, cloth limp, 2*s.* 6*d.*

Hanky-Panky : Easy and Difficult Tricks, White Magic, Sleight of
Hand, &c. Edited by W. H. CREMER. With 200 Illustrations. Crown 8vo, cloth extra, 4*s.* 6*d.*

Hardy (Lady Duffus).—Paul Wynter's Sacrifice. Post 8vo, bds., 2*s.*

Hardy (Thomas).—Under the Greenwood Tree. Crown 8vo, cloth
extra, with Portrait and 15 Illustrations, 3*s.* 6*d.* ; post 8vo, illustrated boards, 2*s.* cloth limp, 2*s.* 6*d.*

Harwood (J. Berwick).—The Tenth Earl. P. 8vo, 2*s.*

Harte's (Bret) Collected Works. Revised by the Author. LIBRARY
EDITION. In Nine Volumes, crown 8vo, cloth extra, 6s. each.
Vol.   I. COMPLETE POETICAL AND DRAMATIC WORKS. With Steel-plate Portrait.
   "   II. THE LUCK OF ROARING CAMP—BOHEMIAN PAPERS—AMERICAN LEGEND.
   "   III. TALES OF THE ARGONAUTS—EASTERN SKETCHES.
   "   IV. GABRIEL CONROY. | Vol. V. STORIES—CONDENSED NOVELS, &c.
   "   VI. TALES OF THE PACIFIC SLOPE.
   "   VII. TALES OF THE PACIFIC SLOPE—II. With Portrait by JOHN PETTIE, R.A.
   "   VIII. TALES OF THE PINE AND THE CYPRESS.
   "   IX. BUCKEYE AND CHAPARREL.

The Select Works of Bret Harte, in Prose and Poetry. With Introductory Essay by J. M.
    BELLEW, Portrait of the Author, and 50 Illustrations. Crown 8vo, cloth extra, 7s. 6d.
Bret Harte's Poetical Works. Printed on hand-made paper. Crown 8vo, buckram, 4s. 6d.
A New Volume of Poems. Crown 8vo, buckram, 5s.   [Preparing.
The Queen of the Pirate Isle. With 28 Original Drawings by KATE GREENAWAY, reproduced
    in Colours by EDMUND EVANS. Small 4to, cloth, 5s.

Crown 8vo, cloth extra, 3s. 6d. each; post 8vo, picture boards, 2s. each.
A Waif of the Plains. With 60 Illustrations by STANLEY L. WOOD.
A Ward of the Golden Gate. With 59 Illustrations by STANLEY L. WOOD.

Crown 8vo, cloth extra, 3s. 6d. each.
A Sappho of Green Springs, &c. With Two Illustrations by HUME NISBET.
Colonel Starbottle's Client, and Some Other People. With a Frontispiece.
Susy: A Novel. With Frontispiece and Vignette by J. A. CHRISTIE.
Sally Dows, &c. With 47 Illustrations by W. D. ALMOND and others.
A Protegee of Jack Hamlin's, &c. With 26 Illustrations by W. SMALL and others.
The Bell-Ringer of Angel's, &c. With 39 Illustrations by DUDLEY HARDY and others.
Clarence: A Story of the American War. With Eight Illustrations by A. JULE GOODMAN.
Barker's Luck, &c. With 39 Illustrations by A. FORESTIER, PAUL HARDY, &c.
Devil's Ford, &c. With a Frontispiece by W. H. OVEREND.
The Crusade of the "Excelsior." With a Frontispiece by J. BERNARD PARTRIDGE.
Three Partners; or, The Strike on Heavy Tree Hill. With 8 Illustrations by J. GULICH.   [Sept.

Post 8vo, Illustrated boards, 2s. each.

Gabriel Conroy.	The Luck of Roaring Camp, &c.
An Heiress of Red Dog, &c.	Californian Stories.

Post 8vo, Illustrated boards, 2s. each; cloth, 2s. 6d. each.

Flip.	Maruja.	A Phyllis of the Sierras.

Haweis (Mrs. H. R.), Books by.
The Art of Beauty. With Coloured Frontispiece and 91 Illustrations. Square 8vo, cloth bds., 6s.
The Art of Decoration. With Coloured Frontispiece and 74 Illustrations. Sq. 8vo, cloth bds., 6s.
The Art of Dress. With 32 Illustrations. Post 8vo, 1s.; cloth, 1s. 6d.
Chaucer for Schools. Demy 8vo, cloth limp, 2s. 6d.
Chaucer for Children. With 38 Illustrations (8 Coloured). Crown 4to, cloth extra, 3s. 6d.

Haweis (Rev. H. R., M.A.), Books by.
American Humorists: WASHINGTON IRVING, OLIVER WENDELL HOLMES, JAMES RUSSELL
    LOWELL, ARTEMUS WARD, MARK TWAIN, and BRET HARTE. Third Edition. Crown 8vo,
    cloth extra, 6s.
Travel and Talk, 1885-93-95: My Hundred Thousand Miles of Travel through America—Canada
    —New Zealand—Tasmania—Australia—Ceylon—The Paradises of the Pacific. With Photogravure
    Frontispieces. A New Edition. Two Vols., crown 8vo, cloth, 12s.

Hawthorne (Julian), Novels by.
Crown 8vo, cloth extra, 3s. 6d. each; post 8vo, Illustrated boards, 2s. each.

Garth.	Ellice Quentin.	Beatrix Randolph. With Four Illusts.
Sebastian Strome.		David Poindexter's Disappearance.
Fortune's Fool.	Dust. Four Illusts.	The Spectre of the Camera.

Post 8vo, Illustrated boards, 2s. each.

Miss Cadogna.	Love—or a Name.

Hawthorne (Nathaniel).—Our Old Home. Annotated with Pas-
sages from the Author's Note-books, and Illustrated with 31 Photogravures. Two Vols., cr. 8vo, 15s.

Heath (Francis George).—My Garden Wild, and What I Grew
There. Crown 8vo, cloth extra, gilt edges, 6s.

Helps (Sir Arthur), Works by. Post 8vo, cloth limp, 2s. 6d. each.

Animals and their Masters.	Social Pressure.

Ivan de Biron: A Novel. Crown 8vo, cloth extra, 3s. 6d.; post 8vo, Illustrated boards, 2s.

Henderson (Isaac). — Agatha Page: A Novel. Cr. 8vo, cl., 3s. 6d.

Henty (G. A.), Novels by.
Rujub the Juggler. With Eight Illustrations by STANLEY L. WOOD. Crown 8vo, cloth, 3s. 6d.;
    post 8vo, illustrated boards, 2s.
Dorothy's Double. Crown 8vo, cloth, 3s. 6d.
The Queen's Cup. 3 vols., crown 8vo, 15s. net.

Herman (Henry).—A Leading Lady. Post 8vo, bds., 2s.; cl., 2s. 6d.

Herrick's (Robert) Hesperides, Noble Numbers, and Complete
Collected Poems. With Memorial-Introduction and Notes by the Rev. A. B. GROSART, D.D.
Steel Portrait, &c. Three Vols., crown 8vo, cloth boards, 18s. 6d. each.

Hertzka (Dr. Theodor).—Freeland: A Social Anticipation. Translated by ARTHUR RANSOM. Crown 8vo, cloth extra, 6s.

Hesse-Wartegg (Chevalier Ernst von).— Tunis: The Land and the People. With 22 Illustrations. Crown 8vo, cloth extra, 3s. 6d.

Hill (Headon).—Zambra the Detective. Post 8vo, bds., 2s.; cl., 2s. 6d.

Hill (John), Works by.
Treason-Felony. Post 8vo, boards, 2s. | The Common Ancestor. Cr. 8vo, cloth, 3s. 6d.

Hoey (Mrs. Cashel).—The Lover's Creed. Post 8vo, boards, 2s.

Holiday, Where to go for a. By E. P. SHOLL, Sir H. MAXWELL, Bart., M.P., JOHN WATSON, JANE BARLOW, MARY LOVETT CAMERON, JUSTIN H. McCARTHY, PAUL LANGE, J. W. GRAHAM, J. H. SALTER, PHŒBE ALLEN, S. J. BECKETT, L. RIVERS VINE, and C. F. GORDON CUMMING. Crown 8vo, 1s.; cloth, 1s. 6d.

Hollingshead (John).—Niagara Spray. Crown 8vo, 1s.

Holmes (Gordon, M.D.)—The Science of Voice Production and Voice Preservation. Crown 8vo, 1s.; cloth, 1s. 6d.

Holmes (Oliver Wendell), Works by.
The Autocrat of the Breakfast-Table. Illustrated by J. GORDON THOMSON. Post 8vo, cloth limp, 2s. 6d.—Another Edition, post 8vo, cloth, 2s.
The Autocrat of the Breakfast-Table and The Professor at the Breakfast-Table. In One Vol. Post 8vo, half-bound, 2s.

Hood's (Thomas) Choice Works in Prose and Verse. With Life of the Author, Portrait, and 200 Illustrations. Crown 8vo, cloth extra, 7s. 6d.
Hood's Whims and Oddities. With 85 Illustrations. Post 8vo, half-bound, 2s.

Hood (Tom).—From Nowhere to the North Pole: A Noah's Arkæological Narrative. With 25 Illustrations by W. BRUNTON and E. C. BARNES. Cr. 8vo, cloth, 6s.

Hook's (Theodore) Choice Humorous Works; including his Ludicrous Adventures, Bons Mots, Puns, and Hoaxes. With Life of the Author, Portraits, Facsimiles, and Illustrations. Crown 8vo, cloth extra, 7s. 6d.

Hooper (Mrs. Geo.).—The House of Raby. Post 8vo, boards, 2s.

Hopkins (Tighe).—''Twixt Love and Duty.' Post 8vo, boards, 2s.

Horne (R. Hengist). — Orion: An Epic Poem. With Photograph Portrait by SUMMERS. Tenth Edition. Crown 8vo, cloth extra, 7s.

Hungerford (Mrs., Author of 'Molly Bawn'), Novels by.
Post 8vo, illustrated boards, 2s. each; cloth limp, 2s. 6d. each.

A Maiden All Forlorn.	A Modern Circe.	An Unsatisfactory Lover.
Marvel.	A Mental Struggle.	Lady Patty.
In Durance Vile.		

Crown 8vo, cloth extra, 3s. 6d. each; post 8vo, illustrated boards, 2s. each; cloth limp, 2s. 6d. each.
Lady Verner's Flight. | The Red-House Mystery. | The Three Graces.

Crown 8vo, cloth extra, 3s. 6d. each.
The Professor's Experiment. With Frontispiece by E. J. WHEELER.
Nora Creina. | April's Lady.
An Anxious Moment.
A Point of Conscience.

Lovice. Crown 8vo, cloth, 6s.

Hunt's (Leigh) Essays: A Tale for a Chimney Corner, &c. Edited by EDMUND OLLIER. Post 8vo, half-bound, 2s.

Hunt (Mrs. Alfred), Novels by.
Crown 8vo, cloth extra, 3s. 6d. each; post 8vo, illustrated boards, 2s. each.
The Leaden Casket. | Self-Condemned. | That Other Person.
Thornicroft's Model. Post 8vo, boards, 2s. | Mrs. Juliet. Crown 8vo, cloth extra, 3s. 6d.

Hutchison (W. M.).—Hints on Colt-breaking. With 25 Illustrations. Crown 8vo, cloth extra, 3s. 6d.

Hydrophobia: An Account of M. PASTEUR's System; The Technique of his Method, and Statistics. By RENAUD SUZOR, M.B. Crown 8vo, cloth extra, 6s.

Hyne (C. J. Cutcliffe).—Honour of Thieves. Cr. 8vo, cloth, 3s. 6d.

Idler (The): An Illustrated Monthly Magazine. Edited by [illegible] [E.]
Nos. 1 to 48, 6d. each; No. 49 and f[...] each;

Impressions (The) of Aureole. Cheaper Edition, with a New Preface. Post 8vo, blush-rose paper and cloth, 2s. 6d.

Indoor Paupers. By ONE OF THEM. Crown 8vo, 1s. ; cloth, 1s. 6d.

Ingelow (Jean).—Fated to be Free. Post 8vo, illustrated bds., 2s.

Innkeeper's Handbook (The) and Licensed Victualler's Manual. By J. TREVOR-DAVIES. Crown 8vo, 1s. ; cloth, 1s 6d.

Irish Wit and Humour, Songs of. Collected and Edited by A. PERCEVAL GRAVES. Post 8vo, cloth limp, 2s. 6d.

Irving (Sir Henry): A Record of over Twenty Years at the Lyceum. By PERCY FITZGERALD. With Portrait. Crown 8vo, 1s. ; cloth, 1s. 6d.

James (C. T. C.). — A Romance of the Queen's Hounds. Post 8vo, cloth limp, 1s. 6d.

Jameson (William).—My Dead Self. Post 8vo, bds., 2s. ; cl., 2s. 6d.

Japp (Alex. H., LL.D.).—Dramatic Pictures, &c. Cr. 8vo, cloth, 5s.

Jay (Harriett), Novels by. Post 8vo, illustrated boards, 2s. each.
The Dark Colleen. | The Queen of Connaught.

Jefferies (Richard), Works by. Post 8vo, cloth limp, 2s. 6d. each.
Nature near London. | The Life of the Fields. | The Open Air.
*** Also the HAND-MADE PAPER EDITION, crown 8vo, buckram, gilt top, 6s. each.

The Eulogy of Richard Jefferies. By Sir WALTER BESANT. With a Photograph Portrait. Crown 8vo, cloth extra, 6s.

Jennings (Henry J.), Works by.
Curiosities of Criticism. Post 8vo, cloth limp, 2s. 6d.
Lord Tennyson: A Biographical Sketch. With Portrait. Post 8vo, 1s. ; cloth, 1s. 6d.

Jerome (Jerome K.), Books by.
Stageland. With 64 Illustrations by J. BERNARD PARTRIDGE. Fcap. 4to, picture cover, 1s.
John Ingerfield, &c. With 9 Illusts. by A. S. BOYD and JOHN GULICH. Fcap. 8vo, pic. cov. 1s. 6d.
Prude's Progress: A Comedy by J. K. JEROME and EDEN PHILLPOTTS. Cr. 8vo, 1s. 6d.

Jerrold (Douglas).—The Barber's Chair; and The Hedgehog Letters. Post 8vo, printed on laid paper and half-bound, 2s.

Jerrold (Tom), Works by. Post 8vo, 1s. ea. ; cloth limp, 1s. 6d. each.
The Garden that Paid the Rent.
Household Horticulture: A Gossip about Flowers. Illustrated.

Jesse (Edward).—Scenes and Occupations of a Country Life. Post 8vo, cloth limp, 2s.

Jones (William, F.S.A.), Works by. Cr. 8vo, cl. extra, 7s. 6d. each.
Finger-Ring Lore: Historical, Legendary, and Anecdotal. With nearly 300 Illustrations. Second Edition, Revised and Enlarged.
Credulities, Past and Present. Including the Sea and Seamen, Miners, Talismans, Word and Letter Divination, Exorcising and Blessing of Animals, Birds, Eggs, Luck, &c. With Frontispiece.
Crowns and Coronations: A History of Regalia. With 100 Illustrations.

Jonson's (Ben) Works. With Notes Critical and Explanatory, and a Biographical Memoir by WILLIAM GIFFORD. Edited by Colonel CUNNINGHAM. Three Vols. crown 8vo, cloth extra, 3s. 6d. each.

Josephus, The Complete Works of. Translated by WHISTON. Containing 'The Antiquities of the Jews' and 'The Wars of the Jews.' With 52 Illustrations and Maps. Two Vols., demy 8vo, half-bound, 12s. 6d.

Kempt (Robert).—Pencil and Palette: Chapters on Art and Artists. Post 8vo, cloth limp, 2s. 6d.

Kershaw (Mark). — Colonial Facts and Fictions: Humorous Sketches. Post 8vo, illustrated boards, 2s. ; cloth, 2s. 6d.

King (R. Ashe). Novels by.

Knight (William, M.R.C.S., and Edward, L.R.C.P.). — The Patient's Vade Mecum : How to Get Most Benefit from Medical Advice. Cr. 8vo, 1s. ; cl., 1s. 6d.

Knights (The) of the Lion : A Romance of the Thirteenth Century. Edited, with an Introduction, by the MARQUESS OF LORNE, K.T. Crown 8vo, cloth extra, 6s.

Lamb's (Charles) Complete Works in Prose and Verse, including ' Poetry for Children ' and ' Prince Dorus.' Edited, with Notes and Introduction, by R. H. SHEP-HERD. With Two Portraits and Facsimile of the ' Essay on Roast Pig.' Crown 8vo, half-bd., 7s. 6d.
The Essays of Elia. Post 8vo, printed on laid-paper and half-bound, 2s.
Little Essays : Sketches and Characters by CHARLES LAMB, selected from his Letters by PERCY FITZGERALD. Post 8vo, cloth limp, 2s. 6d.
The Dramatic Essays of Charles Lamb. With Introduction and Notes by BRANDER MAT-THEWS, and Steel-plate Portrait. Fcap. 8vo, half-bound, 2s. 6d.

Landor (Walter Savage).—Citation and Examination of William Shakspeare, &c., before Sir Thomas Lucy, touching Deer-stealing, 19th September, 1582. To which is added, **A Conference of Master Edmund Spenser** with the Earl of Essex, touching the State of Ireland, 1595. Fcap. 8vo, half-Roxburghe, 2s. 6d.

Lane (Edward William).—The Thousand and One Nights, com-monly called in England **The Arabian Nights' Entertainments.** Translated from the Arabic, with Notes. Illustrated with many hundred Engravings from Designs by HARVEY. Edited by EDWARD STANLEY POOLE. With Preface by STANLEY LANE-POOLE. Three Vols., demy 8vo, cloth, 7s. 6d. ea.

Larwood (Jacob), Works by.
Anecdotes of the Clergy. Post 8vo, laid paper, half-bound, 2s.

Post 8vo, cloth limp, 2s. 6d. each.
Forensic Anecdotes. | **Theatrical Anecdotes.**

Lehmann (R. C.), Works by. Post 8vo, 1s. each ; cloth, 1s. 6d. each.
Harry Fludyer at Cambridge.
Conversational Hints for Young Shooters : A Guide to Polite Talk.

Leigh (Henry S.).—Carols of Cockayne. Printed on hand-made paper, bound in buckram, 5s.

Leland (C. Godfrey). — A Manual of Mending and Repairing. With Diagrams. Crown 8vo, cloth, 5s.

Lepelletier (Edmond). — Madame Sans-Gène. Translated from the French by JOHN DE VILLIERS. Crown 8vo, cloth, 3s. 6d. ; post 8vo, picture boards, 2s.

Leys (John).—The Lindsays : A Romance. Post 8vo, illust. bds., 2s.

Lindsay (Harry).—Rhoda Roberts : A Welsh Mining Story. Crown 8vo, cloth, 3s. 6d.

Linton (E. Lynn), Works by.
Crown 8vo, cloth extra, 3s. 6d. each ; post 8vo, illustrated boards, 2s. each.
Patricia Kemball. | **Ione.** | **Under which Lord ?** With 12 Illustrations.
The Atonement of Leam Dundas. | **'My Love!'** | **Sowing the Wind.**
The World Well Lost. With 12 Illusts. | **Paston Carew,** Millionaire and Miser.
The One Too Many.

Post 8vo, illustrated boards, 2s. each.
The Rebel of the Family. | **With a Silken Thread.**

Post 8vo, cloth limp, 2s. 6d. each.
Witch Stories. | **Ourselves :** Essays on Women.
Freeshooting : Extracts from the Works of Mrs. LYNN LINTON.

Dulcie Everton. Crown 8vo, cloth extra, 3s. 6d.

Lucy (Henry W.).—Gideon Fleyce : A Novel. Crown 8vo, cloth extra, 3s. 6d. ; post 8vo, illustrated boards, 2s.

Macalpine (Avery), Novels by.
Teresa Itasca. Crown 8vo, cloth extra, 1s.
Broken Wings. With Six Illustrations by W. J. HENNESSY. Crown 8vo, cloth extra, 6s.

MacColl (Hugh), Novels by.
Mr. Stranger's Sealed Packet. Post 8vo, Illustrated boards, 2s.
Ednor Whitlock. Crown 8vo, cloth extra, 6s.

Macdonell (Agnes).—Quaker Cousins. Post 8vo, boards, 2s.

MacGregor (Robert).—Pastimes and Players : Notes on Popular Games. Post 8vo, cloth limp, 2s. 6d.

Mackay (Charles, LL.D.

McCarthy (Justin, M.P.), Works by.

A History of Our Own Times, from the Accession of Queen Victoria to the General Election of 1880. LIBRARY EDITION. Four Vols., demy 8vo, cloth extra, 12s. each.—Also a POPULAR EDITION, in Four Vols., crown 8vo, cloth extra, 6s. each.—And the JUBILEE EDITION, with an Appendix of Events to the end of 1886, in Two Vols., large crown 8vo, cloth extra, 7s. 6d. each.

A History of Our Own Times, from 1880 to the Diamond Jubilee. Demy 8vo, cloth extra, 12s. LIBRARY EDITION, uniform with the previous Four Volumes.

A Short History of Our Own Times. One Vol., crown 8vo, cloth extra, 6s.—Also a CHEAP POPULAR EDITION, post 8vo, cloth limp, 2s. 6d.

A History of the Four Georges. Four Vols., demy 8vo, cl. ex., 12s. each.   [Vols. I. & II. *ready.*

Crown 8vo, cloth extra, 3s. 6d. each; post 8vo, illustrated boards, 2s. each; cloth limp, 2s. 6d. each.

The Waterdale Neighbours.	Donna Quixote. With 12 Illustrations.
My Enemy's Daughter.	The Comet of a Season.
A Fair Saxon.	Maid of Athens. With 12 Illustrations.
Linley Rochford.	Camiola: A Girl with a Fortune.
Dear Lady Disdain.	The Dictator.
Miss Misanthrope. With 12 Illustrations.	Red Diamonds.

The Riddle Ring. Crown 8vo, cloth, 3s. 6d.

'The Right Honourable.' By JUSTIN MCCARTHY, M.P., and Mrs. CAMPBELL PRAED. Crown 8vo, cloth extra, 6s.

McCarthy (Justin Huntly), Works by.

The French Revolution. (Constituent Assembly, 1789-91). Four Vols., demy 8vo, cloth extra, 12s. each.   [Vols. I. & II. *ready;* Vols. III. & IV. *in the press.*

An Outline of the History of Ireland. Crown 8vo, 1s.; cloth, 1s. 6d.

Ireland Since the Union: Sketches of Irish History, 1798-1886. Crown 8vo, cloth, 6s.

Hafiz in London: Poems. Small 8vo, gold cloth, 3s. 6d.

Our Sensation Novel. Crown 8vo, picture cover, 1s.; cloth limp, 1s. 6d.

Doom: An Atlantic Episode. Crown 8vo, picture cover, 1s.

Dolly: A Sketch. Crown 8vo, picture cover, 1s.; cloth limp, 1s. 6d.

Lily Lass: A Romance. Crown 8vo, picture cover, 1s.; cloth limp, 1s. 6d.

The Thousand and One Days. With Two Photogravures. Two Vols., crown 8vo, half-bd., 12s.

A London Legend. Crown 8vo, cloth, 3s. 6d.

The Royal Christopher. Crown 8vo, cloth, 3s. 6d.

MacDonald (George, LL.D.), Books by.

Works of Fancy and Imagination. Ten Vols., 16mo, cloth, gilt edges, in cloth case, 21s.; or the Volumes may be had separately, in Grolier cloth, at 2s. 6d. each.

Vol.   I. WITHIN AND WITHOUT.—THE HIDDEN LIFE.
,,   II. THE DISCIPLE.—THE GOSPEL WOMEN.—BOOK OF SONNETS.—ORGAN SONGS.
,,   III. VIOLIN SONGS.—SONGS OF THE DAYS AND NIGHTS.—A BOOK OF DREAMS.—ROADSIDE POEMS.—POEMS FOR CHILDREN.
    IV. PARABLES.—BALLADS.—SCOTCH SONGS.
   V. & VI. PHANTASTES: A Faerie Romance. | Vol. VII. THE PORTENT.
   VIII. THE LIGHT PRINCESS.—THE GIANT'S HEART.—SHADOWS.
   IX. CROSS PURPOSES.—THE GOLDEN KEY.—THE CARASOYN.—LITTLE DAYLIGHT.
,,   X. THE CRUEL PAINTER.—THE WOW O' RIVVEN.—THE CASTLE.—THE BROKEN SWORDS—THE GRAY WOLF.—UNCLE CORNELIUS.

Poetical Works of George MacDonald. Collected and Arranged by the Author. Two Vols., crown 8vo, buckram, 12s.

A Threefold Cord. Edited by GEORGE MACDONALD. Post 8vo, cloth, 5s.

Phantastes: A Faerie Romance. With 25 Illustrations by J. BELL. Crown 8vo, cloth extra, 3s. 6d.

Heather and Snow: A Novel. Crown 8vo, cloth extra, 3s. 6d.; post 8vo, illustrated boards, 2s.

Lilith: A Romance. SECOND EDITION. Crown 8vo, cloth extra, 6s.

Maclise Portrait Gallery (The) of Illustrious Literary Charac-

ters: 85 Portraits by DANIEL MACLISE; with Memoirs—Biographical, Critical, Bibliographical, and Anecdotal—illustrative of the Literature of the former half of the Present Century, by WILLIAM BATES, B.A. Crown 8vo, cloth extra, 7s. 6d.

Macquoid (Mrs.), Works by. Square 8vo, cloth extra, 6s. each.

In the Ardennes. With 50 Illustrations by THOMAS R. MACQUOID.

Pictures and Legends from Normandy and Brittany. 34 Illusts. by T. R. MACQUOID.

Through Normandy. With 92 Illustrations by T. R. MACQUOID, and a Map.

Through Brittany. With 35 Illustrations by T. R. MACQUOID, and a Map.

About Yorkshire. With 67 Illustrations by T. R. MACQUOID.

Post 8vo, illustrated boards, 2s. each.

The Evil Eye, and other Stories.	Lost Rose, and other Stories.

Magician's Own Book, The: Performances with Eggs, Hats, &c.

Edited by W. H. CREMER. With 200 Illustrations. Crown 8vo, cloth extra, 4s. 6d.

Magic Lantern, The, and its Management: Including full Practical

Directions. By T. C. HEPWORTH. With 10 Illustrations. Crown 8vo, 1s.; cloth, 1s. 6d.

Magna Charta: An Exact Facsimile of the Original in the British

Museum, 3 feet by 2 feet, with Arms and Seals emblazoned in Gold and Colours, 5s.

Mallory (Sir Thomas).—Mort d'Arthur: The Stories of King

Mallock (W. H.), Works by.
The New Republic. Post 8vo, picture cover, 2s.; cloth limp, 2s. 6d.
The New Paul & Virginia: Positivism on an Island. Post 8vo, cloth, 2s. 6d.
A Romance of the Nineteenth Century. Crown 8vo, cloth 6s.; post 8vo, illust. boards, 2s.
Poems. Small 4to, parchment, 8s.
Is Life Worth Living? Crown 8vo, cloth extra, 6s.

Marks (H. S., R.A.), Pen and Pencil Sketches by. With Four
Photogravures and 126 Illustrations. Two Vols. demy 8vo, cloth, 32s.

Marlowe's Works. Including his Translations. Edited, with Notes
and Introductions, by Colonel CUNNINGHAM. Crown 8vo, cloth extra, 3s. 6d.

Marryat (Florence), Novels by. Post 8vo, illust. boards, 2s. each.

A Harvest of Wild Oats.	Fighting the Air.
Open! Sesame!	Written in Fire.

Massinger's Plays. From the Text of WILLIAM GIFFORD. Edited
by Col. CUNNINGHAM. Crown 8vo, cloth extra, 3s. 6d.

Masterman (J.).—Half-a-Dozen Daughters. Post 8vo, boards, 2s.

Matthews (Brander).—A Secret of the Sea, &c. Post 8vo, illustrated boards, 2s.; cloth limp, 2s. 6d.

Meade (L. T.), Novels by.
A Soldier of Fortune. Crown 8vo, cloth, 3s. 6d.; post 8vo, illustrated boards, 2s.
Crown 8vo, cloth, 3s. 6d each.

In an Iron Grip.	The Voice of the Charmer. With 8 Illustrations.

Dr. Rumsey's Patient. By L. T. MEADE and CLIFFORD HALIFAX, M.D. Crown 8vo, cl. 6s.

Merrick (Leonard), Stories by.
The Man who was Good. Post 8vo, picture boards, 2s.
This Stage of Fools. Crown 8vo, cloth, 3s. 6d.
Cynthia: A Daughter of the Philistines. 2 vols., crown 8vo, 10s. net.

Mexican Mustang (On a), through Texas to the Rio Grande. By
A. E. SWEET and J. ARMOY KNOX. With 265 Illustrations. Crown 8vo, cloth extra, 7s. 6d.

Middlemass (Jean), Novels by. Post 8vo, illust. boards, 2s. each.

Touch and Go.	Mr. Dorillion.

Miller (Mrs. F. Fenwick).—Physiology for the Young; or, The
House of Life. With numerous Illustrations. Post 8vo, cloth limp, 2s. 6d.

Milton (J. L.), Works by. Post 8vo, 1s. each; cloth, 1s. 6d. each.
The Hygiene of the Skin. With Directions for Diet, Soaps, Baths, Wines, &c.
The Bath in Diseases of the Skin.
The Laws of Life, and their Relation to Diseases of the Skin.

Minto (Wm.).—Was She Good or Bad? Cr. 8vo, 1s.; cloth, 1s. 6d.

Mitford (Bertram), Novels by. Crown 8vo, cloth extra, 3s. 6d. each.
The Gun-Runner: A Romance of Zululand. With a Frontispiece by STANLEY L. WOOD.
The Luck of Gerard Ridgeley. With a Frontispiece by STANLEY L. WOOD.
The King's Assegai. With Six full-page Illustrations by STANLEY L. WOOD.
Renshaw Fanning's Quest. With a Frontispiece by STANLEY L. WOOD.

Molesworth (Mrs.), Novels by.
Hathercourt Rectory. Post 8vo, illustrated boards, 2s.
That Girl in Black. Crown 8vo, cloth, 1s. 6d.

Moncrieff (W. D. Scott-).—The Abdication: An Historical Drama.
With Seven Etchings by JOHN PETTIE, W. Q. ORCHARDSON, J. MACWHIRTER, COLIN HUNTER,
R. MACBETH and TOM GRAHAM. Imperial 4to, buckram, 21s.

Moore (Thomas), Works by.
The Epicurean; and Alciphron. Post 8vo, half-bound, 2s.
Prose and Verse; including Suppressed Passages from the MEMOIRS OF LORD BYRON. Edited
by R. H. SHEPHERD. With Portrait. Crown 8vo, cloth extra, 7s. 6d.

Muddock (J. E.) Stories by.
Crown 8vo, cloth extra, 3s. 6d. each.
Maid Marian and Robin Hood. With 12 Illustrations by STANLEY WOOD.
Basile the Jester. With Frontispiece by STANLEY WOOD.
Young Lochinvar.
Post 8vo, Illustrated boards, 2s. each.

The Dead Man's Secret.	From the Bosom of the Deep.

Stories Weird and Wonder

Murray (D. Christie), Novels by.
Crown 8vo, cloth extra, 3s. 6d. each; post 8vo, illustrated boards, 2s. each.

A Life's Atonement.	A Model Father.	Bob Martin's Little Girl.
Joseph's Coat. 12 Illusts.	Old Blazer's Hero.	Time's Revenges.
Coals of Fire. 3 Illusts.	Cynic Fortune. Frontisp.	A Wasted Crime.
Val Strange.	By the Gate of the Sea.	In Direst Peril.
Hearts.	A Bit of Human Nature.	Mount Despair.
The Way of the World.	First Person Singular.	

A Capful o' Nails. Crown 8vo, cloth, 3s. 6d.
The Making of a Novelist: An Experiment in Autobiography. With a Collotype Portrait and Vignette. Crown 8vo, art linen, 6s.

Murray (D. Christie) and Henry Herman, Novels by.
Crown 8vo, cloth extra, 3s. 6d. each; post 8vo, illustrated boards, 2s. each.
One Traveller Returns. | The Bishops' Bible.
Paul Jones's Alias, &c. With Illustrations by A. FORESTIER and G. NICOLET.

Murray (Henry), Novels by.
Post 8vo, illustrated boards, 2s. each; cloth, 2s. 6d. each.
A Game of Bluff. | A Song of Sixpence.

Newbolt (Henry).—Taken from the Enemy. Fcp. 8vo, cloth, 1s. 6d.

Nisbet (Hume), Books by.
'Ball Up.' Crown 8vo, cloth extra, 3s. 6d.; post 8vo, illustrated boards, 2s.
Dr. Bernard St. Vincent. Post 8vo, illustrated boards, 2s.

Lessons in Art. With 21 Illustrations. Crown 8vo, cloth extra, 2s. 6d.
Where Art Begins. With 27 Illustrations. Square 8vo, cloth extra, 7s. 6d.

Norris (W. E.), Novels by.
Saint Ann's. Crown 8vo, cloth, 3s. 6d.; post 8vo, picture boards, 2s.
Billy Bellew. With a Frontispiece by F. H. TOWNSEND. Crown 8vo, cloth, 3s. 6d.

O'Hanlon (Alice), Novels by.   Post 8vo, illustrated boards, 2s. each.
The Unforeseen. | Chance? or Fate?

Ohnet (Georges), Novels by.   Post 8vo, illustrated boards, 2s. each.
Doctor Rameau. | A Last Love.
A Weird Gift. Crown 8vo, cloth, 3s. 6d.; post 8vo, picture boards, 2s.

O'''-'ant (Mrs.), Novels by.   Post 8vo, illustrated boards, 2s. each.
Primrose Path. | Whiteladies.
Greatest Heiress in England.

Sorceress. Crown 8vo, cloth, 3s. 6d.

O'Reilly (Mrs.).—Phœbe's Fortunes. Post 8vo, illust. boards, 2s.

Ouida, Novels by.   Cr. 8vo, cl., 3s. 6d. ea.; post 8vo, illust. bds., 2s. ea.

Held in Bondage.	Folle-Farine.	Moths.	Pipistrello.
Tricotrin.	A Dog of Flanders.	In Maremma.	Wanda.
Strathmore.	Pascarel.	Signa.	Bimbi.	Syrlin.
Chandos.	Two Wooden Shoes.	Frescoes.	Othmar.
Cecil Castlemaine's Gage	In a Winter City.	Princess Napraxine.
Under Two Flags.	Ariadne.	Friendship.	Guilderoy.	Ruffino.
Puck.	Idalia.	A Village Commune.	Two Offenders.

Square 8vo, cloth extra, 5s. each.
Bimbi. With Nine Illustrations by EDMUND H. GARRETT.
A Dog of Flanders, &c. With Six Illustrations by EDMUND H. GARRETT.

Santa Barbara, &c. Square 8vo, cloth, 6s.; crown 8vo, cloth, 3s. 6d.; post 8vo, illustrated boards, 2s.

POPULAR EDITIONS. Medium 8vo, 6d. each; cloth, 1s. each.
Under Two Flags. | Moths.

Wisdom, Wit, and Pathos, selected from the Works of OUIDA by F. SYDNEY MORRIS. Post 8vo, cloth extra, 5s.—CHEAP EDITION, illustrated boards, 2s.

Page (H. A.).—Thoreau: His Life and Aims. With Portrait. Post 8vo, cloth, 2s. 6d.

Pandurang Hari; or, Memoirs of a Hindoo. With Preface by Sir BARTLE FRERE. Crown 8vo, cloth, 3s. 6d.; post 8vo, illustrated boards, 2s.

Parker (Rev. Joseph, D.D.).—Might Have Been: some Life Notes. Crown 8vo, cloth, 6s.

Pascal's Provincial Letters. A New Translation, with Historical Introduction and Notes by T. M'CRIE, D.D. Post 8vo, cloth limp, 2s.

Payn (James), Novels by.
Crown 8vo, cloth extra, 3s. 6d. each; post 8vo, Illustrated boards, 2s. each.

Lost Sir Massingberd.
Walter's Word.
Less Black than We're Painted.
By Proxy. | For Cash Only.
High Spirits.
Under One Roof.
A Confidential Agent. With 12 Illusts.
A Grape from a Thorn. With 12 Illusts.

Holiday Tasks.
The Canon's Ward. With Portrait.
The Talk of the Town. With 12 Illusts.
Glow-Worm Tales.
The Mystery of Mirbridge.
The Word and the Will.
The Burnt Million.
Sunny Stories. | A Trying Patient.

Post 8vo, illustrated boards, 2s. each.

Humorous Stories. | From Exile.
The Foster Brothers.
The Family Scapegrace.
Married Beneath Him.
Bentinck's Tutor. | A County Family.
A Perfect Treasure.
Like Father, Like Son.
A Woman's Vengeance.
Carlyon's Year. | Cecil's Tryst.
Murphy's Master. | At Her Mercy.

The Clyffards of Clyffe.
Found Dead. | Gwendoline's Harvest.
Mirk Abbey. | A Marine Residence.
Some Private Views.
Not Wooed, But Won.
Two Hundred Pounds Reward.
The Best of Husbands.
Halves. | What He Cost Her.
Fallen Fortunes. | Kit: A Memory.
A Prince of the Blood.

In Peril and Privation. With 17 Illustrations. Crown 8vo, cloth, 3s. 6d.
Notes from the 'News.' Crown 8vo, portrait cover, 1s.; cloth, 1s. 6d.

Payne (Will).—Jerry the Dreamer. Crown 8vo, cloth, 3s. 6d.

Pennell (H. Cholmondeley), Works by. Post 8vo, cloth, 2s. 6d. ea.
Puck on Pegasus. With Illustrations.
Pegasus Re-Saddled. With Ten full-page Illustrations by G. DU MAURIER.
The Muses of Mayfair: Vers de Société. Selected by H. C. PENNELL.

Phelps (E. Stuart), Works by. Post 8vo, 1s. ea. ; cloth, 1s. 6d. ea.
Beyond the Gates. | An Old Maid's Paradise. | Burglars in Paradise.
Jack the Fisherman. Illustrated by C. W. REED. Crown 8vo, cloth, 1s. 6d.

Phil May's Sketch-Book. Containing 54 Humorous Cartoons. A
New Edition. Crown folio, cloth, 2s. 6d.

Phipson (Dr. T. L.).—Famous Violinists and Fine Violins:
Historical Notes, Anecdotes, and Reminiscences. Crown 8vo, cloth, 5s.

Pirkis (C. L.).—Lady Lovelace. Post 8vo, illustrated boards, 2s.

Planche (J. R.), Works by.
The Pursuivant of Arms. With Six Plates and 200 Illustrations. Crown 8vo, cloth, 7s. 6d.
Songs and Poems, 1819-1879. With Introduction by Mrs. MACKARNESS. Crown 8vo, cloth, 6s.

Plutarch's Lives of Illustrious Men. With Notes and a Life of
Plutarch by JOHN and WM. LANGHORNE, and Portraits. Two Vols., demy 8vo, half-bound 10s. 6d.

Poe's (Edgar Allan) Choice Works in Prose and Poetry. With Intro-
duction by CHARLES BAUDELAIRE, Portrait and Facsimiles. Crown 8vo, cloth, 7s. 6d.
The Mystery of Marie Roget, &c. Post 8vo, illustrated boards, 2s.

Pollock (W. H.).—The Charm, and other Drawing-room Plays. By
Sir WALTER BESANT and WALTER H. POLLOCK. With 50 Illustrations. Crown 8vo, cloth gilt, 6s.

Pope's Poetical Works. Post 8vo, cloth limp, 2s.

Porter (John).—Kingsclere. Edited by BYRON WEBBER. With 19
full-page and many smaller Illustrations. Second Edition. Demy 8vo, cloth decorated, 18s.

Praed (Mrs. Campbell), Novels by. Post 8vo, illust. bds., 2s. each.
The Romance of a Station. | The Soul of Countess Adrian.

Crown 8vo, cloth, 3s. 6d. each; post 8vo, boards, 2s. each.

Outlaw and Lawmaker. | Christina Chard. With Frontispiece by W. PAGET.
Mrs. Tregaskiss. With 8 Illustrations by ROBERT SAUBER. Crown 8vo, cloth extra, 3s. 6d.
Nulma: An Anglo-Australian Romance. Crown 8vo, cloth, 6s.

Price (E. C.), Novels by.
Crown 8vo, cloth extra, 3s. 6d. each; post 8vo, Illustrated boards, 2s. each.
Valentina. | The Foreigners. | Mrs. Lancaster's Rival.
Gerald. Post 8vo, Illustrated boards, 2s.

Princess Olga.—Radna : A Novel. Crown 8vo, cloth extra, 6s.

Proctor (Richard A., B.A.), Works by.
Flowers of the Sky. With 55 Illustrations. Small crown 8vo, cloth extra, 3s. 6d.
Easy Star Lessons. With Star Maps for every Night in the Year. Crown 8vo, cloth, 6s.
Familiar Science Studies. Crown 8vo, cloth extra, 6s.
Saturn and Its System. With 13 Steel Plates. Demy 8vo, cloth extra, 10s. 6d.
Mysteries of Time and Space. With numerous Illustrations. Crown 8vo, cloth extra, 6s.
The Universe of Suns, &c.
Wages and Wants of Science.

Pryce (Richard).—Miss Maxwell's Affections. Crown 8vo, cloth,
with Frontispiece by HAL LUDLOW, 3s. 6d.; post 8vo, Illustrated boards, 2s.

Rambosson (J.).—Popular Astronomy. Translated by C. B. PIT-
MAN. With Coloured Frontispiece and numerous Illustrations. Crown 8vo, cloth extra, 7s. 6d.

Randolph (Lieut.-Col. George, U.S.A.).—Aunt Abigail Dykes:
A Novel. Crown 8vo, cloth extra, 7s. 6d.

Read (General Meredith).—Historic Studies in Vaud, Berne,
and Savoy. With 31 full-page Illustrations. Two Vols., demy 8vo, cloth, 28s.

Reade's (Charles) Novels.
The New Collected LIBRARY EDITION, complete in Seventeen Volumes, set in new long primer
type, printed on laid paper, and elegantly bound in cloth, price 3s. 6d. each.

1. **Peg Woffington;** and **Christie John-stone.**
2. **Hard Cash.**
3. **The Cloister and the Hearth.** With a Preface by Sir WALTER BESANT.
4. **'It is Never Too Late to Mend.'**
5. **The Course of True Love Never Did Run Smooth;** and **Singleheart and Doubleface.**
6. **The Autobiography of a Thief; Jack of all Trades; A Hero and a Martyr;** and **The Wandering Heir.**
7. **Love Me Little, Love me Long.**
8. **The Double Marriage.**
9. **Griffith Gaunt.**
10. **Foul Play.**
11. **Put Yourself in His Place.**
12. **A Terrible Temptation.**
13. **A Simpleton.**
14. **A Woman-Hater.**
15. **The Jilt,** and other Stories; and **Good Stories of Man and other Animals.**
16. **A Perilous Secret.**
17. **Readiana;** and **Bible Characters.**

In Twenty-one Volumes, post 8vo, illustrated boards, 2s. each.

Peg Woffington. | Christie Johnstone.
'It is Never Too Late to Mend.'
The Course of True Love Never Did Run Smooth.
The Autobiography of a Thief; Jack of all Trades; and James Lambert.
Love Me Little, Love Me Long.
The Double Marriage.
The Cloister and the Hearth.
Hard Cash | Griffith Gaunt.
Foul Play. | Put Yourself in His Place.
A Terrible Temptation.
A Simpleton. | The Wandering Heir
A Woman-Hater.
Singleheart and Doubleface.
Good Stories of Man and other Animals.
The Jilt, and other Stories.
A Perilous Secret. | Readiana.

POPULAR EDITIONS, medium 8vo, 6d. each : cloth, 1s. each.
'It is Never Too Late to Mend.' | **The Cloister and the Hearth.**
Peg Woffington; and **Christie Johnstone.**

'It is Never Too Late to Mend' and **The Cloister and the Hearth** in One Volume,
medium 8vo, cloth, 2s.
Christie Johnstone. With Frontispiece. Choicely printed in Elzevir style. Fcap. 8vo, half-Roxb. 2s. 6d.
Peg Woffington. Choicely printed in Elzevir style. Fcap. 8vo, half-Roxburghe, 2s. 6d.
The Cloister and the Hearth. In Four Vols., post 8vo, with an Introduction by Sir WALTER BE-
SANT, and a Frontispiece to each Vol., 14s. the set ; and the ILLUSTRATED LIBRARY EDITION,
with Illustrations on every page, Two Vols., crown 8vo, cloth gilt, 42s. net.
Bible Characters. Fcap. 8vo, leatherette, 1s.
Selections from the Works of Charles Reade. With an Introduction by Mrs. ALEX. IRE-
LAND. Crown 8vo, buckram, with Portrait, 6s. ; CHEAP EDITION, post 8vo, cloth limp 2s. 6d.

Riddell (Mrs. J. H.), Novels by.
Weird Stories. Crown 8vo, cloth extra, 3s. 6d. ; post 8vo, Illustrated boards, 2s.
Post 8vo, Illustrated boards, 2s. each.
The Uninhabited House.
The Prince of Wales's Garden Party.
The Mystery in Palace Gardens.
Fairy Water.
Her Mother's Darling.
The Nun's Curse. | Idle Tales.

Rimmer (Alfred), Works by. Square 8vo, cloth gilt, 7s. 6d. each.
Our Old Country Towns. With 55 Illustrations by the Author.
Rambles Round Eton and Harrow. With 50 Illustrations by the Author.
About England with Dickens. With 58 Illustrations by C. A. VANDERHOOF and A. RIMMER.

Rives (Amelie).—Barbara Dering. Crown 8vo, cloth extra, 3s. 6d.
post 8vo, illustrated boards, 2s.

Robinson Crusoe. By DANIEL DEFOE. With 37 Illustrations by
GEORGE CRUIKSHANK. Post 8vo, half-cloth, 2s. ; cloth extra, gilt edges, 2s. 6d.

Robinson (F. W.), Novels by.
Women are Strange. Post 8vo, illustrated boards, 2s.
The Hands of Justice. Crown 8vo, cloth extra, 3s. 6d. ; post 8vo, Illustrated boards, 2s.
The Woman in the Dark. Crown 8vo, cloth, 3s. 6d.

Robinson (Phil), Works by. Crown 8vo, cloth extra, 6s. each.
The Poets' Birds. | The Poets' Beasts.
The Poets and Nature: Reptiles, Fishes, and Insects.

Rochefoucauld's Maxims and Moral Reflections. With Notes

R . . . . x . . . . . . al **Warriors who**
Colours, 5s.

Rosengarten (A.).—A Handbook of Architectural Styles. Translated by W. COLLETT-SANDARS. With 639 Illustrations. Crown 8vo, cloth extra, 7s. 6d.

Rowley (Hon. Hugh), Works by. Post 8vo, cloth, 2s. 6d. each.
Puniana: Riddles and Jokes. With numerous Illustrations.
More Puniana. Profusely Illustrated.

Runciman (James), Stories by. Post 8vo, bds., 2s. ea.; cl., 2s. 6d. ea.
Skippers & Shellbacks. | Grace Balmaign's Sweetheart. | Schools & Scholars.

Russell (Dora), Novels by.
A Country Sweetheart. Crown 8vo, cloth, 3s. 6d.; post 8vo, picture boards, 2s.
The Drift of Fate. Crown 8vo, cloth, 3s. 6d.

Russell (W. Clark), Novels, &c., by.
Crown 8vo, cloth extra, 3s. 6d. each; post 8vo, illustrated boards, 2s. each; cloth limp, 2s. 6d. each.

Round the Galley-Fire.	An Ocean Tragedy.
In the Middle Watch.	My Shipmate Louise.
A Voyage to the Cape.	Alone on a Wide Wide Sea.
A Book for the Hammock.	The Good Ship 'Mohock.'
The Mystery of the 'Ocean Star.'	The Phantom Death.
The Romance of Jenny Harlowe.	

Crown 8vo, cloth, 3s. 6d. each.

The Tale of the Ten. With 12 Illustrations by G. MONTBARD.	Is He the Man? Heart of Oak.	The Convict Ship. The Last Entry.

On the Fo'k'sle Head. Post 8vo, illustrated boards, 2s.; cloth limp, 2s. 6d.

Saint Aubyn (Alan), Novels by.
Crown 8vo, cloth extra, 3s. 6d. each; post 8vo, illustrated boards, 2s. each.
A Fellow of Trinity. With a Note by OLIVER WENDELL HOLMES and a Frontispiece.
The Junior Dean. | The Master of St. Benedict's. | To His Own Master.
Orchard Damerel. | In the Face of the World. |

Fcap. 8vo, cloth boards, 1s. 6d. each.
The Old Maid's Sweetheart. | Modest Little Sara.

The Tremlett Diamonds. Crown 8vo, cloth extra, 3s. 6d.

Saint John (Bayle).—A Levantine Family. A New Edition. Crown 8vo, cloth, 3s. 6d.

Sala (George A.).—Gaslight and Daylight. Post 8vo, boards, 2s.

Saunders (John), Novels by.
Crown 8vo, cloth extra, 3s. 6d. each; post 8vo, illustrated boards, 2s. each.
Guy Waterman. | The Lion in the Path. | The Two Dreamers.
Bound to the Wheel. Crown 8vo, cloth extra, 3s. 6d.

Saunders (Katharine), Novels by.
Crown 8vo, cloth extra, 3s. 6d. each; post 8vo, illustrated boards, 2s. each.
Margaret and Elizabeth. | Heart Salvage.
The High Mills. | Sebastian.

Joan Merryweather. Post 8vo, illustrated boards, 2s.
Gideon's Rock. Crown 8vo, cloth extra, 3s. 6d.

Scotland Yard, Past and Present: Experiences of Thirty-seven Years. By Ex-Chief-Inspector CAVANAGH. Post 8vo, illustrated boards, 2s.; cloth, 2s. 6d.

Secret Out, The: One Thousand Tricks with Cards; with Entertaining Experiments in Drawing-room or 'White' Magic. By W. H. CREMER. With 300 Illustrations. Crown 8vo, cloth extra, 4s. 6d.

Seguin (L. G.), Works by.
The Country of the Passion Play (Oberammergau) and the Highlands of Bavaria. With Map and 37 Illustrations. Crown 8vo, cloth extra, 3s. 6d.
Walks in Algiers. With Two Maps and 16 Illustrations. Crown 8vo, cloth extra, 6s.

Senior (Wm.).—By Stream and Sea. Post 8vo, cloth, 2s. 6d.

Sergeant (Adeline).—Dr. Endicott's Experiment. Cr. 8vo, 3s. 6d.

Shakespeare for Children: Lamb's Tales from Shakespeare. With Illustrations, coloured and plain, by J. MOYR SMITH. Crown 4to, cloth gilt, 3s. 6d.

Shakespeare the Boy.

Sharp (William).—Children of To-morrow. Crown 8vo, cloth, 6s,

Shelley's (Percy Bysshe) Complete Works in Verse and Prose.
Edited, Prefaced, and Annotated by R. HERNE SHEPHERD. Five Vols., crown 8vo, cloth, 3s. 6d. each.
Poetical Works, in Three Vols. :
Vol. I. Introduction by the Editor; Posthumous Fragments of Margaret Nicholson; Shelley's Corre-
    spondence with Stockdale; The Wandering Jew; Queen Mab, with the Notes; Alastor,
    and other Poems; Rosalind and Helen; Prometheus Unbound; Adonais, &c.
  „ II. Laon and Cythna; The Cenci; Julian and Maddalo; Swellfoot the Tyrant; The Witch of
    Atlas; Epipsychidion; Hellas.
  „ III. Posthumous Poems; The Masque of Anarchy; and other Pieces.
Prose Works, in Two Vols. :
Vol. I. The Two Romances of Zastrozzi and St. Irvyne; the Dublin and Marlow Pamphlets; A Refu-
    tation of Deism; Letters to Leigh Hunt, and some Minor Writings and Fragments.
  „ II. The Essays; Letters from Abroad; Translations and Fragments, edited by Mrs. SHELLEY.
    With a Biography of Shelley, and an Index of the Prose Works.
  ₄ Also a few copies of a LARGE-PAPER EDITION, 5 vols., cloth, £2 12s. 6d.

Sherard (R. H.).—Rogues: A Novel. Crown 8vo, cloth, 1s. 6d.

Sheridan (General P. H.), Personal Memoirs of. With Portraits,
Maps, and Facsimiles. Two Vols., demy 8vo, cloth, 24s.

Sheridan's (Richard Brinsley) Complete Works, with Life and
Anecdotes. Including his Dramatic Writings, his Works in Prose and Poetry, Translations, Speeches,
and Jokes. With 10 Illustrations. Crown 8vo, half-bound, 7s. 6d.
The Rivals, The School for Scandal, and other Plays. Post 8vo, half-bound, 2s,
Sheridan's Comedies: The Rivals and The School for Scandal. Edited, with an Intro-
duction and Notes to each Play, and a Biographical Sketch, by BRANDER MATTHEWS. With
Illustrations. Demy 8vo, half-parchment, 12s. 6d.

Sidney's (Sir Philip) Complete Poetical Works, including all
those in 'Arcadia.' With Portrait, Memorial-Introduction, Notes, &c., by the Rev. A. B. GROSART,
D.D. Three Vols., crown 8vo, cloth boards, 3s. 6d. each.

Signboards: Their History, including Anecdotes of Famous Taverns and
Remarkable Characters. By JACOB LARWOOD and JOHN CAMDEN HOTTEN. With Coloured Frontispiece and 94 Illustrations. Crown 8vo, cloth extra, 7s. 6d.

Sims (George R.), Works by.
Post 8vo, illustrated boards, 2s. each; cloth limp, 2s. 6d. each.

Ring o' Bells.	Dramas of Life. With 60 Illustrations.
Mary Jane's Memoirs.	Memoirs of a Landlady.
Mary Jane Married.	My Two Wives.
Tinkletop's Crime.	Scenes from the Show.
Zeph: A Circus Story, &c.	The Ten Commandments: Stories.
Tales of To-day.	

Crown 8vo, picture cover, 1s. each; cloth, 1s. 6d. each.
The Dagonet Reciter and Reader: Being Readings and Recitations in Prose and Verse,
selected from his own Works by GEORGE R. SIMS.
The Case of George Candlemas. | Dagonet Ditties. (From *The Referee*.)

Rogues and Vagabonds. A New Edition. Crown 8vo, cloth, 3s. 6d.
How the Poor Live; and Horrible London. Crown 8vo, picture cover, 1s.
Dagonet Abroad. Crown 8vo, cloth, 3s. 6d. ; post 8vo, picture boards, 2s.

Sister Dora: A Biography. By MARGARET LONSDALE. With Four
Illustrations. Demy 8vo, picture cover, 4d.; cloth, 6d.

Sketchley (Arthur).—A Match in the Dark. Post 8vo, boards, 2s,

Slang Dictionary (The): Etymological, Historical, and Anecdotal.
Crown 8vo, cloth extra, 6s. 6d.

Smart (Hawley), Novels by.
Crown 8vo, cloth, 3s. 6d. each ; post 8vo, picture boards, 2s. each.
Beatrice and Benedick. | Without Love or Licence.

Crown 8vo, cloth, 3s. 6d. each.
Long Odds. | The Master of Rathkelly. | The Outsider,
The Plunger. Post 8vo, picture boards, 2s.

Smith (J. Moyr), Works by.
The Prince of Argolis. With 130 Illustrations. Post 8vo, cloth extra, 3s. 6d.
The Wooing of the Water Witch. With numerous Illustrations. Post 8vo, cloth, 6s.

Society in London. Crown 8vo, 1s.; cloth, 1s. 6d.

Society in Paris: The Upper Ten Thousand. A Series of Letters
from Count PAUL VASILI to a Young French Diplomat. Crown 8vo, cloth 6s.

Speight (T. W.), Novels by.

Post 8vo, illustrated boards, 2s. each.

The Mysteries of Heron Dyke.
By Devious Ways, &c.
Hoodwinked; & Sandycroft Mystery.
The Golden Hoop.
Back to Life.

The Loudwater Tragedy.
Burgo's Romance.
Quittance in Full.
A Husband from the Sea.

Post 8vo, cloth limp, 1s. 6d. each.

A Barren Title. | Wife or No Wife?

Crown 8vo, cloth extra, 3s. 6d. each.

A Secret of the Sea. | The Grey Monk. | The Master of Trenance.
A Minion of the Moon: A Romance of the King's Highway.

Spenser for Children. By M. H. TOWRY. With Coloured Illustrations
by WALTER J. MORGAN. Crown 4to, cloth extra, 3s. 6d.

Stafford (John), Novels by.

Doris and I. Crown 8vo, cloth, 3s. 6d.
Carlton Priors. Crown 8vo, cloth, gilt top, 6s.

Starry Heavens (The): A POETICAL BIRTHDAY BOOK. Royal 16mo,
cloth extra, 2s. 6d.

Stedman (E. C.), Works by. Crown 8vo, cloth extra, 9s. each.
Victorian Poets. | The Poets of America.

Stephens (Riccardo, M.B.).—The Cruciform Mark: The Strange
Story of RICHARD TREGENNA, Bachelor of Medicine (Univ. Edinb.) Crown 8vo, cloth, 6s.

Sterndale (R. Armitage).—The Afghan Knife: A Novel. Crown
8vo, cloth extra, 3s. 6d.; post 8vo, illustrated boards, 2s.

Stevenson (R. Louis), Works by. Post 8vo, cloth limp, 2s. 6d. ea.
Travels with a Donkey. With a Frontispiece by WALTER CRANE.
An Inland Voyage. With a Frontispiece by WALTER CRANE.

Crown 8vo, buckram, gilt top, 6s. each.

Familiar Studies of Men and Books.
The Silverado Squatters. With Frontispiece by J. D. STRONG.
The Merry Men. | Underwoods: Poems.
Memories and Portraits.
Virginibus Puerisque, and other Papers. | Ballads. | Prince Otto.
Across the Plains, with other Memories and Essays
Weir of Hermiston. (R. L. STEVENSON'S LAST WORK.)

Songs of Travel. Crown 8vo, buckram, 5s.
New Arabian Nights. Crown 8vo, buckram, gilt top, 6s.; post 8vo, illustrated boards, 2s.
The Suicide Club; and The Rajah's Diamond. (From NEW ARABIAN NIGHTS.) With
Eight Illustrations by W. J. HENNESSY. Crown 8vo, cloth, 5s.
The Edinburgh Edition of the Works of Robert Louis Stevenson. Twenty-seven
Vols., demy 8vo. This Edition (which is limited to 1,000 copies) is sold in Sets only, the price of
which may be learned from the Booksellers. The First Volume was published Nov., 1894.

Stories from Foreign Novelists. With Notices by HELEN and
ALICE ZIMMERN. Crown 8vo, cloth extra, 3s. 6d.; post 8vo, illustrated boards, 2s.

Strange Manuscript (A) Found in a Copper Cylinder. Crown
8vo, cloth extra, with 19 Illustrations by GILBERT GAUL, 5s.; post 8vo, illustrated boards, 2s.

Strange Secrets. Told by PERCY FITZGERALD, CONAN DOYLE, FLOR-
ENCE MARRYAT, &c. Post 8vo, illustrated boards, 2s.

Strutt (Joseph). — The Sports and Pastimes of the People of
England: including the Rural and Domestic Recreations, May Games, Mummeries, Shows, &c., from
the Earliest Period to the Present Time. Edited by WILLIAM HONE. With 140 Illustrations. Crown
8vo, cloth extra, 7s. 6d.

Swift's (Dean) Choice Works, in Prose and Verse. With Memoir,
Portrait, and Facsimiles of the Maps in the "Gulliver's Travels."

Swinburne (Algernon C.), Works by.

Selections from the Poetical Works of A. C. Swinburne. Fcap. 8vo, 6s.
Atalanta in Calydon. Crown 8vo, 6s.
Chastelard: A Tragedy. Crown 8vo, 7s.
Poems and Ballads. FIRST SERIES. Crown 8vo, or fcap. 8vo, 9s.
Poems and Ballads. SECOND SERIES. Crown 8vo, 9s.
Poems & Ballads. THIRD SERIES. Cr. 8vo, 7s.
Songs before Sunrise. Crown 8vo, 10s. 6d.
Bothwell: A Tragedy. Crown 8vo, 12s. 6d.
Songs of Two Nations. Crown 8vo, 6s.
George Chapman. (See Vol. II. of G. CHAPMAN'S Works.) Crown 8vo, 3s. 6d.
Essays and Studies. Crown 8vo, 12s.
Erechtheus: A Tragedy. Crown 8vo, 6s.
A Note on Charlotte Bronte. Cr. 8vo, 6s.

A Study of Shakespeare. Crown 8vo, 8s.
Songs of the Springtides. Crown 8vo, 6s.
Studies in Song. Crown 8vo, 7s.
Mary Stuart: A Tragedy. Crown 8vo, 8s.
Tristram of Lyonesse. Crown 8vo, 9s.
A Century of Roundels. Small 4to, 8s.
A Midsummer Holiday. Crown 8vo, 7s.
Marino Faliero: A Tragedy. Crown 8vo, 6s.
A Study of Victor Hugo. Crown 8vo, 6s.
Miscellanies. Crown 8vo, 12s.
Locrine: A Tragedy. Crown 8vo, 6s.
A Study of Ben Jonson. Crown 8vo, 7s.
The Sisters: A Tragedy. Crown 8vo, 6s.
Astrophel, &c. Crown 8vo, 7s.
Studies in Prose and Poetry. Cr. 8vo, 9s.
The Tale of Balen. Crown 8vo, 7s.

Syntax's (Dr.) Three Tours: In Search of the Picturesque, in Search of Consolation, and in Search of a Wife. With ROWLANDSON'S Coloured Illustrations, and Life of the Author by J. C. HOTTEN. Crown 8vo, cloth extra, 7s. 6d.

Taine's History of English Literature. Translated by HENRY VAN LAUN. Four Vols., small demy 8vo, cloth boards, 30s.—POPULAR EDITION, Two Vols., large crown 8vo, cloth extra, 15s.

Taylor (Bayard). — Diversions of the Echo Club: Burlesques of Modern Writers. Post 8vo, cloth limp, 2s.

Taylor (Tom). — Historical Dramas. Containing 'Clancarty,' 'Jeanne Darc,' 'Twixt Axe and Crown,' 'The Fool's Revenge,' 'Arkwright's Wife,' 'Anne Boleyn,' 'Plot and Passion.' Crown 8vo, cloth extra, 7s. 6d.
⁕ The Plays may also be had separately, at 1s. each.

Tennyson (Lord): A Biographical Sketch. By H. J. JENNINGS. Post 8vo, portrait cover, 1s.; cloth, 1s. 6d.

Thackerayana: Notes and Anecdotes. With Coloured Frontispiece and Hundreds of Sketches by WILLIAM MAKEPEACE THACKERAY. Crown 8vo, cloth extra, 7s. 6d.

...mes, A New Pictorial History of the. By A. S. KRAUSSE. With 340 Illustrations. Post 8vo, picture cover, 1s.

...ers (Adolphe). — History of the Consulate and Empire of France under Napoleon. Translated by D. FORBES CAMPBELL and JOHN STEBBING. With 36 Steel Plates. 12 Vols., demy 8vo, cloth extra, 12s. each.

Thomas (Bertha), Novels by. Cr. 8vo, cl., 3s. 6d. ea.; post 8vo, 2s. ea.

The Violin-Player. | Proud Maisie.

Cressida. Post 8vo, illustrated boards, 2s.

Thomson's Seasons, and The Castle of Indolence. With Introduction by ALLAN CUNNINGHAM, and 48 Illustrations. Post 8vo, half-bound, 2s.

Thornbury (Walter), Books by.
The Life and Correspondence of J. M. W. Turner. With Illustrations in Colours. Crown 8vo, cloth extra, 7s. 6d.

Post 8vo illustrated boards, 2s. each.
Old Stories Re-told. | Tales for the Marines.

Timbs (John), Works by. Crown 8vo, cloth extra, 7s. 6d. each.
The History of Clubs and Club Life in London: Anecdotes of its Famous Coffee-houses, Hostelries, and Taverns. With 42 Illustrations.
English Eccentrics and Eccentricities: Stories of Delusions, Impostures, Sporting Scenes, Eccentric Artists, Theatrical Folk, &c. With 48 Illustrations.

Transvaal (The). By JOHN DE VILLIERS. With Map. Crown 8vo, 1s.

Trollope (Anthony), Novels by.
Crown 8vo, cloth extra, 3s. 6d. each; post 8vo, illustrated boards, 2s. each.
The Way We Live Now. | Mr. Scarborough's Family.
Frau Frohmann. | The Land-Leaguers.

Post 8vo, illustrated boards, 2s. each.
Kept in the Dark. | The American Senator.
The Golden Lion of Granpere. | John Caldigate. | Marion Fay.

Trollope (Frances E.), Novels b...

Trollope (T. A.).—Diamond Cut Diamond. Post 8vo, illust. bds., 2s.

Trowbridge (J. T.).—Farnell's Folly. Post 8vo, illust. boards, 2s.

Twain's (Mark) Books.

Crown 8vo, cloth extra, 3s. 6d. each.

The Choice Works of Mark Twain. Revised and Corrected throughout by the Author. With Life, Portrait, and numerous Illustrations.
Roughing It; and The Innocents at Home. With 200 Illustrations by F. A. FRASER.
The American Claimant. With 81 Illustrations by HAL HURST and others.
Tom Sawyer Abroad. With 26 Illustrations by DAN BEARD.
Tom Sawyer, Detective, &c. With Photogravure Portrait.
Pudd'nhead Wilson. With Portrait and Six Illustrations by LOUIS LOEB.
Mark Twain's Library of Humour. With 197 Illustrations by E. W. KEMBLE.

Crown 8vo, cloth extra, 3s. 6d. each ; post 8vo, picture boards, 2s. each.

A Tramp Abroad. With 314 Illustrations.
The Innocents Abroad; or, The New Pilgrim's Progress. With 234 Illustrations. (The Two Shilling Edition is entitled **Mark Twain's Pleasure Trip.**)
The Gilded Age. By MARK TWAIN and C. D. WARNER. With 212 Illustrations.
The Adventures of Tom Sawyer. With 111 Illustrations.
The Prince and the Pauper. With 190 Illustrations.
Life on the Mississippi. With 300 Illustrations.
The Adventures of Huckleberry Finn. With 174 Illustrations by E. W. KEMBLE.
A Yankee at the Court of King Arthur. With 220 Illustrations by DAN BEARD.
The Stolen White Elephant.
The £1,000,000 Bank-Note.

Mark Twain's Sketches. Post 8vo, illustrated boards, 2s.
Personal Recollections of Joan of Arc. With Twelve Illustrations by F. V. DU MOND. Crown 8vo, cloth, 6s.

Tytler (C. C. Fraser-).—Mistress Judith: A Novel. Crown 8vo, cloth extra, 3s. 6d. ; post 8vo, illustrated boards, 2s.

Tytler (Sarah), Novels by.

Crown 8vo, cloth extra, 3s. 6d. each ; post 8vo, illustrated boards, 2s. each.

Lady Bell.	**Buried Diamonds.** **The Blackhall Ghosts.**

Post 8vo, illustrated boards, 2s. each.

What She Came Through.	**The Huguenot Family.**
Citoyenne Jacqueline.	**Noblesse Oblige.**
The Bride's Pass.	**Beauty and the Beast.**
Saint Mungo's City.	**Disappeared.**

The Macdonald Lass. With Frontispiece. Crown 8vo, cloth, 3s. 6d.

Upward (Allen), Novels by.

A Crown of Straw. Crown 8vo, cloth, 6s.

Crown 8vo, cloth, 3s. 6d. each ; post 8vo, picture boards, 2s. each.

The Queen Against Owen.	**The Prince of Balkistan.**

Vashti and Esther. By 'Belle' of *The World.* Cr. 8vo, cloth, 3s. 6d.

Vizetelly (Ernest A.).—The Scorpion: A Romance of Spain. With a Frontispiece. Crown 8vo, cloth extra, 3s. 6d.

Walford (Edward, M.A.), Works by.

Walford's County Families of the United Kingdom (1897). Containing the Descent, Birth, Marriage, Education, &c., of 12,000 Heads of Families, their Heirs, Offices, Addresses, Clubs, &c. Royal 8vo, cloth gilt, 50s.
Walford's Shilling Peerage (1897). Containing a List of the House of Lords, Scotch and Irish Peers, &c. 32mo, cloth, 1s.
Walford's Shilling Baronetage (1897). Containing a List of the Baronets of the United Kingdom, Biographical Notices, Addresses, &c. 32mo, cloth, 1s.
Walford's Shilling Knightage (1897). Containing a List of the Knights of the United Kingdom, Biographical Notices, Addresses, &c. 32mo, cloth, 1s.
Walford's Shilling House of Commons (1897). Containing a List of all the Members of the New Parliament, their Addresses, Clubs, &c. 32mo, cloth, 1s.
**Walford's Complete Peerage, Baronetage, Knightage, and House of Commons

Waller (S. E.).—Sebastiani's Secret. With Nine full-page Illustrations by the Author. Crown 8vo, cloth, 6s.

Walton and Cotton's Complete Angler; or, The Contemplative Man's Recreation, by IZAAK WALTON; and Instructions How to Angle, for a Trout or Grayling in a clear Stream, by CHARLES COTTON. With Memoirs and Notes by Sir HARRIS NICOLAS, and 61 Illustrations. Crown 8vo, cloth antique, 7s. 6d.

Walt Whitman, Poems by. Edited, with Introduction, by WILLIAM M. ROSSETTI. With Portrait. Crown 8vo, hand-made paper and buckram, 6s.

Ward (Herbert), Books by.
Five Years with the Congo Cannibals. With 92 Illustrations. Royal 8vo cloth, 14s.
My Life with Stanley's Rear Guard. With Map. Post 8vo, 1s.; cloth, 1s. 6d.

Warner (Charles Dudley).—A Roundabout Journey. Crown 8vo, cloth extra, 6s.

Warrant to Execute Charles I. A Facsimile, with the 59 Signatures and Seals. Printed on paper 22 in. by 14 in. 2s.
Warrant to Execute Mary Queen of Scots. A Facsimile, including Queen Elizabeth's Signature and the Great Seal. 2s.

Washington's (George) Rules of Civility Traced to their Sources and Restored by MONCURE D. CONWAY. Fcap. 8vo, Japanese vellum, 2s. 6d.

Wassermann (Lillias) and Aaron Watson.—The Marquis of Carabas. Post 8vo, Illustrated boards, 2s.

Weather, How to Foretell the, with the Pocket Spectroscope. By F. W. CORY. With Ten Illustrations. Crown 8vo, 1s.; cloth, 1s. 6d.

Westall (William), Novels by.
Trust-Money. Post 8vo, Illustrated boards, 2s.; cloth, 2s. 6d.
Sons of Belial. Crown 8vo, cloth extra, 3s. 6d.
With the Red Eagle: A Romance of the Tyrol. Crown 8vo, cloth, 6s.

Westbury (Atha).—The Shadow of Hilton Fernbrook: A Ro-mance of Maoriland. Crown 8vo, cloth, 3s. 6d.

W\ \ \ st, How to Play Solo. By ABRAHAM S. WILKS and CHARLES F. \ \DON. Post 8vo, cloth limp, 2s.

W\ \ \ te (Gilbert).—The Natural History of Selborne. Post 8vo, printed on laid paper and half-bound, 2s.

Williams (W. Mattieu, F.R.A.S.), Works by.
Science in Short Chapters. Crown 8vo, cloth extra, 7s. 6d.
A Simple Treatise on Heat. With Illustrations. Crown 8vo, cloth, 2s. 6d.
The Chemistry of Cookery. Crown 8vo, cloth extra, 6s.
The Chemistry of Iron and Steel Making. Crown 8vo, cloth extra, 9s.
A Vindication of Phrenology. With Portrait and 43 Illusts. Demy 8vo, cloth extra, 12s. 6d.

Williamson (Mrs. F. H.).—A Child Widow. Post 8vo, bds., 2s.

Willis (C. J.), Novels by. Crown 8vo, cloth, 6s. each.
An Easy-going Fellow. | His Dead Past.

Wilson (Dr. Andrew, F.R.S.E.), Works by.
Chapters on Evolution. With 259 Illustrations. Crown 8vo, cloth extra, 7s. 6d.
Leaves from a Naturalist's Note-Book. Post 8vo, cloth limp, 2s. 6d.
Leisure-Time Studies. With Illustrations. Crown 8vo, cloth extra, 6s.
Studies in Life and Sense. With numerous Illustrations. Crown 8vo cloth extra, 6s.
Common Accidents: How to Treat Them. With Illustrations. Crown 8vo, 1s.; cloth, 1s. 6d.
Glimpses of Nature. With 35 Illustrations. Crown 8vo, cloth extra, 3s. 6d.

Winter (John Strange), Stories by. Post 8vo, illustrated boards, 2s. each; cloth limp, 2s. 6d. each.
Cavalry Life. | Regimental Legends.

Cavalry Life and Regimental Legends. LIBRARY EDITION, set in new type and handsomely bound. Crown 8vo, cloth, 3s. 6d.
A Soldier's Children. With 34 Illustrations by E. G. THOMSON and E. STUART HARDY. Crown 8vo, cloth extra, 3s. 6d.

Wissmann (Hermann von). — My Second Journey through Equatorial Africa. With 92 Illustrations. Demy 8vo, cloth, 16s.

boards, 2s. each

Wood (Lady).—Sabina: A Novel. Post 8vo, illustrated boards, 2s.

Woolley (Celia Parker).—Rachel Armstrong; or, Love and The· ology. Post 8vo, illustrated boards, 2s.; cloth, 2s. 6d.

Wright (Thomas), Works by. Crown 8vo, cloth extra, 7s. 6d. each.
The Caricature History of the Georges. With 400 Caricatures, Squibs, &c.
History of Caricature and of the Grotesque in Art, Literature, Sculpture, and Painting. Illustrated by F. W. FAIRHOLT, F.S.A.

Wynman (Margaret).—My Flirtations. With 13 Illustrations by J. BERNARD PARTRIDGE. Crown 8vo, cloth, 3s. 6d.; post 8vo, cloth limp, 2s.

Yates (Edmund), Novels by. Post 8vo, illustrated boards, 2s. each.

Land at Last.	The Forlorn Hope.	Castaway.

Zangwill (I.). — Ghetto Tragedies. With Three Illustrations by A. S. BOYD. Fcap. 8vo, cloth, 2s. net.

Z. Z. (Louis Zangwill).—A Nineteenth Century Miracle. Cr. 8vo, cloth, 3s. 6d.

Zola (Emile), Novels by. Crown 8vo, cloth extra, 3s. 6d. each.
His Excellency (Eugene Rougon). With an Introduction by ERNEST A. VIZETELLY.
The Dram-Shop (L'Assommoir). With an Introduction by E. A. VIZETELLY.   [Shortly.
The Fat and the Thin. Translated by ERNEST A. VIZETELLY.
Money. Translated by ERNEST A. VIZETELLY.
The Downfall. Translated by E. A. VIZETELLY.
The Dream. Translated by ELIZA CHASE. With Eight Illustrations by JEANNIOT.
Doctor Pascal. Translated by E. A. VIZETELLY. With Portrait of the Author.
Lourdes. Translated by ERNEST A. VIZETELLY.
Rome. Translated by ERNEST A. VIZETELLY.

SOME BOOKS CLASSIFIED IN SERIES.

• *For fuller cataloguing, see alphabetical arrangement, pp. 1-26.*

The Mayfair Library. Post 8vo, cloth limp, 2s. 6d. per Volume.

A Journey Round My Room. By X. DE MAISTRE. Translated by Sir HENRY ATTWELL.
Quips and Quiddities. By W. D. ADAMS.
The Agony Column of 'The Times.'
Melancholy Anatomised: Abridgment of BURTON.
Poetical Ingenuities. By W. T. DOBSON.
The Cupboard Papers. By FIN-BEC.
W. S. Gilbert's Plays. Three Series.
Songs of Irish Wit and Humour.
Animals and their Masters. By Sir A. HELPS.
Social Pressure. By Sir A. HELPS.
Curiosities of Criticism. By H. J. JENNINGS.
The Autocrat of the Breakfast-Table. By OLIVER WENDELL HOLMES.
Pencil and Palette. By R. KEMPT.
Little Essays: from LAMB'S LETTERS.
Forensic Anecdotes. By JACOB LARWOOD.
Theatrical Anecdotes. By JACOB LARWOOD.
Witch Stories. By E. LYNN LINTON.
Ourselves. By E. LYNN LINTON.
Pastimes and Players. By R. MACGREGOR.
New Paul and Virginia. By W. H. MALLOCK.
The New Republic. By W. H. MALLOCK.
Puck on Pegasus. By H. C. PENNELL.
Pegasus Re-saddled. By H. C. PENNELL.
Muses of Mayfair. Edited by H. C. PENNELL.
Thoreau: His Life and Aims. By H. A. PAGE.
Puniana. By Hon. HUGH ROWLEY.
More Puniana. By Hon. HUGH ROWLEY.
The Philosophy of Handwriting.
By Stream and Sea. By WILLIAM SENIOR.
Leaves from a Naturalist's Note-Book. By Dr. ANDREW WILSON.

The Golden Library. Post 8vo, cloth limp, 2s. per Volume.

Diversions of the Echo Club. BAYARD TAYLOR.
Songs for Sailors. By W. C. BENNETT.
Lives of the Necromancers. By W. GODWIN.
The Poetical Works of Alexander Pope.
Scenes of Country Life. By EDWARD JESSE.
Tale for a Chimney Corner. By LEIGH HUNT.
The Autocrat of the Breakfast-Table. By OLIVER WENDELL HOLMES.
La Mort d'Arthur: Selections from MALLORY.
Provincial Letters of Blaise Pascal.
Maxims and Reflections of Rochefoucauld.

Handy Novels. Fcap. 8vo, cloth boards, 1s. 6d. each.

The Old Maid's Sweetheart. By A. ST. AUBYN.
Modest Little Sara. By ALAN ST. AUBYN.
Seven Sleepers of Ephesus. M. E. COLERIDGE.
Taken from the Enemy. By H. NEWBOLT.
A Lost Soul. By W. L. ALDEN.
Dr. Palliser's Patient. By GRANT ALLEN.
Monte Carlo Stories. By JOAN BARRETT.
Black Spirits and White. By R. A. CRAM.

My Library. Printed on laid paper, post 8vo, half-Roxburghe, 2s. 6d. each.

Citation and Examination of William Shakspeare. By W. S. LANDOR.
The Journal of Maurice de Guerin.
Christie Johnstone. By CHARLES READE.
Peg Woffington. By CHARLES READE.
The Dramatic Essays of Charles Lamb.

The Pocket Library. Post 8vo, printed on laid paper and hf.-bd., 2s. each.

The Essays of Elia. By CHARLES LAMB.
Robinson Crusoe. Illustrated by G. CRUIKSHANK.
Whims and Oddities. By THOMAS HOOD.
The Barber's Chair. By DOUGLAS JERROLD.
Gastronomy. By BRILLAT-SAVARIN.
The Epicurean, &c. By THOMAS MOORE.
Leigh Hunt's Essays. Edited by E. OLLIER.
White's Natural History of Selborne.
Gulliver's Travels, &c. By Dean SWIFT.
Plays by RICHARD BRINSLEY SHERIDAN.
Anecdotes of the Clergy. By JACOB LARWOOD.
Thomson's Seasons. Illustrated.

THE PICCADILLY NOVELS.

LIBRARY EDITIONS OF NOVELS, many Illustrated, crown 8vo, cloth extra, 3s. 6d. each.

By Mrs. ALEXANDER.
A Life Interest. | Mona's Choice.
By Woman's Wit

By F. M. ALLEN.
Green as Grass.

By GRANT ALLEN.
Philistia. | The Great Taboo.
Strange Stories. | Dumaresq's Daughter.
Babylon. | Duchess of Powysland.
For Maimie's Sake, | Blood Royal.
In all Shades. | Ivan Greet's Master-
The Beckoning Hand. | piece.
The Devil's Die. | The Scallywag.
This Mortal Coil. | At Market Value.
The Tents of Shem. | Under Sealed Orders.

By MARY ANDERSON.
Othello's Occupation.

By EDWIN L. ARNOLD.
Phra the Phoenician. | Constable of St. Nicholas.

By ROBERT BARR.
In a Steamer Chair. | From Whose Bourne.

By FRANK BARRETT.
The Woman of the Iron Bracelets.
The Harding Scandal.
A Missing Witness.

By 'BELLE.'
Vashti and Esther.

By Sir W. BESANT and J. RICE.
Ready-Money Mortiboy. | By Celia's Arbour.
My Little Girl | Chaplain of the Fleet.
With Harp and Crown. | The Seamy Side.
This Son of Vulcan. | The Case of Mr. Lucraft.
The Golden Butterfly. | In Trafalgar's Bay.
The Monks of Thelema. | The Ten Years' Tenant.

Sir WALTER BESANT.
All Sorts and Condi- | The Revolt of Man.
tions of Men. | The Bell of St. Paul's.
The Captains' Room. | The Holy Rose.
All in a Garden Fair. | Armorel of Lyonesse.
Dorothy Forster. | S. Katherine's by Tower
Uncle Jack. | Verbena Camellia Ste-
The World Went Very | phanotis.
  Well Then, | The Ivory Gate.
Children of Gibeon. | The Rebel Queen.
Herr Paulus. | Beyond the Dreams of
For Faith and Freedom. | Avarice.
To Call Her Mine. | The Master Craftsman.

By PAUL BOURGET.
A Living Lie.

By ROBERT BUCHANAN.
Shadow of the Sword. | The New Abelard.
A Child of Nature. | Matt. | Rachel Dene.
God and the Man. | Master of the Mine.
Martyrdom of Madeline | The Heir of Linne.
Love Me for Ever. | Woman and the Man.
Annan Water. | Red and White Heather.
Foxglove Manor. | Lady Kilpatrick.

ROB. BUCHANAN & HY. MURRAY.
The Charlatan.

By J. MITCHELL CHAPPLE.
The Minor Chord.

By HALL CAINE.
The Shadow of a Crime. | The Deemster.
A Son of Hagar. |

By ANNE COATES.
Rie's Diary.

By MACLAREN COBBAN.
The Red Sultan. | The Burden of Isabel.

By MORT. & FRANCES COLLINS.
Tra

By WILKIE COLLINS.
Armadale. | After Dark. | The Frozen Deep.
No Name. | The Two Destinies.
Antonina. | The Law and the Lady.
Basil. | The Haunted Hotel.
Hide and Seek. | The Fallen Leaves.
The Dead Secret. | Jezebel's Daughter.
Queen of Hearts. | The Black Robe.
My Miscellanies. | Heart and Science.
The Woman in White. | 'I Say No.'
The Moonstone. | Little Novels.
Man and Wife. | The Evil Genius.
Poor Miss Finch. | The Legacy of Cain.
Miss or Mrs.? | A Rogue's Life.
The New Magdalen. | Blind Love.

By E. H. COOPER.
Geoffory Hamilton.

By V. CECIL COTES.
Two Girls on a Barge.

By C. EGBERT CRADDOCK.
His Vanished Star.

By H. N. CRELLIN.
Romances of the Old Seraglio.

By MATT CRIM.
The Adventures of a Fair Rebel.

By S. R. CROCKETT and others.
Tales of Our Coast.

By B. M. CROKER.
Diana Barrington. | Village Tales & Jungle
Proper Pride. | Tragedies.
A Family Likeness. | The Real Lady Hilda.
Pretty Miss Neville. | Married or Single?
A Bird of Passage. | Two Masters.
'To Let.' | Mr. Jervis. | In the Kingdom of Kerry

By WILLIAM CYPLES.
Hearts of Gold.

By ALPHONSE DAUDET.
The Evangelist; or, Port Salvation.

By H. COLEMAN DAVIDSON.
Mr. Sadler's Daughters.

By ERASMUS DAWSON.
The Fountain of Youth.

By JAMES DE MILLE.
A Castle in Spain.

By. J. LEITH DERWENT.
Our Lady of Tears. | Circe's Lovers.

By DICK DONOVAN.
Tracked to Doom. | The Mystery of Jamaica
Man from Manchester. | Terrace.
The Chronicles of Michael Danevitch.

By RICHARD DOWLING.
Old Corcoran's Money.

By A. CONAN DOYLE.
The Firm of Girdlestone.

By S. JEANNETTE DUNCAN.
A Daughter of To-day. | Vernon's Aunt.

By G. MANVILLE FENN.
The New Mistress. | The Tiger Lily.
Witness to the Deed. | The White Virgin.

By PERCY FITZGERALD.
Fatal Zero.

By R. E. FRANCILLON.
One by One. | Ropes of Sand.
A Dog and his Shadow. | Jack Doyle's Daughter.
A Real Queen. |

Prefaced by Sir BARTLE FRERE.
Pandurang Hari.

GARRETT.

THE PICCADILLY (3/6) NOVELS—*continued*.

By PAUL GAULOT.
The Red Shirts.

By CHARLES GIBBON.
Robin Gray. | The Golden Shaft.
Loving a Dream.

By E. GLANVILLE.
The Lost Heiress. | The Fossicker.
A Fair Colonist. | The Golden Rock.

By E. J. GOODMAN.
The Fate of Herbert Wayne.

By Rev. S. BARING GOULD.
Red Spider. | Eve.

By CECIL GRIFFITH.
Corinthia Marazion.

By SYDNEY GRUNDY.
The Days of his Vanity.

By THOMAS HARDY.
Under the Greenwood Tree.

By BRET HARTE.
A Waif of the Plains. | A Protégée of Jack
A Ward of the Golden | Hamlin's.
  Gate. [Springs. | Clarence.
A Sappho of Green | Barker's Luck.
Col. Starbottle's Client. | Devil's Ford. ['celsior.'
Susy. | Sally Dows, | The Crusade of the 'Ex-
Bell-Ringer of Angel's. | Three Partners.

By JULIAN HAWTHORNE.
Garth. | Beatrix Randolph.
Ellice Quentin. | David Poindexter's Dis-
Sebastian Strome. | appearance.
Dust. | The Spectre of the
Fortune's Fool. | Camera.

By Sir A. HELPS.
Ivan de Biron.

By I. HENDERSON.
Agatha Page.

By G. A. HENTY.
Rujub the Juggler. | Dorothy's Double.

By JOHN HILL.
The Common Ancestor.

By Mrs. HUNGERFORD.
Lady Verner's Flight. | A Point of Conscience.
The Red-House Mystery | Nora Creina
The Three Graces. | An Anxious Moment.
Professor's Experiment. | April's Lady.

By Mrs. ALFRED HUNT.
The Leaden Casket. | Self-Condemned.
That Other Person. | Mrs. Juliet.

By C. J. CUTCLIFFE HYNE.
Honour of Thieves.

By R. ASHE KING.
A Drawn Game.

By EDMOND LEPELLETIER.
Madame Sans-Gène.

By HARRY LINDSAY.
Rhoda Roberts.

By HENRY W. LUCY.
Gideon Fleyce.

By E. LYNN LINTON.
Patricia Kemball. | The Atonement of Leam
Under which Lord? | Dundas.
'My Love!' | Ione, | The World Well Lost.
Paston Carew. | The One Too Many.
Sowing the Wind. | Dulcie Everton.

By JUSTIN McCARTHY.
A Fair Saxon. | Donna Quixote.
Linley Rochford. | Maid of Athens.
Dear Lady Disdain. | The Comet of a Season.
Camiola. | The Dictator.
Waterdale Neighbours. | Red Diamonds.
My Enemy's Daughter. | The Riddle Ring.
Miss Misanthrope.

By JUSTIN H. McCARTHY.
A London Legend. | The Royal Christopher.

By GEORGE MACDONALD.
Heather and Snow. | Phantastes.

By L. T. MEADE.
A Soldier of Fortune. | The Voice of the
In an Iron Grip. | Charmer.

By LEONARD MERRICK.
This Stage of Fools.

By BERTRAM MITFORD.
The Gun-Runner. | The King's Assegai.
The Luck of Gerard | Renshaw Fanning's
  Ridgeley. | Quest.

By J. E. MUDDOCK.
Maid Marian and Robin Hood.
Basile the Jester. | Young Lochinvar.

By D. CHRISTIE MURRAY.
A Life's Atonement. | Cynic Fortune.
Joseph's Coat. | The Way of the World.
Coals of Fire. | BobMartin's Little Girl.
Old Blazer's Hero. | Time's Revenges.
Val Strange. | Hearts. | A Wasted Crime.
A Model Father. | In Direst Peril.
By the Gate of the Sea. | Mount Despair.
A Bit of Human Nature. | A Capful o' Nails.
First Person Singular.

By MURRAY and HERMAN.
The Bishops' Bible. | Paul Jones's Alias.
One Traveller Returns.

By HUME NISBET.
'Bail Up!'

By W. E. NORRIS.
Saint Ann's. | Billy Bellew.

By G. OHNET.
A Weird Gift.

By Mrs. OLIPHANT.
The Sorceress.

By OUIDA.
Held in Bondage. | Two Little Wooden
Strathmore. | In a Winter City.[Shoes
Chandos. | Friendship.
Under Two Flags. | Moths. | Ruffino.
Idalia. [Gage. | Pipistrello.
Cecil Castlemaine's | A Village Commune.
Tricotrin. | Puck. | Bimbi. | Wanda.
Folle Farine. | Frescoes. | Othmar.
A Dog of Flanders. | In Maremma.
Pascarel. | Signa. | Syrlin. | Guilderoy.
Princess Napraxine. | Santa Barbara.
Ariadne. | Two Offenders.

By MARGARET A. PAUL.
Gentle and Simple.

By JAMES PAYN.
Lost Sir Massingberd. | High Spirits.
Less Black than We're | Under One Roof.
  Painted. | Glow-worm Tales.
A Confidential Agent. | The Talk of the Town.
A Grape from a Thorn. | Holiday Tasks.
In Peril and Privation. | For Cash Only.
The Mystery of Mir- | The Burnt Million.
By Proxy. [bridge. | The Word and the Will.
The Canon's Ward. | Sunny Stories.
Walter's Word. | A Trying Patient.

By WILL PAYNE.
Jerry the Dreamer.

By Mrs. CAMPBELL PRAED.
Outlaw and Lawmaker. | Mrs. Tregaskiss.
Christina Chard.

By E. C. PRICE.
Valentina. | Foreigners. | Mrs. Lancaster's Rival.

By RICHARD PRYCE.
Miss Maxwell's Affections.

By CHARLES READE.
Peg Woffington: and | Love Me Little, Love
  Christie Johnstone. | Me Long.
Hard Cash. | The Double Marriage.
Cloister & the Hearth. | Foul Play.
Never Too Late to Mend | Put Yourself in His
The Course of True | Place.
  Love Never Did Run | A Terrible Temptation.
  Smooth; and Single- | A Simpleton.
  heart and Doubleface. | A Woman-Hater.
Autobiography of a | The Jilt, & other Stories:
  Thief; Jack of all | & Good Stories of Man
  Trades; A Hero and | and other Animals.
  a Martyr; and The | A Perilous Secret.
  Wandering Heir. | Readiana: and Bible

THE PICCADILLY (3/6) NOVELS—*continued*.

By Mrs. J. H. RIDDELL.
Weird Stories.

By AMELIE RIVES.
Barbara Dering.

By F. W. ROBINSON.
The Hands of Justice. | Woman in the Dark.

By DORA RUSSELL.
A Country Sweetheart. | The Drift of Fate.

By W. CLARK RUSSELL.
Round the Galley-Fire. | My Shipmate Louise.
In the Middle Watch. | Alone on Wide Wide Sea.
A Voyage to the Cape. | The Phantom Death.
Book for the Hammock. | Is He the Man?
The Mystery of the | Good Ship 'Mohock.'
  'Ocean Star.' | The Convict Ship.
The Romance of Jenny | Heart of Oak.
  Harlowe. | The Tale of the Tea.
An Ocean Tragedy. | The Last Entry.

By BAYLE ST. JOHN.
A Levantine Family.

By JOHN SAUNDERS.
Guy Waterman. | The Two Dreamers.
Bound to the Wheel. | The Lion in the Path.

By KATHARINE SAUNDERS.
Margaret and Elizabeth | Heart Salvage.
Gideon's Rock. | Sebastian.
The High Mills.

By ADELINE SERGEANT.
Dr. Endicott's Experiment.

By HAWLEY SMART.
Without Love or Licence. | Long Odds.
The Master of Rathkelly. | The Outsider.

By T. W. SPEIGHT.
A Secret of the Sea. | The Master of Trenance.
The Grey Monk. | A Minion of the Moon.

By ALAN ST. AUBYN.
A Fellow of Trinity. | In Face of the World.
The Junior Dean. | Orchard Damerel.
Master of St. Benedict's. | The Tremlett Diamonds.
To   vn Master.

By JOHN STAFFORD.
Do   d l.

By R. A. STERNDALE.
The Afghan Knife.

By BERTHA THOMAS.
Proud Maisie. | The Violin-Player.

By ANTHONY TROLLOPE.
The Way we Live Now. | Scarborough's Family
Fran Frohmann. | The Land-Leaguers.

By FRANCES E. TROLLOPE
Like Ships upon the | Anne Furness.
  Sea. | Mabel's Progress |

By IVAN TURGENIEFF &c
Stories from Foreign Novelists.

By MARK TWAIN.
Mark Twain's Choice | Tom Sawyer, Detective.
  Works. | Pudd'nhead Wilson.
Mark Twain's Library | The Gilded Age.
  of Humour. | Prince and the Pauper.
The Innocents Abroad. | Life on the Mississippi.
Roughing It: and The | The Adventures of
  Innocents at Home. | Huckleberry Finn.
A Tramp Abroad. | A Yankee at the Court
The American Claimant. | of King Arthur.
Adventures Tom Sawyer | Stolen White Elephant.
Tom Sawyer Abroad. | £1,000,000 Banknote.

By C. C. FRASER-TYTLER.
Mistress Judith.

By SARAH TYTLER.
Lady Bell. | The Blackhall Ghosts.
Buried Diamonds. | The Macdonald Lass.

By ALLEN UPWARD.
The Queen against Owen | The Prince of Balkistan.

By E. A. VIZETELLY.
The Scorpion : A Romance of Spain.

By WILLIAM WESTALL.
Sons of Belial.

By ATHA WESTBURY.
The Shadow of Hilton Fernbrook.

By JOHN STRANGE WINTER.
Cavalry Life and Regimental Legends.
A Soldier's Children.

By MARGARET WYNMAN.
My Flirtations.

By E. ZOLA.
The Downfall. | The Fat and the Thin.
The Dream. | Rome.
Dr. Pascal. | His Excellency.
Money. | Lourdes. | The Dram-Shop.

By Z. Z.
A Nineteenth Century Miracle.

CHEAP EDITIONS OF POPULAR NOVELS.

Post 8vo, illustrated boards, 2s. each.

By ARTEMUS WARD.
Artemus Ward Complete.

By EDMOND ABOUT.
The Fellah.

By HAMILTON AÏDÉ.
Carr of Carrlyon. | Confidences.

By MARY ALBERT.
Brooke Finchley's Daughter.

By Mrs. ALEXANDER.
Maid, Wife or Widow? | Valerie's Fate.
Blind Fate.

By GRANT ALLEN.
Philistia. | The Great Taboo.
Strange Stories. | Dumaresq's Daughter.
Babylon. | Duchess of Powysland.
For Maimie's Sake. | Blood Royal. |piece-
In all Shades. | Ivan Greet's Master.
The Beckoning Hand. | The Scallywag.
The Devil's Die. | This Mortal Coil.
The Tents of Shem. | At Market Value.

By E. LESTER ARNOLD.
Phra the Phœnician.

BY FRANK BARRETT.
Fettered for Life. | A Prodigal's Progress.
Little Lady Linton. | Found Guilty.
Between Life & Death. | A Recoiling Vengeance.
The Sin of Olga Zasson- | For Love and Honour.
  lich. | John Ford; and His.

By SHELSLEY BEAUCHAMP.
Grantley Grange.

By Sir W. BESANT and J. RICE.
Ready-Money Mortiboy | By Celia's Arbour.
My Little Girl. | Chaplain of the Fleet.
With Harp and Crown. | The Seamy Side.
This Son of Vulcan. | The Case of Mr. Lucraft.
The Golden Butterfly. | In Trafalgar's Bay.
The Monks of Thelema. | The Ten Years' Tenant.

By Sir WALTER BESANT.
All Sorts and Condi- | To Call Her Mine.
  tions of Men. | The Bell of St. Paul's.
The Captains' Room. | The Holy Rose.
All in a Garden Fair. | Armorel of Lyonesse.
Dorothy Forster. | S. Katherine's by Tower.
Uncle Jack. | Verbena Camellia Ste-
The World Went Very | phanotis.
  Well Then. | The Ivory Gate.
Children of Gibeon. | The Rebel Queen.
Herr Paulus. | Beyond the Dreams of
For Faith and Freedom. | Avarice.

By AMBROSE BIERCE.
In the Midst of Life.

By FREDERICK BOYLE.
Camp Notes. | Chronicles of No-man's
Savage Life. | Land.

BY BRET HARTE.
Californian Stories. | Flip. | Maruja.
Gabriel Conroy. | A Phyllis of the Sierras.
| A Waif of the Plains

TWO-SHILLING NOVELS—*continued.*

By HAROLD BRYDGES.
Uncle Sam at Home.

By ROBERT BUCHANAN.
Shadow of the Sword.
A Child of Nature.
God and the Man.
Love Me for Ever.
Foxglove Manor.
The Master of the Mine.
Annan Water.
The Martyrdom of Madeline.
The New Abelard.
Matt.
The Heir of Linne.
Woman and the Man.
Rachel Dene.

By BUCHANAN and MURRAY.
The Charlatan.

By HALL CAINE.
The Shadow of a Crime.
A Son of Hagar.
The Deemster.

By Commander CAMERON.
The Cruise of the 'Black Prince.'

By Mrs. LOVETT CAMERON.
Deceivers Ever. | Juliet's Guardian.

By HAYDEN CARRUTH.
The Adventures of Jones.

By AUSTIN CLARE.
For the Love of a Lass.

By Mrs. ARCHER CLIVE.
Paul Ferroll.
Why Paul Ferroll Killed his Wife.

By MACLAREN COBBAN.
The Cure of Souls. | The Red Sultan.

By C. ALLSTON COLLINS.
The Bar Sinister.

By MORT. & FRANCES COLLINS.
Sweet Anne Page.
Transmigration.
From Midnight to Midnight.
A Fight with Fortune.
Sweet and Twenty.
The Village Comedy.
You Play me False.
Blacksmith and Scholar.
Frances.

By WILKIE COLLINS.
Armadale. | AfterDark.
No Name.
Antonina.
Basil.
Hide and Seek.
The Dead Secret.
Queen of Hearts.
Miss or Mrs. ?
The New Magdalen.
The Frozen Deep.
The Law and the Lady.
The Two Destinies.
The Haunted Hotel.
A Rogue's Life.
My Miscellanies.
The Woman in White.
The Moonstone.
Man and Wife.
Poor Miss Finch.
The Fallen Leaves.
Jezebel's Daughter.
The Black Robe.
Heart and Science.
'I Say No!'
The Evil Genius.
Little Novels.
Legacy of Cain.
Blind Love.

By M. J. COLQUHOUN.
Every Inch a Soldier.

By DUTTON COOK.
Leo. | Paul Foster's Daughter.

By C. EGBERT CRADDOCK.
The Prophet of the Great Smoky Mountains.

By MATT CRIM.
The Adventures of a Fair Rebel.

By B. M. CROKER.
Pretty Miss Neville.
Diana Barrington.
'To Let.'
A Bird of Passage.
Proper Pride.
A Family Likeness.
Village Tales and Jungle Tragedies.
Two Masters.
Mr. Jervis.

By W. CYPLES.
Hearts of Gold.

By ALPHONSE DAUDET.
The Evangelist; or, Port Salvation.

By ERASMUS DAWSON.
The Fountain of Youth.

By JAMES DE MILLE.
A Castle in Spain.

By J. LEITH DERWENT.
Our Lady of Tears. | Circe's Lovers.

By CHARLES DICKENS.
Sketches by Boz.

By DICK DONOVAN.
The Man-Hunter.
Tracked and Taken.
Caught at Last !
Wanted !
Who Poisoned Hetty Duncan ?
Man from Manchester.
A Detective's Triumphs
The Mystery of Jamaica Terrace.
In the Grip of the Law.
From Information Received.
Tracked to Doom.
Link by Link
Suspicion Aroused.
Dark Deeds.
Riddles Read.

By Mrs. ANNIE EDWARDES.
A Point of Honour. | Archie Lovell.

By M. BETHAM-EDWARDS.
Felicia. | Kitty.

By EDWARD EGGLESTON.
Roxy.

By G. MANVILLE FENN.
The New Mistress.
Witness to the Deed.
The Tiger Lily.
The White Virgin.

By PERCY FITZGERALD.
Bella Donna.
Never Forgotten.
Polly.
Fatal Zero.
Second Mrs. Tillotson.
Seventy-five Brooke Street.
The Lady of Brantome.

By P. FITZGERALD and others.
Strange Secrets.

By ALBANY DE FONBLANQUE.
Filthy Lucre.

By R. E. FRANCILLON.
Olympia.
One by One.
A Real Queen.
Queen Cophetua.
King or Knave ?
Romances of the Law.
Ropes of Sand.
A Dog and his Shadow.

By HAROLD FREDERIC.
Seth's Brother's Wife. | The Lawton Girl.

Prefaced by Sir BARTLE FRERE.
Pandurang Hari.

By HAIN FRISWELL.
One of Two.

By EDWARD GARRETT.
The Capel Girls.

By GILBERT GAUL.
A Strange Manuscript.

By CHARLES GIBBON.
Robin Gray.
Fancy Free.
For Lack of Gold.
What will World Say ?
In Love and War.
For the King.
In Pastures Green.
Queen of the Meadow.
A Heart's Problem.
The Dead Heart.
In Honour Bound.
Flower of the Forest.
The Braes of Yarrow.
The Golden Shaft.
Of High Degree.
By Mead and Stream.
Loving a Dream.
A Hard Knot.
Heart's Delight.
Blood-Money.

By WILLIAM GILBERT.
Dr. Austin's Guests.
James Duke.
The Wizard of the Mountain.

By ERNEST GLANVILLE.
The Lost Heiress.
A Fair Colonist.
The Fossicker.

By Rev. S. BARING GOULD.
Red Spider. | Eve.

By HENRY GREVILLE.
A Noble Woman. | Nikanor.

By CECIL GRIFFITH.
Corinthia Marazion.

By SYDNEY GRUNDY.
The Days of his Vanity.

By JOHN HABBERTON.
Brueton's Bayou. | Country Luck.

By ANDREW HALLIDAY.
Every day Papers.

By Lady DUFFUS HARDY.
Paul Wynter's Sacrifice.

By THOMAS HARDY.
Under the Greenwood Tree.

By J. BERWICK HARWOOD

Two-Shilling Novels—*continued*.

By JULIAN HAWTHORNE.

Garth.	Beatrix Randolph.
Ellice Quentin.	Love—or a Name.
Fortune's Fool.	David Poindexter's Dis-
Miss Cadogna.	appearance.
Sebastian Strome.	The Spectre of the
Dust.	Camera.

By Sir ARTHUR HELPS.
Ivan de Biron.

By G. A. HENTY.
Rujub the Juggler.

By HENRY HERMAN.
A Leading Lady.

By HEADON HILL.
Zambra the Detective.

By JOHN HILL.
Treason Felony.

By Mrs. CASHEL HOEY.
The Lover's Creed.

By Mrs. GEORGE HOOPER.
The House of Raby.

By TIGHE HOPKINS.
'Twixt Love and Duty.

By Mrs. HUNGERFORD.

A Maiden all Forlorn.	Lady Verner's Flight.
In Durance Vile.	The Red House Mystery
Marvel.	The Three Graces.
A Mental Struggle.	Unsatisfactory Lover.
A Modern Circe.	Lady Patty.

By Mrs. ALFRED HUNT.

Thornicroft's Model.	Self-Condemned.
That Other Person.	The Leaden Casket.

By JEAN INGELOW.
Fated to be Free.

By WM. JAMESON.
My Dead Self.

By HARRIETT JAY.

The Dark Colleen.	Queen of Connaught.

By MARK KERSHAW.
Colonial Facts and Fictions.

By R. ASHE KING.

A Drawn Game.	Passion's Slave.
'The Wearing of the	Bell Barry.
Green.'	

By EDMOND LEPELLETIER.
Madame Sans-Gene.

By JOHN LEYS.
The Lindsays.

By E. LYNN LINTON.

Patricia Kemball.	The Atonement of Leam
The World Well Lost.	Dundas.
Under which Lord?	With a Silken Thread.
Paston Carew.	Rebel of the Family.
'My Love!'	Sowing the Wind.
Ione.	The One Too Many.

By HENRY W. LUCY.
Gideon Fleyce.

By JUSTIN McCARTHY.

Dear Lady Disdain.	Camiola.
Waterdale Neighbours.	Donna Quixote.
My Enemy's Daughter.	Maid of Athens.
A Fair Saxon.	The Comet of a Season.
Linley Rochford.	The Dictator.
Miss Misanthrope.	Red Diamonds.

By HUGH MACCOLL.
Mr. Stranger's Sealed Packet.

By GEORGE MACDONALD.
Heather and Snow.

By AGNES MACDONELL.
Quaker Cousins.

By KATHARINE S. MACQUOID.

The Evil Eye.	Lost Rose.

By W. H. MALLOCK.
A Romance of the Nine...

By FLORENCE MARRYAT.

Open ! Sesame !	A Harvest of Wild Oats
Fighting the Air.	Written in Fire.

By J. MASTERMAN.
Half-a-dozen Daughters.

By BRANDER MATTHEWS.
A Secret of the Sea.

By L. T. MEADE.
A Soldier of Fortune.

By LEONARD MERRICK.
The Man who was Good.

By JEAN MIDDLEMASS.

Touch and Go.	Mr. Dorillion.

By Mrs. MOLESWORTH.
Hathercourt Rectory.

By J. E. MUDDOCK.

Stories Weird and Won-	From the Bosom of the
derful.	Deep.
The Dead Man's Secret.	

By D. CHRISTIE MURRAY.

A Model Father.	By the Gate of the Sea.
Joseph's Coat.	A Bit of Human Nature.
Coals of Fire.	First Person Singular.
Val Strange.	Hearts.	Bob Martin's Little Girl
Old Blazer's Hero.	Time's Revenges.
The Way of the World.	A Wasted Crime.
Cynic Fortune.	In Direst Peril.
A Life's Atonement.	Mount Despair.

By MURRAY and HERMAN.

One Traveller Returns.	The Bishops' Bible.
Paul Jones's Alias.	

By HENRY MURRAY.

A Game of Bluff.	A Song of Sixpence.

By HUME NISBET.

'Bail Up!'	Dr. Bernard St. Vincent.

By W. E. NORRIS.
Saint Ann's.

By ALICE O'HANLON.

The Unforeseen.	Chance? or Fate?

By GEORGES OHNET.

Dr. Rameau.	A Weird Gift.
A Last Love.	

By Mrs. OLIPHANT.

Whiteladies.	The Greatest Heiress in
The Primrose Path.	England.

By Mrs. ROBERT O'REILLY.
Phœbe's Fortunes.

By OUIDA.

Held in Bondage.	Two Lit. Wooden Shoes.
Strathmore.	Moths.
Chandos.	Bimbi.
Idalia.	Pipistrello.
Under Two Flags.	A Village Commune.
Cecil Castlemaine's Gage	Wanda.
Tricotrin.	Othmar
Puck.	Frescoes.
Folle Farine.	In Maremma.
A Dog of Flanders.	Guilderoy.
Pascarel.	Ruffino.
Signa.	Syrlin.
Princess Napraxine.	Santa Barbara.
In a Winter City.	Two Offenders.
Ariadne.	Ouida's Wisdom, Wit
Friendship.	and Pathos.

By MARGARET AGNES PAUL.
Gentle and Simple.

By C. L. PIRKIS.
Lady Lovelace.

By EDGAR A. POE.
The Mystery of Marie Roget.

By Mrs. CAMPBELL PRAED.
The Romance of a Station.
The Soul of Countess Adrian.
Outlaw and Lawmaker.
Christina Chard.

By E. C. PRICE.

Valentina.	Mrs. Lancaster's Rival
The Foreigners.	Gerald.

By ... RD PRYCE.

Two-Shilling Novels—continued.

By JAMES PAYN.

Bentinck's Tutor.
Murphy's Master.
A County Family.
At Her Mercy.
Cecil's Tryst.
The Clyffards of Clyffe.
The Foster Brothers.
Found Dead.
The Best of Husbands.
Walter's Word.
Halves.
Fallen Fortunes.
Humorous Stories.
£200 Reward.
A Marine Residence.
Mirk Abbey.
By Proxy.
Under One Roof.
High Spirits.
Carlyon's Year.
From Exile.
For Cash Only.
Kit.
The Canon's Ward.
The Talk of the Town.
Holiday Tasks.
A Perfect Treasure.
What He Cost Her.
A Confidential Agent.
Glow-worm Tales.
The Burnt Million.
Sunny Stories.
Lost Sir Massingberd.
A Woman's Vengeance.
The Family Scapegrace.
Gwendoline's Harvest.
Like Father, Like Son.
Married Beneath Him.
Not Wooed, but Won.
Less Black than We're Painted.
Some Private Views.
A Grape from a Thorn.
The Mystery of Mirbridge.
The Word and the Will.
A Prince of the Blood.
A Trying Patient.

By CHARLES READE.

It is Never Too Late to Mend.
Christie Johnstone.
The Double Marriage.
Put Yourself in His Place.
Love Me Little, Love Me Long.
The Cloister and the Hearth.
The Course of True Love.
The Jilt.
The Autobiography of a Thief.
A Terrible Temptation.
Foul Play.
The Wandering Heir.
Hard Cash.
Singleheart and Doubleface.
Good Stories of Man and other Animals.
Peg Woffington.
Griffith Gaunt.
A Perilous Secret.
A Simpleton.
Readiana.
A Woman-Hater.

By Mrs. J. H. RIDDELL.

Weird Stories.
Fairy Water.
Her Mother's Darling.
The Prince of Wales's Garden Party.
The Uninhabited House.
The Mystery in Palace Gardens.
The Nun's Curse.
Idle Tales.

By AMELIE RIVES.

Barbara Dering.

By F. W. ROBINSON.

Women are Strange. | The Hands of Justice.

By JAMES RUNCIMAN.

Skippers and Shellbacks. | Schools and Scholars.
Grace Balmaign's Sweetheart.

By W. CLARK RUSSELL.

Round the Galley Fire.
On the Fo'k'sle Head.
In the Middle Watch.
A Voyage to the Cape.
A Book for the Hammock.
The Mystery of the 'Ocean Star.'
The Romance of Jenny Harlowe.
An Ocean Tragedy.
My Shipmate Louise.
Alone on Wide Wide Sea.
The Good Ship 'Mohock.'
The Phantom Death.

By DORA RUSSELL.

A Country Sweetheart.

By GEORGE AUGUSTUS SALA.

Gaslight and Daylight.

By JOHN SAUNDERS.

Guy Waterman.
The Two Dreamers. | The Lion in the Path.

By KATHARINE SAUNDERS.

Joan Merryweather.
The High Mills.
Heart Salvage. | Sebastian.
Margaret and Elizabeth.

By GEORGE R. SIMS.

The Ring o' Bells.
Mary Jane's Memoirs.
Mary Jane Married.
Tales of To-day.
Dramas of Life.
Tinkletop's Crime.
My Two Wives.
Zeph.
Memoirs of a Landlady.
Scenes from the Show.
The 10 Commandments.
Dagonet Abroad.

By ARTHUR SKETCHLEY.

A Match in the Dark.

By HAWLEY SMART.

Without Love or Licence.
The Plunger.
Beatrice and Benedick.

By T. W. SPEIGHT.

The Mysteries of Heron Dyke.
The Golden Hoop.
Hoodwinked.
By Devious Ways.
Back to Life.
The Loudwater Tragedy.
Burgo's Romance.
Quittance in Full.
A Husband from the Sea.

By ALAN ST. AUBYN.

A Fellow of Trinity.
The Junior Dean.
Master of St. Benedict's. | To His Own Master.
Orchard Damerel.
In the Face of the World.

By R. A. STERNDALE.

The Afghan Knife.

By R. LOUIS STEVENSON.

New Arabian Nights.

By BERTHA THOMAS.

Cressida.
Proud Maisie. | The Violin Player.

By WALTER THORNBURY.

Tales for the Marines. | Old Stories Retold.

By T. ADOLPHUS TROLLOPE.

Diamond Cut Diamond.

By F. ELEANOR TROLLOPE.

Like Ships upon the Sea. | Anne Furness.
Mabel's Progress.

By ANTHONY TROLLOPE.

Frau Frohmann.
Marion Fay.
Kept in the Dark.
John Caldigate.
The Way We Live Now.
The Land-Leaguers.
The American Senator.
Mr. Scarborough's Family.
Golden Lion of Granpere.

By J. T. TROWBRIDGE.

Farnell's Folly.

By IVAN TURGENIEFF, &c.

Stories from Foreign Novelists.

By MARK TWAIN.

A Pleasure Trip on the Continent.
The Gilded Age.
Huckleberry Finn.
Mark Twain's Sketches.
Tom Sawyer.
A Tramp Abroad.
Stolen White Elephant.
Life on the Mississippi.
The Prince and the Pauper.
A Yankee at the Court of King Arthur.
The £1,000,000 Bank-Note.

By C. C. FRASER-TYTLER.

Mistress Judith.

By SARAH TYTLER.

The Bride's Pass.
Buried Diamonds.
St. Mungo's City.
Lady Bell.
Noblesse Oblige.
Disappeared.
The Huguenot Family.
The Blackhall Ghosts.
What She Came Through.
Beauty and the Beast.
Citoyenne Jaqueline.

By ALLEN UPWARD.

The Queen against Owen. | Prince of Balkistan.

By AARON WATSON and LILLIAS WASSERMANN.

The Marquis of Carabas.

By WILLIAM WESTALL.

Trust-Money.

By Mrs. F. H. WILLIAMSON.

A Child Widow.

By J. S. WINTER.

Cavalry Life. | Regimental Legends.

By H. F. WOOD.

The Passenger from Scotland Yard.
The Englishman of the Rue Cain.

By Lady WOOD.

Sabina.

By CELIA PARKER WOOLLEY.

Rachel Armstrong; or, Love and Theology.

By EDMUND YATES.

The Forlorn Hope. | Castaway.
Land at Last.

By I. ZANGWILL